MULCH

STEPHEN SCOTT WHITAKER

MONTAG

A Montag Press Book
www.montagpress.com
Montag Press
777 Morton Street, Unit B
San Francisco CA 94129 USA

Montag Press, the burning book with the hatchet cover, the skewed word mark and the portrayal of the long-suffering fireman mascot are trademarks of Montag Press.

Printed & Digitally Originated in the United States of America
10 9 8 7 6 5 4 3 2 1

"*Mulch* is a daring sprawling work reaching back into the colonial past and captures a seedy underbelly of the Eastern seaboard rife with magic and narcotics, of mermaids and madmen. *Mulch* inhabits a universe that is one part tall-tale, two-parts supernatural thriller imbued with gritty realism. A potboiler through and through, with poetry upon its shimmering pages."

—Gabriel Boyer,
author of *Devil, Everywhere I Look*

"*Mulch* is a dark magic that conjures secret things better left unknown but impossible to resist. Whitaker's Eastern Shore, a lonely, mythic anachronism, exists in a place just to the left of both time and reason, full of monsters both human and magical, reeking of moonshine and the redolence of genocide. *Mulch* will eye-gouge and skull-fuck you to death with its transgressive vision of corruption, family, and memory."

—Paul D. Miller,
author of 'Albrecht Drue, Ghostpuncher"

"What is so great about the American novel? Its potential for change, spiritual transformation, is what you find in Whitaker's *Mulch*. Like an old hymn, the syntax does battle with that persistent lunar quality: the immersion of the reader is complete. The syntax, packed with overcharged undercurrents, reveals a momentary but eternal world. Bizarre, twisty, *Mulch* is an utterly digestible yarn chronicling the alchemy of existence, the magic of sinking."

—Walker Zupp, author of *Martha*

AUTHOR'S FOREWORD

This book is **not** an accurate representation of the Eastern Shore of Virginia and Maryland, Boston, or Amsterdam. I have taken great liberties with names, geography, and history in creating this universe.

This book is not about nice people (see the website for TWs). This is a book about corrupt souls, and losing agency over one's mind and body, and this book is about memory, as well as it is about friendship, love, and storytelling. Inspired by comic books, cartoons, westerns, and Shakespeare, to say nothing of Stephen King, *Mulch* was the project where I taught myself how to write fiction.

I began the novel when I was a grad student at Boston University in 1996. I continued it while working as a teacher at EF International in Brighton, MA, and later finished the novel while I was teaching in Northampton County, Virginia. The first draft was completed in 2002. My former students from EF International in Boston, Northampton High School in Virginia, and Pocomoke High School in Maryland will recognize many Easter Eggs.

I was a different human when I wrote *Mulch*, amid an active addiction, one that I did not recognize nor address for some years, to say nothing of denial, anxiety, depression, and dysphoria lying underneath my addiction. I almost didn't make it out of my 30s. I'm in a much healthier place now. Revising the novel has been a fascinating tour of my younger voice. My voice has evolved since this book was written, and I have evolved since this book was written. I thank my family for their continued love and support, as well as the Montag Press community of writers, editors, and artists who have been supportive from the jump.

From the bottom of my heart, thank you.

Enjoy.

Visit https://mulchverse.wordpress.com/
for trigger warnings, character lists, maps,
and character playlists.

For those who are powerless

"Shadow is the means by which bodies display their form."

—Leonardo Da Vinci

JUNE 22

Maria tried to stop the fire. And I see her, sweat soaking her shirt, rising flames spreading over her back like wings. The veins on her forehead popping as she lugged the water bucket into the living room. Water sloshing dollops as big as quarters on the old rugs Granny inherited from her mother after the war.

Mulch had broken her hands with a skillet and left her flailing on the floor to die. He poured gas on her too. What a shitty thing to do your lover. Maria, poor Maria.

When Maria tried to handle the buckets, she dropped them. She never even got as far as the living room. Barely managed to crawl out the door.

I saw her. I have that in my head, and my head is filled with light and sometimes I feel as if I am all the light there ever was in the world.

Where was I? Where was I?

Smoke appeared as a brutish, purple cloud, the kind that exists in story books. The clouds seemed to move all at once as if they were some inky paint spilled on a sheet of paper that was pulled invisibly to the end of the world. The kind of clouds you see only once in your life. The kind that don't seem real.

I couldn't move. My head hurt, but I felt something, thunder I thought. The steady beat of lightning rollers coming in from the sea.

It was our horses, five of them and the cattle striking their way towards the corn fields where I lay.

But I didn't know this. At first, there was just my bleariness, corn pollen like golden snow caught on the wind tail, dragging down across my nose and lips. It was a kind of bliss, I think. The corn pollen collected on my chest. My breath scratchy, my legs itching where husks, bobbing in the wind, scraped my flesh. I remember thinking of Adam and the box Pembroke put me in, but mostly I stared at the sky. I thought it was going to rain, and I remember thinking back then that was fine with me.

It was the kind of sky you'd expect in a movie, or a storybook, not the kind of sky that was your family gone to smoke and ash. The tearing sod of the stock escaping to the wilds. Maria in the yard raising her broken hands to the sky cursing Mulch in Spanish, in English, and calling for rain.

PROLOGUE

June 7th, 3:37 AM

The fog crept out of the woods, slow, building, and so thick and dense it curled up and curled away from itself as it swelled through the air. And if anyone would have seen it, they would have thought that the fog moved like an animal. Something cold and reptilian out of the cold and dewy forest. And if anyone had seen the fog, they would have noticed that when it crossed the road to the little house on the other side that it did so by creating a series of roped fog- feet, much like a centipede, or like a dragon. But being that this is the Eastern Shore, one probably would have thought crab, the way the fog crabbed across the road, the way it continued to foam out of the woods like how a crab appears suddenly out of sea-green bubbles, alert, ready to lunge for meat.

And if someone were to have seen the fog, it is even possible someone might have seen the profile of a great stag, and the fluttering of black muscular wings hidden in the fog's breath, in the trees. The head ragged with moss, the eyes focused toward the salt-box house, the winging of birds moving behind its head like a squirming brain.

BOOK ONE: JUNE 7

"When the fog appeared, the sailors shouted and screamed that a sea devil was upon them...We could not mistake the feeling of dread, like a shroud covering their countenance in darkness... Even after they calmed and the captain had set them back to work, the devilish fog remained, whispering as it glided across the deck."

—from the diary of Samuel Moses Johnson,
passenger on the Wildflower from England
to the King's Creek Plantation on the Eastern Shore

"Take away a person's body. Take away that agency. There's no worse prison than one's own body."

-Sofie Xeon, speech on March 29th "
Intersections Between White Supremacy, Climate Change, Immigration,
Black Lives Matter, & Transgender Equality"

"Adam Taylor, my boyfriend, probably wants to sleep with my best friend. This is a fact, journal. Stone cold fact. Next time Macy and I have drinks, I'm turning on the bitch jets."

—from the journals of Virginia Maria Hayes

CHAPTER ONE

1

The box, a perfect cube sixteen feet by sixteen feet, had been built by Mulch himself out of swamp oak planes and sealed with pitch to outlast sun, surf, and weather. The bottom, outfitted with black pontoons so the box could be floated into the creek, could plow through ocean seas and storm seas alike. It had taken Mulch a year to build it, designing small models and testing their buoyancy.

On the outside, the box looked like a building block, except for the two narrow slits on two opposing walls that allowed sun and air to ventilate the inside. On the outside, on parallel sides were O-rings where a heavy rope would be attached, so that the box could be dragged by boat to sea. In building it, Mulch had wanted the box to float out of his life forever.

The walls were an inch thick, reinforced with oak cross planks and steel brackets, and built to withstand the heavy winds and powerful waves of hurricane season. Cut on top of the box was an opening six by six inches, that could be double locked from the outside by one large sliding bolt. The bolt was twelve inches long and three-quarters of an inch thick. Through this hatch, food could be lowered and jars of waste collected by a simple leather sling, also of Mulch's design. On the outside of the upper hatch was one large eyehole and latch where an industrial-sized padlock would be attached.

The box was built to hold Marina, Mulch's eldest daughter. She was incredibly strong and had been known to snap 2x4s without straining. Mulch looked at his box as loving protection, the kind only he could give. Mulch knew that both Pembroke and Cilia wished the girl could be flown to Amsterdam, but they underestimated what Marina was capable of. This was the only way.

It was the inside of the box that Mulch was most proud of. He had crafted a large bed made of driftwood that curled up at the ends like fingers. The fingers held two comfortable feather mattresses. The bed itself was bolted to the floor to prevent shifting and to prevent Marina from using the bed as a stepstool to see outside her box.

His favorite feature? The carvings.

Sea Hag and Marcos Silva crafted the interior walls so that Marina would have something to see and touch as she tossed and bobbed around the sea, and of course, the carvings were magic, though they all would have been horrified to know that their home spun magic did little to comfort Marina as she suffered in her prison, but there was no way to know that as they poured their love into their work.

Marcos had cut the swells and crescents of the tide into the walls so one could feel the tide coming in. One could touch the gentle angles small at the top of the wall and slide one's hands down the carving feeling the waves grow larger and wider as they approached the floor. Marcos had loved Marina since the moment he glimpsed her moony form swimming the back creek. Entranced, he had watched her night after night, looking for the subtle ripples of her wake as she dipped and played in the warm water. That's how he created the designs for the waves, by watching for her wake and memorizing the coastline's pull and drag. Marcos imagined Marina standing on her toes to reach as high as she could and then sliding herself down to the bottom, feeling the carved waves increase in size and detail as they crashed onto the rough floor. On the opposite wall, Marcos carved a silhouette of a wide, tall flame that would radiate heat, like the sun on warm afternoons. He loved her and wished, as he carved, that his fingers could press into the wood the heat and light she would need to survive.

Marcos and Sea Hag believed she would be rescued.

Sea Hag spent months on the interior, working beside Marcos, carving not the sun and the waves, but the delicate folds and spines of sea plants and dolphins, whales, and jellyfishes. She carved the creatures of the back creeks and creatures of the bay. She carved the plants of the Atlantic and its fishes. She left a small rough patch of wood to remind Marina that outside of the cube there were beaches to roll on, instead of walls and floors. The opposing wall was spooned and pitted like coral. Sea Hag had glazed the relief with ground coral and clam shells. It was finely ground and the powder gave the wall a glow that was matched by the ceiling.

Mulch had paid migrant children five dollars for every jar of lightning bugs they could collect. He subtracted twenty-five cents for every dead bug in the mason jar, because he said, "Dead bugs are good for nothing except spider food." But really, he docked their pay to be mean, because he then ground all the poor bugs, living and dead, into a paste and mixed the paste with luminescent paint and the result was a ceiling that glowed with star light and anyone sleeping on the bed could rock away to waves and the hushed, dim wattage of hundreds of massacred lightning bugs.

And Marcos and Sea Hag, together with Mr. Bill bound the box with magics and bound the box with protection. Mr. Bill threaded each magic together so that Marina could not be hurt by outside forces, by men or by weather, or by opposing magic. Mulch had insisted on it, and being the loyal man he was, Mr. Bill saw to it.

Marina, of course, knew nothing of their endeavors. She spent the day basking in the sun and swimming the shallow creek, blank as a wave.

2

If Nick Adams had woken up in his little house on the morning of June 7th and had known that his life would have changed completely from then on, that he had been placed on the wheel of some great journey and he either had to foot it, or get crushed, he would have gone back to sleep, or maybe have gotten drunk, or perhaps cut off his left foot, or something even more drastic just so he wouldn't have to deal with the facts as they presented themselves over the next few weeks. Nick lived a simple life and even though many would think it an empty life, or even unambitious life, he was happy until he found the painting, and then everything began to drift towards the inevitable conclusion.

But that morning, Nick awoke to a sunny daybreak, the grass beady with dew from where the morning's fog was dissipating, the thermometer climbing towards 85 so early. Something wasn't right. Things didn't smell right, and there was a sharp acetone bite to the air. Nick couldn't move. There was something heavy and cold sitting upon his chest. His crotch was ice cold and his sex had crawled up into his body. From outside he heard the cawing of a crow. It was then that Nick saw that his hands were smeared with blood.

Startled, he shouted and whipped himself out of his bed. The blood-red on Nick's hands were smeared along his thighs and boxers. A small, dried pool of it lay at the foot of the sheets. He saw that his toes had swashed the red gunk in broad strokes from kicking and turning in his sleep. He checked himself, looking for evidence of cuts. For a second, he thought that there might be a body. But whose?

Mine, of course. Stop that, Nick. Must not think bad thoughts, must not think bad thoughts.

The red was real, but it didn't feel like blood, more like paint. Then he noticed the painting.

Nick would later look back on that June morning when he awoke and saw on his wall the painting that made him sigh and freeze, as the moment that turned his life sideways. Outside, the cicadas revved up and down, a swelling that always reminded Nick of engines. The sun broke through in ribbons across the floor and one big slice of sun cut the bottom half of the wall in two. He remembered later how the sun seemed to slow everything down, and the cicadas too, how their song was like a theme for breakdown. Slow-motion sounds, slow-motion heat.

"Jesus."

Nick's whisper sounded amplified in his suddenly creepy bedroom.

Something is wrong here, he thought. *No shit Sherlock. What did you do?*

His wall had been painted a violent red with streaks of purple. The strokes, so forceful and thick, had erased the white. The colors swirled upwards. Someone had used a broad brush and several gallons to layer the paint-like clothing. It rippled like water. He went to touch the painting which lay thick on his wall. *How?* He thought. *Why?* Layers of purple and red folded over a bit of black. Nick couldn't look away from it. His brain squirmed in his skull, but he couldn't look away. He estimated that the painting was about six feet tall. It began two feet off the floor, continued to the top of the wall, and was about five feet wide, nearly covering that entire side of the wall. As he touched the strands thrown up in thick splotches and strokes, Nick knew that he had painted it in his sleep. *What in the actual fuck?*

"Nobody paints in their sleep, I mean maybe like Picasso or Monet, or somebody like that, but not me." Nick pronounced Picasso like Pick-ass-O and Monet like Moan-et, pronouncing the silent t. *Now you are fucking talking to yourself. Damn. How much did I drink last night?*

The painting crisscrossed with purple and black paint blended and mashed together to create the idea of smoke, or darkness. In the right corner, at the very top, a figure in white with blackish hair floated as if carried aloft by wind. It looked like a woman. And above it, something bird-like floated, but maybe it was a storm cloud, Nick couldn't tell.

"Yep, that's pretty weird all right," George said as he rubbed his jaw.

"What the hell is it?" Nick replied, lipping his cigarette like a movie gangster.

"Well, it could be a bad attempt at impressionism."

"Don't fuck with me, George."

"I never fuck around with impressionism." George painted ducks, and waterfowl, a champion at the state fair no less. "This isn't something I would do or could do, for that matter. It's a little out of my league." George kept studying the painting, turning his head this way and that.

"I'm not asking for your opinion."

There was a faint smell of alcohol bleeding through the smoke stench, but George was pretty sure it was coming from his arm pits. Nick's little house was unusually hot that morning. George's hairs were curling from the humidity.

"Well." George scratched his red curly hair. "I can say that it's pretty weird."

"What the hell is it?"

"Well." George sniffed his shirt. "Okay. Well. Hmm."

"George stop sniffing yourself," Nick said.

"Sorry," George said shifting his hips to the right. George gave the painting another good once over, all the time scratching his goatee which never seemed to grow, no matter what, past the heavy stubble stage. "It is odd, that's for sure."

"Can't you say any more than that?"

"Hey man, as I said, this is a little out of my league. Ducks and billboards are one thing."

Striking a match, Nick held it up to his nostrils and inhaled the sulfuric smell. "Well, I was hoping you'd tell me what the hell it is, cause I have no clue."

"Nick, I don't know how many times I have to tell you, I paint ducks and seascapes – plain stuff, you know. This here is like real art or something."

"What do you mean *real* art?"

"You know like abstract and stuff. Museum art."

"Oh."

"Never mind. Bad analogy. This kind of thing is more like a psychological thing than an art thing." George didn't know what else to say, but that sounded as good as anything. George looked at his buddy out of the corner of his eye. "Come on we're going to be late," he said, slapping Nick on the shoulder.

3

The Eastern Shore is an unusual place, and if you ask any of the from-here's why that's so, they'll pretty much tell you and won't be shy about it – isolation – and the from-here's like it that way. A 'from-here' is a native. A 'come-here' is someone who isn't. And a 'come-back' is someone who's lived on the shore and left and come back for some reason. Not that natives are unfriendly, not at all. Sure as a chicken is to cluck, natives are willing to invite you to church, out to fish, and over to quilt, maybe even to can some preserves. Come-here's are quickly indoctrinated into the local religious life faster than you can say,

"Jesus Died For Me." That's because church is the social cell of the shore. And yet isolation makes the shore what it is. Twenty-dollar bridge-tunnel fares both ways keep the urban sprawl that is Va. Beach, Hampton Roads, Newport News, and Norfolk, over *there* across the bay. The bridge keeps it all from crossing the Chesapeake. Which is a good thing, the natives will tell you because things are pretty much settled in terms of who has what and who's going to get what. We're talking pure nativist economics where the old boy network is still running strong. Even today, when you drive through the idyllic peaceful farm towns that line beautiful and tranquil Northampton County, you don't suspect that the whole county is run by a bunch of old guys who sit at the Lazy Titty in the back woods and dice things out.

On the shore, there's an underground, and an underground to the underground, which is run by Mulch Hayes.

Take Cheriton, for example. Old Selma Hoggs lives on Cherry Creek Road and when you drive down Cherry Creek Road, you'll see a leaning house that is missing its northern exterior wall. You can see right inside up the stairs and into her bedroom. You can see the busted lamps her son broke when he threw them at her one afternoon. You can see her stacks of winter quilts on top of cedar chests. Between the floors, like a white strip of cookie filling, you can spy the insulation. You can see her rabbit ears on top of her TV. If you drive by at night you can see Selma watching her game shows. If you've got pretty good vision you can make out the pictures on the wall – they look like potato-headed children, and they are potato-headed children. You can see them clear as a bell, if your vision is okay, from where your vehicle sits on the road. When the state turned off her electrical power, the old boys down at the power station just turned it back on again. Seems Selma's boy, Isaiah, knew somebody at the power plant and he wasn't going to let his mother live in her broken-down house without power. He was going to let her live anywhere she pleased, the state be damned. To celebrate, she had her grandson come to string X-mas lights, the big bulb kind grandparents always seem to have. You can see them too, like frozen fireflies stuck in amber goo. Then HUD got involved and they were going to fix Selma's house, only she'd have to go somewhere else for six months or so while they went through all her stuff. Selma told them to stuff it. The HUD boys didn't like that at all, and Turner called in a favor with Mulch Hayes and suddenly Selma was on her own.

If you know the right people in town you can get out of your speeding ticket. If you know the right people you can buy large quantities of hydroponic weed, you can have your oil changed for free. The oil company will not charge you late fees and will not charge you extra for coming out on Sundays. If you are the right type of person Mulch Hayes will give you a loan with low interest, Doc Snyder will come out to your house, and Principal Steve Custis will call you first before disciplining your cuss of a kid.

If you know the right people you can get your county sticker (for your car – a small fee) for free and have the county write it off for you as a tax expense, you can get your groceries at a 15% discount at Food City Markets in Cape James or in Lonely, you can have someone muscled around, you can have someone whacked, you can purchase cocaine, crack cocaine, meth, heroin, LSD, XTC, locally grown mushrooms, Cuban cigars, kiddie porn, and stolen antiques (a real high-market item in terms of supply and demand. With demand always exceeding supply which is why so many people fuss and fume over who's getting what in the underground's shady and sometimes violent antique business). If you know the right people you can get a hunting license for free, not to mention a fishing license, commercial crabbing, oystering, clamming, and fishing license, all for free or at least without the hassle of government red tape. If you know the right people the coast guard will look the other way, Sim Smith will come out to your property and spray all sorts of sordid chemicals onto your lawn that will kill mosquito larvae and cut down considerably on the mosquito bites you'll get on your thighs, earlobes, forehead, arms, neck, privates, etc. But the spraying will never eliminate all the mosquitoes, ever, and Sim will tell you that up front before he even gets the chemical sprayer out, just in case you're environmentally conscious (most people around here aren't so much environmentally conscious as they are environmentally over-stimulated. You simply don't think about it when you're up to your neck in mosquito bites and you have to cut the lawn three-time a week).

If you know the folks at the florist's you can get your flowers on credit and at any time, even when the store is closed, and it is V-Day and all the roses are cut and secured to other folks, they'll find you some and wrap them up real nice. Bill at Bill's Bar will let you into the kitchen and let you cook up whatever it is you want, for free. Mulch Hayes might not kill you if you cross him. Judge Ferris will sign off that you have participated in a drug rehab even if you are off on a bender. Most importantly though, you can bet the church ladies won't gossip so bad if they know you – all if you know the right people.

Because it's so isolated the come-heres tend to get restless. Now there are only about 45,000 people on the shore, or about the size of the undergraduate population at Virginia Polytechnic Institute in Blacksburg, VA, which is a seven-hour drive away and the only football college team watched around here, unless you're African-American, then it's Tech *and* Norfolk State, which is single-A but is close enough to go see live when you're desperate for helmet crunching action, which pretty much means that college football gets stratified by class.

In everything on the shore, at the end of the day, it all boils down to class. Most white folks say they aren't racist and most black folks will tell you white folks are okay, but racism is alive and well, growing fat with fear, too. It doesn't take much to stir the pot, and between the media, the politicians, and the bizarre way human beings tend to behave, fear is growing wild.

And there's plenty of bizarre behavior as well. For instance, when the Ugly Mother goes shopping at Bayshore she usually rides with the other migrants on the big blue school bus Mulch pays Shiny Morris to drive. Shiny's forehead is always a gleam with shiny wax, thus his name. The Ugly Mother is always telling Shiny in Spanish that she's gonna bottle that wax of his and it's gonna make her rich. The Ugly Mother likes to screw with the shoppers and does so by conjuring a parade of white kittens to follow her around the aisles. They don't do much, the kittens, but they mew and follow her around and mew and climb all over everything. Little kids go ape-shit when they see them rushing to pet all the different cats. The little kids tend to get clawed and bit a lot by them, especially at the grocery store. When the Ugly Mother is around kids tend to come out of Bayshore Market with hands wrapped in rags, covered in Band-Aids, their cheeks bleeding. The little kittens are quite ferocious, they also tend to get lost in other people's groceries. If you're not careful you'll end with a kitten in your grocery bag, a kitten in your car trunk, sometimes in your purse, if you're not careful that is. There must be hundreds of white kittens running around the shore, hundreds of feral cats living by their wits, stealing into purses, cars, or shopping carts without warning. The Ugly Mother thinks this is funny, the children bleeding from their fingers and cheeks, the mothers running terrified through the aisle at the sight of a fur ball of a kitten. Most people haven't noticed that it's the Ugly Mother who brings on this phenomenon. The few who have point and blame and shriek as if they have seen the devil.

Oysterhaus had become smaller and smaller each passing decade until all that existed was the PO, a branch of the local bank – Farmers, Seamen & Merchants – and Sea Hags Clam Fritters, a small fish fry next to the dinky, splintered dock blasted gray from sun, sea, and wind. At one time, by the dock, there had been an oyster shucking house where watermen had hauled in clams, and oysters via nets and baskets, and shuckers had shucked open the mussels with the broad base of a thumb and their oyster knife. During those days – the oyster days – Oysterhaus had been rich, very rich. Refrigerated cars had taken local catches as far north as Boston. A general store had once graced the main drag, and in the summer, there were farmer's markets and ice cream stands. Traveling stage shows arrived by boat, pitched a stage by the wharf before pulling up anchor and going to another town. First, the oyster market bottomed out, then the railroad dried up, and now the town barely moved under the sun. Only a handful of watermen remained to work the waters, most of the local traffic consisted of sport-fisherman and the occasional hobby-clammer. Mulch Hayes had shut the shucking house down in the '70s and tore it down a decade later, leaving only a tower of shells fifteen feet high and thirty feet in diameter, a monument of sorts, bone white. From a distance, the puckered calcium appeared to be human bones. From a distance, the puckered mound could have been anything.

Like other local money, Hayes had invested in a newer port, south of Osyterhaus, closer to the tourists who shuttled across the bay bridge for a little local color. Through the newer port, Mulch Hayes operated his smuggling business, using commercial fishermen to bring in the goods. But Mulch didn't go down there much. These days Mulch sticks close to home, close to his daughters, for whom he has plans.

Of the twenty-two homes in Oysterhaus, only twelve remained occupied. Once the shucking houses shut down, the town started to dry up. Today some of the folks live beyond the town's incorporated limits, on the back roads and along the creek, but they still get their mail-in town. Sea Hag's place is out on the marsh, an old oyster cabin grandfathered and protected. She came ashore in a small skiff to operate the fritter and fry house, each morning through the marsh channels and each night back out again. Her sputtering little two-cylinder engine sounded like her bad cough, and in the winter, it became hard to tell which was which. Just outside the town's limits were the Hayes' Feed and Shore Supply Store, a dumpy building slanting to one side attached to a boxy compound of outbuildings, sheds, and supply depots that served the few farms that Mulch didn't own. In it, Hayes sold seed, feed, farming supplies, and some hardware. Behind the store was a large bay loading dock and packing & storage area. Inside the feed store was a little office with a bigger office in the storage building. The old-timers and retired farmers met each day at the store to drink the free coffee and complain about the latest government fuckery and generally be grumpy old men while their wives were off somewhere being productive and generally satisfied old blue heads. As it so happened, Mulch Hayes owned eighty percent of the land in and around Oysterhaus, a lot of it shoreline jagging and zipping along the Atlantic. All the while the marsh grass sang and the wind blew all out its memories.

The old Hayes home was tucked at the end of a neck among tall white pines that kept the house in shade and shrouded from scrutiny. It was one of those old country farmhouses that were two medium-size houses, and two small houses built onto one another over time; the tourist guides called them telescopic houses. Telescopic because the oldest section of the house is the largest, usually on one end, or in the middle and the newer sections are small sections expanding from the main house out like a telescope. The first part of the home had been built in the early 1700s by one of Mulch's ancestors, who had for a time, built hidden crawlspaces and hallways to hide all the bootleg rum and sugar. Just two hundred yards away, down a sloping hill of sorts, lay a saltwater creek that emptied into the Atlantic. The creek could even be accessed through the basement by a deep underground channel, which was originally dug for bringing rum and sugar into the house to hide. Over the years more additions were made to the house, and now there were more rooms than people and Mulch liked the privacy the old house gave his family, or so he said. But most of all he needed his own space to rot and stew, his brain squirming like mud under a man's boots in boiling rain.

4

Adam Taylor worried that he was going to be late, and he couldn't be late. He'd had this itching feeling that Mulch was pissed at him. It was the way Mulch looked at Adam, like he was meat, hell, like he was Virginia, and that bothered him. He liked being the predator, the one on top.

He wasn't fucking Virginia because she was a good fuck, or not just because of that anyway. He'd known ever since he was a kid that Mulch was the one who made things happen around Oysterhaus.

It had begun innocently enough. Adam had approached Mulch in his feed store, thinking it was the best way to a) get his attention and b) show that he was serious. Sometimes Adam thought they were the same things, getting his attention and showing he was serious. Billy Squared Rickenhouse was the one who suggested that Adam swagger up to the feed store counter and demand to see Mulch. When Mulch showed up he was to be polite and then in private beg for a job. Adam didn't think it was such a good idea. For one thing, he didn't think he'd have enough balls to do it, the begging at least. And the other was that it wasn't much of a plan.

"Look, Tom Nunn told me that the best way to get Mulch's attention is to demand it. He won't look at you otherwise. When you see him, then you can get all polite and kiss-ass. But before then act like you're mad and crazy as hell and maybe, just maybe they might let you see him." Billy Squared's head was actually shaped like a square, a fact Adam always thought about when he hung with Rickenhouse.

"Whoa. Who's they?" Adam hadn't liked the sound of 'they.' *They could mean muscle, like that big native American fellow,* Adam thought.

"Well, they *is* Mr. Bill, of course. The old heads call him Indian Bill on account there was more than one Bill on Mulch's payroll back in the day. We call him Mr. Bill. And I'd watch out for him. But sometimes Huck and Buck Winston are up there, and you want to watch out for them too. They will fuck your eyeballs and finger your ears."

"Great." Adam sighed.

"Not to mention half the farmhands up at the trucking docks would probably bash your head in just to get a nod from Mulch."

"This plan of yours is sounding better by the minute."

Fortunately, he hadn't had to do any such thing. He'd met Virginia Hayes at a party the very night she returned home from college. They hit it off from the beginning, but not as lovers, as friends. Initially, Adam had been interested in Macy, Virginia's friend. Virginia had seemed out of his league. That night as Virginia was leaving the party, she'd promised to set up a meeting with Mulch. He'd heard all sorts of things about Virginia. How she was crazy like her old man. How she was a druggie and like to sleep around. How she'd gone and gotten herself stuck-up at that school in Boston. That she was no better than the snobby trash living up high on Bay Bluff Heights while everyone else squatted on land they didn't own in their trailers or the old homes or worse. Adam wanted respect and power and a nice house. And of all the people around, he thought Mulch was the one who could give him the keys to that kingdom.

When he finally met Mulch, he was surprised at his silence. The old man didn't speak, he scowled and jerked his head towards the back and turned on his heels quietly. His boots echoing in the suddenly silent feed store. Mulch didn't speak till he sat down at his desk and put his heels up, his blue denim shirt made his eyes sparkle. "Speak boy. What can I do for you?"

And like that, doors opened.

His first assignment was to deliver drugs to a Virginia Beach associate and return with the money. That first assignment had been easy because it turned out that he'd already met the associate at one of Billy Squared's parties, and better yet, they'd gotten along. Soon he was running drugs and money all over the shore and as far inland as Williamsburg.

Then Mulch had asked him to take his daughter out. To set up a hidden camera and fuck her hard and record it and to send the files to him. Adam knew better to fuck around with the boss' daughter, and the suggestion felt like more of a test than a request. But when he saw that Mulch wasn't kidding and that Mulch had planned out the first date, well then hell he thought; *who didn't want to get paid for fucking?*

That had been well over a year ago and Mulch had given him bigger and bigger jobs. Still, Adam hadn't killed anyone yet, nor had he run the gauntlet, nor had he handled a deal on his own, but that was to come. *Yes, sir,* he was sure of it. *Soon, he and Mr. Bill will bring me out to the field and let me run their stupid gauntlet and I'll be a made man. I'll be running the skiffs and working the boats out of the southern harbor.* Thus far there had been only one screw-up. Well maybe a tiny second one, but he didn't think Mulch knew about that one. *Mulch couldn't know everything,* not even with Mr. Bill on the payroll. See, Adam had been coked up at one of Billy Squared's parties, where he and Billy had been doing lines and bingers all afternoon, and Billy was in one of his moods when he liked to strip to his waist and get crazy – run around jumping on top of the furniture and calling his son's high school girlfriends over for a whirl on the old dick stick. Billy had called everyone in his little black book because, goddamn it, he hadn't thrown a party in almost two weeks. Then Adam had called everyone in his little black book too and soon enough there was a full-blown, five-alarm party raging in Billy's shitty double wide. It had spilled into the backyard and the road and though Adam wasn't drinking too much he sure was talking a blue streak about his special assignment video-recording him and Virginia doing the horizontal mambo. He didn't remember how he started to talk about it, or how many people he'd told. He knew it couldn't have been many. A few at most. And maybe one of those people had been Buck Winston, he couldn't be sure of that because after a certain point everyone had that streaked *oh-my-god-I'm-fucked-up* blur to their faces that made them look like they were being seen through a filthy windshield.

And if that hadn't been bad enough, he'd run his mouth again the very next night. This time at the Lazy Titty. But he didn't think Mulch knew about that one, either. He hoped to God he didn't because if he did, he was probably as good as dead. *I better keep my eyes peeled for a blade or maybe a gun.*

5

"It'll take just a minute!" George yelled over his shoulder as he stepped into his house. The kitchen air was a mix of stale smoke and paint thinner, and he winced at the foul odor. Outside, he saw Nick staring at the window. All the way over Nick had been babbling about his painting. *The 'painting' if you could even call it that.* George himself had talked about experiencing something like a trance while painting, but that had been when had been awake, but it was more like being in the zone, like when he was a kid at the little league park. Nothing like what Nick had described.

In the bathroom, at the top of the stairs, George found his deodorant and lifted his shirt to apply a thick white layer. He hated to worry about his appearance, but he did not want to stink while they painted Mrs. Enfield's house. Mrs. Enfield, legally blind, could smell a chicken farting upwind from three hundred paces, according to Huck down at the feed store. George worried about the sharp way his sweat peeled off him, like paint thinner. *Why can't I just be normal?* George thought. Mrs. Enfield's solid word-of-mouth praise could bring him plenty of work. "Keep it together," George, he said to his reflection, "Nick, don't talk about it all day." *Especially not today,* as Mrs. Enfield, herself a notorious gossip, would happily trash talk anyone. George was the fifth painter in a long line of workers involved with the upkeep of the Enfield home which was to be bequeathed to Mrs. Raquel Tyson, Mrs. Enfield's daughter, when the "old blind bitch," kicked the proverbial bucket, again according to Huck down at the feed store. Enfield was as good a meal ticket as you could find.

6

Along a narrow dusty road leading to a thick band of woods that thins onto the shoreline and opens out onto a weedy beach where the Indian caves lay, Mulch's pickup truck idled near a clump of honeysuckle bushes. Flies and mosquitoes moved back and forth in waves. Heat shimmered off the dirt road and the sun clocked in over the scrub pines. Mulch stared off into the small field of tomatoes that had grown considerably despite the intense heat and lack of rain. Sitting there, he smoked his cowboy killers like he was angry at them, and when he killed someone he always felt the urge to smoke and then drink, in that order.

For Mulch, killing Taylor was business. But killing Taylor was also personal. He'd miss the videos, but he had the recordings. Thinking the whole thing through, he bit the end of his left pinkie.

Farther down the dirt access road, Mulch saw Taylor's truck rumble and bounce its way over the pits and guts in the road. Mulch watched as the tires kick up spirals of dust behind them. *Taylor always drove too fast,* Mulch thought, *Taylor did everything too quickly. Which was the real reason I'm killing this prick, right? Because he moved too fast. Way too fast motherfucker.* Huck had told Mulch that Taylor wanted to run the gauntlet, to which Mulch snorted, *like hell.* Taylor had one real job. fuck his daughter and deliver recordings to him every week. Plus, there was all the talk about "the scandal."

At least, that's how Mr. Bill busted Mulch's balls, "the scandal." In truth, it was only a stupid, drunken indiscretion, something mentioned after way too many beers at Billy Squared's party, something that could have been forgotten and forgiven, written off as young man's folly. *You're lucky Billy Squared is your bitch,* Mulch thought. *If Taylor had told anyone but Squared, there would have been immediate repercussions; gossip would have spread.* But Taylor screwed up more than just the once, he screwed it up the next night, at the Lazy Titty. This time he wasn't drunk and from what Mulch had heard, he'd gone into way more detail. He'd named Mulch's name, which was the real reason Taylor was getting axed now, a week and a half after the fact. The bartender, an honest to god witch, Lark Mariner, had called Mr. Bill with the info. "This fool's down here at the bar, the backroom bar, and he's talking shit about Mulch and his daughter." Luckily, Lark curtailed Taylor's movement by buying him rounds, at Mr. Bill's expense.

Taylor slowed his truck and pulled up next to Mulch. Sweat rolled down from Taylor's blonde hair. A mosquito landed on his forehead, and he swatted it back. Taylor, according to Mulch's youngest daughter, was a sweater, as in he sweated through shirts, through ball caps, and his pants even. Virginia had said something to Mulch about how Adam had to bring two dress shirts with him when they went out because one would be dripping after dinner. *Well, he wouldn't need them any-more where he was going,* Mulch thought.

"Hey, boss," Adam said.

Mulch nodded but kept silent. He wanted to see how much Taylor would run off at the mouth before he bought it.

Looking him over, as if for the first time, Mulch saw that Taylor was a big handsome lug, built like a football player, Taylor was everything Mulch wanted in a son-in-law save for Taylor's stupidity and his public duplicitous nature. Taylor should have played the suitor if he had been a smarter, and more honorable, and more sinister criminal. He could have set Virginia against her old man. *That would have been something, Taylor. But no, you had to be a dumb ass,* he thought.

"So I've got the latest batch for you. And man, let me tell you, VA has got the best ass I've had the pleasure of tapping. That's saying something, Mulch, let me tell you. Because when I was in high school, I was the *MAN*, and I was offered asses a-plenty. VA is it."

Mulch hated the way Adam insisted on calling his daughter VA when she wasn't around. He nodded, keeping his sun wrinkled face calm. To keep cool,

Mulch thought of ice and imagined snow. *The best magics are the simplest magics,* Mr. Bill liked to say. Mulch smiled and manifested an iceberg in his mind. For such a hot day, Mulch felt downright cool in his blue jeans and short-sleeved white button-down. Then the two men got out of their vehicles and just looked at each other.

Adam Taylor knew it too; Mulch would later recall to Mr. Bill. That moment when Adam stopped yammering and his voice dissipated and there was only silence between them. No wind. No insects. Nothing but sun and heat and Mulch staring him down. A moment of unease passed between them as Taylor reached for Mulch's hand, to hand him the memory drives and Mulch remained stony and cold, and when Mulch finally spoke, he was all animated and slapped Taylor on the shoulder and looked into his eyes with what Taylor thought of as kindness and almost familial love but what was Mulch's cold selfish neutrality.

"I'm sure you've done a good job, no doubt about it."

"You should see how she gets this time. Lots of screaming, just like you wanted. I got all the files cleaned and edited from the last two weeks, just ready for you."

"I'm sure."

Taylor felt Mulch's cool fingers as the handshake continued. He thought Mulch was about to give him some encouraging words and a nice fatherly pat on the neck, so he didn't have time to react when Mulch slammed his other hand against his skull, right above the ear, which echoed and popped and Adam brought his hands up to his head to protect himself, and Mulch reached over and broke his neck. Taylor fell to the ground with a soft thump. Normally Mulch would have had Mr. Bill handle work like this, or maybe Huck or Buck Winston, at least the clean-up, but Mulch had to see this one through himself. Mr. Bill was busy with Marcos and Sea Hag and Huck and Buck were indisposed. Besides, he didn't want them too involved, anyway. They were all getting old and less able to handle a situation like this if it went wrong. But Mulch had handled Taylor just fine. *Just fine indeed.*

The tomato plants at the far edge of the camp fields, where the migrant workers were free to cultivate, were already as high as his thigh, much too early for June, and big green spheres had begun to appear on the plants, some as large as his palm. It took him two hours to dig far enough down to drop Taylor's body in. He planted him between the rows of tomatoes, the earth soft, the digging easy. Still, he'd worked up a sweat and felt the crawl of sunburn over the back of his neck and arms. He had sweated through his shirt and his pants, but he wasn't tired, he couldn't afford to be. He dumped Adam's body and covered it up. In the woods behind him, he heard the caw of a crow. The sun blanched the high marsh just off the road. The mosquitoes and bugs thickened, buzzing up to where he was digging the grave. At least it wasn't the fog, or the crows, or the horned shaggy stags, and only the insects, – the horseflies, deerflies, noseeums, mosquitoes, and chiggers- hundreds of bugs that fed on people's blood and misery. They were nothing more than scavengers awakened by the scent of blood in the air, moving with a breaking crawl out of the thicket.

Come get your meal, you bastards. Mulch chuckled. *Come and get your blood.*

7

Nick drummed his fingers along the edge of the steering wheel and thought about the painting and how he'd come to paint it. He made a mental checklist of things that might have sparked his midnight painting madness – stress, lack of sex, alcohol abuse, insanity, or X-the unknown. Stress seemed unlikely, he had a few bills and had steady enough work through George to pay them. He wasn't the king of the hill, but he wasn't a pauper. Besides he had the little house his parents had left him. It was not much, but it was something to start with.

So, sex then? He hadn't dated in almost a year, since Olivia left him for the trucker with his new rig and a fancy new double-wide on the water. He heard she was pregnant, and by all accounts happy.

Hmm, maybe, Nick thought. Was that what was bothering him? *She's happy without me!*

They had been together for over two years and lived in his two-story salt-box. At first, things had been great. She had kept flowers in the back and even grown some tomatoes. Her father, the old hippie, supplied them with his home-made wine and homegrown dope. Olivia had worked as a waitress to keep her share of the bills paid. They didn't have satellite TV but they never needed it. They had each other and the occasional paperback thriller thrown in to boot. So what if they hadn't had a new car or the newest smartphones. They hadn't needed them. Most of all, they'd been happy, too. At least until the roof started to go soft and tar paper shingles peeled back like scabs, falling to the ground in every heavy gust of wind. That's when Nick remembers Olivia getting rest-less. *About the same time as the roof.* He had known something was wrong when instead of hunkering down in front of the stereo for a joint, a beer, and a game of cards, she'd pace their one downstairs room like a caged tiger, hissing at him every time he asked what was wrong, bitching about the leak in the attic. She had said it was nerves.

Then Olivia cheated on him. At least she'd been honest about it. It had happened one October evening, Ironically Nick had been too tired from finishing up patching the roof, and he had refused to go to the party with her. She had told him that if he didn't go with her, she might end up going home with someone else instead. Scrubbing his hands Nick had laughed, course he couldn't believe his little sweetie would do something like that. But then, as it turns out, she did. George later told him he should have kept his eyes open, telling him:

"Buddy, I know you don't want to know, but she's a terrible flirt."

"What does that mean? What makes that so bad?"

"Because she wants to act on it, the flirting. You can tell. She's a desperate flirt. Attention, attention, attention."

"She isn't."

"She is."

"She was probably drunk. Lay off it George. I don't want to talk about it anymore."

And because George is a good guy, he didn't.

So if it's not sex or stress, I must be going insane, he thought. He didn't want to let himself think about the unknown. *Just like dear old dad, right? But adopted sons cannot inherit madness, can they?*

His father had been going a little soft in the skull before the accident. He'd spend his mornings tracking the fog, which he claimed was the ghosts of a great herd of deer, a local legend. A legend that they told to campers from across the bay when they came to Camp Occahoneck in the summer. "Watch out for the fog," they'd say in hushed tones. "It hides the great stag that hunts men and beasts," and so on. His father, a Baptist minister, had believed firmly in spirits. Tracking the fog, he'd haunt local cemeteries and farms in the early hours, hoping for a glimpse of the herd. His mother never understood, but it turned out she was taking Valium and Percocets like candy, so what did she know. After the accident, Nick had found a shoe box full of pills under her dresser. He'd spent the next two weeks following the winding roads to their funerals in a chemical haze. He's first met Olivia in that haze. It had been Olivia who finally got him to shake his mother's pills.

Insanity is heredity, isn't it? How is my inheritance anything but?

When his father had been at the height of his obsession with the herd, rising at three in the morning to chase fog and record his adventures Nick had been doing his own kind of joyriding. He'd been playing Irish. His father, Randall "Randy" Adams, had become interested in the ghost herd the same summer that Nick had converted to Catholicism.

Nick had surprised his old man by exclaiming that he wanted to convert to Catholicism to explore his Irishness. Nick had found out that previous Christmas that his birth father and mother were from Ireland, and over the winter his desire and curiosity about Ireland had simmered to a boil. At school, he'd spent all of his free time in the library looking up facts about Ireland. Up to then everything he knew about Ireland fit on the head of a U2 album. He knew that he needed to know more. It had all exploded shortly before supper when he had announced that he was converting to Catholicism.

"What?" Randy's face had immediately gone into defensive overdrive. He'd made a series of bizarre facial expressions that ranged in expression from anger, sorrow, to remorse.

"Catholicism. You know, I want to become Catholic, to explore my roots, or something like that." Nick remembered trying to remain cool. In truth, he was just really interested in the idea of doing something to acknowledge his birth mystery. He wasn't doing it for spiritual rewards, or the lifestyle, but rather to find common ground with his blood parents. If you were to have asked Nick back then, he would have told you that he was serious about it all, the religion, the Irish lifestyle, and the common ground with his real parents. Later he had learned there was a language he could learn, a dying one, and one that was a bitch to master, but by then his interest in his Irishness had become limited to his regular consumption of Guinness.

When he had announced his intention to join the Catholic fold, Randy's tongue refused to move for about twenty seconds. Nick then remembered the later silence to be more pronounced, more dramatic. Underneath the silence, Nick had heard an ominous humming. He had felt it too, in his teeth, a soothing hum under everything, like the whole house was resonating with his statement of fact.

"You most certainly will not, young man."

"But I..." Nick felt like most of the time he was saying "But I..." to his mother or father.

"Really, it's not a good idea."

"Then I'm just going to do it."

"You know you've acted this way before, and it's only gotten you in trouble."

"I'm joining a church, not a gang." Nick had done his best to be positive.

"The Catholics are kind of like a gang, son. You have to admit it. A gang not unlike the one you already belong to, our church son, the one where I deliver a sermon every Sunday morning, the church where you grew up and the church where you still go. We're a gang. Your gang."

The argument continued, and lead to more fighting over dinner. A dinner which Ginger Adams had described to her mother, Nick's adopted grandmother, as a "meal that ate like a marathon," because afterward her jaw, and back and hands had ached from the stress she had held inside of her, and which had made simple things like handling silverware during washing the dishes, laborious and painful. There had been no resolution.

"How would it look if he left his father's church?"

"What would people say?"

"They'd say something's wrong in the preacher's house, that's what they say."

Randy knew it. Ginger knew it. Nick even knew it. But then there was Nick's newly discovered heritage. *What could be done about that?*

That night, so long ago, as Nick had prepared for bed, his father had left the house to investigate all the talk of the ghost herd which some people had said had just been seen in the Fall Creek Baptist Church's cemetery. When he returned he promised Nick that he'd give the whole Catholic issue serious consideration. But first and foremost, he announced, there was the more pressing issue of the fog.

"There's something there, Nick," he had pleaded with his son, "Something truly supernatural. Not from God, or of God."

And like that I'm written off as an accessory to my father's occupation, Nick had thought at the time.

Since then, it was always the fog with his father. His mother would sit dumbly and listen as he described how thick the fog had been that day, and how that thickness must have held the ghost herd hidden inside. How he heard them, the ghost herd, moving through the undergrowth, their breath the very fog itself.

Mind you Randy Adams never actually saw the ghost herd, only the thick fog, which may or may not have been "the fog". One night he claimed to have glimpsed figures moving in the dense soup – figures that had defied natural laws. He'd even claimed that he had floated above the ground for a few seconds while in the fog, as if he were walking on toes that behaved like snakes, or serpents, carrying his body above the ground. He'd tell Nick stories about feeling his mind give way to another intelligence as if the fog was alive, coiled with tentacles and menace.

Sweat had begun to run from under Nick's cap. He wished George would hurry up. He nervously tapped his fingers along the edge of the truck's steering wheel. The memory of his father faded away. That was the last time he'd remember anything about both his parents, for a while, other than a dull haze.

The first wave of nausea hit him when he turned the radio on, hoping to catch the tide report or weather. Nausea started in the pit of his stomach and bubbled up his esophagus. He barely had time to open the door. But what came out wasn't vomit. He knew the taste of his bile well, but what he tasted this time was fish and the stink of the creek. Which was impossible because he hadn't swum in the back creek since the previous summer.

Whatever it was, it was a ghost of a smell and had the taste of raw fish. Nick didn't know how he knew the fish was raw, only that he did. Again his stomach buckled and again nothing came out but green bile, bile reeking of back creek water and fish.

8

Ignoring the bumps and washboard bounces, Mulch kept the odometer at a steady sixty-five, making his way off the dirt road and onto the black-top winding around the back of one of his many fields. Off in the distance, the migrant workers bent like half-moons in the dust. On the seat next to him was Taylor's phone. He checked his watch; he would be two minutes early. He massaged his penis; he had a feeling he wouldn't get through half of the files before Virginia would go. Marina was on her way out tonight. Virginia would not be far behind because *Virginia always had a way of sniffing things out.* He thought, *she could be very dangerous even though she couldn't lift her luggage, let alone tear a man apart.* She wasn't like her half-sister at all. Pembroke believed that Virginia could be tamed and turned so she could take over the family business, allow Mulch to open operations west of the shore, possibly even in Europe, depending on how Virginia took to it. Mulch didn't think she needed too much prodding, *not his little love bumpkin.* Pembroke wanted to breed her, but Mr. Bill didn't like the idea and had offered no council. Not that Mulch would have listened, Mulch wanted to play this out on his terms and see what happened after he stirred this hornet's nest.

Mulch kept his eyes on the phone on the seat next to his. He couldn't wait to see what was on it. Whatever it was that Taylor had videoed, it was occupying a corner of his brain and was sure to interfere with the rest of his thinking for the afternoon. That is unless he could get home, just for a quick peek.

9

When George stepped out the back door, the driver's side of his truck swung open and Nick fell out and doubled over, the sound of his retching like that of gravel being kicked. The sound almost made George feel green, but he held it back. *Damn, that doesn't sound good. At all.* At least, he thought, he was spared the smell.

"You okay." He didn't think Nick looked at all OK.

"'s'allright." Nick wiped his mouth. "Just dry retches."

"Maybe you should take it easy on the sauce."

Nick nodded. "Nah, it's just the heat, I think."

"Yeah. That'll do it to ya."

"You know what, George?"

"What's that?"

When George helped Nick to his feet, Nick's hands were cold as if he'd just come back from swimming. George wiped his hands on his jeans.

"A second ago. I thought I tasted like sea water – the barfing." Nick shook his head, almost in an awe-shucks kinda way. "Isn't that strange?"

"Come on we're late." George bit his lip and prayed Nick would hold out the afternoon.

As George drove to Mrs. Enfield Nick's stomach leveled out and he started to feel better. On the drive, George let Nick be, he didn't want to be thinking about Nick, anyway, and Nick didn't want to do any of the talking. Nick felt a tingling in his neck. He associated it with the rush of blood to his head when he was dry heaving. But when the tingling spread slowly to the base of his skull, he felt like he was thinking underwater, as if his skull was submerged. It felt muffled and amplified like when one sinks their head under a pool and listens to the kicking of feet and splashing hands above. The tingling nerves felt like the hard nails of a pretty girl scratching down your neck on a hot night, giving you the chills.

Then suddenly, the uneasy feelings vanished as quickly as they had come, and when it left him Nick Adams promptly forgot whole chunks of his life. He didn't realize it at the time, or what was happening when it happened. He was just sitting in George's truck as the world sped by, staring out the window at two pretty girls sunbathing by their above-ground pool, drinks in hand, their chins angled upward at just the right degree to catch the last of the day's glorious sun.

10

Mrs. Enfield wanted two of her spare bedrooms painted. She had three, she'd told George over the phone, and a fourth bedroom in the old servant's wing, she had added with a snarl. George had said No problem, and depending on the size of the rooms, they'd probably be finished in a day or two. Mrs. Enfield had said, "That's fine," and "Why not come by tomorrow," while she and her daughter lunched at the Turner's, "of Turner Chicken," she added, again snarling.

Mrs. Enfield kept a fine house, circa 1840, complete with an out kitchen which her late husband had modernized and built a wing onto. They were not to touch anything in the house, she had told George. The two upstairs rooms were to be painted white. She would only pay for the cheapest kind of paint.

"So what's up?" George wiped his brow and looked up the ladder as Nick listlessly rolled paint across the ceiling. The strokes were half-assed as if Nick wasn't putting any muscle behind it.

"I'm just too tired from that damn painting all night. Maybe" Nick said.

The paint seemed kind of off-color from the rest of the wall, but George assumed it was the sunlight. *It's always the changing sunlight,* he would tell the clients.

"Hey?" George called to Nick again and Nick turned, his face dazed and pale. *You are one hungover dude,* George thought.

"What's that?"

"I said what's up? How's it going? How's it hanging?"

"Fine," he said and with a sharp twist of his neck, he returned his gaze to the ceiling.

George could tell that Nick was thinking about the midnight painting session in his house. *Like who wouldn't be?* "Hey man, if you don't want to talk about it, fine, but I'm here for you man, just let me know," he said.

Sighing, Nick dropped his arms, sending a few dozen paint beads from roller to drop cloth beneath. He descended the ladder, gently looking George in the eyes. "I can't get it out of my mind, I mean it's like I was there, but I wasn't, and I remember it, but I don't remember it. You know? Like just right now I felt something in my hand, as I was doing the trim?"

"Like what?"

"Like déjà-vu, but it was in my hand. It was weird. A physical déjà-vu, like déjà-feel, if there's even such a thing." Nick didn't like to think too hard about anything, it made his head hurt. "You don't suppose I'm dying or something?"

"That won't happen for at least a week." George laughed. "You gotta build up to that."

"Thanks, funny," Nick laughed, "So what do you think?"

"What am I? An expert on paint-related unidentified psychotic phenomena?" George scratched his head and sniffed the air around his underarm. "Just relax. I would only worry if it happens again.

"Look, once my cousin got up in the middle of the night and fixed an entire three-course meal, ham, eggs, biscuits. In the morning he woke up on the couch in the living room. Said he had a dream about cooking. He then ate a hearty breakfast, his second in as many hours, and forgot about it. It's probably just a little sleep walking is all. Stress at the office and all that shit. So he slept walk, you sleep paint. Big deal."

"I've never slept-walked before."

"Well, one sure-fire cure for that is plenty of drinks after we quit." George, said as he provocatively raised his eyebrows.

"That sounds good." Nick seemed relieved at the idea and resumed rolling the paint out, and as George looked up at him, he saw that Nick's jaw was still clenched, and he was grinding his teeth, to which George thought, *Yeah, I'd grind my teeth too.*

Nick had always been a little strange. As a young teenager, Nick had been prone to nightmares. Once while spending the night at George's, Nick had woken up the whole house. He had shouted *The Gilligan's Island* theme over and over, in his sleep. And then there was that one time with the tooth dreams. Nick had told George about weeks' worth of dreams involving dental pain and psychic frustration, about how Nick had traveled up the road to the dentist each week just to be assured that his teeth weren't falling out. George hated to hear those dream descriptions, about how Nick would awaken in the middle of the night sure that one of his molars hung by a bloody nerve, jabbing his fingers into the back of his mouth to find it. Then there were the times that Nick told George about the dreams where he would be falling face-first into the curb of some street. In those times Nick would dream about swallowing half his mouth, and Nick would scream out of sleep, his voice ripping him out of the psychic nightmare that emptied his pores, drenching Nick in thick night-sweats. He always swore to George that he felt the bloody pulp of a nerve in his gaping mouth with the tip of his tongue just before tearing away from the dream and back into his sheets. *So yeah, this night painting stuff was nothing new,* George thought.

CHAPTER TWO

1

By many, the Shore is considered a quaint little strip of land, a peninsula, surrounded on one side by the Atlantic, and on the other by the Chesapeake Bay. Lying as low in the water as it does, some fishermen like to say that it's flatter than a pancake, and it is too, for the most part, save a few hills in the earth, mostly caused by flooding. There's not a lot of beaches either, mostly just coastline, or marsh. What little beach there is private with *OFF LIMITS* signed everywhere and even that isn't very big. This is why so much of the coastline is up for sale and the Eastern Shore so undeveloped and primitive, as far as East Coast waterfront property is concerned. The truth is that the shore is mostly for sport fishing and hunting. Birdwatchers come in the fall to get wet and to get their rocks off on any unusual migratory sightings, plus the rare bald eagle and the thousands of blue herons who dip, pivot, and pluck fish right out of the shallows. Plenty of owls, and seagulls, there are seagulls everywhere.

Only a handful of people live on the Virginia side, relatively speaking. Maryland's got a bit more, and Delaware is pretty heavily populated in comparison to the lower Virginia end. More students are attending Virginia Polytechnic Institute than there are in both counties of the Va. Eastern Shore, combined. The people there like it that way, it suits them just fine.

You would be hard-pressed to find a better place for seafood, and fresh produce though. The watermen who keep up the old traditions have passed down their most evil recipes; oysters wrapped in bacon, double-dipped flounder, pastry-fried shrimp, clam chowder like you've never tasted. The produce grows up rich and fat all summer.

The shore is an old place. It is old, in terms of settlements, court records, and history. With the most complete records in all of the states, it's just a hop-skip and a jump to Jamestown. But it is also old, old as in dying. So much so that most of the real shore is dead, or well on its way. Most of the new life springs up by the highways, the Hardees, McDonalds, and Shore Stops. Away from those businesses, the small communities struggle to keep their store front windows from being busted, not to mention open. If you ask the kids, they hate the place. They'll tell you that nothing new ever happens, and the kids are all about new, even when it comes to the shore. The churches are the needle in which all of the local traditions are threaded. Most of the longtime native colloquialisms have been phased out by the baby boomers. Not many of them choose to work the land, or the water the way they used to in the old days.

But in the back fields, and along the backroads, the traditions are still being passed along. It runs like kudzu all over the back legs of the counties, where it thrives in the fields, on the sunburned necks of the farmers. The African American churches are as inspired as they ever were, and in some circles still hold some of their old magic which is still practiced in hushed tones and passed down from preacher to child. In the migrant communities, that magic, from various traditions is alive and well, and practiced daily, right under the white farmer's noses. Around every bend, there are small but vibrant communities of Meso-American pagans and Santeria groups, voodoo doctors, and witches of every variety. Most of them herbalists really, who on occasion toss the bones to tell a mother what kind of kid she's gonna have. Sometimes there's a little black magic to put the hurt on a double-crosser, or a binding ritual to keep a wandering John and Jose faithful. Among these small communities' powerful practitioners of magic can be sought out to heal, or to kill. Most people wouldn't know it if they ran over one of these spellcasters, but there are tales about them if you listen. Listen closely and you'll hear legends about the old Native American Indians, giants, who could bend the sea water to their will, fog banks full of ghosts, stories about old African American men who could turn into crows, stories like that. Not to mention the Ugly Mother's magic, which most days took the form of old folk wisdom she'd share about camp unless she took to vomiting a vegetable or conjuring kittens, which she was known to do. Most of the people ignore the folklore and worry about their neighbor's business instead. It's like the bit about the fog and the great herd that hides inside it, or the story about the white cats that appear on farms across the county. There's plenty of ghost stories concerning Revolutionary war soldiers, wronged sailors, and rum-running pirates. Most of the people around here turn their heads away from that kind of nonsense, where their God, down here, is definitely white, very old, and hangs out in the clouds. Ghosts, on the other hand, haunt the tombstones and wrecks, preferring to keep their noses up to the sky.

2

Rick "the Dick" Bell laid out a fat line of cocaine on the Formica countertop. He licked his thumb and smiled as his gums went tingly and numb. Macy screwed herself up against him in the small trailer bathroom and smiled, her face all doughy and her eyes taking on that horny, lively look. As she watched him work, her eyes bounced between the line and the bulge growing in his pants.

"That looks like some good shit," Macy said.

Rick looked behind him through the curtained window. The sun was blasting through the sides and down the middle where the camel-colored material didn't meet. He guessed it was late afternoon.

"Man, this shit is real preemo, babe. Let me tell you. Get it from Mulch?"

Macy looked into Rick's reflection; their eyes met in the small mirror medicine cabinet screwed to the wall. Macy cocked her ear, thinking she heard the phone. Virginia was supposed to call in her an hour ago.

"Yup. I bet you get this stuff for free?" Macy grinned. She licked the bottom of her lip, "I'd fuck Virginia's daddy for a free trip around the world." Macy leaned over and inserted the glass straw in her nostril. She loved the feeling of the glass against the inside of her nose. It felt like security. The white crystals kicked her heart into party mode. "Baby I know you'll take me around the world with you."

"Was there ever a doubt in your mind?" Rick took the straw from his girl.

Macy reached over and began to massage Rick's crotch as he blew the back of his mind out with the loaded straw.

3

George liked to shop. He preferred to buy the weekly supplies for Nick and himself because there was a girl at the hardware store who really had him pulled. Her name was Lilly. She was of Mexican descent and George could flirt in Spanish just enough so that he hoped he'd stand out from the other guys who came in. George had it so bad for Lilly he would act out conversations with her in the cab of his truck. So when Nick popped the last can of Industrial White # 4 paint, George excused himself to get more, leaving Nick sweating in the upstairs spare room, alone, chewing on his teeth.

"Do you need anything buddy?" George jingled his truck keys and pulled on his sticky T-shirt.

"Nah." Nick turned and smiled, his teeth flashing dully in the sunny room.

"You sure?"

"Maybe a break."

"Why don't you eat lunch. I'll be back in an hour."

Mrs. Enfield had left with her daughter mid-morning, so she wouldn't be listening in, in case Nick had an episode or something, George thought. *That had to be worth a day's work.*

Nick nodded and kept on working.

Hammer 'n Nails was a twenty-minute ride up the road into the town of Lonely. This gave George time to rehearse how he was going to ask Lilly out. Lilly, younger than he by five years, was Oaxacan and her folks were farm migrants. She lived in a small apartment a few miles from the Hayes migrant camp. Other than the fact that she worked at Hammer 'n Nails, George knew little about her, he had only engaged in conversation with her a few times, things like "How are you doing this afternoon?" and "Do you have any 3/4" plywood today?" The fact that she was Oaxacan made his stomach twist with worry. *What if her pops only allowed her to date Hispanics? What if her mamma spoke no English? How would he communicate?* He knew this was an irrational fear. Fear kept him from doing so many things. How long had it taken him to start his own business? Years, because of fear. *Fear. Yes, she was an immigrant.* He thought, *yes, she came from a different culture. So what? Love is love. Right?* His fear flashed, faded. Like any fool in love, his mind was full of bright light. *Have faith in love,* George thought, and then without realizing it, he scoffed aloud. Lilly Aguirre was five foot four, give or take a little, depending on how high she wore her hair. Other times Lilly would wear her hair down and her curls lapped the side of her cheeks which had a shine only those with perfect skin knew. Her face would illuminate any room and glow behind the counter of Hammer 'n Nails, which drove George crazy, her glowing beauty. What George didn't know was that Lilly too mooned over him because he was cute and funny, because he never really knew what to do with his hands, always playing with the air as if he were going to pluck a rabbit out of nothingness. Lilly had a bit of the witch in her from her mother, which George didn't know about either, and like all witches, she seemed to attract both men and dogs who sensed their innate ability to care for and nurse the wild, the feral, and the broken.

As George crunched his breath-mints, he tried to decide if he should cut across one of the Hayes fields to get to the store faster. George wanted to fold the old road in half so that he could be at the Hammer 'n Nails in seconds, and not minutes, but the best he could hope for was that he push his truck past 55 over the washboard ruts ahead of him.

Meanwhile, outside the store, Lilly was feeding a dog who had been stalking the parking lot of the store for a week. It was a big old St. Bernard half-breed with attentive brown eyes that seemed to know all feeling. Some days ago, she had decided to call him Rufus. She thought it as good a name as any for a dog.

"Here you go Rufus," she said, stooping low.

Rufus sniffed at the Alpo goop that was mushed flat. Rufus nudged the bowl with his large head before sitting on his haunches and letting out a singular bark.

"Don't be picky, you're lucky to get any food," Lilly said as she pulled her bangs back out of her eyes. She laughed and threw her head back as Rufus gobbled up his food.

Rufus barked again and settled down onto his front paws, his head resting on the tops of his feet. He looked up at her with sad eyes, although Lilly wasn't buying it.

"Go ahead now and be a good dog." Rufus drooled into his bowl and barked, one paw raised as if to shake.

4

"Do you want them to stay?" Mr. Bill asked, gesturing to Marcos and Sea Hag, who packed their gear at the edge of the clearing. Mulch nodded no.

Mr. Bill smelled of his homegrown, which had a kind of rabbity scent to it, like hay. Mr. Bill looked less rabbity than his smell would tell. He was a large man, in a compact way that made Mulch think of a relaxed muscle as if Bill had not yet been flexed, and that at any moment he could become more imposing than he already was. Mr. Bill stood 5'11, but solid, with skin so weathered and cracked that he looked more like a relief map than a man. Now, he stooped, tired from giving the box the final test. He'd been using magic all day.

"How does it look?" Mulch asked locking eyes with Mr. Bill who looked especially rubbery at that moment.

"I wouldn't lie, boss."

"So it looks good?" Mulch turned his gaze out onto the field.

"I wouldn't lie." Mr. Bill pulled his long hair back into a ponytail. Mulch had been watching him do that since he was a kid and Mr. Bill had been what? 50 then? 60? The old man looked the same to him as when Mulch was a boy. He didn't appear to have aged a day. To Mulch, Mr. Bill was constant, loyal, and unchanging.

"Marcos and Sea Hag want to leave. I don't think their hearts can stand the wait any longer." Mr. Bill's voice always sounded somewhat robotic to Mulch, anytime Mr. Bill was involved in something serious he tended to become monotone. *He's all business,* Mulch thought, *the perfect weapon.*

"Where is it?"

"It's back in the woods a bit, on a trailer. We tested it this morning. These two," Mr. Bill gestured over to Sea Hag and Marcos, "are exhausted. I think they're getting sentimental."

"Jesus Christ, what a bunch of whiners," Mulch shrugged. "No getting sentimental!" he shouted, "Understood!"

Mr. Bill chuckled. Sea Hag shot a look to Marcos who rolled his eyes. Marcos carried his carving tools towards the battered old Ford Sea Hag drove, and from the distance, his hands looked like clawed, palsied things. Sea Hag's rags flowed about her, and she looked the same as always, wet and leathery like turtle's skin. Mulch drew a long swallow from his flask.

Marcos prodded his toe about in the dirt. His feet were muddy from the creek and his jeans were rolled up past his calves. Mulch spotted his tattoos, his markers, a brightly colored snake coiled thrice down around both calves. The head of the snakes rested over the bonny knob of his ankle.

"She'll never live through it." Sea Hag's voice was rough like sand and had a coughing hack to it. She waved her hands which were bony, and spidery, about her chest. "I don't know if *you'll* live through it either."

"Well, we'll just see about that now, won't we," Mulch said under his breath. "Now, both of you, get out of here." But nobody moved. The tension in the air was tinny. Mr. Bill felt it. Marcos felt it. Sea Hag and Mulch sure as shit felt it, but they kept on staring each other down like they were about to duel.

"You got no right." She spat and shuffled to her truck.

Marcos sighed and sucked in his lips. "I'll meet you tonight. To take her out," he said.

"Thank you, Marcos."

"No. Thank you, Mulch, for allowing me to help."

"It's no problem. No problem at all." Mulch's egg yellow teeth looked fierce behind his smile, which Marcos couldn't help but think was reptilian and not at all to be trusted.

5

Nick's fingers smelled of peanut butter and grape jelly. "God, I love peanut butter."

With his right index finger, he dragged a paint lid about an inch closer so that he could ash into it. *No sense messing the place up,* the thought. He lit the cigarette and took a sharp inhale.

Nick had been trying to remember what he had dreamed about last night. He remembered a figure floating at the corner of the painting. Perhaps it was a girl, perhaps a woman. As far as he knew there was no way to tell. She was white, almost alabaster, without any details, yet there was something unmistakably feminine about her. George had recognized the figure instantly, the wavy dark brush strokes at the top like a swath of thick hair down a back, and possibly thinner hair caught in a wind. *And then the dark cloud behind her, like a bird or something.* Nick saw it perfectly in his mind but couldn't imagine that he had painted it.

"Maybe someone else snuck into the house and painted it?" he had said to George.

"No way, you know it was you, the paint on your foot, the fact that your bedsheets were covered with paint. Forget it, it was you," George had said with a gruff guffaw.

"Forget it? How can I forget about it?"

"I meant the theory of the other man."

And Nick didn't have anything to counter George with on that point. Shortly after that, George had pulled Nick into the yard and then into the car to go painting, even though Nick hadn't felt much like doing any work.

With George in Lonely for a while here was his first chance to meditate on the fact that he couldn't remember anything about the day before either. He only remembered things from this morning on, which bothered him. The not remembering, even with things that he should so easily remember, like what his parents had looked like, what his high school commencement was like, his first day at college, all of which seemed like they were at the bottom of a very deep and dark well which he could get to. He knew it was there, but it was just way down in his head, far out of reach. And all the thinking was making Nick's head hurt. He felt like he had been partially erased.

It also occurred to Nick that he wasn't the least bit tired, and he tried to convince himself of that fact as he began to feel himself droop into sleep. *That girl, she must have been running away from something,* he thought. Nick's head grew light, and his eyes became fuzzy. He would remember later how he felt oddly awake and wired as he knocked off into deep sleep that afternoon as if he were preparing for a great, heroic feat.

6

Along the upper seams of the box, ornate symbols had been carved along the outside trim like lace, or latticework, and between the lace-like squares, curly-qs and triangles within triangles were carved between runes that Mulch did not understand. However, his cousin, Cilia, would have a field day with such a lavish script. *Mr. Bill didn't fuck around,* Mulch thought. Three different interpretations of magic had been threaded together to give the spells muscle. The box was hinged on the side, a door of sorts, that would be magically sealed once Marina had been placed inside. *Human traffickers would have a time penetrating the box,* he thought. *Good. She needs to be protected until she gets to Cilia. Would the spells protect Marina from Cilia?* Mulch wasn't sure. He looked over to Mr. Bill who seemed business as usual. *Something to consider,* he thought.

"Hey, Mr. Bill, do you ever think of Eb?"

"Eb?"

"Yeah Eb? I do. God. Sometimes when I think about him all the time and I start to get the feeling that he's watching me from somewhere, judging me, watching me act out a part in my play. He never did give two shits about me."

They often spoke like this. Mr. Bill acting as a kind of wall for Mulch to bounce conversation off of. Sometimes Mr. Bill would engage, but mostly he hung back on the conversation and let Mulch just talk, or mutter, as the case would be.

"About you?" Mr. Bill repeated.

"Jesus. I want to get this over with – this cleansing, this exfoliation, whatever the fuck it is."

"Exfoliation." Mr. Bill sighed. "You're just cutting everyone out of your life is all."

"Yeah, I've been calling it a cleansing, of sorts, an unraveling, giving myself a whole new skin to live in, so to speak."

"New skin?"

"You've been around the block several times. I know you know what I'm feeling."

Mr. Bill did not feel what Mulch was feeling. Mr. Bill had long ago reached some kind of plateau in terms of feeling. Mr. Bill was simply waiting to remember. He was the only remaining Native American from the nation that originally populated the Eastern Shore, the Nassawatucks, led into the woods by old Debedeavon, the Laughing King, whom the white man eventually corralled out of sight, and historically, out of mind. Mr. Bill reminded people that there was a secret history to the land, one whose history had been erased by those who had come after them. And Mr. Bill knew that this made many people uncomfortable, emotional leverage he leaned on.

"What you're feeling?" Mr. Bill repeated. "Men make their own mistakes. I've made plenty." Mr. Bill rapped his knuckles across the inside trim of the box. A mosquito buzzed Mr. Bill's ear and dipped into the shadow cast by the box's walls and its open mouth.

Mulch stared at the dark floor and then up at the ceiling. Sometime that night it would alight with the crushed hulls of lightning bugs. The bed, itself, a dark insectile thing, its spiny driftwood fingers cradling the mattress. *She's going to love it*, Mulch told himself. *She's going to be all right.*

"I can personally vouch for the bed." Mr. Bill commented. "It is like sleeping on the surface of the creek." Bill touched the left corner of the bed with his toe. The bed was the only fixture in the box.

"Good." Mulch pressed his hand on the mattress. Firm. He'd half expected it not to be real. So much didn't seem real anymore. Mulch touched the purple downy quilt, soft after years of being turned over by children's hands, by the rough bark of Maria's fingers as she folded the quilt back over Marina's bed each morning. Each spring when she put it in the attic Maria would remark how it felt softer than last year.

"This is one of Marina's favorite quilts," Mulch observed.

"You don't have to do this you know?" Mr. Bill had never once, ever, tried to talk Mulch out of what he planned to do, regarding his daughters, or the family business. "It'll destroy you."

"Yeah," Mulch sighed, standing up. "I know."

Outside the cicadas revved up and down and the heat shimmered across the field, the morning dew lay still in the cupped leaves of the maturing crop.

7

"Hey Lilly," George's smile felt like it was all angles on a rickety fence.

"Hey yourself," Lilly leaned over the counter as George smelled her perfume.

"Hay is for horses," George regretted saying it the minute it flew out of his mouth.

Lilly leaned even farther across the counter and gave George eyes that gave him goosebumps. *Lilly's feet must be dangling behind her*, George thought. *She must be floating.*

"Well, I like horses, Mr. George."

Oh boy, George thought.

"So tell me, what's up?" George said, his voice wavering.

"Not the temperature," Lilly's smile so bright that George thought he could power solar cells with it. "Buck turned on the AC and it's dropped below freezing. Bastard. That's why I have to wear these thick T-shirts, so I don't advertise," Lilly pulled on her T-shirt down below her collarbone which made George's heart beat a little faster. "Buck can be a real asshole."

George felt himself fumble.

"He likes to watch my nipples get hard," Lilly whispered and pulled her T-shirt tight so her nipples stood out. George blushed, stepped back, and turned around on his heels before re-planting himself, his blood heating his face, and in doing so he nearly knocked over the Gorilla Glue display behind him.

"Sorry, I'm a little slow, you know paint fumes can be a real doozy."

"I can tell." Lilly tugged again on her T-shirt, "The physical hazards of being a woman in bitterly cold air- conditioning. Who are you painting for this week? Mrs. Enfield?"

Lilly spread her legs out behind her, so she seemed to grow shorter behind the counter.

She remembered my job, that's a good sign, George nodded.

"Szo you've come for ze' paint szir," Lilly said in a mock German accent. George had heard her speak in a mock French accent on many occasions, but never a German one. Lilly seemed prone to silliness.

"Yes I must have it, or the army is finished." George had trouble making the German sounds come out. *Don't fuck it up, George.*

"It szounds like you needz szome help, no?" Lilly pushed her legs back together which made her rise above the counter, her thick black hair bounced a little.

"Yes, lots of help. The army is uh, um, well, bureaucratic?" George dropped his accent, he felt foolish, self-conscious. "I need 10 gallons of Industrial white # 4 or the army is finished!"

"An interesting choice for a house." Lilly dropped her accent and picked a piece of white lint off her shoulder. Lilly's hair was so black it ran blue in streaks like the feathers of a grackle or a purple martin.

"She's blind, legally, she wanted something white, but not too expensive." George felt suddenly mean, saying those words, the way he did.

"Okay then. I'll check." Lilly shuffled around the counter towards the paint section. Lilly was a bit disappointed and a little hurt. She had had several dreams over the last week that George was going to ask her out, in the store, but the dreams had not been specific as to when George would gather up his courage and ask her out. When Lilly got to where Industrial white # 4 sat on the shelf, she smiled at the thought and hoped. George followed, playing with his fingers. He didn't realize that he twiddled with the air, like a kid playing with an imaginary toy. George's face beamed a mixture of a grimace and a nervous grin, which made George look kind of like a person who has just eaten something sour or bitter. Lilly turned to George, her face sweet and smiling. Taken aback by George's odd expression. "I don't have any ten-gallon buckets but have ten one-gallon cans. If you'll give me a hand, we can bring them to the counter together."

"Okay then," George's face now more of a grin than a grimace. He followed Lilly down the aisle, his hands swinging with the weight of three gallons of paint in each.

8

I looked at my best friend and wondered for the second time in the last hour if she was sleeping with my boyfriend.

"The problem Jenny is that you're a whore." Macy giggled as she sipped her drink.

"Virginia, call me Virginia." I inhaled sharply on my cigarette. Macy is the whore. I'm *whorish*, and there's a big fucking difference if you ask me. "Macy your problem is that you don't know your shit from your shinola. I know Adam is sleeping around. I know he's a sleazy son-of-a-bitch. And I know you want to fuck him. You think he's got a cute butt, but sister, stay away from him. Stay far away. He's nothing but T-R-O-U-B-L-E."

"Jesus, cool your bitch-jets, the plane has like already taken off." Macy snorted as she turned away from me. The hot afternoon was getting to her, it always does when she combines vodka and sun tanning. Add cocaine and you get the picture.

"I'm sorry Macy. I'm not in the mood."

Macy's pool glimmered, and beyond the lattice screen alive with rosebuds, her father mowed the lawn far away, half-drunk himself. He's probably trying to catch a glimpse of us through the wooden checkerboard, young cute girls, half-naked in his backyard. It hardly matters that Macy is his daughter, they never speak anyway.

"You know as soon as things are going great with Adam he does something to totally fuck things up."

"So true."

"God, I mean just yesterday's he's all like wanting to settle down and now barely 24 hours later he's AWOL."

"Tell me about it, Virginia."

"It's bullshit."

"Bullshit." Macy hit her vape. "So when is Adam supposed to pick us up?" Macy asked as she drained her margarita.

"After five, we got plenty o' time." I lit a fresh cigarette and flicked a mosquito off my right forearm. The air hung still and fat; it was still incredibly hot and it showed no signs of cooling down.

9

The dragon-backed irrigation pumps crawled straight down the middle of the field, the bright azure sky framing the spiky spine in a blue so blue it was like a Technicolor Sea. The metal glinted like wet scales on a hot rock near the river. The pick-up truck that pulled the irrigation pump, dwarfed by the high pipes that brought rain to the crops during dry spells, looked like some kind of prey trying to outrun a giant skeletal reptile. The adjacent field would be popping with cotton by fall, and the cotton would be like bright white ashes blown from the dragon-backed pipes across the dirt road. In recent years there was more king cotton and more corn. And a whole week of watermelon patches. The corn gave off static sounds in the high breezes. Tomato plants sizzled when the wind blew hard across the ground. Mulch employed close to a hundred migrants and owned four buses to transport them to the fields and back to camp, a sprawling community of pine and plywood shacks, picnic tables, bonfires, and bathhouses. The gardens grew back towards a stretch of field that Mulch allowed the migrants to cultivate. He had strips of land all over for his employees to work as they want, and work them they did, growing gourds, corn, cucumbers, and peppers of all kinds. Beans grew up the cornstalks and flowered among the sister crop, and squash rose up like brown nuts, even in early summer, the gardens and fields so taken care of throughout the day and week. In-between the many fields, Mulch had planted apple and peach trees which offered shade during break time, and fruit for snacking. Mulch didn't care to have them harvested and instead allowed his workers to make wine and brandy from the fruit. The smell of the fruit on the tree was Mulch's private get-away. Early dawn would see the clouds open and the stars peel back, and Mulch would be sitting in a peach tree sniffing blossoms and sucking the juice from a peach. It was there among the bite sweet peaches that Mulch conceived of the box, how to get rid of his daughters and the end of himself completely. And it was there under the sickly smell of rotting fruit that Marcos and Sea Hag came into the fold of his plan.

Mulch had pulled the box up out of the creek and into a dark grove where it would wait before he moved it the last time. Afterward, Mulch and Bill ended up walking towards the trees. The sun bright, and still made the air shimmer with ghosts. For a second Mulch thought he saw a flock of dark birds settle in a tree.

"Do you think she suspects anything; she can be quite perceptive you know?" Mr. Bill puffed on his pipe which he offered to Mulch. Mulch took the pipe and inhaled.

"Possible. You know how she gets in the summer, all milky and mooning over the water." Bill snickered. "It's been a strange year with her like you said it would."

They had reached the strip of peach trees that separated the tobacco from the corn and cotton. Mulch stared into the glare that came off the irrigation that spined the field.

"You could do that you know, instead of this? Send her *out there,* the sea?"

"She wouldn't leave, Bill. I think she's too familiar with the environs here to want to go anywhere else. But how is she going to find a mate? Who will protect her?"

"I could talk to her."

"There's like no such thing as a mermaid dating club, or would it be *mating* club?"

"Perhaps she could be persuaded to seek greener pastures, boss."

"Furthermore, she's very dangerous. A lot more than you or I think. If she sticks around, I'm liable to hurt her."

"Greener pastures being a metaphor, of course."

"Bill, you can do many things, but you can't reach her. She has to want to be reached."

"Perhaps if we only showed her a map with the Canary Islands highlighted or marked with the proverbial X."

"Talking to her is like talking to an alien. She doesn't really listen to you and half the time she plays clumsily."

"Perhaps a long talk over tea."

"Her mother should have never left. I could have used that kind of woman around. But I didn't really get her either, come to think about it. But I didn't have a clue. How was I supposed to know what to do with a mermaid half-breed?"

"I'm sure Marina has an opinion."

"Didn't she know she was trusting our daughter to me? A normal human?"

"Yeah, but it's worth a try, talking to her."

"I've got tomatoes, cotton, corn, tobacco…. not to mention…"

"A very profitable industry."

"…Okra, kale, green beans, peanuts, and some fruit, enough to make any family rich."

"Don't forget potatoes."

"I own most of the arable land in the county."

"And carrots, boss."

"Over half of the unusable land, a huge house, a store, stocks in computer companies."

"Not to mention the unmentionables."

"Not to mention the unmentionables. And it's all rotten, Bill." Mulch leaned over to spit, his face ruddy with sun, his eyes alert and bouncing back and forth in his skull. "I'm worried."

"You think she saw?"

"No Bill, probably not. If she did, she wouldn't think anything of it."

"She is curious, no?"

"Are you going to take care of that business today?" Mulch gestured to the area of field that Mr. Bill used to send smoke signals.

"Yes." Mulch inhaled on Bill's pipe and passed it back. The smoke took drift in the breeze and snaked through the tree limbs.

CHAPTER THREE

1

My father grows some of the best weed on the shore. Near the marsh. Out where it's no-man's land. It grows thick and green and potent from the deep humus of earth that's packed there.

Oh yeah, he also imports coke and smack. The drugs, from what I understand, come through the new shucking shacks he owns on the creek and the feed store.

When I was younger, we'd go in the store and there were always people lined up to see Daddy. Scary people. I'm talking guys with tattoos and heavy metal hair. You could smell city on them. Like scorched oil. The few times Marina came with me we huddled together, afraid of the people who waited in nervous groups to talk to him. Marina and I would play on the grain sacks and run around the parking lot, jumping on big rubber tires and stuff. All while Daddy brokered coke deals inside.

Of course, I learned much later it was drugs that Mulch made his money from, not seed and feed. I later learned that Mulch traded weed for coke and sold smack and crack. Oh sure, he's got a legitimate feed business, a pretty successful one at that. But it's a front and he has a staff that will graciously set you up with fertilizer and seed and other assorted farming needs.

It is awful boring around here, on the shore I mean. Real boring. It's easy for kids to get lost in dope. Yeah I know, it's a cliche. Here it becomes something of a tradition.

There are a few ways to buy dope from Mulch. Now keep in mind Mulch mostly sells to middlemen, who sell to smaller buyers. If you're a middleman, you don't go to the store. The store is for the big shots. The store is for city folks. The store is also a front. If you work for Mulch as a pusher, you wait for the smoke signals. Another one of my father's brilliant ideas. He got it from watching cowboy films on that Western app on the Roku TV. Mr. Bill probably hates it, but he doesn't say squat about it. Mr. Bill gets his smoke signals going and that gets the attention of the pushers, who all live in Oysterhaus. Mulch only deals with locals. Real locals. Nobody from up the road or down the road or any of that bullshit. He's the main guy. He sells the crack and coke that supplies Hexmore. He sells the weed that supplies Cape James. The pushers all come barreling down the fields, towards the source of the smoke. Money and drugs are exchanged. Now the genius of the smoke signals is, is that from far away it looks like somebody's burning trash. And when the pushers meet in the field there's nobody around, and from far away it looks like a bunch of hicks checking out the acidity of the soil or some shit. Pretty ingenious, I'd say.

Steven Rickenhouse told me that when his father lost his job his father came to Mulch and asked to sell drugs. Steven's parents were getting a divorce and his mother and father were both shacking up with other people. Sue Ellen, Steven's mother, was fucking Larry Stiles her old boyfriend (who happened to have some kind of snuff fetish – Steven skipped school one day and came home to get his dope and found his mother playing dead with her boyfriend doing all kinds of weird stuff to her. Like fake blood all over her chest and Larry's standing over her with a knife. Bleeck!) and his father, Billy William (no shit – Bill Squared is what most call him), was shacking up with the Williams twins. Both of them, according to Steven. Anyways, Steven said his father started selling weed and pills at first. He'd get his dad to sell him some and he'd refer his friends to his father. Billy Squared ran with a younger crowd that way and got to the point where he could unload cocaine and hash, and a bit of horse on the weekends. Nice profit. Pain in the ass, but worth it, according to Billy Squared. At the time I was in the seventh grade and not of age to be around such party people. Steven, two years older than I, saw a lot more. One night at this party (Steven's there too, drunk as a skunk and trying to get his father to hook him with a dime) Billy stole some of Mulch's primo stuff. Super white powdered coke. Something new. Something special. Steven didn't know how Billy Squared got a hold of this stuff, his father being notoriously awkward around stern figures of authority. Mulch shows up around midnight when the kids are getting wild. Billy's got a sixteen-year-old in the bathroom ready to give him a blow job when Mulch busts in and grabs Billy by the throat. The girl doesn't know what's going on and runs out the door with a look of terror that Steven described looked something like a cross between a monkey and squirrel being chased by something large and ferocious. In the tiny closet of a bathroom, Mulch throws Billy's face into the mirror, takes his coke off Billy Squared, and leaves the party. Billy Squared got all sorts of quiet and weird and spent most of the night drinking Southern Comfort out of a thermos and walking in circles in the backyard. Steven said the next night Mr. Bill shows up (let me pause to say that Mr. Bill is very scary. He's not very tall but he feels big, you know. Like he could grow a few feet and really whop you one. Plus, he's wide and muscular. I used to be scared of him; Marina and I used to think he'd beat us if we were bad.) and calmly states that if Billy pulls a stunt like that again, he's gonna cut Billy's dick off and force-feed it to his son.

I didn't believe Steven. First Steven is a notorious liar, tall tales and all. But Steven says it's true. Said he was standing on the other side of the door, listening, hoping his dad wouldn't be killed. Steven sells weed and pills for Mulch now. He says he sells the pills to smoke weed for free.

2

Mulch has a ritual he goes through when his daughter Virginia is home. He'd rifle through her dirty laundry looking for panties, bras, and possibly sexy lingerie, sniffing everything in her pile for a catch of her scent. Doing this, he'd be transported back to his childhood where his father, Eb, old Ebeneezer, used to skulk in the hallway of the house, listening to his wife screw his brother, Leon. Mulch would peer through the keyhole and spy his father listening intently and watching his wife, and his body would juice up in fear, and he'd peer through the keyhole for hours it seemed, aroused and fearful at the same time Mulchie would cower in his room, right across the hall and listen to his mother screw his uncle and listen to them call each other 'baby', 'dear' and 'doll', which made little Mulchie sick to his stomach. Sometimes they would sneak off to Leon's room, right above Mulch's room and they would make love all night, and Mulch would listen, aroused, angry, and scared all at the same time. And later, barely eighteen, when Mulch stabbed Leon again and again, he thought of his mother, and it made him sick and aroused again, the memory of their coupling. And now, Mulch finds himself fondling Virginia's dirty underwear and can't seem to stop until she comes home from wherever she is or decides he needs to masturbate to just simply get rid of the urge so he can get on to whatever is on his agenda for the day, which is usually sordid in and of itself anyway. The sniffing of the soiled undergarments, which reminded him of Eb, with a flask in his hand, schlumping around the yard, while Leon was inside with his wife, his mother. This is how Mulch feels when he compulsively sniffs his daughter's underwear and imagines that he is somehow like Eb, and that Virginia is somehow like his mother and that he can re-live some sort of twisted sexual urge that had long ago snaked into his subconscious and laid eggs. So when his daughter does come home, he first makes sure Maria has enough chores to keep her busy so she can't do the laundry, so he can check the hamper for the clothes that his daughter brought back with her. If he finds something new he'll lock the door and inhale the sweaty-dried smell of his daughter for sometimes twenty minutes or more. Once he finds a used pair of panties or a slip that he likes, that didn't make it into the hamper, he smells it and rubs his face in the material. When he's in her room he doesn't stay long. He counts to forty in his head before re-folding her item of clothing and placing it back in the drawer, or on the floor, or back in the hamper, before getting on with the rest of his day. And the busier he is, the more he finds himself wishing he could smell her clothing. And so when he came home, June 7th, in the afternoon to eat, he made sure Maria was good and busy so he could lock himself in the bathroom and relieve all the tension he'd built up over the morning.

Maria doesn't suspect anything. Though she's seen Mulch come and go from Virginia's room many times. She doesn't think anything of it. This is good because Maria's been growing very tired of Mulch Hayes.

When he comes and goes, he barely says a word to Maria. When the children were younger Maria expected this, his silence, his macho heart. When his whores came to stay she kept silent herself. She too has a macho heart and can refuse his love as easily as he refuses hers. She loves the children. And if she knew that Mulch spent enormous amounts in his head planning ways to sniff his daughter's unmentionables, she'd probably have at him with a kitchen knife. Mr. Bill, or no.

Maria loved his girls, they were as close to her as family, even closer than her family, or any of her relatives in camp. Virginia and Maria had always been close. But Marina. *Marina was special.*

At first, Maria didn't think she could love Marina. Believing was the hardest part. Believing that a half-mermaid had been born in the basement of the house. She didn't believe it. Even when she witnessed it she didn't believe it. Couldn't believe it, even when Mr. Bill held her down, whispering to "look, look at the child. See the child. Love her so that you will tell no one."

Mr. Bill had vowed to keep Marina safe from harm and would not tolerate Maria's denial, or possibility of betrayal.

Marina was so innocent. A filmy baby, whose milky skin gave off a flinty green glow. A baby whose fingers and toes were webbed; and strong. A crushing grip for a newborn, fierce and determined to hold on. The mother left shortly after Marina was born and was never heard from again. Maria didn't mind because she was alone with Mulch, for the first time. She had hoped they would grow closer. But instead, Mulch brought Virginia's mother home, a leggy young woman half his age, who spent her days locked in her room, reading magazines, fighting off morning sickness. Before she moved in, Mulch had kept her in town, in an apartment he owned. She was only to stay for a few months until the baby came. Maria didn't like her, but she loved baby Virginia, who came nine weeks after her mother arrived. And Maria didn't question Mulch when the baby stayed, and the mother moved on. Didn't question it at all because once again Mulch would come to her in the night, and she would take him. The other women never stayed. Only her. He comes less and less to her room, now, and pays even less attention to her, too, as if she is simply the maid and not the de facto matron of the house.

But lately, Mulch has been nice, polite, even. This is why when Mulch came home, breathless, eager to watch his new videos, Maria left him alone, thinking he had great work to do. She wanted him to be pleased with her so he would want her. She didn't notice or would have cared when Mulch slid in and out of his daughter's room.

3

Several weeks ago, Mulch severed all ties with a DC family who sold Mulch heavy narcotics. They were a nasty outfit that specialized in smack, coke, and political blackmail, run by a short Italian guy who went by the name of Sunday Comics because he strutted like a comic book don full of cock and swagger and liked to flash his money. Sunday dealt with Mulch because his cousins had dealt with him in the sixties. But Sunday didn't like the Native American, nor the way Mulch looked at him like Mulch didn't know what he was doing. Sunday had the notion that Mulch didn't like Italians. But Mulch had run a real hush-hush operation Sunday wasn't clear about (and didn't want to be clear about) and had garnered real respect, almost close to fear, from the rest of the family. You didn't fuck with sleeping dogs, Sunday reasoned, no matter how much you hate the dog. He didn't understand why he was so respected though, this creepy old redneck farm hood. But he didn't have a choice. And when Mulch and that scary ass Mr. Bill visited him and told him they weren't distributing for him anymore, Sunday had almost had a heart attack, from relief. Muling the stuff down from DC had been a pain in the ass, and often costly. The entire Eastern Shore is a red-light zone in terms of cell phone use and is monitored by the State Police, ATF & DEA constantly. The mules had to use CB radios and code words for drugs and pick-ups. Route 13 was ideal for smuggling, being that it's so idyllic, so quiet. No one had any idea that over beyond the cotton fields, heroin, cocaine, XTC, LSD, marijuana, and crystal meth was being sold and disseminated throughout the southeast, via boat, car, and bus. Sunday and his captains had been expecting this change-up for a while now. Mulch was getting old and they sure as hell weren't going to deal with the creepy Mr. Bill, that was for damn sure. Every time they were together, Sunday felt like his head was being measured for a scalping.

Then promptly after severing ties with Sunday Comics, Mulch gave Mr. Bill a job. "Get rid of these loose ends, willya."

Purging anything could get ugly. Mr. Bill understood it, better than anybody. If the body needed to get rid of something it did so in an ugly and vile way. Purging usually smelled bad in Mr. Bill's experience. And this was going to stink.

Mr. Bill had six men on his list. One as old as 62. One as young as 15. All of them would have to die. And he couldn't do it his usual way. He'd have to be sly and stealthy because even though the sheriff's department wasn't the FBI, they'd see a pattern if he left one. Especially since all the men lived in or around Oystehaus' corporate limits. Almost all of them lived on the back roads that snaked and backtracked along the creek and marsh side.

Thinking this through, Mr. Bill rose from where he had stirred up the fire pit. Around him in the restless woods, small animals and insects crept around the deadfall and dried leaves. Somewhere in the woods, farther back in the dark than Mr. Bill could see, black muscular birds took notice of his activities, and the thin threads of a late afternoon fog wrapped around the base of trees.

He built a fire, smoked his pipe, and waited.

He didn't have to wait long.

They all came. Tom Nunn and Billy Squared, his kid, Lila Coates, Johnny Miller, and Warren Dean. All on time. All with the usual slow list to their stride, which usually meant some drugs or just on the drink. Mr. Bill had packages for them all. And bonus money, too (except for Billy), for a good spring, and here's to a great summer and all that bull malarkey.

Other than the beer Steven Rickenhouse bought when he left the buy, none of them had time to spend any of the money. And none of them noticed how Mr. Bill had laid the evil eye on each of them as he handed them their backpacks, stuffed to the gills with bills and drugs.

4

That afternoon, in a small Cape Cod, on rural route 345 in Oysterhaus, Tom Nunn had a heart attack. It was shortly after three o clock and Tom had been fiddling with his fishing poles, which he hadn't used since last year when he'd started using crystal meth. Like most dealers, he dipped out of his distribution supply once in a while, more so lately Burly and wild, Tom liked to show his wife a good time and they partied like it was a Friday every night. Tom Nunn was Mulch's number one dealer. Top shelf customers paid top dollar for his coke, smack, XTC, LSD, weed by the pound, and Cuban cigars. Tom Nunn whom Mulch would drink the occasional drink with, whom the girls still thought was cute, at 48, living: THE. LIFE. Poor dead Tom. Anita Nunn who at 38 was notoriously skinny, found him slumped over his fishing poles in his shop. She came out to the garage with a lemonade and a joint and a randy nerve for a quickie on the wet patio furniture. She knew he was doing more meth than he should. She wouldn't nag because that's what wives are supposed to do, and she didn't want to be that kind of wife. Poor Anita found him slumped over the worktable. She'd thought he'd crashed and prodded him with a screwdriver. When he didn't respond, she pulled at his head and saw that his eyes had rolled up in his skull. She felt the weight, which was the dead giveaway. He felt like meat in her hands, and she horrifically thought for a moment that his hands looked like steak. She could even smell the faint whiff of a steak in the garage. She shrieked, promptly went inside, and snorted a line of coke before calling the paramedics. Then she downed three shots of vodka and waited on the front porch, chain-smoking to take the edge off.

Poor old Anita didn't tell anybody what she thought she saw that morning. They'd lock her up, post finding your husband dead stress or no. Poor Anita, whose husband was dead at 48 from a heart attack. She knew it then as she sat on the steps. She just knew it. She had read in Reader's Digest, of all places, that husbands and wives shared thoughts. *Ideas.* She'd read that article waiting for Doctor Scott and the results of her pregnancy test. She wasn't pregnant and knew from the first moment Tom had slipped inside her that she would not bear his child. Knew it like it was a birthday written on a calendar. Just like she knew what she saw that morning was real. It wasn't a dream or stress. She'd sat on the edge of the steps and cried. Big heaving sobs that stopped as soon as they started. In shock, she couldn't believe Tom was dead, she'd been staring off into the tree in her front yard waiting for 911 to arrive. Anita didn't even know what kind of tree it was, she only stared into whorled eyes where limbs had been hacked off when the tree had been young. She'd been staring into that tree forever before the crawling sensation of somebody watching her took over her nervous system.

That's when she saw the very large deer standing in her front yard. The fact that it was a deer wasn't so strange, but the fact that the deer stood as tall as her house, taller even, and she strained her neck to look up at the many points which disappeared into the leafy foliage of the tree she'd been staring at. *What in hell?* The buck's height shimmered, as if the buck's body was both growing and shrinking, an effect Anita would remember forever, the feeling of being prey under an animal that might as well have been a god or a ghost. Unsure of reality she stared as the beast stamped its feet and snorted. She decided the beast was twelve feet up in the air, the head some four feet higher, and the crown, its rack spread up into the sky as if it were made for the holding the sky and clouds and stars. It was a dusty white color, that suggested age because she saw roan underneath, mixed and brushed in with the white. She stared at the beast unable to move, only able to stare at its cold eyes and impossible size.

"This is what happens when we die." She said aloud, unaware she was speaking.

As if answering the buck shook its head, its antlers shaking the trees and sending fresh leaves spinning off into the yard.

"That's what's happened to Tom, isn't it?"

And the buck shook its head again, sending more leaves to the ground, as if to say, 'that's right, baby, we're green once, and then we're shaken to the ground.'

Then buck had moved a little, to look off into the east. And for a second, just for a second, Anita thought the beast was going to scoop her up onto its back and take her away. Her husband had planned on taking her to the Caribbean for their anniversary, which was in three weeks. The thought made her cry, and she turned her face into her hands to let it out. And when the ambulance arrived a few minutes later, she was surprised to find the beast gone. It had vanished, leaving only the stray dead leaves on the ground under the June sky.

5

If there was ever an all-around fuck-up, Billy Squared Rickenhouse would be it. As a child, he had shown considerable skill as a waterman. He'd go out with his father on his skiff and work with his dad, and when work was done, he fished. He could identify forty-seven varieties of fish by the time he was eight years old. Then he started sniffing glue with Tommy Salinger. Tommy and Billy Squared had set up a rather profitable glue trade by the age of ten and were up to peddling warm beers and reefer when Billy went out and bragged about how much money he was making to the principal. He'd thought he'd been called into the principal's office because Mr. Warren, his art teacher, had caught him stealing glue. He'd been called into the office because his mother had fallen down the stairs and was in the hospital. But Billy just went off and told the principal everything about their operation. How they'd steal the good glue from school and sell it for five bucks a baby jar in the boy's bathroom during lunch. The principal suspended him for ten days and recommended a psych workup, which meant that in middle and high school Billy had his prescription Ritalin to sell instead of glue. He learned for a while to keep his mouth shut. But there was always something going on with Billy. He couldn't lie to save his life. He made promises he couldn't keep, and he often pissed Mulch off. The amazing thing about Billy's hit was that it had taken Mulch so long to order it.

To this end, Billy Squared Rickenhouse set himself on fire by burning his trailer to the ground, on the same night Tom Nunn was found slumped over his fishing poles. Billy hadn't moved any product in over a week on account of his girlfriend, Emily, who had been horny lately, since her twin Sally had taken off for god-knows-where. Billy, tooted to the gills, waiting for Emily to come home from Walmart, had fallen asleep in his lazy boy around noon. He had been watching college baseball and smoking cigarettes. The fire chief didn't even bother with an investigation. Billy Squared had nearly burned his hand off the year before bootlegging in his backyard. Plus, Billy was long suspected of being the cook for much of the local meth trade. Billy Squared had a long history with the fire department and when the call had come in, the firefighters began taking bets as to what Billy had done this time. Had he set fire to his car or his yard? Perhaps he'd only cut the gas lines in his house, again, by accident. Or had he gone off and finally set himself on fire, which everybody joked about but didn't think would happen. When they showed up at his trailer and witnessed the melting plastic-like goo and tin that was Billy Squared, his Lazy-boy, and the floor underneath him, nobody had been able to say anything. Only later, after Billy had been cleaned up did the joke start and the speculation begin. Officially it went on record that Billy Squared had fallen asleep with a lit cigarette, despite the protests by Emily, soggy with tears, that Billy Squared had kicked his cigarette habit for a less harmful chewing tobacco habit. The evidence having been burned away with the rest of Billy. The weird thing was, which no one spoke about, was how Billy Squared was melted into a pile of pink and white goo. Not burned to a crisp, like most of the trailer around Billy, but melted like a candle.

6

Billy's spawn, Steven, was better than his father at most things. That included dealing drugs. Steven personally liked hash and weed. Speed made him want to jump out of windows and smack made him feel like a goddamned roach, and he'd seen enough roaches in his life living in his father's trailer to last him forever. He hated his father because his father wasn't good at anything. Not that Steven was a brain surgeon, mind you, it was just that Steven realized that some things in life were meant to be taken seriously. That included drug dealing. What Steven took most seriously of all was his dedication to his car. He was a motorhead through and through. He listened to Ozzy Osbourne and Metallica and liked to turn donuts in the school parking lot, even though he had dropped out three years prior. He sold his dope out of his little shop. Speed freaks would come in for a tune-up and they'd get one, that was for sure.

So when Steven's friends learned that he was killed driving his car, they could only half believe it. Steven wasn't exactly the type to do something quite so stupid. That was his father's style. Still, the apple doesn't fall far from the tree and all that.

Steven Rickenhouse, 19, had driven his Dodge into the oncoming traffic lane on route 13 at the same time that his father was melting into his chair. He'd felt this crazy urge to drive on the wrong side of the road, just a little itch of thought, like the time when he had gotten shot in the ankle and kept on wanting to grind the base of his thumb against the bandage just to see how much pain he could take. He'd passed out several times, just grinding his thumb into the wound. And now he had just wanted to take a little jaunt into oncoming traffic, nothing dangerous. He'd be able to swerve out of the way, was his reckoning. Sure he would. And if he didn't, so what? Somebody else would swerve. They always do. The first few cars he met on the road did swerve. And he laughed at their contorted and pained faces, their mouths open, screaming at him. How funny. How amusing. But when he had stared down the grill of the Purdue chicken truck that appeared out of nowhere, he froze up, his fingers locked around the wheel, his eyes locked ahead, unable to right himself, and his Dodge exploded against the mac, and Steven was no more.

7

Warren Deen, 15, the youngest of Mulch's dealers, shot himself with his brand-new crossbow shortly after dusk. He'd bought it to use that fall when his father came for his yearly visit, which always included a hunting excursion out into Mitchfield woods. His stepfather Darren, a waterman, had teased Warren about the crossbow. Said it was for wimps who couldn't use a real bow, said it was for pussies and faggots. So Warren had gone out to play with it to show his stepfather up. Shoot some cans. Maybe kill one of the stray white cats that always seemed to be sniffing around the shed. *Maybe shoot Darren in the leg. Yeah, that was the fucking ticket. You calling me a faggot, you son of a bitch.*

He was high on gasoline and pot. He didn't drink, Warren Deen. He smoked pot in joints, bowls, bongs, and vapes, and huffed gas, a secret he hadn't shared with any of his friends. Not even Adam whom Warren thought had secrets of his own. Gas had been Warren's friend for a few weeks now. He'd go into the garage and pour gas into a five-gallon bucket and lay a towel over his head and stick his head in the bucket, careful to keep the towel over the bucket's mouth. He'd inhale deeply and get as high as the highest fucking sky. When he got his weekly package from Mulch, he sold everything but half the weed, which he smoked himself. And for a fifteen-year-old, he could move product. He sold crack and smack down in the trailer park from his house. His dumb slut mother and her friends bought most of the blow. He'd even gotten free blowjobs for it, from his mother's slutty friends. His stepfather couldn't say that; Darren didn't get half the pussy that Warren got, that was for fucking sure. Warren knew that whenever his dad was around, Darren and his mother would try to fuck, but one or the other would be too drunk or high and somebody was never able to stay awake, usually both of them. Which was the hilarious thing, Warren Deen thought. That neither could fuck. Warren would dream at night about shitting in Darren's mouth. He'd make his stepfather eat it and like it. He'd heard his father say that there were only two kinds of people in the world, those who shat and those who ate shit. Warren's real father said that Darren was a shit-eater. That anyone married to his mother had to be shit-eater. *I'll show Darren,* he thought. Warren could always kill that annoying crow in the tree. Just because it wouldn't shut up. It wasn't the same as shitting in his stepfather's open dead mouth, but it was close. He'd skipped school to play with his crossbow and he'd be damned to not kill something on his day off. *Might as well be the crow.* And while Warren was playing with the bow, somehow a bolt had shot through his jugular. He collapsed and bled out in the backyard and died three and a half minutes later. And for three and a half minutes he watched that fucking crow laugh at him from above. The crow was fucking laughing at him. 'Haha, you can't fucking shoot. Look at you. You shot yourself in the damn neck, you ass.' And that crow didn't shut up. Laughing and carrying on, and Warren, hell Warren got so mad his heart pumped faster. And the madder he got the more he wanted to get at that bird. But he couldn't, the fucking crossbow was on the ground, and the bolt was through his fucking neck. And the more he moved the more the wound tore and the more blood he lost. Warren began to sink into a hazy daze as he watched the crow snicker at his worthless self. His worthless little body which was nothing now. Nothing but a bled-out piece of meat.

His stepfather found him. Already a chorus of flies had gathered around his neck. Warren's hands held the crossbow, his eyes turned up as if he'd spied something high up in the trees when he died.

8

Johnny Miller, 62, was a friend of Mulch since high school. He was the first official LSD dealer on the lower shore, a grandfather of three, who spent his mornings raising and digging clams and his afternoons selling drugs on the side. He didn't take any hard drugs anymore, didn't need to. These days just getting up felt like a rush, but he always said when he got real old he'd just eat a sheet of magic chemicals and let himself trip on home to death. Johnny wasn't so innocent though, but he wasn't a killer, either. He'd had his share of run-ins with the law, but now he was older and interested in more things than just a fly in the sky with Johnny Paper. A learned man, Johnny Miller read and studied, wrote meaty odes to sex and the shoreline. Terse, angry poems that floated somewhere between Romantic notions and protest poetry. Each morning he'd rise at five-thirty and take his boat out into his clam beds and see what was what. He'd check his crab-pots and his oyster beds and maybe do a little light fishing. All the time he'd be working on a new verse which he'd write down in the afternoon as he waited for his customers to call. He only sold psychedelics, for which business had been brisk, as of late, with all the zoomers micro-dosing mushrooms. Johnny didn't get it, not really, *why take just a little when you can take a whole lot?* He didn't sell heavy stuff. Leave that to Mulch. To him, hard stuff was for the next generation.

An hour before Johnny's death, Johnny had been working at his typewriter. Over the last few days, he'd mostly worked on stream of consciousness writing, which he'd cut up, sometimes, into long fragmented poems. Sometimes they worked, sometimes they didn't. But Johnny was a 'process over product' worker and liked the way his fragments teased at forming whole thoughts and ideas. What had been bugging him for the last two days was the image of a giant graveyard. Not a large graveyard, but a graveyard for giants. The image had come to him when he'd been out in the boat. He couldn't remember exactly what he'd been doing when it came to him, probably smoking his umpteenth joint of his life. It came to him dream-like, blurry at the edges like a kid had gone nuts with black crayon and Vaseline. The image was of three, but he could tell that there were many more, thousands more, giant elephantine skeletons. Not elephants, exactly, but humanoid, with elephant-like features. The drawn-out face, the huge eyes. He'd read somewhere that the ancient Greeks had probably seen an elephant skeleton and mistaken the trunk hole in the skull for a large eye, and thus the cyclops had been born. But these weren't elephants, and they weren't men. *Titans. Ancient giants who had ruled earth long before man came and fucked everything up.* The image resonated with him because to him the image meant the closing of one era and the beginning of a new one. And that's what he was feeling, at 62, like he was starting over. Like he was getting a whole new lease on life.

He wanted to capture the image in his writing and worked hard to describe the tusk and bones protruding from the earth, the clay-colored ribs that fit over a man like a cage. And as hard as he worked on the image, he couldn't do anything with it. What he needed was a narrative, and that's when he saw the giant American Indian. It wasn't Mr. Bill, he didn't think. He'd known Mr. Bill since he was a teenager. Heck, he'd even smoked Mr. Bill's homegrown. The American Indian standing in front of him loomed over seven feet tall, impossible in Johnny's home, a prefabricated trailer. "Mr. Bill?" he asked, but the man did not answer. The American Indian wore face paint, but no headdress, only a headband, and leather and breeches. Johnny hardly had time to ask the Indian his name when the Indian reached out and gripped his mouth with his giant hand. He couldn't shout out and flailed as the big man picked him up and dangled him over his floor, Johnny's head pressed right up against the ceiling, nothing was ever what it seemed. Johnny had kicked and struggled, but he half believed he was seeing things and gave up, thinking, *this is what I get for dropping all that acid.*

He believed it even less when his mouth was being stuffed with paper. But by then his brain was popping like the fourth of July, and Johnny was knee-deep in the Titan's graveyard, knee-deep in elephant shit and human waste. Dwarfed by the impossible size of the figure in front of him. Johnny had made little noise and had gone out like a light.

Johnny's death, of all the deaths known that day, mystified the police the most. His small narrow home showed no signs of forced entry, but the front door had been left open, which meant that the perp had probably left in a hurry (Truth is Johnny just kept his door open, all the time, really.). Johnny was found at his typewriter, slumped over the keys. Stuffed in his mouth were over a dozen sheets of colored paper, that turned out to be nothing but dyed perforated tabs. The kinds used to make LSD paper tabs. His pupils were open like gun barrels and his skin had taken on an orange coloring around the neck. The blood vessels in his ears had burst, and there were no fingerprints save for Johnny's.

9

Lila Coates, the only African American woman who worked for Mulch, and probably the most dangerous employee other than Mr. Bill, handled the nefarious Crack Council. Her main home of operations lay in Oysterhaus proper, but she spent the other half of her energy up the road in Hexmore. The Crack Council was a cul-de-sac way off the main road, just inside town limits, hidden away from the world. Originally built in the 1940s for housing railroad workers, over the years the lonely spot had attracted criminal elements; there's simply no reason to seek out the Council unless you were a junkie. Locals called it "the Council" because every house on the cul-de-sac was in on the operation, plus it always felt like someone was at court, because everyone saw what you were doing there and at any time could act as judge and jury. Everyone who lived on the cul-de-sac was in on it one way or another. It had been that way for a few generations now. All those open porches and buzzing good-looking folk meandering in and off them like there was a game afoot. Lila's folks owned a house on the cul-de-sac, and so did her grandparents. She used their basements as banks and hid all the cash there until it was time to pay Mr. Bill. She didn't have any problems, as far as security went. Once a couple of years back, a hot-head come-here named RL Tooks tried to push in on Lila. He beat and raped her to send a message to her suppliers, which Tooks assumed was just some white guy, not a real threat. RL Tooks had relations on the shore but was from the Bronx and hung his NY street cred around his neck like a giant target. He wanted to take over the Council and "push all them old folks out." Tooks wanted his men to live in all the houses on the Council. He had an idea to build underground passages between them. He imagined the Council as some kind of fort, and the only person in his way was scraggly old Lila Coates. So he took care of her. Tooks beat her with a bottle of lotion in her bathroom. Threatened to get his crew and gang rape her if she didn't leave that very night.

Lila vowed revenge.

Mulch understood that there was always posturing on the Council. Lila had to save face; Mulch had to save face. So he paid for Lila's hospital bills and the night Lila lay in the hospital with internal bleeding, Mr. Bill showed up on the Council, near dusk. Lila wished Mulch hadn't sent Bill, but when she heard what had happened, she was glad he did. Though she had wanted to be there to see Tooks' face as he was taken down. Bill had arrived as Tooks' men milled around the Shakers' front porch, Thomas Shakers and his grandmother, Soma having lived on the Council for years. They didn't sell drugs, though Thomas spent his fair share on weed and the occasional 8-ball. Their job, as a corner house, was to be the lookout. Shakers feared Tooks because he growled, always promising to cut open a throat if you messed with him. Tooks had been taunting Thomas and his grandmother all that week and when Tooks went in and took over the living room, they'd just let him. They all knew what he'd done to Lila. When Bill arrived in Hexmore, as local legend states, "the whole block went silent. Like there was some kind of storm. We knew who he was, but Tooks sure didn't. They came up to him like he was some kinda old white man." Details after that are shoddy. Some say Bill cut each man down with a scythe-like he was the grim reaper. This particular version was popular with the older veterans of the Council. The other version, one that's more whispered than spoken, was that Mr. Bill used magic. Lila didn't see it herself but heard from her cousin that Mr. Bill kept disappearing and reappearing around Tooks' men. They didn't know where he was or where he was coming from. He'd cut all their throats by the end of the episode; twelve throats in less than a minute. He spent the longest on Tooks, they said, cutting his face and groin apart and slicing his throat in six places. This Lila heard from her fourth cousin who worked as a lab tech in the same building the county morgue was in, where they did the autopsies. Her cousin said the man looked like a tiger had ripped him open.

After all that, you'd think Lila would feel grateful to Bill. Not true. Lila had wanted to do Tooks for herself. And Lila hated Bill because he had done what she should have, simple as that. That Bill had somehow damned her as well as saved her, that he knew something about her she didn't want him to know about – a weakness. Somehow, he'd seen inside her, and she didn't like it. She began to have nightmares. Not about the rape, but Bill, and fog, and stags, creepy shit she wanted to tell somebody but was afraid they'd think she was crazy. Like they'd think, "Old Lila cracked up." She believed that if she were to live through this, she should speak about it to no one. She should clam up, not speak, go mute, plead the 5th, become the rock, be strong and silent, show muscle. To this end, Lila had started to wear talismans – crosses, rosaries, good luck rabbit's feet, a necklace her mother had given her made of finger bones and chicken bones. But they didn't work because Lila woke up nightly, sweating, coughing, sure that the fog, and the stag were after her, sure that Bill was waiting in the dark with his knife. She'd sweat through her clothes and her bedsheets. The lack of healthy sleep has had its effects on Lila. More so than the coke and the weed which were her daily bread.

Lila was gunned down by a young fourteen-year-old by the name of Marcus Simpson. Marcus lived on the other side of the Council, behind Curtis DeMonne's house. Simpson's older brother Tamari had fled the week before for Florida and the promise of a recording contract, leaving Marcus home alone. Their neighbor, DeMonne sold out of his garage and crackheads fixed in his attic or basement. Marcus Simpson would stay up late and peek through his blinds for the naked women who would inevitably pass by one of DeMonne's open curtains. Simpson, a low-level recruit, had been itching for action, bugging Lila every week for something to do. His restlessness coupled with his youth made for trouble. Lila had been using DeMonne's backyard as part of a shortcut. The other part being over the neck-high fence and into the Simpson backyard and out onto the street. She'd take that way at night when she would do business with her relatives. Lila would wall up the money and smoke a joint and go looking for some kind of action – sex, or booze, or drugs. Something to let her sleep heavy so the nightmares wouldn't come that night after she drove home. Lila had crept into DeMonne's yard and paused, listening to the happy and whorish sounds emanating from within, thinking *Someone's happy.* And *So, that's what happiness sounds like,* and for a moment a wall fell away in Lila's mind and Lila saw her life free of Mulch and Mr. Bill and drama. A life away from all helplessness.

Meanwhile, Marcus spied Lila creeping through his backyard, *suspicious,* he thought. Her face slack, her mouth open in a sly grin. *Possessed. Something else is alive inside of her,* he kept thinking. His heart pounded in his chest. *Cut it out. Think about something else.* Of course, he knew who Lila was. Everyone knew Lila. She carried a nine-inch blade in her boot and could shoot the eye out of a crow at fifty feet with a Beretta. But Marcus Simpson picked up his pistol, out of nerves, and when he refocused his attention on Lila, he did not see Lila Coates. Instead, a seven-foot-tall bird stood, its muscled breast squirming with worms. It raised its wings, the phalanxes tattered and beating with disease. The bird looked straight through his soul and hooked his guts. Afterward, he would dream about a bird-woman who would force him to suck on her leathery breasts, a bird-woman who tore at his skin and forced his mouth to hers with her beak. He would dream of her rank breath and how she often forced a rotting worm into his mouth as her thorny feet worked their hooks into his abdomen.

He shot Lila through the eyes. Only she wasn't Lila, but the bird-woman coming for him with a fat worm in her beak. Lila probably didn't see him in his window, squatting on the floor, hand, and pistol hanging out the window, taking aim.

10

"So I'll see you tonight?" George said back to Lilly, smiling and blushing. "Around eight, then?"

"Around eight." Lilly looked into George's eyes swelling with tears, *nerves probably*. She decided that George was the kind of man who would cry if he was happy enough, which she thought was too damn cute for his own good.

George waved again, for the third time, and exited the store. Outside a big sad-looking St. Bernard sniffed his truck rims. Its fur was matted around the legs like he'd been sleeping in the woods for a few nights. The dog looked up to George and smiled the way dogs can smile, and as George walked around him to place the last three cans of paint into the truck bed, the dog jumped up and placed his paws on George's stomach.

"Whoa boy!" George said, backing off, the dog's weight knocking him down. The big dog barked a reply and George smelled the faint lingering of a beefy lunch. "Down. Down. That's a good boy," the dog's breath too close for George's liking.

"All right Rufus," Lilly said as she pulled on the big dog's collar. He was so big he almost caused Lilly to fall right over as well. Rufus backed away past the truck plopping down under the eaves of Hammer n' Nails, panting heavily. George got up off the ground and brushed off his shirt, which bore the marks of two huge paws on the front. When Lilly touched George's chest, wiping the paw dirt and tiny little pebbles off, George's head briefly filled with bright light, which disappeared as soon she removed her hand.

"I'll see you tonight, big boy."

"Yeah."

When George started his truck he stared at the dog, smiling the way dogs can smile, as he backed up and left the driveway. George hoped Nick had finished painting the ceilings because he wanted to knock off early to get ready for his date with Lilly.

11

Nick felt like he was being forced into a dank cave, hot iron hands on his neck and fierce breathing in his ear. He listened to his heart's boom and tasted the salt water on his lips, and for a moment he felt like he was watching someone else's dream. He wanted to scream but couldn't like he was gagged. His face tingled at the rushing thought of it. *Could he be in danger?* His tongue felt fat and there was a heavy feeling in his cheeks and muscles. A strange medicinal taste coated his mouth, like bitter roots and chemicals. For a second he was able to get a look at himself and noticed the diaphanous white robes whipping around him. But then his sight failed again, fluttering away like a lightning bug. He was in the darkness and moving with great speed. Someone was still holding him with a hot iron grip.

He said, "Hello." Except he couldn't speak. His mouth went through the motions of forming vowels and fricatives and plosives, but his throat ached and was dry like he had sucked in a hot and terrible wind. He wasn't moving anymore, he was sure of that, yet he couldn't see anything. The iron grip had left him, but he felt where someone's flesh had made a temporary mark on his shoulder. Reaching out with a finger Nick pushed against the air and hoped there was something in front of him, and there was. His blood rushed with surprise. It felt like a door, woody and smooth. Nick pushed the door open, and sunlight flooded his face. His nerves woke him, and he peered cautiously into the light. *Where am I?*

Nick crawled out of the closet and onto the drop cloth he and George had laid down that morning. His first thought was that he had been sleep-walking as his body broke out in shivers. It took him a good second before he recognized the windows and the boxy shape of Mrs. Enfield's house. His hands shook as he went for a cigarette and when he turned around, he froze. Part of the wall behind him had been painted a deep-ruddy green. Hairs went stiff on the back of his neck, and he stared at the squarish block of florin green and fire-engine red which had been haphazardly combined on the wall. In some places, the green had not quite melded with the red, but for the most part, there was a muddy shine where the colors were still wet. "George is going to kill me." He said aloud, his voice trembling, his lips tingling as if coming off a numb.

12

Nick French inhaled the cigarette and glanced over Mrs. Enfield's brown lawn. Mrs. Enfield's kitchen new and shining, sported big bay windows. The lawn needed a cutting, the thin cuticle of pansies around the house wilted in the sun. Nick didn't want to think about the painting, or the dream and instead forced it all into a small box at the corner of his mind. Something weird was happening to him, something dangerous creeping up his spinal column. *Maybe I'm sick. Mosquitoes are notoriously saurian on the shore.* He felt his head, there was no fever, not even warm. Nick checked the clock. Mrs. Enfield would be out for a while still and George hadn't come back yet. By the looks of it, he had slept twenty minutes, or so. And in twenty minutes he'd managed to paint something out of his dream before sitting himself down at the bottom of the closet. *Call the doctor.*

He lit another smoke when he realized he had nearly a fifth of one left, hanging on to the end of his lip. Lucky for him, Mrs. Enfield's daughter was a smoker, she wouldn't notice the smell, probably. He juggled the smokes and rifled through the white pages. Nick had left his phone in George's truck, again. Luckily, Mrs. Enfield had one of those rotary phones equipped with an extra piece, which enabled Mrs. Enfield to hold the phone without her hands under her chin, but without straining and craning her neck. He looked first for doctor's offices and couldn't remember which of the local practitioners he frequented. A fog had settled in his brain. He juggled his half-smoked cigarette with the newly lilt cigarette, desperately wishing he had a bona fide ashtray instead of his Mt. Dew can. He sucked his smoke into his lungs and felt his chest tighten. Absentmindedly he rubbed his shoulder where the iron grip had held him. He still felt the strong fingers of someone carrying his (*dead*) weight. *Had he died in his sleep?* He'd heard that if one died in their sleep they died for real. He couldn't believe that. But before that morning he didn't think he could paint in his sleep, either. In the yellow pages, he found a curious entry for Dial-a-Nurse. Nick ashed the short cigarette in the can and finally only had the one lit cigarette left.

"Dial-a-nurse." The woman's voice, high-pitched, sharp at the edges, sounded like aluminum foil, Nick thought. She chewed gum. Nick predicted that he'd hear her gum-smacking shortly.

"Um. I think I might be sick."

Sighing, the nurse blew a bubble. In his mind, Nick saw it swell large and pink and thin as it grew larger and larger. It popped over the line. He imagined the dial a nurse to have big hair, pink lipstick, and a low-cut nurse out-fit. "Symptoms?" She sounded like she was from Jersey.

"Well uh, I've been sleep-walking some and I've had vivid dreams."

"Oh." There was another pop from her gum. "What kinda dreams?" She giggled sarcastically and cleared her throat. "Come on baby, tell me your dreams."

"Uh. Hmm." *Is she implying what I think she's implying,* Nick thought? "Do I have the right Dial-a-Nurse?"

"Oh yeah, don't worry sweetheart, your quarter is safe with me."

"What?"

"Just tell me your symptoms darling." She drawled 'darling' out, and Nick thought for a second he was being mocked.

"I've been sleepwalking and I'm worried that I might endanger myself."

"Uh-huh. Are you eating before you sleep?"

Nick thought for a sec. "Yes. I ate a peanut butter sandwich this afternoon before I...um before I took my nap."

"Well," she sighed, "That's probably it then. If your "symptoms" persist contact your doctor."

"But couldn't it be a symptom of malaria or something?"

Someone had scrubbed Mrs. Enfield's kitchen with something very lemony.

"Honey, all I can legally tell you to do is contact your physician."

"But I thought you could help?"

"Maybe you did call the wrong number." As she spoke, he noticed that Mrs. Enfield kept jars of licorice, three of them, along the top of her stove. At least they looked like licorice.

"No, it's just that I... well...no... I should go."

"Wait, sweetie, tell me about your sleepwalking."

"Well, I've been doing something in my sleep." Nick heard the nurse sigh on the other end, *wherever dial-a-nurse was head-quartered, probably the Jersey Shore, it was probably drizzling and muggy.* She blew another bubble and this time Nick felt like she was right next to him, big hair, gum, stethoscope, and all. "I've been painting in my sleep."

"Excuse me?"

"Painting."

"You mean like houses, or fences, or what?"

"Well neither." He was pretty sure he was looking at licorice.

"Okay spill it." She popped her gum again. "You've been painting nudes haven't ya!?"

"Not really."

"Oh come on. Painting in your SLEEP. I don't believe it."

"I've been painting walls."

"Pssht. Boring! Come on walls? You've been sleepwalking and painting WALLS? That's it? When can you come over and do my house."

"Aha. Um. Well. It's not like I've been painting walls or anything. They're pictures, but I don't know what they're pictures of."

"Weird." She smacked the gum against her lips. "You're telling me you don't know what you've been painting."

"You think I should see a therapist?"

"Honey I can't tell you much 'cause people are listening, but get thee to a doctor, or a shrink."

"Really." Mrs. Enfield's counters had the look of polished marble and her ice machine looked like it could jam on some ice. Not like his refrigerator. "Are you sure you can't help me?"

"Really."

"Okay. A shrink, then." Mrs. Enfield's wallpaper looked fresh and new, there was no smoke stain whatsoever, which you usually got in the typical kitchen. Nick had a whole new appreciation for Mrs. Enfield.

"So do you think you're painting your dreams?"

"What?" Nick's head began to swim. From the back of his skull came a dull throbbing. "Maybe. I don't know. I don't usually dream a lot."

"By the way, your southern accent is so cute."

"Thanks. Um, have you ever heard about this sort of thing before?"

"Do you drink often?"

"Well I wouldn't call it often, but I'm no prude." Nick couldn't help thinking that his kitchen was way too small, even though he only cooked for one. And that Mrs. Enfield's kitchen was something to marvel at indeed.

"Hmm"

Nick thought he heard dirty surf crashing against the Jersey Shore.

"I wouldn't turn down a cold one, especially with the heat these days."

"You don't by any chance do drugs do you?"

"Drugs. Well, I've known a few in my time, I can tell you."

"Hmm. perhaps you need to stop your substance abuse and actually check into rehab, is what I'm thinking. Sleepwalking aside."

"Well, I wouldn't really call it abuse."

"Painting is very physical you know. Maybe you need to get something out of your system." The operator popped her gum. "I can see right here on my terminal that you're calling from Virginia, though I can't for the life of Christ pronounce the name of the town you're calling from. Watchu-something-or-other. It looks like a bastardization of...something to me."

"I see I'm bothering you. I should let you go. It was nice talking to you."

"I definitely think you should see someone before it gets WAY out of hand, you know, sir?"

"Here comes my boss, I should go."

"Hey?"

Nick heard her gum expand with a fresh exhale of air and before the phone clicked there was the small, deflated pop of her bubble smacking against her lips then dead silence except for the hollow hum of Mrs. Enfield's refrigerator.

13

George took the news of the new "painting" well.

"Shitassfucker."

"George, I can't hear you. You're mumbling again."

"Date with Lilly and you go and paint a closet door."

"What was that?" Nick's neck ached; his upper lip tingled.

"Damnit!"

"That's better. I heard that one, George. For a second I was kinda worried that'd you be really ticked off and all. Especially that this is Mrs. Enfield we're talking about and not your usual client type, per se."

George snorted and kicked at the dirt of Mrs. Enfield's browning lawn. He slammed his fist into the hood of his truck which produced a dull bang.

"George, I'm sorry. I don't know what's come over me. It's weird, too and I really don't know what's going on except for the fact..."

"Shut up."

"...that I might be going a little crazy, here."

"SHUT UP!" George's face gets beet-red, and his cheeks puff out like a little boy's when he is angry.

Nick sucked in his lips and tried not to laugh. Nick tried not to think about what the painting meant. He tried not to think at all because Nick felt like if he started to look at what he was doing he'd fall down a deep hole he wouldn't be able to get out of.

"Help me fix it, and then I want you to take the next few days off. You could use it. Go see a doctor. Get some sleep. Get laid, for Christ's sake."

"But, George, what about you. You need my help."

"Your kind of help isn't what I need."

"Aren't you over-reacting?"

Nick hoped for a smile, something to anchor him, but George only sighed and scowled.

"Why aren't you over-reacting, Nick? Why aren't you?"

CHAPTER FOUR

1

Sea Hag loved the marsh, the loons, the herons, the ospreys. She loved the way the cordgrass raked across the soles of her feet when she crossed it on foot. The way her toes sucked down into the mud, her toes wet with the fertile dead muck of dead organisms. Sea Hag liked to stand in the middle of the marsh against one lone gray pine that listed to the right a bit, from the way the tide pulled it. She liked to lean and listen for the marsh hens and listen to the wind whistle through the saw grass. Her mind stretched out like the horizon and when she concentrated, she became as still as water. She reached back and felt the history, felt the old curve of the earth underneath her, a kind of calm, a kind of meditation.

She often thought of Mr. Bill when she was out there on the marsh. She felt his age. Trying to read his thoughts was like trying to read a tree. There were so many rings, and his rings tended to be thick hard bands. Her trouble was making sense of them. His eyes were sharp, still, after God knows how many years. And all Mr. Bill needed was a moment to look you in the eye. If you caught his gaze he crawled into your skull through your pupil. If he didn't catch your gaze, he was still there like an insect on your face. Either way was contact, and Mr. Bill didn't need to ask you any questions, because he knew. He knew everything about you. Even at his age, which had to be close to a hundred because Bill had been around long before he hooked up with Eb.

"He's old magic," Marcos had said over moonshine at her shack one night. They had decided to drink off the intense energy of their woodwork which pulsed inside them. Marcos had been especially impressed with Bill. "I mean he's old. A shape-shifting, conjuring type that I've never seen before, Haggie."

Sea Hag had remained silent. She knew like everyone else on the shore that when one spoke publicly about someone else, the wind had a way of caring the fact to that person's ears. "Speak softly. The wind has already rattled my windows once."

"Right." Marcos shrugged, clearly embarrassed. "It's just he's so damned strong. Like standing next to a generator, or a really beautiful woman. The heat and energy move the air. It's like he is as powerful as Marina."

"Hmm." Sea Hag said. "Ah yeah." Sea Hag poured them fresh shine and they turned their attention to other matters.

And now, with everything so close, Sea Hag wondered what Bill and Mulch were not telling them. The scent of it was on the wind, like fresh manure on a field.

2

"It's good boss." Mr. Bill swished the potion about in the beaker. The smell of the damp earth hung in the air.

Mulch sat on the bottom basement stair kneading a beaded necklace. A worm of nervousness made its way through his intestines. Mulch drew his eyes over to Bill. The potion looked like grape Kool-Aid.

"It better be, for your sake and mine." Mulch's voice echoed. "She's got the strength of a bull."

"Of a whale."

"Whatever. I just don't want her to wake up halfway through and take my arm off."

"I'm sure she'd aim for your head first, boss"

"Funny."

Somewhere upstairs Maria ironed laundry. He dreaded facing her when the girls were gone. *What could he possibly say that he couldn't have said thirty years ago? Leave it alone, hoss,* Mulch thought. *Leave Maria alone.*

Mr. Bill corked the beaker and set it in what looked like a spice rack stocked with potions and elixirs. Bill would add the purple potion to Marina's tea, which she likes to indulge in after sunset. She'd fall into a deep sleep and then Mr. Bill would use his power to seal the box. And then Marcos would ferry the box and his daughter out to sea.

"The ceiling is particularly beautiful. If the box were for a more, " Bill rolled his tongue in his mouth, "civilized purpose, you'd have yourself a work of art."

"Thanks. A critic with a heart."

"And don't forget taste." Mr. Bill japed.

"Speaking of taste. Has the ice queen contacted you?"

"I suspect she'll wait till later. After the fact."

"She doesn't belong here, Marina. Cilia will be good for her." Mulch nodded like he was trying to convince himself of the fact.

"Don't try to fool me, old man. Cilia is a bitch." Mr. Bill packed his pipe and lit it with a match. "Cilia is evil as can be."

"She'll take care of her. Get her to where she needs to go."

"A nice salt-box coffin made by Dutch sailors."

"Bill, you don't want to fuck with her."

"Tonto wants to know how come Kemosabe knows so much and Tonto so little."

"Let's leave it at that shall we?"

"You're the boss, Kemosabe." Mr. Bill looked wryly at Mulch and then turned away. Upstairs the sound of Maria singing along to the radio floated through the air.

3

George sat back on his haunches and examined the colors smeared on the closet door.

"It's a muddy mess. What is it?" George asked.

"I was hoping you could tell me," Nick replied.

"Again with the questions."

"This is a whole new thing for me."

"I take it you didn't pass Looney Rooney's art class."

"I can't remember anything of what I took in high school."

"No one remembers anything from high school, Nick."

"No I mean I can't remember anything from high school. My old classes. Girlfriends, if I had any. I don't even remember what my parents look like."

"You're shitting me."

"No."

"You don't remember your parents?"

"I know they existed. That I had them. Or they had me. But I can't quite see them."

"See them?"

"Their faces, George. Everything is foggy."

"You don't remember Veronica?"

"Who?"

"Veronica, the leggy Spanish exchange student you hooked up with your junior year."

"Hooked up with?"

"You don't remember?"

"Remember what?"

"How about the time you and I and Big Wally stole that case from the back of the beer truck outside Shore Stop?"

"Again, no."

"Well, I'll be dipped in shit."

"Nope. Nada. Zilch. Zonko."

George sighed and tapped the wall. His finger came away smudgy. "You don't remember your first time at the Lazy?"

"No."

"Do you know what the Lazy is?"

"Mysterious titty bar back in the marsh?"

"At least you haven't forgotten that."

"I wanted to answer the county dump, but that didn't sound right."

"Listen. I know you're feeling under the weather. So take time off. Get a hold of yourself. But I'll tell you something."

"What?"

"You're going to be all right."

"I am?"

"The fact that you're painting nothing but blobs tells me that there is nothing wrong with you."

"Really?" Nick's stomach sprang back into his body as if it were attached to a large bungee cord. It was a healthy springing feel like he had won a contest.

"Yeah sure. If you start painting actual pictures, then you can worry."

4

It took the rest of the afternoon for George to successfully white the green and red out and to blur the extra coat into the rest of the door. The section seemed a bit whiter, or darker than the rest of the wall, depending on how you looked at it. *Mrs. Enfield's daughter probably wouldn't notice it and that was the important thing.* But George thought she probably didn't care if her mother was happy.

While he was blending the whites, Mrs. Enfield and her daughter had slipped into the house. Mrs. Enfield shouted up the stairs. "It smells like you're doing a wonderful job." Her voice had a cartoon lilt to it. George thought that it sounded like Mrs. Enfield was in a good mood. *She sounded, well, nice.*

"We're not quite done, Mrs. Enfield." George politely replied. "We'll have to return tomorrow to finish the trim in both rooms." George lowered his voice, realizing that he was speaking a little too loud. *Mrs. Enfield is blind, not deaf.* "There's also a little touch-up we'll have to do on the ceiling."

"Oh, anything wrong?" Again Mrs. Enfield sounded nice. Polite even. The way she stood at the foot of the stairs, her left hand resting on the banister, her right hand touching her mid-section, it all made her look matronly.

"No Mrs. Enfield, some of the paint we bought was old and dry. I had to go up the road for some more."

Mrs. Enfield leaned on the banister. "I won't pay for goofing off," she said.

Her finger nothing more than bone dressed in skin, no meat, no dressing.

"No. No of course not Mrs. Enfield. I'll come in tomorrow and finish it up at no extra charge."

"I told you I was only paying for an honest day's work." Her voice lifted into a pleasant register. "An honest day's work. Now show yourself out boys. Chop, chop."

George stepped back into the upstairs spare bedroom where Nick stared out into the yard, the window hot from where the afternoon sun blasted in. "Help me take all this stuff to the truck. Leave a can for tomorrow."

5

Journal, I hate my boyfriend.

"Where the fuck is he?" Adam Taylor pisses me off.

Macy flipped her hair back, again, and I wanted to slap her for it. Obviously, Adam wasn't going to show, so obviously, we were going to be late to the party, and I hated being late, so much that I couldn't think straight, or think of anything else besides ticking clocks. Whole rooms of ticking clocks. When I'm late that is. And forget that hip shit about being late for parties. Especially when drugs are involved. You snooze, you lose, and then there's nothing left. And I wanted to get a load on.

"Maybe his car broke down." Macy slurred her words together. Macy can't handle her alcohol, especially in the sun. Which we both have been in, smelling like tanning products and stale cigarette smoke.

"He claimed he was heading to Salisbury to pick up something... Is that him?"

A truck pulled onto Macy's street, and I felt my temperature boil because I knew immediately that it wasn't Adam's truck. It was some waterman whose truck looked like Adam's, except muddier. Adam's truck has a dent in the front left fender, and as the truck passed, I saw that there wasn't a dent in this man's truck, and a few nets and some bushel baskets in the back and plenty of scratches that Adam would never have let go unpolished. Definitely not Adam's.

"Nope, not him."

"So, what if he doesn't come?" Macy's hair shimmered in the sun, so thick and lusty. She always had the most to-die-for hair.

"I don't know, we'll have to call Rick."

"Rick's car is too small."

"And the truck isn't?"

She shrugged and sighed and gave me the 'why-are-you-such-a-little-bitch' look.

"Jenny, I mean Virginia. God, it's so weird since you changed your name."

"I didn't change my name. It was always Virginia."

"Whatever."

"Virginia sounds more adult. We're adults now, Mace. Don't you like it?"

"Should I call Rick, since Adam is so obviously AWOL?"

Macy pulled her cell from her pool bag.

I shrugged, "Yeah sure. Tell him to clean out the back seat."

CHAPTER FIVE

1 July 9th, 1956

The moon, hidden by a scrim of clouds, peeked out half-buttoned when the wind pushed the purple clouds aside and let its golden white burn through. At times the moon looked broken, its ribbons of light splashing on the dark forest floor. It was chilly for July, a cold front had moved in from Canada. Ahead, water lapped the beach as bitter plops of a drizzle sizzled into the leaves and the heavy cover of the woods near the beach.

Mulch ran between the trunks that appeared and disappeared before him. Branches appeared and disappeared as he melted through them. Blood clotted in crusty lumps on his skin where the branches raked him. He felt the scabs forming on his cheek. *How many branches have I run into?* His lungs expanded. His breath locked in perfect unison with his run. Breathing in when his right foot extended, and out when his left foot extended. Mr. Bill had taught him how to control his breathing, how to keep his head low and his nose open to maximize the oxygen. He couldn't believe the difference concentration made on his strike through the woods. He was younger than his prey by nearly twenty years. *I will catch him.* There was no doubt of that in his mind. There was no doubt of it in any of their minds. And he imagined Eb, his father, sitting fat beside the fire, his yellow maw laughing in the camp smoke.

Before him came a crash and whelp. His prey broke before him. And Mulch sped up, gaining on the older man, whose right leg lagged, wounded by a knife swipe before the chase began. Mulch imagined the cut tearing and ripping, the muscle pulling away from itself.

His prey cut right and vanished into shadow.

He had to catch him before he reached the caves. The caves could be lethal.

Mulch, who had been running all-out now for almost twenty minutes felt the burn in his thighs, his calves, but he wasn't out of energy, not by a long shot. *The old man had to be worse off, he had to be. There was no way he could run so far for so long with such a wound.* Leon left him a blood trail to follow. To Mulch's left, the back end of the caves rose out of the earth and stretched nearly a half-mile to the beach where the caves sloped and opened. Looking ahead it was hard to tell where the woods ended and the sky began. The trees materialized out of the darkness and raked his flesh. Somewhere above the two of them the birds moved and shook their branches. Fog spread out like a tall swamp to his right. Ahead, the surf grew louder, and the broken moon filtered through the trees and scattered along the sand. Ahead as well, Leon labored, swinging his arms at the branches that appeared in his face, slowing as he entered the caves. Crashing onto the beach, Mulch also slowed down, reaching his right arm out to grab hold of the slippery rock he knew was ahead of him. He felt for it and almost slipped but managed to hold on and using momentum he swung into the cave opening.

He screamed as he came around. Not so much out of pain, but out of fear. *He'll be waiting for you,* he thought, *he'll kill you when you duck in. He's waiting for you,* he thought, and Mulch steeled himself for a hit.

But the hit didn't come. Leon wasn't there and Mulch's momentum took him three feet into the interior where the damp cave swallowed all shreds of light. Mulch crouched in the darkness. He heard breathing ahead and muffled cursing. Then came sounds of Leon's stumbling. *Leon can't see,* Mulch thought, *neither can I.* Mulch went ahead, slower than before, careful not to trip himself up.

He'd visited the caves many times before with Maria, one of the younger migrant girls working for his father and uncle. She had started in the fields and when his mother grew too sick to help in the house, she had been moved up to help his mother around the kitchen. After his mother had vanished during the winter, Eb had even given Maria quarters up by the attic, a little bedroom, and wash closet that Eb's great grandfather had originally built for a live-in cook ages ago. Maria's hair, dark as the cave, smelled of apples and spice. Once they had slipped into the caves with a bottle of Muscadine wine and a few candles and had made love watching their shadows flicker on the grainy rock wall above and behind them. The caves went about a mile or so into the earth. They weren't very deep, but they doubled back on themselves in a few places, and they ended in an abrupt depression. Indians had used the cave during winter and during times of war. Mulch had never once found an Indian artifact. He had wished for a tomahawk when he had been younger, something deadly and old.

Somewhere ahead a pant leg dragged across a stone. Mulch stooped and stretched his fingers out, feeling for where the corridor branched off into a parallel corridor that met up with the main run a few yards ahead. He didn't want to find a knife next to his throat, so he went cautiously, and low. Leon could double back and catch Mulch off guard, Mulch had to get to him first.

Hoosh, hoosh, hoosh. Hoosh, hoosh, hoosh, Leon's breath echoed. He was close and wet, full of blood; Leon sounded like a wounded animal.

With the tips of his fingers, he felt the floor slope to the left, and he crawled slowly along, feeling with his hands until he was sure he was next to the parallel corridor. Then Mulch scooted himself around the break in the wall, once he was sure he had headway.

Hoosh, hoosh.

The breathing came from farther ahead and faded. It was so black that his eyes began to color and spin from lack of light, bright greens, and reds, a fleeting dash of paleness. Mulch couldn't see his hands, could only hear the lagging breath of his uncle somewhere ahead of him.

"Mulch!" His uncle was very close. "God! Mulch! Don't do this. Jesus. You and I. Your mother. God, please don't bring her into this. I loved her. I didn't kill her! I don't know who did! Your father. We could be partners. Like your Eb and I once were."

Mulch guessed Leon was no more than ten feet ahead, but the caves spun sounds and reverb and Mulch could not be sure. Not if he wanted to live. He continued to creep and crawl, his body juiced with adrenaline.

"Mulch?" Leon's voice, high pitched, sounded laced with copper, with fear. "Look I want you to know that I loved her. We both did."

With the way sound bounced through the cave-like a ping-pong ball, Leon could be three feet ahead, or six. All Mulch was sure of was darkness. Mulch reached for his knife.

"We both loved her, you know that right?"

Mulch wanted to know who Leon was talking about. He sure as shit wasn't talking about his old man. Eb had stopped loving her a long time ago. Now Eb only felt lust and hate, something dirty and sinister. *Leon wasn't talking about him, either* Mulch thought. He had no reason to love his mother, not after the winter.

"Find your way in the dark, I'm here," and for a second, he saw Maria's face, soft and moonish in the cave dark. She appeared from the murky darkness and was gone. *Find your way in the dark, darling.* Mulch heard her whisper and felt her rustle across the back of his neck, his skin broke into gooseflesh. His penis became rigid, and it throbbed in his britches as he crawled forward. And then Mulch's foot skipped a stone and the stone bounced behind cracking against loose pebbles.

"Mulch!"

Leon lay close.

Mulch tried his best to keep his mind blank, blank as the black. But each time he tried to blank his mind out he thought of Maria's neck, the way it responded to his touch. Mulch thought of his mother's face, her mouth making ecstatic Os, as Leon thrust himself against her. His penis throbbed and hurt. Mulch tried to clear his thoughts. Mr. Bill always told him to make like the forest and think of nothing. *Be like wood, but not hardheaded.* Mulch imagined that his breath came loud, ragged, and desperate. Afraid, his heart bounced blood through him and his ribs and legs hurt. He felt a tight pain in his chest like he had been punched. He thought of Maria again. *Follow me, darling. Follow the trail of my clothes.*

When Maria came she made the same staccato sounds his mother made when she came. Maria's voice had the same timbre as his mother's voice. He looked ahead for her, and then nearly laughed. *She isn't in the cave, lover boy. You're dreaming again.*

There was nothing ahead but darkness and silence.

Mulch no longer heard his uncle's breathing. His foot scraped against another stone and before Mulch could think, the swish of swinging wood rushed by his skull. Pain blossomed in his ear. He winced and reeled back, his hands out for balance. His uncle's gurgled cry filled his ear and Mulch reacted, swinging his knife hand up in a clumsy arc.

Mulch's hand connected with air. His uncle swung the club at him again, striking him in the meaty part of his shoulder, knocking him back into the wall, his head cracking against the rock. When he tried to get up a sucker punch caught Mulch in the jaw and dropped him back into the wall. His head filled with ringing and his eyes filled with stars. His uncle scampered off ahead and then there was the crumpling sound of Leon tripping on his own feet.

Mulch lunged ahead, falling onto his uncle's prone, crawling body.

"Goddamn, you," Leon's voice wavered, frantic.

The swinging arms of the two men moved the air. Friction sparked like trails of fireworks against the blackness. Mulch later remembered how it looked as if there were fireflies following the tussling bodies in the black sack of the cave.

"I'll kill you boy," Leon groaned, his voice weak and ragged. He landed a knee square in Mulch's ribs.

PABOOB, PABOOB. PABOOB.

Mulch's heart felt like it was about to explode. He managed to slam Leon's head into the stone floor, freeing his own hands for a moment.

PABOOB. PABOOB.

His heart rocked his ribcage. His head swam, his eyes searched for a target. He put his knees on his uncle's chest and his left hand around Leon's throat. He heard gurgling blood and spit and felt energy building in his uncle's body. His uncle was going to try to buck him. Mulch felt as if he were holding down a bull. The dark felt alive with imagined light, which Mulch thought was chemical. He saw the white of his uncle's head and the bony rise of a pallor arm, and he thought of Maria's throat and how tender it was, how his stubble had scraped and burned her delicate skin. And how in the candlelight her dark skin became milkier and moony. Leon's throat, grizzly with grime, was rough and Mulch felt it chafe his palms as he held his uncle down. Mulch later remembered how the knife took on a pinkish glow as he slammed it into the tough bone of his uncle's sternum. The knife made a wet whacking sound and then his uncle let out a muffled cry and spewed blood into the air onto Mulch's shirt and face. Mulch swung the blade down again, and again until his uncle moved no more.

2

Outside, rain pelted the beach and the wind picked up. Slowly Mulch's sight returned. First a grainy sense of dimension, the firefly colors he experienced in the black blended into the hues of a woody beach at night during a rain. His face was tacky, wet with sweat, sticky with blood. Mulch felt the blood would stick to him forever. It felt alive, squirming on his skin, and all at once, his body enlarged with awareness, hyper-aware of his uncle's blood, his uncle's death, and his part in it all.

3

After Mulch washed his hands in the surf, he kept touching his face, feeling where branches and barbs had cut and bled him as he ran through the brakes. When he re-entered the forest, it took a good forty minutes of hiking through the thicket to get to where Mr. Bill and Eb waited. White fog covered the ground like gauze and the muscled cries of night birds echoed in his skull. Tomorrow Mulch and Mr. Bill would fetch the body and bury it somewhere.

Firelight. First fly I see tonight. Is this how one feels when one has no soul?

From the shadows, where Mulch stood, the campfire twinkled like fireflies. Flickering against the thin and scrabbled shadows of pine and oak-like a jack-o-lantern's teeth; Mulch heard Mr. Bill and his father speaking in low voices.

Even from the shadows, he smelled the whiskey and Mr. Bill's home-grown. It was raining lightly now, and the canopy overhead provided coverage from the precipitation. Mulch wondered what Maria was doing, *sleeping probably*. It was sometime after one AM. The chase had begun nearly two hours ago. As Mulch approached the camp Eb's voice cut through the wood.

"....old boy....and great skies the fish..."

Laughter.

"... I wonder how Mulch is making it?"

More laughter.

Mulch moved forward in a trance. In a daze, he saw Bill stoke the fire. His father drank from his flask, his toadish face turned away from him. Mulch's feet didn't seem to move, yet he moved forward anyway, his body pulled towards his father who sat like a black hole next to the campfire, sucking light and heat and energy into his great stomach. He felt as if he were walking above the ground as if his body floated.

Mr. Bill looked up and caught Mulch in the eyes as he approached camp. Looking towards Eb, Bill pointed to where Mulch was going to emerge from the woods like a spirit attracted to the light.

"He's back," Bill said puffing on his pipe. He said this to no one, though it was meant for Eb. Mulch looked down to avoid Eb's eyes which had grown yellow throughout the summer as if rabid and Mulch avoided them when he could.

"Well now." Eb rocked on his buttocks and raised a mason jar to his lips. His flask rested half in and half out of his front shirt pocket. "Boy goes into the forest a boy. Boy comes out of the forest a man." He snickered and offered the jar to his son. "Something to wash the blood down with?"

Bill looked into the fire and turned on his heels, "The boy has indeed become a man," he chuckled. Somewhere beyond camp a bird shrieked and made Mulch's neck hair stand on end. The bird had sounded like Leon in the cave. Bill muttered something about, "fresh fungus" and stepped into the darkness, vanishing completely.

Eb went off into a giggling fit, rocking back and forth in his already well-worn seat by the fire. His giggling sounded like a mix between a gurgling chicken and a woman's deep belly laugh. Eb's eyes rolled back into his head, "Tell me the gory details, son."

Mulch said nothing. Eb rose, first to his knees and then to his feet, staggering and crossing to his son. The mason jar sloshed with the forward momentum of Eb's drunken weight. "You were born." He took a swig of shine and again offered it to Mulch. "You were born..." Eb began again. "Ah spit." Eb reeled and balanced himself on Mulch's shoulder. His stink, rancid and sharp, brought tears to Mulch's eyes. "Well, it was worth it, wasn't it? That son-of-a-bitch.... stole my...." He mumbled the last bit of his sentence and released his son. Eb turned on his drunken heels like a ballerina and sat down with one giant *whoof*.

"The first time I killed a man was during the war. Saved that there Leon's life. We served together. Don't think I ever told you. Since you're just like me, you gotta become just like me."

Eb's left hand still held the moonshine and Mulch heard the sloshing in the jar. The rain picked up and the fire sizzled from all the drip from the leaves and needles above.

"When I go all this will be yours. All of it," Eb gestured wide with his hands. "And you can't have something you haven't worked for. That ain't right. You sure earned yours tonight."

He looked swollen to Mulch, rotten like an overgrown gourd.

"You know your mother wanted to name you after our uncle, Claude, but I wouldn't have it. Claude was a fucker, boy. He made my father's life miserable. Claude used to come home from plowing all day and get drunk and then beat his wife and sometimes Paw has to go over there and put a stop to it. There were fights. Claude hurt my mother. Shot Paw once. In the foot. Leon was named after Claude. Claudius Leon Hayes. And I wasn't having my boy named after Leon or Claude. Shit. I hated Harry too." Eb looked to Mulch who was glazed in an oily sweat. "Tomorrow, Bill and I are going to bury the body somewhere. The day after tomorrow I'll call the police, say he's missing. But you must get gone, son. They'll start asking questions about your mother again." Eb swung the mason jar up to his mouth and when he drank, some of the moonshine ran out the sides of his mouth. "Drink some of this boy, it'll rot you out." He offered the jar to his son.

Mulch's stomach, light and almost sick from endorphins, cried out for something. Mulch reached out for the jar and swung it to his lips, taking a long swig. It was like heartburn. It was like gasoline and his head went light from the fumes.

CHAPTER SIX

1

I'm the second daughter, Virginia Maria Hayes. Maria Medina, the housekeeper, is not my mother. Nor am I named for her, either. Maria was the "golden girl" of Mulch Hayes' youth, a black-haired goddess who lived in Spain. Or so he says. Again, we're not talking about Maria the housekeeper, either. Maria is Oaxacan. Not Spanish. I know it's a hard concept but keep up people. He, Mulch, slept with her once. Maria, the goddess not the housekeeper. That much I know. Vacation girl, I think. Mulch wouldn't have fallen for Maria, the golden girl, if he hadn't fallen in love with Maria the housekeeper first, who was simply a poor girl at the time, or that's how Maria tells it, the poor girl bit. Although it may be the other way around. She may have fallen for him first. I don't know. Mulch doesn't talk about it. Neither does Maria. The housekeeper, I mean. Mulch's got a thing for names. My sister Marina is named after some woman he slept with years ago before he met Maria and the other Maria. My mother's middle name was also Marina. He named Marina and me after his lovers. Which when you think about it is kinda sick which makes me think Mulch had some real issues. You name children after grandmothers, and grandfathers, mothers, fathers, aunts, uncles, famous people, old army buddies who saved your butt in a particularly sticky situation. You name kids after rock singers, and places and maybe even, on occasion, the rare pet who possibly was the best thing ever to happen to you. You do not name children after old lovers or people who hate and kill and make trouble.

Virginia was his mother's middle name.

Also, where Mulch met these women is a long rambling tale. My own personal mother left Mulch while I was in diapers. Thinking about this makes my head hurt.

2

The strawberry margarita, which George had thought all along tasted like a raspberry margarita and looked uncannily like the curly whipped top of his aunt Regina's head, frothy and thick, yet shiny where the skin, or in this case ice shone through, the strawberry margarita which Lilly had suggested to him for relaxation, toppled into Lilly's lap.

"Christ." Lilly shrieked and pushed her chair back but to no avail. She was soaked.

George jumped up split-seconds after, he half waved his arms in the air, almost like a chicken, his face a bizarre half-shocked half-horrified grin.

Lilly looked miserable in her pretty sundress now soaked with a strawberry margarita. She took a moment to keep her cool, flinging the sticky drink from her fingers and onto the floor.

"I'm so sorry. *Ohmygod.*" George grabbed her a handful of bar napkins as if the flimsy material would be enough to wipe up the booze which had already colored her bright yellow and orange sundress red. George then handed Lilly his napkin, spilling the silverware onto the table.

"No worries, George. I don't think it was your fault, exactly. I'm not sure what happened there."

"It's been a bad day." He looked Lilly in the eye. "Well except for you, it's been one hell of a day."

"You've had a bad day?" Lilly laughed pointing down to the mess. "At least your date didn't spill their drink in your lap. Ha. Ha." Lilly sopped the alcohol from her dress and calves, which were soaked. She wired him a thin smile. "Hey, it's no big deal. Don't worry about it. It was an accident. I don't think you're a klutz or anything."

"Oh god, you *do* think I'm a klutz, don't you? You think I'm a klutz. Oh man, that's just what I need. First Nick, getting all weird on me suddenly, and now I'm making an ass out of myself." *Chill out, George, focus on Lilly.*

"George it's okay." She continued to dab and wipe. She looked up at him between napkins and smiled.

One look from Lilly's big dark eyes and George lost his balance and fell into them.

"George...George?" Lilly said, for a second she stopped her dabbing, wondering why her date suddenly looked so goofy.

"Sorry. Lost in the moment. You look smashing tonight. Your dress. You look wonderful Lilly, and you smell, you smell so...I can't quite put my finger on it."

"You won't until later. It takes time for the fragrance to work its full magic," Lilly laughed.

George laughed; he hated the way his stomach performed Olympic-level gymnastics down in his lower intestine. He didn't think he'd be able to eat if his stomach didn't cease and desist the Olympic-level gymnastics.

"Go get yourself another drink," Lilly said, her voice like water braiding over stones.

"Of course." George rose and managed to get out of his seat without tripping over himself. *What is your problem, George, get a grip.*

Lilly's eyes glittered in the candlelight.

"I'll be back in a minute," George started and then stopped, "Hey, would you like anything?"

Lilly shook her head and went back to stabbing at her dress with the flimsy napkins.

As George walked towards the bar, he felt the anxiety gymnastics switch to a whole new playing field, to his bladder, which always seemed to be full when he got nervous. Nuclear grade nervous, which was now. *Hey, didn't the bar seem dim compared to the glow that was Lilly? I must be seeing things.*

3

What I want to know is, like, where was Adam, my supposed boyfriend? He never did show up. Macy and I had to call Rick "the Dick" Bell. Rick's an okay guy, but he's dense and short-circuited from all the high balls he throws back on Silver & Gold beach up the road from Macy's place. He's got a cabin there, or rather his parents have a cabin there, and we all hang out there sometimes. When Adam didn't show up, Macy and I found ourselves on the way over to somebody's party-shack to get high. P-A-R-T-Y is a verb, noun, and adjective. When I went to college it felt like I had entered rehab cause the party scene was drastically tame compared to here. The last field party I went to on the shore there were two race strips, one for ostriches, the other for souped-up trucks, plus DJ-DJ, the best DJ for miles around.

Rick handled the car like someone who normally drove at high speeds, with his knees. His greasy head of black hair was the only source of direct light in the back seat, and I bet I could have read under the shine his head gave off.

"He said something about your father," Rick said in his dickish tone.

"What?" I leaned forward.

"Yeah, like, Adam said something about going to see your Pop," Rick "the Dick" Bell said.

"Mulch is not a Pop. He doesn't even rank with parent."

"Yeah, he's hell on wheels," Macy said as she fiddled with her lipstick.

"Shut up Macy."

Since I came home, on a semi-permanent basis, Macy and I have not exactly been getting along.

"Like you care," Rick snorted.

Rick's always snorting his nose, and it gets gross when he's been drinking and doing coke cause his nose runs constantly. He says it's a sinus thing. Everybody knows he's full of shit.

"You're so spoiled," Rick's voice modulated between stoner, hyper and styper, which is a weird amalgam of the two. Right now he's speaking in styper.

"Rick, what the hell does that have to do with Adam and my father?"

I am indeed spoiled. I'll be the first to admit it.

"Um." He looked back in the rearview. "I dunno."

It occurs to me that Rick's voice could also be his dick voice, or his *please baby fuck me* voice, and then the raspy hung-over voice which is the voice you'll least likely to hear because he's always somehow awake before anybody and already packing his nose with blow and throwing back his homemade Bloody Marys and the occasional greasy burger which he calls "food for growing boys." Macy and Rick are fucking on the side, but we all know it. It's weird.

Rick took the turn down to Silver & Gold beach so fast that I slid to the right and slammed against the other side. My head dipped low in the back and suddenly the stars appeared at the top of the window as if they were thousands of people pressed together in dark clothes. They all smoked cigarettes and the butts burned brightly in the sky. Then the clouds banked by like so much blown smoke caught in a breeze and the party in the sky vanished.

4

The Lazy Titty is tucked away on a neck in the backwoods of Northampton County and even though the county bylaws forbid adult entertainment of any kind, the Lazy Titty has remained a county staple simply because of its cooking and unsurpassed service. It's a kind of ritual for a young man of twenty-one to be taken blindfolded into the woods near Hungry Horse Neck, led by his peers, who may be older, who may have had older brothers, or who simply may have been lucky to stumble on it by accident hunting the brack for buck and turkey.

It's not easy to find, and most locals don't even know it exists. Lazy Mel, the proprietor, insists upon good manners and cleanliness, and above all secrecy. He pays his girls handsomely, gives them free room and board, if they so wish, for simply taking their clothes off in a public and secret place. He's got a dozen trailers up around the way for them to live in, but he doesn't pressure any of the girls. He considers himself a feminist, Lazy Mel. It's a solid job, the tips can be very good. Plus, since it's the only joint of its kind for miles around, the girls are treated like celebrities. Often when seen in public, the girls might find themselves bombarded with serenades. Once, in the local Food King Grocer, one girl, while picking up a few things, was assaulted with roses. Assaulted as in she filed charges for the dozen or so cuts along her forearms and face from where the short man with a farmer tan had tossed the flowers at her. The girl said in court that he pitched them at her, not to her, which was the difference in her mind between assault and simple admiration and thankful-givings from an admirer. It doesn't hurt the Lazy Titty's business that judges, and bankers, and lawyers, and the whole circle of good-old-boys come in on a nightly basis and throw back a few cocktails or beers and decide county business, like which state or federal contract is going to which local contractor, all while competing for blown kisses by either the red-head or the blonde, whom the good old boy network seems to prefer. This worked in favor of the one girl assaulted by flowers if you get my drift. The Lazy Titty is by all intents and purposes the heart of local government, or at least at the heart of local affairs.

Nick took a long pull off his beer and stared at the redhead gyrating to Hank Williams III upon a small black runway decorated with candles. She was doing something provocative with a long thin rose-colored scarf, but Nick didn't seem to notice, even when the scarf disappeared and reappeared magically, the audience awing and ooing and tossing bills onto the runway like flower petals thrown before a bride. Nick thought about his sleeping problem. He also thought about the frog legs which were on special, and why his head remained so cloudy, *weird, why can't I remember anything?*

Above the beer cooler behind the bar, a homemade sign had been hung. It stated: IF YOU LIKE TO TOUCH BEWARE 'CAUSE WE LIKE TO BITE. We had been underlined three times and there was a small shotgun icon painted underneath the letters. Nick stared off into the sign. George brought Nick here the summer after Nick had turned 21, though Nick didn't exactly remember this. He had barely found his way back to the Lazy. Twice he had gotten lost on the backroads and had almost given up except a logger truck passed him and the look on the driver's face wasn't exactly that of work, shall we say, and

Nick took a chance which paid off. George's father had helped Lazy Mel build the place sometime in the eighties and had even helped wire the kitchen for electricity. Lazy Mel looked a lot like a mushroom. Big head, thin body complete with an earthy stink that Nick associated with garlic and cloves. Lazy Mel had been a cop or something in New York and had come down here on early retirement and saw an opportunity and jumped on it. The first dancers had been local girls, but they hadn't been too popular and had brought their soap opera of a life in with them so that every night Lazy Mel had to endure the drunken rants of jealous boyfriends who thought that it was okay for them to touch the dancers since they were the dancers' boyfriends, which Lazy Mel had to prove wrong night after night with his old Billy club. Now he only used girls from other places, 'come-heres,' the locals called them. Besides the dancers, he had a couple of topless waitresses, who made just as much money as the dancers made. Only lately many of the waitresses were being pinched, fondled and caressed where they didn't want to be, and Lazy Mel had bid them wear tops for a while and had the bartenders and bouncers Rob, Fooks, Becker, Lark, and Beth sling drinks while wearing crossed pistolas like some black-tie revolutionary. Nick liked the people-watching, though Lazy Mel made it clear time and time again not to watch him. Already once tonight, Lazy Mel had shaken his finger at Nick when Nick had tranced off into his head, staring off into Mel's face, which Mel never appreciated.

6

"Hey, pal, you want some sunglasses?"

The bartender wore a pair and George noticed that the six people sitting at the bar also wore them. A generic black Ray-Ban type that gave the men in short sleeves the look of undercover agents. When George turned around to look back at Lilly, George noticed that every waitress, the hostess, and even the couple seated near them, all wore sunglasses. When he turned around the bartender had a pair ready for him.

"Wow. Everybody's got a pair." George said, pointing to his margarita glass, indicating for another one.

"Yeah, a promotion from last summer. Found them in the basement last night. Not a night too soon." The bartender was jocular, a muscular heavy guy with a short haircut and a gun-toting smile. "I'm glad I remembered them."

"Oh yeah, why's that?"

"Isn't it obvious?" He opened his hands in a gesture that suggested what-more-do-you-want-from-me, or that it's raining, George couldn't tell.

"I'm sorry. I'm not following," and George wasn't.

"Your girlfriend man, she's burning everyone's retinas out."

He turned and later remembered it in slow motion, witnessing everyone in the vicinity of Lilly wearing shades and leaning low behind their significant other if they had a significant other, hoping their significant other would block out a bad glare from some powerful track lighting. The single folks ducked and hid and angled their posture, so they were looking away from the bright glow or held their menus up as shields. One man had stood up and was picking up his table, his date holding her up her clutch to her eyes. Not a single light had been turned on in the section where George and Lilly sat, and not a single candle burned, save for the one on their table which George could not see because of the tremendous bright light emanating from Lilly's body.

7

The sub-basement of the Hayes home contained two large chambers. One was Mr. Bill's room, and the other was Marina's. The house had been built centuries ago and originally had only one large basement which had been used to store rum, spices, and sugar smuggled in from the islands. Where the rum floated in served as Marina's "room" or at least her portal to the creek, and the hideaway room, which lay up a slanted wooden plank floor, where rum and sugar were stacked, served as Bill's room. The creek behind the house was deep enough for a clipper ship to pull into. In the past, the creek had been big enough for a huge four-masted ship. Underneath the house there ran an underground channel which was connected to the creek on one end and the sub-basement on the other. When Mulch came back from Spain, he had expanded the original smuggling hole, tearing away large chunks of the clay floor, leveling it so that it became more of a pool. Eb had thought Mulch was crazy. Bill had had an idea what Mulch was doing because he heard the murmur running through Mulch's brain, a slow trickle that said, "prepare for the child." Mulch didn't quite hear it like that, it was more of a daydream he couldn't shake. A dream that dragged Mulch's days into weeks as he dug and prepared the birthing pool, which in Mulch's mind was not a birthing pool but a gateway to another world.

8

"Get out while you can still drive," Lazy Mel drawled.

Nick stared at Lazy Mel's mushroomed head as he wiped the bar down, and chomped on his cigar. Nick wondered how Mel's skinny neck supported such a large head. *Lazy Mel's head was twice as big as it should be,* Nick thought. He wiped his eyes and yawned. The alcohol had given Nick a real sweller of drunk and his vision blurred in and out, like underwater vision, in goggles. The whole bar looked rolled up, the bar bent in on itself. It reminded him of watching television and coming across an old movie squeezed into a TV screen. The bar looked very narrow and stretched out on the top and bottom. Lazy Mel looked warped like in a funhouse mirror. Mel leaned across the bar, and Nick smelled tuna and cigars twisting out his mouth.

"It's early," Mel snorted, "you'll be able to sleep it off with no problem."

Nick looked at his watch which he had to hold close to his eyes to see, ten fifty-eight. Minnesota Sally had just finished up her set, and she was packing away her fishing net and clam rake. Her skin shined in the dim light and several enthusiastic men in the back applauded. About two dozen men sat around the stage which formed a T. As Nick blinked his eyes, the bar warped some more, the floor pitched, and he felt his stomach sink.

"Byjezum crowl, you look awful, Nick," Mel said as he offered Nick a glass of water, which he slid to him. The crowd stood up around the stage as Bratty Paulina strutted on stage in her Catholic School Girl outfit. Motley Crue's "Doctor Feelgood" blasted from the speakers. Nick took a sip of the water and grimaced. There was a faint throbbing beginning in his skull and he had the feeling that if he didn't get home soon, he'd pass out. *Besides,* he thought, *the air would do me good, no?*

9

Bill set the teapot on the stove and turned the knob too high. As he listened to the bubble of the water beginning to boil, Bill opened one of the many drawers in his workroom. He fished through the string and hemp to find a bent copper spoon. He placed it next to the honey jar on the desk. Leaving the tea, he crossed to his army cot and fished out a knapsack from underneath. He rummaged around inside and fished out a leather sack. About the size of his palm, the sack contained ceremonial ashes, which he would scatter when summoning magic later that night.

Next door, splashing, *Marina has returned from her swim.*

He had long thought of this, betraying the Hayes family. He'd been with them so long now, he could barely remember the years and years before. *That's not true,* he mused, *you remember a memory of a memory. They deserve it.*

Bill had raised Marina and he didn't want to see her go. He would not allow her to be harmed either. But what exactly could he do? *I have no agency in his matters.* But he could add protection spells along the box to keep Cilia from using more explosive magics.

Yes. Bind her power. Bind the influence of Mulch, too.

He sniffed the potion; it had a bitter smell.

You'll have to betray her to save her later. It cannot be avoided. Yeah, buddy, keep telling yourself you're not responsible and see where that gets you.

"I got the rest of my life to hate myself." He said aloud without meaning to.

10

At night, especially on moony nights, Marina liked to slip into her basement pool, and swim the narrow underground channel into the creek. While she was shy and didn't like to be spotted, she enjoyed the company of people from the edges of the banks. At night she would swim out to suckle the saltwater and the moony shadows cast upon the winding creek that spilled into the Atlantic, her long frame gliding easily through the water and her long dark hair like a long dark fin when she swam. She had been known to stay in the water for weeks.

Marina's mother, a mermaid, had given birth to Marina in the pool under the Hayes house, and Marina had been raised on the creek water and had grown accustomed to its taste, the smell of the mud and muck, and the gritty feel of the clay and silt that made up the saltwater creek bed. She practically lived on rockfish and muscles, and shark. She didn't like to rob the watermen of their oysters, but she did, stealing one here and one there, never taking more than she needed; and if she fancied a fight, she hunted sharks and rays which would satisfy her urges. She'd hunted a ten-foot bull for a week till she bested it.

She enjoyed the quiet. Sometimes, Mr. Bill would follow her into the Atlantic as a fish, or a turtle. When he came with her, she didn't have to worry about finding her way home, or being seen by fishermen, Bill kept her safe. She didn't like to be in the ocean by herself, it scared her, in the way a shy, nervous girl might be afraid to stray far from her parents. *Besides,* she thought to herself, *why should she leave the creek?* Everything she loved was in the creek, the murmurous sounds of rain, the gentle pull of the tide as it receded, and the give it gave when it came in. She never had to worry in the creek, the sharks were small, rays too, and she'd come home to the wading pool in her bedchambers which were decked with Christmas lights and hung with paper lanterns.

Not that she couldn't handle the ocean. In fact, in the ocean, Marina's strength surged. She could be deep in the North Atlantic in a matter of hours, banking and swimming the swifter currents that she sensed with her skin. But she rarely traveled out of the creeks that were but merely fingers of the sea reaching towards land. She had the strength to tear a shark in half, as well as the senses to detect them coming. She communicated with dolphins and whales, and she was immune to the most toxic marine poisons. But she rarely left the shore. Marina loved her sister, Virginia, and her father, Mulch, and so she preferred to stay close. *Why would I ever leave?* She thought often while swimming on her back in the creek. Her sister sometimes visited her in the dark and skinny-dipped as Marina turned somersaults in the brine. Occasionally Marina swam with her feet, and her sister brought friends, music, and beer. Marina enjoyed these nights, swimming naked in the water with her sister and her sisters' friends who treated her with kindness but distance, a distance Marina didn't mind. She liked to watch them play and she liked the sound of their laughter. Plus, Marina liked to sing and when Virginia brought her friends, and everyone got buzzed, singing was bound to happen.

Sometimes Virginia would come down alone to the bank and watch Marina as she played in the creek. On these nights Marina would whisper across the lapping water to the shore, where her sister smoked and drank. Her whispers sounded like the tide coming in. Her whispers sounded like fog over the marsh.

She swam under stars as the tide went out, or came in. Spending her nights drifting under stars, on her back, while her fin carried her peacefully under the canopy of moss and magnolias on the bank by the boathouse. Stars twinkled through the foliage and Marina felt like she was floating in starlight, melting away into the night sky.

Marina once told Virginia how she would sneak into the back paddles of the creeks, up to where migrants built bonfires and celebrated Saturday night and Sunday. There the migrants sang songs in dialects that reminded Marina of her mother. Songs that sounded like whispers sometimes. At those times Marina would float in the water and listen from a half-mile away, listening to the voices over the water. Marina told Virginia that Spanish dialects that wooed her sounded more and more like a waterfall the longer she floated beyond their sight, a waterfall she bathed in. Marina said it was like listening to the first sounds ever heard in the world.

11

Marina's head broke the surface of the water, and she peered out into the dark. She'd left early in the day and had not lit any candles. There was a dim glow coming from Bill's chambers and the smell of tea. The tea had been her idea, she'd read about teatime in some children's book long ago. Bill drank tea each night before bed and one night she'd suggested they have tea together. He agreed and they'd been doing it since.

She emerged out of the water and sat on the edge of the pool. Her skin prickled with a chill, but she shrugged it off and pushed her wet hair to her back. *Something is weighing on him,* she thought, her thought fading into another thought, *shark,* a large Bull shark entered the creek and all the vibrations of the creek doubled back to her from every movement of every living creature. *A shark comes.*

She got up and turned on her Christmas lights, and the ceiling glowed and twinkled. Purples, baby blues, pinks, all the mermaid's favorite colors.

"How's the swimming tonight?" Bill said as he stepped into her room. "I thought I heard you." The teacup steamed and Bill felt the heat through the porcelain.

Marina sat back down and dangled her feet in the water and turned her head. Her hair shimmered down her back, like moonlight glinting off scales. At times her hair appeared black, at other times dark green, and sometimes a dark blue.

"Hello." Her voice sounded like trickling water, wet and quick, and a bit hoarse. "Is it tea time already?" Marina sounded far away, spacey. She took the teacup from Bill, and he stepped back.

"Mind if I light a candle?"

"Be my guest," she cooed.

The match sent shadows careening to the other side of the chamber wall.

"Yes, it's teatime" Bill's bones felt as if they were made of stone. He moved very slowly. "Yes, tea." Bill sat next to her and felt her heat, her strength. *She could crush every bone in my body,* he thought.

"Of course," Marina said. She was always dreamy, especially when there was a full moon. When she was in contact with water her mind became that of water, uncontrolled, powerful, sweeping. She thought of all things at once, or only one thing. She possessed the strength of the sea. With her, there was no pretense of conversational rules. Often she said little, which was fine because he often had little to say. The few words shared between the two passed with long pauses.

"Something is bothering you isn't there?" Marina's back rippled, her skin flashed.

Mr. Bill stared at her doubled muscles, the layered strength of her mermaid heritage. The quickness of her flesh made a sound that reminded Bill of a snake, a dangerous predator.

Mr. Bill only motioned to her tea, which he'd placed down next to them, on the edge of the pool. Instead, she slipped back into the pool. She transformed, a great ripping sound, and her fin snaked out of the water seductively; the water around her breasts glowed with candlelight.

"Tell me." Her hair flashed with green stripes.

"What I really wanted to do was to bring you some tea." His smile cut into his bones and muscles. *Am I going to do this?*

"Yes, you've said that."

She's reading me, he thought. He felt her mind crawl over his own, looking for a way in. A tickle under the scalp, a tickle across the lobes.

"How's the fishing?"

"Quite good. I can't wait till some of those oysters fatten up." She hummed. "I *love* raw oysters."

"I know you do."

"And there were many boys on the creek, buzzing in their little boats. They're not very powerful, those noisy boats."

"No, they are not. Not like you."

"And they're clumsy as fishermen. Sometimes that gets me upset."

"That they're hurting the fish?"

"No, because they have no style." Marina somersaulted, splashing Bill teasingly, as she did.

12

"Um, Lilly?" George held up his hands to block the light, and as he approached her he couldn't see the light from within her aura. Either the light had faded, or it was he that was in the inner eye of the storm. The rest of the restaurant still had their sunglasses on.

"Is there something wrong?" Lilly asked as she continued to dab her napkin against her dress, the red of the raspberry margarita marginally less noticeable.

"Uh, well," George strained his eyes, he really couldn't see it anymore, the light. Everyone else seemed to, though. *Am I going crazy, too? Did that guy just raise his hand to block the light?* Over near the bar, a waiter stared briefly at the intense light that was Lilly and promptly slipped and spilled a tray of colored drinks. The fallen waiter shielded his eyes from George and Lilly's side of the room as he slunk away, whimpering. "Um, I don't know how to tell you this."

"Spit it out. Did the bartender say something off-color?"

Lilly did seem to glow, figuratively, however. *That's just her beauty, George.*

"He said something about me. Didn't he?"

"Um, I think well…"

"I knew it! Can't go anywhere nice. Thanks, Fox news…"

"Well, it wasn't that."

"He called me a tomato picker, didn't he?"

"No."

"Come on George, out with it."

"Um, you're glowing."

"What?" Lilly said, dropping her napkin.

"Glowing. As in putting off enough solar power to keep Virginia Beach sustained for a year."

"Glowing! Shit."

"Was the bartender's exact words, I believe, before he thrust these cheap-looking Ray-Ban wannabes in my hands."

"Glowing?" Lilly blushed. "Oh my god. I can't believe this."

"Have you ever noticed that you can keep a cheap pair of shades forever and always lose the expensive ones?" George twirled the cheap sunglasses in his fingers. He'd seen the light but now couldn't see it. *Best to move forward with dinner,* he thought.

"This is awful." She rose, her hands suddenly coming to her face. "Excuse me."

George thought he heard tears as she rushed to the bathroom.

CHAPTER SEVEN

1

Nick swayed and almost fell, catching himself on a sappy branch. Thick goo stuck to his bare skin and glued his arm hairs together. Swearing, he tripped over a clump of tangled vines. He barely saw his own hands in the dark for the thick trees overhead. In the distance, a hoot-owl called out and there was some serious scuffling in the underbrush. It wasn't so much that he couldn't see through the blackness, it was more like he wasn't able to see because of some perfunctory disorder, a temporary sightlessness, his hand's blurry ghosts in front of his face. He wasn't having a good day.

There was only one problem with The Lazy Titty. One had to drive unpaved back roads to get there, and then one had to hike through the woods to find it. You had to park fifty yards from the door, at least, in the woods. Most cars, like Nick's, were parked more than a football field away. Lazy Mel insisted on this, so from the air, in case of police surveillance, the cars would be obscured by the trees. Lazy Mel also planted about a dozen different varieties of thorny plants around the perimeter each year, which was why so many patrons bled from the knees down as they stumbled around looking for their cars, drunk. Nick fell, again and again, caught himself on a sappy tree branch.

"Shit."

He didn't think he'd find his car this time. He decided instead to turn around and go back for another drink, but when he pirouetted, hands sticky, gunky, covered in bits of leaf and bark, he saw nothing but deep blackness. No trees. No shadow. No moon. Only blackness. And that's when the voices began.

2

Mr. Bill's voice, like water braiding over stones, over lichen, and slippery moss, had a soothing effect on Marina. "Here. Why don't you tell me about your day." He palmed the hot teacup and set it down. He handed Marina her cup and brushed her hand, cool from the water. Her blood had been known to hold temperatures as hot as 130 degrees, and Bill felt the strength in her blood as her right index finger and middle finger brushed his hand. Her nightgown lay on the floor like snakeskin. She didn't sip but inhaled the scent.

"There's something special in the tea," Marina said as she coyly lowered her head to make her eyes roll to the tops of her sockets, her skin throwing off a majestic sheen of green and her naked body glistening with water. "There's something in here, no?" She kicked off the side of the pool and rolled over like a dolphin. Tea slopped and sloshed over the side of the cup. Her great fin pointed up out of the water.

"Something special?" Mr. Bill remained stock still, counting his teeth with the tip of his tongue, one tooth, two, three. The trick was to remain empty, void.

"Yes, something special." She repeated, moving closer to Bill who had begun to breathe heavily. When Marina moved the water lapped and licked away from her skin and her blue-black hair gave off a low illumination. Marina's eyes fixed on Bill's cloudy but steadfast eyes. She came right up to the edge and rested her arms on the rim of the pool, her skin touching Bill's skin. Touching Marina was like touching a very hot cup of coffee.

Bill kept his body still. Marina's right elbow brushed him, and her heat coursed through him like a fever. She cupped the tea in her hands, smiling. "Thank you." She licked the edge of her cup.

"You're welcome," Bill coughed. "I hope you like it."

"Of course I'll like it. I like everything you do."

"Thank you, dear."

"It's no problem, really," she said as she sipped the tea without hesitation before setting it down on the edge of the pool.

She knows, Bill thought, *she knows.* He felt his breath kick up in his chest.

"I like the flavor. What is it?"

"Wild raspberry and lemongrass."

"Sounds exotic." Marina's voice modulates from hoarse to throaty, depending on the tide and the shape of the moon. "You're a good man, Bill."

"Thank you."

"You know I think of you as a father figure. Is this correct?"

Mr. Bill nodded, "Yes."

"I just want you to know that Bill."

"Thank you." Bill struggled to calm his heartbeat, but he had trouble. She was feeling him out and she had not taken enough of a sip for the potion to be effective. "So, what do you want to talk about?"

"Our next trip to the ocean."

"Really?"

"Yes." Marina floated on her back and rested the teacup on her stomach. "I think I need to explore the ocean more."

"Good."

"But not without you."

"We've talked about this. Mulch and you have talked about this."

"I know, I know." She snatched the cup off her stomach and gulped the rest of the tea. "This is all he thinks about, my leaving?"

"He is concerned you won't find a mate."

"I do not like the big spaces of the sea. You know this. I am not comfortable, there. Yet."

"I know sweetie." Mr. Bill offered her a loving touch and Marina rested her head on his knee. "You'll be out there sooner than you think. And you'll see a lot more."

"Do you promise?"

"Of course, I do." Marina didn't see Bill's grin and his eyes staring at her empty teacup.

3

Nick told himself: *don't move, don't move, don't move.* He squatted in a thorn bush somewhere in the woods behind the Lazy Titty. Far off, he heard the sounds from the stage. His body broke out into gooseflesh listening for the hag whose voice whispered to him from thick darkness.

"Little sea girl, come on out and fetch your jar," The voice hissed. "Come get your jar little wreck before we drop and break your neck." The voice raised the hackles on his neck. It sounded like a cartoon witch. *Where was it coming from?*

Five feet off to his right a twig snapped.

"Fish girl come and eat your kind before we come to clean your mind." The voice shouted before fading into a long volley of laughter, beginning behind him and then coming from the sides.

Pressure deep in his skull rose like a sinus headache. He rubbed his temples and briefly an image flashed in his mind, of a silver-haired older woman standing before a large bay window, outside the window, a large city spread out. He did not recognize it. For a brief second, Nick thought he could speak to the older woman. "Hello?" Nick whispered as he turned his head, hoping he wouldn't find a ghost over his shoulder. "Hello?" His head pounded; his heart began its trip-hammer in his chest.

What the fuck is happening to me? Nick thought. He scanned the darkness of the forest and decided that this forest was not the same forest he had driven into. Strange nausea flowed over him, and he felt his insides enlarge as if a great gulf opened inside of him. The forest around him did not look familiar.

4

George Henderson felt helpless, wearing his Sunday suit, even though he didn't go to church, ever, nervously fiddling his fake Ray-Ban sunglasses as he waited for Lilly Aguirre, who after realizing she glowed like a lighthouse cried herself to the bathroom and hadn't come out for twenty minutes or more. George flicked his lighter on and off with one hand and twirled the glasses with another. He wanted to see how much one tiny flame could influence the light surrounding his table. George had about decided that a single lighter could cast a romantic glow in a small, contained space. He was staring at the romantic glow, desperate for the date to continue, half afraid she would return to the table and demand to leave. He was staring at his lighter when his table filled with a bright light. George's shadow elongated in front of him as Lilly approached him.

"We have to go," Lilly said, her voice wavering.

"Why?" George fumbled with his glasses and lighter, dropping both on his silverware.

"Why do you think? Because" Lilly sneered, "because I'm glowing. This is *not* supposed to be happening."

At the bar, the beefy bartender handed out shades to new patrons wandering near.

"Oh come on Lilly, we don't have to leave on their account."

"Of course we're leaving on their account." Lilly focused all her nervous anxiety towards the front of the bar. "We should leave now." At the bar, someone let out a scream as they caught Lilly's bright gaze in the face. Another woman covered her face with her purse to avoid looking at Lilly. "Now, George."

"Of course." George rose from his seat. "I've already paid for the drinks."

Someone walking in the front door shouted something about suntan oil.

"Okay," Lilly said as she b-lined it to the door before George could say jackrabbit-slim, Menus, purses, sports jackets, and linen were thrown in front of unshielded faces as she passed.

5

I French inhaled. Rick attempted to French inhale.

"Virginia, your father is fucking slave driver man, I heard those immigrants..." Rick coughed as he exhaled.

"Migrants, the term is migrants."

"Yeah, whatever. I heard he's got the migrants sacked out in tents and sleeping bags, sleeping under an orchard so that every time they go piss, they can pick a few pieces of fruit."

Dull laughter filled the room briefly, everybody was too stoned to laugh much. Rick "the Dick" Bell continued. I sipped my warm drink; it had felt like years since I had poured it.

"Yeah, like I don't care if they work, cause somebody's gotta do it." Clyde, our host, interjected.

Clyde changed the subject by passing a bowl of pills around. The green pills were X. The whites were valium. The yellows were speed. The blues were downers. Low-grade cosmetic drugs reserved for such occasions as summer party blues. I was feeling plenty blue, but not that blue. There had to be forty or fifty pills. Some folks took two.

"Yeah, pass the fucking pot," Somebody jived.

Clyde's living room has no couch and the carpet's threadbare and peppered with ash and butt burns. Someone scorched a peace sign the size of my ass into the far corner of the shag. There are floor pillows, though, and a glass coffee table that's usually littered with paraphernalia, and pornography. Mark hung out with Clyde in the corner by the peace sign, smoking a fat one and placing their pills on the end of their tongues, like hosts. Mark's head bobbed each time Clyde asked him a question. Clyde's fly has been wide open for about an hour and his boxers stick out like a tongue. I keep hoping to get some fly-hole action but so far, nada. Katie and Jennifer circled the beer cooler near Wally. Katie's a cutie. If I were to sleep with a woman, it would be with someone like her. She's the type of girl who can show off her stomach and not look too obvious about it. She's got one of those flat stomachs that cry out to be touched. Her hair hangs in a curly brown bounce of ringlets and kinks, and her eyes soak you up when you look into them, they're always so wet and so large. Rick insists she's on something. I think they're just damn pretty. Jennifer hangs out with Katie and is tall, nearly six foot four and she has great legs. That's gotta count for something, the height. Wally looks like a reject from a military school. His eyes are kind screwed up. His eyes looked painted on like he shouldn't have any eyes. His are shallow sockets, and flat eyes, like his face should be without them. They don't fit. Wally seems to be at every party on the shore. He's got the best party radar and can scare up any drug you want, which is why people are fine to have him around. Here, the party is pretty much pooped out, early too. They mill around the keg and chit-chat. Macy slid out of her top about ten minutes ago and onto Luke's lap about the same time that Rick started rolling doobies. Macy and Luke then disappeared into Clyde's spare bedroom where there is a dirty mattress on the floor and not much else. Macy's probably passed out on Luke, she's a sloppy drunk at best. Just after, Ritchie, Kara, Rocky, Tamari, Jaden, some girl named Lacy, and two guys named Vare (rhymes with glare) and Quinn took off to Julie's house down the beach a bit where she's got a keg and an eight-ball. Vare and Quinn looked like two cool motherfuckers, they must be since I've never seen them at the shitty parties down the road. The party keeps threatening to move to Julie's beach house, but so far no one has made it up from their seats, not since the others left.

6

The last time Nick heard the voice of the hag it had been right on top of him. He moved a little, to get behind what he thought was a tree if only to pee, but he had trouble seeing the details of the tree in the darkness, and when he reached his hand out to swipe a branch away, there had been no branch at all. *My mind is all scrambled,* he thought. He noticed that his shuffling feet made no noises. He didn't hear the rustle of leaves and twigs under his shoes, nothing but the noise of his breathing and the voice of the hag. He wanted to get out of the woods, but the fear of the voices kept him from moving quickly, and the more he kept still listening for the voices, the more he thought of the voices as an It, as a thing, a thing with teeth. He wasn't drunk anymore, and the pressure in his head had dissipated.

Then suddenly, up ahead somewhere, perhaps ten feet, perhaps ten inches, a tiny dot of light appeared, a smoldering glow, a small pinprick of light like a lightning bug, something small with a soft light that emanated from a body. Nick felt the air around him rush toward the light.

"Little fish girl." The voice emanated from the pulsing light.

Instantly Nick felt the pressure build-up in his skull, a pounding wail of an ache that made his eyes throb.

"Fish girl, fish girl."

You gotta get outta here, buddy, Nick thought.

He took a breath and stepped forward into the sticky strings of a fresh spider web. He swatted his nose and spat. The light moved in dizzying tumbles. It was a firefly, after all, Nick thought, but he knew it wasn't. The light sped off and vanished behind a tree and then buzzed back around to Nick, touching him on the shoulder before blasting off again towards darkness. It moved farther back into the forest. Nick followed it. Around him, there was only silence. As he moved cautiously, he thought that somewhere beyond a spider had awakened, to see what catch had landed in its web.

7

The parking lot surrounding Lewandos Italian/Argentinean Bar and Steakhouse was submerged under a giant bubble of light. Two figures lurked inside the large bubble of light, which cars on Route 13 saw from over a mile away, across the corn and soy fields; a bubble of light thrown up against the night as if to resist all darkness. The two figures were oblivious to the bubble of light which was both like a cage thrown over the parking lot and a shield. A few people milling about outside the restaurant in Lonely, turning a corner and looking at the suddenly bright refracted light in the windows of antique stores ran screaming. A small dog barked like a maniac in the distance.

George Henderson took Lilly Aguirre by the hand and tried to get her to twirl under his arm, a very brave move on George's behalf since he was neither coordinated nor very confident.

"I honestly haven't seen this parking lot look so damn good," George said and meant it too, as he tried to pull Lilly under his arms like Gene Kelly, or Jimmy Stewart might. George's face was open like an umbrella, smiling at Lilly, who was putting out enough light to guide a ship by. "Really, I mean, damn!"

He smiled, hoping Lilly understood that he didn't care that she glowed like a human power plant. Lilly's fingers became entangled with his fingers, and she kept her feet firmly planted in the oyster shell parking lot. George's middle finger turned under Lilly's finger and ground up against the ring she wore. The pain made George wince. Still, he continued to dance around her.

Lilly said in a very small voice, "I'm sorry George. I didn't mean to ruin our evening." She said evening like even-ning which made George tingle.

George's face twisted up in pain, the ring cut into his flesh, and he tried to let go of her hand, but she continued to hold tight.

"You look great," he managed. "You look like the brightest idea I ever had."

Lilly smiled and released George's hand, leaning in to kiss him on the cheek. The kiss sent a wave of heat through his body and George's head filled with an intense light that made him squint. Across the street someone said something about being blinded by the light of... then there came a skull shaking thrum as that someone collided with a pole across the street. George made out a very dim ghost of a person rubbing his or her forehead. Lilly was so bright that everything outside her bubble of light was fuzzy and grainy, not to mention dark.

Lilly tilted up on her feet and kissed George on the mouth and George immediately began to sweat. He kissed her back as the person across the street hit his or her head again, the skull numbing thrum echoing this time off Lewandos' walls.

"Jesus! It's so bright!"

George imagined that somebody was going to go home and make themselves an ice pack. Lilly laughed and George laughed too, but they continued to kiss, and George felt like he was going to explode into beams of light.

CHAPTER EIGHT

1

Elementary school, that's how long I've known these people. Sometimes, I think I should have stayed in Boston, job, or no job.

"I'm stepping out," I smiled, "for a smoke." No one noticed but the Dick.

"Some fresh air eh, VA?" the Dick smirked.

"Don't call me VA." I quipped.

As I said, I've known these people from way back when. A few I didn't meet till high school, at parties. It doesn't take long for the party kids from the different schools to mix. It gets to be a regular cocktail of people sometimes. Macy had crawled out of Clyde's spare room and was sprawled on the floor next to the couch. Macy's chest fluttered up and down with her breath.

Marina never went to school, thank God, she'd have been eaten alive. Mr. Bill and Mulch taught her a little math and English. Maria did her best with Spanish. Maria would be happy to know that Marina loved to speak Spanish. Even when she screwed it up, it sounded good.

I had to go to school and Marina didn't. That sucked. Talk about major jealousy issues for me when I was young and coming up in the world. Here I am going to school and enduring teases and taunts in middle school, ego-crushing humiliation of maturing so early my friends' fathers and even a few teachers looked at me with predatory interests when I was eleven. Don't forget dating, and the confidence games and the bullshit speeches my mirror-self had to listen to, not to mention menstruation, which I'm not sure Marina goes through. There was some real shady secret stuff I'm not exposed to when it comes to Marina. She got to swim all day and watch TV, which come to think about it never really interested her, except Disney. Marina got off on *Splash,* a movie Mulch had bought for her. That was sometime after Christmas and snow covered the ground, the kind that crunches under your boots when you go outside. The kind of snow that makes houses feel cozier and lamp light warmer. At night the outside becomes like one giant crystal and the moon is everywhere, reflected in the thick hanging bulbs of frozen Magnolia's, the frozen branches, and the black ice of the blacktop. I remember that when Mulch got out of his truck, he had a bag with him. He said he'd been somewhere on some kind of business trip. Marina had been upstairs, when I say Marina was upstairs, I mean she was not in her cave, she was upstairs with us, lying on the couch watching the fire. I remember she wore a T-shirt and sweatpants, and I sat in the seat next to her totally and completely jealous of her thick greenish-black hair. Marina had been saying something about Santa. "Yeah sure. Santa," I had said.

I had a zit on my chin which had been there for five days. Michael Sminks hadn't called me in a week and the snow wasn't going to last forever. Dread hung over me like a fog that I would have to go back to school with the same zit on my chin I had when Christmas vacation began. I think that was the first time I thought about going Delilah on Marina and taking her hair for my purposes. "Santa isn't real Marina," I had said. "You do know that don't you?"

My hands had picked and pawed my chin in a complex tango around the zit.

"No. Mulch looks like Santa," she had replied.

I turned to look at Marina, my jaw and mouth having already formed a look of abject befuddlement when I saw through the frosted window over Marina's thick and shiny black-so-black-you-can-see-your-reflection-in-it hair, Mulch stepping very carefully across the drive to the front steps. And he had looked like Santa, a little, from the window, walking through the snow with a bag over his shoulder.

"But Christmas is over," Marina had said.

I probably glared at the way she swooshed her hair over her shoulders. God, I must have been 12, no maybe 13. She was 17.

Mulch brought us gifts every time he returned from a business trip. Sometimes something small like a keyring, or lighter from some exotic restaurant, or perhaps a T-shirt, or even a hotel towel, which Marina loved. That one winter I got a make-up kit from Macy's department store; Clinique, so cool because nobody in my school had a Clinique bag full of fat fancy lipstick, powders, and eyeliner. Marina got a DVD; *Splash*, starring Tom Hanks, John Candy, and Daryl Hannah as the mermaid.

Marina never watched a lot of television, she hated it, she couldn't keep still, her legs bouncing up and down the whole time. For a while, I thought it was because she was cognitively different. Her face would twist up and became dark and withdrawn when people carried on a conversation on the television, the close-ups of people's faces looking intent on one another. When Marina spoke to other people, she studied their faces to see how intent they were on what she said, which was little. Mr. Bill said Marina probably didn't have the same vision as everyone else. Which took Mr. Bill a long time to explain to me. When Marina saw *Splash* she stayed in front of the television for hours, forcing the family to watch it over and over again. Mr. Bill, Mulch, Maria, and I squashed on the couch while Marina sat Mr. Bill style, wild-eyed and wide-faced at the screen, soaking up every nuance of Daryl Hannah's poor acting and Disney's poor special effects. It was uncanny, with this one movie, she had taken the family and DVD player hostage. This awkward girl who never sat through an entire episode of anything without becoming completely agitated had become obsessed. I realized watching her watch Daryl Hannah that Marina had never once seen her mother.

"It's like she's watching fish in a tank," Mr. Bill had said.

"Better yet, she's in the tank and looking out," Maria had replied.

Mulch only grunted. I didn't care one way or another, I mean, like, I had watched a thousand movies before, and nobody went gaga when I sat down in front of the TV. Shortly after that, the *Little Mermaid* hit theaters for an Anniversary run theatrical release or something. *Little Mermaid* is, like, the make-out movie of all time for 13-year-old girls. Michael Sminks was so over by the time I sat in the back of the theater for that movie and sucked face with Ryan Kellam instead. I don't even remember the movie, but I remember the hickie Ryan gave me, a big purple lopsided quarter. Later, in the hallways at school, we'd touch and the hickey would shiver, I swear. But Marina, she went to see the movie with me. It was the first time she ever left the homestead. To her, it was like fucking pioneer time or something. She had seen the preview on TV while waiting for *Splash* to load one afternoon. I had never seen anyone flip before. Her feet left the ground, and she did these acrobatic somersaults in the air. God, I mean Marina really flipped out over the *Little Mermaid*. Marina had actually left the house to seek it out, and that of course, was how she met her first boy.

2

Marina looked like a sleeping dragon, her skin flashing shiny pink and shiny green. Candlelight played on her body and made her look like a hallucination. The sleeping potion had forced her mermaid body to transform back into its human form, and Bill scooped her from the water and carried her to the bed in the corner of the chamber. He laid her body lengthwise across an old quilt, one of her favorites. Bill folded the old quilt around her, for fear that she would awaken. Then he threw her over his shoulder. His lungs burned quick and true and his muscles strained as carried her up the stairs. Mr. Bill estimated she weighed over two hundred pounds. His feet made a heavy pounding on the staircase, and for a second he thought he was going to collapse. She weighed as much as a large man, despite her thin frame. Her muscle mass was twice that of a man, plus that of her scales, hard scales that were intertwined with her human skin. The steps shuddered under his weight, and the door barely opened.

Bill wasn't moving as fast as he thought he could. He was afraid that there was a possibility that she would wake up, which didn't help, because Bill couldn't move any faster. Mulch was waiting for them outside, and Mulch would be anxious.

3

As Nick moved in the murky dark, he saw the little lightning bug of light ahead of him pulse in time with his heartbeat, the hag's voice steady in his mind. To his left, a fog hissed along the ground, and twice now he thought he'd seen the form of some large crow before him, its open beak ready to snap down on something tender, like one of his fingers searching the inky dark before him. *Like what kind of fucking crows are active at night?*

"Little reeking wreck," the old crone's voice hissed. He still thought the voice came from the light, though he could not make heads or tails of it.

Up ahead the little light fluttered. *Eventually, I would come upon my car, wouldn't I?* Somewhere around the woods, his little, rusty Toyota Corolla had to be waiting for him.

"Who's gonna save you now little fish girl?" the voice shivered. "Who's gonna paint your picture after you've dried yourself up now, hmmm?"

Nick began to think that the voices were coming from his head, and that terrified him. "C'mon son, join me in the nuthouse." He heard his father tease in the darkness. "Shut up," he told himself. "Just shut up." *What if I haven't been moving at all? What if this is all in my mind?*

Then he saw it. What he would later call the 'Thing in the Woods,' a fleeting dash of white going at a very high speed away from him. No longer the size of a lightning bug but shaped like a woman. He had heard it running, breaking the underbrush beneath it, snapping the trees before it. Nick ran too. He had to follow it.

That laugh had come from inside his head. It felt like a fever or a cold settling into his throat. *But if the voices were coming from him, why was he running? What was he chasing?* Then he saw it again, the whitish blur ahead, eight feet, six feet. He saw its arms, white streaks of hair, and the ragged ends of a dress. Trees blurred around him, materializing to his left, to his right. He could discern the woods again, the dull glow of the moon caught in the canopy above. He dodged and ducked and felt his body click in tune with the woods. The whitish blur rippled, its surface mass changing as it flew through the woods. The figure turned right, and Nick zagged after it and grazed a tree trunk. His torso alive with pain, he felt the scrape draw blood. His feet unsure, his head swimming with throbbing pressure. He felt himself spinning as if his feet were no longer touching the forest floor. The figure, no more than two feet from him, turned to face him. Nick tried to stop but couldn't. He realized he hadn't thought about what to do if he caught it. It never occurred to him that he might confront the whitish thing, let alone tackle it, perhaps.

It turned on him and shrieked, letting out a forceful wind from its mouth, smelling of saltwater, dampness, and rot. Nick slammed into it and screamed himself. He went right through the white figure, and it dissipated into smoke as Nick fell to the ground, all the air in his lungs blown right out of him.

"Fetch your jar." The voice echoed all around him now, in the woods, in the treetops. It hung in the trees like some kind of bird, the voice snaked out of the ground and into his ears.

"Who's gonna paint your picture now. All dried up and nowhere to go." The pressure in Nick's skull spiked and Nick's head flooded with intense white light. *It's coming for you, Nick.* Then he passed out.

When Nick awoke his ears burned where trees had scraped them, and his head throbbed. *Where was he?*

Then he remembered the thing, and his heart jumped. He listened for the sounds of shrieking but heard crickets. He lifted his head and turned around. He didn't see anything. But that didn't mean squat. Rising to his feet, his eyes caught a gleam from his right. No more than five feet away, catching all the moonlight in its wheels, lay his car. *What is going on in my head?* Nick thought, panic settling in his chest like a bird.

4

Macy told our senior English teacher that she didn't fear the end of the world because she lived on the Eastern Shore, and nothing ever comes to the Eastern

Shore, not even the end of the world. The Shore is a kind of purgatory. Take this party, for instance, journal, it's the same high school party you attended when you were sixteen, only it's years later.

Clyde's apartment is actually the second floor of a house. It has two bedrooms, a long railroad living room, and an eat-in kitchen. The bathroom is small but there's a kick-ass bathtub, with claw feet no less, and a stained-glass window right next to it. The stained glass is of a dove with an olive branch in its mouth. The window is bright blue with red crisscrosses, and of course, a bright white dove and a bright green swash of branch cutting the blue, which I guess is supposed to be the sky. Clyde says every time he takes a bath, he feels like he's Noah and the bird is perpetually in flight, telling him that the flood is over, to get off the boat, to get out of the water.

Squeals peal out from under the guest bedroom door. Rick "the Dick" is about through with Macy. I recognize his pathetic grunting. Macy might be awake, or at least hopefully she is. Knowing her, she'll hit her second wind and come out coked to the gills and act like it's no big deal. Everybody else has gone out to the Shore Stop, a kind of a 7-11, Store 24 kinda place, where you can get fried chicken and microwavable sandwiches. There isn't a late-night cafe or even pancake house for hours around here. Being single here is like being stuck on an island. We're all heading for the other party at Julie's beach house. I just hope it's better than this one.

5

Bill had only been outside with her for a minute before he paused, his muscles aching something fierce. He leaned on the deck rails wrapping around the eastern perimeter of the house. He'd helped Mulch put the deck in thirty years back. *Yep, your soul is stretched a bit thin,* he thought. Years ago he met Mulch's father, and he remembered how hungry he had been. *Starving. For attention, food. A family.* He looked up into the sky as much to take a deep breath as to seek *what? A Sign? You're a fool old man.* High trees blocked the moonlight, the moon having sunk underneath their tallest caps. Marina's body smelled sweet and warm and permeated the air. She would sleep a dreamless sleep. It should take her about three days to regain her full strength, which by that time she would have been rendered weak and powerless by the box. Or so he hoped. The sleeping potion had not been made for mermaids, but for people, yet Mulch insisted. *Family. Mulch's fucked up idea of family.*

Marina murmured. *Bill.*

Shit, she's inside my head. Bill's blood turned cold, and fear spread through his limbs. *A tickle,* he thought. *That's how it begins.* Marina had taken possession of him before, but she had been so young and naive she did not even understand what she had done.

Bill. Marina was awake.

Bill.

And suddenly there came an incredible shifting of weight and then Bill fumbled with Marina and there came a great ripping sound of her legs and body shifting into its mermaid form, the quilt he carried her in falling away as Marina's body generated heat and shifted mass.

Got to hurry.

He applied his great strength and held on to Marina like he used to hold onto her when she swam in the bay, unsure, and scared, and Mr. Bill had simply grabbed her by the waist and held her arms as she learned to control her great tail. She had a bad habit of allowing her arms to bank her movement. *She had been what? 7, 8?*

Her body shifted again. And when he saw Marina's legs had returned, Mr. Bill bolted, running as fast as he could with her in his arms. But no sooner than he'd started she shape-shifted again. This time he felt the whipping of her great tail as it arched away from him. *Fuck.* Ahead of him, Mulch's shadow cast a long insectile shape towards them. The single light above Mulch gave the whole yard a sickly grayish look. Beyond the cone of light lay the open box on a trailer, Mulch's Chevy lay draped in darkness. Mulch motioned for Bill to hurry. In his arms, Marina squirmed, her eyes fluttered. *Please go to sleep, please go to sleep.*

6

"Stop here." Lilly pointed to the side of the road and George slowed his car, unsure of where to pull off. George looked into the woods that lay black and fused with volume and undergrowth.

"We're in the middle of nowhere," George half asked, half exclaimed.

"Please, I'll be your best friend," Lilly had stopped glowing once she was in the car, and had not offered an explanation, and George did not prod. It had been the single greatest date he'd ever had in his life and his head was filled with light as if all the light in the world was shining inside him. He didn't want it to end.

"Okay." George eased the car over into the little stripe that passed for a shoulder and kept the motor running. "So what's going on?"

"Nothing," Lilly sighed. "This is where I get off, so to speak. The camp is not far, and I was going to see my mother before going home. We have to take care of something."

George smiled and leaned closer to her, scanning out the window. "Well, what exactly do you have to take care of?" He leaned in for a kiss that did not come.

"Well, it's personal." Lilly angled her body away from George. She smiled, but then stopped, resolved.

"Oh. Sorry. I didn't mean to be nosy."

"George," she had laughter in her voice, "You've been a fabulous date and all, but I have to get out here."

"Here? There's nothing here but us."

"I must be lucky." Lilly leaned in and kissed George, first on the cheek, then on the side of the mouth, then again on the mouth, and for a few seconds, the couple lingered Then Lilly broke the kiss and opened the door. It was sudden and George pulled back. "Call me tomorrow George. None of that make her wait bullshit, either." And with that she stepped out of the car and onto the road, waving as she crossed into the woods "I had a really nice time. Let's do it again, soon."

"Wait," George tapped on the window. "Hold up."

Lilly turned as George rolled the window down. "There's nowhere for you to go."

"Nonsense," she gestured behind her, "there's a path right here. It's the long way home."

George's jaw dropped a little, he was sure that the path she pointed towards hadn't been there before; a little clay strip vanishing into the darkness of the trees.

7

Once, Marina and I were swimming, late in the afternoon. It had been August, or perhaps July. There was this kinda fuzziness in the air and I felt the heat lift off the ground and drag upwards towards the trees. A light breeze blew in from the east. That's when I saw her flippers.

Look, Mulch tried this kind of passive parenting thing he'd read about. So like everything I owned had mermaids on it. Mermaid books and toys and hairbrushes and bathing suits and costumes. Name it and I had it bedazzled in a mermaid form.

When I actually saw my older sister turn into a mermaid, I reacted like every other kid who has ever seen a mermaid, who happens to be their older and prettier sister. I blinked in shock. Several times. I must have been seven, maybe eight. I remember thinking that it was a dream. And for a second I thought it would turn into a nightmare. But it didn't. Marina was 12, or 13. It's kinda fuzzy in my head these days because now looking back on all of it, on all her downright weirdness, it feels like I knew all along that she wasn't completely human. So, when I saw her with her fins for the first time I blinked and stood completely still, squishing the mud underneath my toes. What I remember most was how beautiful she was, her hair thick and dark, full of glow, and her skin, her skin like glazed porcelain. It gave off light and heat, it made the water seem all that prettier.

Marina had turned and winked at me, before vanishing under the surface.

I remember seeing her great fin break the surface of the creek. My whole world changed at that moment.

8

Mulch didn't like to watch Bill work his magic. There was something about watching the man conjure magics that made Mulch vaguely sick. It reminded him of junkies, the mix of pain and euphoria that Bill expressed with his body. Mulch didn't understand what Mr. Bill said during the incantations if he used them. Sea Hag used chanties; Marcos employed chants from his own people. He'd watched Bill turn himself into a great turtle once, and a few times he'd seen the man explode trees with a crackling whip of electricity that he manifested in his hand. Most of the time, Mr. Bill worked alone, and Mulch was glad of it, for Mr. Bill's body when it used power affected Mulch to the bone.

Mr. Bill had managed to get Marina inside the box before she fully awoke, and the two men screwed the box shut and sealed the seams with pitch. There was one spell left to perform and it was Mr. Bill's to perform alone. By the time they had physically sealed in Marina, the girl had slipped back into unconsciousness.

Mr. Bill had once commented that commanding magic was like riding a bicycle for the first time. "You can't think about it, you can only think in it, but not of it. Like when you're going to sleep and you can feel sleep take over, but if you think about the sleep that's coming, even for a second, you break the sleep spell."

The box blazed with blue light, electricity crawled over the box, its oaken planks covered in intricate runes and markings, which in turn, flashed blue and white and green before fading.

For a second Mulch thought he heard screaming, and for a second Mulch thought he saw through the box, for the spell ended in a brilliant white light that shone forth like a lighthouse, and for a moment Mulch saw the inside of his creation, Marina's back arching up, her heavy legs still drugged, her arms limp at her side, her throat bringing her entire body up in a howl. She was in great pain. Then she was gone again. The light intensified. He held his hand up to his face to see and stepped inside Marina's prison.

9

Marcos and Sea Hag had returned to her shack and were waiting for midnight when Marcos would slip back to meet Mulch. "But is it good for anything?" Marcos asked, his dark face peering over Sea Hag's shoulder.

"Maybe warts, but only if they're new warts. It's rather weak," Sea Hag said as she stirred the potion.

"Like the coffee?"

"Hey!" Sea Hag's teeth were crooked like a fence after a hurricane and yellow. When she closed her lips, one of her cuspids remained on the outside like a single fence post. "Get me another cup." Sea Hag said, her mug held out to Marcos. When he took it she resumed knitting a long black and shiny scarf, a bit like velvet, and a bit like silk, but which was neither.

"What blend is this?" Marcos asked, still damp from his shower, rubbing the back of his freshly shaved neck.

"Green Komodo Dragon."

"Ah, yes," Marcos arched his eyebrows in approval, his black hair shining in the dim candlelight of Sea Hag's shack beside the sea. "From the isles."

"No, from Starbucks."

"Yuk, Yuk." The coffee pot lay parallel to the one window in her kitchen/living room that afforded the only view of the marsh and the sea outside which seemed so big and so clean to Marcos. The sea, a promise of a new start. "So how cold does it get in the winter, out here, in the middle of nowhere?"

"Colder than my tits in December," Sea Hag guffawed. She liked to drag her laughter out till it was almost like a cough. "There are no trees here in the marsh, just mud, clay, sand, and a lot of wind. So as you can imagine it gets very cold. The wood stove is nice, but I have to bring fuel in from the mainland on my skiff. I burn driftwood when it washes up."

Marcos sat back down at the card table across from her. *She looked even greener in the candlelight*, he thought, then he realized that it was the candle which was green. "Seaweed?" He pointed.

"What? The candle?"

"Yeah."

"Tallow and seaweed. You can use it to see the future. It has that kind of property."

"Oh really?" Marcos reached over and nudged it.

"You stare into it, Marcos. Pyromancy."

Her shack had three rooms. A kitchen/living room that acted as her workshop, a bedroom that was more of a storeroom for herbs and potions, her hammock covered in quilts and bedding, stretched across the back end of the room. Her bedroom had no windows. The bathroom was equipped with an old coppery tub, and she had a shower on the deck outside. She didn't have a toilet. Use the sandpit, it's natural, she told her few guests. The sandpit lay ten feet from the back of the shack. During a storm, the sandpit washed away, and Sea Hag used a bucket. She had a smokehouse for her fish next to the shed, and both were built onto the same platform as her shack, which stood six feet above the mud. The platform itself a marvel, hand-built during the oyster wars and kept up since Sea Hag took advantage of living on top of the water and had laid crab pots and bait traps up and down the pitched oak pylons of her home. She seeded oysters on one side, and clams grew along the banks. She grew herbs and vegetables in plastic buckets, and she'd bring them inside when the storms proved too powerful. She didn't want salt water washing into her greenery. The inside of her home was tidy in the messiest of ways. Sea Hag favored the waxy large produce box as both shelf and crate. The only furniture was a dusty wardrobe that sat against a wall next to the washtub and the drying rack.

"How do you find anything here?" Marcos had wanted to laugh when she showed him in, but out of respect, he'd kept his mouth shut. He gestured to the cluttered table full of spools, thread, odd material, beads, teas, jars of herbs, spices, ground-up things. Crumpled rags she mended her clothes with.

"How do *you* find anything? I've been to your place, it's so sanitary."

"Funny."

"Things find me when I need them. I simply leave them here, to sleep, if you will and when I need them, I find them."

"You sound like the Ugly Mother."

"I do not know this individual, though Mr. Bill has mentioned her name to me."

"She is a nosy old woman who can wield some very old magic. We worked together in Texas and Louisiana many years ago when I began to work for the feds. We would do good to have her help."

"That is not my job, Mr. Bill recruited us. He can recruit her if he wishes."

"I think Mr. Bill and her have discussed other plans. I think."

"Look into the candle and tell me what you see," Sea Hag teased.

"I can divine, you know," Marcos joked.

"Your accent, what happened to it?" Sea Hag asked.

"Schooling. My father won a fortune on a game show in Brazil, and I grew up in Boston."

"Oh," Sea Hag said as she looked up from her sewing.

"Boston has a large Portuguese and Brazilian population. I grew up in Allston alongside Irish rednecks, bums, heroin addicts, and fresh-off-the-boat immigrants. My father drank his fortune away when I was a small boy. I grew up a street orphan, almost, running with other children whose parents were too busy chasing the American dream to be parents. I turned out okay though."

Marcos yawned and looked out the window. Outside the tide had begun to come in. By the grim light that came through the grimy panes of Sea Hag's shack, he estimated that it was after midnight, almost one, maybe two.

"You should go," Sea Hag sighed, exhausted.

For the last few months, they had sat across from each other many times discussing the box, and Marina. Sea Hag had only agreed to help Mulch out of love for the mermaid. Marcos loved the girl; he could not hide it from anyone.

"What will happen?" Marcos' voice sounded like soft leather rustling against skin.

"How should I know?" Sea Hag squinted to thread the needle. "You should go. She'll be ready."

Marcos rose from his seat and rubbed his neck. "I'll try to get her this far, at least. And then if she hasn't destroyed the box by then, we go up the coast. I must see the Ugly Mother before I leave."

Sea Hag only nodded; her stomach had begun to cramp. She nodded and prayed that Mr. Bill's potion would knock Marina out, she prayed that Marcos would live through the night.

CHAPTER NINE

1 December 18, 1989

The Christmas lights reminded Marina of fireflies and algae when the algae were under the loom of the moon; how the Christmas lights took on a presence of their own which made Marina think the lights were sentient, and if she closed her eyes and squinted just so the lights would flutter and twinkle. Much like how in low summer, fireflies hovered and skipped along with narrow marches of creeks and marshes. The algae that simmered all spring broke apart in large sheets and drifted out from the banks to the deeper creek. The moon is kind to algae and sprinkles upon the oblong sheets bits of glow and shimmer.

"The lights are. Hmhf."Marina pressed her lips together so that they flattened out like a frog's face. "The lights are, like, friendly, you know?"

Marina pressed her face against the cold windowpane, looking for snow, which was absent. *If I think really hard it might start,* she thought. She loved snow. *Snow, snow, snow.*

"Friendly lights." Mulch said, turning from her face which was lit to the bone from hanging icicle lights bouncing against the windowpane. He looked back towards the fireplace. He looked back to his daughter who had mashed her entire body up to the window. "I like that," he said. "Friendly like, uh, Santa Claus."

Marina thought it would be wonderful to hang the woods along the creek with lights. She had been bringing it up since she thought it last Christmas.

"Oh, it would be like fireflies frozen in the branches. Frozen because it's winter."

"Oh, I don't know. That's a lot of work," Mulch said looking over his daughter. Her bones sometimes shifted under her skin. *A wonder, she is. Jesus,* he thought.

"The woods along the creek... like a giant Christmas tree."

"Christmas trees."

"Trees, yes, and it would be so pretty to float out underneath them, like stars hanging overhead. It would be like we had stars so close and stars so high." She pulled away from the window and stepped out from under the window shade and curtains. Through the lace and heavy plastic shade, she saw the lights shining through. *It would look like the sky dripping down from outside, like a waterfall of stars.*

"I hate hanging lights," Mulch said as he looked at his oldest with warmth. Mulch already felt his anxiety spike. *Fuck, a chore.*

"I don't. I love hanging lights!" Marina screamed.

"So shall we take a look, eh?" Mulch sighed.

"Oh, can we?" Marina squealed and hurried to the door before Mulch stepped away from the window. Marina giggled like a five-year-old.

2

"Let's get the fuck out of here," Rick "the Dick" Bell mumbled as he shuffled by me, wobbling a bit to his left and right. "This party's dead."

"Sure," I said. He was still drunk, still a bit coked up; his nose ran like a spigot. Rick and Macy had been in the spare bedroom for an hour while I made small talk at the second lamest party we attended that night. All the cool folks had left.

Macy followed Rick but stumbled in the doorway, pulled her top on, and flashed me in the process. Her breasts jiggled and I spied where Rick had chewed a fresh hickey the size of my palm into the side of her left breast.

"Oh, man. I don't feel so hot," Macy said as she held her face with her hands.

"Hungover Macy?"

"Yeah like a fucking train hit me," Macy rubbed her forehead like she had a headache. I don't think she saw the hickey or the bite, or whatever it was, Macy, glazed like a fine pastry and just as numb.

"God, Macy you two really went at it."

"Is that so? I don't remember most of it." She came towards me and kinda leaned on my shoulders for balance. Her lipstick had long been smeared into a blush around her mouth. Her hair, a tangled bunch, hung in front of her face. I spied actual handprints in the moussed hair. "Cool party, huh?"

"Yeah, love. Way cool."

3

Nick's salt-box house, set back into shadows cast by pine trees on the eastern side of the house, looked downright evil. Nick stood in his driveway afraid of his own house, the whisper of the Thing in the Woods fresh in his mind. Fog boiled out of the forest. He felt the stillness of the damp air and listened for the voice. *You're crazy, Nick. There's no way whatever that was followed you home.* He knew the house was empty, but there was something off. *The painting.* The painting in his bedroom. The painting was inside. He hadn't looked at IT since this morning, but he felt put off by IT.

He felt bone tired. The sky had spilled its stars. Nick looked about the yard, it was shabby and in need of a cut, but there was nothing suspicious, nothing sinister, just simply an empty yard that even star-glow could not enliven.

He almost felt embarrassed as he entered the kitchen, because he had been so scared just moments before. He leaned against his wall and thumbed through his phone. He checked his voicemail. George had called.

"Nick hey, yeah it's me, buddy. Um, had an interesting time with Lilly. I'll come by tomorrow and clue you in. It was weird though, a good weird. Just so you know. Like, in case you were wondering. Not an icky weird, but a good weird. You know? Not as weird as you painting in your sleep weird. Heck, she glowed man. Honest to God. Having a few beers here now, in case you feel like stopping by. As I said, it was an odd time. A good odd, though. Anyways stay home tomorrow. Let me finish up the job. Sleep in."

Nick nodded, a smile cracking across his face.

"And uh, don't even think about the painting. Anyways, talk to you tomorrow."

The second message started as silence, then static that built up to a high squeal, raising the hairs on Nick's neck. Under the high squeal came the voice of the hag, of The Thing in the Woods, whispering "Who's gonna paint your picture now, little girl?" over and over.

Nick's skin tightened into gooseflesh and his blood turned to jelly.

"Who's gonna paint your picture now, little girl?"

He threw his phone into the couch. He dashed through his house checking every closet, under his bed, in his basement, behind the shower curtain and in every possible niche the voice could hide, just so he could lay down to sleep without worry or cause. He found nothing even, which did not make him feel better, not in the slightest.

4

"Look I'm telling you that's not a swan. It's an egret." Maria said as she peered through the binoculars.

"It's a swan," Estrella insisted.

Maria could tell from her tone of voice that Estrella didn't believe her. But Estrella needed glasses, so what did she know. Her second cousin was a know-it-all.

"I know a swan when I see one, Maria."

"Look at the swoop neck, the way it holds one foot up as if it was a flamingo."

"It's a swan."

"If it was a swan, it would have a mate."

Estrella didn't respond and instead busied herself with her wet hair which had got caught up in her bathing suit strap. She pulled on the dark strands caught under her T-shirt, her mouth fussy and dissatisfied. Ahead of them, Webb's Island stretched out to the gunmetal water. Estrella wiggled in the folding deck chairs they'd brought with them.

Maria could tell that her cousin would rather be at a pool. Estrella was the only relative Maria saw anymore. Estrella was planning to return to Mexico City soon to get married. She was going to follow in the footsteps of her mother, marry young, and die an old woman.

A sharp pang echoed in Maria's gut. She and Mulch could have had kids if he had only been brave enough to love her. *Stop thinking about it,* she thought. *Nothing good comes of it. You've done well for yourself and your family. Think of the people you've helped.*

"So what's happening at camp," Maria asked trying to shake the depression.

"The usual. I wish I lived at the house with you, at least you have Wifi."

"Never say that" Maria looked into Estrella's eyes. "Never say such things."

"About what? Wifi?"

Maria scowled, she pulled down her shades and looked her cousin dead in the eye. "Living in the house. You don't want any part of that dysfunction."

"Auntie, please. Central AC. I know you enjoy it." Estrella sighed.

Few of the migrants spoke to Maria when she came into camp even though Maria had often volunteered to translate for many families, spending hours with immigration officials to work out visa problems and general federal nonsense. Granted, Maria did not come into camp as much as she once had, a fact Maria sometimes worried about.

Somewhere out in the bay, a marsh hen cried out.

"I'm sorry," Estrella finally said, "I didn't mean to upset you, Maria, I just wish we were physically closer, is all."

"I'm sorry, too. I miss being around you, too," Maria reached over across the chair and hugged her cousin and kissed her on the head.

"Then come to camp if you want to get away, you could stay with us, or with Lupe, she has a whole room that's not being used right now. Someone will take it when the rest of the workers come this summer, you should get it while you can."

Maria ran her fingers through Estrella's hair, "It's complicated."

"That's not true," Estrella whined.

But it was, and Maria didn't need Estrella to tell her otherwise, it had always been such, the whispers about her, the disappearance of the Hayes wives. It always circled back to the mystery of Mulch's women, and the mystery of Mulch himself. For Maria, though, it always came down to the fact that she was a Mexican who lived with the white boss, and by that, she was guilty by association.

"Let's go walk around the cove. I bet we find some beach glass." Maria said. She reached out and took Estrella's hands. Estrella, hardly eighteen, like Maria once had, dreamed of being a schoolteacher someday. *Maybe those dreams awaited her in Mexico City,* Maria thought. *They could have been yours too.* Only Maria got stuck in a strange house, in love with a man who hardly said a word to her anymore.

By the time they got to the cove, a half-mile away, Estrella had to ask Maria to stop squeezing her hand so hard.

CHAPTER TEN

1

Ostrich Derby took place every year on the same day as the Kentucky Derby, starting approximately an hour after the winning horse made his/her triumphant cross over the finish line. Ostrich Derby took place on Mung's Farm, about four and a half hours north of the Hayes farm and environs. Jeffery Mung and his wife Fay raised ostriches, two and a half dozen of them usually, sometimes as many as three dozen on a sizable chunk of land on Maryland's Eastern Shore. Mung had begun commercial ostrich farming for eggs, not the actual bird themselves, but the leather, the yolk, the albumin, the shell, the whole of the egg. Ostrich eggs retail somewhere in the high teens, sometimes twenties. There's been rumor that Mung has branched out into farming the birds for meat, which he has yet to publicly confirm, or deny. All in all, it's a labor of love, and Jeff Mung charges admission to local school kids to come to see the ostriches. Mr. Bill often reflects on the day he drove through the lazy Maryland countryside, almost identical to Virginia's Eastern Shore in terms of vegetation, animal wildlife, etc., when he saw out the passenger's window a large almost saurian looking bird running at high speeds round and round a fenced section of land. Mulch had casually remarked, "Oh yeah, ostriches," and slowed so Mr. Bill could see the birds. Then even more casually Mulch remarked, "We're coming here next weekend for the derby." But Bill hadn't heard that remark, he had been too busy admiring the stride of the birds, the large nine-foot body, the long sloping necks, and the head which reminded him of an old balding man. Bill then saw several other birds in orbit inside the black screened fence, high as an elephant's eye. Bill, for a second, was transported somewhere else, a real honest to god mind-warp. Mr. Bill never forgot that moment, the odd, but quick black and white cartoon-like bird cutting, zipping across the long stretch of fenced-in green yard, backed by a row of large blocky shed-like things, which housed the dinosaur's closest relative. For a moment Bill thought he was in another country. Where was the desert savanna, the palm trees, the Egyptian oasis? There was only Maryland humidity and hot summer sun.

Since then, Mr. Bill looks forward to Ostrich Derby the way most people look forward to the Super Bowl. He's got a special black baseball cap adorned with a white silhouette of an ostrich, head in the proverbial sand, one leg kicking back the way a dancer might kick a leg back for balance. Mr. Bill's also got a special cooler, also black, with special deep drink holders that hold four specially treated ostrich egg cups that he drinks beer out of. Ostrich derby is in fact the only day Mr. Bill will drink what he still refers to secretly as firewater, a word he learned from westerns, mind you. For Bill, it is a day of relaxation and a chance for him to admire one of nature's strangest birds. Ostrich Derby was also Bill's first real meeting with Pembroke, Mulch's distant cousin, and the brother of Cilia.

Jeffery and Fay Mung spend weeks preparing for Ostrich Derby. It's a huge event for them, profit-wise. They give over most of their farm to it. People start coming in on Thursday night, camping in one of the Mung's fields, and by Saturday, Kentucky Derby time, the Mung Farm has somewhere between five hundred and a thousand residents. At ten dollars a pop for the derby, plus the ten-dollar fee to camp per tent – (camper vans are 25, RVs 50) and a BYOCD/CB rule (bring your own covered dish and case of beer), it all adds up to make Ostrich Derby a pretty profitable weekend for the Mungs. On top of that Jeff runs the betting circle and takes a straight 10% vig off every bet.

The Mung's farmhouse is a quaint ranch-style house located next to pen number one, where the ostriches eat, sleep, defecate, make eggs, etc. About a half-mile away there's a huge field with a football-sized track in the middle of it. Around the track, Jeff and Fay set up portable bleachers and folding deck chairs, of which they have hundreds because so many drunken revelers leave their chairs behind year after year, as well as underpants, hats, shirts, dishes of all shapes and sizes, baseball gloves, whiffle balls, a merry widow and horse crop, and countless other items that adorn the Mung barn wall of shame and forgetfulness which is kind of a museum for die-hard fans of Ostrich Derby.

The racetrack isn't tended to very well, but it is serviceable. Race fans can also set up their chairs, coolers, etc if they wish, but it's not necessary, the Mungs are exceptional hosts. Behind the portable bleachers rest a volleyball net. Down the way, a badminton net, and farther down, near the edge of the racetrack, horseshoe sand pits. On the other side of the track, opposite from the portable bleachers are the tents and tarps Jeff sets up late Friday night, usually with the help of one of the racing fans. The tents are where you put your food, where the kegs are crowned, usually twenty kegs, light and regular, (paid for by Jeff), the t-shirt bins (one for every race, complete with this year's ostriches listed on the back and the list of winners from last year, plus stats like time, number of times the ostrich lays down and hides, etc.), the bar (unmanned – it's pour it yourself – mix it yourself), the bong and about two pounds of Maryland's finest, home-grown weed. There's another gigantic field adjacent to the field where the race is set up, twice the size of the other fields where the people camp, eat, fornicate, and set up many varied musical jams which last late into Sunday morning.

Up at the ranch house, behind the barn, is a newer barn, used only for one thing, Ping-Bong, which begins right after the Ostrich Derby finishes. Ping-Bong is a separate sporting tournament altogether, conceived by Jeff after the first Ostrich Derby ended in two minutes flat when all the birds lay down in the middle of the track and hid, refusing to move when prodded. Ostriches, according to popular myth and paraphernalia from the first Derby, do not bury their head in the sand, instead, Ostriches lay down, to hide.

Ping Bong goes like this: There are four ping pong tables in the barn and you have to sign up in advance to play. There's a whole separate t-shirt involved and whole separate food and drink/pot table. The only rule is you must take either a shot of liquor or a bong hit before you play. Thus the name. Other than that, it's a standard table tennis tournament. Losers are shuffled off to play for the loser's cup, the winners advance and compete until around five in the morning when somebody emerges victorious. It's interesting to note that winners have only ever taken bong hits before a match. Those that go out early have usually opted for the shot. Only about fifty or so people participate in Ping Bong, though its numbers grow by a few each year.

The nice thing about the Mung farm is that it's isolated, right on a neck, on the water, you have to hike through woods to see the water, so there's never a problem with any cops and the nearest neighbors are six miles in any direction. 90% of the spectators are influential businessmen, respectable lawyers, cops, family men and women, teachers, principals, farmers, contractors, veterinarians, watermen, restaurateurs, waitresses, waiters, pilots, doctors on vacation (an entire family practitioner's office shuts down for two days just to attend the event), doctors on call, nurses, and pretty much the entire spectrum of respectable jobs on the Eastern Shore of both Virginia and Maryland who do not wish to have themselves arrested, jailed, or warned by any kind of lawman. This is why fishing and hunting, and firearms are strictly prohibited. Maryland's department of fish and wildlife are rabid compared to Virginia's department of fish and wildlife.

So what generally happens is that around midnight Friday, before the races, most of the campers have arrived. At that time, a few campfires burn, and the people around them sing drunken frat songs. Many joints are rolled and smoked, though not of Jeff's homegrown, – he doesn't set that up till Sat. morning. Bottles are passed, and birds are toasted. Arguments and discussion groups meet and pass e-mail addresses and social media handles and talk into the night about the strange land bird.

Jeff mysteriously doesn't sleep all weekend. His paunchy face and beer belly jiggle as he jogs back and forth between the barn, the racetrack, and the ostrich house. Saturday mornings are spent with the birds, he and Fay coo in their ears and coax them with food. They have to be taken two at a time, by ostrich trailer, which is basically a large horse trailer, to a temporary holding pen at the head of the track. There Fay's niece and daughter, 23 & 18 respectfully, coo and coax the birds and keep them company until all the runners arrive. In the second year of Ostrich Derby, the Mungs tried to use horse jockeys. Horse jockeys would, in the Mung's mind, keep the birds from laying down, and ending the race prematurely. Horse jockeys, appalled at the idea, turned their nose up at the Mung's request. One by the name of Sammy Seward, hooked up with about a dozen jockeys in training, in someplace like Montana, and agreed to jockey the birds for the hell of it. During the first leg of the race one of the jockeys, a Spaniard, was thrown from his bird and run over by the lapping, aging Road Runner (a three-time jockey-less champion). The Spaniard suffered a broken leg, and three cracked ribs, and got a face full of ostrich feces. During the last leg of the race, Sammy was thrown from his bird and was dragged for the last leg. Luckily, a doctor in the stands was able to set the Spaniard's leg and pump him full of morphine. Sammy spent the next week getting a skin graft on his back, which had been completely stripped of skin. For a while, the whole jockey idea was in jeopardy. Sammy's speedy recovery and the Spaniard's endorsement of the wildest ride a jockey could ever hope for kept the torch burning. Only once has a near fatality occurred, when one jockey, a New Yorker, kicked his bird in the shin. The bird replied with a kick of its own that sent the jockey flying back fifteen feet into a wooden fence, which splintered. The jockey suffered six broken ribs, and a punctured lung, and nearly had a heart attack on the way to the hospital, fifteen miles away. Now, it's impossible to say, year to year, how many birds will run. It was Fay who decided that only eight jockeys would be used, as handicaps, so to speak, on the younger, faster birds. Older birds would run jockey-less, which makes the whole betting system a nightmare for Jeff. And for the last seven years, Sammy Seward and seven jockeys in training (sometimes there's a retiree in the mix, too) arrive at the Mung Ranch house, for which Jeff has built a special room equipped with eight jockey bunks stacked four by four in the room, which also includes a television and an entire library of ostrich videos, books, etc. The jockeys are not permitted to practice with the birds, which adds a whole other element to the race, plus a new whole thing spectators can bet on. But Jeff has generously set up an ostrich simulation for the jockeys. The simulator is a stuffed ostrich that's hooked up to a system like that of a bucking bull machine, just like you might see on TV, or say *Urban Cowboy*. The jockeys get to spend an hour each on the machine. Usually, the jockeys are whipped around like a lasso, their arms like an umbilical cord connecting them to the simulator. Lots of bets get passed on the sim too.

Overall, Ostrich Derby is a wild and exciting weekend. Mulch likes to go for Ping-Bong, while Mr. Bill likes to watch the birds, which he's decided are his public trans-continental spirit guide (his real one is a secret). Mr. Bill sits in one of the Mung's folding chairs and smokes his own homegrown and watches with fascination the birds' swift running. The race is three miles long and takes about fifteen minutes give or take. What Bill likes is the unpredictability of the race. The derby should take less than two minutes, but it doesn't. The birds stop and feed off spectators' plates, dig holes, snip and bite at jockeys, and some even lay down and hide. Bill has witnessed six of the fifteen races, and once watched Road Runner and Lola, a virgin runner, run neck and neck, angling their sides enough so that their jockeys knocked skulls and eventually keeled over and off the birds. There's always something unusual happening, and Bill likes a front seat to it all.

It was during the most recent Ostrich Derby that Bill had his first mournful look at his relationship with the Hayes family, one that has spanned over seventy years. Mr. Bill sat in a gray and white folding chair, the newest Derby t-shirt pulled over his plaid long-sleeve button-down, his first Budweiser popped and poured into his ostrich egg cup, his special ball cap riding a little back on his head, when he looked over at Mulch sporting his fake work smile he reserved for the feed store and sometimes his daughters. As Mulch chatted up another spectator, he gently rubbed his finger against the side of a baby's face saying something cute and trite about his brood. Watching this, Mr. Bill's head filled with Mulch's lascivious thoughts about the mother's breast, swelling with milk, and how the baby in just a few years would be as fuckable as the mother. For some reason, that one particular thought jerked Mr. Bill's brain into depression. Eb, Mulch's father, had also been one ornery son of a bitch, ruthless, heartless, and evil. Mulch was twice the bastard as his father, and Mr. Bill had seen Mulch do worse things. For one, Mulch had deep issues with women. But, if Mr. Bill had to choose between the two evils, he would have chosen Mulch over Eb, for at least Mulch had heart. It was the way Mulch's index fingers poked the pudgy cheek of the baby girl, like the way he poked at the meat to check its freshness, Bill thought. Just like the way he touched Virginia sometimes, usually after he'd snuck in through the house's hidden passageway and watched Virginia undress, or dress, or fall asleep, sometimes sneaking into Virginia's room to poke and caress her face, wishing the face of his daughter was the face of his mother. Mr. Bill knew by the way Mulch eyed the young mother and baby girl that he wished he could watch them bathe together, watch the young mother's face turn gooey and sweet as she washed her child. Mulch's fetish with young women's faces, his daughter's in particular, during coitus, or post-coitus was alien to Bill. He didn't understand it and it was then for the first time he thought that perhaps he should pack his bags and hike it out for greener pastures. It wasn't normal for any man to be like that, not that Bill knew anything about normal.

Bill had finally jerked out of his depression when one of the ostriches bucked his or her jockey off his or her back and into a huddle of young adults, giving them an up-close eye-full of the fastest land bird in the world. The jockey screamed something in Italian and landed on top of a large blonde sporting a bedazzled cowboy hat. Once the jockey mastered his bird again, Jeff and Fay Mung stepped onto a set of portable stairs, not unlike the typical high school band directors use, and spoke into their megaphone.

"Um, uh, hello race fans."

A big cheer went up from the crowd. Fans at the food, drink, and drug tables turned and raised a glass, plate, or joint. A few Frisbee throwers raised their Frisbees.

Jeff handed the megaphone over to Fay.

"We've got a new jockey this year. Sammy's brought this one in from Italy!" Fay gestured to the jockey who'd just been bucked, who was still rubbing his lower back, mumbling to himself. "And I see he already had his first taste of spunky Os." The crowd laughed. Fay often referred to the birds as spunky Os. "Let's hear it for Giacamo Fortelli!" The crowd gave Giacamo a warm rowdy race applause. A lady wearing a bright yellow sundress yelled out something in Italian that made Giacamo blush.

"This year we've had to retire Road Runner from the race." Many of the crowd booed and hissed and more concerned noises echoed from around the track. Bill, grimaced, he liked the old bird who always seemed to come in either second or third, jockey or no. "No worries. He'll be back next year. Slight infection of the beak is all." Fay's high and sweet voice cheered the fans up.

Jeff took the megaphone from Fay's hand. "All bets are in, just so you know. I see you, Johnny, over there, trying to make it to my son, but you're too late Johnny, Benny's closed up." Johnny's face, already sunburned, wrung with disappointment.

"For all you first timers out there," Jeff continued before Fay took the megaphone out of his hand.

"For all you virgins in the audience." This remark always induced a low-level groaning that Mr. Bill did not think of as sexual in any way shape or form. "We want you to know that our Ostriches are egg layers, period. Of course, we do pluck their feathers out from time to time. None of the racers are farmed for food." Fay continued. "Just so you know. We have started farming ostrich meat, but those birds don't race, only our layers do."

Jeff hoisted the megaphone out of Fay's hand. "You'll find that and all sorts of other fascinating facts about ostriches on the back of your program."

Mr. Bill's favorite facts are that it takes two hours to boil an ostrich egg and that a single ostrich mother can lay up to one hundred eggs a mating season.

Fay took the megaphone back. "This year we've think we finally figured out how to keep the numbers to stay on the birds, for the entirety of the race. No more confusion as to who wins." To this, the crowd cheered louder. Many fans, presumably bet holders, nodded their heads with pleasure.

"If you're all ready to go, and you've got your programs, which I must add, my youngest daughter designed this year while at Delaware State."

Again the crowd cheered, and Bill even offered a mild hand clap.

"If you're ready...." Jeff raised the starting gun over his head. "On your mark.... get set.... go!" And he fired the gun.

With a slam, Jeff and Fay's niece and daughter opened the gates and the birds and jockeys bolted out of the doors.

There's not an official sports commentator at the races, however, Jeff and Fay have encouraged their nephew, a budding broadcast journalist, to run commentary throughout the race, although it's very hard to hear exactly what's being said because there's so much *ooing* and *awwing* over the birds as they make their way around the track. The commentator's voice always sounds tinny and remote.

From where he's seated, Bill spied the back of Mulch's head as he leaned over the folding chair of a young woman whose sundress was open enough to reveal the tops of her pearly bosom. Part of the reason Mulch comes year after year is to hob-nob with some old family friends, cohorts from an earlier age in the Hayes dynasty.

Mr. Bill saw the eighteen birds fly out of the gate, three jockeyless birds leading the pack, racing at top speed, at at least forty miles an hour. To Mr. Bill, the ostriches always looked hungry, something about the way their camel-like faces hung slack-jawed and how they ate up the wind when they ran.

Mulch moved on to the right, shaking hands with a beefy-looking Italian in a sports coat. Mulch had hinted that perhaps his cousin, a very distant Dutch cousin, would be in attendance.

So far none of the jockey-laden ostriches have made it up to top speed. The one called Desert Storm whipped his jockey about, bee-lining towards a twenty-something blonde guy who was eating a leafy sandwich. Sammy's bird, Jackie O moved at a slow trot.

Mr. Bill met Pembroke, Mulch's cousin, only once before, and Pembroke's skin, when Mr. Bill shook it, had been covered in a slick oil that chilled Mr. Bill's spine.

The lead ostrich, Johnny Gentle, came to a dead stop in the middle of the field, commonly called no-man's land. Sammy, with a chance to take the lead, heeled Jackie O into a light trot, lapping Sid Viscous, who nibbled at a waffle ice cream cone he snatched out of a spectator's hand.

Mulch and the Italian exchanged grins before sitting down to what appeared to be Sambucas.

Desert Storm won the sandwich and chased the young blonde kid off as the jockey desperately tried to heel Desert Storm back onto the track.

From behind Mr. Bill came sighs and gasps.

Johnny Gentle lay down face first in the dirt, spreading its legs and oblong body into the ground. Mr. Bill can't see why the ostrich would think it was hiding, laying down like that, especially with the fat, egg-like body it's got. Susan B. Anthony now led the pack and had lapped both Sid Viscous and Jackie O. Bill Gates was clocking in second, at what Mr. Bill was pretty sure he heard to be 46 mph over the loudspeaker. Jockey's Gift, jockeyless since he kicked the New Yorker, was running a close third.

From behind him the sighs and gasps ran over Mr. Bill's head and ears, and he looked back, unable to resist the commotion behind him because who knew what was going to happen at the Ostrich Derby, and walking very high over the audience came Pembroke, wearing an all-black suit, and a monocle, his wild hair tossed and flipped like it had been combed with salad forks. The last time Mr. Bill saw Pembroke van Hazen was in Pembroke's newly acquired townhouse on Monument Avenue. The house, Bill recalled, vibrated and hummed and replayed sound and sight memories recorded in the wood and marble over and over again, like a record or a DVD, the house's memories visible and audible to one sensitive to them. The house had given Mr. Bill a headache, so many noises overlapping and sights replaying, hundreds of apparitions haunting you at once. The last time Bill saw Pembroke van Hazen he hadn't walked on his toes as he did now.

Pembroke moved through the throngs of spectators eyeballing Sid Viscous chasing Desert Storm, who chased a young man with the leafy sandwich around the perimeter of the track, of which Mr. Bill wondered how that was going to wash when the bets were finally tabled. The crowd simply parted for Pembroke as if he emanated some kind of psychic wave about his person. A few gasped and awed at his feet, which were taffy-like. The toes stretched out like ungainly poison sacks. The nails, hard and talon-like, moved with the rubbery, spider-like toes so that his feet appeared to snake along, which they did. Mr. Bill noticed that his legs remained still and that the spidery toes, each at least three feet in length, propelled Pembroke above the crowd.

"Good afternoon, William." Pembroke looked out to where Sid Viscous nipped the tail feathers of Desert Storm. Sammy had tempted Jackie O into a full-blown run, Sammy's head bent forward, mouth flapping in the air.

"Pembroke." Bill's head tended to swell when he was around Pembroke. He had so much energy, kind of like being around Marina for too long; one felt drained.

"Not exactly the Kentucky Derby?"

"Better," Mr. Bill replied as he looked up at Pembroke, his icy face concealed in a glare. "Have a seat."

"My pleasure." Someone behind them uttered something obscene about how Pembroke's toes could substitute as a male sexual organ.

Out on the track, Randy New Newman and The Boss ran neck and neck, their jockey's dangerously close to each other.

"Where is your master?" Pembroke settled himself in a wicker chair Mr. Bill wasn't so sure had been there before.

"I prefer employer," Mr. Bill said.

"Do you?" Pembroke scanned the audience, nodding to those few who stared at him. Mr. Bill remembered admiring a fake leather plastic weave chair that looked very comfortable, definitely not a wicker chair. And he was pretty sure it was four feet away, not right next to him.

"Don't bother, Pembroke, you'll get a headache trying to read him in this mess." Mr. Bill pointed over to his right to where Mulch moved very slowly towards the food and drink tables.

"He's got you trained well."

"Now I remember why I don't like you."

"Now, now, William. We're of different times."

"You mean ages."

"If you prefer."

Randy New Newman and The Boss's jockey pushed each other away from each other, but their legs seemed to be entangled. Jackie O was way ahead of both Desert Storm and Sid Viscous.

The blonde kid had disappeared into the crowd.

Bill couldn't tell if Susan B. Anthony or Bill Gates was ahead, Jockey's Gift danced above Johnny Gentle's splayed body in no man's land. All the birds' numbers, apparently safety-pinned to clumps of feathers, flapped in the wind.

"So what did you drag yourself here for?" Mr. Bill knew deep down he could take Pembroke in a fight.

"I'm here to talk about taking Virginia off your hands," Pembroke's voice seethed ice.

"I thought that was all arranged. Changing your mind?"

"William, William, William, why the distasteful sheen to your voice? Are you not your master's henchman?"

Mr. Bill didn't respond and stared off at Bill Gates and Susan B. Anthony heading into their third and final lap. Jackie O had been heeled up to what must be about forty miles an hour.

"William, just so you know, it isn't my idea to, how should we say? Train? Yes, train Virginia. Take it up with your employer if you don't approve."

Mr. Bill looked down at Pembroke's toes, which snaked around in the grass like blood worms after a rain.

"Pembroke, would you like a drink?" Mr. Bill opened his cooler.

"Sure, but what I like is one of those fetching T-shirts." Pembroke laughed and tossed his head back, his toes stretched up and wrapped around the cold can of beer, bringing it to his thin, almost feminine lips.

Just as Susan B. Anthony leap-frogged Bill Gates, Johnny Gentle arose from hiding and leaped the fence into the crowd, running for the food table. Spectators shouted and shoved each other out of the way to avoid the crazed bird.

Mr. Bill had stood and moved away from Pembroke, who was giving him a headache. He didn't feel like being caught in conversation with Mulch and Pembroke, who would no doubt pour over the seedy details of Virginia's personal life. It was his day off, for Christ's sake. When Bill looked behind him, Pembroke had followed him, thinking Bill was going to report to Mulch. The crowd didn't seem to care that Pembroke walked on his toes, or that his toes hissed through their rubbery nails. Mr. Bill got as many stares as Mulch's nearly seven-foot "cousin".

Susan B. Anthony crossed the finish line two feet ahead of Bill Gates. Several of the birds milled around the fences, which Bill had noticed had been added on the betting sheets as an option to bet on, that the bird would fence, instead of race.

Mr. Bill felt Pembroke's mind edging into his mind. Mr. Bill thought only of frost. Pembroke wouldn't be able to read much of his thoughts, Bill had a strong defense system of his own. Pembroke was about ten feet behind him, and Bill could tell Pembroke was trying to read him, not Mulch. Mr. Bill sat down at an empty lawn chair, some fifteen feet back from the tracks, and took out a quill pen.

"From one of the birds?" Pembroke appeared at his side instantly, his toes hissing like snakes.

Mr. Bill didn't answer the Dutchman.

"William, we must talk, sooner or later, about Virginia. I will need your assistance."

"I'm too involved with the other sister to offer any help," Bill replied as he removed a small bottle of ink from his jeans.

"Yes, I'm aware. Cilia is seething at the thought."

"I bet." Mr. Bill dipped his quill pen into a bottle of India ink and began to draw on the flesh above his ankle.

"Mulch and I are going to hammer out the details today."

"I bet."

"We will be ready for the box later this spring."

"Good for you."

"What are you drawing on your ankle?"

"Wings."

"In tribute to the feathered, but flightless birds here on display?" Pembroke's head was again mired in a glare.

"Not exactly."

"What are you doing then?"

"I'm going to draw these wings on my ankles and then run with the birds, to get away from you and Mulch, for a while."

"I see," Pembroke's head nodded.

Mr. Bill could barely see Mulch's John Deere ball cap in the crowds. On the track, Susan B. Anthony was about halfway through her fourth, and unnecessary lap. Bill Gates had laid down on the ground, shying away from countless flashes from cameras and phones of all sizes.

"I don't think you do," Bill replied, standing up. He ran in place for a second before vaulting away from Pembroke at an easy 30mph. Mr. Bill leaped the fence easily, considering his age, and kicked up dust, running to catch up to Susan B. Anthony, who didn't seem surprised at all to be running neck and neck with a man holding his black and white baseball cap to his head, the hand-drawn wings on his ankles flapping and giving Bill flight.

BOOK TWO: JUNE 8TH

"Stories come out of a hole in the ground, you know like fucking rabbits. Everywhere you go you run smack into one."

—Stephen Reynolds, actor,
from "Actors speak the truth." Dramatics on the Edge:
Young Actors Speak About the Craft.
Edited by Berman, Burto, Cain, and Douglas, 2008

"What exactly would you do if you found out your boyfriend had a secret relation-ship with your father?"

—from the journal of Virginia Maria Hayes

"On her first visit to my practice, Virginia Hayes claimed that she was kidnapped by her father, which had my full attention."

—Dr. Savannah Garvan, personal notes

"Memory? Memory is constructive."

—Dr. Elizabeth Loftus

CHAPTER ONE

1

Mulch dreamed the kind of dream where it's half-memory, half special effects, the kind of dream where memory enlarges and becomes a spectacle more real than memory itself. So much so that Mulch would later remember the dream as the memory. The dream would replace the memory, much like in his childhood when dreams of his mother were more real than the mother herself. As he dreamed, Mulch's eyes clocked back and forth under his lids, somewhere back where his blood throbbed up from his heart and back into his brain, ripples passing through his eyes, and through his face, tiny ripples of electricity tripping the brain through his REM sleep.

Mulch would later remember the dream like a rabbit hole. He moved through the earth, only it didn't feel like earth, it wasn't hot, or cold, or moist, rather it was dry and cave-like. It snaked along until it opened into a forest, a piney smell with a bitter cold breeze. It was a forest, only there was a light like that of a parking lot diffused through the trees, a bright bubble of light somewhere far off, slowly breaking apart, as the light moved through space towards him.

As he walked, he felt the cold but was not cold and he smelled the pine trees but could not feel their needles when they brushed and slapped against his face. His skin felt young and fresh, and a bit chilly, tight against his skull, his body humming with vigor. When he looked down, he saw child-size boots, and child-sized footprints, yet Mulch felt like he was only standing next to the body of a young boy, instead of inside it.

Ahead a shotgun echoed. Eb trailed a wounded deer across the stream. Mulch was expected to follow. He knew that he should follow.

Then the light began to snow. That's how he saw it and that's how it felt. The light began to snow down on top of him. It was like snow but wasn't snow, it was light, falling on him in flakes, melting against his flannel jacket, the one his mother stitched up every year with black thread.

When it became dark and the pixel light ceased its snowing and Mulch felt the weight of the darkness come upon him, like a blanket, he thought, and then he was in the tunnel and knew no more of the forest.

Here there's a break in the memory, a sharp break from where Mulch entered the tunnel and where he left it again, a fuzz, a bit of static if you will.

He knew he wasn't in the forest anymore. But he knew he was still with his father, that distinct sense of security small children feel around a parent. Then he was pressed against the ground. His father pushed him to the ground. He didn't recognize the surroundings. Eb was lost too, and they both looked out of the trench, or ditch, they crouched in. Eb placed his hand firmly on Mulch's skull and held him to the earth.

Mulch felt like he should panic. He was afraid he wouldn't be able to breathe. His nose filled with the piney peel of tree roots and hummus around him, it was a thick smell. Mulch felt tiny bits of leaf in his nose, grainy soil in his mouth crawling down towards his windpipe. Then there was another skip, and Mulch no longer felt the dirt in his nose or his mouth but instead the sharp, acidic, sour of hot liquid. Eb was holding a tin cup to his mouth, "Here this will keep you warm." His jacket had the same odor, only softer, and rubbed in. "Here son, don't let me down." Mulch didn't want to drink it, that much he was sure of, not then, or now, and then a slow itching crawl began in his hand and traveled up his arms and into his mouth.

2

In a small woody catch, an inlet really, but so overgrown and moss-covered that the trees' canopy hung way down into the water creating a tunnel that nearly covered the entire embankment, Marcos hid most of the box under its shade. He hadn't been able to go far with the box, not at all. Mulch would be pissed if he knew. Marcos had hoped to make as far as Sea Hag's the first night so he would be able to make it up most of the coast the following night, but he hadn't.

Several times the box had gotten caught up in crab pot lines and a few oyster baskets. Each time one of the pontoons got snagged on a line or a wire cage, Marcos had to get out of the boat and swim back to the pontoons with a flashlight and unhook the damn thing and then swim back to the boat, get in and get it moving before somebody spotted him.

He'd felt lucky enough to find the inlet when he did because he spotted the game warden on his boat out looking for crab pot poachers. Luckily, there had been somebody out screwing around with the crab pots because the game warden didn't follow Marcos as he chugged the enormously gargantuan box down the creek towards the Bay. From there he had to navigate Cape James and shoot into the Atlantic.

"It's gonna be hot to-day." He said to Marina but knew he spoke to no one. He looked up at the sun which was barely cresting the trees.

"I wish we had more of a better start than what we did, but I guess it's good enough."

Mulch owned the land around where they docked, which had been a surprise for Marcos. He was never very good with charts and though he knew there was a safe inlet on the way he never in his life thought he'd be able to find it, and therefore when he ran across the inlet, he thought it luck till the next morning when he looked at his charts in broad and stupefying daylight and saw that there was little chance he could have missed it, to say nothing of unwanted visitors. Still, as he settled in for the night, he hoped that the foliage would provide enough coverage to keep him, and his cargo hidden. If not, Marcos could easily scare anyone off with a shotgun. Though he didn't think the authorities would care two shits about his shotgun, not with the pressure on the Coast Guard these days.

What Marcos was concerned about was the box. The heat here would be unbearable and there was little chance of a breeze in the catch. Marina would be too hot.

"Tonight we will hit the Atlantic and be gone like a wink," He whispered to the box. *She's still drugged,* Marcos thought. Otherwise, she would have tried to escape.

The plan was for Marcos to sail out into the ocean, far enough out to avoid the coast guard patrols that cruised the recreational waters, and far enough in to avoid most of the commercial fishing fleets. If he played his cards right, he'd have no trouble. He guessed that it wouldn't be more than a four-day jaunt up the Atlantic coastline. *No more than four days, for sure.*

"You know what I mean girl? No one will find us. I will make sure of that." But he didn't know what to think as he patted the box like a dog, staring off at the gnats that clouded the still water.

3

Marina drifted out under the sky and felt her heart bunch up with excitement. The trees skirting the banks of the creek were full of them: hundreds of icicle lights dangling down into the branches, and along-side bare trunks. The whole edge of the wood dribbled with electricity. Marina could barely make out the tangled line of cords that connected the forest to the house and her home to the forest.

The water was cold, but she hardly felt it. Her thick skin retained so much heat that Marina could stay outside all winter if she so desired. To Marina, the lights meant the water looked like it was full of shattered stars whose bits and pieces had fallen to the earth.

Her father peered out the one dark window on the third floor, Maria's room, squinting to see her among the rippled water. She didn't notice. Above the melding of the lights, a blurriness came over them and the clear dark patches of sky. It was a familiar feeling, like that of looking at a mirror. She felt déjà-vu. It all stirred together, and it all came apart.

4

I'm trying to sleep, though I know I can't, as Macy's guest bedroom is too uncomfortable, and it's like sleeping on a hard sack of feed. When I was a kid, Mulch allowed me to hang out at the feed store with him when he went to work. There wasn't much to do but suck on peppermint sticks and make forts out of the empty produce boxes in the back. Marina would sometimes come too, but mostly it was just me, as she didn't like the smell; it was too hot for her. We often sat in Mulch's office, her and I, which had a fan and a water cooler. She'd stare into the water like it was going to explode or something. It seemed like her head was going to pop, just like a balloon; she stared at it so hard. Her neck muscles would tense up and the room would take on a queer edge. Then there would be a fine salty smell in the air, like tepid ocean water. Years later I learned that it was her sweat that smelled like seaweed and creek mud. As far as I know, she only got like that one more time, when at the movies, when she saw the *Little Mermaid* at the theater in Belle Haven.

God was she beautiful, even then. She wore a loose t-shirt that clung to her taut body. Still, she walked funny, like wasn't used to walking, her limbs so long that she looked like someone had stretched her out on a rack and she hadn't snapped back yet. I was meeting Ryan Kellam at the theater that night and I felt so hideous in my sweater and jeans next to my gangly, unreal sister. She had a certain energy, and you couldn't help but be drawn to her. I knew Ryan would stare at Marina, and there was no doubt that she looked beautiful in her tight jeans, that loose T-shirt, and an old jean jacket that came from God knows where; her hair had a mind of its own. There was something about the way it kinked up around the collar of her jacket. Her hair flowed down heavy, the thick washes of the sides flipped and shimmered with the slightest movement of her shoulders. She was nervous to be out and stood behind me in line at the theater and I sensed that everybody had an eye on her. The ticket boy, who was struck with a bad case of acne, just about drooled on our tickets as he stared out at Marina so hard that I thought it might hurt him.

"One, two, three passes." His voice was monotone and low. He looked right through me as he laid the tickets on top of my change.

"Can I help you miss?" He asked Marina as he edged in closer to make sure that she heard him, his tongue hanging to the side, his shirt collar wet from where drool had either slid off his lips or he had wiped the drool from his mouth onto his collar. When I turned to see her reaction, she was nervously glancing about her. The tacky, almost sticky glow of the neon-trimmed popcorn counter gave the whole scene a pinkish, nauseated tinge. Marina looked like she was about to burst into fish squeaks.

"Can I help you miss?" The ticket boy said louder, smiling and brushing one hand up to his hair which was a mop and cow licked in the back, his lips shiny with spit.

"She's with me," I said, pulling Marina out of line as she began to chirp to herself. The ticket boy's mouth went slack, and his eyebrows raised high over his racine features, her chirps sounding vaguely dolphinish.

I swear to God, for a while the two of us sounded like this:

Me: Are you okay?

Marina: Chirp, squeak, blat, vague farting squeal. Deep breath. High pitched Yarp.

Me: What?

Mar: Chirp, squeak, blat, vague farting squeal. Deep breath. Two high-pitched Yarps and a chirping trill that hurt my head.

Me: Would you stop it?!

Mar: Chirps and squeals and the worst kind of shrieks and click combinations you've ever heard.

Until that is, I kinda freaked out and grabbed her by the arms, shaking her out of her chirping fit. We both felt embarrassed as hell, and I was a little pissed because come on, my reputation was at stake, not hers. Now I feel ashamed thinking those horrid thoughts about my sweet half-sister, but then, journal, I was a bit savage. When she finally calmed down, she was able to speak. She wasn't walking very well, but at least she was speaking English.

"When does it start?" Marina said, half chirping, her eyes huge Os, her long arms knocking against each other, her jacket sleeves rustling together.

"Soon. Do you need to use the bathroom?" I hoped she didn't.

"Yes, please." She didn't seem to notice everyone checking her out, a few of the people who were bound to recognize me, people who were bound to know that Mulch had two daughters, and a few who were bound to put two and two together. But hardly anyone outside the household had ever seen Marina before. They'd heard about her and speculated and spread gossip but hadn't laid eyes on her.

Still, I was excited, and not just because I had a date, but because Marina and I were doing sister stuff, actual sister things were happening, finally.

Let me pause here to explain how utterly strange it was having Marina as a sister. She was cool, and that was the problem. But also, I wasn't a mermaid, so I always felt like I was bothering her. Like a mother or something. I'm the baby of the family. She didn't seem to mind me hanging out with her, but it wasn't like there was much for us to do. She liked to swim and eat raw fish and mussels, and I didn't. I mean, we swam, sure, in the hot months, but it wasn't like we did that every day, at least I didn't.

That night I took her into the bathroom, and we crowded the one sink and mirror. I applied a fresh layer of lipstick, which I don't think I needed because Ryan later complained about how plasticky my lips tasted and about how it made his lips ruddy and a bit glossy. There were three stalls, and the bathroom was very chilly. She watched me apply my lipstick before shying her way into one of the stalls. Marina gasped at the feel of cool porcelain. The other two stalls were empty. I started having visions that the two of us would share kissing secrets and double date hunky Broadbay guys who had their own cars. Just the thought of it excited me, finally being able to do something with my sister. My mind raced with the possibility that Marina and I might actually start shopping for clothes and even hanging out. I don't think she'd ever listened to a radio before. Slumber party plans cooked in my cerebellum. I finished applying my lipstick and checked my hair. I knocked on Marina's stall, "Meet you outside," I said.

"Okay." Her voice still had that awkward chirp to it.

She kept me waiting for almost fifteen minutes. Meanwhile, moms and several bratty girls in pigtails came and went from the bathroom. Some of the boys ganged up around the counter for licorice and popcorn. There was a hint of lemon in the air from the lemon Cokes and sour heads consumed by their many munching mouths.

Ryan was late, and Marina was beginning to worry me.

When I re-entered the bathroom, I overheard a small girl asking her mother questions about mermaids, for the toilet in Marina's stall flushed over and over again. It was either broken, or Marina was flushing the toilet over and over again. I shuddered at the memory of her flooding the kitchen back home because she liked to watch the sink fill with water.

"Hello," I said to the little girl who twirled to face me.

"Hello," the mother said. "Say hi to the nice girl, Rae." Rae smiled and turned to hug her mother's knees. The mother smiled and led her daughter out of the bathroom, all the while eyeing Marina's stall. "I think someone is sick, or the toilet's broken."

"Yeah?"

I waited until she turned her back before knocking on the stall door. "Marina? Is something wrong?"

The stall door opened, Marina peeked out, her eyes wide as half-dollars.

"They've been talking about me," She mouthed as she nodded towards the door where Rae and her mother had gone. Marina let out a tiny chirp that sounded pathetic and lonely. "They were talking about mermaids!"

Her eyes were moist.

5

"Marina! Are you all right?" Marcos peered into the box from the top hatch, but he could only make out a shadowy shimmer of a figure on the bed. It looked like a shadow, or it could have been Marina. He couldn't tell. The tree cover provided little light. "Hope you're okay?" His instructions said only to give her water, but she hadn't moved since he had taken control of the boat. "You know I have cool water up here. You can have some if you wish."

Nothing. Just hot air and darkness.

Marcos began to wonder if he was just dragging a coffin to Boston.

6

When Nick awoke and saw that he hadn't painted anything in his sleep he let out a whoop. He danced to the toilet. He sang while brushing his teeth and slapped his hands together. But that was before he stepped out into his yard to get the morning paper.

It was hot, but the sun had not yet begun to broil. Nick hopped from the concrete steps onto the grass so his feet wouldn't burn, but they did anyway – he hated that. Even the air was burned, dry, and still around the house. The air hung about the trees like the skin of an old man. *Almost a light mist,* Nick thought. The spiky grass jabbed at his soles as Nick walked to the paper/mailbox ten feet from the house. Nick seldom read the paper but kept the subscription to pretend to know what was happening across the bay.

While Nick didn't think of himself as a paper reading kind of guy, this morning he was fucking psyched to be reading the paper, or anything for that matter, because he hadn't painted anything in his sleep. At this time, the paper had become an emblem that whatever happened to him yesterday was simply yesterday's news. The hot metal box squealed as Nick opened it.

"Dag gone. Ouch," He squealed jumping from foot to foot as he slid the paper under his arm. As he hopped back towards the house, he kept his head lowered so the sun stayed out of his eyes. Because of this, he almost didn't see it, he almost didn't look up.

It was the ladder that first caught his eye. The ladder lay against the house, the side that faced the woods, so there was no way for him to notice it from an inside window, or from where he had trotted out to get the paper. Only coming back was he be able to notice the metal ladder refracting the sun. Of course, even if he hadn't seen the glint of the ladder, he would have eventually seen the painting. There was no way he could have missed it.

CHAPTER TWO

1

Abdullah, the genie, last surfaced in 45 BC on a mountain top in Japan, where he found himself face to face with a bearded old man wearing a clay pot on his head and nothing else. The little man's naked unwashed body gave off an obscene stench. The little man's first wish was for a robe. And Abdullah snapped a robe out of the air and handed it to his master, bowing, and complimenting him, and swearing his allegiance, while offering a free rain shower to cleanse his new master's body Abdullah didn't recognize the nation the little man belonged to. Nor did he know he was in Japan. He had no idea how he had come to be where he was, nor any idea who the little man was, as the old man hadn't introduced himself.

When Abdullah bowed to his master and began to introduce himself as Abdullah, djinn, master of the spirits, warrior of worlds, the arm of Sultans, and guardian of gold, the little man only waved him off and ordered him back into his lamp. It appeared that the little man wanted to meditate on his lot in life, wishing to uphold an honor to his land and people. He couldn't make a decision on his other wishes for weeks, he said to the genie. The old man thanked him, politely refused the rain shower, and showed him the door, so to speak.

During that time, Abdullah grew bored. Genies, to endure centuries of boredom, had a rich inner life. But being sent back to his lamp so soon depressed him. Abdullah had forgotten how much he liked being free of the lamp. The old man, afraid of Abdullah, had hidden the lamp in a cave wall, in a hole he covered with a rock. It was strange for Abdullah; he wasn't allowed to come out of his lamp and sit in council with his new master. This new master bewildered him. Though he doubted *this* master kept a harem, Abdullah hoped he did, because he wouldn't be allowed to experience the harem girls, either, if this master was the celibate kind, Abdullah theorized. This was a different master altogether, Abdullah had thought, and a poor one at that. Poor masters always made poor choices, as far as wishes were concerned, and Abdullah was forced to sit until called.

Everybody knows how genies work. If you happen to be one of the lucky people who finds a lamp, and if you happen to be one of the very lucky people who recognize a genie lamp, then you could be that lucky person to rub the lamp and summon the genie. Now while Abdullah was a particular old cuss, he enjoyed most of the masters he served and even liked a few, but Abdullah came alive when his master was genial, loquacious, and fond of adventure. A lover of food and pleasures of the flesh, a plus, though not necessary, what Abdullah liked to do was talk and learn new customs and traditions that had passed him by while he was in the lamp. When it came to wishes, Abdullah, like all genies, was extremely generous. Abdullah tended to favor those wishes that were original or at least fun. He grew bored of stealing riches for his masters and wiping out their enemies, and equally so, finding virgin brides But these were the wishes most people who summoned him wanted and he granted them without prejudice. He tended to stick close to his masters who had the spark and nerve to wish for something different, like for special skills or an elaborate construction project. He tended to stick around longer with those masters, allowed to freely walk the earth to do his masters bidding. Then he could mingle with humanity and experience the sensations all living things craved, food, booze, and sex. Abdullah's magic allowed him to be fluid, and he often swapped his body for a more pleasurable one, morphing throughout the courtship and the act to experience the greatest pleasure. But most of all, Abdullah wished for friendship and camaraderie. He loved to swap stories, which to him was the big payoff for his service – conversation.

While he waited as the old man meditated in his fine new robe, Abdullah stared at the wall of his lamp. To amuse himself he performed crude imitations of former masters and other humans he'd met, and of animals he had encountered along the way. The old man meditated a lot, it turned out, and Abdullah was just beginning to think that his master had died when he was again finally summoned. The little old man's robe was dirty with leaves. Twigs stuck out of the man's hair at odd angles, and there was curious and suspicious soiling both in the front and back of the robe, the old man's rank odor clouding about him. His master still had the clay pot on his head, and it hung a bit to the left. Still, it made his master's head look three sizes too small. From everything that he saw, Abdullah surmised it had been a very long time since his master had made his first wish. He hoped he would make the other two right off the bat, so Abdullah could be free and figure out where he was and find somebody else interesting to attach himself to.

Gesturing with his pinkie finger, the little old man beckoned Abdullah closer and whispered in his ear, "I wish to have a little temple up here on the mountains. I wish to have this temple so the people may come here and ponder the time it took them to climb up this mountain, just for them to see this little temple and think about their climb." The old man's smile was short a few front teeth. And because genies can read their master's mind, the temple appeared just as the old man with the clay pot on his head had envisioned it. A marvelous one-story temple, complete with two wings, a fine garden in the back, adorned with bells, wind chimes, a few birdbaths, and even a little fountain with a statue of the little old man with a pot on his head. The fountain water spouted out the little old man's nose and sometimes from his penis as well. Seeing his temple built, and knowing this to be a good wish, the master smiled with pleasure and ordered Abdullah back into the lamp and placed the lamp into the hole in the wall of the cave, and again covered it with a rock.

2

And so Abdullah sat in the hole in the wall until the old man summoned him again.

Most of all Abdullah hated to wait. Most humans, quick to wish, fortune, fame, women, would have tossed the lamp to some relative by now, thinking themselves smart for their brilliant scheme of keeping the lamp in the family, but that never actually worked out for the better. Still, Abdullah, with no new master, and nothing else to do, pondered the whiteness of the lamp's interior about him and thought about his name. It was kind of a ritual to him, and kind of a game. He thought about his name, given to him by his first master, the first time he was summoned. Abdullah was named after his first master which was a fact that was neither sentimental nor ominous to him. He liked his name. Waiting, Abdullah pronounced his name over and over again so that it began to sound less and less natural. He found that his name sounded ridiculous when repeated at high speed. The more he said "Abdullah" the more he thought that "Abdullah" wasn't his name, that Abdullah sounded heavy, that Abdullah sounded unreal.

In all the time that he waited, he didn't once think about his current master, or who his master was, or how his lamp had come up into the mountains, so far away from the sultan's nation. The last thing he remembered before this strange new master was the silent face of Petra's walls at dusk, the flickering candles set back in stone and hidden from the desert road.

When he was finally summoned for the third, and last time, the old man was balancing himself on a cane, his robe hung on his body in ragged tatters. The old man looked up at the giant form of the genie and said, "I wish this mountain was not so high so that people could climb up here to ponder the time it took them to climb up here and think so that more of the people could come and enjoy this space."

"Done," Abdullah said and leveled the mountain with a snap. And when the dust settled, he saw that the old man was laughing and full of joy.

"Why is it that this makes you so happy little Master?" Abdullah asked, expecting to be thanked for his selfless work.

"Genie, it has taken me ten years to think of the right wishes, and now I can see that my death is near," said the little old man, who, still wearing a clay pot on his head, collapsed like a showboating cobra after the snake tamer's music died.

Abdullah poked the old man's tiny ribs, but the old man did not move. Looking about, Abdullah discovered that the temple was empty, there was nobody around, there wasn't so much as one piece of firewood in the fireplace, or water in the baths. The incense burners were unscorched, and the alter dusty. Birds had made nests in the wings. The old man's chambers were bare and only a few crumbs of bread could be found. The untended garden sprouted wild like some giant spider's web and from what Abdullah could tell, no one but the old man had ever been here, and it didn't look like the old man had bothered to keep the place up.

From what the genie could tell the mountain was now a respectable hill in the middle of nowhere, where only little old men with clay pots on their heads would ever go. Seeing all that was around him, the genie felt a pang of bitterness and jealousy, and he pined for Rome or Alexandria, Petra even, cities where he had been allowed to confer with royalty and dine on dinners and enjoy the company of educated men. He had smoked with mystics and poets and learned all of the new songs. His previous master, a camel trader, had taken Abdullah over the desert to secret cities in the dust where candlelight and music crept from the sand and rocks like tiny leathery creatures. Abdullah had been allowed to ride camels and spit dried fruit with his master's sons. Abdullah had been allowed to swap stories with the shepherds and the guards and drink their bitter water. All along the way, music had dripped off the men's tongues and songs smoked from their mouths.

Out of respect, he buried the little old man with the pot still on his head. Abdullah pummeled a hole into the earth and went down so far that he smelled salt crystals and the rich clay of the Pacific table. There Abdullah dropped his master's body at the bottom of the hole. The little old man crumpled up at the bottom. As he had dug this grave Abdullah hadn't realized that he'd inadvertently dropped his own lamp down the wide and deep shaft. The old man had been holding it in his death grip when he had collapsed, and Abdullah hadn't noticed. Instead, he'd been thinking about kings and queens, figs, and apricots and olives, and all the wonderful fruits he'd tasted so many masters ago. So, as Abdullah caved the sides of the old man's grave in, he inadvertently sucked himself up inside his lamp. And so back into the lamp he went, and before he was able to discover where he was and how he'd gotten there, he was back in his lamp world, and the little old man with a clay pot on his head was a screamer of an impersonation, only Abdullah had no one to show it to. To make it sound just like the old man, he'd exaggerated the voice to make it sound like dried leaves rubbing together. In time he grew bored with making fun of the little old man and began speaking into a small, silver hand-mirror one of his master's had given him. He spoke to his mirror for a long time and in time grew bored with it as well and eventually took to staring at the walls. All the while, all around him the Pacific rim reinvented and re-sculpted its coastlines.

The hole Abdullah had dug was about an eighth of a mile from the coast in an area that had previously been cold most of the year because of the high altitude. No one had wanted to live there because the mountains had been too high, especially along the coast. And most of the men made their living from the sea. The men of the seas made up stories about dragons populating the cliffs and mountain caves and swore never to go there. Finally, years after Abdullah had leveled the mountainside, men began to settle the area. No one believed the old tales of fierce dragons anymore, for there was no mountain left, and only an old, dilapidated temple on top of the hill that was roost to many a delicious bird. It was a beautiful sight, with broad green trees and tall grass. The dramatic, young cliffs afforded a view of the Pacific none had ever seen before. At night men and women could drink rice wine and listen to the surf which to them was like that of a hissing dragon. The old stories were retold of a dragon that had once lived in the mountain and the warriors in the sky that had struck the dragon into the sand and buried him under his mountain. This was how the people explained how the once ancient mountain had become a hill.

Long after Abdullah had inadvertently buried himself with the clay potted old man, a small fishing village prospered near the site. The men who lived there could easily walk down the hill each day to their boats and come up the hill in the evening with baskets of fish and seaweed. It wasn't a far walk, for the land sloped away from the cliffs into a gradual plane that formed a very convenient, natural harbor. Waters around the hills were warm in the summer and were an excellent site for bathing and fishing, especially fishing. But more than fish, the waters provided a prodigious number of oysters.

Over time, the renovated temple was used as a meeting place for leaders of the village and a gathering place for festivals and revelries. Weddings, funerals, religious ceremonies, and divinations were all performed there under the same roof, just like the old man had hoped for.

During the village's first decade several small earthquakes ripped the ground open in some places and filled other places in. At approximately three hundred paces from the village, towards the cliffs, one fissure opened. It was twenty paces long and ten paces wide. You could jump over it if you got a good enough run. It formed a straight line between the village and the cliffs, which dropped dramatically to rocks and surf below. The villagers began to use the fissure as a dump for their oyster shells, fish remains, and all sorts of other refuse.

For many years the villagers dumped their remains and refuse into the fissure and soon it began to fill and though you could not see the shells, you could smell the fishy remains in the village. The shells made a terrible racket when dumped by the basketfuls. It sounded like the pile was only ten feet below, but the pile was over three hundred yards below the surface, but the sound echoed up something awful and the fishy smell escaped when the wind cupped into the fissure and brought up the rancid breeze. Villagers began to tell obscene jokes about the smelly hole and eventually, the smell became so bad that the villagers elected the village idiot to bring the garbage to the hole.

So each week the village idiot and his dog, Kyoto, hauled a cart-full of oyster shells and miscellany, to the hole for dumping. Kyoto would bark at the smell and each week the village idiot would say to Kyoto, "Next time we will see the top."

Hundreds of years passed, some years bringing fresh quakes that gradually shortened the distance between the fissure and the coastline so soon the fissure was fifty paces from the cliff, where generations before it had been over a hundred. One night in the early 1900s a small tremor split the ground and ruptured the ground open like an egg.

The ground had grown weak around the fissure, and issuing forth from the crack, a great rattling sound came as hundreds of years of shells and the bones of fish and animals cascaded below, forming a huge mound at the foot of the cliff below. The village trash can had been permanently broken. There below, at the base of the cliff, amid the bones of animals, the shells of oysters, and the old man's pulverized skeleton, Abdullah's crushed lamp remained for decades, the tide slowly widening and submerging the pile more and more until the year 1972 when the Nakagawa Gofun Enogu Factory discovered the mound.

The Nakagawa Gofun Enogu Factory produced the whitest paint in all of Japan from aged oyster shells. Scouting teams had been set off to each island to buy refuse from commercial fisheries, local fishermen, and restaurants. Factory teams scoured the coastlines for rural oyster dumps and paid handsomely for information leading to profitable findings. The whitest shells were then aged twenty years and then ground to powder and mixed with animal glue and used to paint Hina dolls in ancient court dress, Hina dolls being all the rage in Japan, a tiny piece of the old world that survived in the modern Japanese home.

Throughout the world, museums in America, England, France, Italy, and even Korea paid handsomely for Hina dolls. To many, the dolls represented the best of Japanese physical and artistic beauty. Considered pure, and perfect, Hina dolls were required by tradition to be bone white, and the Nakagawa Gofun Enogu Factory made the only paint considered suitable for Hina dolls, which is how the owners pretty much built the company.

Dirtier, less aged, more "corrupt" shells were crushed into powder and turned into commercial house paint.

One day the Nakagawa Gofun Enogu search team had come to the hill that had once been a mountain. They had heard that there were some shells to be found nearby and spoke to a local fisherman about the history of the area. The fisherman told the story of a village idiot, Yoshiro Takeguchi, who near the turn of the century had caused a great earthquake when he had dumped a cartload too many oyster shells into the village dump. The dump had been a hole in the earth and for years the dump had been filling up until it popped open that one evening and nearly killed Yoshiro. Upon further questioning, the fisherman revealed that the dump had been there long before his great-great-grandfather could remember and that for generations the village idiot had been the local garbage man responsible for the dumping of the shells and bone waste of the village watermen. Hearing all this, with their interest peaked, the research team bid the fishermen take them to the fabled site.

It was by boat that the mound was found for the sea had eroded the sandy base of the cliff and caused shifting that made it impossible to reach by land and thereby the mound had gradually leveled out underwater. The Nakagawa Gofun Enogu Factory sent for a large fishing boat with dredging gear, and the company spent a week hauling in over ten tons of oyster shells. All in all, everyone agreed that it was a most wondrous find. After the shells were sorted and dried in the sun, they would be crushed for paint, eventually. First, they had to be sorted into pure piles and dirty piles.

It was no surprise that no one from the factory wanted to sort ten tons of trash into piles. Shells, if gathered by the truckload, were manageable. Larger piles like this were too daunting. But still, it had to be done, for animal remains, human remains (more than just that of the old man), and the occasional broken brass, or tin trinket lay among the coveted oyster shells.

But why bother with all the sorting? Wouldn't it be just a big waste of energy? The scout team had wondered to themselves.

At that time there was a great abundance of Hina paint already in many of the warehouses and it was decided that the mixed shells from the hill that was once a mountain should instead be crushed for commercial paint.

All the while Abdullah did not notice when his lamp was crushed around him and was ground to a powder, boiled and tamed with industrial chemicals and acrylics, cooled, and poured into aluminum buckets. He was doing his best imitation of a camel when our George popped the lid off a can of Industrial White # 4 and released him. Upon Abdullah's release, there had been no warning, only a loud thunderous crack, streaming sunlight, and a startled red-headed caucasian male who held something burning in his lip.

Excerpt from Ship's Log: Dated June 8th. 10:35

Marina still does not answer my calls. I grow worried that she did not survive the potion. It occurred to me that perhaps Bill had poisoned her. I don't think this is true, but it could be. I do not trust Bill, especially now. When we worked on the box, I felt his eyes above me. Even now I feel his power. I know I am being silly and stupid. It is because I cannot drive the boat as well as I bragged! How I wanted to be with Marina. To brandish my love! Oh, we could run away together. Live among the Canary Islands with her people. I must stop writing now. I hear a motor on the creek.

Marcos

CHAPTER THREE

1

Marina didn't even really know what a boy was until that night Maria dropped us off at the Idle Hour Movie Theater. I mean she probably knew that boys existed, probably, but she didn't know boys existed in her heart, or her mind, or even her libido until that night. I've never seen her so rattled, first, it had been the little girl and her mommy in the bathroom, they had been talking about mermaids, and Marina actually thought they were talking about her, then moments after we left the bathroom, as we were going into the theater, she saw him. I didn't know who he was.

My father sent me to the private school, Broadwater Academy, not public school. Mulch said that public schools were full of disease. He said that shit often. I was six when he first sent me, and I thought he meant that I was going to catch cold or something at the public school. But Mulch didn't mean the cold, or the flu, he meant me being around trash.

So, I started life in the private school, and rarely did I mix with the pubies. Macy coined the phrase, not me. So, it was no wonder that I didn't know this kid, he was a pubie. He was cute though – kinda tall, but rib skinny.

He leaned against the inside wall, blocking the entrance to the aisle on the right. He was right inside the door when we opened it up and light from the screen flooded his face. Light bounced off our faces too, and he and Marina locked eyes for what seemed like a minute, but it had to have been only a second. They locked eyes and just stared deep into each other.

At least his mouth didn't hang open. Instead, he looked composed, 16, or 17-like, though no more, and no less. Marina just paused in half-step. She smiled, but it wasn't her pretty smile, more of a lopsided drugged smile, maybe more of a grin that had gone bad. She's got better, and if she were here I'd prove it.

On-screen, the promos for "disposing of your trash in the proper receptacles" were playing and were halfway through their song and dance – the singing cups, and popcorn boxes, although they served popcorn in bags at the Belle Isle. Now here's the weird thing, when he saw Marina, the pubie, he nodded his head in a kind of cool-guy way. Now mind you I was a young teenager, and he was cute, the fact that he was a pubie notwithstanding. I must have been half-overcome with his cuteness, he had a nice little butt in his jeans, even though he was skinny. When he said hello, it sounded to me like he said it with an accent, British, or something. It doesn't sound weird now, but back then, oh man, it was off. Well, then Marina went all moony. Cutie-pie raised one hand and waved at us and Marina shuddered. Thinking back on it now, she might have been having a mermaid orgasm, or whatever it is that they have. I mean she hadn't even spoken to a guy, like ever. She shuddered and in the flickering light of the screen which had changed to a greenish hue, her skin began to glow, fucking glow, right there in the damned doorway, with snotty runny-nosed kids piling up behind us like we're a fucking train car or something and cutie-pie and Marina are totally eye locked and she's blasting out this weird green mermaid light and shit and it's like the guy doesn't notice it. I remember hearing the kids behind me did, "Mommy what's wrong with that woman? Is that what radiation looks like? Mommy, I scared! Hold my popcorn!"

That's when I tugged her and dragged her to a seat, any seat. The previews had started and I felt scales popping out of her skin as if she were in the water.

When I looked back he was gone. Marina's glow faded, thankfully. I shouted something about the flashlight app on her phone which I hoped would throw off the stink.

Marina just stared up at the screen. She leaned over once to whisper, "Do you know his name?" When I answered "No," she cocked her head back up to the previews. She wasn't going to ask any more questions. She was a little out of her element.

Once the movie started I snuck out to the candy counter. Ryan was buying some popcorn. Cutie-pie was nowhere to be seen. So I shuffled back into the cave-dark with Ryan. We sat behind Marina, and though I didn't really watch the movie, I was pretty sure Marina didn't take her eyes off the screen, not even once.

But she must have sensed the passion between me and Ryan. Passion? Teen passion? Yes. Remember Romeo and Juliet were also only teenagers after all. Maybe she was feeling the first whiskers of curious sexuality showing itself. Heck, maybe she just heard us making out. Maybe it was the damn hickey or the way I had to adjust my bra afterward. But that night, after we were home after Mulch had bitched us out and practically scared Marina to death, she started asking me all kinds of questions.

See, I did have my sister moment, journal, just not how I thought.

I was in my pajamas, and she was just in a T-shirt. She came up to my room to ask me to brush her hair, which was something I normally would have to beg her to do, so I knew there was something way up. She really came up to ask me her questions. "Do you think that boy we saw at the movies was cute?" She played it cool and pretended not to be all moony. I was clued in by the tone of her voice and the fact she was flipping through my biology book.

I remember I giggled. I was on cloud 9.

"Why? Do you think he's cute?" Sister situations, double dates, popped in my mind like popcorn. "All that matters, sis, is that you think he's cute," I told her.

"Really?"

"Well, also you don't want to date an asshole, or a jerk, or anything like that. That's the only real rule. You can't date someone who will abuse you or make fun of you to their friends. But if you think he's cute…that's all that matters."

It occurred to me that Mulch probably wouldn't dare to tell Marina about the birds and the bees, he wouldn't have the guts. After all, I had to read a freaking book to find out for myself and I doubt that there was a book detailing the ins and outs of mermaid/people sex. So, I asked her what she knew about boys and sex. She kinda gave me a look, a nervous one. She shook her head no; she didn't know anything.

"Sex?" she finally managed.

"Okay." I stopped brushing her hair and pulled her on top of my bed with me. "Get comfortable," I told her everything. I tried not to be dirty about it, you know. I wanted her to have a positive attitude towards it, towards sex, and surprise, surprise, turns out she knew something, you know, the basics. She said that her communication with marine life had taught her that life reproduces, life recreates itself, life creates. But she didn't know about boys, or about passion, she didn't know about that at all. And after what had happened to her in the car on the way home, I was very surprised to hear that.

2

The backside of Nick's house was completely covered by the painting. In his sleep, Nick Adams had risen and stalked down the stairs to the kitchen, and then out the door. Nick kept a small shed where he stored his push mower, hurricane shutters, and paint. Over the last year, he had gathered several gallons of yellow and navy gray paint. He had bought the yellow, a bright canary, on a whim about a year ago. He got six gallons for two dollars and figured he could use it to paint birdhouses, or maybe a new paper-box, but hadn't even gotten around to thinking about it. The navy came from an old job the previous spring where he and George were contracted to paint the new bunkhouses at the 4-H camp down at Silver & Gold Beach. In his sleep, Nick Adams carried the paint out of the shed and plopped them by the little square of concrete in front of the back door. He retrieved his ladder from the back of the shed, extended and secured it, and painted the entire backside of the house.

His first thought was: *I didn't do this. No way did I do this.*

Standing in the grass Nick's feet itched, the morning newspaper slipping from his grip, and as it did, he couldn't bring himself to grab it and it plopped into the grass below, his mouth suddenly drying up. It was at that moment when it clicked that he was in some serious trouble. He felt in his arms, in his shoulders, in his back, all the painting he had done in his sleep, the soreness, the strain, his body screaming for sleep. It was at that moment, feeling the soreness in his limbs rise to the surface, that he felt his life turn forever away from him, rolling away like some tire breaking loose from a crashing car. It felt to Nick like someone had stretched his insides tight and then snapped him like a giant rubber band.

"Something's waiting for you, my boy."

A memory of his father flashed in his mind, but it faded. *Why can't I remember?* He was going crazy, painting in his sleep, his body told him that much, that and the giant moon he'd painted on the side of the house.

Covering the entire back of the house, the lunar face was pocked with craters and shadow. Ringing the moon was a pale yellowish fuzz forming a kind of halo and Nick could see that he had sponged the paint to create the aura-like effect of moonglow. How he had managed the craters, he was not sure. The moon lay against a deep gray sky and at the bottom center of the moon, which happened to be right above the back door, he had painted a black cube. It looked as if someone had cut a small square block out the bottom of the big old cheese-in-the-sky. He wasn't sure what the cube was, or even if it was supposed to be a cube, he was too busy taking it all in, him going crazy and all. He might have run out of paint as far as he knew, but by the look of the blockish thing, and the feelings in his hands, he remembered taking the smaller brushes and painting the lines of the square shape so the lines of perception angled back to create the resulting cube effect. It was a cube, Nick half-decided, half-felt. *But what is it?*

The cube floated on water, or at least on what looked like water. A frothy field dominating the lower half of the house. The lower half could be ground, but the way the edges had been sponged, reminded Nick of water. The gray almost looked purple in some places, and there were what looked to be white caps cresting and breaking against the cubic thing, but Nick wasn't sure. He wasn't sure about anything.

His feet itched terribly. It felt hotter than it was minutes ago. Nick's feet felt like they were itching from the inside out, but he couldn't move to itch them, he had to look at the wall. He had to take *it* all in – the purplish water, the hovering cube, the wide and impossible moon drowning everything in its yellowy wash.

There.

It appeared to come out of the cube or was on top of the cube and slumping forward. Nick's head filled with the image of a dying man on a battlefield, and he stepped closer and as he stepped onto the hot concrete steps to stand on his tipsy toes to see, he recognized it. It was a figure of a person, either climbing onto or off the cube. *Definitely a person,* he thought. *But who?*

3

Maria listened to the wind chimes and thought of singing. She used to enjoy singing a great deal, but she had not had an occasion to sing lately. Mulch was ignoring her again. *You can leave anytime.* The voice of her cousin, Estrella, echoed in her head. *Yes, I could, but what about the girls? That is how abusers trap you. With guilt, shame and children. What had she said I had? Stockholm syndrome?* Maria shook her head. Estrella was right, of course. Maria knew it. *You can always go home again, right? Just pack up and ship off with Estrella when she wraps up the summer.*

Maria had been born in Monterrey, Mexico, in a sunny borough called San Martin. She and her brothers occupied a room in the back of a small shack on the top of an adobe roof, their parents and grandparents lived in the rooms below. The three-story home had been plenty big enough, the kitchen lay in the shallow basement and the chimney rose straight up the home so that the entire house radiated heat. Unbearable in the hotter months, the family spent their free time on the roof. Uncle Marcos had given her parents a lemon tree on their wedding night. The lemon tree bloomed in the courtyard below, just outside the front door. It was the only tree on the block and the lemons were like caged canaries that sang when the wind rustled the many hanging chimes that her father made in a factory in Monterrey and hung in the boughs of the lemon tree. She'd sit on her father's lap in the evening as he smoked his pipe, his rough hands resting on her shoulders or combing her hair. Sometimes he'd carry her around on his back as he chased her brothers around the roof.

On some days, the neighbors came with beer in tall brown bottles or Mescal. Then the roof became a stage where guitars were picked, tambourines were rattled and Maria sang old folk songs with her older sister, Constance, whose voice braided through the air. People would stop on the street below to listen or bellow out a chorus in return. Maria saw then how the men watched Constance, only sixteen. How they watched her body as her voice was pulled out of her by some unseen spirit. It was the way her hair lifted when her neck tilted in the part of the song where the woman realizes that she must leave her husband for her true love, the way her bosom heaved when she finished her lament, and her true love was dead. The men watched the way Constance held Maria's hand, squeezing it when she reached a high note as if her singing would be her undoing as if her passion would consume her.

Maria's voice was weak and childish compared to her sister's. When she sang with Constance, she often found herself stoppered, her voice caught on the roof of her mouth.

In time, Constance found herself married to a young man who worked with her father, and she took her singing elsewhere. Maria hadn't seen her in fifty years. Constance had stopped writing when their mother died. The last time she wrote Constance had wanted her daughter to come to Virginia and live with Maria, but since her niece had fallen in love young, like her mother, she had stayed in Mexico City with the one daughter of her own.

There is nothing for you to do but wait. You will survive. You will be happy. Just listen to the chimes, Maria, sing.

After her sister had moved away, the stage had been for Maria alone, and she found her voice had matured, though she did not move the neighbors the way her sister had.

Her father had given her a pair of wind chimes to hang on outside her window, and she would stay up at night and hum and sing and harmonize with the chimes, her body vibrating with happiness.

Here, at the Hayes house, Maria had collected over a dozen wind chimes, five of them in one tree alone. Her favorites were the wooden ones, mostly from Africa. Mulch had bought them for her from across the bay, for her birthday. It had been a complete surprise. Maria rarely received gifts. The wind chimes had set her body a flutter.

Maria listened to the chimes, sipped her lemon tea, and looked for the cats. He'd been so strange lately, Mulch. The previous week he'd been drinking, far later in the evening than he normally started, and he had cornered her in the kitchen, whispering in her ear about the old days when their blood had mingled freely in the caves. Mulch had long ago prohibited Maria of talking of those days. He hadn't wanted to remember what his father had done to him, or what he had done to her.

Then he had abruptly ended his flirtation, and took his bottle of whiskey to his room, leaving Maria alone. *What had that been all about? Money, likely.*

Two days ago Maria had heard old woman Winters talking about the closing of the Feed Store. She was in the Food Lion, on the dairy aisle and old woman Winters had been talking to Susan Henderson. Maria had interrupted them. "No that's not true. The store is making lots of money." But old woman Winters had insisted that the feed store was closing. Her husband had heard it from Mulch himself and later that day when Maria asked Mulch he had replied, "bout time I closed that fucking store."

Close the store? That wouldn't be good, in any way shape, or form for Maria, she didn't think. Estrella had said that she had heard that the cats had been seen, as well as the creature in the water. The creature in the water was Marina, Maria knew, and the cats likely the conjuring of the Ugly Mother, but the fact that people were talking about both made Maria nervous. Plus, there was the white fog forming every morning in a different spot in the fields – fog forming when fog shouldn't form, it is far too dry for fog. The kind of mist that flowed in rivers and streams and eddies, a fog full of shadows taking flight, banking through the fog to roost in treetops.

The wind chimes rattled and made music; Maria felt cold inside.

4

Mulch had never really understood Adam's fixation to try to make professional porn out of what Mulch thought of like a secret diary. He listened for Maria's footsteps to fade off the porch and onto gravel. She was in the back listening to her chimes. Mulch's index finger rubbed the mouse on his laptop. The shades had been drawn and his door was secure. Virginia wasn't home. He wouldn't dare it any other way, her ears were far too good. *She might hear her voice and the jig would be up.* It occurred to him that he didn't know where Bill was. Adam's videos were sometimes a waste of time, depending on how Virginia and Adam had their sex. Lately, it had been very unsatisfying for Mulch, for Virginia's face had been turned away from the camera, from him, and it was her face that he wanted to study – the way she bit her lower lip when Adam entered her. Once when she had been 16, wearing a halter, Mulch felt the urge to pull Virginia's top down just to see her nipples pop hard from the cold. At sixteen Virginia's body had been so perfect it could have bounced around the world. Mulch had already begun peeking through the slat-board wall that made up much of the old house. He'd hide in the hidden passageways and smuggler's lanes his great great great grandfather crisscrossed the house with. The slat walls had mostly been filled in with insulation, but there was a passageway behind his bedroom wall that led to one that hadn't been filled that went up into the second floor, up a narrow wooden ladder, alongside Virginia's room. She didn't know of it. He'd wallpapered over the seams ages ago. And when he hid in the walls he'd taken great pains to see that it didn't open while he pressed against the wood, inches from her as she undressed. He'd stand stock still in the dark and dust, one hand at his crotch, as Virginia, wearing only her panties, made herself up in the mirror. *Mamma Mia, Holy Saint Francis, and Mother Mary,* is what he'd say to himself, if for reasons of comfort, forgiveness, or whatever.

Adam's cheesy blocking from behind left him with only a view of a swollen nipple and the side of her rib cage, which reminded him of farm rows laid neatly apart. Lately, Adam's blocking had been completely off the mark. Mulch wanted to see Virginia's eyes roll so far back into her head that Adam was forced to grab her hair and pull her towards him to get them to roll back. He wanted to see the blush on her neck and watch her lips quiver as she moaned. He wanted a repeat of the April 19 footage. That performance was burned in Mulch's mind. Virginia had been particularly wild and Adam had been particularly clever, angling Virginia towards the camera lens instead of away from it, which is what he did most often, getting her to look right into the disguised lens, moaning into it, begging the lens, harder, faster, crying out for more as Adam took her from behind.

"Well, I'm not gonna tell her to like, model or something. She'll figure it out what I've got going on." Adam barked when Mulch complained of his staging.

"But that's what I'm paying for."

And Adam would roll his eyes and tug on his ear, "Maybe I'll start by rearranging the furniture?"

But Adam never did.

It bothered Mulch that Adam never understood that he wanted to watch her eyes, her mouth, and her neck. It reminded him of his mother when he had been a young child and had hidden himself in the dusty dark corners of his mother's room, under the bed sometimes, or hidden at the bottom of her closet. His hands covered in the fine silt and dust that she never swept up, his penis a stiff little branch in his pants that radiated heat, his mother's neck and mouth arching up as Leon pulled her on top of him, Leon's hands covering her breasts, his mother happy, satisfied, clearly in love as Leon rocked her to orgasm and oblivion. And like those days when he'd watch Leon and his mother from his dark corner, on April 16, Virginia's face came rushing and screaming into perspective, her merry widow ripped down the front, her left nipple like a hard raspberry hanging out of the ripped cloth, her face twisted into ecstasy and perfectly framed in the camera lens.

Buying Virginia underwear was another particular thrill Mulch indulged. He'd handle it before wrapping it to give to Adam, who would, in turn, give it to Virginia as a gift, who would un-wrap it, sneak off to change into them, and present herself as a gift to Adam for the unwrapping. He did this with all her gifts: jewelry, clothes, accessories, but mostly Mulch bought her lots of lingerie. And when he watched Virginia take them off he would think to her, towards her: *Do you know who has touched this, who has seen this, who has smelled this?* But, there was no way she could know. No way at all. And that idea made his prick rock-hard, being so close and involved to her, without her knowledge.

The very first tape he had ever gotten from Adam had been sloppy and tasteless. Upon seeing it, Mulch had cuffed Adam on the ear for his ignorance. He hadn't understood. Adam had thought Mulch wanted something else.

"But you can see her get wet and open up. You can see her pussy real good."

"I'm interested in her expressions you twit. Her face. I want to see her face. It's her face I love."

Mulch called them his video diaries, and he kept them stored away, though never once had Virginia, Maria, or Bill has gone through his room looking for secrets. Maria changed his sheets, of course, and picked up his hamper, but other than that, no one came into his room, as far as Mulch was concerned. The only bad thing about taping his daughter have sex was that Mulch was forced to watch Adam too, and that irritated him. He would often close one eye to imitate the sensation of watching his mother from under the pile of dirty laundry from in her closet, a pair of moist underwear hanging off his forehead, partially blocking his view. Sometimes Mulch wondered why his father had never intervened. Why had Eb heaved around the farm, drunk, a mere shadow of himself, while his wife, whom he met and courted for years and finally took to alter, fucked his brother, in his bed, loud enough for his son to hear? Why hadn't Eb, not till the end anyway, ever intervened?

Mulch pressed play on the newest video file. His tiny laptop, resting on the bookshelf of his bedroom, flickered, and the screen filled with the image of his daughter removing a bra, a black lacy bra that scooped her chest up into a fine cleavage. It was a super-bra, Mulch believed, one from the Victoria's Secret line. She was already stripped below the waist and Virginia bit her lip as she grabbed Adam's penis in her fingers. Virginia had a habit of biting her lips when she was excited. As Virginia placed her mouth on her lover's cock, Mulch's heart skipped a beat. The door behind her, behind Adam, next to the bed, was cracked open, just like his mother's had been so many years ago. He projected himself into the sliver of darkness where the door was open a bit. It looked like the same closet door his father had refused to paint and fix. It never shut all the way and it seemed to always be open a sliver, and there it was, in Adam's house. As Virginia placed her hands on the base of Adam's dick, the hidden camera auto-focusing on Virginia's red lips sliding up and down Adam's shaft, the back of Mulch's brain began to itch. Through the sliver in the door, he spied his mother's hair, penned up and coming undone, ringlets falling in front of her face.

Leon held each of her breasts in his palms. Mulch watched him squeeze and he heard his mother moan, her blonde hair falling around her neckline. She moved between him to climb on top of him and Mulch inched very slowly away from the door, the blackness in the closet swallowing him up. It seemed to swallow them up as well. Falling backward into the darkness, beyond his sight, he heard his uncle grunt, his mother sigh. When he found the strength to inch his way back towards the door, he caught a slice of his mother's naked back riding up on Leon's lap, Leon's hands pressing down hard into her backside. The itching in Mulch's brain stopped and Mulch felt himself snap out of a trance as Adam turned Virginia around, facing her away from Mulch's view. From there he saw her right breast droop down and Adam's hairy butt and thighs. He clicked the file off. Nausea pooled in his gut. He closed the laptop and slid into his bed and scooted his head up and under the sheets.

Excerpt from Ship's Log:
Dated June 8th. 11:00

The boat never came into view. My heart practically beat itself out of my chest as I waited. Marina did not notice. I kept expecting her to cry out. Whatever it was passed by us, quickly and safely. I have yet to venture off the boat, btw.

Charts show that Boston harbor is a little more than four days ride from where we are. If I didn't have the box behind me, I might be able to make it in half that time. The wind is with me.

Let me confess. I hate piloting these things. This trawler is large and clumsy. Maybe it's the heat or the fact I'm stuck under this heavy canopy waiting for the freaking sun to go down. I am going to try to wake Marina soon.

I sang Marina a song. A folk song I learned when I was little. About a girl who loves a boy who does not remember her, or knows she exists. I hope she likes it. Afterward, I fell asleep up there, listening for her.

I whittled a purple finch out of driftwood, it fluttered and sang and kept me company. How I hoped it would bring her comfort but when she has stirred it has been in fever and sleep. How foolish I was. How foolish I continue to be.

Marcos

5

Nick Adams stared at his house and tried to remember painting the moon. He couldn't, but he felt it in his muscles. The cube looked clumsy as if a child had rendered it. It was a cube though, or a box of some kind and it did look like it was floating on the water. *Maybe it's a boat,* he thought. Nick half-felt he could trust himself and half-felt he was going out of his mind, his mind flickering. He watched it as it flickered as if he were observing himself think. The painting of the moon on the side of the house looked to him like a shimmery illusion, its canary face breaking up and becoming pixels and the pixels hovering just above the surface of the wall, like fireflies on a warm summer night, floating above still water. The dark gray sky and the dark gray water broke up as well becoming a shadowy pixel mud around the canary face of the moon, which looked more and more like a face. As soon as that thought popped into Nick Adam's mind, very much like a lightbulb, did the moon's features become clear again, the face vanishing.

That face! I know it. Don't I?

She was pretty, but canary yellow because of the paint, and Nick couldn't tell much more than that about her. He knew she had dark hair, even before the gray pixels that were the sea and the sky swarmed to the top of the canary yellow face to form long shiny black hair.

In his mind a series of grainy pictures that swirled and whorled together into a delirious soup. He wanted to sleep. But he worried that he would paint again. Nick felt his muscles gathering in a kind of union, organizing, ready to paint again, waiting for the brain to go asleep so it could raise a coup.

What was he to do? Stay awake forever. That was crazy impossible.

6

Virginia had one of those faces that mutated to suit her needs. Mulch knew this and therefore did not trust his daughter. She didn't trust him either, and that was fine with him because he knew all about her, and she didn't know squat about him. Virginia came into the kitchen wearing a big T-shirt and skimpy cut-off shorts. She had slept through lunch. The pockets of the shorts hung down below the fringy bottoms of the shorts like saggy cheeks. Mulch thought he would look a lot like those shorts one day, saggy, and clinging to his skinny bones.

"You look tired," Virginia said, her hands in her pockets. Her eyes were perky, but the skin underneath was puffy, and red. She'd been up at it all night again.

"Didn't get much sleep last night," Mulch said, his back turned to her. Virginia leaned in to kiss him quickly on the cheek. She smelled of soap and toothpaste. "You just wake up?" he asked.

"Yeah. Couldn't sleep at Macy's. Came home late, or rather early." She turned away from him and Mulch directed his gaze towards the fine curve of her back, buttocks, and legs, her body so perfectly tuned to its frequency. Virginia moved toward the refrigerator, and as she began to open it she paused and removed her hand from the handle. Mulch felt nausea itch his stomach and he willed it away by staring at the golden aura of Virginia's hair as she poured her coffee and toasted her bagel.

7

Mulch looked at me like he always does, like a stranger. This morning he gave me his befuddled Daddy look – something like half-twisted lust and half-twisted disgust. Ever since I was old enough for sex, he's been looking at me all-weird and what-not. He thinks I don't notice it, journal, but I do.

I said to him, " Did Adam call, or something, while I was at Macy's?"

He replied, "Adam?" his lips uncurling from his half-disgust, half-lust bow to form a blank, flat sneer. His worst look, in my opinion. "You know I do think I saw him yesterday, going down Gospel Chicken Road, down towards the dump."

"By the fields?"

Mulch has a field down by Gospel Chicken Road. Corn, I think.

"Yes. You know how Mr. Bill dumps fish heads in that one field down there."

"Yes, I know. You saw him there, or did Bill see him there?"

"Yes."

He wasn't paying attention to me. I should be used to this by now. "Yes, what?"

"Yes I saw him there."

"Are you lying?"

"No."

He was emphatic. And hiding something because he looked down towards the table before looking back up at me, his face tensing up.

Clearing my throat I said again, "You wouldn't lie to me, would you?"

And he cleared his throat and said, "No."

He looked me dead in the eye when he said it like he was daring me to not believe him and for a second, I thought I saw Adam's reflection in his eye, as if Adam was standing behind me, only Adam's reflection looked frail, sickly, nearly dead.

8

Abdullah felt sped up, energized. He'd been inside his lamp for so long he almost didn't recognize the sun. He had spent so much time in all that whiteness, whiteness which was so bright and enveloping he'd almost lost himself completely, a fact he later thought of throughout his adventures with George. In front of him stood a red-wily-haired young man who held a smoking stick in his mouth. He recognized the smell, possibly. The sun shone with fierce, desert-like teeth, but a wet, almost rotting, smell hung about the air. His new master stood slack-jawed, breathing heavily.

"Hello," Abdullah smiled. He hoped he got the language right. He'd never been wrong before, still, he hadn't spoken with anyone in ages.

George just stared at the seven-foot blue giant as he processed Abdullah and unconsciously downloaded the information before him which seemed like a hallucination, and which after his date with Lilly, could very well have been one. He later recalled a smell, a very distinct charge in the air.

"Hello," Abdullah repeated as it occurred to him then that his accent might be a bit off. This language possessed none of the beauty of the Arabic or Roman tongues he had encountered in the past. "Hi," George said, unaware he had spoken.

"Hi," Abdullah mimicked George's response. "Hi," George said again. George noted how the man's muscular build made the man's shirt look tight, plus the giant man had a potbelly, *a jolly pot belly, right above his broad, vaguely pirate-like, belt. And a shirt my high school drama teacher favored. What in the hell?*

Abdullah curtsied, "I am known as Abdullah. I am what you would call 'a genie' and now that you have freed me from my prison I am in the position to grant you three wishes, in the manner of your choosing."

Upon hearing the word "genie," George began mouthing the word to himself over and over again, to make sure it was real. "You said you are a 'genie'?"

"Yes, that is correct."

"Genie?"

"Yes"

"Excuse me, one second."

George walked to the side of Mrs. Enfield's house, into the shade where he had parked. He looked back at where he had sat down his gear. *Yep, still a big blue guy standing over there.* The only vehicle in the driveway was his. Mrs. Enfield was out with her daughter, doing God-knows-what. *Thank God, for small favors.* George looked down at his cigarette and inhaled.

"Tastes like tobacco. Smells like tobacco."

George stepped to the backyard again, where Abdullah stood over the paint can and appeared to be trying to ascertain something or another, his big shoulders and head cocked forward so he could, presumably, look at the ground. George pinched himself. It was not a small pinch, but a screamer of a pinch. He used his dirty fingernails like small blades to dig in. He had to make sure he wasn't dreaming.

CHAPTER FOUR

1

The sun sank behind the row houses, the canal walks crawling with tourists, the canals themselves dotted with water bikes. The sound of bicycles on the streets rang out, echoing sometimes across the canal. From Cilia van Hazen's home, which rose five stories, and had its own annex above, and sported lively views of the city, which for a person like Cilia was important, for she could siphon that energy into her magics and had been doing so since she had been a child. As Cilia van Hazen's computer blinked and downloaded information, a couple dressed in blue turned their canal bike around and around in circles to get their bearings. Cilia spied them from where she stood at her desk waiting for the downloads to finish. Cilia had to fight the urge to run to the window and sneer something off-color, deciding it wasn't worth the energy. Instead, Cilia let a cackle fly from her throat, the kind of cackle one might hear in a storybook, the cackle of mean old witches and stepmothers, a real hair-raiser. Cilia loved to cackle. It was one of the few things that made her smile; it gave her a lift in the old heart, the effects it often had on listeners a bonus. Once she had belted out a cackle that made a poor child drop its teddy bear and tear-ass away from dear old mommy who bolted after her child, screaming. Another time a bicyclist turned back to see who laughed and collided with a tree that cracked the kid's neck and dislocated his shoulder from the cartoon way he mashed up against the tree.

Come on, fucker. Cilia stared at her computer wishing her magics could affect it. Cilia hated her computer. Her twin brother, Pembroke, loved his, which was so typical of her twin, careening off in the opposite direction. She often thought he worked at being good at things she was bad at just to piss her off. She had gotten the e-mail early in the morning, right about when she had risen to take her potion. Mulch had kept it simple and forwarded the transport's license and radio channel, in case she had needed to track Marcos and Marina as they trudged up the coast to rendezvous with the Van Hazen cargo

154

ship in Boston Harbor. She had told Mulch she wouldn't need a radio channel, or charts, or license numbers, that she would track Marina by other means. *That poor fool, thinking he's better.* Still, she would use the information when she took command of her men on board the ship.

She had preyed on the shipping company for months, focusing her power to learn the habits of the captain and the men who would oversee Marina's voyage to Amsterdam. She had taken over their minds on more than one occasion, and she'd learn to control the lot of them at a time, which had taken practice, the better part of a year. Her brother and she had invested several million euros into retrofitting the ship with a new engine, to say nothing about buying up the hold so that when the boat left Boston it would sail half-full so that the ship could make it across the Atlantic in about two days, instead of the usual four.

At her computer, she was waiting for a spell to download, something her brother had found a month or so ago, a document he'd discovered in North Africa. *Genies, brother? Really?* But it hadn't been genies, no a tome from some state archaeological dig he stumbled upon by accident. Pembroke's search for genies had been in vain; *so far,* he always likes to add when Cilia teased him. Pembroke liked to be helpful when it came to his sister. Cilia liked to think it was out of devotion, but it was out of fear. Cilia relished it. She didn't think the spell would be worth the time. Still, the runes might be useful for extracting the mermaid's power. *Or not.* Pembroke wasn't half the academic she was. She'd been adding spells to her repertoire all year in anticipation of feeding on the mermaid or dealing with complications that arose from trying to harvest the girls' hormones.

Handsome didn't go far enough describing Cilia. She had been ravishing as a younger woman, long blonde hair that had ashed into white as she aged, her figure retaining its girlishness, well into her sixties. But her temper had grown into something powerful and fearsome instead of mellowing. A lot of it had to do with the magic, it took its toll on her spiritually and physically, and like her brother, it had only twisted what was inside as her body bore the brunt of the malicious energy. Pembroke's entire physiology had changed when he'd discovered the snake hormones in Myanmar, a curious magic ritual Pembroke performed every month, at least, if not more. *His toes,* she thought. *He beat me there, damn him.*

Cilia could kill without lifting a finger, she could probe minds like she was reading an advertisement, with grace and speed. And when she had entered the mind of a subject, she could operate the body with more efficiency than the original spirit pushed to the side and dominated by Cilia's power. That was how she killed her parents, she simply broke into their minds, ripped out the controls, and did away with them.

2

"One more time. Did you say you were a genie?" George was pretty sure he smelled himself again. "You look more like a pirate, and not like a genie. It's that belt, I think. You did say that you were a genie, right?"

George didn't want to look at the hallucination. *Keep it together,* George.

"Yes master, I did," Abdullah replied, his face all squinched up as he tried to enunciate. "Three wishes I can give you, because genie I am, yes, I am a genie."

George pinched himself again, harder this time, and this time he was forced to scream, a red welt rising out from his skin.

"Master? Why keep do you cutting yourself with nails of a finger, what can Abdullah do for you?"

"To make sure I'm not dreaming."

"I will remember this, for next time *I* am dreaming, as you say."

Abdullah looked down at George and leaned forward. The two of them drew close together. From afar they looked like they were going to kiss or touch noses. George saw the genie had a thick, handsome head of hair, jet black and flowing back and up, a mind of its own, almost, and eyes which were brilliant blue made all the more diamond by the white of the genie's eyes.

"Did you just say that you, a genie, dreams?" George willed himself to look at the genie. He smelled his underarm odor creeping out. He hoped he wasn't going to see Lilly while he stunk like this. *It's nerves, maybe I have one of those conditions, either that or it's the fact a giant blue guy is standing before me.*

Abdullah blinked.

George blinked.

They blinked together.

"Yes, master. My dreams are dreams of gods and kings and queens and poets, the moon opens its eyes for me, master."

"What do you dream about?"

George's body tingled.

"What the moon reveals, sir, the crown of stars fading into blue until it fades into a great hall of lamps, like minarets reaching for the sky, virgins with hair of fire and kisses of gold, roast goat, and lamb, mounds and mounds of jewelry, reaching to the sky, all of it shrinking to the eye of a hawk perched on a tree watching its prey. And sometimes I dream of rabbits."

"Rabbits?"

"Once master, a long time ago, Abdullah knew rabbits."

"Meaning you ate them?"

George noticed that the Genie's legs ended in a fine mist, he could not see any toe twinkling out of them. He couldn't much see the ground underneath him either. *I swore he had legs just a few minutes ago.*

"Not eat. Speak, master. Rabbits and I talk much about rabbity things."

"You spoke to them?"

George noticed that when Abdullah spoke, his lips curled forward which made the big man look like he was thinking very hard about every word before it left his mouth.

"Master, yes. Many times we have spoken."

"How nice."

"Nice. Very nice, you say."

Abdullah looked at the ground between his legs, his eyes darting back and forth. The mist materialized into a pair of legs, wearing a pair of black pantaloons.

"Pardon me, sir, perhaps this is less distressing." Abdullah asked, "Also, have you seen my lamp, master?"

"Lamp?"

"Yes, lamp from which I, Abdullah, sprang forth to exist in space with you, my new master, master."

Abdullah bent completely forward, his upper body folding down so that his skull nearly rested on the grass so that his eyes could search the ground without difficulty or question. George didn't think it was physically possible for anyone to fold down like that.

"A lamp? I don't know what you're talking about, Abdural."

"Abdullah, master. My lamp, where I come from."

"Gold, eh? Trust me if I had seen a lamp made of gold, I'd have remembered it."

"Yes, a lamp forged of djinn gold."

"Babies from coals, eh?"

"Genie lamps are of great power. Master, you opened the lamp, why am I explaining this to you?"

"Well I don't know anything about a lamp, Adgural, especially not one that travels."

"What is this?" Abdullah asked as he pointed his huge finger to the can of paint.

"Industrial White # 4. I bought it yesterday from Hammer n' Nails in Lonley. I got the receipt in the truck."

"Master, where did I come from?"

"All I know pal was that I was opening a can of fresh paint, and the next thing I knew you were like standing there kinda looking like that Robins Williams cartoon, only a little more menacing, frankly, that beard is rather intimidating, if I might say, compared to..."

"Cartoon? What is this cartoon you speak of?"

"Jesus? How much can you deadlift?" George mentally made a note that he needed to hit the Y later that week.

"Abdullah, master. Jesus I do not know of and neither do I know a deadlift, though many dead men can I carry with one arm. What is a cartoon?"

"Your shirt," George said as he pointed to the genie's chest. "See how it's so puffy? Reminds me of a cartoon pirate. It's cartoony. Puffy shirt, you know, like in a Shakespeare play."

"Shake a spear, the pirate?"

"Forget about the pirate. Forget about cartoons. Forget about Shakespeare." George put his hands on his hips. "So this gold lamp, is it worth much?"

"Yes, master. The lamp is magic."

"See here's my problem. Genies are supposed to wear hats and funny shoes. Genies are supposed to carry curved swords and come with a lamp. You have no lamp, no sword, and you're wearing what appear to be very comfortable-looking palazzo pants, for God's sakes. You don't look like any genie I know."

"What does this genie look like? Which genie did you meet?"

"Never mind, I haven't really seen a genie. I mean, one that wasn't on TV."

"Why is master try to trick Abdullah?"

"I'm not trying to trick you."

"So have you seen a genie before?"

"No, not a real one."

"Now you have!" Abdullah exclaimed grinning ear to ear.

3

Lilly woke up in the middle of the pine grove, the air above her face thick with flies and mosquitoes. She lifted the netting over her face and sat up. As soon as she raised her head, she saw Rufus lying near, cleaning himself and gnawing at fleas. Rufus turned and twisted himself to get at the itches which annoyed him. Once Lilly began to make small noises: popping bones, and groaning ankles,

Rufus ceased cleaning himself. He smiled only the way a dog can and trotted over to her.

Lilly had a tremendous headache, right before passing out she had been in a trance. She had the faintest idea that Rufus had met her at the pine grove, but she could not be sure, everything was muddy. She felt like she had a hangover. Rufus licked her face and wagged his tail. He put one paw up to her chest as if to say, "Hey person, I like you."

"I love you too, Rufus," She whispered as she rubbed the dog's head trying to stand herself up. Her legs creaked under her, and her knees made a dry popping sound as she stabled them. *What was that last night? Had George provoked that from me? I'll have to ask mother.* Her brain felt a little fried, and she didn't like the feeling one bit.

The sun shone directly above through a little O in the treetops. By her guess, it was after nine in the morning, perhaps ten. Thankfully she had the day off. She took a step forward, and finding her footing secure, swaggered off into the woods. Rufus followed, wagging his tail.

She recalled summoning her mother to the pines before she had passed out but did not have the energy to continue it. Luckily, she had carried a bug spray stick and the face netting in her clutch. Had her mother met her she would have brought sustenance.

Did I cast the spell? She couldn't remember. They had been playing the game all summer. Lilly, trying to learn how to communicate with her mother over long distances. Mother, ignoring her daughter unless she transmitted a strong clear thought. Lilly knew what that meant, that her mother was going to go back to Mexico and leave Lilly here, to the life she wanted, probably at the end of the summer. Despite feeling like she had failed her homework, hope fluttered in Lilly's chest. George had something to do with it and the fact that she had produced enough light to blind someone, a level of power she had been trying to achieve for some time.

4

The best thing about having a mother who is not your mother is that that person can give you advice and mother you in a way that isn't like a mother, or what I imagine a mother must do. But without the hang-ups. I'm projecting all of this mind you. Why? Because I didn't have a mother around. Both Marina's mother and my mother were long gone before either of us could remember. Marina claims she doesn't remember my mother, but sometimes I think she does remember something, impressions perhaps. Marina's not sure how old she is. I asked her once and she got foggy and kinda stared off into space. Mr. Bill said once that he thought Marina developed slower than normal children do, which would make her younger than me, I think. You do the math, journal.

Macy's mother is a pest and never gives her any privacy. Macy said when she was a kid her mother took the door off her room, "so there wouldn't be any secrets between them," she had said. Macy's mother is overly motherly, correcting everything she does. Everything from the way Macy unscrews a toothpaste top, to the way Macy sprinkles salt into her soup bowl, Macy's own personal soup bowl, her personal soup, her dinner for crying out loud. Not into the family pot of soup, but simply into her soup, her dinner. And there Macy's mother tells her to sprinkle the salt from North to South, and then East to West, to be sure to cover all grounds of her soup. It's no wonder Macy's like a zombie around the house. Macy can't have a feeling without her mother telling her how to have it.

On the other hand, Maria just tells me to make a quarter-sized mound of salt in my palm and to throw it into the pot. It seems like a lot of salt when I do, but it isn't. It is a thick broth, an old family recipe. Maria's hands are ropy, callous, but sweet, and I'm continuously amazed at what they can do around the kitchen, around the house, and around my heart.

Sometimes I think she'll tell me about her and my father, other times I don't.

"What's wrong with Mulch, anyway?" I asked her.

Maria didn't say much, she only smiled, and that meant that she didn't know the details, but that she knew more than I, and that was enough. Maria quickly scooted away from the stove and disappeared into the dining room.

"We'll need to add a bit of chicken blood to the broth," she said from the dining room, her voice sounding doleful.

Bill had told me once that only Niagara Falls could douse Maria's passion for her family. Which family Bill meant, I'm not sure. Maria was one of those people who loved and loved and loved even when the love sucks them to the bone. *She is one of those people who must love.* Bill had said that at one time Maria was the love of my father's life. Now Mulch never talks about Maria and Maria never talks about Mulch. Bill also said that Ebenezer, my grandfather, who died way before I was born, had come between them, and that's why they never talk about it.

5

When Maria first laid eyes on Mulch the wind whipped off the water and blew pollen up in great dusty swirls as the wind marched through the forest on the Hayes property.

Mulch had been working the bean fields and was dipping a tin cup into the water barrel when he saw her.

Maria moved along the side of the field, whistling, smiling up at the sun, when she caught his gaze. She wore a light blue shirt which had been Constance's and her hair was pulled back into a simple braid. She was new to camp this year and had been recommended to Eb as a house-hand, fresh off the road from Mexico, bright as a cactus flower. Hardly a woman, she had the dainty bounce of a schoolgirl, wild with the new country and new language that surrounded her. She looked happy. Mulch had heard her whistling. He was a fine whistler too, but he was unfamiliar with her song when he heard it.

The memory of their meeting is as crisp as a film to both of them still, and Maria often thinks back to Mulch's electric, steeled gaze, and how for a second saw herself from his eyes, her blue shirt rippling in the stark breeze, her ponytail swinging behind her.

Mulch, young and muscular, sweaty and stinking of work, his hands the color of mud, and his face streaked with pollen and dust, just looked at her and smiled, a big grin that showed the whites of his teeth, his eyes excited, bright points of light. Behind him, in the adjacent field, Eb and Leon, the owners, her employers, tilled up the soil in great tearing sods. Eb and Leon were tiny, little twigs of people lording over their fields far and away, but Mulch was flesh, and she couldn't rip her eyes away from him. Mulch couldn't tear himself away, either. They locked eyes for at least ten seconds, long enough to ignite a fire in them both. Maria broke their gaze first. All the way home flies and mosquitoes hummed wedding songs in her ear and promised her love and beautiful children. Her heartbeat below the surface of her skin, a wild animal ready to tear through her chest. Her heart's beating made her brow break out in a fine haze of sweat which the flies and mosquitoes drank as they continued their tiny symphony.

She never forgot that moment or the first moment she walked into the Hayes kitchen, the woman of the house hung midair, suspended by what Maria could not tell. Ruth Hayes floated stock still before the stove. From her mouth issued rusty sounds of mechanical failure. What she later remembered as bone grinding against bone, a jaw clicking and clicking, gears slipped out of place, by what, by madness or bad luck. Maria put her basket down and simply climbed up on a chair, mosquitoes, and flies singing their arias to her, making her blush as she tugged on the woman's clothing and pulled her down to the kitchen floor. Ruth gargled when she tried to speak, strangled by her swollen tongue, and Maria knew from that instant that she was never leaving the house. What her family had said was true: the Hayes family was cursed.

6

It's always the sun, always, Maria thought, un-pegging the wash from the line and folding the shirts into a flat crisp square. *The sun rises and we follow, the sun sets, and we sit down for the night like the sun.* Inside, Mrs. Hayes laid in the bed sick, dying perhaps, though nobody thought that was true. Eb and Leon fought over the care of the woman, with Maria caught in the middle, for she served as mistress of the house now. *Talk about moving fast.* The strange thing was that it was all so familiar. *It's like I'm moving through water and watching my reflection move with me.*

The sight of Mrs. Hayes suspended in the air had given her chills, then nightmares.

Mrs. Hayes's body had grown ice cold while she had been suspended mid-air, her blood pressure had been dangerously low when the doctor examined her hours later. The doctor praised Maria's quick actions and the Hayes men responded in kind. Maria, lauded as a hero, had been given accommodations in the main house, the entire upstairs which had at one time been used by the live-in cook some generations before. Maria had been given work, and Maria had responded, recognizing her chance, and energized by the attention paid to her.

How Ruth Hayes had been suspended up in the air remained a mystery. The Hayes men refused to speak of it, and the mysterious Mr. Bill seemed puzzled or troubled or both.

Maria's nightmares started immediately, she'd slip into a sweaty tunnel of dreams that ended with her body rising in the kitchen, her own body suddenly next to Mrs. Hayes's suspended form.

In the daytime when she checked in on Mrs. Hayes, she'd find herself leaning over her, drawn to look into her face. Her breath smelled strange, and so did her skin, a rankness tempered with sweetness. Inside Ruth's eyes, strange fish floated.

Back in camp, the Ugly Mother had warned her to keep to herself if she could and avoid the mistress unless she had to change her sheets or help her to the bathroom. *Avoid her.* The camp had many names for her: Her real name was Ruth, Mrs. Ruth Hayes. No matter which name was used, it came with the same distaste and mistrust of the woman. *A curse. The Hayes family is cursed.*

No woman could be so bad, Maria thought.

It was known that Ruth cuckolded her husband. She had been seen with local farmhands, and at least once, a migrant, if the stories were to be believed, a pretty young man no older than 18. Rumor told of her escapades with Juan Fernando, but no one had seen the two of them together, much less making love. If the stories were to be believed, Leon had caught her with a black man once. The Ugly Mother had told her one night at camp that Leon beat the huge man with a horseshoe wrapped around his fist and had to be pulled off by Mr. Bill *if the stories were to be believed*. The Ugly Mother said that Ruth did this because her soul longed to escape her body, which was sick with love, and that Ruth had been like this for a long time. Everyone in camp seemed to know this. Maria saw the way Ruth strutted about the house, refusing to pitch in with chores, the way Ruth tossed her hair, and flirted with Leon openly around her husband and the others, especially, Leon. If the stories were to be believed, the sounds of their lovemaking and bed squeaking through the night sounded like the wheels on a child's toy. The squeaking never seemed to stop and that was funny to Maria, funny and sad.

As Maria pulled Mulch's good work-shirt off the clothesline, he appeared from behind the honeysuckle bushes between the yard and the dirt road. Mulch beamed light despite being dirty and sweaty. She forgot to breathe every time he showed up, but even though she had been working in the house for nearly a month, he hadn't said a word to her, a few hellos and goodbyes notwithstanding.

The Ugly Mother had told her, "Do not talk to that family, stay quiet, work quickly. She is sick, the lady of the house, and when she goes the men will need a wife. But do not get involved with him."

The Ugly Mother often contradicted herself, something Maria found very annoying, but the Ugly Mother was not to be discounted, and Maria did what she was told. All the while Ruth's health deteriorated. She was allowed out of bed, as long she was accompanied by Maria, giving Maria yet another chore, and another opportunity to be closer to Mulch. Because Maria's English was improving, she discerned that Ruth spoke nonsense. Ruth's eyes often had a faraway look to them; she had a habit of staring off into nothing for a time before coming back to life to chatter away about something known only to her. Dinners with the family were the worst as Ruth was either yammering or silent with

Eb, Leon, and Mr. Bill quietly sitting at the table, eating their food like the dead, as if everything in the house was normal.

Maria's experiences with Hayes men, and the white men who worked for them, were eerily similar. They spoke in slow cadences, stared at her directly, and when she answered their questions, they would look her over, head to toe, which at first made her skin crawl and now simply angered her because the men reminded her that she was powerless. They remained quiet during times of unrest, during dinner, Ruth being the only one that spoke back to her husband and Leon. Mulch often ate his meals elsewhere, with Mr. Bill, if the stories were to be believed. If the stories were to be believed, the house was dangerous, but still, it was many weeks after moving in that Maria learned that Eb beat Ruth across the head with wooden spoons. Maria learned to tell when Eb was eager to hurt her because he gripped his spoon like a hammer and swatted it into the bowl of his palm in trying to make his point clear. He would do this at dinner, as Maria removed dishes from the table, as she poured iced tea. The Ugly Mother said that cruel men beat women because they believed it would make them better, and Maria believed her. The Ugly Mother was right about that one.

But other times Ruth didn't seem sick, she seemed full of joy and life. She'd whistle and whirl around the kitchen like a little girl singing old songs out the window. Leaning her face against the newly installed screens, she'd whistle and sing and slur her words. She told Maria in passing that she was singing to the spirits, the spirits in the trees.

7

Nick's teeth felt loose. Each time his tongue came up to touch an incisor he swore they jiggled in his jaw. *I've finally done it,* he thought. *I've finally ground my mouth apart.* He'd woken up from what, a nap. He didn't remember laying down. He sweated profusely, the sun sitting on his chest like a warm fat cat waiting to snatch his breath away. He didn't want to get up because getting up meant that he had to look at it again and looking at it again was admitting that he was crazy.

But he did all the same. The moon he'd painted was bigger than he remembered it. He stared and felt the sun evaporating and the cool drapery of the night fall against his sides, the velvety touch of summer nights.

How long have I been laying here? He didn't know. Nick had been staring at the cube thing at the bottom of the painting when he had fainted, or so he thought.

What's happening to me? His vision briefly doubled and then cleared. The hairs on the back of Nick's head stood on end and he felt a pull inside him, a drawing towards something larger and as immovable as the moon itself. Clockworks ticked inside him, and Nick imagined that instead of guts and blood he was full of levers and gears and that the little old man upstairs who ran the works was finally awake. The little old man was telling Nick to paint in his sleep so his brain couldn't argue, the machinery within him having been turned on.

The moon was much bigger than he remembered it and he felt his arms draw up towards the painting. Somewhere in a little corner of his brain, a flicker of something silver played and rewound and played again, a memory unspooling itself from the reel, and for a second Nick inhaled the thick heavy scent of movie theater popcorn. *Why can't I remember anything?*

8

Marina felt like she was moving through water, for her body seemed suspended, only she felt dry on the inside, like her lungs and her heart had been sucked up into a great cloud. Yet it felt like she was floating, rolling on ocean waves. She could tell this by the way the long wave of the ocean felt so pleasant and true. Marina could feel water, but she wasn't wet.

Float, all I want to do is float, she thought. Her mind drifted off and for a second she was horrified by her powerlessness. She was sick. She had never been so sick in her life, and she felt the infection inside her like a bad thought repeating itself.

Spanish dialects fell out of the air about her, and moonlight, and water, except it wasn't wet. She wasn't sure if it was a memory or a dream, it felt like both. Then it began to whirl around her like a whirlpool. She watched herself float in the back paddles of the creek. She saw the heads of the migrants as they moved about one another on the high banks of the creek. It was the end of summer, the water was warm, and the fireflies were in abundance. She watched herself float in the creek, her hair floating about her head like a giant lily tiara. Her fin edged out of the water and came gently down. Marina watched herself swim away. Her vision swirled and she felt herself being plucked out of it.

All at once the image swirled again, like around a drain, she thought, and it opened up into a long tunnel. Marina knew it wasn't a tunnel, but it felt like one and she was flying through the tunnel towards a bright *something* at the end. It wasn't just a light she saw coming towards her, but the face of a boy, one she hadn't seen in a very long time. She could barely see him because of the dark. Something silver flashed to her left. The boy smiled and waved hello.

9

"Master, if it pleases you, may I give you a wish now?"

George thought about it and shook his head, no. "I'll think I'll wait. I have to finish..."

"Oh," Abdullah nodded his head and bit his lip. George couldn't help thinking the huge man with giant arms looked depressed. *The lamp. It has to be the lamp.* Then denial, that old chestnut of a coping mechanism threw a wall up in front of him. *George, there are no such things as genies. You're insane.* But who then was the blue giant in front of him?

"Master, my master previous he took a long, long time to make wishes. While he waited to make wishes, Abdullah was hidden away. Let me out, he did not. Not this master, master. Abdullah only asks for companionship. To be counsel and general, friend, companion, like the days of old. My old master made me hide in rock-cave. And I am too beautiful to be hidden away, do you not think so?"

"Whoa man, hold the phone." George put his hands up to emphasize. "First I have to finish *this* job. Have to. Absolutely fucking have to finish this job before the lady gets back." He pointed towards the front of the house. "She's a mean one and can ruin my reputation with just a word of hers around here."

George saw the big guy wasn't getting it cause the big guy's eyes squinted and screwed themselves up. And George wasn't exactly sure what to do, only that he needed to finish this job and like ASAP. His anxiety whirred into overdrive.

"Ah, yes, reputation." Abdullah paused. "Master must think of reputation. Best master in all land." Abdullah held his hand up to the side of his mouth. "Shall I call out to the land of master's great reputation now, master? Shall the world know of great deeds of my master?!!?"

"Look you wanna come help me? I'm almost done, we can talk, or something." George figured it was best to get inside, genie, or no. With any luck, the genie would disappear by afternoon, the byproduct of a bad strawberry thrown in his drink by one sick or lazy bartender. *Perhaps revenge for bringing in Lilly, and her brilliant light, Oh, Lewandos will get a nasty letter from me, indeed.*

CHAPTER FIVE

1

At the age of twelve, Cilia was already an accomplished witch and a damn good one. She had taken her father's mind away with the help of her twin brother Pembroke. Pembroke, unlike Cilia, excelled at potions and transmogrification, which would take years for Cilia to catch up and finally excel at as well. At the age of twelve, Cilia was already pretty good at getting into people's skulls, making salads of their brains, and such. She viewed her and her brother's failure to kill their father while they were in the womb as an affront to their power. Shortly after their twelfth birthday, they took their father's mind away from him with no intention of ever giving it back.

The family had just moved back to Amsterdam, into a small house off Prinsengracht. It wasn't too fancy, the home, but their parents had been quite excited at the possibilities. The building was handsome but old, and the nicks in the brick and woodwork reminded Cilia of chipped teeth. There were plenty of trees growing along the canal near the house. They considered themselves lucky to be in an area that survived the war better than others, for much of the city was in the process of being torn down and then rebuilt. Her parents had moved out of Amsterdam during the occupation for fear the secret police would begin seeking out more than Jews, so the Van Hazen's spent the war years in Gouda, a small rural community famous for its cheese. Some ten years later, the Van Hazen's had hardly started unpacking their suitcases in the new house off Prinscingracht, when Cilia, eager to make good on a promise she made in the womb, left her skull to invade her father's mind. Later that morning, she invited her brother to join her inside and they had had a field day with Da and then later their poor Ma, that winter they moved into the new house in Amsterdam.

2

Cilia and Pembroke were the kinds of eerie twins that villagers would have surely stoned in the Middle Ages, long ago. They were the kind of twins that would have been killed in the backwaters of the world because something was unsettling about them. A smell perhaps, a hormone only the twins emitted. The strangeness began before their birth.

The week their mother began her last week of pregnancy, their father lost control of his bowels and lost control of his drinking. Their father, David, wasn't a drinker, usually. He had the occasional beer or wine after dinner, or perhaps after work, but the last few months had been downright unnerving for David. Something was wrong with his wife, and he was sure it was the baby she was carrying in her womb.

When the doctor announced that two heartbeats could be heard through the stethoscope during his wife's latest check-up, Anne assumed the news would cheer her husband up. However, it did the opposite.

Their father had sensed it crawling about the edges of his brain for the last few weeks. A presence, he wanted to call it, or better yet a kind of knowledge. He felt two minds in the belly of his wife, who complained, blissfully almost, of a humming sensation in her womb, which David sensed when he touched her belly.

Shortly after David began to experience a series of violent fantasies where David cut off his testicles, or both his testicles and his penis. The thoughts entered his mind at the most unusual times. Sometimes he fantasized about what it would be like to fuck a knife with his cock. He'd even gone as far as placing the sharp end of a kitchen knife into his pee hole and sliding the point in carefully so not to cut but to feel the sensation of a blade against his skin, an action David woke up to in the middle of, which shook him to the bone.

When David tried to talk to his wife about the strange violent thoughts that were trying to overrun his brain, she only teased him and accused him of being a nervous father. Of course, he didn't explicitly detail his thoughts, no that would disturb his wife. He didn't want to disturb her, did he?

Lately, he wasn't so sure. He'd think about telling her at dinner, simply saying he wished to mutilate himself. Sometimes the words were so close to coming out his body reacted with adrenaline. He finished the dinner shaking and confused.

Once she was in the hospital, he tried again, pleading with her that there was something wrong with the babies inside her. However, by then she was too rife with pain, too pregnant to know anything other than the hospital bed. She bore them after nine months and nine days. His wife didn't even know he'd lost his mind.

During the week before their birth, David's sleep was incessantly disrupted by the twins hissing in his head, and it had begun to make David edgy. He continued to insist that something was wrong. He told his doctor that he dreamed of twins, of monster twins that were more scale than skin, that hissed, and bit and spit poison. He insisted that Anne would die delivering the babies. Eventually, David was sat down and prodded and poked. The doctor claimed David suffered from nerves and stress, that he should go home and rest and not worry his wife.

Six days before they were to be born, David drank out of every bottle in the house, Alcohol, cooking sherry, water, fruit juices, milk, and cream, everything that could be drunk was drunk. But David wasn't the drinking type, and once all the liquid in the house had been drunk, he went out and bought dozens of more bottles to satisfy his unquenchable thirst. He purchased alcohol mostly, for that's what felt the best. The booze dulled the anxiety and booze was cheaper than bottled water, or fruit juices.

On the second day of his binge, hung-over, and wearily drunk, diarrhea started. *It was the booze,* he thought, *just his nerves, as the good doctor had said,* he thought. But diarrhea kept coming and coming, and his stomach was kicked in the gut over and over again by the terrible gas pains and his wild, constricting intestines. At night he cried into his pillow as his wife slept the sleep of a narcotized mother-to-be. *The twins were making it happen,* he had thought. *The babies are punishing me.*

When he did sleep David dreamed about the bottom of the ocean. In one dream, David was turned into a pile of wet goo. A pile of goo with eyes and teeth and ears growing out of the wrong places. He dreamed of sleeping at the bottom of the ocean and of floods that carried his home to him at the bottom of the sea. In one dream, he woke up as a giant jellyfish, he had no agency over his body, or his motion, he simply floated and wanted to float and cared to do nothing but float. *Float, just float away,* he kept thinking.

At the end of the third day of drinking and shitting, when he went out to fetch a very large bottle of whatever, he found himself peering over the edge of the harbor docks staring at his reflection in the water. If it hadn't been for a stevedore's yell he would have stared at his reflection, fascinated, all afternoon.

A light had gone on (or out) of David van Hazen's brain. It was the light that led to his wife and children. All he thought about was drowning himself and ending the throbbing in his head, ending the voices, the malicious whispers of his unborn children.

Anne, safe in her hospital bed, was in pain, passing in, and out of consciousness, repeating the names of their two unborn children in her delirium. David, nowhere to be found, was in communication with his wife, only he did not know it.

David heard his wife's mumbling in his head, and in his head, it sounded like the voice of the dead, rather than that of his wife. Murmuring beneath the voice of the dead was the serene lap of the icy Atlantic. The hypnotic lap of the sea calmed him. The sea before him lay serene, still, in the winter sun. David thought that if jumped in he'd be happy. He'd sink like a stone and wouldn't think of 'It' anymore, of 'Them,' of 'The Twins.' That was when the stevedore's howl shook him from his trance and fearing that he might fall in if he were to continue staring at the sea, David shuffled off in search of another liquor store.

His bowels gave out on him as soon as he left the liquor store causing him to nearly drop the vodka on his foot, but he managed to catch it. What he couldn't catch was his stomach. His rear, and the back of his legs, were suddenly wet. There was a wet, plopping noise on the cobblestone behind him. Instinctively his hands went to cover his butt, and he felt how wet he was through his long coat. Liquid oozed into his shoe, his stomach grew sick from the sour, flatulent, sulfuric smell that snaked into his nose.

From there David walked home. He couldn't run, afraid he wouldn't have enough control over himself to make it back without soiling himself again.

When he arrived home he stripped his soiled clothes, his stomach unleashing another wave of diarrhea. He was amazed at the pain and the amount of fluid in his body. He didn't think there could be anything left inside him.

Such a good Da, Da needs a drink.

David paused, his sopping pants in hand, "Who said that?"

Such a good Da, Da needs a drink.

Da needs a friendly push.

All David could do was fight the urge to be sick again, his stomach cramping. He heard laughter in his head. They mocked him, his children. He shook his head to clear their thoughts and walked up the stairs, heading straight for the bathroom. It occurred to him that the twins were competing, to see who could kill him first.

David wasn't educated, but he was literate and was pretty good with figures. He wasn't religious and didn't believe in evil. He survived the war, the Nazis, and pistol-happy Americans who thought Dutch people were Germans.

David didn't believe in evil, dumb stinking luck maybe, but in evil, no way. And in his bathroom, half-drunk, his head full of visions of taking a long sleepy dive to the bottom of the sea, sure he was going to shit himself to death, while tiny voices, baby voices, malicious, bent on his destruction, whispered to him, only then did he begin to believe in evil.

And so he began to pray to it, and he cried for a long time on the bathroom floor. When he stopped he was naked, the bottle of vodka unopened at his side. He knew he shouldn't, but he couldn't bear to hear the voices again, so he opened the bottle and proceeded to drink himself into another ill-conceived stupor.

Years later, David van Hazen looked back on that week and remembered little. He drank like a camel for the next three days. He wouldn't let himself get sober. He couldn't, for if he did the voices would surely come back, he was certain of that.

Back at the hospital, his wife worried, she hadn't heard from him in days. A nurse was dispatched to their home to fetch David. She found him in the bathroom, naked, on the floor, in a pool of his waste. She showered the feces and vomit off his body, dressed him, and shouldered him to the hospital. While at the hospital, an orderly followed David wherever he went, but he hardly noticed, he had survived, though sick as a dog, but alive. Later, he would look back on it with shame.

As the babies grew into small children their strange influence only increased. They were strange babies, often not crying for days. When they did cry, they seemed to plan it so that Anne and David got no rest. Sometimes animals died in their presence. Sometimes people said strange things to them when they were out. The Van Hazen twins were weird kids, even his wife thought so

"Dear, don't you think the children are odd, the way they look at each other?"

Anne always spoke of the children with a tender and delicate tone.

"Oh yes, especially the boy. Or at least with me anyway," He would reply.

They would prattle on like this, with pauses between their diagnoses that would last hours, or in some cases weeks. Each time the children came into the room, they would change the subject only to resume it later that night, together in bed, sometimes days apart.

"Do you think the children eavesdrop on us?" He might say, in a low conspiratorial whisper. "Sometimes I can feel it in the air, like the smell of gunpowder after a shot."

"Hush now, David. They are only children."

But she would nod, pointing her finger towards the headboard, through the headboard to the wall that separated their room from the twins.

3

The morning the Van Hazens moved into the new house in Amsterdam was a happy one. David had come early to settle things with the movers and to start his new job at the bank. That morning, as his family unpacked boxes and moved their belongings around, his mind began to bubble, *like champagne*, he thought. David felt himself grow small, like he did that terrible week before the twins arrived, small, and helpless, riding a mound, or mountain slide of brown mud. He glided on top of the mud, barely keeping himself from drowning, the effulgence taking all power from his body. His vision went out on him for a second and he felt his heart skip a beat.

"Hello, Daddy."

It was his daughter's voice, and it rattled around inside his head. All he could think of was his baby girl squashing his brain like a pancake. Then it was over like it never happened. His children were playing in the new rooms, weren't they? His wife was unpacking the silver in the kitchen, right? The house was quiet. David's skin bristled with goose flesh.

When they were in the womb, they tried to drown me, he thought, having half-forgotten the mortifying feeling of being small and out of control, his body weak and sick and running riot. He clenched his fists and ground his teeth. If they were trying to kill him, what was he to do?

4

The twins weren't competing, not exactly, Cilia wanted to kill her mother and Pembroke wanted to kill his father. Both were immediate and instinctual choices that they felt during the third trimester. Before they left the womb they had begun to plan it, dream it, even. Cilia knew, even as a baby, that she must wait to kill her mother. They would need her milk and her protection. They could, however, begin on their father before they left the warm, watery womb. Later, in college, where they enrolled together – in every class, they giggled at Oedipus, laughed at it even. The professor could lecture all he wanted to about the psychological implications, and importance of separating the self from the parent, and the later desire to kill the parent, the Electra, the Oedipal urge, the final stage before becoming a man or a woman, but both

Cilia and Pembroke knew that the Oedipal and Electra complex rang true on a murderous level.

They had started murdering at a young age – rats, and mice, at first.

Pembroke and Cilia killed the animals by leaping into their little brain. It was just a matter of imagining what the creature was seeing from its point of view. Imagination was the key, and once they managed to wiggle their way inside, they could bid vermin to do anything they wished. Because they rather liked animals, and animals liked them, at first they didn't kill them, that seemed obscene somehow. Animals were easy, there was no challenge. The two of them could easily break the mind of a dog, cause it to kill itself by eating glass, or shut its organs down by taking control of the brain's other functions.

Adults proved to be more fun.

So it would be, dogs and cats first, looking at the world through their animal eyes, smelling the many odors unknown to the human nose. The twins cut their teeth playing with them, perfecting the skills they would later use to control others. They'd often snuggled up together after they were sure their parents were in their bed. They'd lie together and keep each other warm while giggling and hatching terrible plans for their father.

The winter before their parents died, Pembroke began to enter his father's mind and take control of his husbandly duties. Pembroke had spent many days at work with his father, observing the way men interacted with subordinates and superiors. At night, when Pembroke would take control of his father, he forced David to sing songs off-key and to make violent love to his mother, whispering obscene things to Anne during lovemaking. And sometimes, suddenly he'd cease the lovemaking, forcing his father to fall asleep, cruelly, on top of Anne, his mother, while he remained inside her, pinning her to the mattress of their shared bed. Cilia liked to do similar things with her mother, kissing the milkman, swearing very loudly in the library, kicking small children in the flower market. Cilia wore Anne out like a ragdoll.

5

The Dutch police simply left parts of the criminal report blank. David van Hazen had walked out of his house on a Sunday afternoon, dressed for church, though he'd never been known to go, and right into a canal. Witnesses claimed that he held his head under, before a boat, having not seen him, ran him over with their propellers. One witness had said it seemed intentional, but strange as if he were trying to baptize himself. There was no other way to explain it. The boat pilot, a veteran sea captain, said he didn't see the man, he'd only heard a thump, then a horrible scrape as the rotors sliced David van Hazen's skull open like ripe fruit.

"Suicide?" The police had wondered.

"Perhaps." Had been the only answer.

Friends reported that he'd been distracted lately. His grandfather had died recently and left him a sizable fortune. He'd been happy about that.

"Suicide?"

It didn't seem likely, but on the same afternoon, David's wife walked herself right out the top floor window of their house. The Van Hazen house was an old house, built in the 1600s, and like most Dutch homes, the windows swung out wide so furniture could be pulled up, via a pulley and thick rope, to the proper floor, and hauled in through the window. The children had said that she told them that she had wanted to air the room out, even though it was freezing outside. The children had begged her not to. Then it happened, she had stepped out the window as if she were stepping into another room, falling three stories to land face-first on the cobblestone with a wet smack. According to the children, this had happened moments after their father had run out on an errand.

The children, if you could call them children, were almost twelve but they looked nearly twenty and were sent to go and live with their aunt Hille, in Maastricht, in the south. In time, a public servant declared the children to be the sole heirs of their father's estate, and that of their great-grandfather's estate, which included:

one house in Amsterdam on 12 Prinscingracht

a house (cottage really) in Rotterdam

another cottage in Utrecht – just outside the city

various bits of furniture

clothing

a small cache of jewelry (their mother's & great-grandmothers)

327.25 guilders in a savings account at the ABN AMRO bank near City Hall

and one small (but profitable) engineering firm in Utrecht, currently run by a feeble old man named Joost.

CHAPTER SIX

1

Nick Adams felt like throwing up. It wasn't just nausea, but a sense that he wasn't of himself. He was ravaged and a little freaked out. His head hadn't exactly been playing fair for the last few days, and he didn't know how much longer he could keep it up.

Nick sat at his round, brown, Formica kitchen table, his head in his palms, wishing everything would just swim away. He needed to eat but knew that were was nothing in his cupboards. Nick settled on Miller Ice, hoping it might settle his nerves.

He craved fish. Nick could taste it, *the delicate, tender way a chef could prepare fish, with butter, a dash of garlic, and lemon.* He desired clams, too, *Little Necks with some green pepper sauce. Might as well throw in some shrimp, too.* Nick's mouth watered, drooling practically onto the can of Miller Ice. If he didn't eat fish before noon he would go crazy.

He grabbed his keys and chugged his half beer before stepping out.

2

Sea Hag's Fritters, a small dump of a place where grease hung in the air like fat water moccasins on marsh deadfall. Greasy, black streaks floated over the fryer and coiled around the kitchen before snaking out the little swinging western door separating the kitchen from the dining room. The greasy streaks lined the perimeter of the dining room, running around the ceiling's edges, instead of covering the ceiling as they did in the kitchen. Sea Hag wasn't much for scrubbing, although she did bleach the floors every night, and made sure the trash was taken out. Bathrooms too, though truth be told, if the state regulations didn't explicitly say so, she probably would have forgone cleaning the floors and the bathroom and would have left the trash for the dogs.

Sea Hag's specialty was fritters, clam, and oyster varieties, plus shrimp, steamed clams, baked fish, fried fish, and deep-fried shrimp served over oysters wrapped in bacon. She also served several varieties of fish including, rockfish, flounder, and red and black drum. Sea Hag had three deep fryers and one convection oven where she baked the occasional potato, or fish as well. But her specialty was her breading that she seasoned with onion, garlic, and a secret ingredient that Sea Hag would take to her grave.

The Fritter shop hadn't been "busy" in twenty years. Only during late spring and summer when the watermen and recreational fishermen itched for longer days, did Sea Hag have much business. Sometimes though, when it was busy, Sea Hag's packed, little shack looked like a squid of elbows and arms, the giant head the long countertop, the tentacles reaching back to the screened windows, homemade beer foam slung from toasting red plastic cups like so much ink. Winter months were just plain dead, and Sea Hag didn't even bother opening. The fall was okay, swinging between slammed and empty, a winding down kind of time. Sea Hag related to the changing leaves, the time of sleep near, but early summer was her favorite when it was hot when everyone came by to eat a bite and gossip.

The four tables lay jammed against the wall, a narrow aisle separated the seats from the counter which was jammed with seven bar stools. In the summer months, the old men meandered in after ten o'clock when Sea Hag put a fresh pot of coffee on. Old men like Huck and Buck Winston (no relation,) Dooley Morgan, and Captain Hawes Murdock, who once saved Huck and Buck's life during a summer squall when they flipped their small outboard running marijuana from Maryland down to Cape Charleston. The old men all looked alike, wore jeans hitched up to their waist, with buttoned-down short sleeves whose pockets were packed with Basic cigarettes. They kept Sea Hag in business because they would blab on and on about her cooking prowess to the few tourists who shacked up at Ballard's B&B, the only profitable business in Oysterhaus that wasn't owned by Mulch Hayes.

Sea Hag was breading her shrimp and some flounder in her dark beer batter when Dooley came in that morning. The kitchen counter allowed her to watch the front while she prepped her food in the back. She never hired help, except for in July when the Hattie girls came home from college. This year was the last year for Hattie's youngest daughter, also Hattie, who went by Hat, instead of Hattie, and Sea Hag didn't know what she was going to do the next year without her. Just thinking about it made Sea Hag's head hurt. She had thought it time to call Hattie about Hat when Dooley lifted his green dusty John Deere cap off his head and sat down. His head had a permanent ring about his skull where a John Deere cap had sat for the better part of his sixty years.

"Morning Hag."

"Dooley."

"It's going to be a hot one. Weatherman says 99, maybe 104. Hell, it ain't July yet. Say ol' Hat coming back this season?"

"Yup. Last one too. I was just thinking about her too."

"Great minds, Hag, great minds."

Sea Hag dipped the eight-inch-long fillet in the brownish-yellowish batter.

"How bout your granddaughter, could use a little help next summer. Tips are 'kay if she's polite."

She mashed the fillet in the breadcrumbs, and cracker meal, pressing firmly to get an even breading.

"Well maybe," Dooley responded. "I'd ask ol Capt'n about his daughter's kids. Dot says that Mo'reen is headin' out o' state for college. Some school in Georgia where they teach the kids how to draw." Dooley arched his back, his left hand balancing his weight on his butt. He took a cigarette out of his soft pack, which was crumpled, and lit it.

"Coffee, Hag?"

"It's already brewed. Help yourself if you don't mind." Sea Hag lifted her hands, covered in batter.

Dooley nodded, and got back up and poured himself some coffee.

And that's how most mornings passed, Sea Hag breading her food, heating the fryers. Dooley, or one of the other old boys coming in with small talk.

Before Sea Hag knew it, she was prepped for the day – a dozen fish breaded to go and the fryers were piping hot, the hushpuppies formed, lined up in rows like bullets, fritters stacked to go in the refrigerator. Now she could smoke and wait until someone got hungry.

Captain Murdock was the second customer in that fine, hot morning. Sea Hag smoked her cigarette with her right hand, and with her left, she reached down into her apron pocket and rubbed crystals together for Marcos. Crystals he had given her when he had left to take Marina to Boston. "For luck," he had said, before taking his little outboard back into the paddles of the creek to meet Mulch.

"Hag, didja hear that Mulch was closing down the feed store?" Murdock's voice was like sand gurgling down a drain, deep, and throaty, half biological, and half caused by the filter-less cigarettes he smoked. "Hey Hag?"

"What?" She had been thinking about Marcos, she felt a million miles away. "Sorry I didn't get much sleep last night."

"Hope it was worth it?' Dooley said, half to himself, half to his coffee.

"Shut up Dooley, a woman's private life is private," and she gave Dooley a gentle slap on the back of the hand, as she reached for the coffee pot. "Refill, Dooley, Capt'n?"

Capt'n Murdock nodded, right hand still poised in a point for effect, "I said, didja hear Mulch is closing down the Feed Store?"

No, she hadn't heard that, but that was intriguing, "Capt'n, are you sure?"

"Hell yes, I'm sure. Ran into Daisy last night, at K-mart."

"Doing a little shopping, Capt'n?" Dooley ribbed Murdock with his elbow.

"Hell yes, best beer prices in town. Also heard he was gonna cut loose the migrant help. Anyways Daisy was lookin' upset 'bout something, so I say to her, What's wrong? And she says that Mulch is shuttin' the store down, and even though he was givin' her husband a heck of severance check, he was going lose his insurance, and have to look for a new job."

"Her boy still in school?"

"No. He's up the road, working for a Baptist Church. Organist, I gather. My sister who sings in the choir tells me so," Dooley said as he sipped his coffee. "Damn shame, I tell ya. Though, to be honest, I have spent all my Christmas wishes hoping that damn Mulch would just dry up and blow away."

"Well Dooley, maybe your wishin' paid off," Murdock grunted, swiveled his butt on his stool so he could look down the road that passed right by the feed store.

It was right about then that Huck and Buck Winston came round the corner and into Sea Hag's. Huck's eyes were raisins and Sea Hag could tell that he was already high as a kite. Buck looked a little hungover and walked with his shoulder slumped forward, which he did when he took in too much drink.

"Morning," Huck wheezed, Buck nodded.

"Ask them. They used to work for old Mulch. Ask 'em. They outta know," Murdock looked at Sea Hag, then back to Huck and Buck.

"Ask us what?" Buck replied, settling down next to Murdock. Huck sat down beside Buck and let out a little whimper of a fart.

"Excuse me," Huck said.

"Capt'n here thinks Hayes is closing down the feed store," Dooley's voice sounding a little snaky.

"Think nothin', I know," Murdock's cigarette held an inch-long ash at the tip.

"That feed store, I don't know anything about the feed store," Huck looked up at Sea Hag. "Some coffee please."

"Me too, Hag. I haven't seen Mulch in over a week."

"But you know about the store?" Murdock had always suspected Huck and Buck to be a little bent towards the crooked. His suspicions had grown towards proof. He followed them around for the better part of that summer, sure that Hayes was the one who bankrolled the drug and numbers operation they ran out the back of either Huck's truck or Buck's boat. One day Murdock was gonna spill the beans on Mulch.

"I know nothing, Murdock. Hell." Buck said, fiddling with his lighter.

"Everybody knows you and Huck ran that numbers game for Hayes," Murdock's pale blue eyes held a bright shine for someone so old.

"That was twenty years ago," Huck interjected. "Besides since the state lottery what we were doin' has become legal."

"That's hogshit," Murdock spat into his handkerchief and rolled his eyes.

"Capt, we're straight with Hayes. We don't know anything," Buck said.

"It's just another old business gone belly-up. Been happening since your grandpappy was spitting before you," Huck gave Murdock a steely look and went for a cigarette. " No different than anywhere else in this country. Hard for normal folks to have normal businesses, is all. That's all. He's probably shutting up before he gets shut up."

"Yup," Buck leered. "Probably so."

Sea Hag stepped back into her kitchen; she had heard enough.

3

Oysterhaus depressed Nick, always had. The houses all looked haggard. Paint peeled away in quarter-size chips, and the grass never seemed to be kept up. Oysterhaus, like dozens of other townships on the shore, had been whittled away to nothing by highway 13. Cape Charleston experienced a resurgence of growth, so had Onancock up the road, and Lonely, but Oysterhaus was nothing but a shell of a town. Nick wasn't even sure Sea Hag's was even open when Nick pulled his old Corolla into the parking lot that surrounded Sea Hag's Clam Fritters like a cuticle on an old nail. As Nick shut his door and walked up to the screen door he heard the conversation inside drop to a whisper.

Nick didn't just walk in, he strode in, aggressively, as if he were on fire for some of Sea Hag's goods. The men nodded and Dooley said "Howdy," without even looking up from Sea Hag who was busy frying up some hush puppies and flounder.

"Mornin'," Sea Hag said from the back of her kitchen. "There's some coffee if you like and I'm fixin' these old men here some lunch. Would you like an early lunch?"

There was something about the way the young man looked to Sea Hag that suggested that something was bothering him other than his stomach. Nick looked about the dining room and decided on the farthest stool, two over from Huck. When he sat down he nodded to the men and took out a cigarette.

"Give me a sec."

Nick nodded towards Sea Hag and looked up above the counter where the menu had been painted about a hundred years ago.

"You'll need this buddy," Huck said as he grabbed one of the gold tin ash-trays Sea Hag kept along the rim of the counter and shot it over to Nick, who nodded a thank you and promptly ashed in it even though he didn't need to.

"I think I'll go for the battered flounder. Two pieces if you don't mind, and a side of fries," Nick hollered.

"Done deal," Sea Hag replied as she turned back to the prep table.

Nick heard the fries drop in the basket, the sizzle and the pop sounded like gravel on an old tin roof.

It was hot, and the old men were complaining about it more than usual. Dooley had practically sweated through the front of his shirt, not to mention the underarms, which were soaked. Capt'n Murdock had taken off his hat, which he never does and his pitiful white wisps of hair seemed to rise off the top of his dome-like fog. Huck and Buck seemed to be the only ones completely comfortable, continuing to drink their hot coffee, even after their meals were in front of them. The young man kept flashing his eyes back and forth between the kitchen and Huck who was giving him the once over.

"So tell us your name buddy," Captn' Murdock said. "It's too damn hot of a day to be strangers. Shit, it ain't even noon. I'm Murdock, but most people call me Capt'n. Over here is Dooley, but he's kinda soft in the egg sometimes."

"Shuddup Murdock," Dooley piped in, turning to look at Nick for the first time. "I ain't soft, but I am sweet on Haggy here." He gave Sea Hag a whistle and turned back to staring off at her upper torso that seemed to float above the counter.

"And these two are Buck and Huck Winston, no relation," Murdock said as he rolled his eyes at Huck and Buck.

Nick nodded politely, "My name is Nick, Nick Adams. I live off Bayside"

The old men nodded and turned back to their hushpuppies, French fries, and breaded fish. Murdock took a bite and looked back. The stubble on his face suggested he hadn't shaved in a day, or two. "You aren't any relations to old Pastor Adams. He used to live out by Silver & Gold Beach."

Nick wasn't sure what to say. His brain locked, and for a second all Nick thought of was the painting on the side of his house.

"Yeah, he's my uncle."

Nick didn't know if that was true, but it felt like it had the ring of truth to it.

"Good man," Huck said.

"Sorry about your uncle, he was a right nice fellow. Gave good sermons too," Dooley said. "Ain't that right boys," Dooley looked to Huck and Buck. "Oh, I forgot you all ain't the church-going types," Dooley let out a little howl.

"We're a bunch of old sinners Nick, pardon us," Huck said.

"Don't worry about it. Don't go myself these days," Nick replied.

Sea Hag stepped out from behind the counter with a paper plate full of food for Nick in her right hand. In her left, she held a brown half-gallon jug. Ice had formed around the neck, little crystals of cool.

"Sea Hag's gotta little surprise for you boys. Seein' as I didn't get hardly any sleep last night, and seein' that Huck and Buck are still high from their nocturnal activities, and being that is hot as hell, I figured we should drink some very cold, and some very dark beer."

Nick grinned; his anxiety had faded since he had walked into Sea Hag's Fritter shop. Cold beer sounded great.

"That's just what the doctor ordered," Nick said. "Give me a tall glass."

"You're a tall drink of water yourself, honey," Sea Hag smiled and showed some of her crooked teeth. Nick thought she had a fine smile, an ugly one, but one with a nice, warm countenance, despite her wrinkles and the green shade of her skin. "You boys should watch it now, this stuff is strong, but it will lower your temperature. I guarantee that," Sea Hag said as she waved the jug like a trophy.

"Yeah, it is hot all right," Dooley said as he smacked his lips together, his mouth watering as he watched the beer pour right to the top of his red plastic cup.

"Damn unusual," Capt'n Murdock said. "Goddamn, I don't remember the last time it was this hot this early in June."

"That was the year we had them two big hurricanes. Tore Cape Charleston up something proper," Sea Hag reminded Murdock as she smiled at Nick.

Nick smiled back; things were going to be *just fine*.

4

"Somehow I think that you are a...uh...um..." George's tongue licked the roof of his thirsty, dry mouth. "...well it's just that I don't think you're real."

"Real?" Abdullah's eyes seemed a bit hurt. "Real am I."

"Look I'm sure that you are just some spoiled pieces of fruit that ended up in my margarita last night." Except George remembered that the margarita mix came out of a bottle, a plastic one. He'd seen the bartender pour it. "Maybe a bit of sunstroke. Maybe heat exhaustion. It is hot out here."

"Hot yes. Heat makes men of boys. Move indoors we shall."

George blinked several times hoping each time he opened his eyes again the genie would be gone, but each time George blinked his eyes open, all he saw was Abdullah looking down at him, though looking quite friendly with his big smile and funny clothes. Abdullah looked a lot like some little kid's imaginary friend, or what George imagined an imaginary friend might look like.

"Look buddy, I have to get to work. I don't have a lot to do, but I have to finish it. Would you mind coming back later?"

"Master needs help?"

"Help?"

"Yes, master I will help you. In all the land..."

George raised his right hand, stopping Abdullah mid-sentence. "Come inside, I have some trimming I need to finish, and you can talk and keep me company."

"Master, thank you for your generosity."

"No problem, just don't touch anything. And if Mrs. Enfield comes home and finds you here, don't say a word, I'm going to be up shit creek without a paddle."

Abdullah didn't say anything, he was too busy smiling.

5

George had to finish the trim to make everything look precise and clean, and neat. But Nick's little sleep-induced painting fiasco had turned a one-day job into a two-day job. *And now with a genie?* A figment of his imagination? Not to mention his obsession with Lilly's glowing, a murmuring loop under all his thoughts. *It didn't seem strange last night, but in the sunlight of today...bizarre.* George felt invisible gears turning him in a direction he wasn't sure he wanted to go. To be sure, George reached out and grabbed Abdullah by the wrist.

He felt real enough. Abdullah's skin was tough. He felt strength in Abdullah's arms, and he found that strength reassuring.

"I want you to first sit on the floor while I check things out. Talk to me. You can tell me your story."

"Master, a question I have?"

"Yes."

"What is a Mrs. Enfield? What is the master's occupation with Enfield? Is master a farmer?"

"Enfield doesn't mean anything, I don't think. Mrs. Enfield is a very old and very blind lady who is giving me a very nice sum of money to paint two upstairs bedrooms that Mrs. Enfield does not even use." George tapped the wall with his index finger. "This is Mrs. Enfield's house."

"Palace?"

"House. There are no palaces in this, um, kingdom."

"Master has not a palace?"

"No, Ab....Ab...Ab..."

"Abdullah, master, master needs a palace. All great men need a palace in their kingdom. Even a genie has an empty can of paint to curl up in after a day of work with Master. This must be your first wish. For a palace. But this is simply a suggestion, mind you, a palace."

"It's all right. I have a house."

"A large house?"

"For one person it is rather, large, I guess. But I think I'll hold off on the old wisheroonis for a while, Abracadabra."

"It's Abdullah, master."

"I got it." With that George moved into the room and Abdullah followed, his big head barely clearing the door. George noted the size of Abdullah's arms was twice the breadth of the door frame.

"Tell me about yourself. I wanna hear you talk, while I work, understand?"

"Master, yes. Where should I start?"

"I don't know, tell me something, anything."

The genie sat with a loud thud and the china rattled in the cupboards downstairs. George peeked at his work from the previous afternoon. He was looking for paint ghosts, missed spots. He didn't want Mrs. Enfield's daughter to find anything out of place. He felt doubled, in his soul, reality as he knew it folded outward, or inward, he wasn't sure.

"Master? Is anything wrong?"

"No."

Except for the fact that Genies do not exist.

"If Enfield woman is blind, how come she wishes master to paint her house?"

"She likes to have someone to lord over, Ab"

"Abdullah, master. Lord over, I do not understand the meaning of the words. Do you mean she is a God to be worshiped?"

"No. No, Ab. She's rich. She likes to be in charge. It means that Mrs. Enfield likes to boss people around."

"Then master George is a lowly slave?"

"No, no Ab, there are no slaves in this...er kingdom, not technically, anyway."

"How work gets done, then master, without slaves to whip and beat and build monuments to master's greatness, isn't this how all of man's great endeavors get accomplished? At the suffering of others?"

"Slavery is against the law, my friend, and people kind of trade one thing for another, here. I trade my skill; she gives me money in return. Slavery is god-awful evil, my friend."

"Master is artisan then?"

"Yeah, I guess."

"Makes Abdullah happy to work with a skilled master of paints and brushes."

"Tell you what, you sit here for a second and I'll be back and show you what I do for a living. But when I come back you'll tell me a story about yourself, deal?"

"Agreed. Abdullah has remembered a story for master to hear and enjoy."

6

George carefully and precisely measured his brush to the edge of the ceiling, as Abdullah began his story. And as Abdullah told the story, George saw it, not just in his mind, but along the wall and in the paint, like a film that played across his field of vision, blurry images from Abdullah's mind transmitting to his own. He fell into such a trance that George forgot he was painting, when in fact he was engaged in the most accurate and exquisite trimming he had ever done in his life. Abdullah explained that many genies blamed the humans for their exile from the sky and vowed to trick humans. Many genies wished for the luxury of their former sky palaces and wished to find a master who would grant them the opportunity to join them in their human realm, as a fellow. He explained that many humans made their wishes very quickly, always for love, wealth, or large physical endowments. Abdullah explained that Genies could not grant true love but could only arrange for certain 'situations' that appeared as love at first glance. The men who wished for this never came to understand this and when their promised love failed to materialize, especially disastrously so in Arabia, time and again, then often the genies were carried far out into the wilderness to be cast into the unknown so no human would be able to find the cursed lamp. Abdullah then explained his frustrations with one day being found by the little old man with a pot on his head. Abdullah told that he hadn't spoken to a human in a very long time and that it felt good to finally be able to talk, and how the act of unconsciously rubbing his vocal chords together was quite pleasant. However, whenever a genie did appear it was a sign of great power and often resulted in shifting of power among the ruling class, which was why some masters longed to have a genie as a lifelong friend, reserving their final wish until they were on their death bed. Abdullah explained that he had never seen another genie while he had been in the service of a master, and what he remembered of his former cloud chambers was fuzzy and full of light.

7

Twisting, and knotting, Nick's stomach grew hot and expanded, then grew cold and shrank in on itself, shrinking in on the fried fish that had been masticated by his mouth and was ready to be processed by his gut. Nick's head felt like someone had used it for a soccer ball. It even felt soft, where someone would have kicked it for a goal. His skin felt dry and patchy. He was sure, absolutely sure that it had been the fish.

The old boys had left to go drink beer down at the dock, to take a dingy out to bottom fish for croaker. Since then no other customers had come in and Nick was left by himself at the counter with one hell of a stomachache.

"You feeling okay?" Sea Hag asked as she bit the end of her pinkie nail.

No, not really, he thought. But Nick wasn't able to respond since his stomach was twisting in on itself. He felt like he had a temperature. Sea Hag shuffled around the counter to sit next to him. Nick smelled brown ale on her breath and grease on her clothes. Underneath that smell was a pleasant, soothing odor, one he couldn't place, but one his mind knew.

"Jesus, you're burning up," she said, "I can feel you from here."

Nick's skin felt both cold and clammy and hot and feverish. Nick felt like he had swallowed a wrench. Something hard and cold and metallic was making hell out of his stomach works.

"Oh, God. Jesus." Nick doubled over and started to puke.

Out came the fried fish, out came the homemade ale, out came the French fries. It was wet, and hot and made a soupy pile on the floor next to his shoes.

"Shit on a shingle."

Sea Hag rushed to the back and grabbed a bucket. She flung it into the sink and began to fill it up. Dumping a cap full of bleach in, she added a bit of detergent. She opened the little drink cooler and grabbed a ginger ale. Grabbing the bucket, the mop, the soda in her pocket, she came back around the counter.

"Here you go sweetie, this should settle your stomach." She popped the can for Nick, and as she did, he vomited again, this time a dry heave. "God, you aren't well, are you?"

Nick couldn't think, his head full of green needles of light. A voice in his head told him, rather quietly and calmly, that he was going to die. He couldn't feel his skin, he only felt the untwisting and twisting of his stomach. Nick felt like he was being scooped out with an ice cream scooper. In the middle of the pain, a thought bubble rose in his mind. *You need to be wet. Get to water. Get to water, now. If you want to live you must get to water.*

"So hot," he groaned.

"What's that dear?"

"Hot. I'm hot." The panic left him momentarily, then washed over him again.

Sea Hag felt his forehead again. *Jesus, I hope this guy didn't get sick from my food. Christ*, she thought. She was calm at her center, by which her instincts had guided her thousands of times before.

"Come on, put your head down a bit. Have some soda. Let me clean this up, and I can drive you to the hospital."

Nick nodded. He felt like someone had started a gasoline fire in his belly. Again, the panic had receded, from inside his guts, he felt a stab of pain, the sweat on his forehead a thick blanket of sweat. As Sea Hag slopped the puke into the bucket, Nick had to move his feet. As he did so, he took a sip of soda, and immediately he began to feel better. As the heat left him, he felt his insides untwist and the soreness from his deep retching fade. But what replaced the heat, the fever, and the cold, clammy icky feeling on his forehead, was the intense, ravenous desire to find a chunk of raw, cold, fish and to eat it whole.

8

Journal, when we came home from *The Little Mermaid*, Marina was so excited, she was busting out of her skin. She couldn't wait until we got home, she just had to get into the water. *The Little Mermaid*, to a little mermaid, was the grandest story anyone could have ever imagined. Have you ever thought about what it would be like to be someone so unique that it was possible that all through your life you would be so alone because no one, not your parents, not your half-sister, no one, could really, truly understand the way that you are? How lonely Marina was and so excited she was about that stupid cartoon. But what I didn't know was that instead, she had gotten herself all excited over that dumb boy we saw. Marina had fallen head over fins for that guy. I mean, I knew she thought he was cute. But love? On the way home, she was so excited that I could tell that she would transform, right there in the car, if she could. Maria was driving us and wasn't paying much attention to us girls in the back seat. She liked to listen to dance music while she drove; she hummed it to herself while we girls were left to "girl-talk" in the back. Marina kept pulling on my shirt, which was pissing me off, cause it was pulling it out of shape. She tugged on it like she was desperate to get my attention.

I was hot myself; the way Ryan had felt me up in the movies. I liked the way his fingers had cupped around my breasts. It was the first time a boy had touched me like that, and I hadn't wanted it to stop. Through my reverie Marina kept distracting me, tugging on my clothes. She kept talking to me about how cute that boy was. What wonderful teeth he had. How much fun it would be to swim with him in the creek. Maria wasn't listening to a word, just whistling and about to turn off 13 when Marina transformed. The sound of Marina's jeans and underwear ripping apart, plus Marina's howling, was enough to send Maria driving clear off the road.

"Oh my God!" Maria shouted from the front, the car swerving onto the shoulder, the tires catching the dirt.

All the back roads are crowned so the car was leaning more towards my side, with Marina's fin sliding on top of me. I thought for sure that the car was going to flip. Her fins felt like dry scales. And they were. It was all too weird. I remember her face, as she stared out the window and up into the sky. Her jeans ripped apart, fell off her green shiny skin. The temperature in the car had risen twenty degrees, and there was this faint odor of fish in the air, dry mud, and salt. It was both revolting and mesmerizing at the same time. Her flesh was wet with sweat, but her scales were dry. I do not know how to say this, but her flesh pulsed, like a fish. I couldn't help thinking that her fin, her skin below her waist was alive in a different way from the rest of her body, for she seemed not to know that she had transformed, or if she did, she did not care. Her tail askew, Marina just sat there, twirling her hair in a kind of dreamy school-girl way.

Swearing in Spanish, Maria gunned the motor. She was freaked out, and now so was I. I was trying my hardest to scamper to the one side of the car, to get away from the heat and strange feeling that Marina's skin gave me, but Marina couldn't, or wouldn't hold herself up, and so she slid on top of me, staring out into the sky where she wished for all of her luck.

My mind was being filled like an aquarium with thoughts which I was sure were her thoughts, Marina's, like radio stations from two different states bleeding together at the border. All I thought of was swimming, of submerging myself into water and never coming out again. I could smell him, that boy, his cheap cologne, the popcorn, and the faint burn of cigarettes. I wanted to slip into the creek and sink, and just let myself float out into the blackness.

9

Then, before I knew it, we were home.

Maria ran into the house screaming for Bill and Mulch. Bill came first like he always does, and pulled me out of the car by my armpits. Mulch carried Marina from the car and down into her chambers.

They all wanted to know what had happened. Maria was crying into a ratty kitchen towel, and Bill was smoking his pipe. I had trouble talking. I remember having to cough a lot as if I had been underwater. Mulch was furious. He held Marina's jeans by the crotch, from where they had split. He kept gripping the zipper and would toss the jeans back and forth between his two hands, and I couldn't help thinking that Marina had just been raped or something. But mostly I was overwhelmed with the sensation that I was underwater. One touch from Marina had been like a touch of God, something more powerful than any of us, something vast and unfathomable, and I was lost in it, submerged in the feeling that Marina must constantly live in.

Mulch sat me down and turned the desk lamp so that the light struck my face, just like in some cornball cop movie.

"What happened?" Mulch asked as he passed the jeans back and forth in his hands.

I didn't say anything at first.

"What the fuck happened?"

Suddenly the feeling of being underwater was gone, and there was a terrible silence in my head. Everyone was waiting for me.

"She met a boy."

"A boy!" Mulch ranted, stomping about the living room. Maria continued to sob, and Bill looked calm.

"And where were you when she met this boy?" Mulch pointed his fist at me, the jeans still in his hands, the legs hanging down limply and the waist folded back over his forearm. "Did you see her with this boy?"

"Yes. But she only just spoke to him. All he did was say 'hello.'"

Furious Mulch threw the jeans at my face. The zipper stung when it clipped my cheek. For a moment I thought he was going to hit me.

10

The only thing Marina heard was the lapping of the waves against the boat, a gentle scraping of water against wooden planks, gentle, and consuming, white noise on which all things built their foundation, a gentle sound like that of a heart, beating away.

Marina could not tear herself away from the darkness that was the back of her eyelids, she simply couldn't open her eyes, *and that was just fine.* She was warm and she was near the water, she felt it. *The tide's coming in.* Crabs and small fish gathered below her, she heard them as they picked the cool mud for food, but their vibrations were muted.

Inside Marina's eyes, her mind played a movie on a giant screen. There was the smell of popcorn and the squirmy feel of the movie theater seats against her back. Marina sensed him somewhere in the darkness, feeling her out. She knew the memory well; it was one of her favorites. Mulch was never to let her out of the house again, but she didn't mind, she knew that he would seek her out and that he would find her. She knew it. There was no question in her mind.

On the boat, Marcos watched the sun move across the water. He had caught a short nap, and after a lunch of soggy crab cakes and pickles, contemplated a second. Marina hadn't responded to any of his calls, and he did not hear her moving below. The only thing he heard was the rocking of the boat and the sounds of water lapping the sides.

11

Marcos was tired, exhausted, he had slept all afternoon, but somehow still wasn't rested. His naps were the nebulous time-sucking kind of naps, instant and devoid of dreams. He'd run across no driftwood and had already run out of scrap wood to carve and keep him busy when the autopilot was engaged. It did not bring him peace. Instead, it brought him anxiety. His matchstick carvings of tiny totems, little faces of owls, and birds, and bears did not please him. They moaned and groaned and whined, his anxiety and worry poured into them. Marcos tossed them overboard, one by one, each little whittling more anxious and depressed than the last until Marcos had carved all the wooden matches onboard up.

Marcos hoped that Marina was sleeping well. He guessed that she probably was, the potion being strong. He also hoped the box was comfortable, safe, and pleasant. The thought of it all made him wonder why he had agreed to help Mulch in the first place.

He'd been asked to carve a flame into the wall to serve as a light source. He had also carved waves onto the opposing wall. Marcos was fond of that wall because he imagined Marina would caress that wall while locked inside. That she would lovingly run her hands down the waves that grew bigger as they dipped towards the floor. She would not be able to touch real water for a very long time, if ever, and Marcos hoped that this would help her keep even just a little bit of her sanity.

Mulch, you are a cruel father, he thought.

What could Marcos do but obey? He had given his word and with it, Sea Hag had given her word. At first Mulch's plan had seemed loving.

"Take her home," he had said. "Take her back to where she comes from."

"But why must she be caged?"

"Because she cannot help herself. She will die here. She must be returned to the waters of her kind. For mating. For the better."

But now Marcos saw the truth of his love, a cruel selfish love that destroyed.

12

George finished up the trim in the upstairs room and carried his ladder to the room next door. Abdullah followed, helping. In his hand, the roller pans looked small and inefficient.

"Master, may I ask a question?"

"Sure," George propped his ladder up and stepped to the top. "Can you hand me the roller pan, the one with the little bit of paint in it?"

"Yes, master."

"What did you want to ask me?"

"Why does master paint rooms so blandly? Why not paint the room like a room for a king? Why don't you make works of kingly art, instead of bland white rooms of houses of women who cannot see? Why not gold? Glorious gold?"

"Well let me tell ya, Ab. I paint art for kings when I can, but I have to make a living somehow, you know put food on the table," George felt his stomach sink as he explained it, he felt like he was riding an elevator down, suddenly his business sounded stupid and small, and he knew he was capable of better. "I own my own company. I am the king of my own business, my trade so to speak. My buddy Nick helps me out in the busy summer months. And in the winter, I get to paint all the landscapes...um...er the kingly kind of art that I want."

"Landscape? What is landscape?"

"Pictures of beautiful places, mountains, seascapes, that stretch for miles. I ain't good with people. When I paint people it always looks forced, but when I paint the tides coming in, I succeed in making kingly art."

"Land escapes bring riches to your kingdom of paint trade?"

"Well sorta. The Savings & Loan in Cheriton bought three of my paintings last year and the G & S sandwich shop has got a real fine rendition of one of my ospreys above one booth."

"If you let me, everyone would want one of these fine landscapes in their homes, or businesses. Shall I pronounce your great kingly art for the world to see, master?"

"Well around here, people don't go for that kind of thing. You have to let them come to you."

"Ah, like a marketplace."

"Exactly," George snorted. "I don't think I would have made it in art school, though I wanted to go, you know. Just to see what it was like."

"I see, master."

"My parents couldn't afford art school. I enrolled, had a work-study plan and all, but I dropped out."

"Master fell from a high place?"

"Um, sorta. I quit. I wasn't good enough. I didn't fit in. When I got to school in the fall, uh in autumn."

"What is autumn."

"Harvest time."

"Yes master, I see."

"I found myself all alone. In class, I just painted what I saw every day. I still try to. I read about all the masters, and the greats, but I couldn't paint anything inspiring. It was like I had the technical skill but no verve."

"Verve, master?"

"Yes, imagination."

"I see."

"I saw people all around me succeeding and going to higher levels in their craft and new places in their head."

"Master, I do not understand how one goes somewhere in the head."

"They changed, Ab."

"This is very interesting master. May I see master's paintings?"

"Yeah sure. I'll show them to you. That'd be great."

It was then, as the words were escaping his lips, the paintbrush filling in the edges with a perfect stroke, that George began to think that he was insane. That may be, he was talking to himself. *That's certainly a possibility.*

CHAPTER SEVEN

1

The funny thing about the Eastern Shore is that there is very little beach. Oh, there's a few strips of sand here and there, but no real beach, none to speak of anyway. A few of the townships have muddy marshes, and a few towns have sandbars, not that far out, that can be imagined into a beach at low tide. All you need is to know where to take a boat out into the creek and sink an anchor in the mud and wait. When low tide comes in, the sandbars rise out of the water like a submerged humpback whale. Sandbar parties are fun in the young haze of summer when all anyone wants to do is wet themselves down with a wet rag or stand in front of the air conditioner vent and let the icy air blow, blow, blow. But there are no beaches, not really. A few people are lucky to own some shoreline where there is a bit of a beach, a stripe of beach, but those are private. Of course, everybody *knows* where the good sand is, and everybody knows that you have to be careful sneaking out to the good sand because nobody wants to get ticketed for trespassing and runoff. So, when Nick reached over Sea Hag's greasy counter, grabbed her hand, and horsed out the words "Get me to a beach," Sea Hag knew that she could sneak him down by the old Indian Caves on the Hayes property, which was less than five miles away.

Sea Hag didn't know what was wrong with her new friend and patron, but from the way Nick's eyes bulged out and the way his forehead looked like it was getting ready to sprout a new forehead, she figured she better listen to him. *She'd better listen and move quickly.* And Nick, Nick was having one hell of a migraine. His head felt as if a thin band of his skull was slowly shrinking, popping into his brain. All Nick thought of was fish. He fell forward and rested his head on the cool counter.

"I need to get to the water." Nick's voice came out strained and high-pitched, and it resonated in Sea Hag's ears. Sea Hag whipped around the counter, her apron flying off her shoulders. Something about Nick's distorted voice was familiar, but she couldn't place it.

"Gimme your keys, gimme your keys!" she shouted and seeing that Nick wasn't moving, came up behind him and thrust her hands deep into his pockets. She felt Nick bucking against her and while she fished, her ears pressed against his back, so that when he spoke his voice resounded deeper, full and familiar, itching at Sea Hag's brain. *Something's happening here, what?*

"Help me," Sea Hag pulled back, keys in hand. *Act quick, old woman.*

She was forced to pull his weight towards the door and the car. He seemed drugged, his eyes rolled up into his skull, and Sea Hag began to wonder if there was more to his case of food poisoning than met the eye. *Think, Haggie. Think.*

"We're going to the hospital," she hollered as she thought about calling 911, but then thought again. The last time they had responded to anything in Oysterhaus it had taken them over an hour, and the man had died while waiting. She would have to take him herself.

2

Sea Hag hadn't driven a stick shift in years and as she drove Nick's little car towards the main roads, she couldn't help but feel sorry for the poor kid who kept flopping around in the front seat. He reached up and grabbed her arm.

"What did you eat boy?" Sea Hag gunned the motor a bit.

The car swerved off the road and into the gravel. She felt the car tilt and the tires dig into the soft earth of the ditch before coming back out onto the pavement again. When she looked down at Nick, he was still holding her arm.

"Take me to the water. NOW!"

He tried to holler the last bit, but his lungs didn't have it in them. Sea Hag smelled a thin waft of saltwater on his breath – brine. When she looked down into Nick's face, she saw something she had never seen before. Inside of Nick's eyes, floating behind his pupils, lay a second set of pupils, a second set of color, a superimposed picture of two sets of eyes, both intently staring through to her. One set was Nick's, the others were ebony, and Sea Hag was sure as hell that they weren't Nick's.

"Please. No Doctors. Water. Beach," his voice sounding odd, doubled as if he spoke with the voices of two people.

"The beach then," Sea Hag shouted. When Sea Hag was almost to the turn-off, she would have to stop and open the gate, maybe even carry him down to the beach, if the rest of the road was too bad.

"It wasn't any of my cooking, I can tell you that! C'mon."

3

Once on the turn-off, Sea Hag had to drive about a mile to the old cattle fence that Mulch kept shut by tying an old necktie through the eye. It didn't keep anybody out, Mulch's reputation usually did that.

Sea Hag felt her pulse increase as the wash-boarded road knocked the car as she sped over it. The gate lay straight ahead.

Nick began to dry heave, and in between the dry heaves, Sea Hag heard a faint scratching noise that sounded like fingernails being dragged over a wooden wall. She didn't know what was worse, the sound of Nick's stomach emptying its purse, or the horrid scraping sound that was not human, nor from Nick's stomach, but from inside Nick's body. As she brought the car to a stop, she heard Nick's voice calling for water, yet it wasn't the voice he had used in the Fritter Shop. It was the voice of a person who had not had anything to drink in weeks. She began to wonder if Nick was going to die right there in his fucking car. *This feels like magic*, Sea Hag thought to herself as she pulled Nick's car to a stop.

The tie's red and black stripes had long faded into a muddy, bally, fuzz and as Sea Hag untied it from the gate, she expected the gate to swing out, but instead, it just sank with a lump into the mud below.

"Dammit." Sea Hag looked back at Nick, as he dry-heaved again.

She tried to swing the gate back towards the car but had to stop because she had pulled the car up too close.

"Mother fucking shit-ass fence."

When she got back into the car to back it up, Nick was crumpled into the floor with his head laying on the seat where his ass should have been.

She backed up the car and got back out to open the fence again. The gate swung back easily, and she didn't bother to shut it, since she planned on coming back through very soon. She jumped back in the car and gunned it down the road.

4

It wasn't until she stopped the car at the weedy path that would lead them out to the beach, did she think that maybe she *should* have brought him to the hospital instead.

Nick kept falling into the dirt, tearing great chunks of grass and soil loose as he went. Fat horseflies swarmed his mouth and stung Sea Hag as she scuttled alongside him, like a crab, trying to bring Nick back to his knees.

"Get up, get up," Sea Hag whispered as Nick coughed and dragged her down into the dirt with him. Each time she stood up, he fell forward and whispered something unintelligible while she yanked him back to his feet again.

The pounding inside Nick's head increased; something tore inside him. His stomach felt like someone had pulled all his insides out and stretched them, only to stuff them back in without care. Under the pain was a ravenous, intense desire to eat fish. and he sensed fish beyond him, in the water. Nick wanted to go into the bay and sink into the mud. He wanted to nibble on scales. He wanted to lie at the muddy bottom, and yet there was something else tearing inside him and he felt it as he struggled to keep his balance up, struggling to move towards water. It felt like someone else was pushing into his brain and taking over his body.

Nick felt fingers behind his eyes, pushing his own eyes out of the way to make room for new eyes. Someone's foot reaching through a tear in his back and pushing down into his legs and feet, arms struggling to stretch his skin to take control of his like a finger does a puppet.

"Please, water," he said, his voice different, stretched and torn in a way that would never heal.

He felt something in his throat, not just the dry pain of the vomiting, but another voice rising to the surface, overlapping his voice. Somewhere in his brain, the sound of the hag rustled like dry leaves. He barely heard himself cry to be let go as he fell face forward into the wet grainy earth. Sea Hag panted, nearly out of breath as Nick crawled into the water. He felt her come up from behind and follow along, making sure that he would not drown. Nick only wanted to feel the water envelop him, the warm sunny water that had been heating in the sun all morning.

As Nick crawled, his head and shoulders above the water, his nose breathing air, his eyes half-closed, he saw sandbars thirty feet out, gulls crying above. Already the damp weight of his fever felt lighter as if being in the water was enough. Sea Hag thought he looked like a snake, the way he crawled across the three-foot "beach" and out into the surf. As he went farther out Nick left a trail behind him, with Sea Hag wading out behind him, careful to watch for any sign of trouble.

"I ain't never seen food poisoning like this before," she muttered, the sound of Nick's doubled helix voice echoing in her ear. *And you never will again,* Haggie thought.

Ahead of Nick, the waters shimmered. The waters were clearer at low tide, but still muddy, and Nick saw something ahead of him in the tide pool. A fish turned circles no more than two feet from him. There Nick sank himself into the mud, his muscles primed for a spring, his eyes narrowing on the small trout waiting for the tide to come in. The fish seemed to grow more and more clear to him as he stared at it. He opened his mouth and sprang.

5

Marina's mouth was full of the most delicious wetness she had tasted since the previous spring when she and Mr. Bill, who had trans-mutated into a large turtle and had swum headfirst into young saltwater trout. The taste of fish was like being dropped from a high cliff into a very cold pool of water. It was shock and glory at the same time Marina had been dreaming about fish, and now the taste of fish and cool, cool water in her mouth, and it felt like she was submerged in coolness, and wetness that was as deep as her birth and old as the oceans. Marina didn't know she was curled up in a fetal position upon the great feather mattress her father had placed in the bottom of a very dark box. If she had been able to see, her vision would have been a cloud of doubles, the fish and the water she tasted upon her lip's hallucinations.

6

Sea Hag knew that at that very moment as she waited with her young charge, somewhere along the creeks, tucked away under a canopy of moss and leaves, Marina and Marcos awaited darkness. Sea Hag knew that Marina was unconscious, still in the throes of the potion's spell; and that she must be drying out. Knowing this, Sea Hag knew that Marina would become unhinged. The very early trappings of her insanity would begin before she ever woke up, while the chemicals of the potion would dry her out in her sleep and under the heat of the sun. After the first day, when Marina would not be able to enter the water, her thirst for it would grow exponentially. Sea Hag understood just now, how quickly change would come, because the young man in front of her, this Nick Adams, was himself quickly become a raving lunatic before her very eyes, crazed for fish like Marina would be. She did not, however, connect the two persons in her mind.

Entering the waters, Nick had caught a small trout, one that he had caught in a tide pool, only with his bare teeth. Before he had gotten it, Sea Hag had seen the fish swimming about, and had seen that the fish could have gotten away, should have gotten away, under normal circumstances.

But Nick had crawled stealthily towards the tide pool with tenderness and caution, and when he lunged and he had caught the fish with his teeth, he had brought the fish out of the water like a bear cub at his first fishing hole. When he did, his eyes were unlike before, instead of seeing the two sets of pupils superimposed upon each other, there was just the one pair, Nick's. Sea Hag saw where the man in those eyes had gone out, leaving behind only the dull matte of instinct as he ate the fish raw now. Again, she thought, *this was magic, something strong beyond knowledge.* This was witchcraft, *this was possession.*

7

Lilly's mother wore a terrible scar that zipped across her left cheek. She never said from whence the scar came, but whispers in camp told of old Mexico, the desert, and a terrible love. She was called 'Madre Fea,' or 'the Ugly Mother' by all the migrant workers. The workers loved her because she refused to speak the English she had mastered, not even to Mulch. She only spoke English to her favorite federal government employee, Marcos, and the small children whom she helped tutor, "*for them she would speak English,*" she would say to anyone who would listen. She spoke four dialects, and some Portuguese that Marcos had taught her, as well as her magical language. Despite the dry haggard look of her face and the ugly scar that looked like a bulgy zipper on wrinkled jeans, she had a kindly appearance. With her, there was an instant trust that both animals and idiots understood. She was plump because she ate grease right out of the pan with her tortillas. On weekends she'd balance a bottle of bathtub tequila on her tight, round belly and sing songs as she rocked in an old rocking chair that she had once carried on her back across Mexico. La Madre Fea had been fifty when Lilly was born. Lilly had been born on her birthday, during a great drought, during a time when the workers had nothing to do but sit around, fuck, and wait for the rains to come, or so the stories told. The truth was no one had witnessed Lilly's birth save for her father, who vanished into the floorboards some years later.

As Lilly had grown up her mother had shrunk and grown more wrinkled and plumper with each birthday, or so it seemed to the migrants in camp, as if Lilly sucked the height, and youth out of her mother each year. Lilly had not lived with her mother for some years, though the Ugly Mother kept her room up, just in case Lilly came to visit. Lilly's apartment was bare and white and so American, her mother had complained. *How could Lilly catch a husband if she had nothing to catch him with,* she had asked. The Ugly Mother pestered her daughter with love.

If Lilly's place was as neat as a candlestick, then the Ugly Mother's cabin was cluttered and full of surprise. The Ugly Mother's table was scattered with Tarot cards and bone fragments that long ago had been polished to white by her use. She was reading tea leaves, a wet pile of them bunched at the edge of the table when Lilly stepped into her cabin that morning after her date with George.

"I saw in my sleep last night that you shined on your date." The Ugly Mother's eyes gleamed. Lilly didn't understand why she wanted to live in such a cramped box. "A special one, no? This American?" the Ugly Mother laughed.

"Yes," Lilly replied as she turned. She did not want to look at her mother's eyes. Madre Fea tapped her fingers against the table.

"This American, no?"

"Yes. I told you, mother."

"I am teasing. We must love whom we love."

Lilly stayed quiet. She didn't want to bring up the fact that she had lit up the whole restaurant. It was bad enough that George had seen her, though George didn't seem like he had been bothered by it.

"We should continue to work on your spirit language and continue to work on controlling your mind. The men here are saying that they have seen strange things out in the fields. Who knows what awaits us like a bright candle in a storm. You must be prepared."

Lilly groaned, she hated the arcane way every strange American tick and habit became ominous and important in the eyes of some of the older migrant workers. Lilly lived in both worlds, and both worlds needed to learn some empathy and some compassion for each other. *Fear needed a face,* she thought. Word spread quickly among Mulch's workers and there always *seemed* to be something happening in one of Mulch's fields.

"They say a great beast has been locked in a huge wooden box."

"Mother, the men are always talking. The men talk more shit than the women, that I can promise you."

"This is different child."

Lilly sighed and pulled pine straw off the hem of her dress.

"You slept in the pines?" The Ugly Mother asked. "You must have been exhausted. I did not hear you calling."

"I don't even know, mother. I collapsed pretty much as soon as I got there. It was hard to focus."

"The men say..."

"They say the tomatoes are poisonous because Mulch buries bodies under them, that Mr. Bill can turn into a fish, that Mulch is the devil incarnate. A box? What box, mother? It was probably just a tool shed. We sell them at the store. Remember the time Juancho thought he saw lights in the sky? Or the time Loco thought for sure someone was coming into camp to burn it down? That was bad enough, us calling the police. And let's not forget the time when you, mother, got the women all riled up over Consuelo's dead goat?"

"You're right, of course. But then again if you can light up a room in a bar why can't the men see the things as they are?"

Lilly scowled at her mother.

"Marcos came by to see me last night." The Ugly Mother said this as if she were hurt at Lilly's outburst.

"Oh." For a while, Lilly had thought that Marcos and her mother were having some kind of weird affair. Nobody else believed her.

"He's gone. He didn't say where to. North. But he needs our help. That much I know. He told me to prepare to go north."

"What do you mean 'our' help?"

"My wisdom may be needed in the north."

Lilly snorted. *Typical. Marcos probably just wants to use her translation skills. He's done that before.*

"Maybe Marcos will pay you this time for your wisdom."

The Ugly Mother laughed, dismissing her daughter with her hands as if she would take money from one of her own.

And there it is, Lilly thought. *Just build a bridge and get over yourself, Lilly. Your mother will never be normal. You'll never be a normal girl, either.*

8

Macy once said that I was too mean and too whorish to land a husband. "Whores are selfish. You are selfish." Her exact words to me. A real philosopher, that one. She wasn't done, either. "You won't be able to have true love because you are always fucking your way out of love. I should know because I've been doing it all along myself."

Oh, such an exact self-diagnosis, Mace.

Because I had built this party girl reputation up for myself, Adam went crazy out-of-his-skull jealous whenever I even so much as looked away from him. At a party, he once tried to beat up these scrawny skater types that I used to score dope from in high school because I so much as said hello. But over the last few months, Adam hadn't acted jealous, not even once. Then I found out about his cousin.

Journal, I knew right away he was fucking her, and his cousin is really pretty. All bitchiness aside, if I was Adam and she came up to me, I'd fuck her too. I would.

By then I was fed up with his whole act anyway. His tired way of buying me underwear and presenting it to me time and again in a box. At first, it felt like a cool ritual. At first, they were like rocket fuel to our sex lives. Later it just became this thing. A thing that we did. It was like going to the mall. Something you did and forgot about the same afternoon.

The sex itself was okay. I had no major complaints. But while we were doing it, I felt him slip out of himself and go far, far away. I felt him not be there.

Sometimes I heard him whisper to himself, though I could never make it out. Whenever I asked about it, he'd get defensive and tell me to shut up. When no one had seen Adam for two days, I figured he'd shacked up with his cousin. How fucking common can you get?

CHAPTER EIGHT

1

November 13, 1956

Each time Eb took Mulch out for a weekend hunting trip it seemed to rain. This year's trips were no different, with a late-season hurricane sending thunderheads pealing towards the Eastern Shore, they were already drenched.

"Come on boy," Eb said, his coat drenched, and he looked like a muskrat, his whiskers hanging damp around his countenance. Eb coughed into his hand. "Come on."

"Shouldn't we head to the caves?" Mulch asked, his body shaking with chills.

Eb shook his head. "Nah. The caves are out of our way. We'll build a fire."

"But we'll freeze," Mulch whined.

"We'll be dry by nightfall."

"I think it's best we get out of the rain."

"Dammit boy!" Eb's face turned crimson.

"Mr. Bill would agree with me," Mulch said, his arms crossed across his chest.

"Mr. Bill isn't here is he? And neither is your uncle, so don't go crying tears."

They had been walking for hours, Eb getting drunker with each mile. Mulch wanted to go home, to go anywhere where his father wasn't. They hadn't seen one deer all day. Mulch paused here and there to check the ground for prints but hadn't spotted any. Mulch was sure his father wasn't even looking. The radio had said that rain was supposed to last all weekend and to batten down the hatches, but Eb had insisted that they strike out for game instead.

Once again Eb had walked in on his wife, Ruth, and his brother Leon. But instead of beating her as he normally would have done, he only pointed his finger at her, then at his brother, as if he was making a judgment or a promise. He had caught them upstairs, and though he didn't hit her or him, he did scream loud enough to bring Mulch from downstairs to see what was going on. After shouting and screaming, Eb didn't say a word and when he brushed past his son he whispered, "Let's go hunting." And no amount of arguing could assuage him of their current course of action. Mulch, pulled by the gravity of his father, followed.

Eb slipped and held onto a branch. The undergrowth looked like a pile of live snakes, roots, and branches jutting out and tangling with one another. Mulch miserably looked on. It was too wet outside, and already his trousers had rubbed his crotch and upper thighs a painful pink raw.

Over the last few years, as the farm grew, and as more and more migrants came to work, there had been less and less for Eb to do. That summer Leon had hired a kinder, gentler man to manage the workers, and field production had increased. Buck Winston did a fine job and everybody seemed happy, except Eb who spent the summer on the new porch Leon had built, getting high-drunk on homemade whiskey. Summer had been miserable because between the heat, mosquitoes, and his father's drunkenness, Mulch's mother had started to act strangely, and Mulch had begun to think she was downright loony. Twice Leon and Eb had to get a ladder to fetch Ruth off the roof because she had climbed up there in fright, screaming something about corn, crows, and butterflies. Sometimes Mulch thought she was crazy from love. He blamed it on Eb. He blamed it on Leon. Lately, he began to wonder if all of them weren't cracked to be living together under the same roof. His skin crawled to think of it. Even Maria had noticed.

"Come on boy, don't lag," his father hollered. The rain created a haze that half-dissolved Eb in mist. Eb stopped, and as Mulch crept forward, he saw that Eb had stopped at the edge of a gully. Water rushed along below them.

"We'll camp here."

"Here?"

"Above the gully, dumb ass." Eb pointed at two fallen trees that rested at an angle, supported by an even larger third tree, which had created something like a natural lean-to. Mulch guessed it was no later than three-thirty or four in the afternoon, but lack of light made it hard to tell. Night was coming soon.

"Start gathering wood," Eb gruffed, squatting below the crisscrossed trees. Mulch wanted to say something about the caves but didn't. The caves were a good half-day hike from there, at least, but the caves would have been dry.

2

By the time the fire was lit, darkness had crossed over them. Overhead, the wind howled and stirred up leaves that scuttled into the campfire like little crabs. Sparks shot out past them and into the woods beyond. Rain dropped on the tarp in steady beats.

"It was too wet to start a fire, ha!" Eb said, swigging more of his whiskey and staring off towards the zinging sparks which looked like fireflies.

"Hope we find some game tomorrow," Mulch said, eager to start a conversation.

Eb nodded and spat into the fire.

Mulch had found them two broad logs to sit on, so their rear-ends wouldn't get so muddy. But Mulch's butt had begun to hurt nearly an hour ago, and since he was soaked anyway, threw the log into the fire.

"Got us some good sitting log and you threw it away. You'll throw it all away, I bet." Eb remarked, using his flask to gesture. And that was all Eb said before passing out with his head and his rifle propped up under the treefall.

3

Mulch barely slept for the dreams; he kept dreaming of a herd of deer charging at him in a dead run, trampling the campfire and his father underfoot. Twice he awoke with a jerk, his face wet from rain. Twice he re-started the fire, Eb snoring under the log lean-to. Mulch heard him shiver and cough. He sounded sickly, weak. *Maybe the bastard will die out here. Maybe he'll die and I can leave him here like trash.*

Mulch fell asleep wishing death upon his father, the fire sputtering and hissing. Before dawn, the last dream came to him in the form of a giant twelve-point buck. Its god-like body loomed over him. Wet decayed matter hung upon its antlers, and its bloodshot eyes lay deep in its skull. Mulch raised his rifle, but when he pulled the trigger there was only a wet click. When he looked, the rifle had turned into a stick, and when he looked up the buck lowered his antlers towards his chest and impaled him.

He awoke with a start. The woods lay quiet. He couldn't hear the wind and the rain had stopped. Overhead the sky was the color of deep coal. The sun had not come out, but the remaining clouds would have obscured the light anyway. *The hurricane.* Mulch leaned back and listened for the wind to come. He heard it, like faint crying. Far off was the thunder.

From behind him, a branch snapped.

"Come on boy, piss on that fire, there are some tracks back here."

4

Eb walked along the gully they had camped next to and reached a point where the gully sloped and narrowed. He jumped across and kept going. Mulch could barely see, but followed, making the jump himself. Mulch guessed it was not even six AM yet. He felt like he was retreating into night with each step, for Eb plunged them farther and farther into darker woods. All around, Mulch saw patches of blackness hanging in the trees like strange birds. The saturated ground sucked and pulled underneath him.

Eb led him into a dense fog bank that rose out of nowhere. The trees were thicker here, and Mulch couldn't hear the far-off thunder. The fog swallowed everything whole, including sound. *The hurricane is going to catch us.* They walked for another fifteen minutes before Eb slowed, looking for tracks. Mulch, already exhausted, bore the brunt of the work. Mulch carried the food, the extra clothes, the ammo, the pack, the shotgun, and his rifle, Eb walked with his flask in hand, rifle slung. Sometimes he would stop, stare off into the forest, the forest staring back, the fog staring back. By now they had walked deep into the fog bank and Eb looked like a shadow, hardly there, vanishing into and out of the fog as they moved into and out of it. Eb shivered, his breath coming out in long white puffs that added to the dense white around them. Mulch paused, listening for sounds of deer, but only heard the labored breathing of his father a few feet away.

Then he couldn't see Eb anymore. He couldn't see anything.

Mulch shivered, gooseflesh covered his body, and he felt his testicles crawl up inside his groin. The fog glided over his skin, his clothes, and caressed him, loved him. Somewhere in the back of his brain the urge to run, kicked and died. He wanted to escape, but the fog soothed him, and he felt it crawl over his body with fascination.

The tops of the trees melted into the mist. He no longer heard his father's breathing, and the sound of his own heart was faint and far away. Looking down, his legs vanished into a thick, white soup below his knees and when he held his hand up in front of him, that too disappeared. He could only see his fingers inches from his nose.

"Father," he half-whispered, half-called out.

It felt like minutes before he heard a faint reply.

"A little farther," his father replied, sounding like a ghost.

Stepping slowly and cautiously, Mulch moved toward the sound of his father's voice. His heart beat faster now, and he saw the faint outline of his father appear in the fog. Eb held his rifle upright, his head cocked out to the left. He didn't move or speak until Mulch was right next to him.

Eb nodded towards the left and mouthed the words, "Over there."

Mulch raised his rifle in response and nodded.

Eb motioned for him to follow before taking long, quiet steps into the fog ahead of them. Mulch paused; his body screamed danger. *What if he were to shoot his father?* Part of him wanted that possibility to open up like a bog for him to fall into, part of him didn't. He gulped and tried to build up his courage. Mulch forced a swallow and stepped into the thickness ahead of him.

How Eb was able to track the deer, Mulch didn't know. It had not been foggy when he had woken up, and it shouldn't have been this foggy way back here. The coastal winds should have blown the fog away. Mulch squinted to make out his father's shape, and as he did his dream came back to him and he half-expected to come upon a herd of giant deer who'd charge at him and tear him to pieces. Absentmindedly he tapped his rifle, hoping it would fire when he needed it to.

Eb had stopped next to a swamp oak whose branches lay shrouded hidden in whiteness. The fog did not conform to the topography as much as it swallowed what it could. As Mulch surveyed the area his spine prickled and his testicles crawled up into his chest. From ahead, and all around, the hoofing and breathing of deer, a herd, by the sound.

Mulch didn't dare breathe. He listened to the short, forced inhalations of his father and wondered if the old man was going to make it. The fog obscured the heads of most of the parcel, but they could see them in the murk and gloom.

As if we aren't here, Mulch thought, *as if they aren't here.*

Directly ahead of Eb stood a fourteen-point buck whose shaggy thick neck reminded Mulch of his dream, the buck's mane wild and thick with bits of thorn and leaf. The buck snorted, acknowledging them. This was by far the biggest buck he'd ever seen in his life, and from the look on his father's face, he guessed it was the biggest he'd ever seen, too. The buck pushed the fog away from his head, it seemed, for the fog reeled back in curlicues and spirals from the buck's regal face. The back of Mulch's neck tingled. *The buck manipulated the fog.* He couldn't explain how or why, but he knew this was true. Mulch tasted the metallic tang of fear and adrenaline coursing in his veins. For a second, he thought the fog enabled him to read his father's mind, *nonsense,* Mulch thought.

But then Eb raised his rifle.

Mulch saw it happen in slow motion. When Eb stood to shoot, Eb let off two shots and re-loaded. The buck did not recoil upon the hit. Eb fired again, and again, but the buck did not fall. He didn't even seem to be hit. When the rest of the herd began to bolt back into the woods, Mulch raised his gun and fired, as much by reflex as a conscious action. He turned to a smaller buck to his left, where he re-loaded to fire again. As he got off his second round, his father got off his fourth, but by then the herd had vanished.

"I hit him, son, I know I did," Eb said as his teeth rattled and his frame shook.

Mulch nodded. When they began to look for blood to trail, they found no tracks, and no blood for the ground appeared untouched; not a single twig or branch shook from where the herd had run by. The only sign of the animals, the thick white fog, slowly moved away from them, deeper into the forest, behind the deer, as if the fog was the very breath of the herd.

5

Thunder boomed and Mulch wondered why he hadn't heard it before. The fog had obscured them from the hurricane and now that the fog was retreating into the woods, rain had begun to fall.

"Come on, boy!" Eb shouted behind. Eb was running now, wheezing with each step.

Mulch followed, they were in the tail-end of the fog, which was fine, because if they could see the fog, they could track the herd. Overhead, lightning zippered the sky and for a brief second Mulch spied dark patches of shadow that shook like huge blackbirds in the trees overhead. The shadows blinked.

But that couldn't be, right? Could it?

When the next batch of lightning illuminated the sky, the shadows shifted again. *They're tracking us,* he thought as he pushed his body harder. Even though they had only been running for a few minutes Mulch felt pain throughout his body. He couldn't imagine what his father felt tearing through the trees. The fog, ahead of them now, moved fast, deeper into the woods. Mulch didn't know where he was, but he hoped Eb did. Looking up into the trees again, he saw one of the black patches grow.

It's only your imagination.

Mulch checked again, just to be sure. This time one of the patches of black took flight and sailed ahead of him. Mulch turned his head to follow it and ran right past his father into a thick wall of brambles and thorns that rose out of the woods around a knot of deadfall.

"Didn't you hear me say stop," Eb wheezed?

"I didn't," Mulch wheezed. "I didn't hear anything."

His arms and hands were cut and bleeding and his leg was tangled in the thick squiggle of vines. He tore his trousers as he yanked himself free, blood flowing from the small and numerous cuts on his body, but he didn't care. Mulch kept watching the branches above him. He barely heard Eb's hollering, "This way boy!" for Mulch was so concentrated on the black shadows around him. They hung, suspended in the tree limbs. Mulch's neck hair prickled, the shadows lay everywhere, little patches of deep black against the dark storm overhead.

Eb didn't seem to notice them.

Eb pulled Mulch close, "We're gonna have to run. Are you up for it?"

Mulch nodded.

The rain came in strong cylindrical torrents, sheets of rain funneled through the trees forming powerful jet-like blasts that smacked against their backs as they ran. Mulch wasn't sure if they were heading in the right direction or not, and the darkness of the storm made it difficult to tell.

They had given up on the herd. Which was fine with Mulch.

Neither of them had had any breakfast, and Mulch felt his energy reserves depleting. When Eb disappeared ahead of him, Mulch stopped, relieved almost. He could not hear Eb, only the sound of the wind and rain that ripped the last of the needles and roan leaves about his face, swirling in the wind like a world draining away. He called out for his father.

Nothing.

The shadows must have got him.

Mulch pushed the thought aside. He inched ahead, his rifle pointed at the ground. His father could be unconscious, fallen behind a tree that he couldn't see, or waist-deep in quicksand. He paused. Either the sun was peeking through the clouds, or his eyes were growing used to the dim forest light, because ahead of him Mulch saw his father standing in a gully, waving his arms above his head like a madman. The old man probably needed help up the embankment.

"Hey!" Mulch shouted, the wind and rain drowning out his voice. "HEY!"

Eb looked up at him and smiled, his flask to his lips.

"You okay?"

"WHAT?"

"YOU OKAY?"

"Yeah." Eb cleared his throat, "I'M ALRIGHT. NOW GET DOWN HERE."

Suddenly, Mulch felt a flash of pain. Something heavy slammed into his back, knocking him into the gully. Water forced itself into his mouth and Mulch tasted the tangy mud and leafy wash of the run-off in his throat. He tried to spit but started to cough. Eb yanked him back out of the water and slapped him on the back repeatedly until Mulch raised his hand in protest, "I'm okay, I'm okay."

Eb grunted, "Shit boy, I didn't mean for you to fall in with me."

Mulch panted, shaking his head, "You didn't see it?"

"You could have drowned."

"Did you see it!?"

"See what?"

"What hit me!"

"I didn't see anything," Eb said as he turned to the steep bank and began to climb out the other side. "C'mon we've got to get out of here."

"Why don't we follow the run-off back out?"

"Cause it don't go anywhere."

"So?"

"We didn't follow it in did we?" Eb growled.

Mulch nodded, he supposed that was as good of an answer as he could expect. As Eb tried to get a footing in the clay, Mulch spotted a place a few yards down that would be easier to foot it up and out of the stream. He turned back to call to his father and saw out of the corner of his eye a dark shape flapping. Mulch's skin rippled with goosebumps, his heart a solid fist of ice. He tracked his eyes back up the gully. No more than thirty feet away a giant black bird stared directly at him. The bird was at least four feet tall, its large shiny black eyes locked onto his own. Mulch's breath came in short quick bursts. He felt the animal thinking, its eyes ringed in yellow stared back through him.

Not a vulture, not a hawk, not any crow that I've seen. Instead, the bird looked like a combination of those birds, a mutated raptor.

Oblivious, Eb struggled up the embankment. The bird stood sentinel, silent, then it opened its wings. If Mulch was almost six feet tall, the bird's wingspan was at least eight feet wide. Its ragged cowl reminded Mulch of a tattered black cape a bad guy might wear in a bijou picture. He couldn't tell what kind of bird it was. Its head was far too large and crow-like to be a turkey-buzzard, yet it wasn't a crow, it was too big, and the beak was more falcon-like. He wanted to see it up-close, but his reptilian brain was too busy telling him to run for his life. Yet, the bird was calming, like looking at something majestic and beautiful, something one would like to touch, to hold, to keep. He stepped forward, unaware. He *wanted* to gaze into the bird's eye, and as he got closer, he smelled the rot, the smell of death and spoiled meat, like rotting fish left in the heat too long. Even at four feet, the giant bird was bigger than he had imagined, its talons thick and hooked, and as the giant bird shifted its weight the talons tore the ground apart. Mulch felt the bird analyzing him; the way the bird's eyes moved up and down his body, appraising him, looking for a place to hook its claw.

Mulch no longer heard the wind, nor felt the rain, he felt numb, cold at the core, barely there at all. With each step, the bird became blurry and harder to see. He tried to shake himself out of it. The howling wind and the rain not bothering him anymore. His chafed groin didn't bother him anymore, and the fact that his mother was going crazy didn't bother him either. He only wished to pet the bird and feed it. Except it wasn't so much of a bird anymore as a shifting black mass. It flashed into a bird with the eyes of a man and then flashed back into just a bird again, like it couldn't make up its mind what it wanted to be – a crow, an eagle, a fishhawk, and then back to a crow again.

Mulch's mind filled with the fluttering of wings, and as he came within the final few feet of the bird, Mulch reached up to touch it. Worms squiggled in and out of its oily feathers, its face continuing to shift and flutter between being bird-like and being that of a bird. Sometimes the beak looked like it had teeth. Mulch felt hollow like he had been scooped out. Mulch later remembered that staring at the thing was like looking through someone's eyeglasses; a world shrouded in a shifting blur.

When the bird opened its wings, a blast of black mites and mosquitoes peppered his face. He felt the bugs working their way into his ear, crawling towards his brain. It opened its beak and began to shriek. He felt the need to recoil from the piercing cry but couldn't. He could only stare the beast in the face and feel its worms work their way into his body. The bird's call sounded like a siren in Mulch's ear until a rifle blast shook Mulch from his trance. Eb missed the bird by a few inches, and it took off, only to Mulch it seemed that the bird had folded into the woods around it, disappearing instantly.

"Come on, boy," Eb said as he pulled Mulch back. Mulch wiped his face of crawling mites and lice. "It's gone, flown away!" Eb shouted.

"Where" Mulch shouted in reply. He felt like he was going to vomit. "What was it?"

Eb shook his head. He didn't know. "Let's get out of here before this hurricane blows us down."

Something in his father's voice made him look up. The spaces between the trees were once again filled with fluttering darkness. Hundreds of black shapes flung themselves from tree to tree and back again.

"Come on," Eb said as he jerked Mulch up the embankment and into the woods. "Let's get out."

Eb studied the forest floor beneath them. Mulch checked the trees, and then Eb began to holler. The trees above were quick with dark wings. Mulch's blood ran cold, the fog bank right in front of him, with Eb leading them inside, "It's the only way." Mulch couldn't help to think that the forest wanted them dead, that the forest had gone insane, like his mother, when Mulch's vision was plunged into the white.

6

Half-running, half-stumbling, Eb and Mulch screamed as they ran. The fog felt like another world encapsulated in the mist, a world they were lost in like children. Around the faint grunts of deer and the shrieks of birds created a thick layer of white noise. After a while, they stopped screaming. They no longer heard the grunting noises and the shrieks. They only heard thunder. Mulch thought that meant that they were coming to the end of the fog. He had no idea how long they had been running.

"See that, boy?" Eb shouted. Beyond the fog, rain came down.

"Look," Eb pointed, but Mulch had already seen it. Eb's voice sounded hoarse, broken from all the screaming. Mulch nodded before checking the trees for any sign of activity. The trees were empty, bare.

"Had to," Eb panted. "Had to scream so I could see," he mumbled. "Like it was the only way to get the fog out of my eyes." Then he grabbed Mulch by the shoulder and pushed him ahead. When they broke through the fog wall, the sound of the hurricane crashed upon their ears like a train.

Above them, the trees were devoid of blackness, and the only thing that seemed to move between the trees was the wind that bent the trunks to the ground. Behind them the fog hung, motionless, despite the gale forces tearing through the forest.

It took them another hour to find the edge of the wood. There they came upon a cotton field. The wind was still strong, but the brunt of it had blown over and they walked out onto the field under the bluish, clear sky of the storm's eye. The remnants of the hurricane were a line of tattered-looking clouds to the southeast. The back end of the storm which would bring more rain and wind would be upon them soon.

"Is this our field? I think this is our field," Eb's voice sounded bloody, like his face. His shredded clothes hung about his shoulders and elbows, and he was covered in mud from the waist down. Eb shivered as he emptied the last bit of whiskey from the flask. From his hip pocket, he took his bottle, and seeing that it too was empty, tossed it aside.

"Perfect timing," he said.

"Yeah," Mulch knew where they were – about a two-hour walk from home. Ahead of them, the fields joined to form one giant shallow lake. The roads would be washed out. "At least there ain't any fog," he replied.

"Yup. Sure enough," Eb said as he started walking south, which by Mulch's account would take them across the cotton field to an adjacent cornfield. Beyond that, a bend in the neck and then home. Neither Mulch nor Eb saw the black bird fly from a far oak down the field, back into the woods which had swelled to the edge with thick fog even as they walked farther from the woods, over towards the access roads, which connected all the fields like a chain.

CHAPTER NINE

1

Adam hid his SD cards in a cardboard box under his bed. What a fucking obvious place to hide his shit, journal.

It was after 1:00 PM when I let myself into his house. It smelled like stale heat and air. A small stack of dishes in the sink had become covered with a hard and dangerous crust. I stared into his sink trying to read something in the flaky red sauce sheeted over three medium-sized plates. Pizza. Spaghetti. Adam loves anything with a tomato sauce. I think I was trying to divine where he was, who he was with. I thought I spied lipstick stains on the corner of a coffee mug. It was pizza sauce. All the dishes looked to be several days old. He hadn't collected his mail, either. It lay in pile by his door.

It was about 2:00 when I started rifling through his belongings for clues about his disappearance.

How upset was I?

Anger is a cage, you know. And that afternoon, the cage door was wide open. I walked in on my own accord. When I found the box of homemade porn, I had concluded that he had run off with his cousin; it seemed to be the only logical answer.

I pulled the old shoebox out, whatever was on the inside fell over with a clack. There were about fifty SD cards inside, each one labeled and ranked by stars – one being the lowest – five being the highest. There was no "half-stars," I note without irony, journal. At the very bottom of the box, there was a wrinkled bar napkin. On the other side of the bar napkin was my father's private phone number scrawled in heavy ink.

2

I always knew that he was holding secrets from me.

Mulch, that is. Adam too, but I'm talking about my father here, journal.

I mean, my God, I didn't know about Marina's secret until I was in puberty. He never spoke a word to me about my mother or Marina's mother. Maria might have known something, but if I was to find anything out, I knew I would have to go straight to Mr. Bill.

It was almost sun-down when I left Adam's house. I had watched a few of the videos and was thrumming with electricity. There I was, me, half-naked, full-naked, semi-naked, and engaged in just about anything you can think of. Some of the SD cards had little notes carefully lettered on them, "screaming", "screaming for daddy", "messy", "bad quality", "bad angle", etc. In hindsight, I was both aroused at the power I had over Adam and terrified at the idea that my father's phone number was in the bottom of a box of homemade *freaking* porn. Checking again, the napkin *was* indeed written in Mulch's scrawl, the napkin that was at the bottom of a secret box full of sex videos of me.

Jesus, was it on the internet?

Fuck him. What bothered me was my father's phone number.

The house was lit with soft light as the sun settled behind the pines. A vision of my sister flashed in my mind. If Mulch fucks with her there's going to be hell to pay. Now, how I was going to get Mr. Bill to tell me everything?

3

Pembroke van Hazen sneered as he drew back the curtains of his three-story townhouse in Richmond, VA. He hated his uptight neighborhood, but he loved his American base of operations. It was an old marble and stone townhouse that bespoke Southern genteel riches, an antebellum snobbery and solid American craftsmanship one didn't see too much anymore. Pembroke had bought the house as soon as he saw it. He had to possess it; it had called to him. Rather, it sang to him.

When he had walked by the house he had been on his feet for an hour, and his toes wanted to be out, to be free. He had been fantasizing about killing his real estate agent in the next house he showed him. His toes were bulging against his shoes, and pretty soon if they didn't get some air, they would begin to chew through the leather, which he had so carefully polished just the other day. Then he heard it, a faint sad sound. Pembroke almost mistook it for a radio playing. The agent had not heard the music and gave Pembroke a befuddled gaze when he'd asked the man, "Isn't that music? My god, where is it coming from?" And then, "Somebody has a miserable voice, don't they?"

The realtor, Mr. Toby Snead, mentioned casually that the house was for sale, and that if Pembroke was interested, he could contact the agent that represented the seller and set up a meeting.

As they passed it by, Pembroke rushed back and leaped over the iron railing fencing the hedge. He hooked his fingers around the windowsill and hoisted himself up, just to peek inside.

"What are you doing?" The realtor had asked. Having just received his license, he was nervous enough around Pembroke, whom he perceived to be a snobby German and a little odd. "What are you doing?" he had repeated, his voice revealing his consternation.

As a reply, Pembroke hummed the tune he was hearing in his head.

"We can get in trouble for this!" Toby Snead looked up and down the sidewalk in panic. A woman across the street had come out to fetch her mail and stared at the very tall figure hanging onto the window ledge. "Sir, I have to insist that you step away," Toby had whined.

Pembroke continued to peek, humming the same tune all the while, his mind filled the aural ghosts of past residents. Delighted, Pembroke bought the house that same afternoon.

The music he had heard emanating from the house was in fact songs, sung and played in the old house, and wailings of woe and wailings of terror that had been imprinted into the building itself. The house was a veritable record of the years, and Pembroke imagined that if a person were to cut into the fabric of the house – the plaster, the moldings, the brick, the marble mantel, the redwood timbers, that person would discover rings, like that of a record, a recording of every sonic happening in the old bugger.

The first night Pembroke explored the basement which lay two stories underneath the main floor. It was a crude basement, hand-tooled, smooth, with a stone that stretched the length of the house and under the house next door. A lone lightbulb hung from the ceiling, and upon the catacomb-like walls hung sconces for flambeaux. It predated the Civil War, Pembroke was sure of it, and likely used for shelter during the war. There were pulleys and eyehooks, perfect for suspension wires; and he was beside himself with joy, finally a workspace gothic enough for his sensibilities. That night he had felt tickled to be evil, so full of himself that he felt like a teenager dancing around in his underwear. He decided there and then that he would bring Virginia to the basement, often. He would bring her there and break her.

4

"There's gotta be a law, or something, against unlimited wishes?" George asked, though he honestly hoped that there wasn't. The genie's head was bent low to fit into George's messy truck cab. Anyone passing them would see a very large blue man taking up most of the space in the cab. George would be able to fit a dog, maybe, but not another person, so big was Abdullah's body.

"Yes, Master. Very clever of master to think so, but Genies are smarter than masters, I have explained all of this already, sir, when you were painting." Abdullah said as he rubbed his belly. "Master, may we eat something? Abdullah is hungry."

"Really? Can't you just like you know snap your fingers or something and make food appear?"

"Yes, certainly we can, but Abdullah likes to try, how-you-say 'local' foods. To better understand master George like Abdullah understands himself."

"Local?"

"Yes, 'local.'"

It was near dark, and they had finished Mrs. Enfield's trim and were driving carelessly about the peninsula for lack of any better thing to do. George had decided that he had needed a drive, to clear his head and hopefully to make this genie of his go away. He was having no luck so far.

"You like seafood?"

"Yes," Abdullah replied as he reached his arm out of the truck window and made a wing of it.

"So how about crabs? Fish?"

Abdullah *weed* and *woahed* as he stuck his face in the wind.

"Master's flying carpet of iron is quite nice."

"Steel not iron. It's called a truck."

"A truck?"

"Just truck," George said as he looked at Abdullah. "So you say you like seafood?"

"Abdullah likes to see food, yes, very much, the eyes are the windows to taste."

"No, seafood, as in food that comes from the sea, the oceans, the big waters."

"Oh, food from the ocean?" Abdullah wondered as he stuck his head back inside the cab. "Master's flying truck is much better than any magic carpet! Only too small!" He laughed.

George rolled his eyes. He wasn't sure where he was going to take his giant friend. It had best be somewhere where they wouldn't be noticed.

5

Nick Adams was feeling clammy. *Are you eel? Feeling Crabby? Can ya' tuna a piano?* His mind searched for a pun with sharks. His stomach, after having eaten raw fish, felt surprisingly good for having snaked along the sand and killed a fish with his bare teeth. He felt so much better now that he was back at the Fritter shop.

"Somebody's out to mojo you, darling," Sea Hag said as she pulled a puff on her cigar. "I've seen possession before, but yours my friend, takes the cake."

"Mojo? You mean as in 'I got my mojo working?'"

"Yes dear, just as in 'I got my mojo working.'" Sea Hag said as she moved to the back of the shop. "I do think that if you eat, you'll feel better."

Nick coughed.

"So what the hell is wrong with me?" he asked Sea Hag.

Sea Hag's hands pressed and mealed the fish fillets and laid the fish in a plastic Tupperware dish. "I believe that someone has cast a spell on you. I can smell it on you."

"Magic-like? Yeah, right."

"I'm being serious."

"Okay, how can you smell it on me?" Nick asked as he wiped his sweaty brow.

"Magic shows up as a kind of glow, or sometimes a smell. It's different for everybody. It's on you like a tick on a dog, sucking at your core. There's someone very powerful working you to the bone. I almost missed it, but I didn't." She threw her head back and snapped off a laugh.

Nick looked Sea Hag in the eye. He grew hungry again.

"Magic huh? What if I don't believe in magic. I mean it's just a bunch of bullshit, isn't it?"

Sea Hag flipped the fish steaks and stared across the grill into his eyes.

"It's hard to believe, especially around here. But there are very powerful people living in this world. And I don't mean money or power. I'm talking about elemental power, manipulating nature, that kind of thing. Trust me, some people can curse you that live only a few miles away from here, spooky people," Sea Hag said as she raised her eyebrows up and down. "Haven't you ever been out into the woods at night and felt that things were wrong, known that something wasn't right? Maybe the woods were too quiet, or maybe the woods were tingling. You know what I mean when suddenly the hairs rise on your neck and there's this chill over everything, like a fog almost, except it's invisible. Or maybe you're alone in the yard, and you know that there's nothing there. You know that the woods around your house are empty of life. You've watched them for weeks for deer, squirrel. Nothing. Yet you can feel something staring back at you. Something that has eyes. Something that has teeth. Same when you're on the water. Suddenly it gets still, and you can't breathe."

"Oh come on, this is bullshit."

"Nick, you know what it is that I'm saying. Have you ever noticed that around here there's a church like every twenty feet?"

"Yeah, so."

"Well, the Christians know it. They can sense it. They call the energy God and pray to it, but it has no ears and no eyes. The energy has to be pulled out, tapped, and used. It's alive and crawls out of the soil. It crawls out of the mud."

"It's evil then?"

"Nah, it ain't evil. It's whatever you want it to be."

To Nick, this was sounding all too much like a cheap matinee flick, where the hero is introduced to mysterious forces beyond his understanding or his control, and then the hero is asked by some old gypsy, to take a leap of faith, or to believe in the monsters under the bed.

6

In her sleep, Marina chased a bird. She was cat-like, feral, on the run. The bird, high in the sky, looked like a child's kite, the way the tail swooped and dragged in the wind, a long feathery-plastic thing. Marina felt her legs underneath as she chased the feathery-plastic thing but knew instinctively in a dream-knowledge/ dream-faith kind of way that she was in her mermaid form, that she didn't have legs, that she had fins. Then the feathery-plastic thing seemed to stall. She felt cat-like again as she readied herself to catch it. But it didn't fall. It remained in the air, suspended.

Then, she saw her sister.

"Hey, wake up!" Virginia said as she snapped her fingers. Marina knew this was a dream or fever or memory, for Virginia was the pre-teen Virginia that made other girls cry and made boys cry even harder when she slapped them for pulling her hair. "Wake -up!" Virginia ran ahead of her, in the air and the water at the same time, waving her hands and crying out to her.

Marina heard the lapping of waves against the side of the box. Her eyes fluttered. For a second, she was awake, and her dream was far away. She called out to her sister once before falling backward into sleep.

"Don't go back to sleep!" Virginia shouted, snapped her fingers, and waved her hands in the air. "Don't go back to sleep, I need you!"

Deep in Marina's primitive brain, the potion worked, relentless, and aggressive. It slowly worked on the mammal brain and the upper brain functions as Marina lapped in and out of deep hallucinatory sleep like a kid with a fever.

7

Marina's mother was a golden beam of sunlight streaking through clear, blue, seawater, long and green and beautiful. Then, her mother was sitting next to her bed, on what Marina could not tell. Propping herself up on her palms, Marina looked about the dark, hot room. She heard water around her, yet she knew, felt she wasn't in her room. Her mother was not there, but there all the same.

"Mother." She whispered. "Are you there?"

There was a second of silence before a wispy reply. The sound of dry kelp rubbing together.

"Yes."

Feeling her throat lump, Marina cried out. "Mother, I miss you."

Again silence precipitated the wispy response. "I miss you too dear."

Closing her eyes, Marina felt relief. She felt safe. The magic continued to work.

When Marina opened her eyes again, her mother flickered like a motion picture and for an instant, she looked golden. She saw her mother as any child might, sitting like a queen without a crown, without a throne, simply golden, glowing, and eerily translucent, there to love her child, but her mother's apparition did not stay. Again, her mother flickered, as on a TV screen and vanished. Marina closed her eyes and opened them, sure her mother would reappear, but when she opened her eyes she found an older, white-haired woman, gaunt and skeletal, sitting next to her bed. The old woman sucked the room's air into her maw. Marina's skin dried as the air and moisture from her body were pulled from her and into the dark whorl of air that was the woman's mouth. Marina let out a scream, a little one, and the scream was pulled into a long taffy-like tongue that extended from her mouth and into the white woman's maw, which grew larger and more grotesque as it continued to pull all the air and sound into her mouth. Marina watched the woman swallow the tail of her voice, sucking it in taffy-like.

"Fishgirl gonna have problems," the woman croaked in a high cackle. And like that she was gone, and she was in another dream, a dream where she was hot, and sitting down on a chair, or stool. She wasn't sure which. Someone handed her a warm plate of lightly cooked fish.

8

Mr. Bill sat at the small round brown coffee table in the Hayes sunroom behind the kitchen. It was a good room for house cats and dogs and Mr. Bill liked to sip coffee and watch the sunset and sunrise.

Outside the sun sank behind the trees. The runny colors, orange, yellow, and a ribbon of purple swirled in a commodious river around the giant orange ball, which reminded Bill of bubbly orange soda. Why exactly it reminded him of orange soda was something he was searching his brain for when Virginia came in by the side entrance.

"Hey," Virginia said as she slung her purse onto the kitchen counter and stepped into the sunroom. There were fine beads of sweat on her upper lip.

"Hey." Mr. Bill replied.

"Can I get you a drink?" Virginia seemed nervous, her face a mixture of anger and annoyance.

"No thanks." He gestured to his coffee. "Why don't you get a drink and come sit awhile."

"I will."

The refrigerator door chunked open, and Bill heard the pop and hiss of a beer can. He knew it was beer because Maria had taken the last Diet Coke, Virginia's favorite drink, about an hour ago. Virginia sat down across from him and steeled her eyes as best she could.

"What's on your mind?"

"Okay," Virginia said as she leaned back into her chair, her eyes steeled, determined. "I need to ask you a few questions."

"Okay."

"They are strange questions, I admit, but I need help here."

"Okay." Mr. Bill said recalling a composition Virginia had written her senior year entitled: "Mr. Bill, the man, the myth". She had not interviewed him for the paper, and if he remembered it right, she painted a picture of him as some kind of gypsy who had run away from the circus.

"You know Adam, my boyfriend?"

"With the sweat problem?"

"Glandular problem."

"Boy sweats like a water glass left out in the sun."

"He doesn't sweat that bad."

"Sometimes."

Bill recalled that Virginia received an A on her made-up composition. Mulch had found it in the trash can and had shown it to him.

"What's the relationship between my father and Adam?"

"I didn't realize there was one."

"I've found things," Virginia said trying her best to sound confident and in control.

"What kind of things?"

"I don't know if I feel comfortable sharing them with you."

"Okay." Mr. Bill tried to look surprised.

"Okay, what?" Virginia stared him squarely in the eyes.

"Okay that you don't share them, but I don't know if I can help, though."

"It's kinda weird."

Bill sipped from his mug. "Do you know why I like coffee?"

"What?"

"Do you know why I like coffee?"

"No."

"I like coffee because it's bitter. It's a lot like tobacco. Not like marijuana. Weed is sweet. Tobacco is bitter. Bitterness has an appeal because it's like life, don't you think? I'm not trying to be coy, or cute, or even grandfatherly, because when you get down to it, life is made up of people who are mean to each other, people who put themselves first. Don't you think?"

"What the hell kind of bullshit is this?"

"It's not bullshit."

"What?"

"Don't you think people are basically mean to each other?"

"Look, I didn't come looking for a lecture on freaking human nature."

"Yes. But you must see that people are commodities to be used, abused, and eventually tossed aside. The best of friends are like products you use for life. Toothpaste. Diet Coke. Toilet paper."

"So you're saying that my boyfriend is like toilet paper."

"Yes and no."

"What are you talking about?"

"Look, all I'm saying is that maybe your relationship with this Adam isn't the healthiest. Maybe Adam viewed your relationship as transactional."

"What's the relationship between Adam and my father?"

"You'll have to ask Mulch."

"That won't do, you and Mulch are best friends."

Bill interrupted. "Well, just to be clear, we do not have a friendship, per se, it's more like an obligation. If it weren't for this obligation, I don't know..."

"Look, what I want to know is, how are my boyfriend and Mulch related?"

"Maybe you should talk to your father about that."

"Look, I've found things."

"You've said. What kind of things?"

"Adam is videotaping us having sex."

Bill blinked.

There was a second of silence before Virginia continued.

"Without my knowledge. He's got them labeled by date. There's a rating system. He's got handwritten notes. The angle of my face, the quality of the film, what I say during sex."

"Conversations?"

"No!" She blushed. "What I scream out before orgasm."

Bill's face remained unmoved.

"I found my dad's phone number in the box of SD cards, his private number. I'm worried that Adam is trying to embarrass my father, or blackmail him, or get me in trouble with dad, though that doesn't seem likely."

"I have to show you something," Bill said abruptly.

He headed into the kitchen and the hallway and up the back stairs. He did not wait to see if Virginia followed him into Mulch's room. As Virginia followed her temper sharpened.

"What are we doing? Where are we going? Is Adam here? Where's Mulch?"

"Mulch is not here. I do not know where Adam is. I need to show you something. Something you will not like to see." He looked her in the face. "You will understand what I mean when I say to you that Mulch has been *buying* you for quite some time."

"What are you talking about, buying?"

Mr. Bill knew that when he clicked on the file history's play button's arrow, the arrow would be like an arrow through Virginia's heart. He waited until Virginia was sitting looking at the laptop screen.

Virginia made some protesting grunting noises. She didn't know why she was in her father's study, but she used the time to scan the room for any signs of Adam. She barely paid attention to Bill and his fumblings with her father's computer trackpad, and if she had paid attention she might have asked the right questions. When Mr. Bill clicked the video and a computer fan whined up to speed and she saw her naked body and Adam's naked body together on the screen, only then did she feel faint, all her protest and rational thinking went out the window.

"I should not be telling you this, but I'm sorry to say that your father has had an interest in these things about you for some time."

The crawl space under Mulch's bedroom was originally built by the smuggler Kasper van Hazen as a wedding present for his virgin bride Virginia. The son of a Dutch privateer, Kasper had been schooled in smuggling and piracy by his father. Kasper smuggled rum and sugar from the islands to the colonies where he would bob them in the creek and tether them to his dock. Back in those days, it was common for traders to store goods in the water, provided the barrels were waterproof. Kasper, a Dutchman, was an excellent engineer and knew that his occupation might warrant careful hiding places and sneak-a-ways. Kasper hated to lose, and Kasper hated being caught. The idea of serving jail time for providing services and products to people who wanted them seemed absurd. Jail the rapists, the murderers, he would protest. But to jail a businessman, that was unthinkable to him. And so he built the house with the idea that one day he would be forced to hide.

In the common room, behind the fireplace, there was a lever that when tripped would open the floor in front of the fireplace to a low, shallow hiding place where a few barrels and a few sacks of sugar or grain could be stored. The hiding place could also hide a person, two if they didn't mind intimacy.

Along the back of the master bedroom was a false wall which led directly into a narrow service passage that allowed for free movement about the first floor's original rooms, as well as a narrow, steep stairwell that both climbed to the second-floor passageway that snaked around the upper bedrooms, as well as it dropped down into the basement where one could escape into the underground water channel.

So when Mulch had the house renovated, he made sure the secret passageways were all undisturbed. He'd originally discovered the hideaway when he spied his mother sneaking out of a hole in the wall in her bedroom. It took him a week to figure the latch. He had been fifteen at the time.

It was by squeezing himself into this secret sneak-away built by Kasper van Hazen that Mulch eavesdropped on his daughter, watching her during slumber parties when she was just a teen. Watching her undress, watching her sleep, all the while he was there, in the walls, as Mr. Bill explained the recordings and explained Adam to his daughter. Mulch listened and rubbed his erection. His blood flowed like hot oil, and he was eager to confront his daughter and send her packing.

"You see, you look like his mother." Mr. Bill explained, trying to be both calm and soothing. "I only found out recently."

Virginia sniffled. Her mind stuttered.

"And Adam, you see, he was paid to tape you. It was an agreement between Mulch and him."

Mulch could almost hear the bones of his daughter's fingers snap as she squeezed her hands together. He heard the friction of her skin as Virginia rubbed her palm together, her jaw tightening.

"Because of this, your father had him killed."

Mulch steadied himself. It was all in motion now, just like he had planned. If she were to be broken, Mulch would have to bring her to the edge first himself. There could be no other way.

CHAPTER TEN

1

Captain John Smith, *the* Captain John Smith, who by his talent (some say talentless) and wits (some say witlessness) navigated and commanded (this too is also in question) a small group of settlers to the Eastern Shore of Virginia, whereupon landing in 1608 (the actual date is debated by both local historians and Smithophiles – one group says that the settlers came ashore on June 2nd of that year – Smith's diary states that he came ashore on the 8th) he was met by a group of giant Indians. Just where exactly he came ashore is also in debate, since Captain John Smith was both a flagrant self-promoter and a fantastical storyteller. But bones of seven-foot-tall Natives have been allegedly found in various pockets on the shore leading many local historians to believe that the descendants of the legendary and dreaded Amazons (a hotly debated topic in local crypto-historical circles) had migrated northwards and settled in what is now rural Virginia by as late as 1500.

Mr. Bill had only been a little boy when Captain John Smith had come ashore. If anyone were to ask him what he remembered of the day he would have told you that the white men smelled like the burning of wet leaves.

2

In the subsequent years following the Jamestown settlement and the colonization of the Eastern Shore Mr. Bill matured into a young man and learned magic as his father's apprentice. Mr. Bill knew the creeks and the back paddle bogs and necks that littered the Eastern Shore by heart, and he like many of the youth, lived a carefree life, that was until the white man began to see the Indian as a liability, rather as a partner.

Then it all went south.

Just as the brain can furrow new passages for the firing of synapses, and re-grow cells and whole areas that have been ravaged by nature, or chemicals, the brain is also able to scar, and cover areas of memory that a person does not wish to access. In this way, whole areas of memory can be covered over, like bricks or wood can be covered by ivy.

Mr. Bill managed to do this.

He simply forgot.

3

That morning so long ago when Mr. Bill woke up by the river, he could not remember much of anything. He remembered the name the white man had given to him, "Bill," William, but the great stretch of his life behind him lay cloudy, shrouded in fog.

The tide was high on the river, and the morning appeared promising, already the sun crested the trees and the birds had begun their choruses. But he could not remember.

He didn't remember his past the next day or the next.

Mr. Bill stayed in the woods near the great Machipongo River for almost a year. He built a sturdy lean-to and fished, he gathered herbs, he gardened. He hunted. He got up every day and lived, all the while he felt as if the inside of his head had been scrubbed with sand.

From that moment on it was only while in a trance, or in a dream that Mr. Bill remembered anything from his childhood. And even then, only once in a while.

4

Mr. Bill began to shrink. At his peak, he towered over seven feet tall, but now he barely reaches six feet in boots. It's all a fog. He retains vague memories of his father standing four sometimes five heads over the colonists who squirmed and pissed themselves out of fear. Because of his size, his senses were heightened, and the smell of the white man was enough to turn his stomach. The white men were lazy and threw their waste behind their residences where the sun and heat cooked it into almighty stink that kept animals away. You could always tell a white man's house by the stink and the piles of shit around the edges.

When Mr. Bill came back into white society it was 1774, some hundred and seventy years after the massacre of his people, and the colonists were preoccupied with Mother England to pay him much mind. He had shrunk to about an even six and a half feet at that time. He elicited gasps and grunts from anyone who saw him and found himself seeking the refuge of the islands, the same islands the chief's son had sequestered himself to, over a hundred years earlier. But instead ended up in the white towns to learn his way about the new world. Because he was lonely, because he needed a connection, even if it were colonists.

It had taken Bill several years to perfect his white speech and several more to learn how to read and write the white man's language. He did this by listening, eavesdropping from the woods, or taking odd jobs, mostly working on cotton and tobacco plantations. His strength and size guaranteed him any manual labor job and later when he reintegrated with society his size guaranteed him the fights. Big white men wanted to prove their strength against him and for a while, Mr. Bill enjoyed his notoriety on the local boxing circuit. Other white men and women wanted to teach him so that he would lose his 'savagery'. Still, other men and women wanted to show him the only path to righteousness. Quickly Mr. Bill saw that it was natural and essential that he blend in with the white men, as they were growing stronger, and that he preserve his height and strength inside of him, but not show it on the outside. To do this his bones compacted in on themselves, growing shorter, stronger, and thicker, as his skeleton shrunk a few millimeters each year. With this, his memory shrank and compacted into a small ball somewhere in his brain, somewhere it could roll around away from his conscious mind.

5

"I am not taking you in there," George said as he tried to block Abdullah from the Lazy Titty's door, Abdullah who successfully looked over George's relatively small body.

"Master, merchant's sign says 'open.'"

"I see that. I've changed my mind. There's no way you're going in."

"But master, Abdullah very hungry."

Again, George moved to counter Abdullah from peering into the screen door of the Lazy Titty. George looked like a little kid trying to block his NFL-sized father from seeing the mess he had just made of his room.

"Master, what is Lazy Titty?"

"Long story."

"Abdullah smells tasty roast meat."

"You can't go in."

"Why not?"

"You won't fit in the booth."

"Sign says no one under 21. I don't know what 21 is."

"Look you just can't go in there looking like that."

"Like what, master."

"You need a disguise."

"Who is this guy."

"No disguise."

"Abdullah will dispatch this guy for you master."

"Disguise."

"Is this guy an enemy of master?"

"Disguise. Dis. Guise. Means you need a costume to go inside."

"Costume?"

"Funny clothes."

"Funny?"

"You know, like a hat to cover your freakishly large head. Or your blue skin."

"A free fish?"

"No, never mind. Can you know, change your appearance?"

"Ah, Abdullah can make himself look very different. White and not blue even, if that is what pleases you."

With that, there was a finger snap and a blinding flash with the smell of burnt hair and smoke, and George found himself looking at a short, strange man.

6

"So what you're telling me is that some bitch," Nick said *bitch* emphatically, "has got her mojo working on me. Something like that?"

"It could be a man too you know." Sea Hag nodded. "No need to be hating on females. And this person, man or woman, is making you feel certain ways, see certain things, and generally making my life miserable."

"Yes."

"And this person is doing it by some kind of magical and paranormal means beyond my understanding."

"Yes."

Nick scooped the last bit of fish into his mouth. *She sure can cook,* he thought. The fish made him wish for a cold beer. But she was out of her mind, good cook, or no.

Sea Hag sighed, "Look you may not believe me, but there is a world swimming right under your nose – a dangerous but wonderful world."

"Blah, blah, blah."

Nick didn't know what to believe, but he wasn't going to believe in magic. That was for loonies, like his father. Was his father crazy, he couldn't remember.

"I know you don't believe me, but I want you to be careful," Sea Hag said as she laid her hand over top of his and squeezed. "Promise me that Nick."

Nick didn't respond. He was trying to remember something his father had said about ghosts. *Everything is so fuzzy. What's happening to me?*

"Nick?"

"Sorry. I was just thinking of something."

"Or was someone thinking of you?"

7

"You look like Tattoo."

"Like what?" Abdullah's voice was the same, only it was amusing now because it was so deep, and his short, squat body was so tiny. "Who is Tattoo?"

"He was the small person from Fantasy Island. Great TV show. They made wishes come true."

"Then it's appropriate then?"

"Yeah, I guess." Abdullah's clothing had been transformed into what George thought of as Miami-Viceish - white shoes, and pants, and a light blue t-shirt – a very 80s look. "It'll do."

As they entered the Lazy Titty, Abdullah noticed how big everything looked from such a small body, his tiny heart pumping away, the tiny penis swinging between his legs, tables and chairs coasted just above eye-level, and the bar was too tall for him to approach without the feeling that he was about to squished.

The man behind the bar looked down at Abdullah and nodded. He whispered to George. His master responded, "He's okay, Alex. He's just from across the bay. Mel would approve." The bartender nodded and finished their drinks before he disappeared into the back. George looked down on him, "Come on man, Sheila's just about to go on." George then handed Abdullah a drink. "This is Long Island Iced Tea. We're lucky, there's nobody else here and we've got the place to ourselves," George said as he moved to one of the booths close to the stage.

That! wasn't entirely true. A few truckers were eating fried chicken in the front. The breast and thigh special had George thinking that was a good idea. Abdullah squirmed up onto the booth's bench and sipped his drink.

"Oooo. Strong tea, master."

"Yeah. It's a doozy."

"Master, what is a Sheila?"

George pointed to a tall, busty blonde stepping onto the stage. She wore what appeared to be a belly dancer's costume.

"That, my friend, is a Sheila," George clapped and hollered. "Go ahead, girl."

"Yes, go get a head." Abdullah cried.

Sheila waved to the group of truckers who were removing their singles from their wallets.

"Is she?" Abdullah wiggled with excitement. "A belly dancer?"

"Yes, Abdullah. Hey, do you mind if I call you Ab?"

"Master, yes. You can call me whatever you wish."

"Thanks, and while we are on it, you can call me George."

"I don't understand, would you like me to call you Master George?" Abdullah's lips grew slick as he moved his tongue back and forth over them.

"While we're here. In this place, just call me George."

"Yes sir," Abdullah said as George rolled his eyes.

On stage, Sheila began to gyrate to the thin sounds of belly dance music. Mel tended to let his girls try out new personas in the off-hours. When it was busy, which George guessed would be in an hour, or so, the girls all danced to popular music.

"Those are some lights made by many candles in a fine glass."

"Lights?"

George sipped his drink.

"Master, what is Lazy Titty?"

George coughed into his palm. "The Lazy Titty is a woman's breast."

"Woman's breast? People eat woman here?"

"No!" George said as he looked over to the truckers who didn't seem to have heard a thing.

"Keep your voice down. We eat chicken and fish here, not women. Women take off their clothes here. That's where the breast comes from."

"Very slowly? Lazy-like?" Abdullah had worked his lips into a frothy foam of spit and Long Island Iced Tea. He seemed to like the beverage, and George hoped it would mellow him out.

"Abdullah should make women work harder for you master. So that they are not lazy." He said as he stood up on the seat.

"Get down!"

This time the truckers did look, and they laughed at the little man too. So did Sheila who puffed out her lips and squeezed her left nipple. Abdullah dropped back in his seat, his eyes the size of saucers.

"This here is a strip club, Ab."

"A strip club?"

"Yes, strip. Women here take off their clothes for our pleasure."

"I don't know about this strip club."

"It's like a belly dancer, but better."

"Nothing is better than fine belly dancers, master."

"We should come here in the morning for the eggs and legs special."

"Master, please, she is coming over to us."

"You know, that's not a bad idea, eggs, and legs. I can take Nick here tomorrow morning, and I can bring you too."

"Master, Sheila, is almost here and she looks at me like she wants a husband."

"Speaking of Nick, maybe you and I are having some kind of hallucination brought on by paint fumes."

"Master. I...." Abdullah gurgled.

"This could be a lawsuit. A big one. We could be rich."

Abdullah wiped his brow and finished his Long Island Iced Tea. Sheila pranced in front of their booth, her hips bucking back and forth. Abdullah stared into her breasts, occasionally looking into her eyes.

"Hey there baby," Sheila cooed. Her hands caressed her mounds and slid between her legs to rub her crotch. "Wanna private dance? I could make your little man stand tall?"

Abdullah bit the edge of his glass and shattered it, grinding the glass under his teeth.

"Wow. That's sexy, little man," Sheila said as her eyes batted back and forth.

George reached out to keep Abdullah from drinking any more out of the broken glass, and to keep the little man from touching Sheila, which he never thought would happen. But it did. Right as he got the glass away from his hand, Abdullah grabbed for Sheila's waist.

"Hey, let go of me!" Sheila squealed.

With that, it didn't take long for the truckers to lunge out of their chairs towards the two of them.

"Let's go!" George shouted, pulling Abdullah behind him as they beat it out the door.

8

Virginia appeared unconscious; Mulch couldn't be sure. He'd come out of the very wall behind her and when she saw him she fainted. Feisty as she was, he'd expected more out of her. He poked her with his finger.

"I've watched you grow up into a young woman and a strong one at that. I guess you should thank your parents for that. For your genes and whatnot. Don't you agree?"

She didn't move.

He poked her again. Nothing. *She must be out. Good.*

"What do you want me to do boss?" Mr. Bill looked uncomfortable. Mulch didn't care for his sneer.

"Tie her up." Mulch retorted. "You were playing a little too nice for my taste, Bill."

Bill didn't respond, instead, he took the coil of rope from his back pocket and tied her up per Mulch's earlier orders. He had made sure that the knots were tight but not uncomfortable. Through the ordeal, Virginia would probably struggle and make them tighter and more painful. The ropes tied around Virginia's waist and legs were ridiculously thick against Virginia's skinny and muscled body.

"Genes aside, what you lack Virginia is not good breeding, but good manners. Plain old respect for one's elders," Mulch half-laughed at himself.

Mr. Bill shifted his weight and in doing so shifted the balances of the shadows on the walls. He looked at his boss with something that approached caution.

"Darling don't ever tell anyone that I didn't love you." Mulch purred peeling his lips back into a wicked smile. Mulch leaned over and kissed his daughter squarely on the mouth, something he had never done before, penetrating her mouth and licking her teeth, before recoiling his tongue back into his serpentine smile.

"She's a good kisser, my Virginia. Got to keep an eye out for my girls, even if it hurts me sometimes. Just to be sure, to protect you, I had to hire Adam on as your boyfriend when you got home from school. Had to make sure you were okay. Can you blame me?"

Mulch scooted a stool from her computer desk in front of her and leaned forward, kicking the stool up on its two front legs. "Parents are supposed to love their children and nurture their children. Don't you agree?"

Virginia snorted back a tear.

"Look at this!" Mulch squealed. "She's awake. My little girl is awake."

"Fuck you!" Virginia spat heaving with sobs.

"Don't go crying tears baby. See I knew it, Bill. I knew she would be awake. Ah hell, Virginia, Eb wouldn't have had any crying from me. Oh no, that shit is for babies. You're my child, from my seed, and you're going to get what I got."

To Virginia, Mulch smelled of fever, coffee, cigarettes, the stink rushing against her face. His breath fluttered against her eyelids.

"I killed for my father. What do you do for me!?" He screamed. "Leon was first. I don't know who was dumber. Leon for fucking mother and being so stupid to think it would go unpunished!" Mulch stood up, his fist clenched. "Or me for killing him cause I was told to. Stabbed that motherfucker right in the chest.

"Then I left home. You know killing a man is a strange thing to go through. I didn't handle it well but let me tell you it felt better and better the next few times I shot somebody or cut 'em caused they were giving Eb a hard time. Muscle, that's all I was to him."

Through her haze, Virginia prayed that his ticker would quit on him. She wasn't in any better condition. Her heart pounded against her constricted chest. She had trouble breathing. There was a sharp pain in her groin. *Did my father rape me?* She forced back tears.

"Adam didn't see it coming either. That stupid mother fucker thought we were *friends*. For all it's worth baby, he didn't love you. But I do. I care about you. All I wanted to see was your face. Like my mother's. God, she was something."

The slap came out of the shadows and rung Virginia's head back; she heard her vertebrae popping. Her mind was being shredded by fear and shock for the man who had cared for her whole life was beating the shit of her.

9

Huck and Buck Winston leaned against the Hayes Feed & Supply Store loading dock wall. Huck smoked a nasty piece of cigar and Huck chewed on some Red Man, occasionally spitting into the dirt.

"Sure is a pretty sunset," Huck said.

"Yup."

The sunset had almost drained away, the tail end of the runny orange now a deep red and purple. Night filled in the spaces and in the trees across the road darkness had already made a nest for itself.

"Now what the hell are we here for again?"

"Special delivery."

"Special delivery. That's right."

Huck coughed and spat out a slimy piece of tobacco leaf.

"You know Buck?"

"What's that Huck?"

Buck longed for a folding lawn chair.

"The boss seemed a little off."

Huck also thought about a chair, a leather recliner. The older he got, the more he liked the idea of having a recliner.

"Yup."

Buck spat into the dirt.

"He's been talking about quitting."

"He said that when he took over for his pappy. A mean son of a bitch that one was, boy I tell you."

Huck snorted and kicked a pebble off the loading dock and into the dirt below.

"Remember that time he had that Negro fellow hung up in his barn cause he had been out stealing the opium plants."

"Yeah, he kept saying, 'Wasn't me boss. I stole 'maters. 'Maters boss.'"

"Eb dragged that fucker out of his own house and tied him up in his back yard."

"Yup. Seems to me that the Negro's bitch was there too."

"No, you're thinking of the time we ran that crack-head off Poole's Bluff."

"Yeah, that's right. Tied that fool up too, right?"

"That son of a bitch fell right outta that truck and split his head open."

"Yeah, that's about right."

Huck re-lit the end of his cigar. The cigar was sour now, and the smell of it was wet and soapy and begged to be squashed out. It smelled like heartburn, but Huck figured he could get another good pull. Maybe three.

"Eb was mean, boy. I tell you."

"Yup. No need in telling me."

"Mulch's pretty mean too. Wouldn't cross him neither."

"You remember when Mulch was still young, and he took a hammer to that there hippie."

"Shit, Summer of '71."

"That hippie sure as shit wasn't gonna pass another joint with that arm again."

"Or jerk it."

Buck made a cock-in-hand gesture and laughed. Huck laughed too.

"You think he killed that girl there?"

"Maria? That was her name, right? Yeah, he killed her. I'd bet my life on it."

Huck shifted his feet around on the loading dock, which made a swish-swish sound.

"It's getting to be pretty fucking dark out to see any smoke signal."

"Yup."

Sighing, Huck chewed on his butt and crossed his arms.

"I wouldn't mess with no Mulch, Indian, or no Indian."

"Indian Bill. Mr. Bill. Huh. He scares me right fierce."

Buck squinted and even stood straight a bit to peer further out into the murkiness. "You don't suppose that's our signal?" He pointed off in the distance. Smoke rose from what could have been the Hayes place, though it was hard to tell in the late light. Smoke signals, used to alert buyers and pushers, were usually thicker, more controlled. Mulch liked it when Mr. Bill made it look like the movies. This one was thin; one might even say starved for body.

"Could be," Huck squinted. "Mighty thin for old Bill. Must be in a hurry."

"I don't know, could be some cracker and a tire fire."

"But there ain't nobody over there but the Hayes', right?"

"I guess."

"I guess we'll find out."

"I guess we will."

Buck glanced at his wristwatch and spat at the dirt.

10

George threw the truck into gear and reversed, yanking the wheel hard to the right. He nearly cut down one of the men chasing them, and the man kicked at the truck as George pulled away. "Shit, fuck, damn." He muttered. Somebody threw a bottle which exploded in the bed, glass pinging off the back window. "Never. Ever. Never, ever, touch a dancing woman," he shouted over the truck's gunning engine. "Never!"

"Yes, master."

"Say it! I want to hear you say it."

"Never touch a dancing woman, master."

"That's *fucking* right!"

George slowed down when he was certain that he wasn't being followed, his heart kicking back into normal gear. He was pretty sure he wouldn't be allowed back in the Titty for a while. At least not with Abdullah. Suddenly the thought occurred to him, what with all the commotion back at the titty bar, that he wasn't hallucinating this guy – that Abdullah was real; that he had reached out and grabbed Sheila. Thing is, he'd always wanted to do that himself. He thought about the possibilities as he drove to his house. First, he wanted something to eat, and he needed a drink, something strong too.

They pulled into his driveway without a word. Abdullah had changed back into his normal self and was taking in the sights. He seemed unphased by their flight. *Probably happens all the time,* George thought. *Being that genies can do anything, the regular world must be so boring for them.*

"You know, Ab, I think I want to try for a wish." He turned his truck off and stared off into his yard, unsure of what was going to happen next.

"Really? A wish? Well, what is it that you wish for?"

"I would like to see what Lilly is doing right now."

George turned to see what Abdullah would say to that, but Abdullah was gone and instead, he found himself looking down the bone of a giant pork chop.

11

The white Ford Econoline van used by the field hands to transport water and first aid supplies out to the migrants, or to carry potted plants to the store, was other times used to carry dope to a buyer out in the fields after Mr. Bill's infamous smoke signals. Tonight, it would be used to transport Virginia to Richmond, into the arms of her distant cousin, Pembroke van Hazen. The floor of the back of the van was full of dried mud, dirt, and a nail or two that rolled around and made tinny noises on the ribbed floor as it bounced over the ruts. There were twigs and bits of leaf caught between the ribs and Virginia saw this from under the bandanna tied around her eyes. She lay in pain, her eyes breaking into pinpoints of light each time the van bounced across her bruised ribs. In truth, Virginia expected Mr. Bill to save her, to say or to do something, but he seemed to have been switched off. Virginia did not understand it. Mulch, on the other hand, bubbled over with energy and was practically foaming at the mouth. He had struck her twice before punching her squarely in the stomach, which had knocked the wind out of her. Then she was hogtied and carried out like fresh kill into the back of the field van. Virginia discerned she was being driven away over the field roads and dirt roads that crisscrossed around the farms, and not the county roads. She wasn't sure where they were taking her but she had a feeling from the turns that they were taking that they were heading towards the store. Despite her father had turned on her and beat her, she felt a deep calm. Eerily so. Her heart beat steadily and surely and her brain calmly made a list of resources available to her:

(1) *I'm not dead.*

(2) *My father is insane*

(3) *Aim for the balls.*

(4) *Aim for the eyes, too.*

(5) *Don't scream. Spit. Swallow. Conserve water.*

Thinking back to her room, she couldn't remember where her father appeared from, just that he appeared out of nowhere and wrapped his thick arms around her. She had been turned away from the wall when she heard a click and when she had turned around, a door had been cut open in the wall. Mulch had smelled foul and sick and when he grabbed her and put his hand over her mouth she had fainted dead away.

Had the whole thing with Mr. Bill been a decoy?

The wall, the wallpaper...it was cut and torn from where...My father and his secrets.

The van down-shifted and gravel kicked back onto the fenders – large gravel, not oyster shells, not clamshells, but gravel. It sounded like the gravel her father had laid the store parking lot with.

Outside there were voices, muffled male voices.

12

George was pretty sure that it wasn't a giant pork chop he was looking at. It did look large from where he was sitting, but he didn't think it was gigantic. He didn't care much what it was, it smelled so good. Then he was eating the pork chop, devouring the pork chop, practically inhaling the pork chop. George would have liked to have some salt and pepper, and a little horseradish, but it tasted fine all the same. Around the pork chop, there was the rich smell of caramelized onions and feet, a mild braid of perfume, and body odor. Trying to look around to get a better idea of where he was, George found it hard to break his gaze away from the pork chop. It was too good, and besides the rest of the room was dark. Somebody had been spitting loogies on the rug for a long time. He smelled so many scents, his mind distracted by the taste of the pork chop and the smells of the room. Then somebody walked in front of him.

George tried to speak but it came out unintelligible, monotone, and monosyllabic. The old woman seemed to notice that he was trying to say something and reached out to him. She was huge, taller than the genie. When the old woman scratched his ear, he heard a bark that came from within his head. He was a dog.

The old woman said something to him, but George did not understand the Spanish. Another person entered the room and patted his head. Sniffing her hand as she rubbed his head, George locked onto Lilly's scent. He couldn't see too well, but he knew that there were two people in the room and one of them was Lilly, not just from her scent, but because he could see her glow. A bright halo of light shone around one of the figures. George smelled the pines where she had slept the night before. He could smell wax upon her skin, and the scents of clay from the pine grove soil, cosmetics from Lilly's apartment, the old woman's scent, beans, and coffee. Lilly's scent was multi-faceted, honeysuckle mixed with buttery pastry, with many layers that peeled away from each other like sheets of skin, and at the heart of it a warm waxy smell, like that of a fancy candle.

He'd never been inside a migrant's shack before. He could smell the outside and more people. There was an unusual quality about the voices that George couldn't quite figure. George heard the rattle of dry beans in coffee cans. Egg-shells were crushed and scattered across the yard that sounded like light rain on a tin roof. When Lilly bent down to mess his face up and blow cutey-pie kisses at him, a lifetime of her scents invaded his brain at such a pace that he felt elevated and enlarged. He was pleased that Lilly called him a "good dog."

The hairs on Lilly's arms smelled of pine and earth, and George could smell her sleep self, the tangy mess of sweat and pheromones, and George also smelled himself, though George took a lot longer to recognize it. George saw himself, the day before touching Lilly's shoulder and smelled himself on the dress she still wore, which reeked of tequila, that he had dumped in her lap by accident. George imagined this is what it was like to die and to go to nose heaven. He smelled meat that reminded him of hot dogs. He smelled Lilly's older scents among the shack's layers and layers of scents. Lilly had been smoking a lot, which George could tell from the strong bite of it on her fingers. Lilly was also happy, but nervous. She had recently been in an argument. George wasn't sure how he knew this, but as a dog, he wasn't so much interested in the argument she'd just recently had, but rather where the vague hot-dog like smell was coming from, and whether he, the dog, would get any of it to eat.

Lilly moved away from his direct line of vision and George found himself trying to get the dog to move. Thinking at the dog he said, 'move, follow that girl.' Only the dog didn't seem to know what a girl was. It was only by relaxing and imagining that he was in control of a giant robot that he was able to elicit any kind of control over the dog at all, and only marginally so. Later George concluded that the dog may not have responded to his command, but rather simply followed the smell of the hot dog on Lilly.

Even more infuriating was the fact that George didn't understand what Lilly and the very old woman were saying. When the women spoke their voices had a pinched quality to them. He was able to tell/smell that they had been arguing about the same topic all day. When Lilly and the old one's heartbeats rose, Lilly's pheromones spiked, and the tiny room blossomed with her scent. George tried to imagine his arms were the front legs of a dog and tried to will himself to trot on over to Lilly and lick her hand. Trying to do this George had the odd sensation that time was speeding up somehow.

When Lilly stormed out into the yard George was able to get the dog to follow behind her. The smell of roasting meat and ripe fruit hit George like a truck, his mouth overflowing with thick strings of saliva. He trotted alongside Lilly's hand which reached back and scratched his ear. He felt an urge to push his head into the scratch. Lilly's perfumed clean scent was losing its angry edge in the smell tapestry outside. George bee-lined it straight to a little twelve-year-old girl who held out a thick chicken leg that she'd dropped in the dirt. Chewing on the delicious dirty meat, George couldn't help hoping that the little girl would scratch him behind his ear.

13

The smell of his kitchen slapped Nick when he pushed the door open. The doorknob sweated with humidity, and the smell of pine, scorched matches, and fresh paint hit him in the face. The kitchen smelled sour and wet and dry all at the same time, a cake of smells. He was sure he had left the windows open when he'd left. He deposited his six-pack in the refrigerator where he placed one of the bottles of Rolling Rock to his forehead before ascending the stairs while wiping his brow with the bottle.

"It's so freaking hot," he said to himself, and as soon as he said it cold fear crawled up his spine, something wasn't right.

The upstairs rooms were glowing.

He dashed up the stairs and into his bedroom where the painting pulsed as it moved and rippled and raged. Light shone from the whitish figure blurred at the top of the painting, as the painting breathed, pulsed with light. All of a sudden his ears felt stuffed with cotton, and he couldn't hear anything. It was as if the sound had been eaten up by the light while the light fattened the room, and enlarged the air, thickening it like rising bread dough.

The Rolling Rock in his hand grew hot, and the beer began to boil in the bottle, its white foam gushing over his hand. He winced and dropped it, but the bottle hung in the air, suspended somehow, just for a moment, before falling to the floor, and shattering to pieces.

Nick's arm rolled with sweat. He stepped back into the hallway where it was a little cooler, his shirt soaked to the skin. His skin tingled, he could hear things in the hallway – the sound of his wet shoes against the floor, his heavy panting, even the blood in his ear. *Weird. This is too much.* He peeked back at the bottle of Rolling Rock. It remained smashed on the floor. The beer didn't seem to be boiling now that he was outside the room.

The other room upstairs served as a kind of TV room, though he didn't do much TV watching in there. He was about to go downstairs and drink all the beer in the fridge and get royally fucked up when he saw a small box of light in the corner – it was maybe four feet by four feet – a cube of light that made little squares flare in his eyes when he closed them.

This is way too much for me. He almost went downstairs anyway, but decided, what the hell, he wasn't dead yet, only spiraling into insanity, why not investigate the glowing cube in his living room. *Fuck it.*

When he stepped inside the room his skin flared with pain. His cigarette hanging on his lip flared to life and he inhaled sharply. If the room was hot enough to light his smoke, the room was hot enough to burn him, he thought. Cautiously, he stepped closer to the box, feeling the temperature rise. He was going to have one hell of a sunburn. He was about two feet from the cube when the box began to vibrate and hum.

CHAPTER ELEVEN

1

Nick's cigarette butt flamed like a torch, and he tried to spit it out, but it was glued to his lip. The vibrations and thrums came through the floor and shook his bones. They reminded Nick of an engine as Nick's knees knocked together and his chest felt like a drum. The vibrations increased and rattled him like a heartbeat. The smell of the burning tobacco was strangely absent. For a brief second his head hummed with a sweet and smooth voice and a taste rollicked and smacked against his gums and tongue. He didn't know what the taste was exactly, but he supposed it was the taste of the hum. Nick never thought about a sound having taste before. He was about two feet from the box and thought he could make out a shape inside the cube, a hunched figure inside of it. As he approached, the humming went silent. There was a darker, or perhaps lighter, shape in the center of the cube. Again he tried to spit the smoking butt from his lips, and again nothing. He was going to be smoking his lips soon. He looked down the smoking filter and then back to the box again.

The cube flashed and pulsed with his heartbeat. There was that smell in his head like that of warm water and warmer skin. There was something vaguely popcornish about it. He pushed hard against the cigarette butt with his tongue. The figure in the box had a womanly shape, and it was either pressed to the wall of the cube looking towards him, or the figure's back was pressed into the wall looking away from him. The smell of burning flesh ballooned in front of his face. His tongue moved slowly against the cigarette butt and the acrid smoke snaked up his nasal cavity and into his brain. Then the humming began again and this time the voice lapped against the inside of his skull like ocean waves. Combined with the flickering the box was doing the humming made it very hard for Nick to think and to move. Pulling out his brain through a hole in his head and then dribbling it on the floor would have been more pleasing. Fear

241

settled into his bones. *This was it.* He was going shit-house rat-crazy in his living room staring at a box. *A box that isn't even there.*

Then the box either shrunk or moved away from him, he couldn't tell. As it moved, the flashing intensified, and his heart fluttered in syncopation. The end of Nick's tongue began to burn. The voice murmured now and Nick was no longer sure if it was just in his head or not. The walls seemed to vibrate when the voice made a sound, his mind playing footage of a long stretch of beach. The burning cigarette filter remained perched on the edge of his lips, ready to fall. At the end of the beach was a giant wooden box, like a giant building block except it was all black with a huge sail on top. In the surf, kids and parents pointed and snapped photos. A very large muscular white man, and a small thin black man stood among a pile of cameras, snapping photos. After each photo, they'd chuck the clicked camera into the sand and fetch another camera, and they did this over and over, slowly. Just as Nick's lips started to sizzle, the cigarette butt finally fell, albeit slowly. He could see the box move towards a giant windmill in the ocean. The blades on the windmill turned slowly, and there was a dull rusty wrenching squeal as it made lazy revolutions. In the background, the flash of the many cameras continued. The butt hung in the air before him, and he felt its heat in front of his chin. Then without warning the voice in his head drained away, pulling the pictures of the beach with it. The images looked like colored candy swirling into a sink as Nick passed out.

2

Huck and Buck Winston snapped to attention when Mulch backed the van up. Mulch tore open the door and whipped the back open revealing a blindfolded, hog-tied woman.

"Your cargo boys." Mulch gestured inside. "Do what you have to do to keep her quiet."

Leaning into the van's maw, Huck got a close look at the cargo. She was skinny. Buck also stuck his head into the back hoping for a glimpse of the woman's face.

"Do what you have to do to keep her quiet. Get her to Richmond." Mulch repeated. "Here, in advance. Don't spend it all in one place."

The manila envelope was plump with bills.

Huck wiped his mouth of drool.

When Mulch left the men, he smiled wide with pleasure.

3

George, groggy and hung-over, stared into his greasy reflection in the microwave. The house was quiet.

"Holy crow, what a dream," he said as he slid off his seat. He'd had the strangest dream. He opened his fridge and scooped a Coors Light into his hand. The beer felt cold and real to him.

"Dreamed I was a damn dog." He wasn't sure what to think anymore. Something in his food, probably. "Nick will be thrilled he isn't the only one having fucked up dreams."

From his living room there came a voice that slapped him across the proverbial face.

"Master, ducks are lifelike and fantastic."

Not a dream, he thought. *Fuck.*

"Ducks," Abdullah snapped his fingers. A mug of ale appeared in his hand. "Paintings of feathery creatures who have a face like one big lip," Abdullah spat his words out.

"Are you drunk?"

"Nonsense, master."

"Yes, you have been drinking, haven't you?"

"How did master like his wish," Abdullah chuckled. George spotted several empty beer cans on the table behind Ab.

"Thank you very much for trapping me in the head of a dog. It's not what I asked for. I didn't know what was going on."

Abdullah waddled back into the living room, commenting on George's paintings as he went. George's living room was decorated in late 70s bachelor-style with a leather recliner and a matching leather and wool sofa of a muted brown and beige color. On top of a low coffee table, several copies of dated *Field & Stream* and *Virginia Wildlife* magazines were laid out at catty-cornered angles. Abdullah stooped so his head wouldn't knock against the low ceiling, which it did when Abdullah belched.

"Excuse me, master."

"Uh, no problem," the stink a mixture of perfume and beer yeast.

"Ab, did you know that dogs don't speak Spanish?"

"Abdullah like this one." He pointed and gestured to a painting of Colin McNair decoys. His mug sent ale sloshing over the side onto one of the magazines.

"That one?" George looked up with detachment. "Why?"

"Duck looks so friendly." Abdullah brought the mug of ale to his lips. "You see," Abdullah said as he pointed at the duck's bill. "Affirmative. The duck looks like he's made the most important decision of life. And this one," Abdullah hooked George by the arm pointing at another painting on the wall, "this duck here is very handsome."

George nodded.

"Yes, very handsome like both master and Abdullah. The bill, is this the right word? Yes? No? The bill, it's all in the bill. Like woman tonight, how she removed clothing as if we were the only men around. Only men allowed to witness her bare of clothing."

"That's what she's paid to do."

"Yes. Same with ducks. Ducks make me think I am the only one who sees them and feel for the tiny, feathered creature."

"Thanks, Ab. I appreciate the compliments on my paintings. Sometimes I just don't know. I spend hours working on a painting and most times I don't sell it. Sometimes I don't want to. Sometimes I do, though. I wish I was better, or dead."

"Wish to be dead? Master does not wish to be dead?"

"Dead artists are the most famous artists."

"This does not sound good to Abdullah."

"It's how things work."

"Abdullah thinks master's kingdom works in ways that are very funny."

"I paint nature, it's kind of niche market – few people think to buy it."

"Friendly ducks with shiny feathers?"

"Yes, but some people make sculptures, and other people make movies."

"Abdullah knows about sculptures, but not moovays."

"I'll have to treat you to one. How long did you plan on staying, by the way?"

"As long as master still has wishes, Abdullah stays with master."

4

Nick knew he wasn't swimming, that it was a dream, or a hallucination, or a fever, but he was swimming, relaxed; he felt like he was taking a bath, almost. It was Caribbean swimming, cruise ship swimming, the water the blue of LA pools on TV. Ahead of him, the tail of a giant fish swayed up and down. He was relaxed and swimming, he was underwater, but he had no problem breathing, everything was AOK. He didn't think of his house, of the strange heat and light coming from the strange cube, he dreamed. Nick swam without a care in the world.

When he turned around he jerked out of his tranquil relaxed state – his legs were gone.

For a hot second panic seized him, and he floundered in the water before his muscle memory propelled him forward.

He had fins, or rather, a fin that stretched out behind him and cut through water with power and strength that ran through his body and filled him with euphoria and peace. The sand jetted by underneath him as he cut across the ocean floor. *Whoa.*

The speed at which he traveled marveled him, and his body responded with a rush of goosebumps that he felt all over the human portions of his body. It took him a moment to get a look at his new body, covered with spiny fins that allowed him to cut the water, and ridges at his elbows and wrists that reminded him of miniature marlin crowns, so precise and rounded the small spines were. His breasts jiggled in the water as he swam. He touched one gently and a tingle ran through his body. He stared down at the breasts again. *Whoa.*

He continued to swim, his eyes on the fish in front of him. Perhaps they were also a mermaid or a merperson. He felt his body try to communicate with the figure swimming before him. Communication with the merperson/fish seemed unlikely for they were both under tons of water, but he felt his body react.

Then Nick opened his mouth.

What came out wasn't like anything Nick had ever heard before. It bounced in his head like a soupy echo, deep and amplified, on the bass end. Driven by an unconscious urge, an urge that felt alien, he continued to speak. He imagined the sound to be like sonar waves he'd seen on a PBS special about Navy subs.

The figure ahead of Nick was most definitely a mermaid too. Her naked bosom appeared each time the fin turned up and the torso turned down. Her hair flowed back like long, luscious kelp. The figure whirled partially back to the left, and then cut forwards, before somersaulting to face Nick close enough that he could have reached out and touched her. The mermaid clicked and chirped a response that sounded like a cross between dolphin chatter and whale song. Interspersed among the mermaid's chatterings and clickings, Nick heard the roll of the strange language that sounded a bit like every language Nick had ever heard in his life. The mermaid in front of him was beautiful, striking, with high cheekbones and luminescent skin. She motioned Nick forward and he followed, her hair flowing back towards him like a fin.

Nick was sure he was going to wake up any minute now because this was the kind of dream that he would always wake up from just as soon as he was ready to do something cool. Nick always jerked out of sleep right before the climax of a cool dream and was pretty sure even as he approached two boats on the surface above that he was just going to pop right out of his sleep.

Any moment now.

Attached by a heavy rope, the slack between the boats hung in the water like an umbilical cord. One boat's underside lay dark and dagger-like, the other boat floated on pontoons. Nick thought the shapes looked like a typical trawler-sized boat pulling a catamaran. The other mermaid circled the pontoon boat, and Nick got a pretty good look at her whole body in motion. Her top half jiggled, as the lower half made forward and back motions, her arms hanging to the side, her elbows bending slightly out to move her laterally. The tail curled and pushed against the water; her muscles sprung and taught as the mermaid slowed her ascent. Her scales, even at this depth, shimmered with the shattered sunlight filtered through the water.

Following her lead, Nick began to circle the second craft as well. Nick decided this was the coolest dream he had ever had and was sure, positively sure, that he was going to snap out of it at any second. He even closed his eyes, expecting to open them again in his bedroom covered in a sheen of night sweat. But when he opened his eyes he saw neither his room, nor the cool blue water, but a bright, hot, head-splitting sun spearing down upon his face. At first, Nick thought he had worm holed into another dream, but instead, he was staring at the boats floating on top of the water. The lead boat was a double outrigger trawler with a dual cabin below and a forward and aft deck. He'd seen one like that before. A boat like that typically went out far into the ocean to fish. Nick didn't see anybody on board. The other mermaid clicked and squawked at him, and Nick didn't even recognize the language now that he wasn't hearing it through the filter of water. Now it sounded roughly like someone spitting and cursing like they had just smashed their thumb with a hammer, the mermaid's throat pulsing in the sunlight. *Was that a gill?* He couldn't be sure.

The other boat wasn't a boat or a catamaran at all, but rather a medieval-looking box. Nick thought it looked like a giant wooden jack in the box. The other mermaid disappeared under the surface. Nick followed. The other mermaid drifted underneath the bottom center of the floating box, she hung there and looked up. She stared at something very intently there. *What is going on?* Nick cruised underneath next to her. Her eyes transmitted sadness and weight, a weight Nick did not understand, but one he identified with. *Loss.* It was as if her eyes had been wrung out from grief, put to hard labor, and then retired. She pointed up at the box. *Up,* she seemed to say, *up.*

Nick was sure he was about to snap out of the coolest dream ever when a small portal opened above him. At first, he thought they were going to swim through it, but then he realized that it didn't so much open as the wood above him turned to glass. He was pretty sure the clear portal hadn't been there before. *Magic? That's what Sea Hag would say, Magic.*

There was something painted or hung on one side of the box, it appeared to be a flame, but Nick couldn't be sure. It wasn't as dark as it had been seconds before. *There, a figure.* There was something familiar about the figure's gait, and the figure's shape. There was darkness in the figure, Nick felt it pulsing, reaching for him. Heat beat through him; heat fattened his senses.

Then Nick Adams stared up at himself. Nick the mermaid watched his human face on the other side of the magic portal contort and twist in confusion. His face looked like someone had twisted it and tied it off with a rubber band before untying it and letting it snap back into place. The water rippled and rolled across Nick the mermaid's face and subsequently across his face above, and when the wave rolled by he saw his whole body and the whole inside of the box shimmered and shadowed.

Then the insides of the box changed color. It was dark again like a curtain had been drawn across it. Nick's confused face became a scared beautiful female face staring back at him with big open help-me-eyes. Another wave ripped across and again and the portal closed, at which point, Nick jerked out of sleep and back into his own sweaty body.

5

Doc, when I heard that son-of-a-bitch father of mine say to Huck and Buck Winston to do what they had to do to get me to Richmond, I almost puked. I was pissed, to say the least. Mr. Bill had blindsided me. It felt like I had been dipped in oil. I felt it all over me, shame, humiliation. I just wanted to crawl away and die, for the love of God, my spine bunching itself up like an accordion. That fucking van, mind you. Ever been bounced around the back of a van moving at 60 miles per hour? It's no picnic mind you.

It was good that Adam was dead. I only wished I shot him myself.

All I thought about was how I was going to survive. If I did, the first thing I was going to do was kill my father."

6

Marcos smiled into the wind and caught a mosquito in his teeth. The bug buzzed briefly before Marcos gnashed it and spat it out. He kept his fingers crossed that no one would see the giant box he towed behind him. Luck had been with him, and the tide, and though he saw plenty of sportsmen far off ahead of him, no one appeared to pay him any mind. If he'd been stopped in the creeks, he could have lied and said it was a duck blind, but as the creek opened into coastal waters, the knot in his stomach twisted tighter. Once he was out to sea there would be no good excuses.

Marina hadn't stirred all day and that concerned Marcos. *Just how powerful were the drugs?* He didn't know, and Sea Hag seemed to think that the girl was in danger. *Why would Mulch put his daughter in danger?* Sea Hag had practically nibbled her nails away to nothing worrying about the poor girl. He steered North, with his luck he'd probably avoid the Coast Guard, but something in the back of his mind made him think that his luck might be running out.

If he only knew.

7

Richmond was an hour and a half drive from the Hayes homestead if Huck didn't hit any traffic on the interstate and if traffic on the bay bridges were light. The dark waters of the Chesapeake below them stretched out and away. The Bay Bridge wasn't busy and Huck kept the van at a steady 60. He didn't want to be pulled over with Buck in the back pumping the dark small shape of their cargo. Virginia didn't move, didn't budge, didn't make a sound. When they had found out who the cargo was, Buck had clapped his hands in glee and removed his shirt. He had climbed into the back and was now smacking her thighs as Huck drove the van into the first of two tunnels. Suddenly Huck felt his stomach sink, it wasn't the speed of the van, nor the slope of the road dipping into the tunnel.

Mulch's daughter? What the fuck? Why wasn't Mr. Bill doing this? Huck had done plenty of awful work for Mulch Hayes, often bloody work, but he had never had to do something that felt so wrong. Huck felt like he was driving too fast for the bridge, but he wasn't, just a steady 62 miles per hour.

Buck had started by hitting Virginia pretty hard across the nose. He probably broke it. Could have lodged a shard of bone in her brain for all they knew. When Buck stood up in the back, bracing his arms against the side of the van to kick Virginia, the van tipped to the side a bit. *If a bridge cop was paying attention...*

this wasn't going right, not at all. Huck felt it in his stomach, the way it had bottomed out when Buck had raped her, twice and done God knows what to her when he wasn't looking.

"Did you kill her? For God's sake?" Huck's voice wavered.

Buck only grunted.

"Jesus, you think you could have waited till we stopped," Huck said as he tried to laugh. Buck didn't respond.

There was a rest stop coming up in a few miles, best if he'd pull over and check the girl's pulse.

"Just drive the car, Huck. Don't you worry your pretty little pussy about this girl here?"

Huck gulped and reached into his shirt pocket for a smoke. It was a smoking kind of night, eighty miles more, at least, and then back home again.

8

On his second day, Marcos made good time. The boat handled well, given the fact that he was hauling heavy cargo and he was chugging north into chop. Hours ago, he'd come around the barrier islands hours past, and now they were dark worms behind him and the open sea before him remained clear and rippled with stars. He'd been listening to the scanner all night and the Coast Guard appeared to be busy handling a boating accident farther down the coast. *But it wasn't like the Coast Guard only had one boat.* Still, it did his spirits good to think that he was out of danger since he had no misconceptions that if he were caught he would be arrested for human trafficking. He didn't want to think about the implications, so instead, he tried to enjoy piloting the boat.

For most of his life, Marcos had wanted to be a fisherman. Not because he liked to fish but because he liked the water. Years of living near Boston's harbors had ingrained the smell of the sea into his brain and as a child, he often dreamed of sailing around the world or becoming a merchant marine. When Marcos had been contacted by Mr. Bill a little over a year ago, he'd been contemplating quitting his job working with the migrants to join a boat crew that would afford him a regular trip out to sea. When Mr. Bill had found him his life had been very different.

Among the migrant workers and the many migrant camps splotched along the shore, Mr. Bill was one of the most respected and feared figures. The Ugly Mother preached warnings against what she called the giant in small man's clothes. Of course, Marcos knew the Ugly Mother was a kind of gossip, she was a saint as well, at least to her people, and over the years he had grown to love her. The fact that Mr. Bill had reached out to Marcos through the Ugly Mother was altogether something else for the Ugly Mother was known to not associate with any of the farm bosses, Mr. Bill in particular. Marcos had known the old woman from way back, and even though she had been a kind of mentor to him through the years Marcos had always been wary of the old woman because the Ugly Mother's magics were wholly unlike his own. She vomited vegetables and spoke to spirits from other planes, and if the stories were to be believed, animate life from clay, wax, and mud.

The Ugly Mother had sent her daughter, Lilly, to fetch Marcos one afternoon when he'd been inspecting services and supervising standard visa checks at the Hayes camp. Lilly, curt and nervous, had explained to him that her mother had seemed all out of sorts over him, Marcos. "Out of character," is how she'd put it.

A migrant farmhand had found Lilly leaning up against a peach tree after she'd been walking all about camp asking for Marcos in a daze. He'd been the one to fetch Marcos, who then followed Esteban to where Lilly leaned against a peach tree, stunned. Her eyes were glazed over and at first, Marcos had suspected that the Ugly Mother had put her daughter under a spell, a thought that later nagged him at times. At first, he didn't understand what Lilly meant and thought that she was making some kind of complaint against Mr. Bill, the one person Marcos had expected to be named in migrant complaints but had not been named, but as Lilly went on and on she mentioned a time: 12:30 AM, and she mentioned a place: the edge of the cornfield bordering the peach trees right where she had been found. Then, suddenly, there had been an audible snap, like a finger snap, and she had perked up. When she came to, she'd been surprised to see Marcos, her favorite of government employees, there before her. She hadn't remembered a thing about what had happened to her and what she had been doing in the fields, only that her mother, the Ugly Mother, needed to see Marcos.

That evening, Marcos went to where Lilly had been found and waited against the peach tree there, the sky hung with a blood moon. He hadn't been there for more than a minute when Mr. Bill, not the Ugly Mother had stepped out from behind another tree as if he lived there like he had been waiting that whole time for Marcos to arrive, materialized, was more like it.

"I need your help, Marcos." He had said.

"For what?" Marcos had replied.

"Where is the Ugly Mother?"

"She is eating dinner at her daughter's house, a few miles from here."

"It was her whom I was supposed to meet."

"Not so, she agreed to act as my proxy and invite you here."

"Why?"

"I am responsible for seeing a task to its completion."

"A what?"

"I believe that a life may be in danger."

"I'm not sure I understand how I can help?"

"When you meet her you will," Mr. Bill had said, his face dark with shadow. "In two night's time meet me here. I hear that you have good eyesight?"

"I don't need glasses if that's what you mean?"

"Do you own a pair of binoculars?"

"Um, no, never had any need for them."

"Very well. I'm sure there will be no need. The other parties may require them, and I thought if you owned a pair...." Mr. Bill trailed off. He stared at the moon for a long time. "Do not tell anyone of this." He said. "Keep your thoughts from the Ugly Mother, and her daughter, too. "

Then, Bill had vanished before he could think of a response.

9

Two nights later, Bill drove him out towards the Hayes home. And when Marcos asked about their destination and what it had to do with Mulch Hayes, Mr. Bill had explained they were going to a creek.

"Have you ever been out here before?" Bill asked.

"Once, I was just thinking about it. Drove to one of your boss' camps to interview your Brazilian migrants."

"Brazilian?"

"Yes, there are not too many, but a few. Poor farmers mostly, who fled to the US to escape debt and the coup. Brazil is a country with many financial problems."

"And how did the worker's interview?" Mr. Bill asked as he kept his eyes on the road ahead.

"Very well. They all said that they were happy."

"Happy workers make happy production."

"Mr. Hayes seems to be a fair boss."

"Fair? I don't know about fairness. He understands that happy workers are more productive. How long have you known the one they call the Ugly Mother?"

"For some time. We met many years ago when I was a young man, before my first big government job. She found me, you might say."

Mr. Bill was quiet for the rest of the ride and Marcos stared into the moon glittery fields, the rows of young plants catching the light and reflecting the moon. Far to one side, Marcos caught a glimpse of houselights, honeycombed in a grove of trees. Mr. Bill pulled to the side of the dirt road.

"We're going to park here and walk."

Marcos nodded. Bill was a shadow as he started for the thicket.

"From here on, do not speak. I will speak first if there is to be any talking. Sea Hag are you there?"

"I hear you. You don't have to tell me twice."

A woman suddenly stepped out from behind a tree. She too was like a shadow and Marcos had to squint to make her out.

"Hello," he whispered, afraid that she could not see his nod.

"Call me Sea Hag."

"Okay, then. My name is Marcos."

"Pleasure to meet ya," she said shaking his hand vigorously. "Now, not a word more."

Sea Hag walked slowly behind him, and Marcos heard her step lightly, lifting each foot silently before carefully placing it down in front of her. Mr. Bill was way ahead of them and made no noise. Every step Marcos took sounded like a cow making its way down to a river. It seemed to take forever for Marcos to reach where Bill was stopped and squatting. Below him was the saltwater creek that ran behind the Hayes house and into the Atlantic. Marcos estimated that they were maybe ten feet above the waterline, maybe more, the bank dropping sharply to the marsh below. Marcos had been on many of the creeks before and knew that they behaved like mini bays accustomed to swells of the tide moon and could be very temperamental during hurricane season. Sea Hag reached the two of them and sighed, wiping her brow. The treeline was thinner here, and Marcos could see Sea Hag better now for the moon, which looked like a half of a button sliding out of a buttonhole and cast them in murky, muddy light. She was an old woman whose hair was wild and spiky and unwashed. She smiled at him and nodded toward the creek. Marcos turned to look down at the creek and saw nothing and then turned to Bill who was also scanning the area below them. Along the creekbed, stretched mossy trees and undergrowth, tangled, thick, and black. Marcos looked again to Sea Hag who kept looking out towards the creek, searching for something. Mr. Bill then poked Marcos in the knee and pointed out into the water. Marcos nodded and stared as hard as he could. *What was he looking for? A boat?* As if he could read his mind, Mr. Bill pointed again down into the center of the creek, directly in front of them.

Marcos was sure he was seeing things. There below them was a big fish, the large whale-like back fin protruding out of the water and gracefully disappearing back underneath the glimmering surface. From the looks of it, the fin would have to belong to a swordfish, or a marlin – something large and unusual for the shore. Then he saw the girl. She was being attacked by the fish. It was a big fish. Sea Hag and Mr. Bill saw this too but they were calm and quiet. Marcos imagined the girl being torn in two, swallowed like Jonah, eaten whole. He looked again to Bill and Sea Hag. They were not afraid. Then Marcos saw why. The girl was the fish, she was a mermaid.

She sliced the water and jumped high into the air and back down again and doubled back on herself so quickly that Marcos was sure she had spotted them watching her. This was surely some kind of hallucination. Still, a nagging voice in the back of his head, one that sounded a lot like the Ugly Mother, told him that he'd just witnessed something special, something important. The mermaid began to swim towards them. Her speed alarmed Marcos and he instinctively stepped back. Mr. Bill slowly stood up and turned to Marcos. He whispered, "walk back, slowly," before stepping back into the woods himself, disappearing into shadow.

With the three of them, Sea Hag lead the way back. Marcos was in the middle and found it hard to concentrate on the walking, his mind filled with the sound of gurgling water and a curious cry that reminded him of dolphin, or porpoise squeak. Once they were near the truck, Marcos felt comfortable speaking. "That was amazing!" he breathed rapidly having trouble spitting his words out. "She's magnificent!" Marcos moved his arms excitedly. "Who is she, where did she come from?"

"That, Marcos, is Mulch's oldest daughter," Mr. Bill said as he struck a match and lit his pipe.

"What!?" Marcos stepped closer to Mr. Bill, his pipe flickering like a jack-o-lantern. "How can that be possible?"

"Not for you to know," Mr. Bill said curtly before he looked to Sea Hag. "Are you okay?"

"My head is ringing with the oddest noise. It sounds like squeaking, like mice and river water."

"Yes, me too," Marcos said speaking quickly now. "Except it sounded like dolphins to me. "

"It's something I taught her," Mr. Bill's smoke smelled illegal and sweet.

"A spell?" Sea Hag asked.

"A trick. It disorients those who might see her. Mulch only allows her to swim at night. Though, she swims when she wants to. Still, Marina is somewhat innocent. It's dangerous though, for someone might see her."

"Yes, I can see that is not good," Marcos said, his head feeling like a glass goblet humming with wine.

"Now I've got one hell of a headache, sweetie," Sea Hag said as she rubbed her temples.

"In normal people, the trick would cause nausea, sea-sickness, and temporary memory loss."

"Did she know we were there?" Marcos asked.

They all instinctively stepped closer together, forming a tight circle.

"No. I believe that she did not."

"But Bill, didn't she swim straight toward us?" Sea Hag asked. The ringing seemed to be affecting her more, for she still rubbed her temples.

"I believe she sensed our presence. She has many strange abilities, many of which are surfacing now that she is entering adulthood. Unfortunately, her father knows very little about her mother, and her mother's abilities, so I cannot assess how powerful she will be. I do know from spending much time with her that she is much more powerful when she is in the water."

"That would make sense," Marcos nodded.

"She is a half-breed and rules do not apply to her. She is somewhat of a mixed bag."

"How can we help her?" Sea Hag asked, her breath smelling of brine.

"She needs to be returned to the waters of the Canary Islands, off the coast of Spain and the African continent. That was where Mulch met her mother. "

"Wow. That is all I can say. Wow." Marcos said remembering when he first discovered he could make small objects fly to his hands.

"Yes, she is a miracle. Like you both are, in so many ways," Bill said. "Mulch is concerned that she will wish to mate with a human."

Sea Hag and Marcos blinked in unison.

"But she's half-fish," Sea Hag coughed.

"She can transform and be a full woman when she wishes. A rather pretty one too, I'm afraid."

"What's wrong about her mating with a human?"

"Looking to step up to bat?" Sea Hag teased Marcos.

"No," he replied.

"Marcos, I do not know what is wrong with that. Her father thinks it best she joins her kind if there are any."

"What do you mean if there are any?"

"Mulch has only ever seen one other mermaid," Mr. Bill explained.

"Her mother?" Marcos and the Sea Hag said in unison.

"Yes," Mr. Bill said as he spat into the dirt.

"Is she in danger?" Marcos said.

"Let's first go to the Fritter Shop. We can talk there more comfortably," Bill said.

"I'll make us some snacks." Sea Hag added as they loaded up and followed Sea Hag into Oysterhaus.

The Fritter Shop looked like a dark cocoon and smelled of fried grease and cigarette smoke. Mr. Bill re-lit his pipe and sat on one of the little stools as Sea Hag turned the fryers on. They talked all night, or at least Sea Hag and Marcos did. Mr. Bill listened to them as they talked about ways of transporting the mermaid back to her home waters. Mr. Bill offered up the idea of the box sometime around three in the morning. He had said that it was Mulch who had the idea, but Mulch wasn't sure it would work unless he had some magical help. The box sounded cruel at first, but Mr. Bill explained it would make it easier for Marina to travel.

And now Marcos was towing the damn thing.

The ocean wind cooled him and his mouth smacked with salt. The taste reminded him of the time he had first seen Marina, and it reminded him of a time when he had first kissed a girl, Sheila Davis, whose lips had the same salty wonderfulness to them that always snapped his mind to the sea. She had been a good kisser too, probably still was.

"You're probably a good kisser too, eh Marina?" He shouted back into the wind.

He had only spent a few afternoons and evenings with her. When they'd met it had been with conspiracy, always at night, and always in the same concealed part of the creek. Marina had given off a greenish glow and had seemed so innocent to him. On land, she'd carried herself awkwardly. In the water, her moves were confident, directed.

The first time Marcos witnessed Marina's transformation, he'd nearly fainted. It was also three in the morning and Marina had been swimming and talking to them all evening. Marcos had asked her what it felt like to walk and if it felt different to her from swimming. Marina had then swum over to the bank and pushed her fins up so that he could see them.

"You tell me?" She'd flirted, her voice high and reedy.

"Does it hurt?" Marcos had said, enunciating each word to concentrate on the question since every time he was close around Marina he had to work not to stare at her always erect nipples. In the water, her skin was the color of green phosphorescent light, and she made the water shine around her body. Marcos found the glow very soothing, and his heart swelled when he thought about it.

"I can't imagine that transformation feels good. Does it?" He had wanted to see her change.

"It hurts like a headache might, or a hangnail. You can't place where it hurts, you only know that it hurts. Still, the pressure feels good. Pressure always feels good." Marina had smiled and flipped her fin up at Marcos' nose. "I'll show you if you like?" Marina had giggled and turned over in the water.

Marcos' heart had paced ahead of his thinking and a warm sensation grew in his loins and chest.

"Yes. That would be delightful." Marcos had gulped.

"Ready?"

Marcos had nodded furiously. Then there had been the sound like that of a fresh zipper ripping down. Her skin had shimmered and gave off an enormous amount of heat, which floated up in the air and onto his face. He had broken out in a sweat instantly. In the water she had appeared to shiver, her skin rippling like a water wake and as it did her scales had shifted, folding down to form skin. Her fin had torn in half to form two legs, all the while Marina had winced but did not cry out. Then it was over. It had taken just seconds while all the while his head rang and filled with air so that he had to close his eyes for a moment.

"There. All better," she had said when it was all over. water rushing down her naked body as she had stepped out on land to stand next to him.

Seeing all this, Marcos had gulped and averted his eyes. Marina was never shy about her being naked.

"Did you see it?" Marina had asked with a giggle. Marina then waded back into the water again. There had been the rip of flesh and Marina had transformed back into a mermaid.

"There, did that satisfy your curiosity?" she had asked with a wink.

"Uh. Um. Yes." Marcos had said to his shoes.

He had had trouble looking her in the eyes the next time they met.

10

Marcos had hoped that he and Marina could visit and pass the time together as they traveled the water, but behind him, the box coasted through the water, his passenger silent. He had envisioned them speaking, having long conversations, since when he signed on to pilot the boat he hadn't realized she would be drugged for most of the journey. So far Marina had not whimpered, cried out, or spoken aloud – nothing. Marcos was beginning to think he was transporting a giant coffin and not a treasure box. That afternoon, as he napped, he had dreamed that the box was gift-wrapped and that a cackling old lady in white awaited the package, her long nails clicking together, eager to rip the wrapping to shreds.

11

Richmond isn't a very big city, but it's taller than Virginia Beach and its skyline looked to Huck like a jagged line of Christmas lights. Huck had always loved Richmond. He had only been there a few times in his life. His parents had tried to raise him right, and what was it that he was doing now? *Kidnapping? Accessory in a rape? Possibly murder? I'm getting too old for this shit.* Killing people on the shore was one thing, doing it away from home seemed outright dangerous.

Better do what you are told so you don't end up like the others, he thought. Word around the campfire was Mulch had been pissed at his regular dealers. Most of them were dead. It gave Huck crawling anxiety. Buck didn't seem to care.

Virginia had not moved since Buck had last struck her across the nose. Buck was having trouble finding her pulse. But it was there, fluttering against her skin like a weak bird. Buck had wanted to have at her again before they gave up on her. Huck wasn't having any of it.

"Who the fuck is getting this meat anyway?"

"Some guy. Pembroke."

"Weird name, bubba."

"He's foreign. Mulch has talked about him before. He's German or something."

"Mulch is a weirdo fuck. That whole family is a bunch of weirdo fucks."

"So?"

"Ain't right."

"Ain't right, what you've been doing to her yourself," Huck said, his voice wavering slightly.

"Ain't nothing you ain't never done yourself. Or do I need to remind you?"

"No, you don't."

"Well then shut up."

"You just don't have to be so cruel about it."

"Just shuddup and exit, will ya?"

12

The van circled the block twice and Huck squinted through the murky sepia of the streetlights that diffused through the oaks, poplars, and sweet gums that were slowly rendering hell with the sidewalks pushing up through the concrete. It was driving around Richmond late in the PM that reminded Huck what he liked the most about cities.

He liked the lights.

When he was young, Huck thought city lights looked like fireflies caught in jars. That's all they were, little jars of lightning bugs. There was no electricity, there was no city, only hundreds of jars. Dawn was like someone had let the tops off. Huck never fancied himself an imaginative person, but the city turned an invisible key inside him, and the shutters fell away.

From behind him, Buck snorted. He chomped on a cigar and poked a finger into Virginia's sides.

"Wonder what she did?" Buck sounded sad, somewhat remorseful even.

"You just thinking that now?"

"Yes."

"Fancy that." Huck never cared too much about sex. But Buck seemed to pop every time he got near a girl. "You ever had a steady girlfriend?" Huck asked steeling his eyes at his friend in the rearview; he hoped he looked mean. "You ever had a girlfriend, period?"

Buck didn't answer. He just snorted and spat a loogie into Virginia's hair. "Mulch done knows what I was going to do to her. She must have done something awful to piss him off like that." Buck enjoyed his cruel streak; Huck swore it ran down his back like a skunk's stripe. "We on the right street?" Buck asked as he gripped a tuft of Virginia's hair in his fist.

"Yeah," Huck replied as he scanned his eyes back and forth, searching for potential witnesses.

"Then why can't you find the right damn number?"

Then Huck saw it, the small numbers were hard to see in the light, he pumped the brakes. "We're here," Huck said, "You'd better hope this fella wasn't expecting her to walk in for him."

"With her hogtied like this, there's no way."

Huck continued to wonder what she had done, what Mulch had to be feeling to kidnap his flesh and blood. *The Hayes' always ran a little too high in the blood pressure, that was a fact,* he thought.

It appeared that their arrival had alerted no one. Huck pulled to a stop and the men got out. As Huck stepped up to the house to knock, the door immediately opened and Huck drew backward, pulling from his belt a long folding blade. Buck braced himself and stepped back off the stoop and against the van. For a second Huck expected a monster with a thousand eyes, not the tall thin man before them.

"Gentlemen." The man's voice was curdled, like sour milk. He wore a topcoat and a monocle and looked absolutely out of place in the heat and humidity. The heavy clothes looked like padding to Huck as he stepped up to greet the man.

"You Pembroke?" Huck asked.

"Yes. And you are Huck and Buck Winston, no relation."

Huck guessed that Pembroke was at least seven feet if he was six. Buck snickered and spat on the sidewalk.

"Cover her with this blanket before you haul her in." Pembroke tossed the blanket to Huck, who swore that there hadn't been a blanket there before. Perhaps behind him, or perhaps hidden under the topcoat, but certainly not in his hand.

Huck threw the blanket to Buck who gave Pembroke a hard glance before opening the back doors. Wrapping her was easy and they simply carried her like a piece of meat up the stairs and inside.

The inside of the house was drafty and cool, and it became evident why Pembroke wore such heavy clothes in the summer. The windows were glazed with condensation, which looked suspiciously like frost. The ceilings were tall and high and above them swirled a heavy white mist.

"Great AC," Huck whispered as they followed Pembroke up a flight of marbled stairs in the downstairs foyer. "Why hasn't anyone furnished this place yet?"

"No concern of yours, Mr. Winston."

"Is that fog? Looks like fog to me." Buck said as he and Huck bumped and bounced Virginia against the marble. Pembroke didn't notice or didn't care.

Huck made furtive glances towards the mist as they walked higher towards the next floor. It spooked him how it swirled and hovered. Huck couldn't hear any air-conditioning and wondered how air circulated. Buck, however, reached out his finger to touch the fog floating about three feet off the floor.

"I wouldn't," Pembroke said, his voice cold and sharp.

But Buck's finger was already within the mist and when he jerked his finger back it was black at the tip. It burned cold and hot at the same time.

"I'm afraid you'll lose that tip. Pity." Pembroke said ironically.

Wincing, Buck pressed his finger to his clothes.

The second floor was colder than the first, and the marble floors were covered with a thin layer of frost. There were several doors, each of them closed, a key inserted in each of the keyholes.

"Take her to the last room on the right," Pembroke ordered and when Buck brushed past him, his fingertip fell off and dropped without a sound onto the floor. There was no blood, only a raw stumpy end was left behind that began to throb.

"Fuck." Buck winced. "Goddamn fog took the end of my finger."

Huck's face looked like a mixture of horror and fascination, and as he opened the door to the last room on the right, Huck felt his body twitch with fear. Inside the curtains were drawn, the walls painted a dark gray with black trim. A single candle burned on the bedside table and cast the room in shadows.

"Jeez," Huck said as he looked at the black bed sheets.

Buck dropped his end of Virginia to the floor. Huck let his end go gently and there was a quick whimper and moan and then silence.

"Let's go." Buck winced. He held his finger in his hand, holding it as if that would ease his burning pain.

Pembroke stood at the end of the hallway. The two of them squinted at him, it was hard to see in the infirmed light. The fog on the floor curled about their feet and swooshed about them as they walked. It had been considerably warmer in the bedroom, but not by much, and now both Huck and Buck felt their insides shrinking in on themselves for warmth. Pembroke seemed to float above the hallway floor.

"Let us go downstairs to discuss business."

It seemed darker in the house now, Huck wondered where all the light had gone.

Behind him, Buck had trouble keeping up going down the stairs. His finger throbbed and a fine gauze of cold sweat covered his face.

Pembroke descended the stairs quickly and the mist hardly moved around him. Once he got to the first floor, there was less fog and Huck could see that

Pembroke's feet did not touch the ground. He tried to tell Buck this, but Buck was shaking as he held onto his throbbing finger. He looked feverish and sick.

And all Huck thought about was the strange way Pembroke's face was smooth and dainty, almost porcelain, and how his thin frame and clothes hung on him as they would have on a lab skeleton. Pembroke seemed to have no body, weightless, hovering an inch above the floor as if suspended by invisible wires. *That man is no man*, Huck thought. *God save me from the Hayes family.*

"Thank you for bringing our young charge here," Pembroke said, turning towards Huck and Buck with wide-open arms.

Huck nodded, he wanted to leave, and Buck whimpered behind him. Huck didn't think Buck was paying attention. *The fastest way out is through this man, God help me.*

"The rest of your payment is here in the basement. If you care to follow me." Pembroke gestured behind them to a door under the main staircase in the foyer. "There is a back entrance, and I would prefer that you use that to leave. Lest we continue to arouse the neighbors' suspicions."

Buck eager to leave and go to a hospital, headed straight for the door, whimpering, holding his hand, his mouth a line a woe across his face. Huck followed, his mind scratching at something. *What's happening*, he thought, and then for a second, he felt the cold creep of fear on his spine, like when he was hunting and you are sure you are being followed, hunted, a bear, a panther, a cougar, a coyote, a predator, and as just as Huck's body began to juice itself with adrenaline, all thoughts faded from Huck's mind, and Huck found himself following Buck down the narrow basement stairs. Pembroke flew behind them, his toes scraping the ground as he went.

13

A governor switch had been turned off inside Marina. In front of her swirled a white fog. *Is this the real world?* she thought. Have I been sleeping? She heard the slap of water against wood. *Where am I?*

This is a dream.

There had been a man, a handsome man, somewhere in the fog. The fog was only a few inches deep. It was either very shallow or far away. The perspective gave Marina a headache.

Bill? She tried to call out. *Father!* She tried harder, focusing on the words, but Marina's voice hit her mouth and stopped there. Her voice had weight. Her words were hard and gummy and her tongue discerned shapes of the individual letters – F-A-T-H-E-R – the letters fat and wet, each of them tasting slightly different. The letters then began to swell and grow and push up against the roof of her mouth and down into her throat.

Then suddenly, it was difficult to breathe.

Help! She cried, but her mouth only fattened further, now that the letters H-E-L-P pushed out alongside F-A-T-H-E-R, and B-I-L-L, against the top of her mouth. Her throat tore and ripped. Her head felt like it was going to pop. The leg of an H made its way down her esophagus. Marina's mind flashed danger, her mouth filling with foam.

Panic seized her. She flailed on the bed and tore at her flesh, desperate to escape.

And then the letters were gone.

Marina blinked, she gasped. Before her, the swirl of fog had expanded. It was now at least five feet in diameter and floated in front of her chest. She could see it, the fog, see through it too, a kind of window into another world. *But which world?* Marina felt her strength ebb. In the fog, a boat pulled a large box. On it, a small man moved around the boat, steering it. The box had two slits cut into the sides for ventilation. The box was built to hold something.

You, she thought, *it's for you.*

You have been betrayed.

The fog swirled and for a while Marina watched the fog run circles around the scene. Now and again the cry of a seagull sliced the darkness. There was a new picture, that of a young man lying on a bed in the dark. The young man looked familiar, but the fog swirled around too much, and the angles changed too often for her to tell. She thought for a second that she recognized the room, but she couldn't place it. When the young man opened his eyes, she saw her own eyes staring back at her. There was a popping, rushing noise and then the feeling that she was being sucked away before blackness overtook her again.

14

Mulch stumbled and caught himself. He was drunk, and he felt ornery and mean. He hadn't been mean in a while. He had been too caught up in wrapping things up. Drinking straight from the bottle, he toasted the box, he toasted Bill, he toasted his daughters.

Mulch's taste for booze ran strong and wide and deep, but he often denied himself the taste of it, so when he did indulge, he binged. And when he binged, he grew destructive.

In the secret passage he could access from his room, Mulch had built a shelf to store the overflow of Virginia SD cards. There he kept other secrets, trinkets, trophies, and things to remember. Mulch stared at the shelf while he drank from the bottle. *Mr. Bill is a full-fledged, dyed in the wool shaman-medicine man-priest-wizard*, he thought. *And I have no power. Fuck me.* Mulch had seen Mr. Bill transform into a bear and another time a giant eagle. Bill healed Maria when Eb nearly killed her years ago. Bill made the rains come during a drought. Bill could kill a man just by thinking about it. Mulch tried to focus on the letters written on the SD cards, but couldn't. The shelf held trinkets from his two former wives. There was a vial of sand from the island where he met Marina's mother. Another vial held a single tooth; a reminder that Virginia's mother talked too much. One of Mulch's favorite recordings was of Virginia laying propped up against the vial of sand. In it, Virginia performed alone slowly undressing and masturbating to orgasm, her eyes closed. Adam then interviews her about her sexual fantasies and fetishes. Adam then ends up making love to her doggie style. Adam asks her a list of questions that Mulch had written down for him on a sheet of butcher paper. Adam reads the questions syllable by syllable, slowly and methodically, and every time he watches it drives Mulch nutszo. *You don't have any power, Mulchie*, he thought. *You have no power at all.*

Mulch managed to focus his vision in the low light long enough to put his fingers on that one SD card. It became a whole other venture to plug it into the laptop, but he managed, returned to his room, and sat at the end of his bed, eager and ornery, wanting to watch it one more time, wanting to hate himself again. He fast-forwarded through Virginia's solo show and onto the interview.

Adam: What was your first sexual experience?

Virginia: Macy. Wait? Yes. Macy.

Adam: Nice!

Virginia: Does kissing count?

Adam: No. We're talking nakedness and body contact.

Virginia: Macy, then. There was booze, a lingerie party, a sleepover.

Adam: What happened?

Virginia: Jesus! Really? We got turned on watching each other dress in sexy underwear. We finger fucked each other, licked our fingers, and kissed each other's hootchie. End of story.

Adam: Describe it. In detail.

Virginia: Forget it. Go stream some porn.

Adam: Look who's talking…

Virginia: What's with the questions anyway?

Adam: How about your worst sexual experience?

Virginia: Don't know about that one.

Virginia slid her finger across her nipple, her other hand slid between her legs.

Adam: What? Come on, tell me.

Virginia: It isn't sexual.

Adam: Then it doesn't count.

Virginia: Shut up.

Adam: Seriously.

Virginia: Do you want to hear it or not?

Adam: Go ahead

Virginia: I once thought my father was watching me sleep. I was sick, I had a fever, and I had this fucked up dream that someone was there on top of me, squeezing the life out of me. I woke up and there he was, standing in the corner like an ax murderer, or something. It was the weirdest thing ever like he just appeared out of nowhere. That was my freshman year of high school. God. For a while, I thought he had molested me or something.

Adam: Did he?

Virginia: No, he did not. Next question.

Adam: What's your deepest darkest sexual fantasy?

Virginia: Jesus! Again, with the …

Adam: What?

Virginia: What is this shit?

Adam: I want to make sure I'm satisfying you.

Virginia: Sure, right.

Adam: No really. Think of it as foreplay.

Virginia: (sighs) I suppose every girl wants to have several hot guys pawing her and serving her every whim.

Adam: How many? Three, four? Twenty?

Virginia: You're such a jerk.

On-screen, they began to move towards each other, each of them probing their bodies, Mulch leaned back excited and hard, waiting for his favorite game to continue.

15

Upstairs, Mulch was laughing hysterically and throwing himself around his room. *He was working on a pretty good one,* Mr. Bill thought. Maybe they'd all get lucky, and he'd drown himself before he did any more damage. And when Mulch's roar dulled down Mr. Bill wondered for a second if Mulch was okay. Then he decided it didn't matter. *The old pervert is probably watching one of his videos or practicing his magic.* Mr. Bill laughed to himself, *if Mulch only had the power his cousins had, then he'd be a bigger problem.*

Earlier that evening Mr. Bill had fixed himself an herbal cocktail, and at the cellular level, Mr. Bill's body had started to replicate itself. His cells were splitting off and moving erratically to one side of his body, forming at first a kind of ball, then a kind of battering ram that pushed and shoved against him. It hurt. The kind of pain a mother feels when giving birth. The deep tearing pain of new tissue leaving old tissue. Only Mr. Bill was pretty sure this would hurt more than giving birth to a child. A full-sized doppelgänger was forming inside of him and when it tore free it would take him to new heights of pain. Part of him wanted to see what it was going to be like to give birth. The other part of him wanted to be drunk like Mulch when it happened. The knot had appeared about half an hour prior.

It looked like a bulb or a doorknob and it hurt. Eventually, it began to tear out of his side, right above his hip. How the cells knew what to do, Bill was not sure. The skin around the knot gave way and bled slightly, but only like a minor cut. The knob was like a tumor growing at a rapid pace out of his side and it was the color of blood. The thing then began to take on an oblong shape. It made a crackling and sucking sound as it pulled away from Mr. Bill. Blood, tissue, bone grew inside this oblong bloody thing. Soon it would sprout legs. The smell of the fresh tissue made Mr. Bill's stomach turn.

The legs came first, two nubbins that appeared on the bottom of the fleshy thing, two nubbins that slowly, and as if pulled, reached down to the floor. They were thin legs, scarcely an inch wide, unable to support themselves as it swelled up, six inches wide and three inches thick before Mr. Bill's eyes.

The pain caused Mr. Bill to see spots, and he was pretty sure that underneath all this pain, he would pass out. He didn't think he could carry the burden of such pain but wanted to find out where it would become too much. Because at that point he might be able to have one of his real honest-to-god visions, something that hadn't happened to him since either Marina and Virginia were children.

Then there was a great loud popping crack as the boxy body attached to Mr. Bill's side rippled up and stopped just under the armpit. In a matter of seconds, the thing had grown. Mr. Bill felt the hard muscular tissue attached to his thigh and chest. He felt like he was being gutted. Almost all of Mr. Bill's side was now attached to the thing and his blood flowed freely from where the skin had replicated itself. The blood seemed to serve as a kind of glue between the two figures. Mr. Bill struggled to keep his body erect. The pain made him want to curl up in a ball. He wanted to pass out.

The thing attached to him began to take more of a grotesque humanly shape. It was kind of gray. Its legs thickened, and small toes began to protrude from the stumpy ends. Then the stumpy ends took the shape of feet and ten small moons of nails appeared. One arm nubbin popped out of the far side and immediately started flailing about in spastic circles.

The creation of the head finally did cause Mr. Bill to pass out, and even if he was able to witness the formation of the skull he would have been reviled at its identical features, but he fainted as the skull popped and stretched out of Mr. Bill's underarm, bloody and white. The large round softball of tissue ripped out from under his arm. The bone shone through the thin skin, and the tiny eyes and mouth were fleshy, tenuous meat behind a sticky bloody pink film. The small head lolled back and forth, unable to support its weight.

Mr. Bill's body, curled up into a ball, the doppelgänger's head beginning to balloon in full, taking the shape of an adult-sized head. The final arm was the last bit of the body attached to Mr. Bill. It lacked thickness, hair, and definition. But the other body was stronger now, drawing strength from its host. The doppelgänger placed its feet on Mr. Bill's leg, and using them as a brace, it propped its one arm against Mr. Bill's side. Then it pulled the final arm out of Mr. Bill's body, right out under his socket, like a sword from a scabbard. Mr. Bill's body sealed back shut with a wet plop.

Then the doppelgänger began to scream and howl, a high-pitched yelp. The skin over the body was stumpy and hairy and began to stretch, expanding as bones popped and the new entity cried out in pain as it breathed its first breath. It flopped and flailed its thin wiry body before collapsing on the floor with a wet sticky thwack.

16

Someone had snuck up on Nick and split his head open with a rock. There was no other way he could be in so much pain. He kept checking his skull to make sure there wasn't any blood flowing. His house was hot and stale, his mind cloudy with the images of his nightmare dream. He needed to get some air. Then Nick noticed a funny thing. The windows of his house had disappeared. He crawled from his living room to the hallway, struggling to keep himself upright as he moved to his bedroom. The windows had disappeared there, too. His bed looked soupy, like it had melted, the painting on the wall no longer glowing. His head throbbed. Nick felt like someone was trying to break into his skull. In a half-trance, Nick nearly fell down the stairs and found that the windows downstairs had also disappeared. *That's the most fucked up thing,* he thought. *My windows...*As he stumbled about the house took on the look of something out of the old Twilight Zone television show, everything dusty and in shades of gray, his vision skewed and warped by headache and heat. He struggled to move his feet, they kept slipping under his weight. When he looked down, he saw why. His feet had transformed into flippers.

Nick fainted dead in the hallway.

17

Marina awoke with a start, the water lapping against the outside of her box. The sound soothed her. She'd been hearing it in her sleep. Her head hurt, but the sound of the water soothed her. *How long had she been out?* She wasn't sure, but she felt like she hadn't eaten anything for days. She raised her body up and forward, trying to discern where she was. Soaked sheets outlined her body in sweat.

"Hello?"

Her voice, weakened by disuse, echoed in her chest. She felt far away from herself.

The water was close. There was the distant sound of a motor.

"Hello?"

Marina didn't want to get up off the bed. The bed was incredibly comfortable. All she saw was a glow above her. *It's the blackness behind her eyes,* she thought. When she blinked her eyes, the glow did not dissipate, it grew crisper the longer she stared up at it.

Looking closely, it appeared to be stars, hundreds of small stars shining down on her. Yet, they were unlike the white pricks of light she stared up to from the creek. These stars were yellow. Yellow pricks of light illuminated the room, which allowed her eyes to adjust. Marina stared at the stars, before daring to stand up on the bed and try to touch them. When she stood the bed wobbled beneath her and Marina steeled her knees so she wouldn't fall. Above her, the ceiling glowed and though she couldn't touch it, she could tell it had texture, that the ceiling was no accident, that someone had made it and its glow made Marina long to swim out into her creek and gaze upward at real stars.

Unlikely that's going to happen any time soon. She dropped back down to the bed and sighed. Her body ached. Outside she could make out the sky and the sound of a motor.

"Hello!" she shouted. Marina heard her heartbeat as she waited for an answer. "Hello?"

She finally stepped off the bed and onto the floor. The vibrations of the moving water reverberated through the floor and into her legs and Marina understood that she was being pulled by a large boat. *Where is Mulch? Where is Mr. Bill? Where is Maria?* Her heart hammered in her chest and for the first time in her life, she felt fear. Her mind was fuzzy and cloudy, and Marina could not remember the last time she had even spoken to her father or Mr. Bill. It seemed like it was ages ago.

When she noticed the water bottles on the floor her heart leaped up, her body ached for it. Standing was a problem, for her legs gave out on her almost immediately and she felt swoon. She eventually crawled across the floor to them, taking her time. She had never felt so awful in her entire life.

18

Mr. Bill awoke. The doppelgänger lay still, collapsed on the floor. Mr. Bill's head hurt and his side felt like it had been torn open and glued back up. His eyesight was blurry, and he thought for a moment something had gone wrong and he had bloodied up an eye, but then he removed the bloody gak stuck over his face. It was vaguely skin-like and stuck to his fingers. It felt like mucous. He had trouble standing and did so only with the help of the worktable. The doppelgänger lay crumpled in a heap at his feet. He kicked it and it groaned. That was a good sign.

He turned the doppelgänger over. It looked just like him. Its hair was still growing in and as Mr. Bill examined the body, he saw the hair on the eyebrows pop out one by one. It was like watching someone paint your portrait. The skin color blushed and cooled itself into a light brown and wrinkles appeared below the eyes.

Satisfied with his magic, Mr. Bill gathered his bag. He left clothes out for the doppelgänger. The doppelgänger would know what to do, it would assume his role, it would take his place. He hoped there would be no complications but decided it didn't matter if there were any. The only thing that mattered was that he find Marina and find her before Cilia could get her hands on her. To do this he needed to put a lot of miles between him and Mulch by morning.

Slipping up the stairs, Mr. Bill eased his backpack on his shoulder, he listened for the sounds of Mulch, for Maria. When he heard nothing, he exited the house.

INTERLUDE

"Careful examinations of the indigenous remains found on the Eastern Shore show an evolutionary leap, in terms of bone structure and mass. Either that or a throwback to pre-history. Simply put, the native Americans who lived on the lower shore did not fit the norm."

—Dr. Carol Henderson,
Smithsonian Institute, in a lecture to the
Eastern Shore Historical Society, 6/7/99

1

JUNE 16

A noise woke Maria early – a thump. She lived at the top of the Hayes house, on the third floor, in a small wing that was completely her own. When Virginia was at school, no one lived on the second floor, but two nice-sized guest rooms were never used, plus a separate sitting room. In the old days, Ruth Hayes spent most of her time reading in the sitting room, when she was lucid. Now hardly anyone even went into the room anymore, except Maria, and only then to clean it. Mulch lived on the first floor and Mr. Bill and Marina both lived in the basement. Maria liked being on top. It made her feel in control of a house that had never been controllable her entire adult life, at least not by her. Things weren't as topsy-turvy as they once had been. As she mellowed into her early sixties, Maria was glad that things were slowing down.

Then Virginia and Marina disappeared.

She assumed Virginia was off somewhere and had neglected to tell anyone of her whereabouts, which would not have been out of character. Marina, she assumed, had probably gone out into the ocean. Mulch had told her long ago that that's what she would do when she was older. Still, her instincts told her that something was off.

Virginia would not leave so suddenly. Not in the summer with Macy around. Nor Adam. Maybe Virginia was at the sunroom door? Maybe?

She could ask Mulch where he thought Virginia was, however, Mulch wasn't speaking to her again. When just last week he was so friendly and flirtatious. She thought about asking Mr. Bill about the girls, but lately, he'd become something of an idiot, pretending not to know anything. Just the other day she had to scold him for dumping all the cereal onto the kitchen floor and rolling around in it like it was snow or cash. And he wasn't talking right. *Maybe he'd had a stroke and nobody noticed.*

Which was why she thought the thump had come from Mr. Bill. That he'd finally gone and become old and fallen over like a rotten tree. Then she thought, more hopefully, that it was coming from one of the girls who were just now returning.

When she heard the thump for the third time, she knew she was going to have to go see what was going on. She didn't once think the thumping could be coming from an intruder, because no one in their right mind would break into the Hayes house.

Maria was nearly back to sleep herself when the thump came again for the fourth time. This time it sounded like it came from the outside. *Was someone knocking on the door?* It didn't sound like someone was knocking on the door, it sounded like someone knocking their head against the exterior wall.

2 JUNE 14

Macy Allbright had been Virginia Hayes' best friend for nearly two decades. They had grown up together through middle and high school and managed to graduate with their friendship intact. Both of Macy's folks came from railroad money and were both lawyers even though neither of them needed to work. The Allbrights owned a large plantation house on the outskirts of Eastville, going south, as well as a nice house in the bluffs, right on the old Chesapeake Bay, which was a great place for teenage sun-worshipers like Virginia and Macy. Virginia and Macy would spend weekends at each other's houses, fussing over hair and make-up and scribbling the names of the cutest boys they knew in their notebooks. When they grew older they'd spend the weekend partying with the gang, just grass, and wine coolers at first and then graduating to psychedelics and coke; well just a little coke, at first.

Since the girls had gone to different colleges, Virginia to Boston University and Macy to William & Mary, they had become sort of unglued as friends. For a while, they were just summer break friends. Not even Christmas break, or spring break friends, since both of them, were too busy skiing or visiting newer (and somehow closer) friends from college. Virginia spent Christmas with Amanda Blackstone in Connecticut because Amanda had her apartment above her dad's garage and whoever came to visit could spend the break skiing in Vermont which was only a few hours away. And who wouldn't want to spend Christmas in New England? The junipers and spruces were all shagged with ice, and the sound of nothing and the nothing that is, snow coming down like TV static. And even though Virginia and Amanda didn't speak anymore, social media aside, Virginia felt closer to Amanda because Amanda knew her better, or at least she knew the newer Virginia better.

Macy had her own set of college buddies, sorority friends like Nikki Fox and Nicki Gavin (the Nucks they were called, and not because they were

Canadian, which they weren't) whom Macy would go and visit in Denver and LA, respectfully. Macy got to ski on real mountains, she'd tell Virginia through Snapchat, not like the little ones in Vermont. Colorado had real mountains and big ski lodges and hunky foreign guys with trim bodies and big cocks with lots of money that liked to party with American girls. Nicki had even promised to share an apartment with Macy in Hollywood if she'd just move out there and take a risk to become an actress, or model, or whatever.

But Macy didn't feel inspired to move to LA. To tell the truth Macy didn't feel inspired to do much of anything. When the girls graduated college, Macy spent the summer sunning it up on the coast in the south of France and although Virginia was backpacking through Europe as well, she gave the sunny south of France a wide berth. When they moved back home last summer they fell back into sync, not because they were friends, but because they felt thrown together by somewhat similar experiences and somewhat similar backgrounds, especially when compared to everyone else who had stayed back and *not* gone to college.

Like many young people who go to Europe, or travel a lot, they find that upon returning, their home was just too small for them. *Why look out on Nassawaddox Creek when you can look out on the Seine, or the Thames, or the Colorado River, or even the Charles River? Why eat American cheese when you could eat goat cheese, or Feta, or Gouda? Why would you want to sit on the crappy beach at Kiptopeake State Park when you could sun on the vast beaches of Cannes?*

Macy's mother thought the girls had become snobby (that they were already snobby never occurred to her) because they mooned about Europe and how happy they had been when they were there and living the "good life," though Macy gave Virginia tons of shit about backpacking across Europe like a hobo, with her nappy-headed hippie boyfriend.

Macy had heard at a party that Adam Taylor, who had a cute butt and drove a nice truck which was preemo in their social circle, had a crush on Virginia, and at first, Virginia had not been interested, but after a while when the glamour of Europe had worn off, Adam Taylor began to look a bit brighter to both Macy and Virginia.

Adam mostly hung out with Rick "the Dick" Bell, Tommy Pusey, Zach "the Widge" Widgeon, Micah Watterson, and Nick Genovesi, guys they had gone to school with. And for a while, things were like they had been in high school. Macy and Virginia would spend the night at each other's house like they were teenagers again. Other times Macy and Virginia would go out and party all night with the boys and sleep in all day. And soon, just like high school they were borrowing each other's clothes and dreaming of finding a way to live together on the beaches in Cannes forever. Neither of them worked, not really. And a gap year between college and work became two.

And then Virginia stopped hanging out with Macy so much. She and Adam were clocking serious hours in bed and Macy didn't have a regular boyfriend and found herself wanting one. For the first time, Macy found herself all alone.

This is where Macy started to do a lot of things without Virginia. For one, she started acting again in a tiny community theater group. It wasn't William & Mary, and it wasn't New York or LA, but she felt at home and enjoyed working with the cast and crew. She played three minor characters before Mulch murdered her. She was the maid in a stuffy thriller entitled, *The Deadliest Game*, an air-headed spouse in *Look Ma, I Married a Revolutionary* and a nun in the farce *Praise be to God and Here's to Hoping I Get a Raise*.

The acting helped Macy realize that she wasn't the greatest actress, and she'd long ago given up on her dreams to be a movie star. Macy had also long ago given up on Virginia, which was the saddest thing of all. Macy thought Virginia was adrift in a sea all on her own, while Macy was left behind, on the beach. This is natural if you measure the way post-high school high school friendships peter out.

Macy had also tried to go to church. She knew that something was missing from her life and since she had found herself back on the shore, she tried Johnson Town Methodist (you can't throw a rock on the Shore without hitting a Methodist) and though she liked to sing the hymns, she never really bought into the fact that somebody had died for her sins, even if that man was white (and she had a nagging suspicion that anyone from Galilee would be something other than white). And it depressed her that she couldn't believe in God and the Father and Holy Ghost. Her parents didn't and they had done just fine. Plus, Macy felt guilty going to church. The friendly atmosphere gave her the creeps, because she felt phony, and she felt like everyone knew she was phony but were doing their best to ignore the phoniness. Which made Macy feel even phonier, with the congregation leaping and bounding to make her feel other than phony so that she feels welcome. Which was when Macy quit going to church. It had made her head hurt, and besides, nobody had any fashion sense there. It was all long dresses and shawls which distracted her during the services to no end. Plus it made her feel guilty over being so fashion conscious and thus phony.

The spring before Mulch killed Macy Allbright, she and Virginia had sat down and discussed death, the afterlife, and their future. They had been hitting the vape hard, and the two of them had serious doubts that either of them was being productive in the adult sense. Macy felt her future was black because she couldn't imagine herself doing anything ever.

"Nothing?" Virginia had seemed surprised by this.

"Zippo, babe. Zilch."

"But don't you have like any ambitions, Mace?" Virginia had felt unusually close to Macy that day, she never thought why, not until later, that Macy had been trying to tell her something.

"None. Like I said my future is one big black zero."

"What about us and France?"

"I've been thinking of going back there every year. We've been here for what, two years now and that's all I think about."

"Almost 18 months."

"I mean, think about it, all the people you knew in college have gone off to become doctors and lawyers and businessmen. They are on their way! We're just short of twenty-five and don't even have a part-time job."

"Well...no one is successful from our class. I mean shit. Not unless they are working for their family."

"Neither of us even works for our family, for Christ's sake."

"I don't ever want to work for Mulch."

"I mean, don't you see wedding bells in your future? I like Adam. Don't you think you should be working towards some sort of goal?"

"With Adam?"

"Don't you, Virginia?"

"I like him, too. But I guess I don't fully trust him. I'm certainly not ready to marry him."

And then Macy brought up God and death, which depressed Virginia so much that they started drinking. All that afternoon Macy bounced from one topic to another, dragging Virginia down the length of her mind. And after Virginia had gone off to meet Adam, whom Virginia was sure was sleeping with somebody on the side, Macy thought about Virginia's family and how certifiably weird they were.

As far as anyone knew Virginia didn't have a mother. No one knew what had happened to her. Some weirdo Native American guy lived in her basement with her supremely gorgeous sister who did nothing but swim in the creek. *Like I'm supposed to think that nothing was going on. Please.* They had a maid, Maria, whom Macy liked quite a bit. She had always been kind to the girls, and she was a good maid. A superb cook, to boot. *But what the hell was going on with that family?* Marina, Virginia's "slow" sister, had a different mother than Virginia.

And people said she had disappeared, too. Plus, there was all the talk about Mr. Bill. Then when Adam disappeared Macy didn't think too much of it. Maybe he had gone off somewhere. Got tired of Virginia and split. But when Virginia went AWOL, Macy began to think that her disappearance had to be related to Adam's.

Macy thought she'd get some answers on her own. First, she called the feed store and asked if Virginia was working there. Nope, they said. Virginia hadn't stepped foot in the store in years. Then Macy called Maria. Maria said Virginia had left in the middle of the night, from what she could tell. She had been out visiting with her cousin Estrella, and when she came home, Virginia was gone. A very funny thing though, Virginia hadn't packed any clothes before she left, everything was still there in her room, *like all the stuff she'd take with her.*

Maria went on to say Virginia hadn't taken anything with her, as far as Maria could tell, but Macy could come over and look around if she wanted. Mulch was out somewhere, taking care of business. If she wanted, she could stay for dinner and ask Mulch. Sure, Macy had said. Be right over.

Macy never knew she was in any danger. She had no idea that she was galloping to her death. Before heading over, she had left a scrawled note for her parents. In it, she didn't specify where she was going, only that she was checking out leads on Virginia's whereabouts. She didn't know about staying for dinner, but she did know that she had to ask Mulch a thing or two.

When she got to the Hayes house Macy was struck with the idea that the house was haunted. This was because she felt like she was being watched. *Sure it's my imagination,* she told herself but kept her fingers crossed for luck when she went into Virginia's room, positive that she'd see Virginia's ghost lurking about the cabinets and closets.

"Jesus." She whispered to herself.

"Jesus had nothing to do with it, sweetie," Maria said. "Virginia left with nothing. Which is strange to me. But nobody asks me, I'm just the housekeeper." Maria left Macy alone and when she left, Macy's skin went cold, like someone else was in the room, someone inside the walls. Which was crazy talk. And then she remembered times in high school when she thought she heard (knew she heard) something moving behind the wall in Virginia's room when the two of them were there. She knew that things too often went bump in the middle of the night around the Hayes house.

One evening, that spring, she had woken to pee. She had snuck into the hallway and the bathroom, wearing only her panties and T-shirt hoping no one would see, especially Mulch or that creepy old Mr. Bill. While she urinated, she had looked out the window and seen something that made her stomach cramp and her stream of pee stop. There had been a dark figure holding a globe of light. It looked like a disco ball and it cast light about the yard. She should have been able to see it from the hallway when she came in, but she hadn't. The light was bright, too. The figure seemed to turn towards her, and Macy ducked, forgetting she was still on the commode. She twisted her ankle, slightly and as she fell, her fingers raked the shades, and she felt a smattering of urine spray her thighs. She counted to three and when she looked up, the figure was gone. Her flesh had broken out in bumps and the base of her neck was freezing. She had been half-afraid to go back to Virginia's room. But she had too, and it took her another hour before she had finally fallen asleep. When she woke up she convinced herself that she had been dreaming, half-asleep on the toilet. Except for her ankle, which had swelled during the night.

And that wasn't the only time she'd seen or heard something odd. Twice, during high school, she had been startled awake to sounds of soft breathing coming from inside the wall. The first time it had happened, she'd woken Virginia and the two of them had pressed their ears to the wall but had heard nothing. The second time it happened she let Virginia sleep and crawled over to the wall and just listened, without pressing her head to the wall. For a minute the breathing continued, then it had stopped abruptly. She stayed next to the wall for some time until she crawled back into her sleeping bag.

And now looking over Virginia's room, she half expected a globe of light to appear at any moment, or the breathing to begin from inside the wall. But nothing happened, there was only quiet.

"There's nothing here," Macy said aloud.

Like her own room, there was little left of the frivolity of high school. Gone were the girly ribbons hanging on the bedposts, the ballerina slippers that Virginia used to hide her cigarettes in. Gone were the band posters, Kids on Drugs, Wilco, Lorde, Taylor Swift. Virginia's taste always ran the gamut of polished pop to grunge metal. Macy didn't know what Virginia was listening to these days, but it was probably something different.

It occurred to her as she was looking around Virginia's room and feeling sorry for herself, that she didn't have one clue as to what to look for. She dumped Virginia's purse on the bed, half expecting to find a clue, but found only chewing gum wrappers, tampons, and a cigarette lighter. There was a napkin with a phone number on it, but since there was no name, she discarded it along with the wrappers, and trash. Virginia didn't even carry lipstick with her anymore, which made Macy very sad, because as teens they had always promised to wear

Lip by Lights, a cheesy shiny Hollywood type of lipstick that made them look like sluts. Macy didn't wear it anymore, either, but missed the idea of having a special best friend lipstick.

At first, she was shy about going through Virginia's drawers. But when she didn't find anything interesting on top of her dresser, she became more brazen and began rifling through, looking for anything. She found a variety of sexy lingerie, a vibrator, several pot pipes, all of which she'd seen before. She found a few matchbooks with phone numbers, but they were all from Boston, so she ignored them (it didn't occur to her that Virginia might be in Boston). She found a series of photographs of Virginia, taken by Adam, she presumed, because she was half-naked. They weren't half-bad, and she made sure she replaced the more embarrassing objects under her clothing. No sense in having Mulch find her sex toys, that would be humiliating, missing, or no. After an hour, she exhausted the room. Her closet was a veritable desert of clues. There weren't even any good clothes, everything was last year's styles.

People just don't disappear without a trace. Or do they?

She continued looking and after nearly two hours she had three items that she deemed interesting enough to examine further. Virginia hadn't left with her birth control pills, her Valium, or her journal, which she knew for a fact Virginia carried everywhere. The pills were recent, too, dated last week. She wouldn't forget to take them, especially if she had gone somewhere with Adam.

She wasn't so sure about the Valium. Virginia tended to take it only when she was stressed out. She didn't use it daily, but rather week to week. Usually, she had one on Sunday night to mellow out. Thinking nothing of it Macy took two and dry swallowed them both.

The journal was what made Macy worry the most because Virginia went everywhere with it. She was addicted to journaling and had been since she was in high school. She'd taken creative writing in college and was often coming up with stories. She'd even been writing regularly again if Macy remembered right. If she was on the run she would have taken it and her pills, too. But if she had been kidnapped, or murdered, she probably wouldn't have had them on her person. Macy slipped the journal into her bag.

Virginia was in trouble; Macy was sure of it and she was the only one who knew it.

She had to tell somebody, so she told Maria, who promised to pass on the information to Mulch, who was sure to be very happy to know that Macy was out looking for his daughter – very happy indeed.

Driving home she tried to figure out what happened. Her flair for drama bubbled to the surface and she fantasized that Virginia had stumbled onto something she shouldn't have. That she was witness to one of Mulch's many supposed crimes. Perhaps the creepy Mr. Bill had raped her and dumped her body in the marsh. She chided herself for being so morbid, but she didn't believe her friend was alive. As she drove, she wept and wiped her tears across her hand.

She wanted to get drunk, she wanted to forget herself for a while.

3 JUNE 16

That noise.

Maria hurried out of bed and wiped the sleep from her eyes. Maria left the quiet calm of her bedroom and descended the stairs in a hurry. She didn't want to leave Virginia, or Marina waiting outside for too long. Maria had convinced herself that they were the ones outside making that noise, that they had come home, perhaps a little drunk (at least Virginia) and exhausted. She bounded through the second floor and didn't notice the burly whiteness pressing itself against the hallway window and when she opened the door her first thought was: *My God, the world has been swallowed whole.*

All she saw was white. The mist, or fog pressed against the house like jello pressing against the side of a dish; it had body and texture. It was as if it was solid, because of the way it lay against the house. She peered through the screen door and gasped when she noticed it moving, eddies of swirls moved inside larger rivers of flowing white. Above her layers of systems, each of them varying in thickness, length, and speed moved past her. Some of the layers were wispy, whimsical rivers of fog, others were thick and muscular and slow.

"Holy Mother of Father," she whispered as she closed the door.

To which the fog whispered back, "Mulch."

Maria's already goose-bumped skin practically became scaled.

"Mulch," the fog hissed again.

She froze, only moving when her teeth chattered. It was really cold, and it wasn't her imagination, either. Somewhere in the fog, a cat warbled. She stepped back inside the house, stumbling over her own feet.

"What do you want!" she shouted back into the fog.

There was only the cat's warbling.

She closed the door and went around the sunroom. Through the glass all she spied was whiteness. *One can only be hopeful,* she thought. Still, she found herself pressing her face into the glass, looking out into the white mist, watching, hoping for signs of life.

Then she cracked the glass door of the sunroom, just an inch or so. Just to check if the girls were there. *Just an inch. You are not going out there, Maria, not for the world.*

"Hello?" She cried out.

Nothing.

"Virginia? Marina?"

Nothing.

For a second there was only the faint slide of moisture on moisture, which sounded like a wave whispering against the dock when the tide was out. The fog slid through the glass door and over Maria's face; the touch of the fog made her shiver.

Somewhere in the yard cats started to warble again.

Maria jumped and shut the door, which did little to muffle the sounds of the animals. *There must be dozens of stray cats,* she thought. Their warbling sounded like that of wounded animals. *Was rabies making its way around the shore?* She wasn't going to go out there to find out.

Still, Maria peered into the fog, hoping to catch a glimpse of the mewing cats, or whoever it was that had been knocking. But she didn't see anything. *At least the fog isn't talking to you anymore,* she thought. *That'd be a whole lot worse, Maria, because that would mean that you were crazy. Like crazy old Ruth who floated on air. Like Ebenezer Hayes and Mr. Bill. Like...*

Not knowing what she was doing, Maria's hand slid the door open again.

The thought of the girls being out in the fog was what made her open the door. Again, she shouted their names, and again her shouts were sucked into the fog. The more she shouted the more she felt her breath being pulled out of her lungs and into the fog like the fog was hungry like it wanted to devour her. And Maria was sure that she put so much as a foot into the fog she'd be swallowed whole and never heard from again, so she closed the door and waited.

And for two hours her mind chewed and chewed and chewed. She had decided to go outside because as she chopped the onions for her omelet, she had felt stupid for being scared at some dumb old fog that happened to be pressing into the house so hard she heard it slide over the outside walls with an audible hiss.

How can I be afraid of fog, she had thought, and then she had repeated those words out loud, "How could I be afraid of fog?" *After all, wasn't she Mulch Hayes' household manager? His former lover? Keeper of all Hayes secrets from before and after? Hell yes, she was,* she thought. *What do I have to be afraid of? After Eb, Ruth, and Mr. Bill.* She had witnessed spontaneous levitation, the beatings, and had been threatened at knifepoint? How in the world could she be afraid of fog?

Because it spoke Mulch's name, Maria, it spoke! The fog is alive, and it'll eat you up!

Nonsense.

She had waited till her omelet was made, *just so the fog would recede a bit, of course.* There was no need to go out into it when it was still thick and menacing when a smart person would wait till it was less thick and about as menacing as snow.

When she had finished her omelet and her coffee, the fog had not receded one bit, but it had grown thicker if that was possible, and it had grown louder.

The fog shrieked as rivers of it streaked across the windowpanes. Low shrieks and squeals as it slid across the glass, going back into itself and out of itself like a king coil of snakes.

Seeing this Maria had a mind to go fetch Mr. Bill but decided against it when she poked her head into the basement and heard his deep belching snores. No. Mr. Bill had not been acting himself, lately, and bothering him would be no help. Instead, she closed the door to the basement with a click and sat down facing the wall of fog.

"Dammit," She whispered. *This is what happens to women who don't have children,* she thought. *I should have moved back to Mexico and gotten a job at a bank, had some kids.* She had the English. She had the education, thanks to Mulch and the community college. *Why had she stayed?*

For love? That's a laugh. Mulch Hayes, love someone? Use someone, yes. But love? Never.

He had been nice to her, though, nice enough for small talk, but nothing like what she felt owed to her for her dedication and pain and suffering over all those years. *What the hell was he thinking? What was she to him anyway? Maria now is not the time to hold grudges. You have done well here, maybe it is time for a change.* The thumping resumed against the side of her house which made her jump and splash hot coffee on her robe.

"Dammit," she whispered again.

Then there was the scream, it was a young girl's voice lost somewhere in the fog. Someone called out for help. Marina, Virginia, maybe.

"Hold on!" she screamed. She didn't think about what had happened the last time she'd opened the door. She forgot about the voice yelling for Mulch, or the strange shrieking cats. She was only thinking that it might be Virginia and Marina when she yanked open the sliding door and stepped out into the fog.

"VIRGINIA! MARINA!"

"Help."

The cry came deep from one side. Maria tried to run but stopped dead in her tracks, she couldn't see anything.

"Hello? Anyone?" Maria called.

Nothing. She inched forward, trying to push the fog back with her hands. The fog was so cold it burned. She jerked her fingers to her mouth and breathed on them. Her breath warmed the tips, somewhat and she rubbed them against her chest to get the blood flowing. *It was best to keep them close to her*, she thought. *The fog's hungry. Maybe not hungry for flesh, but hungry for warmth.* And she tucked her fingers under her armpits and called out again, "Hello?"

Nothing.

"VIRGINIA? MARINA?"

There was only the whispered hiss as rivers of fog crisscrossed themselves, snaking back on themselves into something gargantuan and cold.

As she listened for any sound of life, Maria's mind filled with images of stamping hooves – hooves that destroyed the earth beneath them as they tore across a field. It sounded like the animals were angry. But if they were, she'd be able to feel it in the ground, thrumming up her legs to her chest. She listened for the sound of a stampede. The Hayes' kept horses and cattle in a pasture near the house, not enough to create a true western stampede, but if they were about to tear loose, she'd be able to hear them snorting and stomping. But she couldn't hear anything. She didn't even know where she was in the fog.

"Hello?"

There was panic in her voice, she felt it and heard it – the flutter in her throat. She tasted it, like an old copper penny, one that had been stuck on gum on the underside of a picnic table. That's what it tasted like to her. Fear mixed with the taste of being squished like a tube of paint. *Or eaten*, she thought. Too late. Maria's mind replayed every scary movie she had watched with Virginia when the other had been a mere teenager. She hated them, but Virginia had loved them, loved every minute of them. And now she felt as she was participating in some kind of movie herself, one where she was the prey, the victim-to-be.

"Hello? Is anyone out there?"

There was only the fog and her ragged breathing.

Then behind her, to her side, a twig snapped.

"Whoa. Hello? Anyone there?"

Then to her other side a sound of skipping gravel.

She turned one way and then back around the other way when she thought she heard a shirt ruffle. Then it was behind her. And by the time she figured out she was listening to the sound of her clothing rubbing together, her robe's belt dragging the ground, she'd gotten herself twisted around in such a way that she didn't know which way was up. At first, she felt relief because it had been her clothing that had been rustling and not some maniac, but that turned to acid fear when she realized her clothing couldn't snap twigs and she didn't know where she was or which way she was facing. Only a couple of steps from the house and she was lost.

"Shit," she whispered.

Something was out there with her.

"Mulch." The voice boomed in her head and made her temples ache.

"Mulch." The voice hurt her head and made the insides of her womb ache. Maria collapsed onto the damp earth and started to whimper. The fog swirled around her in eddies, sometimes splitting to go around her body as she trembled in the absolute whiteness, sometimes passing over her, or through her mouth and lungs and out again through her nose.

4 JUNE 14

Macy walked through her front door flinging tears off her hands. Her parents sipped their cocktails and watched from their newspapers and magazines in the sitting room. When Macy threw back a shot of whiskey from the kitchen bar, her mother asked if she was all right.

"Yes, mother," she said. "All is well. Just a little upset over my *missing friend*."

"I'm telling you she's shopping in Beantown." Her mother quipped as Macy poured four fingers of whiskey into a glass and slunk up to her room.

"I'm telling you, Gary, she's drinking way too much."

"Hmm. What was that hon? Want a refill, dear?"

Macy's room was her private shelter. She felt like throwing herself away or at least getting incredibly lost. She didn't want to feel anything and right now nothing felt like something, nothing was hurting her quite a bit.

5 JUNE 16

When the cat brushed Maria, she jumped what must have been ten feet in the air. Cursing in Spanish, the cat responded with a deep mew.

"Ah, Christo!"

When she saw that it was just a white stray cat, she felt the air rush out of her lungs. For a second her brain filled with star-pricks, and she thought she was going to faint, but she didn't, and the cat disappeared into the fog only to reappear moments later to brush her leg again, before disappearing once again into the white.

"Kitty?"

For a wild second, Maria thought she should follow the cat back to the house but stopped.

"Stupid cat doesn't know where I live," she said aloud. "Why couldn't you have been a dog?"

Then a tangle of mews erupted in front of her. She couldn't see where they came from, but they sounded mean and spiteful – hungry even. She turned her feet in the opposite direction, careful to make sure she was pointed away from the sounds of the animals. Something about them was off and her body responded by jacking her nerves to maximum. She started ahead in a slow jog her hands in front of her to brace her if she ran into the house or anything else in the fog.

Behind her, the cats continued their terrible warbling, like drunk roosters at dawn. As she jogged blindly, hands outstretched, she feared she was going to run into a great beast whose very breath was the fog itself.

6 JUNE 15, 12:09 AM

Mulch stood in the closet of Macy's room listening to her sip her whiskey. He'd ducked in as a precaution, his nerves high pitched, and his forehead pounding like it had been when he had stalked Leon in the caves. *The Indian Caves. That's where he could dump Macy's body. Or in the swamp.*

His head felt like the swamp now, his eyes boiling in his skull and his forehead dripping with sweat, the shivers had left him sometime after hiding the SUV. No one would notice it. It wasn't that kind of community. Which worked out well for Mulch but wouldn't work out well for Macy.

Macy had left the Hayes' house minutes before Mulch had come home. Maria had greeted Mulch with tears, explaining in that wail of hers, that Macy, Virginia's true friend, had searched for clues of his daughter's disappearance. That she had found things in Virginia's room that she would never leave home without. This when Mulch had contended that Virginia was probably just gallivanting across the country with her boyfriend, Adam, likely visiting relatives along the way, and they'd probably hear from them in no time at all. Of course, Mulch claimed to know nothing for sure, only offering postulations. Maria said that she wanted the police involved.

Mulch promised if they hadn't heard from them in a few days, he'd call the cops himself. 'She'd done this sort of thing before, remember?' he'd said. Maria had been inconsolable. But in the end, he had consoled her, for now. He'd convinced her that he was sure that Virginia was all right, that she was A-OK, that she would be back before you know it, which had calmed her down.

Now there was the Macy problem.

Asking around he'd found out that she'd called the feed store asking questions about Virginia, which wasn't acceptable. *Who else had she contacted?* Mulch had waited till it was dark before striking out for her house. He had no problem entering, for the Allbrights kept their garage door open and the side door unlocked. He'd been inside their house a few times to pick Virginia up and knew which room was which. He'd even had a drink or two with Gary on occasion. Right now, Gary was asleep – both the Allbrights were. He'd spied them heading up to their bedroom around ten. He didn't think they'd be any trouble at all.

He'd been inside Macy's room for no more than ten seconds when Macy came out of the bathroom, wearing only a towel around her head, surprising him. Mulch barely had time to jump into her closet to watch her from his hiding spot as she paraded around her bedroom, drying her hair with the towel. Occasionally she'd burst into sobs before composing herself and returning to brush her hair. She continued to drink her whiskey.

Ribs of dim light made it seem like Mulch was watching her through some kind of movie filter. She threw on a nightshirt and sat down on her bed with a sigh, shifting her weight as she drew up her body into a fetal pose. She slipped her hands between her legs, her arms twitching. The central air conditioning made his arm hair stand on end and his skin bump. He imagined that her nipples were hard as stones.

Her closet smelled of rose and salt. It was filled with silk, satin, and lace. There was the faint haze of sweat on the underarms of several unwashed prom and bridesmaid gowns. *Always a bridesmaid, never a bride,* Mulch grinned inhaling deeply. There was the faint whiff of a crack pipe. There was no mistaking that acetone pinch. He knew Macy had been a wild one, he'd seen it for himself on a few occasions, watching her and Virginia through the walls. He wondered what her parents would say about that if they were to find out she was using hard drugs.

He thought about stabbing her in the heart and leaving the body for her parents to find. They hadn't so much as stirred since he had slipped upstairs; they snored the snore of drunkards in the next room. Rubbing his fingers together, Mulch imagined what it would be like to feel Macy's skull powder under his palms. He'd seen Mr. Bill do it a few times. One only needed to apply pressure to the edges of the palm. "Make it like a knife," Mr. Bill had said as he had rested his hands on the side of Shelley Lumis' skull. Shelley had stolen almost ten thousand from Mulch – right out of the safe in the feed store, right from under Mulch's nose. "Make a quick squeeze, but use all strength, all force" Mr. Bill had said, "imagine you're popping a pimple." Shelley had whimpered underneath the two of them like some kind of dog. Mulch had watched with awe as Bill crushed Shelley's skull with little resistance.

Mulch fingered the ribbed slats on the closet door. He pushed it open, and the door brushed against the carpet shag with a hush sound. His pulse quickened and his penis grew hard as iron. Standing above her, he had the sudden urge to masturbate, to get it, whatever it was, out of his system before he did something terrible. But it was too late for that, Marina was gone. Virginia was gone. They'd all be gone in a few weeks, all of them, and he'd unravel and fall apart like he was meant to. *The sun will come and will melt it all away,* he thought.

And this little bitch had been in his house. This greedy little cunt had been nosing around where she shouldn't have been. Even Virginia had said herself very recently that the two of them weren't even friends anymore. *Tsk. Tsk.* If Macy hadn't made those phone calls, if she hadn't come over and snooped around, then there would have been no need for her to die. As it was, whatever was going to happen was all her fault – Mulch had no control over that.

For a second Mulch wanted to shout. He wanted to wave his arms about his head, screaming through the walls at Macy's parents, "I'm going to kill your bitch! Try to stop me! Come and get me you fucking fucks!" His throat trembled and for a second he thought he was going to do it, but he only mouthed the words, his lips carefully forming the fricatives and plosives of each syllable. A tiny little laugh escaped his lips, and he quickly covered his mouth.

Macy shifted her weight in bed underneath him. She had drifted into sleep. *How convenient.* His forehead felt like it was going to pop. His blood throbbed in the center of his waxy and broad skull. Right in the same place where Maria used to kiss him, where his daughters would kiss him when he kissed them goodnight, back when he was the type of father who kissed his daughter's good night and meant nothing more of it.

Bending over Macy's sleeping body, he inhaled the sharp stink of alcohol and amphetamine rising from her pores. She had been doing coke or speed and recently by the smell of her. There was also the smell of sex mingled in the woodsy shampoo smell of her hair. Macy had always liked sex. He had heard her say it a thousand times in Virginia's room. Where Mulch had watched her disrobe a thousand times too, watched her as she combed her and his daughter's hair. He'd watch them together down at the creek, watch them giggle and splash, bumping into each other in the water. After that, he'd imagined that she had gone home and gotten drunk and high, and finger fucked herself into oblivion. Because he'd seen that too, in his house, Virginia and Macy getting wasted together and collapsing in an exhausted pile of pretty after they'd finished exploring every one of their holes.

He scooped her up like a lover might or like a father would scoop a child. In his thick arms, Macy did not stir, her blood thick with booze, pills, and grief. Her shirt rode up on Mulch's forearms so that he felt her skin as he carried her down the stairs and towards the front door, his hands resting on the backs of her thighs. He felt the heat of her groin on his hands as he passed her parents' room, their snores like the tide. When he was finally out on the front door, he sighed deeply realizing he had been holding his breath the whole time. When he was down the street, to his SUV, his breath came faster and heavier. The whole time he'd been in that house he'd been restricting his lungs and now they struggled to gain the air they needed in the thick humid night. Mulch opened a passenger door and laid her down on the seat and climbed in over the console to take his place next to her. She continued to snore, and he bit his lip as he started up the car, his hand ready to whip over her mouth, if necessary, but Macy didn't move, not until Mulch got her to Pritchard's swamp, on his property, back near the caves.

The swamp seemed appropriate for Macy. The swamp because what the swamp took it didn't give back.

In the end, Macy, when she did move, she only grunted, spilling half words and mumbles out of her mouth as Mulch entered her. She didn't awaken when he came inside her, she only stirred when Mulch failed to crush her skull.

He held her head up with the palms of his hands and squeezed, imagining that his hands were like blades, but he couldn't even manage to crack her skull, it was too hard. That was what woke her finally, roused her to struggle, this poor drug-addled girl that never stood a chance with Mulch. He let her go and she fell face forward in the mud, gurgling and crying, and coming to with a small wimpy moan that seemed almost pathetic.

In the end, Mulch had to break her neck. His hands hurt too much, and he was impatient. He weighted her stripped and naked body down under a log, leaving the job of hiding to the beetles and grubs. It didn't make much of a difference if she surfaced within the year, he'd be long gone by then.

7 JUNE 16

Maria spat the dirt from her mouth. She'd been clipping along at a steady pace in the fog when she lost her footing. She'd gone face-first into the wet dirt and as she tried to get up she felt a pain in her knee. She groaned. Holding her knee, she limped forward. She no longer heard the cats, or the fog, but her head hurt all the same. At first, Maria had found it hard to breathe in the fog. Now she noticed that she was breathing it like it was oxygen. And maybe, she wondered, when she inhaled the fog, she allowed it to enter her mind.

Was that possible? She didn't think it was, but she didn't know what to think anymore. Her mind was full of strange thoughts. She limped ahead, wincing as she went, her knee throbbing in time with her head. If she made it back to the house, she had to find Mulch. Had to get Mulch to get rid of the fog, whatever it was. Ahead of her it thinned, or at least she thought it did, she couldn't tell, the fog was so white and it moved in all different directions at once, but she thought she saw the house in front of her.

Suddenly something moved right next to her and it wasn't a cat. It was large and its breath was deep and heavy like that of a horse, or a big man.

"Hello?"

It was a beast; she heard its hooves tear the sod underneath the fog. *It was probably a horse.* One that had gotten scared and run off into the fog. Or had she wandered into the pasture? *Was that possible? Wasn't there a fence? Yes, there was. Could she have gotten through the fence without noticing it? Not likely.* The horse probably jumped the fence and had wandered into the fog.

"Nice horsey," she stammered.

Maria counted her steps as she went. There were only so many feet between her and the house. And if she could keep track of her distance, she stood a chance of finding it. Only she didn't know where she was, only that the house was out there – somewhere. Her eyes tried to pierce the heavy white veil in front of her but couldn't. When the fog appeared to thin it did so only briefly and immediately thickened again.

Eighteen, nineteen, twenty steps, she counted. Before she had started counting, she hadn't run too far into the fog bank, had she? She couldn't remember.

The house felt like a million years ago. She guessed she'd been out in the milky soup for ten minutes. Maybe more.

Again, ahead of her came the sound of something breathing. She still couldn't tell what was breathing, only that there was *something* breathing. This time it was light and healthy, and perhaps a little tired, or like her, a little scared.

"Hello?"

She didn't know what to expect ahead of her, perhaps Mr. Bill was out looking for her, or perhaps Mulch had gone out to investigate her disappearance (not likely, she thought), or even one of the girls coming home, but what she didn't expect was an enormous white deer standing rock still inches in front of her with six large black crows perched upon his expansive rack.

The beast did not move but the crows did. They opened their beaks and let a hacking cry so awful that Maria shoved her fingers in her ears and ran off, wincing as her knee strained and tore from her momentum.

She ran back behind her from where she had just come and went perhaps three feet before slamming into the wall of the house. *Thank God, the house!* she thought. She slid alongside it until she saw a light slipping through the sliding doors. For a brief second, through the glass, she saw the idiot grin of Mr. Bill pouring sugar into his mouth by the cupful.

8 JUNE 16

When Mick Ellis answered Betty Allbright's call early that morning he'd been picking his teeth with the narrow end of a ballpoint pen cap. Already he regretted coming into work today, he'd forgotten to brush his teeth. *Better double up on the gum,* he had thought to himself. *Otherwise, they'll head for the hills.* Not like he had any customers, anyway.

Mick had owned the Ace Detective Agency for exactly three months and had only worked three cases – a missing dog and two cheating husbands. His aunt, who had convinced him to move down from Jersey to the shore to take over the Agency had moved to Florida. She'd only wanted him on the shore so he could watch over her rental house and the old country store that had once belonged to his uncle and whose upstairs now served as the Ace offices.

He'd been tricked. Still, he kept it up. At least until the fall. Then he'd reevaluate. *And fuck Aunt Susan if she didn't like it.*

When the phone rang, he expected it to be a telemarketer, not a weeping woman.

"Ace Detective Agency, Mick speaking." Mick chewed his Nicorette and slurped his saliva down, hoping to inject his system with a kick. This gum wasn't cutting it. It took a few seconds for the person on the other end of the line to speak.

"I don't know if you can help me," she began.

"Everyone says that ma'am. That's why you called because no one else can help," Mick replied, pleased with himself as he picked up his pencil and began to draw cigarettes on his notebook cover. *Ten to one, the woman is going to ask about her husband.* When he'd been on the Jersey shore he was always busy with cheating spouses, cheating, gambling, and drug-addled spouses. Regardless of what it was, the men always turned out to be sleeping with someone, not always a woman either.

"My daughter has disappeared."

Daughter, eh. So much for so much. "Tell me the story, ma'am."

"I don't know where to begin," she began. She burst into tears and tried to suck them back in.

Mick had hoped it was the cheating spouse. Those were fun. He got to take pictures. Sometimes the women were hot and he got to watch a little freaky-freaky for free. But missing children were messy jobs. Seemed like every state had a high-profile missing children's case these days. *Just where did all the missing kids go*, that was what he wanted to know.

"Look, I can't explain it all. Not now, not on the phone. I'll pay you your money. We have lots of money." The woman's sobs were more controlled now as if someone can control sorrow.

"You should call the police, ma'am."

"I have. They can't do anything."

That seemed unlikely.

"How old is your daughter, mam?"

"23. No, wait. She's 24. She turned 24 at the end of May."

"Oh."

"Can you come over? Now?"

"I think I can fit you into my schedule," he said and as the woman gave him directions, he suddenly felt like smiling.

9

The Allbright's house was a large brick and vinyl affair, with faux Victorian touches for the unimaginative yuppie. Mick imagined the inside was decorated with tacky country knick-knacks and half-assed folk art he'd seen so much of since he moved to the shore. He hated the crafty stuff. That's what his father called his mother's decorating, crafty stuff, and sometimes crappy stuff when he'd had a few beers during the big game on TV.

Before he left the office he called his one local source, his aunt's neighbor an elderly waterman named Captain Murdock. Mick hated calling Captain Murdock because Captain Murdock lectured him. There was no conversing with the Captain – he spoke, and Mick listened. Mick could ask questions, but he'd get the long answer. He couldn't ever introduce new information or change the conversation because the Captain wouldn't have it. It wasn't like the old guy was *trying* to lecture him, he just didn't recognize that a conversation was not one way. *No wonder the old guy wasn't married.*

The Captain told him that the Allbright's were indeed rich. He didn't know much more than that, only that Allbright girl wasn't the only one gone missing lately. A young guy by the name of Adam Taylor had disappeared a few weeks back, and then his girlfriend, Virginia Hayes, had supposedly *just* gone A.W.O.L as well. The Captain mentioned that they all knew each other, were friends together, and hung out. Mick didn't want to know how old man Murdock knew all that, but gossip spread faster than kudzu on the shore. With all that in mind and two more missing people, Mick hoped the family would be able to give him at least a few leads. *Heck, maybe I can be the hero of this tale? Why not you Mick? Why not you?*

Excerpt from Ship's Log: Dated June 12th

This is madness. I'm getting tossed around like a cork in a gin bathtub. I'm surprised Marina hasn't floated out to sea, it's so fucking bad. Really, and slow too. Most of my weight is in food and fuel and though it dwindles daily, I'm not picking up any speed. I'm planning to head closer to shore tonight, which should put me just south of the New York harbor.

I can't believe it's taking this long. Did Mulch realize this was going to happen?

Marcos

10

Mulch did realize that Marcos would have a rough trip to Boston. It was a long way. a lot longer by boat than by car. *That's for damn sure.* And the drag on the box wouldn't make things any easier, which was why Mulch hadn't piloted the boat himself. He hadn't wanted to be bothered dragging that box up the coast. He'd done enough of that exact thing with the Italian families in his youth. Trawlers could take on some heavy seas, but swift they were not. It was also why Mr. Bill couldn't pilot the boat Mr. Bill was needed at the house. Marcos was already in love and expendable and so it made perfect sense to send him. Only Marcos, despite what he thought of himself, wasn't much of a sailor. Mulch knew he would struggle.

Marcos was still worried about the Coast Guard. He worried a lot about the Coast Guard. He didn't want to be nailed for slavery, trafficking, or kidnapping.

He looked back at his charge. He still hadn't heard anything from her. Before he'd left he made sure she had plenty of water and an empty waste jar to eliminate in. He planned to check on her that night.

"Four days in, and I'm only just over halfway there!"

Marcos was being hard on himself. After all, he'd spent most of his first day out hiding under a tree. Then he spent the third day anchored just off the barrier islands, Cobb Island. He was glad he was off the island, too, because while he was there he'd spied a Coast Guard ship.

He'd been grouping water bottles and was on top of the box, lowering them down into Marina's chamber. She was moaning something about her mother and didn't answer his calls to see if she was alright. Sea Hag had said she'd pass in and out of consciousness for a while, probably for days, coming to for a block of time before slipping under again, and that was to be expected. Sea Hag said that she believed her body would do this to protect itself from the madness that came when a mermaid was separated from water for so long. As a result of that, Marcos had been dropping bottles of water down to her as *his* life depended on it. He had no idea if Marina had even drunk them or bathed in them or hoarded them; he had lowered the first bottle ages ago. It was already his third time on top trying to communicate with Marina when he saw the Coast Guard ship.

"Shit." He dropped a water bottle inside the box. It hit the floor of the box with a dull thud and rolled away. Jumping off the box he landed in the shallows and sprinted to his boat. His radio was silent. On his way, his mind thumbed through a thousand spells he'd been learning over the years. Sea Hag had been teaching him a chantey to sing if ever he fell into trouble, but what do you know, he couldn't remember a word of it.

Marcos and his people worked magic with wood, not with words, and the few "spells" he knew were more like illusions, and weak ones at that. But lucky for Marcos, he'd been born with a quick head and a quicker tongue. He was speaking into the radio before he knew it.

"Mayday, mayday, this is DAWN 6, over. Mayday, mayday, this is DAWN 6 over."

"DAWN 6 this is Coast Guard ship 67, over?"

"Taking on water, motor failure. Possible heart attack. Male 67, chest pains, trouble breathing. Advise, over."

"DAWN 6 what're your coordinates?"

Marcos looked down at his finger on the map which would place DAWN 6 twenty miles to the south.

When he began to speak into the radio he watched as the coast guard ship turned and began to head south, no longer a threat to him and his box.

11

Private Dick Mick Ellis stood in the center of a very expensive living room. There were at least a dozen honest-to-god antiques. Mick wasn't sure about the lamp, could be, but could also be a tasteful reproduction. There were three lush oriental rugs over top the hardwood which gave the room its cozy woody color. Two University of Richmond law degrees were framed over the roll-top desk, and what was probably an original Faberge egg adorned the mantle over the fireplace.

Mrs. Allbright sat in her Victorian chair, weeping into her afternoon tea, convinced, rightly so, that her daughter was dead.

She'd managed to explain that her daughter had been searching for clues as to where her best friend, Virginia Hayes, had gone off to. She went onto explain that Macy had been very sorrowful the night she disappeared. She had told her mother that she thought Virginia was dead.

"Had she been that upset before?" Mick asked.

"Before?" Mrs. Allbright managed through her tears.

"Previously that week, I mean. Did she seem upset in the days leading up to her disappearance or only on the night of her disappearance?"

"She seemed worried all week, Mr. Ellis."

Mr. Allbright entered with a beer for Mick and a pill for his wife.

"Can either of you tell me, aside from her friend's disappearance, was there anything else she was worried about, sir?"

"Actually, no we can't. It isn't like Macy's a teen anymore. She doesn't talk to me, or her mother, either. Though I suppose she's closer to her mother. She lives here because she hasn't figured out what to do. This damn job market. I used to support the president.... but three terms...I...Anyway, she's a sweet girl."

"You mind if I nose about her room some?"

"Go ahead. The police were here this morning."

"Did they take anything from the house?"

"No," Mrs. Allbright said, "They assumed she was out early and sure to be coming home because she hadn't taken anything with her when she left."

"They think it's too early to investigate," Mr. Allbright said.

Thinking about the standard 24-hour rule, Mick looked at them confused.

"Mr. Ellis you have to understand that on the shore things move slowly. If it's easier for them to assume that she's off with a boyfriend because of her age, they do that. And besides, until I see evidence stating the contrary, that's what I'm going to assume as well. The police won't get involved unless there is a reason to get involved. Unless there's evidence of kidnapping, or God forbid a body."

Mrs. Allbright burst into sobs.

"You don't think she's been kidnapped?"

"Where's the ransom note? There have been no ransom calls."

"I guess you could be right, but to be sure..."

"Of course I'm right. She figured out where Virginia had gone off to, felt bad at being left behind, and followed. They've done this before."

"Run away?"

"No. Yes. They disappear for a few days here and there and go off to Virginia Beach to shop and pick up men, no doubt. I've heard stories."

"Stories?"

Mick removed his pocket notebook and pen as Mrs. Allbright continued to cry.

"Of their promiscuity."

"They got around, you say?" Mick asked.

"Nothing unusual, if that's what you're implying. No perversions. Just healthy teen rebellion. I know Macy can be wild. We both do. Anyways, the missus thinks you should be getting to work, don't you?" Mr. Allbright said as he gestured upstairs.

12

"There isn't anything here," Mick said looking around the bedroom, but Mr. Allbright had walked off into the hallway leaving him behind. There were no clues, no signs of struggle, no missing clothes, no missing phone. She had left her phone charger, but that wasn't evidence. She probably had two or three of them. He'd have to check with the cell phone company, the credit card company, hell just about everybody. *These girls are probably not missing anyway*, he mused.

The one object that had sparked his interest was a journal he found on her desk. At first, he assumed it was Macy's but when he flipped through it he was surprised to find that Virginia Hayes had written her name on the front cover. He put it in his bag to look at later.

"Mr. Allbright?" Mick peered into the hallway.

"Yes?"

"I'm about finished up here."

Gary Allbright shrugged and let out a long sigh.

"Find what you can. You will want to talk to someone in the Hayes family too."

"Okay?" Mick watched Mr. Allbright descend the stairs and head back into the living room. Mick turned back to Macy Allbright's room and threw his hands up and sighed. *Hayes? Hayes?* His stomach tightened; a feeling of anxious dread descended upon him.

13 Excerpt from Ship's Log: Dated June 16th

Fucking hell, is this water and storm. Eh? What am I supposed to do with this giant fucking box behind me? Forgive me. I must vent, occasionally. This trip is turning me inside out. I am not sleeping well, and the speed Mulch provided me makes my jaw hurt, so eating has become painful.

Imagine, taking trucker's speed just so I can run this harmless girl to Boston so she can catch a ride to warmer waters.

Imagine.

Have refueled off the New York coast and am headed North again. As instructed, I paid the harbormaster $10,000 for no questions. He didn't even look at my face when I gave him the money, let alone take a look at the box like he's done that many times before.

If the weather holds, I should be there in two days.

Marcos

14

Pembroke's basement held an assorted collection of instruments he'd collected over the years, iron rods, long steel skewers, pokers, clamps and hooks, leather spiked gloves, a spiked head cage, whips, one vicious cat o' nine tails, cylindrical devices for stretching orifices, leather shoes with broken glass and bits of nails in the bottom for use on the back, and an actual iron maiden. Plus, he had his electrodes, which he wired to a car battery and then to his victims' bodies. He liked using electricity because the stink of burning flesh tended to drape the room like a ribbon and filled the victim's eyes with knowing helplessness. That's not to say Pembroke didn't like his steel and iron tools and the occasional leather strap. Truth is there were times he preferred the peasant feel of horsehide in his hands as he beat his victims to the end of their wits. Pembroke's electrodes and car batteries and acids tended to make a mess of flesh, which was what he was mostly aiming for, while leather and iron tended to make flesh bruised and tender, which was fine for his sex games, but for real pain and misery alone he always preferred electricity.

Up until now, Pembroke's victims tended to be homeless men and women he'd find laid out in the alley behind his house, like flies caught in a spider's web. His first night there, much to his delight, he'd found a wonderful specimen lying behind his trash bins. Finding a method to his desire he'd offer his victims his place to stay for the night and they often followed down into his home, suspicion boiling their brain and eyes. He knew they thought he was some kind of pervert. "What are you? A homo, a fag", they whispered sometimes as they shuffled behind from the alley, their bags swinging together, the empty bottles within clinking like a clumsy bell choir. The alley behind his Richmond home was a clean, neat alley, perfect for such things, much like ones he'd found in Boston's Back Bay, or Amsterdam's Jewish quarter. It was narrow, cobbled, and lined with vine.

15

Pembroke's snaking, taffy-like toes carried him across the dusty floor of the basement. And as he approached the man tied to a chair at the back of the basement, the man grunted, his mouth stuffed with oily rags. He wheezed in and out of his nose, which had recently been broken and now jutted to the left. The smell floated about him like a beautiful aura. When Pembroke gripped the man by the arm, he at first jerked back before sublimating to his will. Pembroke did not which one of the men he had tied down. He'd dispatched the first one quickly. This poor soul was going to get the full treatment.

"Good evening," Pembroke said, his voice coming out cool as he controlled the pitch and kept it low and mellow.

The man looked up at the sound, his eyes full of sleep. He'd been tied up for days.

"It's okay, remain relaxed, it's so much easier that way." His taffy-like toes reached out like worms and hissed through the nails. To the victim, Pembroke floated like a ghost.

"I'm going to expose you," he said coolly.

The man squealed; the oily rags moved with his mouth movements.

"No. No. Don't worry about your precious body. Or your secrets. Or your mind. I'm interested only in your blood. Exposing your insides. Do you understand?"

The man looked on with wide-eyed wonder.

"I'm interested in your organs. Or perhaps peeling off your skin."

"Mfff Ghhh," the man shifted in his seat, wiggling against the rope.

"Tsk. Tsk. Tsk. There's no need for such an attitude."

Pembroke's toes gracefully carried him over to a small wooden table adorned with long shiny things, which the man couldn't quite make out. In his heart he knew they were knives, he'd handled such shiny flashes before, for his boss, Mulch.

"No, I know that you are not a, shall we say, productive member of our society. And let's say that I know that you have not been the most kind of citizens."

"Mff. Ghh," the man squirmed trying to get loose.

"Now, now." Pembroke picked a small sharp tooth alligator clamp and balanced it in the broad width of his long palms. Sweat, sticky and sweet, poured from his face as Pembroke leaned close and whispered in his ear.

"This should teach you to damage goods promised to me."

With one swift movement, Pembroke thrust the alligator clip onto the man's broken nose. The force snapped the tender cartilage and bone as the clip dug into skin, blood trickling down the man's face.

"Now, now. That doesn't hurt. Quit your moaning."

His victim did not agree. He howled, and his voice filtered through the rags, came out as light grunts. Pembroke reached out for a small rolling cart that housed a small car battery and a series of wires and clamps. His fingers moved quickly. Pembroke pulled a long wire out and gazed at its charged end.

"The best thing about these wires is that I can simply touch you with it, like so." Pembroke grazed the man's side with the wire sending a powerful charge through his body.

"Did you like that? I bet you did. What I like to do is attach the wire to a metal clamp, like the one on your nose. Then I watch the sparks fly and smell the wonderful, delicious smell of burning flesh."

BOOK THREE: JUNE 20

"Archaeological evidence shows that the native Americans began dying off early. Probably due to smallpox, the flu, European sicknesses brought over the Atlantic. However, it's possible privateers waged small wars with the tribes in the Algonquin nation. The amount of trauma the skeletal remains reveal is remarkable as it is disturbing."

—Dr. Susan Randall,
Professor of History,
UVA in a lecture to the Eastern Shore
Historical Society, 6/9/94

"Patient Virginia Hayes, whose birth records are not on file anywhere, it seems, insists that her father, whom I cannot find in a Google search, kidnapped her and sold her to a man whose toes are distended monstrous things with teeth."

—Dr. Savannah Garvan,
personal notes

"There are many ways to punish the submissive. One is to place the slave's head in a box..."

—George Hand-from the Bondage and
Domination Lifestyle Handbook

CHAPTER ONE

1
1607

The Laughing King craned his neck and laughed, his headdress teetered on the crown of his skull, his formal English jacket fit snugly over his imposing arms. The jacket had belonged to the largest and biggest of the English traders, and on the Laughing King, the jacket looked like a child's costume. The warriors standing behind him and the raised dais of earth and logs fidgeted, their fingers lacing and unlacing behind their backs. The English were boring and uncouth. In the back row, someone kicked the ground with the ball of his foot and sent a cloud of dust into the air. The Laughing King pitched forward again with the deep bellow the warriors had grown to loathe recently. The Laughing King, some thought, enjoyed the white men too much. This time the headdress nearly slid off the chief's head, and Kego-tok leaped forward plucking the headdress back onto the Laughing King's head. Three white men who stood in the middle of the longhouse smiled and ribbed each other. The smallest white man was no bigger than a fourteen-year-old Indian boy. The largest one was about the height of an average Indian woman, only stouter. *The white men smell bad too, a deep stink*, Kego-tok thought. *Poison*. His stomach growled, *not friend*. His body tensed, his mind sharpened. The smallest white man carried a parcel on his back. The warriors, eager to see what the white men would bring this time, pressed closer together behind their chief. The Laughing King raised his hands, his mouth open in a hideous grin.

"Gifts. Gifts. Your story makes me happy. Makes me laugh."

Deabdevon's English had improved over the last months and the white settlers understood him. The tallest of the white men bowed, showing his balding skull.

"We bring tobacco, great king, grown in Powhatan's land."

A murmur ran through the warriors and through the few women, who with their children had crawled into the back of the Laughing King's wigwam. The Laughing King waved his arms for silence. Children on the floor wiggled between adult's legs like puppies.

"Pow-ha-tan. Great chief. Many nations bow before Pow-ha-tan." The white man smiled as he spoke.

The odors from the basket of tobacco made Kego-tok's head sing. *They knew just to mention Powhatan and the old Laughing King was your ally,* Kego-tok thought. *Jealousy corrupts.* His stomach barked, *yes.*

"He is a good chief. Though not as great or kind as you, my lordship."

Kego-tok rolled his eyes, this word, 'lordship' really got to Debedeavon. He laughed every time he heard it.

The tallest white man gestured for the smallest white man, who shook when called. Kego-tok thought that they looked all afraid, but he smelled fear on the small one as he placed the basket of tobacco before the Laughing King. Kego-tok got a whiff of the man's smell, it was like horse urine. He also caught the smell of something else – something fragrant and tasty. The smell of this tobacco was one that Kego-tok had never smelled before. It had a sweet bite and reminded him of his own home-grown medicine that he tended to behind his family's wigwam.

"Laughing King, this tobacco is the finest tobacco in all of his majesty's Virginia."

The small English runt took a plug of the sweet-smelling herb and packed it into a pipe, much like the one's the warriors and chief smoked regularly in the evenings. The runt gestured to the Laughing King, his trembling hand held the pipe out.

"Ah. Hmmm."

The Laughing King's giant arms bridged the distance easily. The runt backed off, bowing. Laughing King smelled the pipe and gestured for Kego-tok to light it. Tasting another chief's tobacco was powerful; the symbolism was not lost on Kego-tok.

The three white men clustered together, sweat gathered on their foreheads like a sheet. The men smelled of rot.

There was the whiff of spark and tinder, and the pipe flared and the warriors, and the women and children, inhaled the sharp, sweet aroma issuing from the pipe's mouth. Rolling his head back, Laughing King bellowed a great guffaw and raised his arms over his head, a gesture usually reserved for victory on the battlefield. Laughing King smiled, his glassy eyes canvased the longhouse.

"Pow-ha-tan's tobacco is good tobacco."

The tallest of the white men elbowed his way forward. Bowing he reached inside his flowing heavy shirt and withdrew a skin. The skin was shaped like a kidney, and it sloshed with liquid.

"This, my King, is also for you. It is from my private oaks."

The quiet white man looked nervously about the room. Kego-tok's stomach fluttered like a crow's wings. *Something wasn't right*, he thought. *Bad spirits*, his stomach gurgled.

"It is a drink?" Kego-tok asked, as his mind searched for bad thoughts. The white men's feelings were easy to read.

"Anon."

The tallest white man raised his arms, turning around for everyone to see. He pulled something out of the top of the kidney-shaped bag. There was a pop. He held the small object between his thumb and forefinger and drank from the skin. When he finished he sighed, bowed, and offered the skin to the chief.

"Is it animal blood?" Laughing King said, his eyes cautious and curious.

"Brandy, my lordship. It is made from grapes."

Laughing King didn't smile at lordship this time, the pipe smoldered in his hands.

"Grapes?" Kego-tok asked, peering closer. He found no malice in the man's thoughts, but still, his stomach fluttered like the crow. The spirits did not whisper to him.

"Grapes?" Laughing King asked.

The white man faltered, turning around he gestured to the other white men who looked at him with agog.

"Ah. Um. Ah. Yes. Hold on. Please."

The middle one, the quiet one, sifted through a small pouch hanging from a string from his waist. "I thought...my lord...that you should see...what sweet fruit our Lord in heaven cultivates in our gardens." He then held out a small purple oval fruit between his index finger and thumb.

"Ah! Hinds." Kego-tok said with surprise.

"Hinds," The Laughing King said, his voice lifting to fill the longhouse. "Hinds!"

Unseen, wiggling closer on his hands and knees, just barely a young man, little Kego-tok, yet to be so named, peered at the strange white men and their smoking and dripping gifts and thought to himself that he was on the verge of some great new vista, yet to be seen by anyone, the warriors, his father, the white-men, and even the Laughing King. Little Kego-tok imagined he was on the edge of a whole new world.

2

Maria sighed and counted to ten.

Mr. Bill was rummaging through her underwear drawer, and though Maria had seen Mr. Bill do and say a lot of strange things in her life she had never imagined that he would be drooling over her unmentionables and generally making an ass out of himself. Mr. Bill hadn't heard her come up behind him. He didn't seem to understand anyone these days, much less follow through with a simple request. When she had scolded him for eating sugar out of the sugar bowl he had run away blabbering like a child.

She cleared her throat. "Are you quite done, Mr. Bill?" She stamped her foot down. "I have had up to here with yours and Mr. Hayes' behavior lately." She stomped over next to the dresser to see what it was he was looking for.

Mr. Bill had avoided direct contact with her and Mulch for the last two weeks. He had also avoided bathing, a fact Maria remembered as soon as she stood next to Bill.

"What are you looking for?" She asked through her hand, which covered most of her mouth.

"GhhhG." Mr. Bill replied holding her old bathing suit in his hands.

Great, Maria thought.

Mr. Bill looked at her with bloodshot eyes and stalked out into the hallway.

"Ghhh.AggYUGkk," he said as he pointed to the dresser and then to Maria. "She-blaaat." And then walked stiffly down the stairs.

"Good God!"

Maria surveyed her room and found he had gone through every one of her drawers. Bits of clothes hung out from them like little colored tongues. Blouses and pants were tossed into corners. Bras littered the floor. Maria wanted to scream.

3

Mulch watched Mr. Bill trip over the worktable downstairs in his chambers. Mr. Bill mumbled something that sounded like "Flubbegug." Mulch hoped whatever it was that was bothering his friend would cease and desist, would go away, and would pass through him so he would help him finish everything that still needed to be done. So far, his hopes had been dashed.

"What exactly is wrong with you?"

Mulch picked up a mason jar of dried orange flowers and tossed it in the air. Mr. Bill looked at him and made a gesture with his hands. It looked like he was giving up.

"Are you all right?" Mulch asked.

"Hhhkkklllmm."

"Hmm," Mulch nodded and opened the Mason jar up to smell the orange flowers. "I need something for my headaches."

"Boingjustllotts."

"By all accounts, Marina is awake. Cilia can see her you know. That bitch gives me the creeps." He'd hoped Mr. Bill would take the bait and tell him how Marina was doing. He had only guessed she was awake. He didn't know for sure. Marcos could have been arrested. Cilia would not play nice once the tables tilted in her favor. Mulch needed Mr. Bill, at least for a little bit longer.

"SSSSRRuntsfhy."

"I see. I'll come back when you're feeling better." Mulch placed the Mason jar of flowers back on Mr. Bill's worktable and started upstairs. Mr. Bill fell into his bed and kicked his shoes off. Mulch noticed that they didn't match; they were two left boots.

4

Amanda Blackstone sat behind her desk on West 52nd Street along the Jersey Beach wishing her window overlooked the actual beach instead of a row of second-string fleabag motels. Currently, a trio of floppy blonde college guys was hanging out the third-floor window of one. *They looked like they were prepping for a kind of group guillotining,* she thought. One of them held a bra in his hands.

"God, what a boring job." The nicotine gum had lost its nicotine power and Amanda thought about a cigarette and how easily she could sneak out of the office, *just for a puff.*

"Amanda?" The head nurse called to her from her station, which was more of a real 'office' office, complete with a private bathroom and three computers for simultaneous research. *She gets to do all the cool things,* Amanda thought.

"I need you to field the calls for a while. I don't think you'll get much today."

"Hope not."

"Probably no more than a burn, or a scrape."

Head Nurse Rose Goodman waved and went out the door. Amanda sighed and rummaged through her purse for another piece of nico-gum. She was sure there was another piece down there. *There had to be.* The door jingled and Nurse Rose popped her head back in.

"Do you need anything dear? While I'm out?"

"No."

Amanda didn't even take her head out of her purse.

"Okay. See ya in an hour."

"An hour?"

Amanda snapped her head back up, but Nurse Rose was already gone.

"This fucking sucks. Dial-a-freaking-Nurse my ass!"

Opening the top drawer of her desk cubicle she removed a pack of smokes, her emergency smokes. She was going to smoke, one or three. She deserved it.

"Rose, you fucking always do this to me. It's not like I went to medical school to work here."

But she had. She always came back around to the fact that even after medical school she was stuck at the bottom of the proverbial medical rung. Dial-a-Nurse, whose customers called because they had first aid questions or vaguely icky questions or were drunk and thought Dial-A-Nurse offered a sex service of the role-playing variety.

"Shit."

Amanda couldn't find any matches.

There were two other nurses, Barney and Melissa, who shared the rest of the office with Amanda. They each had a cubicle, which was all in various states of disrepair. Amanda's walls were held up by rope from the ceiling. The staff bathroom was a joke. It had grown over time to be a kind of giant staff break room. Barney kept sports magazines and light girly magazines like *Detective Weekly* in a moldy, sometimes hairy pile next to the commode. Melissa liked flowery perfume and teddy bears and had covered the full-length mirror with teddy bear stickers. Barney had stuck a picture of Jersey General Hospital on the mirror. It was an aerial view and he had scrawled on a sticky note next to the photo: *You Are Definitely Not Here.* Rose, who had her on-suite bathroom, supplied the staffers with outdated medical pamphlets she found in a box somewhere. Cartoon STDs, pre-HIV, sang the benefits of goatskin from men with square sixties haircuts who wore bright white lab coats. Someone had colored in the teeth of the cartoon Herpes Virus, which looked a lot like Casper 'the friendly ghost.' Barney kept matches in an ashtray on top of his magazines and insisted, absolutely insisted that people strike up when going inside to take care of business. Amanda stared at herself in the full-length mirror. She was tall and skinny, and most unlike the girls in *Detective Weekly* who seemed to catch criminals in a two-piece bikini.

"This is my life. Ground Zero."

The phone was ringing when she came back from her smoke break. *Likely a scrape*, she thought, *or maybe a wasp sting*. Barney and Melissa fielded the real interesting calls. Cuts, suicide attempts. Accidental poisoning. They worked the late shift and reported anything fishy to the cops. Their computers could dial 911 anywhere in the country, depending on where the call originated from. She on the other hand was doomed to work the boring dayshift, where she handled the mundane first-aid stuff that made her yawn.

"Dial-a-Nurse, how may I help you?"

"Um. Uh. I need to see a specialist." The voice sounded strained and hurt.

"What's wrong?"

"Well, I don't know where I am, or what's happening to me." The male on the other end of the line had a southern accent.

"Whoa, start again," Amanda readied her Dial-a-Nurse ballpoint and sticky note pad and was ready to take notes.

"Well. It started about two weeks ago when I began to paint in my sleep."

"Wait. Hold the phone. Did you call here before?"

There was a breathy pause. "Yes." The voice flattered. "God. Did I? It feels like a dream."

"You did call here. I talked to you. I kinda teased you about it, remember?" Silence.

"Yes, I think so. My head has been fucking with me lately."

"It's okay. Start from the beginning."

Amanda traced the call to a payphone in Ocean City, New Jersey, approximately 45 minutes from the office. The guy sounded crazed, half-exhausted.

He probably was crazy, but his other one-minute phone call had been the only exciting call she'd ever taken in her 18-month stint at Dial-a-Nurse, just because it was so different. *Original*, she thought. Amanda never expected to hear him again. It was just too weird.

"The last two weeks have been bizarre," he continued. "I wake up and I find that I have painted something. I don't know where I am. Sometimes I paint a place, a location. I go there and wait. Nothing. Then..."

"Wait. You go where?"

"It's different every time. Beaches mostly. I'm probably hitting every beach on the frigging East Coast. I'm going mad, I think. What should I do? Is there a specialist that can help me? Somewhere I can go."

"So why did you call me?"

"Well. I. Uh. You are in the phone book. I needed to talk to somebody."

"What's your name again?"

"Nick. Nick Adams."

"Do you have any money, Nick?"

5

George hadn't been seen Nick in two weeks and from the looks of Nick's house, Nick hadn't been home in two weeks, either. A painting of a giant moon completely covered the back of the house. It had made George's jaw drop.

"Nick must have gone off his rocker."

Ab countered and said he was probably on some kind of spirit quest. George thought Ab was full of shit.

"Cut the crap Ab. I mean really. For goodness sake, he isn't on some fucking spirit quest."

"Master, how you know this?" Ab stood on his tipsy toes to admire the brush strokes. "I say spirit quest."

"Because I'm his fucking best friend and he would tell me that's why, and I'm worried about him."

"Worried? This is a good painting? No?"

"Yes. That's not the point" George crossed his arms in frustration. "It's weird. It's really weird. He couldn't do this in his sleep, could he?"

"Does master wish to know this?"

"No, I do not. I'd rather not think about it. It makes my stomach hurt."

Ab snorted and placed his big index finger against the painting of the sun. His fingertip was the size of a half-dollar, at least. The all too real sun blazed down on them, and George felt his skin baking.

"Master miss Nick?"

"Yeah."

Over the last few days, Nick's absence had haunted George. Ab had been a good distraction, as well as Lilly. Both had assured him that Nick was okay. He'd talked to Lilly several times on the phone, and they'd even had coffee, twice, but they hadn't gone out again. Nick had probably just taken a road trip. Which was something that George could believe. That is until he saw the painting on the back of the house. Now all bets were off.

"Ab, what happened to all the windows?"

"Wind holes, master?"

The windows are gone. They hadn't been boarded up. They had vanished. George felt butterflies in his nether regions.

"Master, do we have any jobs today?" Abdullah said to change the subject.

Jobs? Where was his appointment book?

"Shit."

Jobs had not been on his mind too much, at least not these past few days.

"Are we late boss?" Ab chuckled to himself. He liked using the term "boss" and "chief," "captain" even.

"I hope not."

With Nick on his mind these last few days, he hadn't been keeping up with his books. Plus, Lilly was acting somewhat evasive. They had yet to plan their second date. George assumed it had something to do with her glowing. But that had been so long ago, he barely remembered it himself. Plus, Ab was constantly bugging him to make his second wish.

6

For the first time in a day or two, the wind was at his back and Marcos made good time. He was going to be in Beantown soon, his old stomping grounds, where he grew up, where he had his first kiss: Michele Mancini, under the Maryvale Middle School football bleachers. It was where he saw his first baseball game: Red Sox VS. the Yankees, where Marcos had first learned he could see the future: the beat-up cab had knocked the old woman out of her shoes and into the glass window of the Greek pizzeria on Brighton Ave. He knew that the old woman would cough blood and die. Marcos had seen it all in a cloudy film two minutes before it happened. For a while he'd thought he caused it, the accident, until one afternoon in school, carving a random symbol into his desk with the tip of a pen, the little symbol gave off a light, like fire. He'd shrieked and his teacher had sent him out for using a lighter, despite his empty hands and pockets. His classmates steered clear of him the rest of that week.

By his calculations, he'd pull into the private marina, near the harbor, somewhere out from the airport, the next evening. According to Mulch, someone would be waiting at the Pilgrim marina, who would take the boat into the harbor and arrange for the box to be transported into a holding bay where it would sit until it reached Holland. Marcos, anxious about docking in Boston, had begun to peel at his hangnail. The soreness comforted him in some bizarre way he could not explain. Mulch had bribed the harbormaster so he'd get as much privacy as he needed. He hoped he wouldn't need any. After all, people would notice the box he was towing behind. He hoped the Dutchman would be on time. He didn't want to be too exposed for too long.

The ship that was supposed to lift the box (and presumably the boat and Marcos too) into its cargo hold was run by Captain Van Dijk. His boat shipped Dutch imports to large exporting companies like the one in Beantown. Likewise, it shipped American products to Holland. Once the boat was close enough to Amsterdam, the boat and the box were to be released (Mulch was very unclear about how this was going to work) and Marcos was to pilot the boat into the Queens Marina, where Cilia van Hazen, Mulch's cousin, was to meet them. Or so the plan went. Marcos had been instructed to contact her by radio. He had scribbled the channel on a piece of paper, which by now was a little runny and yellowed. According to Mulch's plan, Cilia was to meet Marcos and hand him a one-way plane ticket to Norfolk International Airport, where Huck & Buck Winston (no relation) would be waiting to drive him home.

7

Two days ago Marina had called out to Marcos. She said that she was hungry and Marcos lowered more food to her. Exhausted and disoriented, she didn't talk, not really. To make matters more stressful, Marina didn't understand what was happening to her. She called out for her sister. She called out for Mulch. She called out for Maria. She called out for Mr. Bill. When Marcos tried to explain to her that she could not make any noise, she did not know what to make of it. She looked at him with blank eyes and then fell into a crying fit that made Marcos' spine pretzel up. She must have been going insane. Just like Sea Hag had said she would.

What have I done? By denying her access to the ocean I am killing her.

Shortly after, Marcos had taken to pouring bucketsful of seawater down into the box. He'd fix the helm on auto and spend a few hours dumping seawater on top of her, only to watch it seep into the bed or through the floor. One afternoon he heard the most horrendous scraping only to find Marina digging at the damp floorboards with her hands as if she could escape. No matter how much he called out to her she would not respond. It was during these times that he cursed Mulch and Bill for forcing him to do this. It was horrid watching this beautiful creature disintegrate. He watched her claw at her clothing, and at her skin. Shouting unintelligibly, she tore her fingers into the box carvings he and Sea Hag had labored on. At night he listened to her scream, even as the box pulled behind him in rough seas. Once he was on the boat, he could spend time soothing her as they traveled to Amsterdam.

8

Cilia van Hazen thrived on Marina's pain. Cilia sucked it out like a vampire. She crept into Marina's sleep and pried open her brain with magic. When Cilia looked about her house, she saw right through the beams and brick and out into the canals and streets beyond them. Her blood fired through her like rocket fuel, her brain eating oxygen like candy. When Cilia breathed, her body shook with energy and power. From far away she was twisting Marina already and hoped to have broken her by the time Marina reached Amsterdam. Then she would mold her, touch her, feel her skin. The promise of touching Marina excited her. She would eat her heart, right out of her chest.

Then you can wear her skin on your feet, she thought. *Or harvest her hormones or whatever you like.*

Only Cilia was troubled by one thing. It was a blip on her radar, nothing. Someone was following the box as it traveled up the shore. Cilia had first dreamed of the young man the night Marina had been placed in the box. She dreamed that she had chased him out of the woods. The dream had come out of fitful sleep, and she had awoken to find that her covers were twisted into a kind of rope. Her hands held the roped blankets around her pillow as if she had been trying to kill someone in her sleep. Later she dreamed of his house and that it had no windows, and that this man was somehow communicating with the mermaid. How Marina and this man could do that, she wasn't sure.

Cilia had long ago stopped asking questions about how she knew things. It was enough that the whispers in her head told her so. It was these whispers that informed her that a stranger was following Marina. Rather quickly too, up the shore and into Maryland. At first, he was simply curious. But by the time the man had reached New Jersey the idea more than annoyed her, it made her angry.

Then there was the fact that high winds had slowed Marcos' progress towards Boston. The box was proving to be more of a burden than anticipated. Dragging the box had not been her idea and it was a terrible one in her opinion.

She had made arrangements with Captain Van Dijk to stay in port a few days longer, just in case Marcos was late. *Mulch! That fool could cost her everything,* she fumed.

But the stranger traveled light and was moving all the time.

What made it all worse for Cilia was that she could not invade this man's head. Every time she tried she was bombarded with images – pictures, of water, of a funny-looking man with red hair, a house with no windows, so many shades of paint, liquid, thick and heavy, syrup-like.

She didn't want to think that this man posed a challenge to her. She didn't want to think about him at all. If he were to become a challenge that would mean the whole playing field of the game would have to change.

And if Mulch is trying to double-cross me? The thought had entered her mind. The man was a distant relative, but God knows he was an American. *Pembroke better be keeping a close eye. Pembroke better come through with Mulch's daughter.*

9

At that very moment, Nick Adams felt like he had been kicked up the East Coast by a very angry pro-football team. He felt every bruise on his body where a pair of cleats had kicked him. Each sore spot felt like he had been stepped on by a heavy linebacker. And somehow thinking about the football team made the pain easier to bear. His arms stiff, his legs sunburned and tight, his face felt like it had been scalped, stretched and beaten, and put back on tight as a kettle drum.

The last few days had been a blur. Nick wasn't even sure how long he'd been walking up the coast, or even if he'd walked the whole way. Nick had hiked his jeans up to his waist. He had lost weight, though he wasn't sure how much, it felt like ten pounds, maybe more like fifteen. His backpack was plastered with paint splotches and he heard the many mason jars of water clank and slosh around inside as he moved. Every day for the last week and a half Nick had been emptying his paint jars from the night before only to find them re-filled again in the morning. He had slept on beaches, and riverbanks, under overpasses, and beside the highway, the vibrating hum of passing traffic lulling his senses. His arms and face were riddled with beach fleas, horseflies, and mosquito bites. His skin was now thoroughly tanned and leathered. He smelled like beach and sweat, his hair tangled and hard. What scared Nick the most was how far he'd gotten in such a short time and how much he'd been painting when he was supposed to be asleep. The paintings were clues. He stopped rationalizing them days ago and had found making intuitive leaps about them more accurate. He felt the sanest at night, just before sleep, when he knew he was going to paint. He was the most vulnerable in the morning, after waking up. This morning was no exception. He had awoken to find himself sleeping on a boardwalk somewhere. He held a piece of cardboard to his chest. On it was a smeared painting of a city skyline. His hands had started to shake, and he had the sensation that his teeth were going to fall out. He felt like the more he traveled the more his brain turned to mush. The painting was a mess and he had most of it mashed into his chest hair. He thought it looked like New York City, but he wasn't sure. Panicky, and lonely he called Dial-a-Nurse.

An hour later he wasn't sure he had done the right thing. He was a mess. He would surely be sent to a mental hospital. He looked like some shipwreck victim, only one who couldn't find his way off the Jersey Shore. He needed a cigarette. There were seven dollars in his wallet and sixty-three cents in the bottom of his backpack. A credit card floated down there somewhere, too.

10

"Doc, I want you to know that I don't remember the horrid ride to Richmond. It's all a dull sort of dream, you know? Did you ever block something out and keep it all to yourself? You keep it so long that you don't even know it's yours anymore, and it becomes someone else's memory, someone like you, but not you. You do that because something that bad couldn't happen to you, right? It's like that – deny, repress. – two of the most underrated verbs in the English language. Virginia, I said to myself, you're a survivor. You'll beat whatever this is, just wait, be patient like Mr. Bill taught you. Wait."

11

Mick Ellis's jaw had developed a permanent hang affectation working on the Allbright case. Seems like no one knew anything. What little he did learn was mysterious and suspicious.

The Allbrights had referred him to the Hayes, who had been anything but helpful. Their housekeeper, Maria something or other, allowed him to search Virginia's room. And of course, he found nothing. Even more nothing than Macy Allbright's room. Mulch Hayes, the father had been very rude and suggested he stuff himself with very large objects.

Virginia Hayes' journal read like a soap opera, complete with drugs and hook-ups and the like. Still, there was very little information in the journal. Half of it read like a redneck Bret Easton Ellis novel. The only one who'd been any help was Captain Murdock and all he told him was rumors and conjecture concerning the Hayes family.

Then there was the matter of Adam Taylor, who had also disappeared, according to his grandmother, with that whore of a Hayes girl. A family friend, Richard Bell told him that he was looking in vain, that if he wanted to find them he should start looking underground. He wouldn't elaborate. He was still waiting for his contact at the cell phone company to get back to him. No one knew anything at the feed store. None of the friends had heard from them. He couldn't investigate Virginia's disappearance without pissing off the Hayes family, which was something everyone he spoke to did not want.

Seems like Mr. Hayes' wife had vanished some years ago. Murdock said Mulch had another wife, one nobody had ever seen. But many had seen this particular woman, only no one could remember her name. To which Murdock said that the memories around these here parts have more holes than Swiss cheese.

So Mick went to the courthouse to check out the records. He found a birth certificate for Virginia Hayes, but no record of the mother. On every document concerning the child, the mother's name had been left off. *Something was going on here, what was it?*

12

After delivering Virginia, Pembroke skinned Huck and left him raw and peeled like a shrimp, hanging from a hook in the basement ceiling. He took his time with Buck; he wanted to make a special trophy of Buck and severed his penis and placed it in a jar of formaldehyde. He disposed of their bodies in the James River. Three days later some kids found the bloated and rat-nibbled body of Buck Winston down by the old Virginia Power plant. Buck had no money, no wallet, no ID. By the look of him, the authorities presumed he was a drifter.

Pembroke placed Buck's penis on the nightstand next to Virginia's bed. When he left he leaned over and whispered a few words in Dutch to her, before kissing her on the forehead.

There was waiting to do, she must heal before the fun began.

CHAPTER TWO

1

"Amanda, you are not meeting him," Tanya said, her voice static over the phone.

Amanda heard a computer whirring behind her somewhere. Tanya's boss was cursing someone out.

"I am too."

"You can't."

"T, give me three reasons why I shouldn't."

"You don't know him."

"You're the one who is always saying, always, that the guys I meet are too friendly."

"That is not what I said, girl. And you know it."

"It is, in a nutshell."

"My ass. Plus, you don't know how freaked out this guy is. You know serial killers, that sort of thing. You have got to be out of your fucking mind, Amanda."

"That's only two reasons, and both are paranoid."

"They are not paranoid."

"Yes, they are. I didn't know any of the guys I went out with very well either."

"Yeah, but you meet them in the Cabana Bar, or at Stinky Joe's, where people know them. You don't meet them on the phone, from far away. What if he's really ugly?"

"Ugly is *in* by the way, didn't you read this week's *Entertainment Weekly*?"

"That's so five minutes ago. Please"

"Listen, Tanya, I've already given him directions."

"He's coming to your office!?!"

"No, we're meeting at Stinky Joe's. We're doing the lunch thing."

"You are fucking crazy, girl."

"What if he's totally cute and sexy and all?" Amanda fumbled with the nico-gum. Her mouth was totally dry, as in Sahara dry.

"Amanda? Remember Ray?"

"Yes. But..."

"Remember what Ray did?"

"Yes..."

"Say it."

"No. I'm over Ray."

"Say it girl, or I'm moving out."

Pause.

"Ray left me for a dog catcher. Look it was more complicated than that!"

"Ray was gay honey. And where did you meet Ray?"

"At the clinic."

"What was that?" Tanya's volume increased. Tanya's boss's voice faded into the white chatter of office noise. "Let's hear it?"

"I met him at the clinic when I was in nursing school."

"And what did you make me promise to do?"

"To bring Ray up whenever I met somebody cute from the clinic."

"That's right."

"You don't have to be homophobic about."

"Don't hit me with that. You made me promise. That's what friends do."

"But this isn't the clinic."

"Yeah. It's worse. It's Dial-a-Nurse honey. DIAL-A-NURSE. People call you up when they have no insurance. Drug dealers call Dial-a-Nurse."

"God. You make us sound like..."

"Porno perverts who think you'll walk over their back in high heels wearing nothing but a stethoscope call Dial-a-nurse."

"We're kind of legit."

"Homeless people don't even call Dial-a-Nurse."

"We offer lots to the community at large."

"Guys with weird things inserted in their butts call Dial-a-Nurse."

"Honestly, just last week we saved a guy's life."

"People with mother issues call Dial-a-Nurse."

"He said we helped more than 911. That we helped him bandage the organ immediately before the paramedics arrived. Saved his life we did."

"Did you say organ?"

"And yesterday we helped an old nun find the best clinic to get free pain killers."

"Serial killers call Dial-a-Nurse. Did I mention that?"

"We have the highest percentage of calls on the east coast."

"Save it, Amanda. Didn't you say, just last night, that you would walk over coals to work at the hospice? At the Public Health Center? Hell, at a nursing home?"

"Um. Yes."

"Then don't get on your high horse to look down at me. Look I gotta go. Randy's looking at me with that stressed-out look in his eyes."

"Look we'll chat at dinner."

"Ciao."

"Ciao."

Amanda felt worse than ever.

2

Nick's hands shook so badly he dropped his quarter into the sandy gravel below. It was hot out. It was his last quarter. He bent over and picked it up and when he stood up again he saw Stinky Joe's. He hadn't seen it before. He didn't think it had been there before, like a mirage. After all, Jersey was a kind of desert. Nick blinked and crossed his fingers that Stinky Joe's would be there when he opened his eyes next. A car zoomed by, and his shirt lifted with the breeze. Someone called him a fucking bum. There was the smell of exhaust and as he closed his eyes again he felt himself waver and begin to fall. But he didn't. He steadied himself and when he opened his eyes again, Stinky Joe's was there. Crystal clear. Just like he had hoped. The reflecting sun glinting off the panes, bouncing back to his dirty shoes. Nick would need new shoes soon, the soles were separating from the body.

Nick stood there for what felt like a long time. He felt like he was coming unglued. Somewhere kicking around his brain was a beautiful woman, a familiar woman. And swimming about in the back of his head was the idea that she was in danger and that he had to save her from harm, from death even somehow. The paintings were the key, Nick knew this, but one side of his brain told him that he was as crazy as a shit-house rat for thinking such nonsense. For the last several days, Nick had begun to think that there was something to that crazy old Sea Hag. Maybe he was cursed by something, the hag woman perhaps, who for some untold reason in the stars had picked his body and soul to split apart by simply yanking his sleep out from under him and forcing him to run and paint.

But where was he going?

Nick crossed the street and looked inside Stinky Joe's. He had to squint through the glare on the glass. It wasn't too crowded; he should be fine. He went inside and took a seat.

It was dim, which he liked, and there was a jukebox playing Hank Williams Sr. very low and it gave the place a down-home sort of feel to Nick, which was exactly what he needed – some down-home comfort. Stinky Joe's was a bar that was also a diner, but probably more of a late afternoon watering hole from the looks and smell of it. The air had a stale beer and cigarette waft, and he noticed that the stools were well worn and shiny from the many asses that had sat upon them. The waitress barely looked at him when he ordered his coffee and a Danish. The waitress scribbled the order and backed away from his table before she had finished. Nick opened his backpack and removed his sketchpad.

3

Amanda nervously popped her gum and pumped up her hair, though the humidity had already turned her dark hair into a droopy mess. She heard Tanya saying, "Don't worry about your hair spray. Worry about your pepper spray."

Stinky Joe's was a white-pinkish building where she and Tanya liked to spend Thursday nights. Thursday nights were FIFTY CENT pitcher nights and Tanya loved a good beer. So did Amanda, but Amanda preferred Tequila to brew. Tanya particularly liked Stinky Joe's because it was as she put it "New Jersey Redneck Heaven" with a gay dance night that boasted the best DJ in three zip codes. Tanya booked talent in gay clubs, comedy clubs, African American clubs, retro-disco bars, and everything else in-between from the Jersey Shore, through Atlantic City, all the way up to New York City, and into Boston. Amanda loved Tanya but liked to be around Tanya because Tanya was the focus of the spotlight and Amanda could get close without having to squint from the brightness. Nothing ever happened to Amanda, she was a boredom magnet, which is the main reason why she'd agreed to meet Nick.

Amanda peered in from the outside. Pointless, she huffed. She couldn't see anything worth a squat. Once inside she ascertained that Nick was either the scruffy skinny thing in the back, or he hadn't come in yet.

"Hey," she said to the bartender, whom she didn't know by name, but by sight.

"Hey," he said hey like he was checking her out.

"Could I get some coffee and maybe a menu?"

"Sure."

The bartender was a young guy with his hair bleached at the tips.

The scruffy skinny thing in the back hadn't looked up, nor did he look like he was going to. He was engrossed in what appeared to be a sketchbook.

"Excuse me?"

Amanda lit up a fresh cigarette. She had purchased a pack on her way over. No way she was going into a potentially dangerous situation without nicotine.

"Are you Nick Adams?"

Nick immediately looked up and nodded.

"I don't know where to begin," he said.

Nick kept his hands below the table, nervously rubbing them together.

"Well, why don't we start with introductions," she said as she sat down and extended her hand. "I'm Amanda. Why don't you start at the beginning.?"

"Okay. Do you want to hear this? Really?"

She nodded.

"Okay. Two weeks ago. God, I can't believe it's only been that long. Feels like more. Anyway, I awoke to find that I had painted this thing. It wasn't a picture; it was mostly just blue. Here, I took a Polaroid of it."

He handed her a stack of Polaroids, and she began to flip through them.

"Not with a cell phone?"

"When you are traveling by foot you don't have places to charge your devices.

"True, true."

"Wait, don't look too far ahead. You have to go through it carefully, to get the whole story. You know."

"I guess," she said inhaling. "Is this your house?"

"Yup. that's my house.

"There are no windows."

"Weird huh?"

"Yeah. I couldn't live in a house without windows."

"It used to have windows."

"So why did you board them up?"

"I didn't."

"Well, who did?"

"Woke up after a night of painting and then they were gone, vanished."

"You're shitting me?"

"No. I'm not."

"Come on."

"Really. Yeah, I did that in my sleep too." He pointed to the large moon on the outside. "There was one in-between those two, but I painted it over."

"Why?"

"I fell asleep on the job and painted some woman's wall green and red. I'm not sure what it was, it didn't look like anything. Anyways, then I painted that one."

"Cool moon."

"That one on my house that very night."

"You're not an insomniac, are you?"

"What? No. Three pictures in twenty-four hours. My arms were stiff and sore like you wouldn't believe. The next day I had an.... *episode*."

Amanda visualized her pepper spray not working. This guy was odd, but he didn't seem dangerous. Desperate maybe, but not dangerous. However, she knew that desperate became dangerous under stress.

"What kind of episode?"

"An episode where I ate a fish raw. Not like I wanted to or anything. Best to leave out the details. And not like sushi, either. I was driven to.... driven as in possessed to. Yes, possessed. That's the right word for it."

"Weird."

Amanda's hair prickled. A chill ran down her spine.

"The second night I came home and had a... dream."

Nick paused. He wasn't sure how Amanda was taking all this. She seemed nice enough. *She probably thinks I'm crazy,* he thought.

"It was the most vivid dream, too. Full of water and boats and a giant box. I dreamed that I was a mermaid and that I was trying to free myself from a huge box. An iron box, I think, I'm not sure. I only know that it's big, really big. It was being pulled by a boat. That was the night I discovered the windows had disappeared."

Amanda lit a second cigarette and scooted back an inch or two from the table. She looked over to the bar. The bartender hadn't noticed the smoke.

"Sounds crazy right?"

Amanda didn't say anything. Nick looked normal. Ragged and sunburned, but normal. A deep stink rolled off him, like sandwich meat long in the sun.

"Tell me if this gets to be too much. Anyways I fainted. I fell dead asleep from exhaustion. Then I took off with this here sketchbook and a bunch of paint. Paint that I forgot I had. You know the cool little vials of paint artists use? Yeah, those. Some brushes. Four in fact. Two small brushes for the pad, and two large brushes for um...er...larger canvases? I also took an old Polaroid camera. The Polaroid had been socked in a box somewhere in my house. It had plenty of film and so I took pictures of the paintings in and on my house and then I took off. I drove to Delaware and was so exhausted I had to check into a motel, at like two 'o clock in the afternoon.

"That's when the real trouble began."

Amanda ashed her smoke and crossed her arms over her chest.

"I painted the hotel wall. I don't know where I got that paint, only that when I awoke later that night, sometime around midnight actually, I had done this."

Amanda looked at the bent Polaroid and her jaw dropped.

"Yeah, that."

It was a beautiful picture of a naked mermaid.

"She's the woman in my dreams."

"Um, that's a mermaid."

Nick didn't reply.

"They don't exist Nick."

It was an exquisite composition. The mermaid stretched over the back half of the wall, over the bed. Nick had removed two floral prints and had set them aside. She spied them in the bottom corners of the picture. Amanda noted that the walls were several shades whiter where the paintings had hung. The mermaid's hair was long and greenish-black. She was positioned face down so her breasts were not exposed, but her head was turned back as if she was looking behind her. Her fin looped up at the end like a comma. The painting had to have been six feet in length.

"It's very pretty, Nick."

Amanda had read in one of her nursing textbooks that if one used someone's name over and over again, an unconscious bond would form between them. If Nick was crazy, then maybe Nick wouldn't want to kill her if he felt comfortable around her.

"It's she that's pretty."

Nick looked at the painting with moons in his eyes.

Okay, head for the door, Amanda. She heard Tanya telling her to leave. T.V.O.R. as Amanda called her – The Voice of Reason. Tanya liked it when Amanda called her that.

"I know it sounds crazy."

"Not really."

"Yes, it does."

"It could be worse."

"It gets worse."

"Oh?"

Amanda couldn't remember the last time she'd tested the pepper spray, much less held it in the ready.

"I awoke from my sleep, from my painting, from my sleep-painting, whatever you want to call it. I awoke in a complete panic, I was freaking out, my heart was exploding in my chest and my head was spinning. I thought I was going to go all exorcist on myself."

"Why?"

"Turns out something had been following me."

"Something?"

"Yeah. A haint."

"A haint?"

"Yeah, like a ghost, since the first night that all this started happening. This white hag-like thing chased me through the forest when I was coming home from the...when I was coming home. And then there are times where I can feel her whisper these weird things to me. I can feel her breath on my body. She says, 'Fish-girl. Come get your food fish-girl.'"

Nick shivered.

"Sheesh. God. Then she was there in the hotel room that night, breathing on me like I had been right about her that whole time. I can feel her now. She feels like a breeze on your skin. Anyways I panicked, I grabbed my pack and ran. I didn't even think to take my car. I ran straight back behind the hotel, which turned out was this field – a potato field. I ran for hours, probably. Then I fell asleep in a ditch somewhere."

"Yuk," Amanda remarked as she tried to keep it neutral.

"Yeah. I woke up with five ticks on me. I'm not sure if the last one came off."

"You've been on foot ever since?"

"Yeah, well I think so, I found myself near the shore. I walked for a few more miles until I got to the coast and followed the Atlantic straight up."

"You walked up the coast?"

"Coastal highways, backroads, and boardwalk and stuff, not so bad really. But yes, mostly, I think so."

"And the rest?" Amanda pointed to the pictures.

"All the way up the shore. There's one that I painted one on the side of a hotel, Security Guard beat me with a flashlight."

Nick raised his shirt and revealed an apple-sized bruise. Three smaller bruises orbited the large one like planets.

"Jesus!"

"Don't have a photo for that one."

"Awful."

"Yeah, but mostly I painted in this sketchbook. Or on large pieces of trash I'd find."

"Very chic."

"I painted something last night on a piece of cardboard. I'm painting on everything."

"Wow."

Then Nick opened his sketchbook and handed it to Amanda. His heart thundered in his chest. He hoped Amanda wouldn't be his undoing. He imagined her spraying his face with mace and calling the cops. He imagined them arriving with a white jacket and sending him to a place with padded walls and no phone calls. He was sure the hag would find him if he stopped moving, that the hag would whisper in his ear until he completely unraveled.

The first sketch in the book was labeled Tuesday 6/10. Nick had used colored pencils and pastels, all of which had run together and across the right upper corner to create a blobby, bloody looking thing that reminded Amanda of a gross experience at summer camp when her tent mate had woken up in the middle of night bleeding from a bug bite on her forehead. The sketch was of a large boat pulling a giant box. The box was all black and there seemed to be a bubble of a voice, or a thought rising from one side into the blobby, bloody smear in the right corner. Amanda thought that the sketch looked like a kid's drawing, but with a little more sophistication. She lit another cigarette only to find that she had not extinguished her last smoke that lay on the edge of the danish plate. Its smoke curled upwards into the air and made Amanda think of punctuation.

"Hey, Dial-a-Nurse," the bartender shouted, "no smoking."

Amanda smiled and nodded but did not extinguish her cig.

The second sketch was labeled DELAWARE 6/11 and had more, *what was the word she wanted to use? Body. That was it.* The sketch showed more artistry and for a second she doubted that Nick Adams, the scruffy skinny man across from her eyeing her pack of smokes like a wolf, was painting and drawing these sketches while he was asleep. They were too good, even though childlike, to be done while asleep. Perhaps Nick Adams, who was practically eating her smokes with his eyes, was stringing her along the proverbial way and was planning to either a) kill her b) rape her c) both a & b or d) invent some new and utterly disgusting way to mutilate her body.

"Would you like a cigarette?"

"Yes." Nick helped himself to her pack, his hands shaking as he fumbled with the matchbook. "Thanks. What about the bartender?"

Amanda dismissed the idea with a wave of her hand. "Never mind him."

The second sketch pulled Amanda's eyes back to the book. It showed a hag-like woman with knife-like teeth reaching down from the sky and gnashing her teeth at a scared little girl hiding under her bedsheets.

"That's the one that did it for me," Nick said, smoke curling from his nose.

Why? Because you are a psycho? Amanda thought.

"Really?" Amanda said politely.

"Yes. See I don't remember much of the dreams. The drawings and the paintings are kind of like my memory, though they are expressionistic. What I mean to say is, that I, Nick Adams, cannot remember what it was that I was dreaming about, only what it feels like when I'm dreaming. That is to say what it feels like when *she's* dreaming. Do you see what I mean?"

"You've lost me here Nick."

"That is to say since I paint and travel in my sleep, these sketches serve as memories of the dreams."

"Okay?"

"And I think I'm dreaming what she's dreaming. I think these sketches are her dreams."

"This little girl is who you are dreaming about?"

"I don't think she is a *little* girl. That's what she felt like in this dream."

"What she felt like?"

"Yes. That thing. That horrid woman that has been chasing me, following me, I should say. I don't know who or what she is. I believe that she is the antagonist of the woman I am dreaming for."

"This woman. This mermaid?"

"Yes."

"This woman, this mermaid. Is somehow communicating with you? Through your, or her dreams?" *If Nick was painting in his sleep, maybe I could get a research grant and get out of Dial-a-Nurse for once and all. Write my own ticket, so to speak,* Amanda thought.

Nick nodded.

Amanda was honestly a terrible Dial-a-Nurse nurse, but she did have a real nose for the odd and weird. Which was why, she thought subconsciously, that she had left the clinic for Dial-a-Nurse, which had been in many ways a draining but enriching experience, the clinic if one liked a chorus line of STDs, and vomit, lots and lots of vomit. If Dial-a-Nurse was anything, it was odd and weird.

"About me, I do a lot of reading, for fun you know," Amanda said gently.

"And?"

"And what?"

"What do you read?" Nick asked.

"Oh."

Nick seemed calmer to her, now that he was smoking. Nick's kind face and lazy drawl disarmed Amanda and she felt herself thinking she could work with this man, this patient.

"I like to read about occult stuff, you know, like magic, or even less magical academic ephemera like Native American mysticism and dream knowledge and tarot cards, and shit like that," Amanda explained as she sipped her coffee. "It's kind of a hobby. My sister was really into astrology way back when. *Aliens in Antarctica* is the last really hot thing that I've been into."

"Right."

"Really. I've read about sisters who have like spoken to each other in their dreams from across the country, from one coast to the other."

"And you think that's what's happening here?"

"Sure, Nick, why not?"

"But I don't know this woman."

"So?"

"So you're talking about sisters. This woman is a stranger. And this woman is not a woman at all. She's more than a woman, she's a..."

"I had a sorority sister like that once," The waitress said, appearing from nowhere, popping her gum much like Amanda did when she was on the phone. "We're tight, Emma and me. I chat with her every other day almost, my sister." She stood with one hip out. "More coffee?"

Nick and Amanda nodded in tandem, and she refilled their cups.

"I painted this one after the problems at the hotel, you know," He said as he raised his shirt to show the bruises.

The third sketch showed a man's blurry face. Nick wasn't a very gifted illustrator, and the face had the crude less-than-professional feel that one might see on the back of notebooks or the tops of desks in high school. The person had a thought bubble that contained a picture of a skyline. At least Amanda thought it was a skyline. It looked like it could also have been the readings on a defibrillator, or an EKG line.

"I've painted that twice now."

"The...er...guy?" Amanda asked.

"No, the skyline there. I don't recognize it. Do you?"

Amanda looked back to the skyline. It could have been New York. It didn't look like New York. It could be Philly. Or Boston. For that matter, it could have been Trenton.

"No. I don't."

"Damn. I think it's meant to mean something."

Amanda flipped the sketchbook pages to a giant fish that appeared to be swimming. The fish had a frenzied scribbling about it. She grunted.

"I'm pretty sure I drew that one standing up. While I was walking."

"What?"

"Well, it was about then that I started walking and running a lot in my sleep. As if I had to get somewhere very quickly. Besides I couldn't lay down because of my bruises."

"Oh."

"In the drawing, the fish is dying because it's out of water."

"How do you know?" Amanda said as she looked down at the fish again. The fish did look like it was in pain, but it looked like it was in the water to her.

"I wrote something on the back of that one."

"Oh." She flipped the sketch over and saw: Walking/Fish/Out of water/ Toe jam.

"Toe jam?"

"My feet were really dirty."

"Eeew."

"Yes. I had lots of mud and sand in my shoes the next day. Something yellow was clinging to my..."

"Don't. Please."

"Ok."

The next sketch made Amanda feel a little uncomfortable. The hag-like woman was back and was tearing bits of flesh from the girl, who still looked innocent and young but was now an innocent and young mermaid, being ripped apart at the tail. The sketch was rendered in lots of reds and browns which made Amanda think of the sepia bloodstains that covered the floors of the waiting room in the public clinic from the migrants who had suffered farm equipment accidents who didn't have the insurance to be seen in the hospitals.

The next sketch, which was the last one, was of a beach. On the beach, there was a little man, which looked a lot like Nick. Nick seemed to be either getting ready to swim or had just finished a swim. He was naked and drawn with impressive anatomical correctness which made Amanda blush a bit.

Nick opened his backpack, and Amanda leaned over to peer in furtively. Inside she saw two Mason jars, which she assumed he used to mix paint, or to wash brushes. She saw the brushes he had talked about, boxes of colored pencils and pastels, a few rolled-up pieces of paper, and one folded-up piece of cardboard that didn't want to completely fold, and what she assumed was the Polaroid.

"Here," he handed her a roll of papers and the half-folded-up cardboard which flopped open before her.

She looked at the cardboard painting first. It had been done with some kind of acrylics, its colors unmixed and straight from the tube. It was the skyline, again. There appeared to be some sort of arrow, or perhaps it was just a brushstroke that looked like an arrow; the arrow/brushstroke pointed to the city, wherever it was. There was a harbor and large skyscrapers. There was a blinking red light far in the distance with lots of gray clouds, and lots of rain, *maybe it was Seattle?* It was a seaport, wherever it was.

Amanda placed the skyline aside. Parts of its blue water were still damp. A bit of the grayish-blue paint rubbed off on her thumb. She tried to wipe it off with a napkin. Nick eyed her cigarettes like they were naked boobs. Amanda pulled two out.

"Take a picture will ya," she said smiling. She looked back at the bartender who had moved up front to pour drinks. "I'll leave him a big tip."

She lit hers and then his, handing him one. Amanda turned to the rolls of drawings. One painting was on newspaper (it was more paint than newspaper, she noted), one was on the back of a red, white, and blue 'Re-elect Sheriff Hasbro' ten by twelve card-stock sign, and one was on the back of a poster that had been at one time plastered on the side of a club wall. The words KITTY CLUB bled through the green and blue paint. Each of the paintings showed the girl. The one on newspaper was of the girl's face in the moon. *Rather romantic,* Amanda thought. That particular painting was gritty. Nick explained he had used sand as an added texture. The one on the back of the re-elect Sheriff Hasbro sign showed the girl thinking or dreaming of fish. Amanda wasn't sure and was sure that Nick wasn't sure himself so there was no use in asking him. In the corner of that picture, there was the face of the hag. The hag seemed to be gnashing her teeth together again. Her lips were a bloody red. The last one showed a giant lighthouse on the shore of some beach. In the distance, there was the box, and it was either coming into shore or leaving the shore. There was no boat. Amanda wanted to know what the box was. She had read stories about freaks who kept their girlfriends in boxes under their beds to make them obedient. Amanda didn't think this was one of those situations. The words KITTY CLUB bled through the bottom, on the beach like some fleeting message a couple of kids would have scrawled with their toes in the sand.

"I was hoping, among the many things that are confusing me, that you might be able to help me figure out which city it is that I keep painting."

"Hmm," Amanda sighed. "I don't know. Honest."

"Let me tell you my theory."

"You have a theory?"

"I have. Well sort of. I think. Somebody wants me to go somewhere. I believe that there is somebody in trouble. This mermaid, I think. I don't know anything about the box. Though I assume that somebody is keeping this mermaid captive in a box."

"Like at the fair."

"The fair?"

"Yes. You know, the freak shows. With those bubbled glass portholes that you buy a ticket to stare down at a girl who is obviously not a mermaid but is dolled up to look like one. You know what I mean?"

"Um. No."

"Never you mind then."

"I think this person is in trouble. I think somebody wants to help her. And I think I'm being possessed to be the one to do so."

"Possessed?" Amanda hated the film *The Exorcist*, hated it, couldn't even watch snippets of it, couldn't even stand to glimpse at Linda Blair. "Don't say possessed."

"Why not?"

"Because it's evil."

"This doesn't feel like an evil possession."

"Say what?"

"This doesn't feel like an evil possession."

"How do you know what an evil possession feels like?"

"I don't. This just doesn't feel evil to me."

"And what does it feel like?"

"It feels like I'm supposed to help somebody."

"Oh."

Nick rolled the loose paintings back up and slid them into his backpack. He placed his sketchbook inside too, and unfolded the cardboard skyline, and drummed his fingers on the top of the fluffy gray clouds that looked like storm clouds.

"Thanks for meeting me here. I know it's sketchy to meet people you don't know, especially strange guys who call you at work. Thanks for talking, or rather listening to me. Are you sure you don't know where this is?"

"Well, it could be New York. But it looks too skimpy to be New York."

"Yeah, that's what I thought."

"It could be Seattle"

Nick groaned.

"Maybe not. I don't see the space needle. Plus, it has to be on the East Coast. Otherwise, you're likely heading in the wrong direction."

Another groan.

"Do you get any, you know, vibes from your dreams?"

"No. It's like the dreams are teaching me what to do, through the paintings. That reminds me, I have to get some more paint. I was using whatever I could get my hands on. Just some shit, excuse me, stuff my buddy George had given me like years ago. George, he's an artist. He gave me some paints to encourage me to start painting, so we could eventually paint together. Never mind. Say you wouldn't happen to know where there's an art supply store around here?"

"Yeah. I think I do."

"There's one a block over. The Muse," The waitress said as she let go of their ticket and watched it float down like a fall leaf onto the grayish skyline. "Yeah, my boyfriend is an artist." She made finger flexions around the word, "artist." She popped her gum. "Cool picture of Boston. Going there next week. Gonna be one hell of a party. Let me tell you."

Nick looked at Amanda and Amanda looked at Nick. Suddenly there was a kind of electricity in the air between them and Amanda's hair began to thicken with static.

"Are you sure it's Boston?" Nick stammered.

"Yeah, of course, I'm sure. My brother's there in college. Some art school." Again, she used her finger flexions around the words, "art school". "Emer-something or another."

"Are you positive?" Amanda looked up into the waitress' eyes, they were red and smoky.

"Yeah. Sure I'm sure. See that red dot in the middle of the painting?" She pointed it out. "That there's the Handycock tower or something. It flashes red or blue depending on the weather. Also flashes when there's a Red Sox game or something."

"Really?"

"Yeah. I go see my brother twice a year, me and my girlfriends. Boston is a real party town. It closes early, but they still know how to throw down," the waitress winked.

Nick looked for a nametag but couldn't see one. There was a pin that looked like it had some dried glue on it.

"Pay for the coffees anytime you want," the waitress said.

"Thanks," Nick said. His heart gunned in his chest.

Amanda grabbed the ticket. "I'll pay for it."

"That's okay. I can pay my way."

"Really. It's okay, I got it."

Nick grabbed for the ticket, but Amanda snatched it first.

"Look it's my good deed for the day. My deposit in the karma bank."

Amanda left a hefty three-dollar tip on a nine-dollar tab, threw a fiver on the bar as an apology for smoking, and joined Nick outside.

"I'm going to check out that art store," Nick said shaking her hand.

"I have to go back to work. Listen what else can I do for you? Anything?"

"Let me think about it. I don't want to impose."

"Stay at my place tonight. No romance, country boy. I want to pick your brain some more, maybe for a grant. Plus, you need the rest."

Nick shuffled his feet and looked down at them. "I don't know. I don't want to make things um...er...inconvenient for you, like if you have a boyfriend or roommates."

"Don't worry about that. I'll kick you out in the morning. First thing. I swear. Also, you could use a shower. Believe me."

"Um..." Nick shuffled on his feet some more.

"You can use my phone, to call home. I'm sure your parents are worried about you."

"I can't remember my phone number or my parents."

"What?"

"Ever since this thing happened, my memory's been all screwed up."

"Oh, shit." The sun glinted off a Lexus windshield and bounced into Amanda's eyes. She held her hand up to shield herself.

"No worries," Nick said.

Amanda thought he sounded remorseful.

"Look meet me here in front of Stinky Joe's at 5:00. We'll have dinner at my place, me and my roommate will show you some hospitality."

"Roommate? You do have a roommate." Nick's stomach went loopy and his brain dropped into his bowels. He didn't think he could socialize with anyone.

"Don't worry about it. A good deed in the karma bank and all that. I may have a few questions about your overall dreams I'd like to ask you, maybe take some notes. She'll be fine with it. Get your paints. Do you need any money?"

"No worries."

"Okay?"

"Okay."

"See you here at 5:00?"

"Yes, see you at 5:00. Right here. At Stinky Joe's"

Amanda waved and turned to huff it down the street. She was going to be late getting back to work. *Fuck it*, she thought. Something stirred inside of her, a feeling of downright goodness. *God*, she thought, *I hope he doesn't think I'm like gonna jump his bones or something. Nah, probably not. He's got it bad for his damsel in distress. As long as this isn't some kind of scam.*

How was Tanya going to take it? That was the real horror.

4

Abdullah followed George as he paced across the lawn. Abdullah didn't so much follow George as he mimicked George. George didn't seem to notice, and if he did, he paid him no mind. George had come outside to smoke a joint, and to get some fresh air. Ab followed behind, wearing the new giant overalls that made him look more like a very large, albeit blue, handyman than a magical genie. Ab had conjured them a couple of days ago when Nick hadn't shown up for work and Ab helped his new master with a series of odd jobs.

The last time George had seen Nick was the day he painted that thing on Mrs. Enfield's closet door. When Nick hadn't returned his phone calls, he and Ab had gone over to see what was going on. *Nick's house had been a disturbing glimpse into the mind of the insane,* George thought in recollection.

The matter of the windows bothered George the most. They were just gone, smoothed over as they had never been there in the first place. The siding looked equally weathered where the windows should have been, a detail that bothered George the most, to say nothing of the giant painting on the back of the house which was truly disturbing because it suggested to George that Nick was not getting the kind of restful sleep that Nick deserved and desperately needed.

On the other hand, Abdullah had loved the moon painting and thought it was wonderful.

George stopped to scratch his head. When he turned around to look at Abdullah, he saw that Abdullah was scratching his head in the same spot that he was.

5

"Doc, the severed penis bedside table beside my new bed did little to ease my state of mind. Doc, it looked like a plastic, rubbery thing, floating in the amber liquid. It was the hair growing on the base of the shaft that made me vomit that first day. Of course, the penis had been attached to someone, but the little tufts of dark pubic hair made it real for me. The hairs curled up like tiny Qs."

My food was left in the hallway and my fresh linens too. My door remained unlocked, though the hallway outside was coated in fog, and the fog whispered along the floor. I bathed at least three times a day for the first few days. They were hot baths. I scrubbed, I cried, and I sweated. I iced my bruises; I took the pills Pembroke left for me. Hey, I'm no fool. The house was so cold that hot baths were necessary to warm throughout the day and night. On the third day, I started to do push-ups and sit-ups, because I had nothing to do. And they kept me warm too.

As I said, the fog kept the house as cold as a tomb. The cold seeped through the floorboards, into the hallway, and my room. I felt that the fog wanted me, it kept calling my name. It's true. That fucking fog rubbed its hands together spoke. I have nightmares about it today.

The wooden windows of the room were bolted shut and behind them, on the outside, were skeletal bars of iron bolted into the walls. The inside of the window panes was covered in heavy condensation, the room being so cold. I cannot tell you how many times in the first few days I jumped, tapped, flailed my arms at the passing pedestrians below. Not one person heard me. After a while, I gave up. In hindsight, Pembroke's scheme was ingenious. At first, I saw nothing of the man. I would wait, my ear pressed as close as I could get it to the door of my room without touching it, waiting to hear just one footstep, one word, one slide of silverware, something, anything I would wait until my stomach was paining for food, and when I opened the door, there my food was, sometimes cold, or just luke-warm, but I never heard him deliver it. It was always vegetables, always bread, and always cheese, but nothing else except the pills. One was an antibiotic; I recognized the code. And the other two were Vicodin. Pembroke also included three cigarettes with each dinner meal, which I eagerly smoked up as soon as the last bite was in my mouth. I supposed he delivered the food when I exercised, but I wasn't sure. Then I thought he delivered it when I bathed since I bathed close to breakfast, lunch, and dinner time. So to try and catch him, I would start the bath and instead of getting in, I'd wait by the door, listening for something, anything. Then I would randomly open the door to try to catch him, just to see what he looked like. But when I opened the door, I only ever saw the fog, which whispered and gleefully lapped into my room like an eager pet.

The room itself had been painted a dull charcoal gray, with black trim. At night the gray took on a black look and a black feel. At first, the color both horrified me first, *who would want a black room*? How was that any good? But the more I stayed in the room the more the color grew on me. The room felt larger because of the black, rather than smaller. At any moment I felt that I could push into the walls and expand the room to fit any size that I wanted.

It was on perhaps the fifth day when I felt that one push was all it would take to make the walls fall back when I heard the ghosts. It was a woman's voice that spoke with a high-Southern Virginian drawl, the type which exists only in the most affluent circles of Virginia. At first, it sounded eerily like one of my high school teachers who was from such a circle, but the more I heard it, the more I realized that it was of course not my teacher. This woman clipped on about the help incessantly. My heart rose in my chest and for a second at the thought that I was finally going to see someone. The voices grew louder and louder until they were right there in my room.

"Very snobby, I thought. What's the word, genteel?

"That's it. Genteel.

"The hairs on my neck and body rose and my skin turned cold and clammy, just like they say it does in the movies when one encounters a ghost. The voices trailed out of the room and back out into the hall. They'd come and go sometimes, sometimes the fog made it worse, sometimes the fog made it better.

"That evening was the first time I heard the screams.

"Now it may seem rather typical for a haunted house to scream or possess ghosts that scream. I know it's all very standard and well documented in books, poems, black and white movies, and old, moldy folk songs, etc. But to be inside a house that has ghosts in it is quite another thing. Now, I never did see any ghosts. There were no funny lights, no green slime monsters, no floaters, no nothing. I did hear all sorts of things, but as I said, I never saw one myself. There were all sorts of murmurings and they seemed to float in under my door via tiny wisps of fog.

"Then it all made sense to me.

"The fog was some kind of amplifier.

"That night I stayed under my sheets and hardly slept. Sometimes I caught snatches of words. Sometimes all I heard were the screams. But there was always the fog, of course, whispering my name and sliding against the door. With nothing else I could do, I re-lit all my butts and smoked them down into the filter, and I counted the hours until morning. I hoped that the light would at least make the noises more bearable.

"It had been six days, six days, and try as I might I had not laid eyes on my cousin Pembroke once."

6

Pembroke's toes stretched like ten fat and ungainly spider legs, the smallest toe six inches in length and the largest almost a foot in length and an inch wide, and at times they moved with the crawl of an eight-legged animal and at times they behaved like snakes, with each limb moving independently of another propelling Pembroke over the floor as if he were floating. The fog lapped up around Pembroke and formed curly q's behind him, thickening the foggy hallway with whispers, obscuring his grotesque feet from view.

He's coming for you pretty one
This one for fun
Like the other

Virginia had awoken to find herself standing stationary at the end of the very cold and foggy hallway, the door to her bedroom, behind her, shut. Her eyes encrusted with sleep boogers. In her sleep, she had been dreaming of Marina, who like her, was somehow in trouble. Virginia stood stock still and very straight, her spine felt like it had been being pulled upwards by an invisible thread, her frozen arms at her side. It was the whispers of the fog that woke her.

Meat for the grind
My look how she pales
Isn't she sweet
All that meat

The fog formed tentacle-like hands and wrapped around her ankles. She felt her body heat drain into the mist. In front of her stood a very tall man with a monocle. She knew that it had to be Pembroke. Seeing him for the first time made her skin crawl, turn cold, and her head ache. Blood throbbed against her eyes, and it felt like someone was pressing a very large book against her inner forehead - like there was a roach that needed to be squashed.

The fog filled up the hallway, and Pembroke's eyes burned through the fog, a steely whitish-blue that flashed to black. It was then when she saw his toes snaking in and out of the fog. Pembroke lifted his leg and the toe shot up to his chin. It reminded Virginia of the Plastic Man cartoon she used to watch as a girl.

"It is finally time we speak," Pembroke said as his big toe scratched his chin. "Your father has given you to me." Pembroke licked the fat toe before it shot back under the fog. Virginia thought she heard the toe hiss.

Virginia noticed more pink things squirming around under the fog. They were toes, *ten snaky toes. Why is my family so weird,* she thought?

"Your father thinks I should break you."

Virginia looked up to Pembroke.

"What do you think of that?" Pembroke said as his eyes flickered in the cool hallway. his thick overcoat swaying like a cape. "You may follow now."

Virginia wasn't sure what was happening to her. Her spine began to crawl, her legs stretched out beneath her, but her arms remained still.

She is ours now, the fog whispered. There was giggling in the fog, an undercurrent of girlish ghouls.

Her trembling started before she knew what was happening and her body shook with convulsions. "It's .... so...cold," Virginia stammered.

"Let's get you warm then, shall we. Follow me, if you please."

Virginia's legs lurched forward, her muscles stiff and still, her head straight and her spine stock straight. It occurred to her as the fog parted and weaved around her body that she didn't know what time it was, or how long she had been out, or even what day it was. Realizing that was not in control of her body, panic exploded in her mind like tiny pinpricks of white flashing light.

7

"The top floors are all bedrooms. Though at one time this may have been a study perhaps, I'm not so sure about it." Pembroke pointed to the first door at the top of the second-floor landing. "The ghosts that live here still have not given up all the clues yet."

"What do you use it for now?" Virginia said, the words leaving her lips before she had time to stop them.

Pembroke stopped short of the first stair.

"Ah, there is a conversationalist in you after all," he said as he rapped her skull with his knuckles and continued. "I'm going to enjoy opening that brain of yours. Nothing yet my dear. I spend too much time in the lower quarters to make use of the upstairs. But we will, my dear, soon *we will.*"

Virginia did not see the way Pembroke's lips curled over his white teeth, but Virginia felt the tinge of evil in the way he said "we will." It made her think of the time a spider camped out in her tennis shoes one spring. She had put her bare feet right on the monster, the hair on its body made her shiver. *Stay calm, Virginia.*

"Large though it may seem, the house is small, compared to more modern mansions. But the high ceilings, and the marble, and let's not forget the wonderful dining room, the living room, the back study, and the delicious, delicious parlor all make it what it is. Such a wonderful parlor area. You can see where there once was a piano. It is *our* house now, darling. Don't forget it."

The fog whispered its way down the stairs and followed Pembroke through the dining room and into the kitchen, which was large and polished like a new pan. Virginia didn't so much walk as she was carried by some invisible force down the stairs. *I can feel him inside my mind,* she thought. *Perhaps through the fog? The way it touches me, perhaps.*

The tour continued through each floor, each room empty as the last. Only the downstairs rooms had much in terms of furniture, her bedroom aside. The office, the kitchen, the dining room, and the parlor had some furniture, but not nearly the kind of accumulation of objects Virginia had been accustomed to.

The living room was the only place in the house that Virginia felt any warmth. The furniture was stiff and Victorian, not at all comfortable looking, much like the bed in her room. It was very difficult for her to concentrate on Pembroke's tour. It was as if her mind was being clouded by the fog, Pembroke, or both.

"I do like the back study there, especially the desk." Pembroke sneered.

Virginia spied her reflection in the polished wood. She looked haggard and used, warped out and weird.

"The desk covers a nasty bloodstain. The realtor tried to tell me it was cat piss. Nonsense. On wood? To go and slander a perfectly good bloodstain like this one is downright scandalous." Pembroke said as his eyes flashed black to whitish blue, his pupils dilating. "You must see it. It looks almost like your sister."

The fog backed out of the room and hovered outside the living room. Virginia spied Pembroke's toes for the first time without the cover of fog and her stomach twisted at the sight of the plump and oozing sacs of flesh. They looked like they had no bones and the flesh looked hard and scaly. When they wiggled and moved under Pembroke; they would tense and Virginia witnessed the toe muscles flex and push against the skin, the skin which appeared swollen with poison. With sick fascination she watched the two big toes push against the old desk, straining at first, then succeeding in moving the old desk an inch, then another, the toes swelling and oozing thick white pus. She swore she heard them hiss like snakes. Virginia's eyes followed Pembroke's toes as they snaked him closer to the stain, which was stretched out like a C, except there were arms at the top of the C and a slight fork at the bottom of the C.

"You see, like a mermaid. Like your sister. See how someone tried to wash the stain from the wood. Silly things, the wood simply faded around the stain, making the stain much easier to see."

Virginia's knees grew weak.

"Oh dear," Pembroke said.

The fog giggled and Virginia knew that it was giggling at her.

Fall, fall

Meat go boom

Hee hee he

Timber goes the tree

The floor spun up towards her and Virginia didn't feel like she was falling at all, on the contrary, she felt as if the house was coming up on end and falling towards her, the fog creeping up towards her twisting her stomach from the cold. Her headache came back worse than before, like a brain freeze headache. Virginia's nose began to run. Then she smacked against the floor and her eyes exploded into pin-prick stars. As Pembroke's skeletal arms scooped her from the floor, she felt like she was a bird flying over the fog and the hard earth below it.

8

Virginia awoke with a start. There was something out in the hall.

She lay in her bed, in the black room, her skin warm and cozy, her eyes struggling to focus. She was completely nude. Her breathing slowed as her eyes adjusted and she ran her hands up and down her naked body. *He's even taken my underwear off,* she shuddered, imagining his hands cupping her breasts. She couldn't get the idea out of her mind. He had left her something on her bedside table in a mason jar. Pembroke had moved the severed penis to the windowsill. Sunlight illuminated the veins and the hairs as they floated. When she looked away from the severed penis, she stared at the mason jar and leaned over to look at it up close. A pickled pair of ears floated in amber, its tiny hairs curled and tight against its once warm skin.

9

Marina balanced herself on the bed and jumped again. She'd tried three times already, with no success. The first time she fell backward onto the bed and saw pinpricks of light. The feathered mattresses didn't give her the tension that would allow Marina to jump high. Once again Marina fell short of the small square hatch at the top of the box and landed on the heels of her palms and knees. She whimpered a bit as she stood up from the floor, not from pain, but frustration. Sunlight streamed in through one of the narrow slits in the box, but the slit was positioned too high up in the wall for her to pull herself up to see out of it. She felt that she could peer *out* of the hole, but she needed something to stand on to be able to do it.

Only there was nothing to stand on. The bed had been bolted to the floor. She'd spent the last hour trying to move the bed, just an inch, but so far nothing.

You can do this. Concentrate. Like Mr. Bill taught you.

She had drunk all the water, and the plastic bottles rolled around on the floor and would shift and rustle when the boat crested a wave. Absentmindedly Marina scratched her arm. Her whole body itched. She desperately needed to swim. *That's it, Marina that's all you need*, she thought. The idea occurred to her all the time now, and more and more frequently over the last few hours. *All I need is a good swim.*

If she let it, her mind screamed water. *Concentrate.*

"Hello!" Marina's shout reverberated against the wood.

Through the slits, the sound of the lapping of waves taunted her. *I am so close and so far.*

Marina laid down prone on the floor and pressed her forehead into the wood. Below her, she felt the water lap and splash against the bottom of the box. There she tried to sleep, but when she did sleep nightmares descended upon her, a laughing white-haired hag with razor-sharp teeth, darkness.

10

Marina had never needed time. Time was something her father spoke about. Time was between seasons and Christmas and moons. Time was for school and children. Time was for people.

Marina turned over to look at the ceiling glowing with the crushed bodies of the fireflies. Sometimes, when she woke from a fevered dream, she felt like she was home. A thought that terrified her. One thought in a chain of thoughts that ended at her death. *Stop being...what was the word? Morbid. That is right. Morbid.*

Ironically, the very thing that would save her life was also the thing she did not want to do.

Sit still and wait.

Mr. Bill's most powerful lesson. *"Sitting on your hands,"* as he said, *"waiting."* He had repeated it so often the words had become funny to Marina. *"Sitting on your hands is the hardest lesson. You're lucky you're half mermaid because it's dominant. What that means for your head and heart, I cannot say. But Marina, the most important lesson in the world is to not do anything. Wait. Panic is no one's friend."*

Mr. Bill could not offer much instruction in being a mermaid, but he taught her to be a human being. To do this they bird-watched, him in a canoe, her in the creek. They'd stay in the creek for hours, moving into the snaky channels that wound through the Hayes' neck, the marsh grass a sea of waving green, the sun's bright chatter upon the water. And they would be quiet for hours at a time. Sometimes they had a conversation that stopped and started and carried on throughout the day.

Once, Marina had been upset at Virginia over Virginia hiding her *Splash* DVD. Marina experienced her first real human frustration. She'd tore through Virginia's room looking for it and had bothered everyone in the house about it. Marina, in human form, was stronger than the average human, and when her temper flared and she lashed out in powerlessness, she crushed the kitchen wall. One second she was cursing Virginia and then poof, her hand went through the drywall. A cloud of dust hung about her like a cartoon.

And Mr. Bill took her bird watching, a fact that infuriated Marina because all she wanted was to get her Daryl Hannah fix, but Mr. Bill wasn't having it. After about an hour of Marina aggressively swimming next to Mr. Bill's canoe, Mr. Bill called her over. "Marina, this is when you have to sit on your hands. When you have no control. Just wait. It will appear."

"You're going to use magic?"

"I was being literal."

"I hear this word a lot and I still do not understand it."

"I simply meant it will turn up, your DVD, that someone will find it."

And the *Splash* DVD did turn up, Maria found it, inside one of Virginia's schoolbooks.

Marina wished she could watch *Splash*, her favorite movie, and sleep. *I am so thirsty,* she thought. Soon, the man would stop the boat and she would listen to him swim to where she was, listen as he climbed atop and opened the lid. She had hoped to have the strength to attack the man, but she could not manage it. Her head hummed with heat and white noise. Sometimes she heard a violent, shrill voice, a voice that cut her mind. When that voice spoke, it spoke words she didn't understand. She almost always passed out when the voice attacked her. *You must remember to save some water. You must remember.* So far she hadn't been able to remember. Marina supposed it was her weakened state, but she also thought it was because of the voice in her head.

Soon the man will come with water.

She spied the man once or twice, though she could not see his face. The bright sun shooting down from topside blinded her. *And the voice, always at the same moment.* If she could keep the old hag's voice from hurting her, she had a chance to either speak or attack the person dropping the water. Maybe she could get free.

Stop thinking. Just wait.

Placing her hand on her chest, Marina listened for her heartbeat.

Her heartbeat made her think of *him*. Her mate.

She had only seen him once. And once was enough. In her mind she imagined him following her down a deserted beach, spying whitecaps for her as she swam beside him. She sighed. Her sister had spoken about kissing boys, but Marina had never had the pleasure. Sometimes at night when the creek swelled with moontide, Marina felt like she knew what it was to kiss a boy, her body tuned to the warm saltwater. There Marina would think of her heart swelling and kissing a handsome man like the one in the movies *Splash*, or the *Little Mermaid*. She'd feel the moontide in her loins, in her whole body, and sometimes all it took was a rub of mud, or sand to send her body into shivers, so sensitive and swollen.

Marina never told Virginia about how she felt tuned to the world like that. How it was all about the moons, the tides, and the ocean for her. Her feelings towards people were more like dreams. Her feelings for Virginia were no exception.

That's not nice, she heard Virginia sass as if she was there with her. *That's not nice at all, especially all that I've done for you.* She had hurt Virginia's feelings plenty of times, though she didn't understand what that was – to hurt someone's feelings.

Mulch had grounded Marina after she had gone to the movie.

Marina didn't know what to feel when Mulch grounded her, but she trusted her instincts not to hate him. Later, Mr. Bill had reminded her that because she was special she had to be extra special around boys. Mr. Bill also reminded her that because she was not of this man's world she had to know how to live in a man's world and that she had to be careful. Mr. Bill and said that and lots of other things like that. *Sitting on your hands is the hardest lesson.*

She stretched her legs in the bed and pursed her lips together and made a chirpy cry with her throat. *It would sound better underwater,* she thought. *The fish cannot hear you when you are not underwater. Don't be so stupid. Stupid.*

Stupid was one of her favorite words. Zipper was another one. She liked how zipper sounded like what it did. Heart too, though she thought the word clipped off at the end too sharply with the 't' to be round and plump like it a real heart was. Water was the absolute best word in the whole wide world. That 't' lapped against the 'er' like the real thing and made her skin prick with goose flesh. Hearing the water made her want to drown herself in the ocean.

You can't drown, stupid. You can't swim, either, stupid.

Not here. Not in this room.

In the back of her mind, Marina pulled open a sticky cola-colored door. Inside, against the wall he leaned, his skin smelling of fresh aftershave and cigarettes. Marina's body tensed as her sister pushed past her. He managed a nervous hello before Virginia pulled her away and into the murky seats of the movie theater.

11

"If you don't stop playing with my pasta I swear to God, I'll bean you with this skillet," Maria countered Mr. Bill as Mr. Bill made a move for the door. Dry pasta shells fell out of his shirt pocket onto the floor. He crushed them under his heel as he leaped through the doorway.

"You son of a bitch," Maria said as she let the skillet fly without really meaning to. It ricocheted off the wall tearing a hole in the drywall before clanging to the floor in the dining room. "Goddammit," she bellowed.

Maria looked out the window and spied Mr. Bill running across the lawn and shoving needles of spaghetti into his nostril.

"Hope you get one in the brain!" she shouted.

"My, my. Maria. That sounds positively evil," Mulch said as he wrapped his arms around Maria's waist, squeezing her before he turned her around, his manhood pressing into her thighs. Mulch smelled of lemon and aftershave and when he bent in to kiss her, she felt her knees go weak. It was a good kiss. Mulch hadn't kissed Maria like that in years. It was the kind of kiss that made the butterflies in Maria's stomach flutter.

"No." Maria pushed Mulch back, breaking the embrace and holding his hands squarely in hers. Hands that had so many times ran through his thick, heavy hair and down his strong back. Hands that had held off Mulch's father for so many years waiting for the son. This was like watching old Eb return. She saw a bit of the yellow creep in Mulch's irises.

"Please," Maria pleaded as she felt the bite of tears in the corners of her eyes. "Not now. We, you and I, are no more." Maria wanted to say more. She wanted to say, 'after years of having me wash your clothes, cook your meals, raise your weird children, you only want me now for a part-time lover!' She wanted to tell him that if 'you were man enough to kill for your father for the love of me, then you should have been man enough to love me, to marry me, to give me the respect that I deserved.'

Where were the other women now? she wanted to ask him. *Where were all the women he claimed to have loved?* Only she remained. And that thought frightened her.

Mulch did not speak. His mouth trembled lightly. He stepped back, the color draining out of his face, The yellow Maria saw creep into his eyes, melted away. In the kitchen, water boiled over.

"Fine," he said before stepping away from her and slipping back into the dining room, his tone bitter and full of ashes.

Maria clenched her fists and strode to the oven. She slammed the pot off the stove and cursed in Spanish.

12

"Maria told me that she worked for my father because she loved him, and though my father treated her good, I know that Mulch did not love her back. I don't think she would have had the same financial success she did with us with any other family. I know how that sounds, but seriously, my father doted on her. She saved a pretty penny, she told me once and sent a fortune back home. She told me that she has a little nest egg saved for when she couldn't work anymore. Once she told me that she wanted a daughter – a little girl of her own. I think she looked at me like her own child. I looked to her as a mother.

"When I was brat...well...I mean, look at me, Doc... I hurt her, I know that now. I didn't know it then. I feel so ashamed thinking back to how I would strut through her kitchen and give her orders. Nothing too snotty mind you, I was only a kid. 'Make me a sandwich. This soup has too many pepper balls – please remove them,' that sort of thing. She'd do as I asked and inquire about my day

at school or about my boyfriends, that sort of thing. Sometimes she'd say something about my father. For a long time, I thought they were getting it on behind
all our backs. But I don't think that now. I don't think my father is capable of
loving another person.

"Mulch took me camping once. I was seven, I think, no, older, eight, maybe.
Marina had not come with us. We hiked through the woods, no more than two
miles from the house, but near the creek, far enough away so that the landscape
was unfamiliar to me. When I was older I would go there often with friends
to get drunk and fool around. There's a place where the trees bend back, and
the earth drops a sudden ten feet to the creek. In places the bank is incredibly, impossibly steep, in others, it's just a gradual drop. We camped about ten
feet from the bank. The smell of the salt and the breeze gave me the chills. The
campfire left a taste in my mouth – it tasted like char.

"I remember waking up in the middle of the night, and Mulch was not in
the tent. He wasn't outside. Mulch wasn't around the fire either. When I called
out for my father he appeared. He'd been in the trees somewhere. He'd been
watching the water, watching for Marina.

"I didn't know that then, but I know it now. It's funny how you can remember details from your past and how they become informed, enlarged by what
you learn in the present. Mulch had taken me camping to spy on my sister. I
know that now."

13 Dover, Delaware

A young man whipped a Polaroid camera out of his bag and focused it on the
dirty, smeared painting haunting the wall of the Sea Breeze Motel and Resort.
The sodium glow of the security lights cast a greasy glare in the camera's lens,
but he's able to make the smear disappear with a little angling of his own. Satisfied with the lighting, he frames the painting – a murky oily black swash of hair
and a beautiful face. The woman looks either sad or perhaps in the throes of
passion. It strikes the young man as lurid, though he cannot say why. He shakes
the Polaroid and slips the picture into his backpack.

CHAPTER THREE

1

Lilly picked through her clothing, collecting underwear, extra jeans, something warm. Ugly Mother insisted on warm clothing, but nothing too heavy. Lilly had to carry the Ugly Mother's duffel bag as well, and she planned to pack light.

Lilly didn't understand what was going on. Marcos had left on some mysterious trip, and Ugly Mother had felt that something was seriously wrong with Marcos – Ugly Mother had spoken to ghosts about it. The Ugly Mother refused to teach Lilly about speaking with ghosts, had been refusing to do so for nearly a decade, which remained a point of contention. *I swear my mother gets excited just saying his name,* she thought. *She loves him more than she loves me.*

"It is because of love. It is my duty and your fate to go," The Ugly Mother had said as they walked through the migrant camp that afternoon. Lilly *did not* want to go. She hadn't felt this way since she was a young child – the lonely holidays, the winters when sometimes she had to leave her friends at school and go to Mexico or follow the crops south. The blue faded bus Juan drove left the taste of rust in her mouth. *Why are you doing this?* she thought. She sighed, powerless to speak her mind. When she was older, she was allowed to stay with Isabelle, Anayelli, and Adrian whose parents owned a small tortilla stand in Lonely. The Ugly Mother had always taught her that it was natural for her to resist her family. The lifestyle was not for every spirit. Her father had always been in the field – away, gone, absent, but mindful of her in the broken chain of letters and postcards he sent from Florida, Texas, and Louisiana, wherever he hung his hat, at least until his death at the Hayes camp some years ago. And when Lilly graduated at the top of her class at the local high school and got a full-time job at the hardware store, the Ugly Mother, recently widowed, had grown even more distant. These days Lilly's life tilted out of control.

She felt like a young child again, having to pack her belongings on short notice, following the blue bus somewhere she didn't know, places filled with dust and endless days of fields.

Lilly rented a single-wide trailer on a small rental lot on the edge of the scrub pines. Some days it seemed like Lilly lived a million miles from her mother and the camp, and on other days the five miles between them felt like it had been folded so that her mother was up in her business at all times. She contemplated walking to camp, carrying her duffel, cutting through the pine grove for a magical attitude adjustment. She decided against it. Best get back to camp quick. *You're doing it again, Lilly, thinking of your mother first instead of you.*

They were going North to Boston. Although Ugly Mother was sure they wouldn't get far before they'd find Marcos. *What was so important about Marcos anyway? He wasn't family. Maybe you're just pissed at your mother. Right. When is it not that? No, it's George.*

Lilly would miss George. They were just starting to get to know each other, and she didn't know how long this trip was going to take. They were due for a second date. Coffee in the hardware store parking lot wasn't going to cut it.

"The trip will be as long and hard as it has to be," her mother had said.

Great, Lilly had thought. *Just great.* As usual, her mother didn't tell her anything. As usual, Lilly was left in the dark.

2

Mr. Bill sucked on his thumb and sniffled. His nose was running again, and he didn't seem to notice.

"You think he hit his head or something?" Mulch wondered as he looked at Maria's disgusted scowl.

Mr. Bill's hair was tied in a lopsided ponytail, with one of Maria's bras.

"Maybe," Maria said rolling her eyes. "Maybe."

"What do you think happened?" Mulch said as he watched Mr. Bill pick through the magazines on the coffee table in the sunroom.

"It was what you did, Mulch."

"What did I do?" For a second Mulch cringed. *Maria did not know everything,* at least he thought she didn't know everything.

"Don't play games with me. You and Bill and that Sea Hag person. And don't think I don't know about the Brazilian with the tattoo on his ankle."

Mulch's stomach tightened. His head buzzed like thousands of tiny insects. His energy level began to rise.

"At the store, I ran into Consuelo. She whispered it all to me, half afraid the rednecks in the store would understand her. Said that the men had seen Mr. Bill in the fields at strange hours."

"They always say that!"

"They say he was acting strange."

"He's always up checking on things that's why!"

"Like this strange?" Maria pointed at Mr. Bill's ponytail.

"He is old, Maria."

"And not likely to suddenly become this blubbering idiot."

As if on cue, Mr. Bill began to make gurgling noises in his throat. His button-down flannel hung on him like an afterthought, and he wore his t-shirt inside out He certainly did not strike confidence in anyone.

"I don't know what they were telling you in camp, Maria. But they don't know anything." Mulch stressed *they*. The migrants. Sometimes Mulch's disdain for them was like a hard diamond, a perfect treasure, other times he almost seemed envious of them.

"They said they could hear the water spirit, your daughter, howling for the dead."

"Nonsense."

"She, the Ugly Mother, spoke your name in her sleep again. They say the Brazilian was a river seer and that he was here to destroy the angry water spirit, your daughter. He even brought a giant box to hold her in."

"A box?" Mulch's eyes popped in surprise.

"Yes. A giant box."

Mulch looked over at Mr. Bill who was licking snot off his index finger.

"What do you know about such boxes, Mulch?" Maria sneered.

Mulch looked at her with hate. Only minutes ago he had kissed her.

Behind them Mr. Bill kicked his left leg out, striking the underside of the coffee table shifting the magazines and coasters lying on top of it. "Fraga-loooma," he muttered.

"He hasn't been able to speak right for a few days now." Mulch said, stepping back into the kitchen and disappearing into the hallway.

Mr. Bill looked at Maria, his eyes glassy, his nose running, his hand covered in a sheen of mucous. For the second time that day, Maria swore in Spanish.

3

Sun broke through the windows in Virginia's room, the black and gray paint absorbing the heat and light. The slats in the curtains left warm stripes of bright yellow on the black sheets on her bed. Already, the fog whispered against the grain of the door, its thick tendrils already reaching a curly finger under. Soon it would, like a centipede, or sometimes a snake, crawl or slither across the floor and then up the legs of the bed before curling up like a cat on her chest, or her face.

Rise and shine
You're all mine
What a pretty pair of ears she has
Better to hear with
My dear, my dear
What ears
You're all mine, sweetie

Virginia had spent much time debating whether or not the fog spoke, or if it were her invention. *Best not think too much about,* she thought. *You have plenty of other things to worry about.*

When the knock came at her door, Virginia jumped. There was only one person it could be. The door appeared to open on its own.

The mind games, Virginia thought.

Pembroke entered; his toes carried his tall frame above the floor. Virginia had come to loathe the way he moved. Today he looked like he could have been a banker, or a CEO, the black wool suit, the waistcoat, except for the shoes. He didn't wear any, his toes remaining invisible under the fog.

"It is time for your first lesson," Pembroke purred.

"Excuse me," Virginia said. She didn't like the sound of "lesson". "Lesson" was a word used by people who wanted to force something on you, something you didn't want to do.

"Breakfast?"

"I'm not hungry," Virginia drew an arbitrary line in the sand. *Don't play along.*

"Please, join me."

Virginia felt an invisible wire pull her forehead and frontal lobe up and out the door. *I can feel him inside my mind,* she thought as she fought against his influence. Against her skin, her bedclothes felt as limp as her will. The fog kissed her feet with its dampness and coolness. She concentrated on following Pembroke down the stairs and into the kitchen; her brain didn't have energy for anything else.

4

Mr. Bill whistled as he walked. He had covered almost twenty miles already and his feet were just getting into their groove. He felt good, A-plus good. The doppelgänger had put the whammy on his system, but the walk had cleared his head and he'd sweated the magic out. He allowed his internal compass to direct him, but he knew where Marcos was heading. Mr. Bill did not fear getting lost, he only feared the clock. He knew what boat Marcos would link up with to carry the cargo across the Atlantic. His only hope was that he intercepts the boat before it sailed for Holland. If he hurried, he'd be able to catch it. The sun overhead seemed brighter and crisper than it had in some time. Now, it was time for him to fly.

5

Lilly paused before dialing George. She hoped George would pick up, so far his track record had been good.

One ring.

Two rings.

Three rings.

Four rings.

Lilly hung up. She wasn't going to leave a message. Looking at her watch she saw that she had a few hours before she had to meet her mother. She hoped it would be enough time. She picked up her duffel and locked up her apartment. She slung her bag and began the walk to meet her mother, humming a snatch of a song her father had sung to her a long time ago.

6

Kevin "Spider" Jones' Basement Workshop, New Jersey

"I don't like these photos. Too much glare." Blockhead pointed at the glare with his giant index finger.

"It's lousy work, too." Spider clicked through the thumbnails.

"Everything can't be New York." Blockhead's head nearly brushed the top of Spider's basement ceiling.

"I can still have my standards." Spider rolled his eyes at his friend.

"Look, this summer's kinda starting worse than we thought." Blockhead rubbed his big hands together. "I have not seen one decent tag in weeks."

"But there's the weird one." Spider retorted.

"You think everything's weird."

"No, that one on the hotel, that one is weird." Spider insisted.

"I thought we agreed that that thing was a political move on behalf of the Rid the Beach Police."

"They only take on new construction projects." Spider said.

"Yeah, they're only active in more natural environments, and Dover is anything..."

"North Carolina, Virginia, Maine, Connecticut..." Spider continued.

"And? So?"

"So we agreed." Spider looked up to his friend, who was at least a full head taller, if not a head and a half.

"Larry spotted another one," Blockhead said.

"Another what?"

"Another fucked up graffiti job. Nothing like shit we're used to seeing."

"So this is some kind of new tag?" Spider asked.

"More like urban abstract expressionism."

"I disagree. It's nonrepresentational." Spider said.

"All I'm saying is that this stuff is different. And if Larry spotted a new one, then maybe we should catalog it." Blockhead argued.

"What if it's a copycat?" Spider countered.

"Then we have a new style that's breaking. Either way, we should find this guy, or girl, gender-fucked individual, and totally do a feature on him, on her, on them. Whatever. That site in the city is light years ahead of us and this art could go a long way to expand our audience."

"They're based in New York. This is Jersey." Spider said, even though he knew Blockhead was right.

"So?" Blockhead's giant body was as big as three of Spider's, if not three and a half. "Our site is as good as theirs. Raw urban angst only counts for so much."

"We should find this guy." Spider agreed.

"Plus New York's got twice as much area to tag."

"Did we have anyone out on the street today?" Spider asked.

"Just Larry. And Zac." Blockhead replied.

"Jesus." Spider retorted. "Call Larry and see if he can confirm this new sighting. Tell him no glare this time."

"No problem," Blockhead said. "Texting him now."

"I'm sick of looking at glare."

"You got it, Spider."

"I mean geez. What the hell. Am I paying for glare here?"

"Yeah, bossman," Blockhead said, his head bobbing as he texted.

"Let's go see this thing in person." Spider said, closing the digital picture editor on his laptop.

"I'll find out from Larry where it's at."

7

When Nick Adams entered the art supply store the clerks immediately began to case him, following him up and down the aisles. This was probably because he looked dirty and smelled like feet. He quickly made his purchases and left. He had a moment of terror when the credit card reader lagged, but after a prolonged pause, his purchase was approved, and he was ready to roll. His bag was heavier now, and it felt good to be re-supplied. It felt even better to speak to someone who, for lack of a better word, *understood* him.

"She'll probably have a paddy wagon waiting for me," he said aloud, imagining that Amanda had contacted the local crazy house and was now lying in wait. Not that he would blame her.

Across the street, a young punk, baby blue hair with pink highlights, leaning against the wall glanced down at his phone. The punk blended into the background, appearing disinterested and aloof like most of the Jersey shore. The punk kept their eyes on Nick as Nick looked up and down the street orienting himself. When Nick walked away from the store, the punk followed. Nick was too busy soaking up the sun to notice.

8

Once again Marina had passed out before the man dropped her water supply for the day. She had hoped to catch his face, at least. But once again the voices in her head had attacked her and she had succumbed to their power.

You must wait. You must rest. Sit on your hands.

But Marina was too frustrated to rest. Instead, she focused her rage on her cage.

Marina punched the floor and again pain raced up through her arm. In the floor below her, there were tiny indentations where her knuckles hammered into the wood. The thirst to swim and to be surrounded by water had elevated into a maddening craving in her. Her head sang and whined, her vision alternating between clarity and unfocused confusion. *One more time,* she thought before smashing the floor with her body.

She managed a few strong punches, rattling the bed on its driftwood frame, but she collapsed, exhausted. Marina licked her upper lip of sweat and returned to her bed. At least on the bed, she felt like she was riding on the surface of a wave. That was something of a comfort, but not much of one.

9

Amsterdam lay in its humidity, a giant surrounded by the fog of its breath. Cilia walked briskly, ignoring her sweat. People stared at her as she went by, she was used to it. Women envious of her dress and hair tended to ogle the old fashions she sported. Victorian, but crisp as a lemon peel. Her silver hair caught the air as she walked, a wisp of hammered light. But most people looked just at her ears, or the lack thereof. Men eye-balled her figure, their eyes crawling over her breasts and waist and legs. Some of the men imagined fucking her on a bed, pillows propping her up any which way. She felt their thoughts as she passed them on the street, and they made her smile. Sometimes when Cilia needed a rush of euphoria, she wore an iron corset equipped with tiny sharp studs on the interior of the bra that left her skin ruddy and freshly pricked that both aroused Cilia and pained her. The corset was her way of reminding herself of the way one can shape a life through rigorous discipline. *People lacked discipline these days*, she thought often.

Cilia had lost her ears ten years earlier when she had decided to expand the family business into prostitution in the Red Light District. Cilia had purchased several homes just on the outskirts of the Red Light District and had rented the lower rooms to prostitutes. This had been before the ban on brothels had been lifted and Cilia had run an illegal brothel in one of her other houses. The international boom to Amsterdam's sex trade had yet to peak.

Cilia was careful with her business. She paid the right cops to keep their noses out of it. And they did until Peter Scholtes took over the city's vice beat. Peter Scholtes had been a boxer for a while and when that didn't pan out for him, he had become a police officer. Peter Scholtes found his true calling in law enforcement because it was there that he could legally beat the shit out of almost anyone. Usually, they didn't put up a fight, the addicts and syphilis riddled bums that he tramped down. As a boxer, Peter had taken his share of hits, and his face had been sculpted by the glove, taking on the look of hardened dough. One of his ears was mangled, bent in on itself like a crude flower. His nose lay flat on his face and the half of his upper lip was permanently swollen to twice the size of the rest of his lip, giving him the look of someone who has just been stung by a bee. He didn't drink, except on holiday, and in his opinion soft drugs were for pussies. His drug was violence.

Peter lifted weights and liked to hit things. Once in the ring, he had knocked a young African so hard in the face that his skull had cracked. He died in the hospital as his brain swelled up. When the newspaper printed news of the young man's death, he'd cut it out and put it on his refrigerator under a mermaid magnet. Until police work found Peter, he had felt that that had been his finest moment. Then Peter had gotten trounced in the ring by a giant Russian whose uppercut had lifted Peter off the mat. He had landed sprawled in the ropes, his head hanging over the side, his feet off the ground, the cartoon birdies circling his head almost visible to the crowd. After that, he lost three more fights and his ranking had fallen, hard. Plus, he never made any money off the fights. His first manager Benny Haast had taken him in, gave him a place to stay in a backroom in the gym, and then stole his money. Peter tried to get it back but had no luck. Benny had spent it all at the casino.

Then Peter had tried to manage himself and that got him nowhere. Soon he bottomed out, no trainer would touch him. He'd been walking alone one night and took a turn down an alley when he stopped short. Some cops were beating up on a girl. The woman had scratched one of the cops down the side of the face and the cop was going at her with his Billy club. He heard her ribs snap. Finally, one of the cops intervened, but the girl was down, heaving, certainly in shock. Watching the cops take this woman to town had increased Peter's heart rate back to where he liked it to rest. His mouth smacked with adrenaline. The next day he applied to the academy, and he never looked back. *It was like something was telling him to join up,* he often told people who wanted to know the story. 'Born to box, bred to police,' he'd joke at the gym where he worked out and sparred when he was off duty. Peter excelled as a cop. He especially liked to catch muggers and pound them into hamburger by smashing their faces against brick walls. This was his favorite thing to do, taking scum and running the man's body against the side of a wall so his face was scraped off on the brick.

His first beat assignment was the area surrounding Rembrandt Park. Then it was the Vondel Park. Then way over on Van Beuningen Plein. then Boerhaave Plein. His arrests piled up like bodies, and nobody complained. The punks he beat up were too scared of him and soon, Peter found himself working Cilia's beat, the Red Light District, and surrounding area.

Peter had no love of prostitutes, but he didn't hate them. He felt that most of them were illegal and were bringing disease to his country. He didn't give two rat cents about the tourists who walked away with their shriveled dick, dragging some disease home to their wives. His peers thought he was nuts, but Peter was just afraid of women, and deep down he knew the only way he'd have a relationship with a woman was to pay one. The fact was that Peter enjoyed bullying women. The look on their faces when they reacted to his presence made his dick hard.

His first tip that the house near Oude Kerk housed illegals was the fact that when Dutchmen briefly flirted with the women outside the women did not respond in Dutch – their words were off, just enough to catch his ear.

Peter stalked the house for a few weeks before entering the house himself where he found like he has suspected, that the whole house hid a maze of interior rooms where illegals traded skin. First, he arrested each of the girls, on different nights, over two weeks. He nabbed an African, three Chinese, four Russians, one Hindi, and three Indonesian prostitutes. Then he arrested Cilia's madam and arrested the woman running the illegal gambling operation. The girls were to be deported, the madam and the house manager heavily fined. The courts had already gone soft on sex trade workers, and even Peter knew that eventually, the law would change to accommodate them, it was all the talk up and down the red light streets, but on his beat, while it was still illegal, Peter cracked skulls.

In response, and having paid good money for protection, Cilia had to come all the way down to the station to get things straightened out with his bosses. She had hoped she'd be able to get there before he filed the paperwork, but Peter had already processed the girls by the time she got to the station. Still, she reached out and entered his mind, controlled him. She saw the station as he saw it. She saw that he had been a boxer and where he got the scars and wounds that made him look like a beaten bulldog. She ordered him to release the girls, to take the rest of the night off, and then she left with the paperwork in her purse. It wasn't a total loss, but the bust did slow down business, for a while, for some of the girls were terrified, one even bolted in the middle of the night.

After Cilia left his mind, Peter found himself at his own home, fully aware that he had arrested some illegal whores and then let them go, all because some strange middle-aged woman had told him too. He understood it intellectually, he just did not understand why he would have agreed to it. He stewed it over for a few days and the more he thought about it the angrier he became. *She must have done something to his head*, he thought. *Like maybe she had dipped her fingers into his brain and made a salad out of his thoughts.* He knew this idea was insane but clung to it. No way would Peter have let those women go. Driven by these thoughts he investigated the brothel's background but he didn't find much of anything. He discovered an impenetrable paper trail Cilia and her brother had left. *He'd have to get his revenge in another way*, he thought.

Peter had no problem jimmying Cilia's lock. The house lay dark and he walked as quietly as he could up the stairs, pausing to listen every few steps. Peter's police training had taught him to walk along the sides of the stairs where the boards are less likely to bow under his weight and creak. When he found her, she was sleeping in a bed three times the size of the one Peter's parents had slept in when he was a kid. As he stood over her, ready to strike, her mind seeped into his. It made him felt sick all of a sudden. He had never puked in his life (not even once when he was ill) but for a horrible second, he thought he was going to vomit all over the woman. Her mind felt like a spider spreading its legs over his brain, its pincer mouth waiting to sink into the meat of his noggin. Then he pulled out his knife from his belt and leaned over the old woman and cut her ears off. The first ear came off without a hitch, she didn't even twitch once. But halfway through the second ear she awoke, and her scream not only pierced his head, but he felt it ripple through his body. Quickly, he jabbed in her the face with his fist, popping her nose open, before clamping down on her throat with the weight of his knee to cut off the second ear, which came off with a little hang-nail tear while Cilia thrashed under his weight.

The only way to get one over on Cilia van Hazen was to surprise her, and she hadn't expected Peter. Once Peter had her ears, she narrowed her pain into a beam of anguish that screwed itself into Peter's skull. The force of her pain threw Peter off her and onto the floor. He landed on the small of his back and curled up like a dead insect, crying out, the ears and the knife scattered on her bedroom floor.

Cilia, like her brother, enjoyed her torture. She knocked Peter out with the blunt end of a bookend and then tied him up tight. When Peter awoke, he found that he had been skinned alive, and peeled back like a shrimp. She had used her best knives, and her mind, her focus pulling tight his body to exact the most precise cuts. He was dead of shock when the police found him in an alley in the heart of the Red Light District. They had no idea it was one of their fellow policemen until the dental records came back. His case became an anomaly in the files of the Dutch police – hot-headed young star skinned alive just months after being on the job.

Cilia was humiliated. She had been taken by surprise, in her own home. She wanted a reminder that she had once left herself vulnerable and to never do that again. So she kept the ears. The strange thing was that they didn't shrivel, or change, or decompose in any way, instead, they remained pliable and soft, but ice cold. She also found that if she placed them onto her head, they would stay there. They'd only ever fall off her head if she walked too fast, or bent over too far forward, so she kept her ears in a leather satchel and carried them with her wherever she went to put them on when she needed them. She found she heard better when she attached them to her ear holes. Besides, it made people that didn't know her more at ease to see her with her ears on, rather than the scarred and warped holes left from her attack. And a predator always wants prey at ease, always.

10

Cilia made her way past the touristy Leidsplein and past the Vondelpark and walked towards Museumplein. She continued just beyond Museumplein, and on to Nicolaas Maesstraat, where The Crystal Ball magic shop was located. The front of The Crystal Ball was for the children, filled with jokes and gags, card tricks, and souvenir postcards. The back of the store was the new-age book-shop, but if the owner knew you, or if you had a reference, you could be admitted upstairs, to the real shop. Henrik Brower's family had maintained the store through Nazi occupation, mostly because the Nazis were afraid of his grandfather. Henrik's grandfather was the only man in Amsterdam, probably the whole of Nazi-occupied Europe, that openly employed a Jew, a mystic who was half Austrian and a deaf-mute. He said Hitler had allowed the man to stay because of his knowledge of the occult. Though Henrik's grandfather managed to keep his shirt during the war, the store flourished in the early 60s and the 70s and it was then that Henrik handed the store over to his only son, Hedrick, whose brow was sloped and thick like a Neanderthal. Cilia had known Henrik well and knew Hedrick from an intimate time during their teenage years before he had gone and joined the Dutch Royal Navy to travel the world before settling down as an entrepreneur.

This day the store was empty but was alive with the smell of fresh garlic cloves and wolf's bane which hung above the shop entrance. Large crucifixes greeted the customer as they walked in. Hedrick had a vampire phobia and even had a cross etched into the bald head of the doorknob. To protect himself, Hedrick had a cross tattoo emblazoned on his chest, one that was blessed by a rebel priest who worked in black market exorcisms. Cilia had often wondered what had made her former lover so afraid of vampires, but Hedrick never hinted, not even once.

"Hedrick, haloo." Cilia cooed.

"Cilia Haloo. Good. Good. Come in," Hedrick waved her in through the beaded curtain to the back of the store and up the steep stairs, talking as he walked.

"All of your supplies have come in. Though I had a devil of a time with those African herbs. I had to go to Spain myself to procure them from a very old and very tenacious woman who did not want me to have them. I bargained for over two hours with her over the price, the old hag." Hedrick's voice rang out in laughter.

"My dear, I hope you didn't get taken advantage of."

"It was nothing. My grandmother was a gypsy. I'm sure you recall."

"Ah, yes. I forgot."

"She taught me how to barter, I tell you," Hedrick said, his breath sharp with garlic and onions made Cilia's nostrils flare.

The cozy upstairs smelled of earth and spices, the hardwood floors creaking underfoot. The entire upstairs was lined with built-in shelves. It had cost Henrik a fortune to install when he opened the store, but it had been very much worth it, he'd even put in secret doors that led to an annex behind the store, a room Hedrick had shown her only once. The walls were lined with old leatherbound books, icons, and charms made of little bits of finger bone and feathers. Masks lined the walls from Asian lands, as well from Africa and Indonesia; the fruits of colonization for Cilia to pluck at will. The counter area was arranged with vials of squid-like translucent flesh of different creatures. Books in locked cabinets sat safely behind the counter and a few select swords and knives rested under glass. Below the shelves, the real dangerous stuff lay in secured drawers of which only Hedrick had the key.

Cilia reached into her purse and removed a flat leather satchel, it was twelve inches long, four inches wide. She unfolded it on the counter. Her ears lay inside the leather pouch like some kind of exotic cheese, pale and cold.

"How's business been lately?" Cilia said as she affixed her ears. They attached with a wisp of suction. Hedrick shivered noticeably.

"We are on the web, my dear Cilia. My nephew just made us up a new web portal. So exciting. That's brought in as many euros as from our usual business."

"Glad to see you're always adapting."

"I suppose it seems obvious that we should."

Hedrick saw the right ear quiver of its own will. *One day it will fall off,* he thought.

"So tell me, what are you doing with all of this stuff?" Hedrick asked as he hefted the heavy brown paper bag over the counter to Cilia; the contents shifted inside, glass clinked against glass. "Harvesting the power of mermaid hormones?"

"Oh, Hedrick my dear. You know that I don't kiss and tell, I never have."

Hedrick's eyebrows lifted as he teased her.

"Oh, Cilia. You must know that you are the reason that I keep this store open every day. In the hopes that I may see you again," Hedrick smiled, his grin forced but friendly.

"And Hedrick my dear, you are the only reason I shop here every week."

Hedrick watched the left ear pulse with life. It appeared to be breathing. *There it goes,* Hedrick thought. Hedrick hated the left ear the most because he thought it was looking at him.

"Tell me something dear?" Hedrick asked.

"Yes, my pet."

"Will you let me see it? When you get it?"

"Why Hedrick, I don't know what you're talking about," Cilia giggled.

Hedrick only smiled warmly and took one long loving gaze at her large bosom, which Cilia fanned kittenishly.

After Cilia left the shop, she whistled her way back to Prisingracht, the heat of his stare lingering on her breasts.

11

Virginia scooped her scrambled eggs into her mouth. She had trouble tearing her eyes away from Pembroke's androgynous face. If she blinked she saw a very thin female face, and if she blinked twice his male face waxed into view. She did this to amuse herself while he continued to lecture, taking up all the air in the room.

"My sister and I have been watching you and your sister for a while now. We are interested in your...well-being. It was your father, Mulch, when he was on some family-tree kick he discovered us. Cilia invited your father over to Holland to visit. It was then that I began to do business in America.

"I have photos if you don't believe me. Sometime later, Mulch began to photograph you and your sister. I'm sure you know that now. Cilia fell in love with Marina. Oh, it was precious the way Cilia mooned and fawned over her.

Your photos glowed with innocence and charm. There's one he took of you in the bathtub, the proverbial naked baby in the tub. Images that become blackmail pictures that mortify teens, and adults alike. I carried that photo with me for years. You see, Mulch promised me that I'd have you when you got old enough."

"Have me?"

"Yes, have you. You see you and I are going to become very close."

Every time Pembroke touched Virginia, she'd shudder and inside her mind, the moment would splinter and in each splinter, she felt her ages, her youngest smallest self, her middle school self, her present self, and the subtle differences in the selves that were to come, an eternity shattered into moments inside her.

12

The fish hawkers in the market barked over the craning necks of the Italian and Portuguese women. The market was getting ready for a busy morning and already a fresh stream of bloody ice water leaked and pooled under stalls, running out in streams under Marcos' feet.

The ship's captain had been out – out getting drunk, out getting laid, the men growled. Though in truth, none of the men had any clue of Captain Van Dijk's whereabouts. Marcos told the men he'd come back, that he'd walk over to his old stomping grounds, soak up the atmosphere, and see how the old neighborhood was doing, so to speak.

Marcos didn't notice the three burly men follow him from the docks to the markets behind Faneuil Hall. He was too busy catching the eye candy of a familiar place, the cobblestone streets of old Boston, the bright yellow cabs, the tall and imposing buildings in the financial district. *I've been away for too long,* he thought.

Cilia's orders to Captain Kasper van Dijk had been very clear, 'Kill the messenger.' The captain had simply nodded, unable to get the buzzing out of his head. He hadn't felt like that since he was a young boy when his grandmother punished him for breaking her favorite vase. Kasper had run around the house and stuck his arms like he was flying out when he shouldn't have, not indoors when he knocked the vase over. When his grandmother got a hold of him she locked him down with a stare, before slapping him hard, back and forth, across the face. His grandmother's stare and her icy cold voice had been enough to make him weak in the legs – the slaps had been unnecessary. Cilia's voice had gotten to him in the same way. He felt like a fish on a line. But the money was good – a real lifesaver.

The Brazilian messenger had come like Cilia said he would. Politely, with shipping orders from a Mister Mulch Hayes. The shipping order had a Virginia address on it. Captain Van Dijk recognized it at once.

The Captain had agreed to take care of the messenger himself, but he was an ancient 56, and by the looks of it, this messenger was no older than 35. So, he had agreed to pay some boys a little on the side, for protection, like insurance, just in case the messenger proved to be too strong for him.

Willie Harmon and Hector Fillman, roughnecks from Southie, knew Boston well and they liked to break heads. *Easy money,* the Captain thought, *easy money. Killing the Brazilian would be no problem.*

13

Around noon Nick began to feel woozy. Around one he had to sit down on the crowded beach where he admired the towels and the colorful umbrellas and thought about going swimming. Only he didn't have a bathing suit and he was sure his boxers wouldn't do. The dizziness seemed to subside as he watched bathers move in and out of the frothy surf, but once he shifted his weight, or moved his feet, the dizziness crept up on him again. After a half-hour on the beach, he started to feel downright sick. The coffee and nicotine inside him reared up and begged for sustenance. Somewhere in his bag, he had a bottle of water. He felt like he should take a nap but didn't want to. The dizziness seemed to draw energy out of his stomach and into his heart. By 1:45 he was painting a large picture of a flapping fish out of the water on the sidewalk near a cluster of dated hotels, their orange and sepia curtains flapping high above him through the open balconies.

14

In Nick's mind, he walked toward a place where the sun shone down in pleasant but powerful streams of light. The sun left pools of light like water, and it splashed upon his legs and calves. The splashing sun warm on his body soothed his chest and throat which felt ragged, raw, and undone. Around him the beach was empty. He passed a few scattered sheets of newspaper, Styrofoam cups, and fast-food wrappers. Walking farther, the hotels melted away and the air grew cooler as he approached a small, hunched figure playing with a sand bucket next to the sidewalk. She was a young girl with black hair, her skin shone in the sun. Nick could tell that she had been oiled up with sunscreen because of the intense light reflected off her skin. The young girl scooped sand into her bucket and turned it over, flattening the top and sides out with her hand. She molded and sculpted the sand into a box shape before filling the bucket with sand again.

"If you use wet sand, you can sculpt it easier," Nick suggested.

The young girl looked up at him and for an instant, her face morphed into that of an older woman with a familiar face before morphing back into a little girl's face.

"I can't get to the water. Will you help me?" The little girl said, her hands upturned in the sand.

Nick watched himself take the bucket from the young girl's hand and turn to the breaking surf. The surf was a good fifty yards away.

"The water's a good ways away. Don't you want to move closer?" Nick asked.

The young girl continued to scoop sand in her bucket and looked up at Nick.

"It's my feet. The hot sand hurts my feet."

"Oh," Nick said. "You should wear flip-flops."

"Yes. So should you."

"I have shoes on."

The girl giggled.

Nick looked down and saw that his feet were bare; the sun had scorched his skin into a dry leather.

Nick giggled. The girl was right, the sand *was* hot under his feet.

He looked out to the surf and then back to the girl, who again, for an instant was a beautiful young woman whose hair flashed green and whose skin gave off heat as warm as the sunlight splashing down upon him.

"I'll be back. With water. For your castle." Nick said as he motioned to the girl.

"It's not a castle," the little girl said.

Nick was already walking to the beach, the bucket swinging in his hand. When he turned to look at the girl, she was shaping a box with her hand and something else, something long and oblong. Nick knew the girl. Nick knew the woman that she flashed into, but something was keeping his brain from remembering from where. He could almost see it, it looked like a wall, a gray stone wall rising before the water. He looked out to the surf. The water was now even farther away than he had thought and as he turned to look at the young girl again, he saw that she too was very far away, now a mere blob on the horizon. When he looked down at his feet, he saw that they had turned to jellyfish tendrils. Then he was neck high in the water and flailing his arms to keep afloat.

15

"Hey buddy, get out of the way."

"I think it looks cool."

"Definitely modern."

"Abstract."

"Impressionistic."

"You don't know what you're talking about."

"I saw this thing on the internet – a graffiti cult or something."

"That's a bunch of Infowars bullshit."

"Oh yeah?"

"Yeah."

"That's what they said about crop circles."

"Fuck Alex Jones."

"Does he have a tip jar?"

"I'm not sure but he ought to."

"Kinda in the way, don't you think?"

"He does have a cute butt, for a homeless guy."

"I'm telling you, he isn't homeless. Part of this cult or whatever."

"It's pretty."

"Does anyone have the time?"

"You'd think he'd choose a less busy spot."

Nick swam under the cool surface of the ocean. Then he swam up to the surface and broke through the water where he expected to look onto the beach, where he expected to see a young girl making a sandcastle. However, instead of a beach, Nick was staring down at a large square of concrete approximately three feet by three feet. He smelled the ocean, and he heard it, down the beach. It was no more than one hundred feet away. The sun was baking his neck and hands and he looked down to see if his feet were burned. He saw his shoes and he saw the charcoal and pastel rendering of a giant blue and green fish flapping out of water. In the background, there was a pool whirling of oranges and reds. People were standing around him, chewing on gum, sucking soda through straws. Nick smelled cigarettes and the faint whiff of rum peeling off the pedestrians watching him. A young punk with blue hair and red highlights aimed a small camera at the painting and took a picture.

CHAPTER FOUR

1

Marcos strolled through the throngs of commuters into the mothball smell of Boylston Street station. Boylston wasn't as busy as Downtown Crossing Station or Park Street station, both of which were closer, but he enjoyed the extra two-thirds mile walk down the length of the Common to get his land-legs back, to catch the scent of flowers blooming along the edge of the Common. From Boylston, Marcos could take the B line into Allston and hop off at Marty's Liquors. Within minutes he'd be able to get some really good Brazilian food in his stomach. He was tired of his diet of peanut butter and tuna fish sandwiches. He wanted something hearty and greasy. Boylston was filled up with students and commuters, but it remained civil. Boylston Street station was known to get hairy sometimes, especially when the drunks got rowdy. Once he witnessed a young girl get a beating from her father when a bum made off with her purse. Marcos remembered the shock he felt along with the other pedestrians. Here was this guy slapping his daughter across the face while some liver-sore bum made it over the turnstiles and up the stairs with her purse and money while he did nothing about it. It was the first time he'd ever seen the dark side of human nature. A few years later he was picking pockets on the red line – Harvard Square mostly, where the drunk college students practically gave their money away. He'd never understood how some of the smartest college students in the world could be stupid enough not to be safer with their wallets. It was while he was picking pockets that Marcos learned to control his abilities.

All it took was a simple suggestion on his behalf and people opened up like clams under the blade. He'd just have to think about the victim leaving the wallet halfway out the back pocket and his fingers did the rest.

He had been such a scrawny kid. The kind with a runny nose that was always running from something. When he wasn't running, he'd carve wood. He could make what looked like anything with a knife and a scrap of wood, figurines that moved their arms when the sun went down, or whistles that blew themselves. He'd carve the wind on scrap wood to cool his skin on hot summer nights. He'd singe lines by pressing his fingertip into it and thinking of only light. He'd force the wood to fall away in large chunks while he whittled, or willed his blade to slice precisely along the grain, or against the grain. Only years later after the Ugly Mother found him and braided his magic with that of the Unhceglia magic tattoo, did he realize the extent of his power. But what had he known as a teenage boy? Nothing. His pickpocketing supplied him with blades. The rest of the money he spent on girls.

At Boylston Station, Marcos waited twenty minutes for the B line. Two Cs and one E rumbled and sparked by. Once on the B line, he managed to get a prized single seat facing forward on the left side. From that seat, he was able to people-watch once the tracks lifted the train above ground. It also gave him a full view of Kenmore Square station, one of the more colorful T stops. From that seat, he was not able to see the burly men dressed in greasy blue jeans and white t-shirts who had followed him. The leader, an older man in his fifties, wore a plaid button-down shirt. They all wore baseball caps, each one of them slightly different, all their jackets stained with fish blood.

2

Captain Van Dijk listened to the buzzing voice in his head. At times the voice sounded like two voices, one a high cackling call and the other a sensuous calm voice. He understood both and did not question them, as if his mind was simply receiving crisscrossed radio transmissions from two different stations like they were radio ghosts he had to wade through to think, radio ghosts that clouded and fuzzed his mind like a good whale of a drunk. Except the voices told him where their prey was heading, their prey named Marcos. The voices told the Captain that their prey headed towards Allston to eat in a little restaurant called Cafe Brazil Rio. They also told him that Cafe Brazil Rio was just off the beaten pedestrian path. Most of Allston's restaurants, clubs, and video stores lined the sides of Brighton, or Harvard Avenue, an ever-buzzing crawl of people. Cafe Brazil Rio was on Prospect Station Street that slid off the side of the main drag like a stray man o' war tentacle. The voices told him that it would be a perfect place to kill this man.

Captain Van Dijk liked the voices. They soothed him and he felt like dozing in the train as it sparked, squealed, and stopped at every Boston University building and apartment building on Commonwealth Avenue. A bright white hum filled him from his toes to his crown. He looked over to Willie and Hector. They knew Allston well, and when he leaned over and whispered to them that he knew where Marcos was going, they didn't question their captain. If Van Dijk got the idea that he already knew where the young man was going, what the young man was up to, then he knew.

Of the two, Hector had, for a brief period in his gray childhood, lived in a one-room apartment in Allston. When he was just barely a teen, Hector had been jumped by a bunch of Brazilian hoods. The zipper scar across his chest was all the motive he needed to cut another Brazilian's throat open like a shark's belly. Willie, on the other hand, just wanted the money. Van Dijk, watching his silent men gape around the train, knew that they must be hearing the same fuzzy voice loop and re-loop in their heads as he heard in his own.

3

Cilia van Hazen licked her lips and tasted the sweat that had gathered on Captain Van Dijk's lips, her armpits growing damp. She smelled the sharp wind of mothballs, body odor, and perfume. Inside her mind, she saw six screens. On each screen there played a different scene with each screen narrated by a different voice. Enduring such a feat would have exhausted her years ago. Now she kept her exhaustion at bay by the promise of her prize. Within hours she would have fewer screens, fewer people to control. The promise of this thrilled her.

Four of her screens played a similar picture, the sights of Boston University bouncing by. One of them would be dark soon. Each of the screens was overlaid by different perspectives, connected via a sinewy cord which allowed Cilia to plug them together. Cilia had been mastering mental models since she hit puberty, ever-expanding her capacity to use her mind as a weapon. The invention of television had been a boon, all the mental energy the world generates regarding TV. All she had to do was reach out and pluck it.

"Two more stops Captain, then you and Willie and Hector will get off. Use the rear exit door. Marcos will stop at the magic shop on the right-hand side of the street. He does not remember the name, but you will see a giant bronze rabbit out front. Next door to the magic shop is a newspaper stand. Go and buy some gum and a paper."

The words threaded into the reels of the men's memories and thoughts. The white hum of Cilia's voice soothed them, enlarged them. Captain Van Dijk nodded to himself and eyed the back of Marcos' head.

Cilia looked at the other screens. One was dark and hot and on it, Cilia saw what Marina saw, the darkened room of her box. Marina was sleeping now, her body twisting restlessly. The sixth screen troubled her, all she saw was white light and a beach, but she could not concentrate on that now. She could not see inside this man's head. All she received was feedback.

Soon, she thought. *I'll get to you soon, whoever you are. And I'll drain you dry.*

4

Pembroke stood in front of the desk which hid the bloodstain shaped like Virginia's sister. He raised his elongated, rubbery toe to his mouth. He scraped the side of his big toe with his teeth and licked the dirt from the head of the toe. His teeth made a sound of bone against hard flesh which rippled Virginia's neck into goosebumps.

I swear he does that to fuck with me, Virginia thought.

"Time for pictures," he said gleefully, his toe slowly stretching back to his foot. Virginia thought his toes looked like cheap rubber snakes at times, and like hard candy at others, and at other times like snakes, distended and fat with pus.

"TIME FOR PICTURES!" he yelled. He threw his hips into the laugh and his toes spread out like octopus' legs to support the shift in his weight. He laughed fully, spittle sprayed the air and Virginia closed her eyes against the moisture.

"TIME FOR PICTURES!" he screamed, his voice piercing the fog that was now beginning to seep in. It braided itself into thick coils that rifled through the bookcases, removing a thick leather album from the shelves. A different trio of braids cleared the desk as the fog laid down the picture album.

The fog controlled him or he controlled the fog, Virginia was not sure.

"This is from the time you were eight."

A fat finger of fog curled around the corner of the album and opened it. There were two pictures on the front page, both were grainy black and white and were dated in the bottom corner. They reminded Virginia of the sex videos Adam had filmed. A thin braid of mist caressed the cheek of an eight-year-old Virginia.

"That's me!"

"Didn't I say that!" Pembroke said as he cut off the end of her comment.

Virginia stared down at the photo and tried to remember it. She was in the bathtub, far past the age when pictures should have been taken of her in the bathtub.

"Your father hid a camera in your bathroom."

The fog flipped the pages. There were several shots of her in various stages of undress. After three pages of photos, the camera angle changed from where Mulch had moved it. In these photos, Virginia was face first and she was older, in her teens. There were lipstick shots, pictures of her singing, cupping her breasts. The fog lingered over her face and cheek, stroking the picture.

"We, my sister and I, agreed long ago with your father's request to take you and your sister for him. With these pictures, we simply wanted to get to know you both before we broke you in."

Virginia remained silent.

"As you can see Mulch was very forthcoming with supplying me with all these photos of you."

5

Marcos walked off the T inhaling the sharp mothy smell of a city in early summer. The summer heat had yet to invade Boston and everywhere Marcos looked he saw people enjoying the balmy temperature. Girls were in shorts and tanks, guys in shorts and sweats. No one carried with them the humiliated, downtrodden look of one who has yet to wade through the heat and wet of a farm day. People were invigorated being outside. This is what he liked about living in the Northeast. Summer wasn't as much of a bitch as it was in the South, whereby now the grass was already brown and wilted. Thinking back, it had been an unusual year, it had been an unusual week. He trotted off up the street. Somewhere ahead of him was Cafe Brazil Rio, the promise of coxinha, and black turtle beans making his mouth water as he pushed through the college students crowding the T stop.

A calm had come over him sometime yesterday afternoon. All the stress he had endured due to Marina and the box was now gone and he couldn't help feeling that he did a bang-up job on transporting her so far. Marina was 862 land miles from her home. Lord knows she could swim it in less than half the time it took Marcos to pull the damn box up the coast, fighting currents the whole way. *Things were going to be just fine.* As he passed some familiar stores, Marcos noticed the old magic shop he used to visit as a kid, and then seriously as a teenager, where he participated in one of their Samhain rituals when he was in his twenties.

The Rabbit's Brow was adorned with a large bronze jackrabbit whose feet were angled out as if the rabbit was jumping over the storefront. The rabbit was jumping over a magic hat, but the magic hat had long been removed, even before Marcos' time. As a boy, Marcos would stare up at the rabbit and wonder what the rabbit was running from. The hat had apparently been removed by some randy college students in the late sixties shortly after the store had opened its doors. Rumor had it that the hat had floated around Boston's various sub-cultures and ended up in Maine, in Stephen King's possession. Marcos stood in front of The Rabbits' Brow, his mouth widened to a noticeable grin. The old sights, the old smells, he'd been away for so long, what had he been thinking? He did not notice the three men trailing behind him. One that kept smacking his fist into his palm repeatedly, the other with his hands in his pockets, fiddling at something, the last bent forward slightly, stalking the front two. All three of them wore caps. They crossed the street and huddled inside the Royal Bee Newsstand next to the Rabbit's Brow, buying newspapers, gum, and smokes.

Inside, the sharp smell of garlic and wolf's bane greeted Marcos at the door and he looked up at the friendly curly-qs of magic script flowing along the woodwork. The script was said to be of Arabic origin, and lore had it that it was a spell that enabled buyers and sellers to agree quickly and without aggression. This is how Bob Van Allen had explained it to Marcos when he was barely fourteen. Now, Marcos viewed the Rabbit's Brow as a white-washed magic shop. Though it had its charms, it remained mostly a shop for children and hippies, and tourists. Still, nostalgia vibrated in Marcos' heart.

He half expected to see someone from the old neighborhood. Bob was long dead, and his children had sold the shop. Still, the smells took him back. Incense, wood polish. He remembered learning how to read Tarot in the back and learning how to dowse for water with Bob's rods, he remembered the potions Bob's wife brewed, the smell of lavender. He noticed that a second crystal case had been added and several local bands were selling their CDs by the register. Soon his hunger kicked back and seeing no one he knew, or that knew him, Marcos pulled himself away from the magic shop and out onto the street.

6

Captain Van Dijk led his men out of the Royal Bee Newsstand.

"How do you want to do it?" He asked.

"Quickly," Hector said.

"Without much notice," Willie added.

"No shit." Van Dijk rolled his eyes.

"In the alley by the fire station." Hector offered.

"Won't someone see?" Willie asked.

"Have to be quick about it." The Captain said.

Marcos cut up the street at a brisk pace and rushed across Brighton Avenue. Captain Van Dijk and his men quickly followed behind. Marcos headed up Brighton Avenue for about twenty paces, just past the White Horse Tavern, and ducked into the narrow alley between the fire station and the youth center. Once in the alley, Marcos felt the hair on the back of his neck rise and prickle. Still, he had not seen the men following him.

Willie lit a cigarette and aimed it for the center of Marcos' neck. Cocking his finger back he chuckled, and Marcos spun on the chuckle, just in time for the cigarette to smack him in the eye. Marcos screamed and Hector produced a thin pen knife blade and attacked. Hector easily got behind Marcos and drew the blade across Marcos' neck deep and wide. Marcos slid to the alley floor, grasping at his throat. The blood came quickly. Willie blocked the alley entrance so no one could see or enter. Hector wiped his blade on a stray newspaper and folded the blade in his pocket. The Captain kicked Marcos in the ribs once, just because, and the three men walked out into the sunny street. No one made a sound. The Captain turned down the street and doubled back to the T.

"Come on, I know where his cargo is docked."

7

Mr. Bill didn't like hypnotizing people. He found the whole process rude, but the large rotund man named Albert was delighted to be giving over his car, to him, Mr. Bill, the kind man who showed him the pretty coin. Albert blanked out like all weak spirits, and Mr. Bill directed him back into the Royal Farms to treat himself to some candy.

The SUV's tank sat on full. *Thanks, Albert.* Mr. Bill guessed that he was about ten hours from Boston, that is if he didn't stop for more than just gas. He knew that the ship was scheduled to leave port in fourteen hours. That should give him plenty of time to find Marcos and rescue Marina. Besides, how hard would it be to find the box in a harbor?

8

Sunlight hammered Nick's face. His skin had dried all up and down his arms. He'd hadn't felt so thirsty in all his life. He guessed there were perhaps a dozen people crowding him in by the rail. His hearing warbled in and out. They seemed to be clapping and encouraging him, but that seemed too surreal and stupid to be true. Then, all the phones, a few cameras, a tall woman in a red ill-fitting blouse waved her young son over to get a photo. Nick felt like he was floating on water. Except he was so thirsty. He was so goddamn thirsty.

"Water," was all he managed to say.

"What's he saying?"

"Sounds like water."

"Does anyone have any water?"

A young punk with the camera produced a small bottle of Poland Spring. Nick unscrewed the cap and gulped the contents down.

"Thanks."

He had never felt cotton mouth like this. The way his body felt drawn and dried out had something to do with the girl. *You need to get out of the sun.* Nick pushed his way out of the crowd and stumbled toward the convenience store across the street.

CHAPTER FIVE

1

Marina slid off the bed and down to the floor. The driftwood itself was bolted to studs which in turn bolted to the floor. The wood blasted to a fine bluish-gray, stretched like fingers to the floor. Gnarled and bent back on itself, partially by weather and sun, partially by nature's ringed design, the old tree looked like a great hand that held the bed frame and the mattress, which had become her home, her safe spot. The bed looked too extravagant to be inside this cell with her. Under the bed, she had hoped to find an opening – something. But there was nothing.

I had a dream. Marina paused, took several deep breaths. *He swam up to a hole in the bottom. Hadn't he? Was it real?*

Marina stood and placed her hands underneath the tines of the old driftwood. She calmed herself first, finding her heartbeat and placing her focus there. As she breathed, she imagined herself ripping the wood from the bolts in the floor. She imagined ripping a hole in the floor. She imagined seawater rushing in filling the room. She closed her eyes and pulled up with all her might.

She strained and held for three counts before backing off, her eyesight spiraling with pricks of light. *You're not going anywhere,* she thought, before sliding back into unconsciousness.

2

Larry Lorquist chewed on his right index fingernail. It was down past the skin and the fingertip was raw and sore from his teeth. He managed to tear a tiny sliver of it off and he removed his baseball cap. Under the brim, behind the sweatband, he produced a small plastic baggie, an old dime bag, and he placed the bit of nail inside where it slid to the bottom with all of the other bits of nail. Satisfied he placed the dime bag back under his sweatband and drummed his fingers against his baggy pants. The guys were coming over and they wanted to see the weird pics he'd taken.

In his senior year in High School, Larry Lorquist and Spider Jones started the Art Thugs website where he and his pals showcased their urban graffiti-styled art, as well as photos of classic graffiti in and around the Jersey Beach area. After a year, they switched up the name, to AT, which was more mysterious and professional and still true to their high school roots. Larry wanted a place to show off his tagging skills and Spider wanted to showcase his photo skills, both necessary to the site. Over the last year and a half, Spider's pics had been purchased by The Source, Vibe, and a record label called POPTHRASH-SWING. Next month, one of Spider's pics of graffiti from a deserted industrial site in East Jersey was going to be featured on the new Snoop Dog retrospective. Business was good.

One of Larry's tags made it into the Village Voice supplement about graffiti in New Jersey. He'd been interviewed even. He hoped he'd get his chance to design a record cover one day too. For a while, Larry thought about ditching Art Thugs for LA. LA seemed to have a whole different take on things. Feeling jealous of Spider's small successes, Larry thought maybe it was time for a change.

But just last week one regular contributor, Lockspray77, or LS77 submitted a pic of an unusual picture found on the side of a beach hotel, a little farther down in Delaware or some shit. LS77, a non-binary performance artist of sorts, had begun a new project where they tagged zombie businesses with natural landscape imagery and had been scoping buildings out for potential sites when they came across what LS77 described as folk art meets suburban dystopia. The artist had left no moniker only a dreamy, clumsy, picture that had a strange hypnotizing effect when someone stared at it too long. The picture had become something of a controversy around the "office," also known as Spider's basement. Some there said it was art, others said it wasn't. Whatever it was it was new to the graffiti scene. For one thing, the artist hadn't signed it. For another, it didn't appear to belong to any one neighborhood or culture. It didn't smack of the street, and yet somehow it did. Even Spider couldn't put his finger on it. The composition looked like a white woman floating by her hair above a swirling ocean where what appeared to be a crow, or raven (there was quite some speculation as to which) above what looked like a big building block.

And now there was another possible hit. Larry hoped it was the beginning of a new style of street art, something different from the tired old stuff seen on every dilapidated wall and sidewalk since forever. He hoped that it was a wave that he could ride to California.

3

"Amanda, you are not having him over for dinner," Tanya clipped.

"It's a little late to take the invite back, T." In the background, Amanda overheard at least two conversations in Tanya's office braiding together.

"No, it isn't. Just don't show up." Tanya enunciated the p in up.

"I can't do that!"

"Yes, you can," Tanya said.

"No, I can't. Aren't you supposed to be working?"

"Working. Skunk Mouth and Fuck are both coming to town, not to mention that whole Bowie tribute thing."

"Right, what's that again?"

"Show at the Met. It's a big deal. Management is bringing in us Jersey suckers to work on it. That's not till next week though."

"Look, I met this guy. He seems okay. He's weird, but there's this vibe coming off him."

"Vibe? Please."

"No really. He was intense. He's the guy who called in and I talked to last week."

"The one with the toothbrush?"

"No. Up his butt? God no!"

"Jesus, Amanda, all of your callers are a little on the crazy side."

"This is the guy who painted in his sleep."

"Oh, right."

Amanda's switchboard lit up, "Look I have to go."

"All I'm saying is be careful. I'll call my brother and get him to come along."

"What for?"

"For protection."

"Tell him to leave that machismo at home." Amanda quipped.

"Aw. He's sweet. Spider always is sweet to you."

"When you're not around he comes on to me. Tells me I could be his girl."

"He's had like a serious crush on you for years."

"I figured."

"Bathroom shower fantasies, I'm sure."

"Gross." Amanda popped her gum.

"Please. Somebody digs you. Dress sexy."

"What?"

"To fuck with the men."

"Oh."

"Not literally, of course. I was just riffing there, kinda." Tanya's voice trailed off.

"Of course."

"But do wear lipstick. That new shade we got last week. It's perfect for a maybe-he's-a-killer-maybe-he's not-night. Wield your beauty like a hammer, right?"

"Perfect." Amanda quipped.

"Cool. I'll bring the mace."

"I gotta go, my board is blowing up."

"It's all you girl. It's all you."

Amanda hung up as her switchboard light flashed out. She stared at it for a second hoping the caller would try again. Amanda didn't receive another call all day.

4

Spider Jones and Blockhead swung out of the cramped Yugo Blockhead bought off his stepfather for a hundred bucks. The crappy little yellow coupe -- barely fit Blockhead and he had long ago busted the seat back so that his legs wouldn't be so cramped against his chest. Spider fit easily into the Yugo. His thin body was like a wire compared to Blockhead, who was an ex-football player turned photojournalist, or rather, a wanna-be photojournalist.

Larry was stretched out on the hood of his brand new Camaro thumbing through his phone. Spider saw that Larry's army boots were scuffing up his wax job. Spider didn't say anything. *If Larry wanted to fuck his car up like that, no problem,* Spider thought. Larry bobbed his head to the steady beat of vintage De La Soul pumping out of his car window. Beyond Larry lay the private world of yachts and yachting clubs. Larry's Camaro was the only car along a long stripe of road that ran like a cuticle along the commercial wharf.

"Larry. LL Wassup?" Blockhead slapped hands with Larry as Larry pulled himself into a sitting position.

"No. Don't get up Larry," Spider said as he hooked hands with Larry and Larry sucked in his teeth.

"It's right over here."

"Here?" Spider pointed down to his shoes.

"Yeah."

"This is the beach?" Spider looked to Blockhead. Blockhead's pale forehead was slicked with sweat already.

"Yup."

Blockhead remained silent. Spider had bitched all the way down to Larry's part of the world. Bitched about Larry's lack of vision, lack of determination, etc. Blockhead only nodded and tugged on a blunt Spider had rolled for the drive.

"So point," Spider said, his arms half upraised in a challenge.

Larry sighed and slid down the length of his Camaro. His boots scraped the blacktop as Larry slipped off and walked around Blockhead to the driver's side.

"Move along," Larry said.

"What?" Spider looked to Blockhead. Blockhead looked out into the ocean. Spider ran his comb through his hair. Spider didn't appreciate his associate's attitude.

"Step off," Larry said as he looked Spider in the eye and hardened his look. Spider and Blockhead stepped cautiously aside.

Larry's Camaro grumbled to life and he moved the car forward six feet. Blockhead noticed it first and slapped Spider in his chest so hard that Spider gasped for breath. When Spider saw the green mermaid, laid down in a fine haze of chalk and oils, he almost choked on his tongue. Particular detail had been placed on the shading of the green scales, and the picture itself reflected the sun as the real thing would have done. The mermaid appeared to beckon them to come forward, to her naked breasts, which were aroused, though not cartoonishly large as most naked breasts in street art tended to be.

"Damn," Spider said.

"Yeah," Blockhead said.

"Somebody put some care into this."

"Yeppers." Larry hooked his hands on his pants.

Blockhead was the first one to notice the previous night's date, as well as the time, 2:11 AM, written in a flat, crayon-like scroll, almost tucked under the painting.

"Larry?"

"Yeah."

"Did you get pictures of this," Spider squinted?

"Sure did, Spider. Backed em up on my phone and everything."

"Weird," Blockhead said.

"Yeah," Larry nodded.

"Looks like the same strokes," Spider said as he stooped to point. "See here. And there, in the corner, where it looks like something floating on top of the water there."

"Yeah, for sure, that's the same brush technique as the other one." Blockhead pointed with his finger, which was roughly the size of three of Spider's fingers.

"Good, Blockhead, good. When did you find this Larry?" Spider said as he looked up to Blockhead scratching his very small goatee.

"This morning. I come out here in the morning to help my uncle scrape barnacles off some of the boats. You know, got to get paid. I came out this morning and saw it right here."

Spider's phone began to buzz. He ignored it and concentrated on Larry.

"Let's see your pics."

Larry handed his camera over, and Spider clicked the camera on. Over the last year, the success of the website had allowed Spider to purchase the most cutting-edge digital cameras, but Larry had always opted for the old HP PhotoedgeX99 with a telephoto lens. To him, they were dependable and durable. But Spider hated the lens flare on the Photoedge line.

"Scroll down two. I had the shakes last night," Larry said as he pointed to the screen.

Spider scrolled down to the photos and smiled. They were good, real professional, and framed nicely. They would look good on the site, right next to that odd, almost psychedelic one Lockspray77 sent in from Delaware or Maryland.

"How did you get the angle?" Spider asked.

"Borrowed a ladder."

"Good boy." Spider said.

Spider's phone buzzed again.

"Blockhead, time to go."

"Sure thing Spider."

"Larry," Spider looked up at Larry, "Go ahead and get these emailed to the office. We'll do a whole piece on this guy, whoever he is."

5

"George, Hello. It's Lilly."

Lilly's voice, bright and happy, filled George with euphoria.

"Hello."

George's excited voice made Lilly's skin ripple.

"So, what are you up to?" George asked. "I feel like it's been weeks since I've seen you." George had seen her the day before yesterday when they ate lunch on the picnic tables outside the hardware store.

"I'm going to visit an old friend of the family," she coughed. "With my mother."

"Oh, with your mother."

"Yes. It's not for fun, I can assure you. We need to go dancing."

"Nice! I'm down for dancing." George's blood rushed to his head and his chest. "Look how long are you going to be gone?"

"That's the trouble. I don't know. My mother is all wound up about this. And I told you about my mother, right?"

"Yes, that was the double coffee morning, remember?"

"Yes! Of course."

"Somebody sick?"

"Sorta." Lilly's mouth moved away from the phone and her voice came from far away.

"Is it serious?"

"Well, we won't know till we get there."

"Oh."

"Yeah. All I can say is that I'm going to miss you terribly."

"It's gonna be lonely around here," George said. The happiness building in his chest had him tapping his toes.

"You'll be all right."

"Yeah," George said. His face was one big smile.

"Nick can take care of you."

"Well, he's kinda out of town, too."

"Really?"

"Well, truth is, I don't know where old Nickola is. He's kinda missing."

"Missing!" Lilly moved her mouth closer to the mic again.

"Yeah, he's been gone for at least a week, though I didn't notice it really till a day or so ago."

"You didn't notice?"

"Well. He wasn't feeling too good, so I gave him a few days off."

"And you didn't check up on him, George Henderson?"

"Well. Not really."

"What if your friend was sick?"

"He didn't seem that sick."

"What if he's in the hospital?" Lilly asked. "I mean have you called?"

"I didn't think about that."

"Maybe you should."

"Not a bad idea at all."

"George."

"Yes, Lilly?"

"I'm gonna miss you."

"Me too."

"I'm sorry we haven't had a chance to get together again."

"It's okay."

"Since I ruined our dinner with my, uh, um, problem."

"Lilly, it's totally fine with me. When you get home we'll spend a week together, I promise."

"Really?"

"Non-stop fun with George."

"You promise?"

"Promise."

"Good," Lilly said. Suddenly, Lilly's body hurt. A dull ache started in her heart and pulsed out through her body. She felt it in her blood – a sense of dread. "I'm sure Nick will be back soon, George."

"I hope so."

"Me too." Lilly felt darkness unfold inside her heart. And an ache rose inside her; she bit her lip to alleviate the pressure building up in her bones. "We'll be staying with Loco's relatives." Lilly was fighting back tears now, the pain coming in sharp throbbing stabs. The metallic taste in her mouth was all too familiar; the trouble ahead had to do with magic, with her mother.

"Oh sure. Call me if you can, I mean, if you want to."

"Of course, George! I didn't want to leave without talking to you."

As Lilly hung the phone up, the sense of dread remained. Her teeth ground together, and her stomach turned somersaults. For the first time in a long time, Lilly Aguirre was afraid, very afraid. *What did the pines say? Wait. Wait. Flow with wind and wait. Fuck,* Lilly thought. For a brief second a picture flashed in her head, of George and of a giant heading north into a cloud that looked almost like a mermaid. Lilly dismissed the idea as simple fancy and went outside to find her mother.

6

"We're taking Loco's truck." The Ugly Mother said, her face pinched and serious.

Mother looks exhausted, downtrodden, Lilly thought.

"Loco?" Lilly repeated. She looked over at him, his big handsome face smiling in the sun.

"He's driving, don't worry. With Loco we will be safe," the Ugly Mother said as she patted Loco on the shoulder. Loco had a reputation as someone who liked to have fun, but she also knew Loco could be very strong and brave, when necessary. The man read poetry and listened to Metallica, *at least he'll be entertaining,* Lilly thought.

"Mind your manners, Lilly. I can read what you're thinking."

"You do not know what I'm thinking, mother."

"Yes, I do."

"But..."

"But nothing. Loco has business to take care of in Boston – a family mess. We are tagging along to see to our own business."

"Mother, this has nothing to do with..."

"No more arguing."

Fine, Lilly thought. *What the fuck am I doing? Again. Lilly? You think it'll be different, that you can have a normal relationship with your mother, but it never happens. You won't. You never will.*

The urge to run swelled up in her heart and for a second Lilly thought she was going to crack in half with madness. She recognized the negative thinking, slowed her breathing, and let her feelings rush over her. *This is why we commune with the pines, Lilly, to learn how to be patient and flexible.*

Loco swung their bags into the back of the pick-up. The pick-up had a king cab and Lilly helped her mother into the front before taking the back seat. As Loco drove them out of camp, Lilly bounced with the truck as it ran over the pitted and pocked dirt roads and onto the smoother concrete road. She gazed out the window at nowhere and nothing and sent her imagination into the forest where she and George ran hand in hand. They would buy a farm together with a house and have a few kids and as many pets as she wanted. She'd keep working at the hardware store and George would make money painting houses in the summer and portraits in the winter. They would even build the Ugly Mother a small house next door. *What can I say? I'm a dreamer,* Lilly thought, as Loco began to play Metallica's *Ride the Lightning.*

7

Back in camp, many of the migrants saddened to see the Ugly Mother go began to speak of leaving for other farms or even Mexico. This began as a whisper after dinner when the families gathered in the open courtyard between the housing. The elders sat in circles in their lawn chairs, and after a few songs, the departure of the Ugly Mother began to bubble up in conversations. Her leaving signaled an end of an era of sorts. Lots of them felt that way about it – Javier, Maria Consuelo, Juan, and Benito, Estrella, and Guadalupe, too. Then talk turned strange. Javier told them of the mosquito giant he'd seen the night before, a big lumbering insect of a man, striking across the fields, his steps the size of a tractor, humming so loud the plants shook around him. Maria Consuelo told them that he had seen the fog again. Talk of the fog led to talk of the bird spirits and strange deer in the fields in the morning – the deer that was afraid of no man.

But no one was sadder to see the Ugly Mother and Lilly go than the big dog Rufus who had been following Lilly around for weeks. No one paid Rufus any mind, so when he trotted out the camp, no one noticed. Led by more than scent Rufus the dog trotted his way toward George's house, toward the one person who could take him to Lilly, whom Rufus was sure, was going to need his help, his mind was filled with soft bright light, and it was his duty to follow.

8

"Spider here."

"Kevin?" Tanya's voice sounded strained like she was biting into aluminum foil.

"Oh." Spider sighed.

"What's that mean?"

Spider looked out of Blockhead's windshield, "Nothing, sis"

"Look I need your help."

"I'm not having dinner with you and mom again, T."

"It's not like that Kevin," Tanya said as she let out an *urrr* of frustration and sighed.

"You two have to work out your issues on your own time," Spider said, casually looking over his shoulder at Blockhead who stared ahead at the nothing that was Jersey Beach. There were a few girls in bikinis and big hair, and a scrawny guy with a backpack. Blockhead's Yugo dashboard had been plastered with stickers, some as old as the car, others new and fresh. He pushed his giant index finger on the loose end of a Mermaid Trans Life Shelter sticker to press the mermaid's head back against the dash.

"Kevin?"

"It's Spider."

"It's Kevin."

"I won't help you, T."

"Fine, Spider. Happy?"

"Very."

"What are you so slap-happy about?"

"Some new graffiti. Some cool stuff too. Very cutting edge, sis."

"You know, Aunt Wanda could get you some serious gallery time for your pics."

"I ain't going to Virginia."

"Ain't? Ain't? Sounds like you done been there already Kevin."

"Yeah, so what do you want?" Kevin liked to make his older sister squirm. He still got twisted brotherly fun out of listening to her grind her teeth and grunt. He looked over to Blockhead and rolled his eyes at his sister. Blockhead's face did not register a reaction.

"Come over for dinner tonight."

Tanya sounded desperate. Spider arched his eyebrows and looked over at Blockhead, enjoying his sister's pain. Blockhead's face did not move.

"Tonight?"

"Yes."

"That's short notice, T."

"Please Spider. It would mean a lot."

"I'll need tickets." Spider slapped Blockhead against the shoulder.

"Fine," Tanya seethed.

"Good. So, what's going on."

"Amanda invited a guy from work to dinner."

"So."

"No. A guy from work. As in he's a patient."

"From the clinic?"

"No from Dial-a-Nurse. She doesn't work at the …"

"From Dial-a-Nurse?"

"Yes."

"That dippy phone first aid and referral service?"

"Yes."

"The phone service with the ads featuring that guy crawling on his hands and knees, bleeding from a gunshot wound, moaning and crying for mother and he's down to like 2% battery and he calls Dial-a-Nurse?"

"Are you high, Spider?"

"And when Dial-a-Nurse answers they tell him how to make a tourniquet with a belt and call him an ambulance while they refer him to a better general practitioner who'll better serve his day-to-day doctorly needs?"

"The very same, Spider," Tanya said with extreme emphasis and indignation.

"They don't have patients."

"I know."

"So what's up with that?"

"She met him on the phone. They met locally."

"Sounds desperate. So Amanda needs my help?"

"Yes, she does. She needs your help."

"Hmm. I'll take that as a positive comment. I'll wear a button-down shirt for this. But you need to put a word in for me, you feel me?"

"Maybe. Meet me at the apartment at like 6?"

"Sounds good."

"Great."

"Great." Spider said as he hung up the phone. He looked to Blockhead. "Tickets, man, tickets."

Spider's phone buzzed again.

"It's Zac." Spider said, rolling his eyes at Blockhead. Blockhead looked away across the street. An old man walked by with his yellow lab.

"Yo." Spider said.

"Spi--I trailed this guy; I mean there was something about him. My stomach, I mean, never mind about that. Anyway, I trailed him."

"And?"

"That there was something about him, something about how this guy would have looked good in his newest urban sprawl/decline montage piece. This guy was totally homeless/bum-looking but with a real powerful electric vibe running through him. This guy would make a great composition, Spider."

"Okay, bro."

"The pics came out washed out. Like there was interference around him. Weird. I mean, I tried more than once to take his picture and you know I'm sly, right. Anyway, I keep following him and he gets all trancey and he paints this amazing, cool, thing on the boardwalk street, in the middle of heavy foot traffic. While in a trance!"

"A cool, amazing picture?"

"As in like the picture on the side of that hotel, that had been sent in by Lockspray77. You know, Spider?"

"Zac, where you at?"

9

Zac gave them directions. Spider googled them and called him back. Zac had given him the wrong street name. Spider googled them again and had to call back again because Zac had again misspoken. This went on, Spider sighing and cussing, and then calling Zac back to confirm.

"Zac saw this guy live." Spider said, sliding his hands across the Yugo's dash. Spider smoothed the mermaid's head back down from where it had peeled up from the weathered plastic.

Blockhead had not moved his head once, since Spider had been on the phone with Zac.

"What?" Blockhead kept his eyes ahead. He started the engine. The little Yugo whined and hummed like a toy.

"Saw him in the flesh. This guy was using paint, not spray paint, brushes, and a pallet. He had a bag with him."

"Wow, brushes."

"Yeah, retro, eh?"

"Yup."

Blockhead didn't move his head to back out. His eyes moved behind his sunglasses, backing the car into the road. "Zac's been wrong before you know?"

"Oh yeah, I know."

Blockhead and Spider crawled out into the bright sunny afternoon, the Yugo, a five-speed stick shift, took about two minutes to get up to 60 miles an hour. Zac lay ahead of them, a possible photo of the mystery artist and then dinner at his sister's. Spider was beginning to think he should play mean and fuck with Amanda's desperate cry for attention, maybe show up and give this weirdo a real scare.

10

Maria did not know exactly why the sheriff was coming over for lunch. Before her stood a sweating pitcher of iced tea. She had ham, cheese, mustard, egg salad, and leftovers from dinner.

As Maria fussed about the kitchen while just beyond the dining room in the dark and cool living room Mulch sat under the spinning blades of the ceiling fan. He muttered something low to himself and rubbed his thumbs together and imagined Maria's head vacant and empty.

Over the years that Mr. Bill had lived with the Hayes family, Mr. Bill had shown both Eb and Mulch how to bend reality. It was a matter of concentration and sometimes a mixture of herbs and flowers, which Bill said were used to stir the senses. When someone is extremely angry, one did not need anything special at all, only the mad blood rushing through them. *Black magic is hate,* Bill said once. *Anyone can do it. All you need is the will to focus your anger.* While Eb had been downright awful at manifesting his energy, Mulch had shown some aptitude at it, although when it came down to raw power, Mulch relied on man-power versus magic. Mulch's confidence was high when he began the spell that would take out the local sheriff and set plans in motion for the rest of the farm, for Maria, and Mr. Bill.

11

Sheriff Thomas Bradford North pulled into the long gravel driveway of the Hayes home and slowed his speed as he wound his way through patches of trees. He'd been up here once before to tell Mulch one of his farmhands had been killed in a knife fight at Sully's BBQ & Beer. He had been struck with the idea that the Hayes did not want to be bothered by the outside world, that Mulch wanted the Hayes homestead to be an oasis to itself. The Sheriff figured that Mulch could use the back roads, the side roads, and field roads to move about his property and never once leave it, his property, not to mention the water access in and out. Thomas Bradford North was again struck by that sensation of isolation.

Maybe this is a waste of time and maybe it isn't. Macy Allbright had disappeared, right out of her bed. The Allbrights had woken up to find that their alarm system had been shut off and their side door unlocked. There were some muddy footprints around the home but no fingerprints other than the family. By all accounts, Mulch's daughter, Virginia, was one of the last people to see Macy socially. North thought it was odd that Virginia had not contacted him about the case, despite several calls to Mulch personally. Odder still was that many of the young people North had interviewed had not seen Virginia in days, as well. Adding to all that it seemed that Adam Taylor, Virginia's boyfriend had also disappeared. Though by all accounts, according to everyone that thought to mention it, Adam was the type of guy to pick up and leave town without notice. *But Macy Allbright wasn't that type of girl. And why hadn't Virginia returned his calls?* Mulch had said Virginia was out of town, visiting an uncle. He said that she had been for a while, that she had left before Macy had disappeared. Plus the nagging Ace Detective Agency was calling his office and asking for information. North was damned if some come-here detective was going to take the lead on this, his case.

Sheriff Thomas Bradford North was a man of the shore and like many locals, he knew of the rich textured pirate history of the early pioneers who dared the mosquitoes, the harsh heat, and the New England chill that winters bring to the backpaddle creeks and marshes. North himself owned a large home in Westville, but nothing like the Hayes home which spread out like a telescope from the original five-room farmhouse that had been built for them in the 1700s. The newer wings were Victorian. Above the doors high windows had been added, as well as several bay windows along the front, affixed with stained glass. A decade ago, the Hayes had built a new kitchen. North's cousin, Marty, had helped install the skylight and a new stove. A friend had worked on the new roof. Other than the few workmen, North had never heard of anybody visiting the Hayes house, socially that is. Hayes didn't go to church. His daughter had attended a private school. When Hayes was at the feed store, he kept to himself. North didn't know what to think of the rumors that Mulch sold drugs or buried corpses in his fields. North had personally busted every so-called drug dealer in town, at least once, and none of them had ever mentioned Hayes. Instead, they had kept their mouths shut and had been bailed out by big-shot attorneys from up the road.

But now all the so-called drug dealers were dead – Billy Squared, Johnny Miller, and Bill Nunn. Even Billy's kid, Steven, a real snot of a brat, had been killed in a driving accident. *Lila Coates, too, come to think of it.*

And now this business with Macy Allbright, the sheriff thought. By all accounts a decent kid who liked to have a good time.

There were stories about the Hayes' Mr. Bill. North had never seen Mr. Bill for himself but had heard enough about the mysterious hired hand who had a way of looking at you that made you feel intruded upon as if Mr. Bill could read your mind. He'd also heard that Mulch drank the blood of workers that betrayed him, that Mulch kept a half-retarded girl locked up in his basement. North regarded most talk as horseshit. The idle gossip of people with nothing else to do, imagining that those who didn't attend regular church service were in league with witches, devils, and perverts. And everybody, not just the blue bus riders, the welfare cheese eaters, and the blue-headed Bible thumpers, everybody, talked shit on the shore. It was how the Eastern Shore world turned. Gossip was sport.

There was the matter of the smoke signals. Warner Williams, his senior deputy swore that Mulch and his Indian weirdo dealt drugs all over the county. He swore that it was done by smoke signals. How in today's day and age someone could get away with sending smoke signals without raising an alarm was anybody's guess. But Warner swore that sometimes, driving through Oysterhaus, he would see the thin dotted, almost morse-code-like puffs of smoke rising from deep out in the Hayes fields. But there was nothing North could do about that. Not without firm evidence anyway. Just saying it out loud was enough to make Bradford pull out his hair. *Where was the reason?*

North drove through a small grove of oaks and there the Hayes house stood, the creek behind stretching out behind. North parked his cruiser in the driveway behind a flashy SUV and Mulch's blue Ford pickup. The house looked cool and inviting in the shade, the creek behind the house flashed a gunmetal blue. North admired the boathouse. *Take it nice and slow, buddy. This guy is a loaded gun.*

"Sheriff." Mulch's voice startled him.

North's first instinct was to go for his weapon, so startled he was, but he did not. *But where is he? Must be inside.* North stepped closer to the porch. He couldn't see Mulch anywhere.

"Over here."

North spun on his heels and looked for an open window.

"No, over here."

North spun again, this time quicker, his spine prickling with fear. He felt foolish and childish spinning like this, one way and then another. His hand went to his holster, and as he did, the front screen door opened and Mulch leaned into the doorway, his tall body blocking the entrance to the foyer.

"Sorry, Sheriff. Just practicing throwing my calls. Be hunting season soon."

"Huh. Right. Be here before you know it," North said as he wiped his hands on his slacks. *Since when were his hands so sweaty?*

"Didn't mean to make you jumpy."

"You didn't make me jumpy," North said as he felt Mulch's eyes on him.

Mulch slid off into the house, disappearing into the relative dark of the inside.

"Come on in Sheriff, I got some lunch made out for us." Mulch hollered from inside.

"You said on the phone..."

"What?" Mulch hollered from the house.

North stepped inside. Mulch had already vanished into the back rooms of the house. Upstairs, North heard light singing. *A woman.*

"I said you said on the phone something about lunch."

North paused at the foot of the stairs, above a woman passed by into a room, her light summer dress trailing behind her like a song.

"Back here, Sheriff."

North removed his hat and weaved his way past a little WC under the stairs, past a small study, the connecting dining room gleamed with crystal. The kitchen was bright. Mulch sat at a small table on the screened porch which was like a little sunroom behind the kitchen. The sheriff looked out onto the deck and the backyard and beyond to the boathouse, open like a dark mouth.

"Sit, Sheriff, some cool tea to refresh you?" Mulch's eyes were bright and reflected the sun into North's face.

"I think I will," North replied as he sat down and admired the spread before him.

"Maria went a little overboard this morning. We have fresh tortillas and beans, excellent fare I might add, Chicken, yellow rice, cold-cuts, and egg salad."

"Wow."

"Yes, she must have temporarily lost her mind." Mulch smiled. "Maria is so exuberant sometimes."

"I guess so."

Mulch placed his two hands under the table and gently rubbed his thumbs together.

"What can I do you for Sheriff? As I said, Virginia has been out of town for some time. Visiting an uncle was the last she told me."

"Well, Macy Allbright disappeared, as you know. I've questioned her friends, all of them except Virginia. None of them know where she is, or for that matter where she *would* go."

"Unfortunate."

Mulch looked into North's eyes and as he did, North thought to himself, *this man is touched.*

"I was hoping that Virginia could shed some light on the subject, Mr. Hayes."

"I wish she was here."

"So do I," North's stomach rumbled.

"You can contact her in Richmond if you like, but I must warn you that she is undertaking a sort of internship with her uncle, a cousin of mine really, but no matter. But I don't know what he's got planned for her. Or even if she is in Richmond at the time."

"So, she's not in Richmond? Or is she in Richmond?"

"The fact is, Sheriff, I don't know."

"What do you mean?"

"Virginia took off to Richmond in a huff. I haven't heard from her since she left."

"Did you have a fight?"

North decided that he didn't need to take notes, that he would be able to remember all the details. North felt crisp and light. Mulch continued to stare at him, but North didn't feel creepy about it anymore. He felt downright okay with it. *This man is quite friendly*, he thought. *I bet it would be fun as hell to hang out with him for an hour.*

"We have been fighting – some, you know how young women can be."

"Oh." North's stomach grumbled, again. "I'm sorry."

"Yes, about my footing the bill for all of her shopping, you know one of those things."

North chuckled, and then he filled his mouth with egg salad. He hadn't realized he'd picked up a spoon. He felt like he could eat the entire table, chairs and all. *So hungry. I didn't even realize it.*

"She takes off all the time, Sheriff, without telling me. I guess I'm going to have to get used to my little girl finally leaving the nest."

North shoved a whole piece of ham into his mouth followed by a spoonful of mustard. He chewed with relish, delight, his mind full of bright light. *This food.*

"I don't know what to do about her, Sheriff. But I guess that's what young women do these days. No more of that staying around the home bit. No. It's see the world, buy the world, you know?"

North mumbled and worked his jaw on the ham. "Maybe," North swallowed. "Maybe, Macy went with her." His stomach rumbled and he rushed to feed it.

Mulch's eyes narrowed and under the table he rubbed his thumbs faster, producing heat.

"It's possible. Anything is possible. Don't you agree Sheriff? Have some beans and some tortillas. They're quite nice. Maria is quite the chef."

"Thanks, I will. I am suddenly so hungry," North gulped. He reached for his ice tea. He gulped a swallow. Then another.

Mulch continued to stare into his eyes and North felt safe, taken care of. Why even downright respected, for once.

"What a good idea you had. This food." North said as he piled the beans onto his fork and shoveled them into his mouth. He folded the tortilla in half and crammed it in, too. Then another scoop of beans. For added measure North found himself reaching for the ham again.

"Sheriff, it's not going anywhere." Mulch laughed.

North's face flushed with shame, but he already had the ham in his fingers anyway and added it to his stuffed, paunchy face.

"Sheriff, I think Macy will turn up soon. Don't you? She's a rich girl and rich girls need money."

North nodded.

"Or rather, Daddy's money."

North was dizzy from the taste of the food. The beans and the tortillas made him light-headed, and he could feel his heart flutter like he was in the presence of incredible beauty. He didn't remember the last time he'd eaten food so wonderful before. *God, it is so divine.*

"Now don't choke Sheriff. I don't know what I would do. I'm kinda clumsy with my hands." Underneath the table, Mulch continued to rub his fingers together.

"Dunwrrie," North nodded. A dab of bean gushed out his mouth and down onto his front. North looked down at his shirt in shame. North had the odd notion that if he didn't eat everything soon, real soon, the food would go away. And North was too hungry for that to happen.

"Let me get you a napkin." Mulch stopped rubbing his hands together for a second and raised them to give North a napkin.

"Goofood," North said. His jaw hurt, but his hunger hurt worse. It throbbed in his stomach. It had a voice, his hunger. A growl and a high-pitched gurgly whine. North made a promise to himself that he and his wife would eat larger dinners from now on.

"Let me get you some more ham, Sheriff." Mulch pushed back from the table and entered the kitchen. He had yet to reach the refrigerator before North began to make gagging noises at the table. "Did you say something Sheriff?" Mulch said gleefully.

North sputtered and flailed.

"I'm sorry, I'll be a second, I don't know where Maria keeps the horseradish. Which I'm sure you'll find to be a spicy addition to your meal."

12

Wilhelmina "Pro-Zac" Evans' gut rumbled and spat. It didn't so much rumble as it growled verbs. Often Zac was sure he heard the words "walk," or "run," or "photo" coming from his stomach. Sometimes his stomach sounded German.

Zac's stomach had been acting up since high school around the same time Zac had begun playing with a non-binary identity and using the shorter male version of their birth name, Willie, which morphed into Billy when Zac started using his/him pronouns, wearing a binder, and cutting his hair short. Pro-Zac, a nickname given to Wilhelmina in middle school because of Willie's crawling anxiety, continued to stick long after Willie transitioned; a name Billy shortened to Zac. Zac's stomach had been pretty much a normal teenager's stomach until Zac's stomach told him not to go to school one day. He skipped not because of his stomach, but because his best friend had scored some killer green bud and they got high and watched anime instead. Meanwhile, at school, Zac's chemistry partner blew up the lab, killing himself and injuring five others. Since then, Zac listened to his guts as a rule; he listened and took notes. In college his stomach told him the answers to four incredibly hard questions on his Economics final; a final he needed to pass. His stomach, like many college student's stomachs, told Zac when to stop drinking. However, Zac's stomach tended to use mono-syllabic words – 'Stop. Drink.' Sometimes the words had a feminine ending like drinking or running.

That morning Zac's stomach told him to *walk* and *photo*, which Zac interpreted for him to take a walk with the camera. Sometime before noon he spotted Nick Adams in front of Stinky Joe's. There had been something in the way Nick stood in front of the greasy spoon that made Zac want to take his picture. Zac trusted his gut and he didn't have to wait too long to see that Nick had been worth the hunch. Zac wasn't sure if Nick was the artist who had painted that thing on the side of the hotel or not, and it didn't matter. Zac also didn't know that Spider and Blockhead had intercepted another mysterious drawing. Zac wasn't stupid and he knew that if he was to get the guys to listen to him that he'd have to bullshit a bit. So, when he spoke to Spider, he claimed that he'd nabbed a photo of the hotel painter. Being brash and bold, Zac hoped only for some recognition, plus some of his stills on their site. Zac hoped and wished and prayed that eventually he could make a living taking pictures and this would be a good start as any. His stomach agreed with him.

13

Spider and Blockhead passed Zac's camera back and forth between them. Blockhead's large hands made the camera look small and toy-like. Spider had a smug look on his face.

"Looks like we got a live one."

"Really?" Zac's stomach agreed with a belchy yes. No one else seemed to hear his stomach, a fact Zac worried about, a lot.

"Really."

"Listen, Zac, you said he took off. Did you see where he took off to?" Spider tapped his feet in anticipation.

"No. I think I freaked the guy out when I took his photo. You should have seen this guy, man, He looked zonked out on something."

"Maybe he was." Blockhead handed the camera back to Zac. If Blockhead thought anything of the pics, he didn't show it.

"It does look like his work. It's hard to tell with him in front of it," Spider said. "You know, there are some good photos in there."

Zac smiled at Spider's comment.

"He does look fucked up." Blockhead's diagnosis was accurate. "You know as in fucked up."

Zac nodded. His stomach roared the word "trance," loud enough for Blockhead to look at Zac's belly area.

"You should have seen him when he snapped out of the trance," Zac said.

"Really? He was in some kinda trance?" Spider asked.

"Maybe, Spider. Hard to tell. The guy was really into his thing and then *bam*. He came out of it and was kinda freaked out."

"He looks high to me."

"Everyone looks high to you Blockhead," Spider said.

Zac bounced up and down on his heels.

"Look, you two hit the streets, see if he's made any other hits today. I gotta go and meet my sister for dinner," Spider continued.

"Is it dinner time already?" Blockhead patted his belly.

"No, but I gotta shower and change first. Maybe tonight I'll finally get Amanda to see me as a man and not her best friend's little brother."

"Fat chance of that," Blockhead said under his breath.

"I heard you," Spider said, but Zac and Blockhead had already started down the street, the two of them striking matches and lipping smokes.

14

Pembroke's eyes rolled, his toes carrying him behind Virginia. He placed his icy cold hands on her neck and leaned in to whisper. "Today we are going to break your mind."

Virginia remained perfectly still, the feeling of Pembroke's breath on her skin revolted her.

"Today you get the box."

Pembroke clapped his hands together. The air parted and folded back on itself and before Virginia, a box the size of her head, perfectly square, appeared before her. Made of wood and leather, and oiled and stained from ages of use, Virginia smelled the residue of pain.

Pembroke snapped his fingers and the fog rose to braid itself around Virginia's arms, pulling them down. When the fog wanted to be solid, the fog felt like rope, cold and indifferent. Virginia couldn't move at all, the ice of the fog penetrated her skin and seeped into her bones. She began to numb. She watched with fascinated horror as Pembroke handled the box and turned it over in his hands. Extending from the bottom was a leather hood that would affix over her head; the hood had two thick leather straps that would go around her arms and keep the box on her head. Pembroke smiled as he placed it over her head.

Inside, the darkness was complete. Virginia's eyes tried to adjust in vain. She heard snapping and the sound of a lock click home. Lost in the darkness, Virginia smelled something sweet and sticky. *Blood? Sweat?* For a second, she thought she might crack up, the box itself beating her panicked breath back against her face.

"From now on you'll need me to get back and forth to your room. You'll need me for most things. I find it's better that way."

Virginia tried to talk, but her words were sucked out of her mouth, her brain firing *run, run, run* as the incredibly hot and moist air closed about her like a tomb. Her mouth felt tacky and dysfunctional. She whimpered, began to cry.

"Now, now my dear, *Hush*. There is no sense in struggling."

15

Nick Adams spied Stinky Joes from the alley across the street. His nerves jumped and jived. Some guy had taken a picture of him. That made him nervous. He didn't want trouble. He just wanted to get to Boston where someone needed him. It was in these moments, heart-pounding, sure and unsure of what he was doing, that Nick felt like he was wasting valuable time. His trance states had brought him this far and he was willing to let them take him as far as they would go. His nighttime ramblings exhausted him, but they always seemed to lead him in the right direction. When he thought too hard about things he stalled. His brain was too much in the way.

Then there was the matter of dinner. He appreciated the idea of food, a hot shower, and maybe a couch. But he couldn't rest. Somewhere there was a woman, a mermaid, who needed him, and that fact eclipsed all others. It was at times like these when he missed George, missed having a friend, a person to talk to.

Already at four-thirty Stinky Joe's was busy, the after-work crowd poured into booths and onto barstools. Nick looked down at himself, his clothes torn and dirty; he felt like a sweaty watchband.

16

Amanda sighed. *Why did I care so much?* She thought, *did she care?* She thought she might. *But why? Because maybe his pain can work for you, that's why. Get a nice research grant, perhaps. Work your way into the system through academics.* These thoughts came to her in the voice of her roommate, good old Tanya, The Voice of Reason.

But Nick needed *her*, or rather he needed someone, and why not her? She needed to be needed. It felt good to be someone's savior. At these times Amanda regretted her decision to work at Dial-a-Nurse. She had always been needed at the clinic, but the clinic had burned her out.

At the clinic, Amanda had worked a good sixty hours a week, without overtime. That had been two years ago and already her memory had turned it into nostalgia. *And love*, according to Tanya, *was what every twenty-seven-year-old professional cute girl should be thinking about.* Besides, a girl like Amanda should work in the hospital and not the local clinic. *The hospital had a union*, TVOR had said. She had taken the job at Dial-a-Nurse instead, for the meantime.

And now I am about to invite a patient into my home, am I nuts?

17

Marina's fingers throbbed; her fingers red and tender at the end from where she had clawed the floor. The wooden splinter protruding from the tip of her middle finger was over an inch long, at least. Her digging had barely scratched the surface of the wood. She had expected the wood to splinter and break under the force of her strength. She had broken wood before. She felt strength inside her, only here the strength hid from her – *it hibernated* – she thought.

She was so thirsty. Underneath her, the sea lapped and splashed against the wood. The box hadn't moved in hours, and she was sure she was docked somewhere. Outside faint far away sounds of other boats, other ships, other people, washed in. Her throat ached. She tried to cry out, but it only made it worse. Marina felt her body shudder. She bit down on the splinter and pulled. When it slid out, blood filled the slender hole. Marina laid down on the bed and sobbed herself into sleep.

CHAPTER SIX

1

The pavement's heat rose to meet Amanda's face and her hair wilted in the humidity. The sun was high above her and was moving into its last arc before settling down for the night. She walked briskly, passing dozens of people leaving their cramped offices and hitting the streets for Vietnamese, Thai, Chinese, Pizza, and the pub food that dominated the streets and boardwalk near the beach. Amanda felt a lift in her walk that was normally not there. She enjoyed the mothy smells coming from the trash that was being hauled onto the sidewalk for evening pick-up. The light body-odor peeling off the bodies of sweating folks made her smile, blush even and she imagined that these people were just like her. They were going home to someone they liked, or loved, and were going to spend a few civilized hours before sleeping into the next day.

At that moment Amanda's mind opened and her imagination crept out of her head and into the heads of those she passed. Her head played a few scenes for her, people stepping off the sidewalk, out of her sightline and into cars and she saw the squashed cigarette filters in the ashtrays and the McDonald's wrappers crumpled on the floors, and she smelled the pine air fresheners hanging off the rear-view of cars and vans and trucks. She even saw into the apartment of a tall handsome mustached man, whom she had seen before, at the newsstand. She had the taste of Camel cigarettes in her mouth as he struck the match.

Amanda did not know what remote viewing was and would have discounted the idea immediately if someone told her that she was experiencing a kind of remote viewing. Amanda was a sensible girl who liked Netflix, Fiona Apple, reading a good medical thriller, pizza on Fridays, a cold beer on a hot afternoon. Sure, Amanda was curious about new-age types of things, but Amanda wasn't even so sure she believed what Nick told her. She wasn't sure it mattered; Nick gave off a radiance that Amanda didn't understand.

But you feel it, she thought. *His radiance. Something is going on with him,* something she didn't quite understand. As she neared Stinky Joes Amanda tensed with nervousness. And there he stood, vacant in the eyes, shirt flapping in the breeze, his dirty face fixed on the window.

In the glassy light, he looked noble, dirty but noble.

"Hey."

Her mouth became instantly dry.

"Hey," Nick nodded, his eyes perking up. "Look you don't have to do this, you know. I'm no weirdo, but you don't have to do this."

Amanda was struck by the Southern accent which she found cute.

"Come on and meet my roommate," she said.

"Are you sure?" Nick asked, his face full of fear and stress.

"Sure I'm sure. Her brother's going to be there. In case you are a weirdo or something."

"Oh," Nick smiled.

Amanda began walking up the street, Nick following slightly behind.

2

Captain Van Dijk, Willie Harmon, and Hector Fillman felt different. Sick, maybe? The men could not agree. Captain Van Dijk was sure it was the subway ride, the bouncing always got to him. After all, he was a sea captain, and it took him a long time to get his land legs back. Willie and Hector didn't seem to be bothered by the bouncing and screeching subway car. But yet both felt a creep of uneasiness in their stomachs.

"Drinks," Van Dijk said. "That will cure all ailments."

The men agreed.

Captain Van Dijk felt a ball of nausea roll into the bottom of his stomach and sit there. He eagerly eyed the front of the train. Ahead of them, dark tunnels began to lighten. At the next stop, he and his men would get off go topside and get drunk. There were a few trashy taverns near the harbor where he could settle his nausea and leave it at the bar, or in the bathroom.

"Willie, Hector." Van Dijk growled; his accent clipped like the rail under them. They turned, each of them glazed and absent. "Drinks on me."

Willie nodded, Hector did not, and turned back to the window and stared off into the grime that leaked and spooged down the sides of the subway, like urine running down an alley wall.

3

Captain Van Dijk and Willie spoke in low tones as the men climbed the stairs up into the light of Boston's cityscape.

"We must find you a nice girl, Willie. One who won't piss you off so much," The Captain said. "This cargo will bring good money to you. You'll be able to buy all the whores you want in Amsterdam. In my city, we will find a nice girl to keep you happy."

Willie threw his head back and laughed, "They don't make women like that."

Hector's brain remained blank and quiet.

Back in Amsterdam, Cilia poured herself a late brandy. In Cilia's mind, there were five television screens. One screen was dark, a small green fish swam in circles through inky water, Marina. Another screen was full of static, the mystery man. Two screens showed the side streets of a dank and seedy Boston wharf. The last one showed the same side streets of the Boston wharf, but the picture remained fuzzy, almost blank. Captain Van Dijk and Willie's screens were focused on getting to the bar, while Hector was hell-bent on hurting a woman. Cilia planned to use that hate to torture Marina. The mermaid was so close she tasted her.

Once inside the bar Captain Van Dijk ordered a round of snakebites and a round of shots. Willie got a shot of vodka. And Hector ordered tequila.

Hector shot back his snakebite and his shot of tequila and slipped out the front. He did not tell his Captain where he was going. He did not signal to Willie that he was leaving. Neither of them noticed.

The noise in Hector's mind had risen to a pitch. It wasn't like it blotted out his thoughts, but supplanted them, his thoughts receding behind those of Cilia.

It took Hector longer than he thought to find Marcos' boat. Marcos had docked a few miles out of town. Hector barely had the cab fare. It was a suburban marina. It was too early in the season for most New Englanders to be using the docks regularly, a bitter chill rose off the Atlantic. Hector knew from experience that the season didn't kick up till the fourth of July, in New England anyway. As it was only the second full week in June and the docks were practically empty, Hector was free to roam for Marcos' boat.

The sun had completely disappeared behind the skyline when Hector walked up to Marcos' ship. It had been relatively easy to find since it was attached to a large box. The funny thing was Hector had not even noticed the box, as huge as it was, floating on pontoons. It was as though he wanted to look beyond it. He found it hard to understand. He was surprised at the size. A trawler, a bit beat up, but in good condition. It was registered in Virginia. The next closest boat was several berths away.

Onboard he found Marcos' personal belongings. He rifled through the clothing and took a scarf which he wrapped around his neck. He wanted to strip the box to the nails and get inside. But a warm itching in his mind told him to wait till it was safely snug in the ship's hull before peeking. Hector had no problem hot-wiring the boat and tugging the box into the inner harbor. He wanted to crack the nut and get a taste of the meat.

4

Tanya was surprised to see her baby brother sporting his best shirt and a tie. He still wore his black jeans and Timberlands and held a brown paper bag in his hand. Tanya didn't think her brother could look so good.

"Spider?"

"Hey, sis."

"Come on in. What's in the bag?"

"Is he here yet?"

"No. Amanda's bringing him. They should be here any minute."

"Smells good, what's on the stove?"

"Baked spaghetti."

"Cool."

"Did you bring wine?"

Tanya and Spider flopped down on the couch.

"No, Tequila."

"You're shitting me?"

"No. Seriously. I thought we might as well get fucked up."

"Fine with me."

"Are you stoned?"

"What?"

"Are you stoned?"

"Hush, baby brother. You'll ruin my mellow."

Spider sat the Tequila on the table. Tanya's living room opened to the dining room, which in turn opened to the galley kitchen. A small counter served as a kind of bar between the kitchen and the dining room. The table was set for four. It was going to be tight.

"Where did you move all your shit?" Spider said as he peeked under the table.

"What?" Tanya moved into the kitchen and began to busy herself, checking the oven. "Oh. I threw it all on my bed."

"You guys have to get a new place."

"Look who's talking."

"Hey, I pay rent."

"Yeah, like Mom and Dad charge the going rate."

"I have my own door."

"You live in the basement."

"I have my own kitchen."

Tanya guffawed. Spider did have more space than she did, and Spider did pay three times less than she did. "How's AT coming?"

"We've begun to pay our freelancers."

"Really."

"Yup. Fifty bucks for single shots. Buck-fifty for a series."

"Not bad. You know, I'm proud of you little brother."

There was clicking and a brief burst of laughter as Amanda pushed the door to her apartment open. Nick followed, his head bowed, his cheeks already blushing. Spider and Tanya stared at Nick, taking in his dirty clothes, his ratty shoes, his sun, and weather burned face while Amanda stalled by the door, staring dumbly back at Spider and her roommate.

"Uh. Hello guys. Didn't expect you so soon."

Tanya tried to smile; she was too busy checking out Nick.

5

Rufus paused for the third time at the vole hole. He had a vague rumbling in his belly. His nose told him the vole had passed by not too long ago but too long ago to be a pre-dinner snack. He resumed his trot. Rufus loved the woods. They scared him sometimes because there were sounds and smells that didn't go with anything. Sounds and smells that sounded and smelled of death, of old coppery things.

He knew that his Lilly, with the bright light, had gone. He knew in his dog brain that he had to follow her. He also had the nugget of thought that George would help him. He wasn't sure why he knew this, only that George would take him to Lilly. He was close now.

6

George and Abdullah sat on George's porch drinking beer and were arguing about names when Rufus trotted up to them. "Look, I know this is going to sound...Fox News aside, we don't get anyone that..."

"Master, Abdullah is not..."

"You look like one..."

Abdullah knocked his mug back. "Master if you want Abdullah to be an Arab, as you say, Abdullah will – poof – be an Arab."

"But you're name. Abdullah. That's Arab, isn't it?"

"Abdullah already told master George. First master gave this name to me."

"So, what's your real name?"

"No offense to Master, but master George couldn't pronounce Abdullah's real name. Abdullah believes he has already informed master George of this."

George wanted to say something clever but found when talking with Ab that all of his clever sayings went out the window. *Stop arguing with a genie, you're just a country kid who doesn't know anything,* George thought.

"Master seems sad lately. I'm sure your friend is fine. Don't you want to know how your friend is doing?"

George did want to know about Nick. He was worried. He also felt that he should give Nick a wide berth. He felt he owed Nick that much. Nick had a rough time a few years back with his parents' death. Sometimes personal stuff required personal space.

"Yeah, I do Ab. I want to know what he's thinking. Especially with all that fucked up painting bullshit."

"Master could. One of two wishes remaining to master."

"I don't know, Ab. I'm worried about Nick and all, but I have this feeling that I should save them, the wishes."

"Okay by me, Master. Abdullah likes how you say "sticking around.""

"So, after I've used up my wishes do you have to leave?"

"In genie world. It would be in good taste for Abdullah to leave and bestow wishes on other mortal men with kingdoms small as yours."

"So, exactly what happens?" George asked as he swatted at a mosquito.

"Abdullah crawls back into a vessel of eternal whiteness and boredom and waits."

"And?"

"Abdullah waits and waits and waits."

"Wow. That sucks."

Ab propped his feet up on the porch railing and looked out into the yard. George imitated his friend. Neither of them saw Rufus trot out of the woods and run alongside the house. It wasn't until Rufus had sat down at their feet that they noticed him.

"Master, strange creature has come," Ab said as he pointed to Rufus.

To Rufus, Abdullah smelled like spices, cinnamon, and pepper.

"Abdullah, that's a dog."

"Master's palace should never be breached without permission. Shall I dispatch small and furry creature?"

"Hey, I know you," George reached down and rubbed Rufus' face.

Rufus' tail wagged.

"Master, do you know this creature? This animal is a carrier of pests. Must be cast out of the kingdom."

"You're that mutt that Lilly hangs out with! Aren't you buddy?" George rubbed Rufus harder and added a round of ear scratching to boot.

"Master's behavior confuse."

"He's a good boy. Aren't you a good boy?" George had Rufus turning over on his back to be belly-scratched. "What do you think he's doing here?"

"Abdullah does not know many kind and benevolent masters such as yourself. I admit this is a little strange, even for Abdullah, this kindness to animals."

"Don't tell me you've never seen a dog before."

"Dogs used by kings to hunt and kill slaves. Children play with dogs. Kings do not."

George ignored Abdullah, his beer warm in his swelling belly. He'd put on a few pounds over the last few days, he and Ab had been hitting all the fast food stops they could think of. As he leaned down, his boozy breath in Rufus' face, George had a crazy thought, *Lassie.*

"Perhaps Abdullah can whip dog to eat an enemy's heart."

Lilly was in trouble. Could it be? Rufus cocked his head, his eyes mooning up to George.

"Perhaps this creature could be useful. I wish to learn, Ab, as you call me. Ab wishes to learn about this marvel, this animal, master."

Lilly was in trouble. But so soon? She'd only left a few hours ago. George quickly pushed the thought out of his mind. *Lilly had just left for Boston. She must have set this dog loose before she left, let him roam around a little, that's all.*

"He's just lonely," George said, the feeling that something was wrong swelled in his stomach like a balloon.

"Master looks content rubbing the long head of the furry creature. Abdullah sees dogs before that were not fat with fur, like big creature here. Ab bent down to rub Rufus' head and Rufus shrunk back from Ab's big hand at first. Rufus smelled the magic on him. Ab smelled a little like Lilly did sometimes. After a second Rufus leaned forward into the pet. Ab's big hand rubbed Rufus vigorously.

"I bet he's hungry," George said.

Rufus recognized the tone of George's voice. That tone meant food. George got up and Rufus followed. He was sure there was something the dog could eat inside – hot dogs at least. And maybe after he fed the dog then the funny feeling in his stomach would go away. *Maybe.*

7

For some reason, Spider was having a brain fart. He'd seen Nick before, very recently, in fact, only he couldn't remember where. *I shouldn't have gotten high,* he thought. Marijuana destroys slowly, but thoroughly, his sister once told him, before selling him a bag.

"Smells great," Nick wasn't sure what to say. The young man named Spider kept giving him the evil eye.

"Only the best," Tanya seemed nervous to Nick.

Amanda fidgeted with the drinks. Nick felt like he should help, but the kitchen was too crowded already. He was the only one in the living room area. Spider kept eyeing him without looking like he was eyeing him, so Nick tried not to let Spider know that he knew Spider was giving him the evil eye. Nick tried to remember his parents. He couldn't.

"So, Nick what do you do?"

Tanya reached across the bar and handed Nick a glass of wine.

"Um. I paint houses."

Nick had become painfully aware of his Southern drawl and how it stood out among the flat, sometimes accentuated city accents.

"Do you own your own contracting business?" Spider asked, his arms crossed. He kept sneaking furtive looks at Amanda.

"No, I work with my best friend."

The girls both erupted with a long soft aw.

"Must be good for you to kick off work for," Tanya paused, "such a long time."

"Well, I'm on a vacation, sorta."

"Hmpf," Spider turned his nose up at Nick. Spider's brain turned circles, *Who the hell was this guy?*

"You look homeless," Tanya snorted and Nick looked down at his clothing with shame.

"Tanya!" Amanda flushed and gave her roommate the eye. Nick noticed there was lots of eye-throwing going on around the cramped little space, and Nick felt each hot stare.

"Sorry. Just a reflex. I have to protect my roomie," Tanya said as she looked at Nick. "She's all I have."

Tanya squeezed Amanda by the shoulder. The look had not been friendly.

"It's okay," Nick said, doing his best not to sound like a hick. "I expect it. If my roommate came home with a stranger who was painting on sidewalks and buildings, I'd be concerned too."

"What did you just say?" Spider's brain snapped up, his eyes sharpened.

Nick shrugged and looked Spider right in the eye.

"Nothing. Just lately I've been painting stuff on the sidewalk."

Spider's mouth dropped.

"That's how I met your friend Amanda."

8

Loco reached over to the glove box, first to retrieve his cigarettes, then to fumble for his lighter, which had caused the truck to swerve in the narrow two lanes of traffic on route 13. The Ugly Mother had said nothing, sitting politely in the passenger seat. The third time, only seconds later, prompted Lilly to pipe up from the back that the Ugly Mother should act as Loco's long arm on the wheel so they wouldn't end up in a ditch, that they wanted to go North and North didn't mean to heaven. Loco laughed hard at the jab and knocked the back of his neck rest with his head. He pumped Metallica, and even The Ugly Mother could not resist tapping her foot as Loco sang along, his voice a balloon of mirth. Lilly surfed the socials on her phone, grew bored, and tried to sleep.

Much later, the Ugly Mother passed around soft tortillas and grape tomatoes. They ate in silence, save when Loco belted out whichever Metallica song moved him. Lilly stopped paying attention after *And Justice For All*.

As night began to fall, Lilly leaned over and tried to talk to her mother. Just a normal conversation. But the Ugly Mother's stomach rumbled, and her head hurt. Lilly was almost convinced that she complained of these ailments so as not to discuss Marcos and what was so important about him. When Lilly laid her head back to rest, she fell into a restless sleep punctuated by Loco's high-pitched yodels and her mother's snoring.

Lilly dreamed of rooms – small rooms, cramped rooms, rooms without windows and doors. She dreamed of rooms she recognized, rooms she didn't. One door opened into another cramped room, which would open into another room. Sometimes she would turn to back out and find herself in a room without a door. One dream worm-holed into another. Her mother's ragged cough woke her up. Loco was rambling on and on about different tomato pesticides, about a new one Mulch used which made the worker's fingers itch. His fingers had begun to bleed the night three nights before from all the hard scrubbing in the sink, trying to make the itch stop. The lights on the side of the highway were like hard bits of candy and they streaked by as if in the rain. Darkness unfolded, yet the end of the sun's day fizzled in the far west corner of the window like a light at the end of a dark field.

9

Mulch shook Michael Greenway's hand and tried to control the giggling creeping up his throat. *Fucking hey, Greenway, Greenway I'm fucking using magic.*

"Thank you so much for trying to save him, Mr. Hayes."

"I'm so sorry I couldn't, deputy. He just kept eating like he was starving or something." *Like he couldn't stop himself,* Mulch thought with glee.

Mulch looked into Michael's eyes. Michael, as a child, had once sold him candy for the local Little League Association. Part of him wanted to grab the deputy and press his thumbs into the man's skull. Another part wanted to laugh hysterical at Michael's grief.

"I know you did sir. There was simply too much in his throat. It's a tragedy." Michael sniffled and looked towards where the coroner's crew were zipping up North's corpse.

"Yes, deputy. A real honest-to-God tragedy."

"He was just so hungry."

"Yes, deputy. An American tragedy. What with so many picnics coming up. The Fourth. Labor Day. Sunny afternoons on the beach."

"Yes sir," Michael Greenway nodded and turned to the other two paramedics lingering in the front door. "We're done here."

Beyond Michael, two deputies mingled on the oyster shell driveway kicking up dust in the glow of the exterior light. They had been polite and mournful at the death of their sheriff and friend. The coroner's crew closed the ambulance. They too had been grateful. They all had been grateful.

"I'll never be able to eat a ham sandwich again. Not without thinking of him," Michael teared up. One of the other deputies looked down shamefully at the driveway. The other sniffed back tears.

Mulch stepped back into his doorway and tried to look sorrowful and waved a meek and hangdog look. Once inside, he began to giggle, a low giggle, almost maniacal. Upstairs, Maria began playing her mariachi music. *She's pissed at me. Perhaps I shouldn't have suggested her cooking was partially to blame.* As if on cue, Maria's mariachi music grew louder, and the jingling of the castanets sounded like the rattle of men's bones.

10

Mr. Bill's mind spread open before him like butter on bread. It spread out of the car and out over the road and ahead of the car and flickered through the minds of the people driving I-95. It wasn't so much that Bill read the minds as he drove up the coast that day as it was that he scanned through them. Mr. Bill moved like a wraith through traffic. He didn't speed too much, keeping a steady seventy miles an hour past the State troopers and their radar guns and the big trucks who didn't like to let anyone by.

Mr. Bill had agreed to help Mulch farm his daughters out to his cousins some years back, and for a while, Mr. Bill had believed Mulch that the girls would benefit from the experience. But he stopped thinking that months ago. Virginia was made of tougher stuff than Marina. Though Marina could tear his head off his shoulders without a thought, Marina was innocent and naive, like a child, and he felt like she was his child. That's what this boiled down to – Mr. Bill protecting his own – turning around what he alone had the power to change. Mulch couldn't have completed the box without him, Mulch had enough magic juice to maybe kill a normal man, but he did not have the power of his cousins or power like his own. Mr. Bill had been an important part of the puzzle. He had been everything. Then there was the matter of Cilia. Cilia would waste Marina away to nothing. Bill wasn't going to let her do that, not on his watch.

11

"The blackness was unlike any blackness I have ever experienced, doc. Only sound penetrated the wood and the moist leather that bonded the box to my shoulder, the leather smelling of sweat and fear and my coppery adrenaline rush. The leather acted like a living thing, stretching when I moved, bending to my shoulders as I bent. Even now, when I wake to find the bed covers tossed about my head, I can't help my tiny, puny shriek.

"You see my voice could barely escape my mouth before being pushed back into my throat. My throat grows scratchy even though I swallow constantly. The moistness of the leather skull cap eating my voice.

"I can't help but think of the way Pembroke summoned it, out of nowhere, out of the fog, I guess. But I don't think even the fog could have produced this dark maw. It felt like a heavy textbook resting on the cap of my head, my skull hurting constantly while I was on inside.

"The whole of my being is locked away – just like that. I understand now why the KKK used bags to cover the faces of the hanged. It wasn't a way to numb the guilty. It's a way to destroy their sense of reality.

"That I could no longer see Pembroke, that was a relief, for his fat and rubbery toes that propelled his stiff legs like gross, squat spider legs gave me the willies. Each time he bent his leg up and the toes stretched out, he'd lick a side, or suck their ends and I imagine how ripe it must have tasted with the grime and dirt of the hallways caked onto the skin. He moved on his toes like a spider, his legs stiff and knees locked, his arms limp at his sides. Troubled as I was by the box, I was glad to not see that.

"Pembroke led me about the house. It was like living in a black sack. "Darling," he'd whisper, his voice wet on my neck. I was constantly afraid he'd try to kiss me. I wanted to scream out. I tried, but when I did my voice came sucking back into my throat and my esophagus threatened to close itself around my deadened scream. My throat would constrict each time I tried to speak. If I managed any sound at all, it crawled out and over my tongue like a bug and was sucked into the darkness of the box around me. It was like living in an ink-black whirlpool.

"The fog took advantage of my blindness. I felt the cold air on my thighs, on my ass, sliding up my leg like a slug. 'Yes, yes. Darling bud. Darling niece,' the fog whispered. I hated that fog – the way it whispered sometimes, the way it didn't at others, the frosty touch as it braided together into a limb. 'Open your legs for me, sweetheart.'

"Pembroke's hand was often on my neck as he led me back to my room. The blackness of the box allowed my mind to wander. There were colors. They appeared with form and shape as I climbed the marble stairs. Pembroke was silent behind me, half pushing me upwards, half caressing my neck under his grip. Each time his fingers rubbed the base of my neck, they dipped down under my shirt.

"'I should lock you in the basement and leave you to the mice,' he said, his breathing increasing as we reached the top of the stairs. 'I should lock you in a closet all by yourself with no one to talk to and you'd forget how to talk and come out looking like a shriveled white mole.'

"Blah, blah, blah. Pembroke would go and on and on about it. Drove me mad, all the time acting like he was so helpful.

"I could tell that the idea of hurting me excited him and I felt his blood pressure increase through his skin. One day when he was leading me around, I acted. I didn't know what I was going to do when I did it – it was instinct, it was stupid. *Where was I to go?* First, I had to get the box off my head before I could do anything. Once I felt the top of the stairs, my feet carefully poking ahead of me without bumping into a riser (I hadn't wanted to be caught blind in the middle of the stairs), I slammed my arms backward into Pembroke's body. My elbow connected with his chest, and I felt him slip, his arm grabbing at mine, and I jerked back with him. I imagined it all there too, escaping, getting the damn box off my head, and rushing out into the streets screaming for help. But as I knocked free of Pembroke, I felt the slimy slick fog on my feet, and my darkness became a brilliant shower of rainbow-colored pixels before I tumbled after him, cracked my head, and slipped into unconsciousness."

12

Spider couldn't breathe. He fumbled his wine and caught it before it spilled on the fresh white linen. He recognized Nick now, he hadn't at first because he hadn't expected him to be here. On film, Nick looked like some kind of deranged homeless man. Or at least his eyes did. In his sister's apartment, he looked like a burnt-out graduate student. His clothes didn't fit him. His face was emaciated, and his eyes were sunken, but he didn't look possessed as he had in the photos.

"You know I've seen your work." Spider said.

Nick's eyes flickered, his face blushed, "My work? There must be a mistake."

"Yeah. Hotels, sidewalks."

"Hotel?"

Nick tried to make himself very small at the suddenly very crowded table.

"Hey don't freak out. I run a website. We specialize in pictures of urban graffiti. Urban art. We've won a few webbies. Google loves us."

Nick remained quiet; he didn't know what to say.

"Look, Nick, one of my compatriots saw your work on the hotel. We scour the crappy wasteland of this consumer-driven coastal culture and look for signs of urban coolness – urban decay, urban art, that kind of thing. Dystopia with an attitude."

"He takes pictures of cool graffiti," Amanda said suddenly, sensing the tension-like humidity in the room.

Nick blinked and looked at Amanda. Tanya plopped large portions of spaghetti onto plates.

"She's right. But it's more than that – the city is a canvas, a museum, posters, graffiti, if in you're in New York, on Sunday, come check me." Spider half-sang, half-rapped. "Man, I love that song," his teeth glazed with red wine.

"Nick, one of my regular contributors works as a delivery person for hotels. They truck food and beds and cleaning supplies up and down the Jersey Shore, into Delaware, into Maryland sometimes. They saw it, your painting, your picture, whatever the fuck you call what you do. They took a photo of it and sent it to us."

"Oh."

Tanya and Amanda stepped into the dining room each loaded with two plates of spaghetti.

"Spider's website is really good," Tanya said. "I can show you later if you want. They'll pay you for your photos."

Spider's eyes twinkled.

"Yeah. I can pay you. I had my boys looking for you this afternoon."

"What?" Nick's mouth dried up.

Amanda's face perked up at this. Spider looked to his sister and then to Amanda and back to Nick again.

"Just this morning one of my guys found something you did down by the commercial wharf, somewhere over by Nathanson Street. It was a wicked cool, man, a mermaid, a fucking mermaid, man. Usually, I think that shit is so cheesy, corny shit for kids, but this thing was like, 'WOW.'"

"Mermaid?" Nick's voice came out like he was in a trance.

"Yeah, he's got a fetish," Tanya said, quickly covering her mouth after it slipped out. "I'm sorry, that was rude."

Amanda flushed.

"Should have seen it, sis. It was banging, tough, the way the scales on her skin glistened. This weird trippy aspect to the whole composition. I don't know what you've been smoking, but I hope you can share."

Nick had a sudden thought that his life was out of control, unmanageable.

"How do you do it, Nick?"

"I don't want to get into it right now, Spider. It's, um, complicated."

Amanda looked down at her spaghetti sheepishly and Tanya's eyes trailed off into the corners of the room. Spider seemed to look through Nick. It was quiet for almost a full minute, which to everyone seemed like an eternity. Nick's body odor began to peel, his nervousness shedding itself in the close quarters, fed by hot food and awkward conversation.

"So Tanya how was work?" Amanda's eyes bobbed to Nick's.

"It's okay," Tanya deflected the question. "How was your day?"

"Fine," Amanda said.

Spider sniffed the air, and casually sniffed his shirt.

"So Spider, how much do you pay?"

Spider's face perked up at Nick. "Um well, we can pay you up to a buck-fifty for a spread. Unfortunately, we can't offer any more than that."

"Do you mean $150 bucks, or one dollar and fifty cents?"

"The former," Spider looked at Nick like he was crazy.

"Good."

Tanya laughed into her wine glass and Amanda giggled. Nick stuffed his mouth with food. He tried not to be too greedy about it, but that was difficult for him. His body ached and for the first time since he had set out on this journey, he felt comfortable.

"So Nick's going to Boston," Amanda said confidently.

"Boston, huh?" Spider wondered how anyone could smell that bad and not bathe. Tanya's eyes watered from the stink.

13

Mulch passed Maria in the hall, her face damp with tears, her eyes puffy and swollen. Mulch reached out his hand to touch her shoulder, but she shrugged away from him. He wasn't surprised. He'd expected her to shun him. After all, he wanted to purge his life and that included his family and those close to him, and that included Maria. But Mulch wasn't sure how he was going to get rid of her just yet. Maria would be delicious.

Pausing before the basement door, Mulch listened for any signs of Mr. Bill. Hearing none, he cautiously descended the stairs.

Mr. Bill's side of the basement had begun to smell like a zoo with a funk that was the byproduct of urine, feces, rot, and the musty damp smell of the basement. And there, in the corner, Mr. Bill fumbled with something, his hands coming together and coming apart. He seemed to be playing with the air and with himself. He issued a low mumbling sound that sounded both magical and nonsensical at the same time. Mulch didn't recognize it, and he usually recognized the pattern of whatever it was that Mr. Bill chanted and sang, a few words anyway, words he didn't know the meanings of, words that sounded like locks tumbling, a metal key scraping against metal as it turned the lock and opened into a wide, echo-filled room.

Mr. Bill's back shook and he turned away from the sound of Mulch's footsteps. His hair hung in ragged clumps. He had not been combing his hair for a few days now and already it seemed like that of a man who had been lost in the woods for a week, the long locks grimy and greasy and knotted like hell.

"Bill?" *This man is not the same man I once knew. Perhaps he's finally gone soft in the head. What was it Bill always said...magic takes its toll...yeah, bucko.*

Mr. Bill turned so that his right profile jutted out of the corner shadows.

"We need to talk." Mulch looked at his friend. *Was Bill my friend,* he thought, *or a means to an end?*

Mr. Bill mumbled. Mulch had trouble making out the words.

"Bill if you're in there, we need to discuss a few loose ends."

Mr. Bill quieted down, but his hands still fumbled and toyed with the air.

Mulch whispered, "Soon we will have to deal with Maria and the house."

"Ayu," Mr. Bill turned, and for a second Mulch saw that Bill's eyes were vacant, *glazed, like a donut,* Mulch thought. Mulch backed away from Bill and headed toward the stairs. He paused before Marina's room – it was quiet, but for a second, he thought he heard Marina's splashing. But it was only water lapping the sides of her pool. He waited for a second before heading up the stairs.

14

Nick felt drunk. Sleep moved into the forefront of his brain, he needed to rest. Spider had promised to call on him first thing tomorrow. Spider had left shaking hands and reiterating what an interesting take Nick had on graffiti – something different, rebellious, selfless, and understandable. Nick didn't know what the hell Spider was talking about, but he liked the idea of getting some money for his anguish.

Then Tanya turned in, leaving Nick and Amanda alone in the living room. They hadn't spoken much during the evening and Nick was happy about that.

The evening had begun to feel like a double date, and he didn't like that, even though Amanda had never once even remotely flirted with him.

"You know they're not that good, the paintings. Not as good as my friend George's paintings." He said as Amanda moved to the lounge chair next to the couch.

Nick seized the moment to kick his legs up. He supposed that his body odor would keep her away, which was good and fine by him.

"They look neat. I could never do what you do."

"I don't know what I'm doing."

"Maybe this is your subconscious telling you that you need to be an artist."

"No. No. No. Definitely not. I don't know what I'm doing now. Here…"

Amanda looked down to her lap, "I'm sorry if I'm keeping you from your whatever."

"Look I don't know what I'm doing. All I know is that now I have to focus on getting to where I'm going."

"I don't know what's going on here either. Maybe you have a chemical imbalance, but you're a good person, I can tell. You're nice, you're polite. God, I can't remember the last time I saw someone with such near-perfect table manners as yours. You can also carry on a polite conversation, which most men can't. I don't know much, but I know that these are important things for me. I'm going to turn in. The shower's ready for you if you want it."

"Thank you for your hospitality."

"Good night, Nick."

The shower felt great, and Nick washed off days of grime and sweat. His skin felt puckered and red, his face a bit swollen from where he scrubbed it with Amanda's pink plastic loofah. When Nick finished, he fell upon the couch, and he was asleep in less than a minute.

15

Mr. Bill liked the sound of the macadam under his car as it hummed along the freeway, the road open before him. He had always liked those Flintstone cartoons – where the cars run on foot power. Watching the invention of automobiles had been a revelation. It was at times like these, behind the wheel of a car, or in a grocery store where one only needed a piece of plastic to buy food, that Mr. Bill felt time slipping by faster and faster. It had been easy not to notice time in the earlier days when there were no clocks, no radio, television, or computers. Machines sped time up for Mr. Bill and he knew it would eventually catch up to him. But for now, there was only the road, and night and the great wheel of stars rolling on by. It had been ages since he'd been on a road trip, Mulch's pockets ran deep, deep enough for Mr. Bill to enjoy vacations wherever he wanted. A sense of freedom swelled up in his heart. He almost felt hopeful. As if he were making changes to his life which he had needed for some time.

Bye-bye Mulch, he thought, *bye-bye creep. You'll never see it coming.*

16

Neither Amanda nor Tanya heard Nick stir. He was out the door with a soft click and down to the street in minutes. Nick's dreaming body moved quickly in and out of the little traffic that zipped along the boulevards. His eyes were open like gun barrels, but the barrels were empty. No one noticed him skirting up the side streets. An idling car sat in front of the Glass Slipper, a reputable strip club. The owner, Tommy Scinilli, was throwing up in the trash can outback. His girl, the featured dancer Double D Diana waited impatiently for her beau to clean himself up. Neither of them noticed the shadowy figure huddling beside Tommy's rumbling Mustang. Neither of them heard the engine rev as Nick gunned it out of the parking lot and down the alley and out into the street.

Nick Adams, asleep at the wheel, headed out of town towards interstate 95 North, which would take him directly to Boston.

CHAPTER SEVEN

1

Marina heard the crane before she felt it. It sounded like death, metal crunching against metal, rust on rust, a giant metal mouth, squealing as it opened its jaws for her. The box shook. Her body flashed hot panic and for a second, Marina's body tensed and rippled, her skin flashing to scale. Then the awful sound of the box lifting from the water, the ocean water dripping and splashing into its mother. Marina clamped down her jaw and steeled herself for what was to come next.

In the wheelhouse of the freighter, Hector pulled the long twelve-inch handle the men called the "shaft" and watched the boat get pulled up like a toy. Marina felt the box pull and jerk as the box was upended and she fell against a side wall, slamming her head onto the hardwood.

Marina gritted her teeth and felt something well up inside her that she had not felt before, an urge to hurt something, to hurt someone. All her life she had never felt such adrenaline and anger before. She had always known it was there, but now it beat violently in her chest. She ripped her nails into the wood floor, enough to hold her fast as the box dangled in midair. She had no idea what was happening. The scraping of metal on metal opened Marina's blood to the fear which was jammed up inside her. Her brain screamed for her to get out. She no longer heard the sea below her, the smell of it fading. She looked for any signs of light outside her box, but she could see nothing.

Then there was a creaking crash and Marina felt the box tremble. Something had fallen hard, and she felt that she would befall the same fate. She didn't know which way was up, or where she was. She clutched the walls of the box and waited. But there was no crash, no breaking, no splintering sound. Oh, how she wished she would break up out over the sea. She was so dry. *How long had it been since I have been in the water?* There was a dull thud as the box came to rest and the metal monster was quiet.

2

George never enjoyed dreaming. For an artist, he found it inexcusable and a little sad. He had considered making his second wish a wish that would allow him to enjoy dreaming, but George was possessed with the idea that if he did so he would become obsessed with sleep and would never want to wake and become unproductive. Being unproductive wasn't in George's nature. George wasn't sure what was worse, not enjoying his dreams, or being obsessed with the idea that if he did enjoy dreaming, he would become obsessed with sleeping.

However, the night Rufus showed up George suddenly wanted to, needed to, dream. Maybe it seemed like an escape, with Nick in absentia, Lilly off to the north, and a big genie living on his couch.

In one dream Nick was carrying a tray of coffee. In the cups were various colors of paint. George knew they were a variety of colors, even though they were all a dull steel gray in his mind. In each coffee cup of paint floated an eye. The eye didn't scare him in the dream, though it did make his spine quiver when he thought about it once awake. In his dream, the eyes blinked and looked up at him with steely reserve. Towards morning he dreamed that Lilly and Nick were holding hands on a beach somewhere – they looked intimate, they looked like something important had passed between them.

When he awoke, George felt confident about what he must do; he was refreshed and eager for a mysterious road trip somewhere.

3

Lilly took her turn behind the wheel as the Ugly Mother snored in the backseat. Lilly's back ached and her legs were cramped from sleeping in the back. Loco zoomed into sleep in the passenger seat as soon as she pulled out of the rest stop. They were ahead of New York and Loco was exhausted. New York always exhausted Loco. He had begun drinking in New Jersey and as they headed into the golden shoulders of traffic, Loco had begun to sputter in broken Spanish to the passing drivers, his lips frothy with whiskey and lime juice, snot, which always came out of him when he drank, dripping down his chin. Lilly didn't say anything and only crossed her fingers. She thought about the shore instead and how all of its wide strange spaces were clean compared to the junky look of I-95 and the Jersey turnpike.

Loco eventually pulled over at one of the mega-rest stops and let Lilly take over. And no sooner had she begun driving did she begin to recall keeping her distance from the other kids at school so the children wouldn't pull her hair. For some reason, a pesky little redhead that all the other children called Macaroni called her Candle Head. Lilly didn't think it was funny and her two friends Sandra and Michele didn't either.

"That's just stupid," Sandra had said.

Michele just scowled and called Macaroni a dirty little bitch, which made Lilly blush. Lilly spent her lunch periods with an English tutor even though Lilly thought her English was just fine, but the guidance counselor had insisted that all migrant children spend an extra hour with a special needs teacher. This meant that Lilly and Benito, Estrella, Mary and Luis (who really couldn't speak English) had to eat lunch with a bunch of slow kids. And so they were called 'retards' on the playground – special ed kids, mouth breathers, the poopee pants people, slope-heads, jelly-brains. Which meant that Lilly had to have a different recess than the rest of the children in her class. Lunch was a drag too because they had to go into the cafeteria and carry their trays out into the hallways and back into the Special Ed rooms. Benito was a year older than Lilly, the oldest, and he would duck out at lunch and spend his time on the playground playing soldier or beating up on Macaroni like the others did when Lilly wasn't around.

One day Macaroni got suspended for selling dirty pictures on the bus. That day Lilly had skipped class. When she skipped past Macaroni in the front hall, Lilly turned her head away from old Mac and Cheese. Mac & Cheese had dried tears on her face. Lilly remembered they looked like dirt. That afternoon, waiting for the bus by the playground, Macaroni had spotted Lilly by the see-saws. Macaroni and three other girls, two of whom she didn't know, only that they had failed a grade and were in Macaroni's slower and much larger group. They were big girls and had big, upturned fists the size of apples. Macaroni led them down to Candle Head, and Lilly just kinda melted into the ground between the see-saws where Lilly stared off into the red flaked paint and waited for the blows. Lilly had been sure that she was going to be hit, she was sure of it. The way that Macaroni was calling her a dirty spic and a bitch. The closer Macaroni got to Lilly the uglier her face grew, spitting curse words as she ground her fists.

"You told on me you little spic."

Lilly had just turned her cheek.

"Hit that little bitch," one of the others said.

"Smash a tomato on her head. She likes tomatoes."

They gathered around her. Lilly shook her head trying to tell them that she had not said anything to Mrs. Boggs and that it was Conchetta, who had a

Mexican name, but was no more Mexican than apple pie was, and who the one who told on Macaroni.

"Liar. I heard it was one of the Spics."

"Yeah, it was one of these greasers that told on you," one of the big, fat girls echoed.

"Smear her face with your fists."

They crowded around her and began to lash at her with their feet to get Lilly out from under the see-saws. Lilly started to mutter something the other girls thought was Spanish. Lilly hadn't realized what she had been saying under her breath and when it came out it made her heart stop for a second as the girls were shoved backward three feet by an invisible hand.

None of the girls had said anything. Macaroni was the first to raise her finger and point at her in accusation. The other two were too shocked to do anything.

Lilly turned and ran to Mrs. Fields, a sweet-smelling older woman whose coffee-colored skin was warm against Lilly's own. Mrs. Fields smelled like perfumed tissues and the last time Lilly had seen her she had still smelled the same.

She hadn't thought about those people in a while and turned them over in her mind as if they were stones in a river. Loco reminded her of those days. Not because he looked like Benito, but because he acted as wild and careless as Macaroni or Luis or Mary who was now a pretzel after driving her car around a tree. Loco and Benito were third cousins. Benito never visited the shore anymore. He worked in a bar in the Bronx somewhere, or maybe in Harlem, or Spanish Harlem, like in the movies.

4

Virginia kept as still as she could. The fog, she was sure it was the fog, hovered over her body keeping her cool and tense with apprehension. She felt deadened, like a sack of meat. She hadn't realized till then how important sight was. She felt stupid for even acknowledging it now – a kind of dumb, obvious thing to say. The satin sheets felt like cool cream each time she shifted her body to get more comfortable. A feeling of cheapness covered her skin like baby oil.

The blackness inside her head-box was complete and total. Her muscles stilled themselves and she felt inanimate like she sometimes felt after smoking a joint with Macy and the two of them just laid on the back deck soaking in the afternoon rays. She'd sometimes get this feeling that if she was perfectly still, for the first time in her life, and that if she could manage to hold that stillness long enough, some great epiphany would come to her. And that maybe now if she could manage complete and total stillness here with the head-box, with the whispering fog and the crazy uncle, then she'd think of a way to escape.

And when she got out, she was going to kill Mulch.

But then she felt the cold tendrils of the mist, and she steeled herself for trauma. She didn't even feel herself begin to rise from her bed.

5

"Inside the head-box, my senses sharpened. Doc, it was like having a screwdriver tool through my skull and into my brain. It was weird, sacked out like a piece of meat, listening to the fog which had long ceased its whispering and become a kind of echo of my thoughts instead – a kind of static, if you will. He drugged me too, needles and psychedelics. Damn, what a fucked-up thing to do to another human whom you want to impregnate.

"I dozed off after an hour of twisting my mind around like a wet dishrag, mopping up all the stray thoughts. I dozed and remained still, my body stiffening, my mind beginning the slow warp of a mind shut off from its main sense. When I awoke, still encased in the box, baby blue light fluttered in the corner of the dark, then a yellow flickering, a hush golden glow, and soft white speckles shot across my blackened field of vision like fireflies."

6

The bright lights flickered in the corner of the box and would flutter close to her eyes and nose which made Virginia tense. She didn't know what they were. Perhaps there was some kind of film or fabric that allowed for air to circulate. She felt a light batting of air on her face, which felt swollen like a sausage. The bright lights felt like the hushed beating of wings, hundreds of small kisses against her cheek.

Pembroke is going to hurt me, very slowly.

The fluttering light knew it. She knew it. The blank-faced fear of the unknown hanging inside her body like a ghost.

The coffin floated on a bed of fog about waist high, and Pembroke moved the coffin into the hallway. The coffin was one of those fancy rich jobs with red satin lining and deep cushions. *Perfect to sleep in,* Pembroke thought, *very death chic. Virginia will learn to love it.*

Using his magic, Pembroke levitated the sleeping form of Virginia, and with the help of the ever-present fog, moved his captive into the coffin. If he had any luck Pembroke would have Virginia crying before the end of the hour.

Years ago, Cilia and Pembroke had taken some little girl, barely out of high school, and dressed up as a dead maid. Cilia forced the girl to wear formaldehyde as perfume. Pembroke liked to rub a long thigh bone across her naked belly. She was a good sport, the girl, docile, broken. Celeste was her name. She liked the humiliation, which is something Pembroke had come to count on, *certain people crave humiliation. Guilt,* he supposed, *they got off on playing the slave, willing, eager to be hurt.* Celeste had worked for free. She had no freedom and would spend hours polishing silver or running little errands, not to mention the sex. Cilia liked to take women and men to the edge of their desire and Celeste had taken everything with gusto. Cilia had tried whoring her out, writing crude words on her forehead, parading the girl around Dam Square, naked and marked with lipstick in the evening. Nothing would break Celeste. Finally, Cilia made the poor girl up as dinner, made her strip naked, and lie on a large serving platter. She stuffed her mouth with an apple, the whole nine yards. She planted a thick spit in her rectum and threatened to skewer her through, which got Celeste crying all sorts of tears and got Pembroke thinking that there was something about being on the bottom of the food chain. *People didn't like that, the idea of being eaten.* Shortly thereafter Cilia let her go. Months later she was a window girl in the Red Light District.

The drugs and the head-box will fuck her up enough, thought Pembroke as he floated the syringe through the air and over the coffin. He stared down at Virginia's body. He heard thoughts running through her head, worrying about her sister, something delicious about Adam, and evil thoughts about her dear old Dad. *Discovering evil in the family is such sweet work, how a mind turns over on itself.* Reading minds was fishy work, one had to know where to cast your line. The human mind bustled with all sorts of things with fears populated on one corner of the sponge, fantasies on another. Memories are like mines; you couldn't help but step on them once you were traipsing around the inside of a skull. Pembroke imagined the brain to be like a ball of twine. It started as an unspooled line, and as it was rolled up, across the floor, it gathered lint and nicks where a cat swiped at it, it rolled up pieces of dirt and microscopic bacteria, small insects, which met their death inside the ball, and once it was all wound up the inside had all the nasty trappings of the house and cat fur and lint mites and all sorts of unmentionables – everything overlapping and crisscrossing, growing hard with age.

"Hello Virginia," he sneered.

She jerked upwards, the fireflies zigging and zagging across her face like electricity. She wanted to cry out, but her mouth was infected with her damp hot voice.

"Don't mind the bugs. They're there to keep you company. Unless they're hungry. Then you should worry."

She didn't respond.

He scraped a fingernail across her chest, pausing at her nipple.

"I do hope things are exciting for you in there."

7

Virginia awoke from her sleep in a panic sweat. Her entire body was drenched. The smell of her piss permeated the air. She felt dried tears on her cheek. She needed to keep her head so she pushed the hot, damp, infected feeling to the back of her skull. A cramped thigh muscle spasmed before calming. *You can get through this*, she thought. *You can get through this. You can do anything you want, girl.* She'd been told that all her life, but she had no idea she'd be in a situation like this one here. *First things first. What do heroes do in tight spots? They case out the joint. Batman always knew what was what. MacGyver, Bond, they all had powers of observation. Buffy, too. Fuck. Wish I had Wonder Woman's strength right now.*

Carefully and with small movements she splayed open her fingers. She had no idea what was around her but there was no sense in risking harm to herself. She knew she had been put somewhere, inside something. Virginia imagined being inside one of those Chinese boxes within boxes within boxes. She slowly spread her fingers out. She didn't want to prick a finger on anything sharp and draw mice or rats. *Creepy houses like this always have mice. Rats. Places like this always have rats. And spiders.*

Her fingers felt the smooth satin cushions under her. Her brain melted like goo. Panic, she feared, lay just beyond the scrim, waiting. The fireflies fluttered like calm points of light at the corners of her box. The cushions below her were batted and deep.

There were about six inches of space on either side of her. It felt good to wiggle her fingers and shake her arms like wet noodles. She stretched her feet down and found that they didn't touch anything, just more satin underneath her. It was comfortable at least. *Where am I? A coffin? No, that was not possible.* The head-box didn't allow for her to rotate her head, but she assumed that her head was near a headboard or something. Raising her arms slowly she thumped into the top cover of her prison. *Shit,* she thought, *I am in a coffin.* She ran her hands along the length of it and guessed that the coffin was longer than she and wider. It was probably built for Pembroke, not for her.

He's going to bury me alive. Fuck. Keep it together, girl. Keep it together.

What kept her going was the knowledge that Pembroke had said that he wanted to break her, not kill her. She didn't have any doubt in her mind that he would kill her if she fucked with him.

How am I going to get out of this? Her mind whirred, panic jumped her nerves. She began to breathe deeply, slowing her mind, and her body's reactions.

8

Brainwashing a human being is a complicated process – it's about a Total Power Exchange or a TPE. Pembroke could manipulate a mind by using his own, but Pembroke liked the down-home feel of using his own two hands to manipulate a person's brain, rather than magic. He liked using his voice and his behavior to plant ideas that would reverberate in the skull of his submissives. He wanted his voice to be a loop they never forgot. Magic did not provide the thrill of watching a body react to pain. Magic was far too kind. Virginia was to be brought into the fold willingly. Now, depriving a subject of sight dehumanizes them, throw in some old-fashioned gaslighting and physical restraints, and time, and like magic, a mind bent all on its own. The headbox and the coffin were Pembroke's morbid fantasy – Halloween in June. In it, she would have to rely on Pembroke for all things. After a week of her in there, he'd take her out and show her the world again, using the headbox only at night or when she misbehaved. He'd take her out to play. If it worked, she would become docile and his. Then it was a matter of turning her into the master he had wanted her to be. To give her responsibility, let her be in control, let her feel her power over another human being.

It was a pity the girl was not talented as magic ran strong in the Hayes line. Still, one can't be picky when there's a mermaid in the family – even a half-mermaid. *Corrupt the pure?* Mulch had *botched that job. Eb had been so much more the animal.*

CHAPTER EIGHT

1 Smith Island, off the coast of Virginia and Maryland, Chesapeake Bay, December 12th, 1936

Ebenezer swung the shovel over his head and into the soft earth. The clay gave and he dumped the dirt to the side. The moist smell of the ocean hit him, and he sniffled, snorting back snot into his chest. He paused before resuming, looking about him. He had a nagging sensation that someone was watching him, had it all day. On the ground below him were his shotgun and the mason jar. The mason jar contained three gold rings, one silver tooth, a gold watch chain, and half a dozen gold Confederate buttons. Eb felt the urge to look at the gold again. He also felt the urge to touch the shotgun. The shotgun was his safety.

Smith Island was flat and took the brunt of the powerful winter gusts the Bay threw at the Shore. In the old days, the natives would fish off the beach. But they knew better than to live on the island permanently. Only the dead lived on the island.

The tombstone said Tankard in broad letters – a Confederate Captain, no less. Eb hoped the body hadn't shifted. The tide tended to do that to a grave. None of the other bodies had been right under their grave, a little to the left, drifting with the tidal sands, a little to the right, one hadn't been there at all. Eb supposed that was why no one built much on Smith Island anymore.

He started again, digging harder, dark was coming soon, he tasted it in his mouth. When the sun went out the wind got sharper. Leon was at home cooking dinner. Maybe tonight he'd go into town to the church social. Maybe meet him a young girl.

The soft ground gave way under his shovel and Eb hit the pine box in no time He felt the shovel push through the softwood, most of the top having disintegrated. His arms hurt and his legs hurt, his throat had begun to smart an hour ago. He was bent over, examining the box, when he heard it – a low singing – coming from the tree line.

Smith Island had one thin craggy line of trees and shrubs. The sandy soil stunted the growth so there was very little cover to hide in. Eb squinted toward the singing. About a hundred yards away a thin man walked towards him. Over his shoulder, he carried a rifle. The man cast an impossibly long shadow. *Big boy,* Eb thought.

Eb crouched and grabbed the mason jar, placing it quickly into his jacket pocket. He wasn't going to share this bounty – *no sir.* He and Leon would just head up the coast, right to Philly, get some cold hard cash, maybe even have enough money to winter it out and start fresh again in the spring.

Things had been going from bad to worse for some time now. Their father had been stabbed in the back, in his stable, no less. That same year, their mother caught consumption and died, and now here he was robbing graves on the island for bits of silver and gold.

The stranger moved slowly like he didn't have anything to prove, or lose. *Careful,* Eb thought. Eb figured it was one of the old Smith Island landowners who come down to see who was digging up the dead.

Eb just might have to kill him somebody, if that somebody proved to be a threat. Then Eb got this crazy notion that it wasn't a man at all, that the man was some kind of revenant, one of the souls of the men he just unearthed. The man walked slowly and deliberately, his song a warbled cry. The song wasn't in English. Eb didn't recognize the sounds of the words. It was a sorrowful song. *A don't dig me up just cause I'm dead kinda song,* he thought. Eb put down the shovel and picked up the shotgun. The gun felt cold in his hands. *Like the dead,* he thought.

Ebenezer Hayes had just turned twenty. He had years left to suffer through and live for. He and Leon had big plans for the farm, *But maybe not. Maybe death has come for you. Death, a long skinny colored person who sang queer songs on an island that was one big graveyard.* For a second Eb saw wings rise and shake on the man's back.

Of course, the man was probably only another grave digger. Eb had heard at Willie's Tavern that lots of the dead had been dug up in Westville and Eastville, and south of Lonely a whole field of Revolutionary soldiers lay newly uncovered, spoiling in the wet air. Someone had made off with all their silver buttons and gold buckles.

The man was thirty yards away now and he now saw that the man was an American Indian. He was old, middle-aged, and looked tough. Eb began to think that maybe he had pissed off some old Indian Spirit and that now he was going to have to die or suffer Indian torture. Indians hadn't lived in these parts for centuries. Eb fingered the shotgun and began to shift his weight back and forth to get a solid footing. The balls of his feet sank in the earth and for a second, he felt the soft earth would open and swallow him whole.

The wind whipped sand up in his face. The whole of mother ocean churned; a storm was coming. The man stopped ten yards from Eb and finished his song. Eb could see the wrinkles in the man's skin. The guy was old, and his age seeped out into the air around him just as the ground sank beneath him. Here was a man whom life had challenged, and a man that had beaten those challenges. The old Indian just stared, and he stared back and he saw the land as the Indian did – eternal – sweeping away the dead in the shifting and cleansing of the soil. The wind picked up around him and sand blew into the craters and folds of the Indian's skin. He wore thick clothing – heavy dungarees and a chamois shirt, a heavy coat, old and ragged with use. His hair was thick and long and tossed about his throat like a scarf.

Eb looked past the Indian at the salt-blasted trees gray and brown from where the saltwater spray hit them and dried, sucking the moisture from the bark and needles.

"Nice song," Eb said surprising himself with his words.

"Thank you," the Indian replied.

Eb looked into the Indian's eyes and sensed the Indian's strength flowing through him. If the Indian had been white, he would have been the kind of white man who walks into a room and stops time. People would stare. Women would fantasize about having him in bed. Men would wonder how much money he had. But he was an Indian and, in this America, powerless and powerful all at the same time. He pictured himself and the Indian walking into town, stirring up trouble in the eyes of the women and old-timers.

"Name's Ebenezer."

The Indian looked at him and nodded.

To give your name meant to give your power up. I gave up mine, now give up yours. Ebenezer thought.

"Call me Bill."

Eb reached out his hand, and Bill stepped closer to shake it. Eb noticed that Bill had also been digging in the ground, his sleeves were covered in clay and mud and when Bill's hand connected with his own, he felt a thrum of power like he had just touched a hot stove.

"Never met an Indian before," Eb said.

"I've known plenty of white men." Bill laughed. He pointed to the earth and produced a small hand shovel from his coat. In this manner, the two of them finished digging up Captain Tankard, pilfering buttons, gold chains, a watch, three gold fillings, and a saber encrusted with semi-precious stones.

2

Marina gripped the side of the box. Fear had taken control of her entirely now, a new sensation for her. She had never felt this metallic feeling before. She felt like she had been skewered and placed on a tin plate. The taste of metal ran through her like a current. Her mouth filled with harsh bitterness, and she was too paralyzed to spit it out.

Outside the box, the world enlarged with sounds – metal on metal and the awful wrenching and slamming of heavy doors. Underneath it, all was the trickle of water draining out of the boat that had pulled her so far.

And deeper under that, Marina felt movement, a murmur of water.

The boat and the box had been pulled up together out of the harbor and placed below. The boat that Marcos had piloted lay on its side, an unused toy on the floor of the cargo hold. The box which held Marina lay upended.

Hector whistled as he skipped down the stairs. He couldn't wait to see what was in the hold. The Captain would be back soon, he knew it. There was a tiny picture in the corner of his head – a black and white TV. He imagined his finger touching the screen, and the screen would flash on and show the bar where the Captain, Willie, and a blonde woman drank. He tasted the salty wash of whiskey and tobacco. Something had happened to him in the last twenty-four hours, Hector saw things that weren't there, he saw what others saw in their minds. The idea frightened him a little and excited him a lot. He felt perched on top of a wave that would take him to a new place in life. But that was for later, now he wanted to see the thing in the hold.

The Captain and Willie had put on a whale of a drunk and had returned to set sail. The ship was quiet save for a few sorry sailors who were carousing on deck or below with a bottle and a porno magazine. A few smoked pot on the port side.

Hector silently pissed a clutch of the men. He smelled whiskey on their breath. They paid no attention to him, only acknowledging him with nods and glances. Lots of the men snuck off to the cargo bay to jerk off or get high. Aside from the wash closets, the cargo bay was one of the few places on board one could have any privacy and so his descent therein suggested nothing to no one.

The cargo hold smelled of stink and bodies, cardboard, and oil. Hector snorted, he hated the smell, it reminded him of prison. The stairs were old and wiggled under his weight. Somewhere in the murk, a rat scuttled away.

In the middle of the floor, somewhat to the left, leaned Mulch's boat. *It looked so small,* he thought and Hector, liking the size of it, hoped to stake a claim to it when everything was done.

Most of the men on board didn't care what Hector had brought up, didn't care that it wasn't normal cargo, not on this ship. To their credit, those who saw and heard anything ignored it.

And it was also a fact that none of the men on board, who saw or heard the cranking arm of the crane lift the boat and the box dangling behind it into the hold, were curious enough to come to Hector and ask him directly, or to peek into the wheelhouse, or to watch as the cargo hold closed its maw over the strange box, or even whisper among themselves. That idea made Hector approach the upturned box on his tipsy toes, his hands out to throttle whatever could pop out of the box, like a jack in the box, prepared to hurt or even kill him.

3

After killing Leon, Mulch had traveled up the coast by rail. He couldn't sleep because of all the noise in his head. The small flask in his jacket pocket dispensed bitter moonshine into his system, but it wasn't enough. In Wilmington, Delaware he had almost run off the train screaming, "I did it, I killed Leon," to the passengers headed for Philly, or New York. But when Mulch got ready to step off the train he was struck with the utter feeling of anonymity – no one there knew who he was, no one knew his kin. The accents clipping out of the broad traveling faces were pinched and foreign. He could have shouted all he wanted to and no one would have had any clue. And it was on that train running north from his family dead that Mulch realized how big of a world it was out there and what little everyone knew about anything.

In Philadelphia, Mulch booked passage on a liner to Spain. Eb had given him the money, but he was afraid to spend it. Mulch had no idea how to budget and was afraid of spending it all. Mulch had never before in his life held his own money. He felt like if he wasn't careful his pocket would unravel and leave a hole big enough for his billfold to fall out of. Mulch walked around the decks holding both his front pockets tight, clutching the money to his person. After the first week on ship, he relaxed, letting himself have a few drinks after dinner, but mostly he stood out alone on deck and looked up at the sky, and into the sea watching for fish. One of the crew had told him to look out for dolphins, and so he did, not knowing of anything else to do.

When the ship approached the Canary Islands Mulch about fell flat. It was the immense whiteness of the sand and the pale baby blue of the water that overcame him. The trees were bright green swashes, like paint across the sky. It was as if the warm sun and the light had burned a layer of grime and ugliness off his skin. He got off at Gran Canarias and booked a cabana near the beach where he laid on the linen bedsheets and breathed.

He had no idea how long he would stay. He paid a month's rent in advance and decided he'd go home when and if he felt secure that it was safe to do so.

4

Mulch spent his first day on the beach, not sure what to do. The hotel people spoke enough English that he was able to get by without Spanish. After three days of sun worshiping, he was bored. The bellhops were about his age and let him hang out with them at night, as long as Mulch bought a round or two. Together they cruised the local clubs, Mulch giving English lessons and learning bits of Spanish in return. He learned that there was an interesting village he should visit to get a real idea of the history and majesty of the islands – Telde, an old gaucho's place. There was even a holy cave, and you didn't find holy caves on every island, don't you know? Mulch didn't know what a holy cave was, and he didn't know enough Spanish to find out. Instead, Mulch decided to give it a whirl and get a truck and go across the island to find it himself. He had wanted to do something, as he missed working on the farm. There, at least, was something that would occupy his time, instead of the hollow sugary space in his body where his guts should have been.

Telde was a nice village, and Telde, like most of the little villages, claimed to have the best beach. Mulch thought they all looked the same. He met an Austrian couple, who told him that he should check out the caves and some of the coves that pocketed the landscape like bomb craters. So he did. His brain was vacant, absent. And he wandered into the jungle-like growth and promptly got lost.

5

Mulch didn't know how long he had been wandering. The heavy canopy of trees swung back and forth, knocking him in the face, slashing his checks with tiny little cuts.

Somewhere off in the western portion of the forest there was a voice, it was Spanish, that of a man. To the east was the water, it whispered through the forest. Above him, shadows of large birds swooped down low. Ahead of him, the earth rose in clay hills and the footing became too steep for him. He turned east instead.

Through the canopy of trees, he caught glimpses of water, there was some kind of creek or stream. He doubted that it was freshwater, rather it would be salt water, like the waters back home. Soon the forest swallowed the blue up and Mulch found himself chasing little slivers of blue as it appeared and disappeared in the undergrowth until the forest broke out of its tangled knot and flattened out into a mossy, grassy bank.

On the bank was a naked woman.

Mulch stood there calmly, his heart thumping in his chest. He watched her skin glisten and ripple in the broken sunlight. Her hair gave off a blackish-green glow and the skin on her back shone in the same eerie light. Suddenly, Mulch felt very hot. The light was playing tricks on him, but he couldn't take his eyes off her. She bathed herself in the stream, dipping her head under and tossing her hair around. It smacked against the flat of her back. It all happened in slow motion, the turning of her head, her flat friendly smile, the beckoning hand. Mulch stepped into the sunlight and walked slowly to her. Her eyes empty of emotion and he found it impossible to read her. He was afraid he'd frighten her if he approached too quickly and scare her off. That or her husband, a gruff voice in the distance, would appear with a shotgun to blow him to Kingdom Come. But she only opened her arms towards him and whispered – a strange whipping of words that squeaked and floated out of her like moans and bubbles. Before he knew it he found himself in her arms. He didn't even remember stepping so close, almost as if he were pulled by an invisible force. She whispered in his ear, her wet tongue and hot breath arousing his blood and calming him, soothing him, so that he finally folded under her and laid down with her in the grass. He understood what she was trying to say to him, she had been waiting for him, she had sought him out and prayed for him, she would consume him entirely.

Her kisses tasted like saltwater and her tongue wrapped around his tongue. He didn't realize that she had taken command of his penis and was sliding it into her. He had been completely caught up in her loamy smell, her whispers. Her body radiated strength and she gave off heat that made him want to climb away from her, but he couldn't. He suckled her breasts, hoping to satisfy her. She gave into his mouth and pressed her sex into his groin.

When she was done, they laid in the grass for a while before she spoke. It wasn't in Spanish, nor English but strange whipping bubbles. He heard it in his head, in his heart, and he understood every word.

When the sun fell below the canopy, he stripped away the rest of his clothing and followed her into the creek. The creek was no deeper than the saltwater creeks back home and they fell into an easy rhythm. She swam before him, laughing and giggling and he swam behind her and admired her breasts when they broke the surface, nipples erect, her bosom full. He spoke to her in soothing tones, communicating as best he could. She seemed to understand him, but he could not be so sure. The knowledge lay in his heart like a fact, though he did not trust his feelings. He followed her out to the sea, some mile from where they had laid, and where they were shot out into the ocean by a pulling drag. The undertow caught Mulch off guard, but he kept his head up and followed her into the swell of a wave, that was when she transformed.

At first, Mulch thought it was a fish – a shark perhaps, or a marlin. He shouted out to her in surprise, worried for the girl, and though realizing that he was vulnerable he did not care about his safety, only for the girl.

She turned around and smiled, her skin catching the green tones of the water and moonlight. She flipped her fin up at him and made a jumping leap beside him and Mulch was able to see the full sweeping motion of her body. His head went light, and he felt the undertow grab him, but he fought it off and swam to the shore where he flopped on the sand and watched, unsure of what he saw, her fin cutting the water like a long double-edged knife. She played in the surf, doing turns and turning her body around and around. He couldn't believe it, but there was that sound in his head – the language that made him calm and aroused at the same time, the language that was like a song, he decided. He felt a little drunk on himself, on her – whatever she was.

6

Over the next few days, Mulch remained immersed in the warm itch of the mermaid's embraces. When they made love his pores opened like tiny mouths desperate to consume her scent and her touch as they moved together. When she kissed him in the water, he heard the language of the fishes and felt the brilliance of the tide as it moved the great sea. Through this all, not once did Mulch see another person.

He didn't know where he was, only that the cave was far away from the tourist beaches. She had carried him, like a bride, to some hidden niche that lay in the crotch of a cliff, the cliff worn away and tangled up in scrub bush and other rough vegetation. They made a cute little spot for themselves, pulling the soft vines from the nearby forest to their den to form a cushion over the hard stone. There she sunned herself on the rocks and he napped on the vines. Eventually, the vines formed an impression where their bodies had lain together. For a few days with her Mulch forgot his old life. When she fed him fish, he often thought that he must have died because the rawness and the zing of the fish made him tingle like he thought heaven must, and fish had never done that to him before, not ever, and he had pulled a lot of rockfish and flounder out of the creeks and the bay near his house. Not one of his fish, fried in the skillet or roasted over a fire, matched the raw silky taste of being fed by such a beautiful creature. He believed time and time again that he must have died somewhere along the way, and this must be his heaven. Only he was pretty sure heaven didn't stock mermaids.

Mulch had to remind himself that she was a creature, she wasn't a woman. She was part woman; she was part fish. The fish part didn't bother him, he was afraid of the woman in her. He came to call her Maria, for he loved that name so, and she didn't seem to mind.

Most days she left in the morning to hunt before the sun grew high. Often, she would stay out till dark. Sometimes he would try to explore the woods around them. He never got too far, the rough, thick tangles of growth made going difficult. Mulch had to climb over twenty-foot walls of vine and cane and tree fall. He'd get a little farther each time he tried but always failed to penetrate a mile into the interior. He'd always come back to their little home among the vines and collapse, exhausted.

At night his brain fell away to the heavenly canopy of possibilities. Maria would wrap her fingers around him and lead him to the water. She'd kiss him on the cheek and slip into the water, a deep drop-off. She'd flare-up in a greenish light for a brief second and dip under, her tail coming out of the water like some great antenna. Mulch would follow her, try to keep up with her and hold her hand as they floated under the stars, Maria's fingers transmitting heat and strength into his hand. He sometimes saw the heat move through his body like some kind of fever, or pulse, *just my imagination*, he told himself. But his hand would seem to glow a sea green and Maria would take notice and would smile, her kisses the taste of the ocean.

The clusters and knots of stars and the warm Atlantic waters nursed Mulch – he felt very alive – somehow fixed in the world, though not of the world anymore. Maria learned bits of English quickly, although Mulch found it impossible to shape his mouth and contort his tongue to her strange vocabulary. He thought it would be easier if he were underwater and often tried when they swam, which caused him to swallow seawater. He never managed more than half a sound before his mouth filled with brine. As the days lengthened, he spoke to himself mostly and figured he'd eventually go home a better man than his father and run the business the way it should – no bootlegging, no killing, just honest farm work. He'd expand the store, maybe look at buying out one of the local fisheries. Mulch felt that he could do it, that he had been so enabled. Of course, his change of heart was all due to the mermaid. It was Maria the mermaid that made him feel so pure.

7

What Mulch didn't know was that Maria's magical nature seeped out of her. It floated about her like a loose flow of hair. Only the hair didn't just caress against his skin, it invaded his skin and fed his body. Just by standing next to her, he was becoming a part of her. It was in this manner that he was bewitched, stuck in a trance as the days went by before he awoke from it.

The final morning Mulch laid eyes on her, Maria had gone hunting as usual, but when dark came, and she had yet to rise out of the water Mulch got worried. By nine o'clock he was hungry. By ten he was pacing the short space between the jungle and the rocky edge of their home. By midnight his stomach was talking to him in grunts and squeaks. He swam out into the warm slip of the ocean and called out her name, but there was only the sound of the breeze and his heartbeat. By noon the next day, he resigned himself to swimming around the island to somewhere civilized. He didn't have any clothes, but he supposed he'd worry about that later.

8

Shark. Mulch thought. *A shark ate my mermaid girlfriend.*

As he swam Mulch checked under him and behind him for a shark every chance he got, resting against the side of a rock or bank to catch his breath.

He couldn't shake the fear of it. He was all alone all again. She had taken him to the remotest edges of the island, around high rock cliffs and thick curtains of vegetation. For a while, he wondered if he was on the same island that he arrived on. He estimated he had swum some miles, at least, when he came to the white pale sands of one of the resort areas. He didn't recognize it, but it didn't matter much anyway. He waited until dark and snuck out on the sand to the shower houses where he stole a robe and a pair of pajama bottoms. He spent the night in an empty cabana curled up on a lounge chair. The next morning, he found a branch of the bank he had deposited his money in. He didn't have his passport to prove his identification but hoped he'd be able to get a new one and at least set up a small line of credit to buy clothing and food. His American citizenship proved to be all he needed, and Mulch was taken care of by management. After a bit of shopping, he spent the rest of that night wandering around looking for booze and hoping to find an American, or Brit, someone to get a meal out of, someone who spoke his language.

9

From the outside, Virginia looked like a magician's helper, a freak show accident perhaps, laying in the coffin encased in a headbox. Pembroke laid his hand on Virginia's upper thigh – Virginia squirmed. She tried to counter Pembroke's hand, but he batted it away.

"Now, now. Let's not get cocky," Pembroke gurgled from the back of his throat.

"You've been in there for some time. No lights but the bugs, no sounds but the ones your body hums," Pembroke imagined his voice floating through the air and hanging about her sheltered head like a ribbon. His prize, his gift from his cousin.

The fog curled around Virginia's chest and slid her robe open. Pembroke reached down and pinched her nipples. Virginia's hand flew up faster than he'd expected.

"Now, now. Mine." Pembroke sneered. "Her legs."

The fog took on a denser shade of white and wrapped itself around her ankles and wrists. Immediately, she began to squirm.

Virginia didn't know what was happening. Her flesh began to burn and then she heard the whispering of the fog as it bound her, pulling her arms and legs open. She felt Pembroke's weight on the sides of the coffin before she felt Pembroke on top of her. He was cold. His skin was soft and cold like velour over marble and her flesh rippled back in goosebumps. Her nipples were rock hard now and she felt his cold breath on them, his hands cupping her sex. It took a moment for her to remember to breathe. She wanted to scream when he entered her, for he was like an icicle and big, bigger than anyone she'd ever been with. Her vaginal walls tore, blood spotted and flowed. She grew numb

– a diamond-hard numbness. The fireflies fluttered awake, circling her nose and eyes, their hot little wings beating against her face in excitement.

10

It took a while before Virginia realized that Pembroke had gone and left her in the coffin. The men who had driven her here, that man had raped her and beat her, he had done much more to her. She had the bruises to prove it, and she considered herself lucky that she didn't remember much of that drive, only its cruel aftertaste, a copper in her mouth, blood rising from her gut, a raw ache from where the disgusting man had his way. Pembroke had not beat her. For that she was grateful. Still, she felt the coldness on her skin where his hands had lain.

She had imagined that he stood over her watching her, which was the worst kind of fear, not knowing where he was, not knowing what his plans were.

Just breathe, Virginia, rest and wait.

11

"Marina wasn't like any old sister, Doc. We didn't have those sister talks. She never combed my hair at night, and she didn't come to me with her problems. With her as my sister, it was kinda like growing up alone, an only child. It was weird, at times.

"Maria was the one I went to when a boy dumped me or when I had girlfriend problems. Boys, to think they cause so much drama in a girl's life. I learned to be the dumper early on. It's much cooler to be the one who walks away. Face it, if you're the dumper and not the dumpee, sunshine is right around the corner at any time. Maria understood that even though she waited for my father to love her back, something that never happened, save for when Mulch needed her.

"No, Marina was not the sister for consoling. Marina was the sister who made me want to be strong. She radiated strength. I don't believe in God because of her. Because in Sunday School they teach you that only God has power. Marina made me doubt God. She made me doubt everything.

"Imagine if your father was a giant that lived in a house on top of a beanstalk. Imagine having to hide the fact that your father was a giant. You couldn't show him off to people when they came over. You couldn't brag about it at school. Even when they said your father was some kind of freak or was some kind of prisoner in his own home, that he must be a freak freakish, or plain out imaginary. Imagine learning about how there are no such things as giants or giant beanstalks. Teachers and Sunday school ladies all telling you that such things belong in the imagination and only in the imagination. That only God has that kind of power and when you ask your question how can my father, the giant, not exist? The answer they give is simply because he can't.

"Mr. Bill told me that I shouldn't listen to my teachers, that the schools had it all wrong, that the churches had it all wrong. He said the whole world was kept together by a band-aid and that at any minute that old band-aid, which was beginning to turn up at the corners with grit and sweat was going to rip open, and then we'd see how big of a wound our world was.

"Mr. Bill was resentful, I think. I don't blame him, not one bit. I always knew he was playing a role just to get by. He had hinted this on several occasions, but I could see that he had tempered that resentfulness into something more powerful. What did I know? I was a vain party girl with a penchant for nose candy.

"But Pembroke was more than I could handle. I could have cried when he climbed on top of me. I could have struggled. But part of me wanted to remember all of the pain so that when I had my revenge it would be true and pure and equal to the pain he was causing me. Does that make sense? You never answer me. I sometimes feel as if I am talking to myself.

"Anyway, when he fucked with me, I would go and visit my sister in my memories.

"Memories Doc, they helped me more than anything. And not just my memories either but will get to that.

"A habit I got into fairly early in captivity, going into my memory. She was on the back porch of the big house. One of those rare moments when she had come out of the water and spent a little time with us. The TV was on and the *Little Mermaid* on repeat.

"She turned to me and said, "Sometimes I can't even stand it." She was talking about the water and how the light warmed the whole face of the creek. How it made the trees look golden and warm. Her eyes were wide, and she looked like she'd just had an incredible orgasm. I had been 17 and I was in love with Billy Street.

"I went over to her and laid my chin on her shoulder. Her skin warmed me through her tank top, her hair brushing my chin. It was soft and full. It smelled of protein and mud. It smelled of sex and my body responded, growing warm and sensitive. I put my arms around her and hugged her tight. She smiled and hugged me back.

"She ate dinner with us that night. Maria made fish. Mulch opened a bottle of wine and let me have some. Mr. Bill joined us. Maria made evening coffee and served up some of her homemade pound cake. Marina laughed and giggled all through the night. Afterward, we all went swimming in the creek. Maria heated some spiced wine and served it to us on the dock under the stars which boiled above us."

12

Cilia awoke with a start. She tasted tequila and whiskey in her mouth from the sailors' bar-soaked outing. In her mind, four images of the television screens remained, all of which were blurred with drink, or sleep save the one screen which was a haze of white and static. Whoever the mystery man was, his impulses affected her so all she saw was noise.

The thought came to her like a shot. *Mr. Bill is working against Mulch. Mr. Bill is the one following Marina up the coast. Fuck.*

Her brother had warned her not to trust the man, for the old Indian wasn't a relative, not that they could trust Mulch Hayes, but at least Mulch shared a common bond of money and power and blood. *Mr. Bill could be trouble. Perhaps I will email Pembroke…* She let the thought linger, drift, and die. *Pembroke will be busy enough. Patience. Focus on the positive. The Brazilian is dead, and your prize is secured on your ship. Trust Mulch to take care of his problems, trust yourself to take care of yours.*

Marina was ripe, her fear swelled and fattened, and by the time she would arrive at Cilia's door, she'd be bursting at the seams. Cilia sensed Marina's weakness, already it formed on her tongue sweet as honey. *Never mind, Cilia, don't worry, your ship has sailed.*

It was past noon already; she had slept late after controlling the minds of the sailors who did her dirty work. Through the window, the tourists were chatting it up on the walk. Cilia heard them – a young French couple. Cilia laid back down on her bed and pulled the covers over her. Her hands floated down her thighs and rested between her legs. She worked her palm over her mound gently. Her fingers pressed down and moved in circles. Outside on the street, the French woman felt her groin moisten. She felt fingers massaging her sex and her head began to loop. Her lover went on and on about the Anne Frank House and how they needed to hurry to avoid the lines. The woman grabbed at his waist and pulled him into her, grinding her crotch into his. Cilia felt the tourist's body yield to the pleasure. *Oh, today is going to be a good one,* she thought aloud before shuddering off into orgasm.

13

Spider tapped his fingers on the counter and dialed his parent's number. Amanda moved through the motions of lighting a cigarette, wrestling with the idea. Tanya read Vibe magazine on the couch. Zac and Blockhead were gassing up the Yugo. Spider hoped his parents wouldn't be home to answer the phone. He looked outside for the car expecting them to come around the corner at any minute. His parent's phone rang. He heard the empty hollow ring of the old rotary in the pale avocado kitchen. The answering machine clicked on, and Spider heard his father's deep teacherly voice.

"No one is here to take your call, please leave your name and number and someone will get back to you."

A tinny saxophone solo followed a bit squeaky and a bit awkward. *His father thought he was as cool as Bird, but he played like a turkey,* Spider thought.

"Hey, guys it's me. I'm going with Block, I mean Willie, to his aunt's house in Roxbury for a while. I'll call when I get there. I'll drop in on Aunt Sally and say hi. See ya in a few days. Text me if you need anything."

He doubted he'd get anywhere near Aunt Sally's house. She lived in Beacon Hill, in a swank house with an enclosed garden. Tanya had spent a lot of summers there, doing internships at the Capital and running errands for Sally who was more or less on tour with *Porgy & Bess* or some such nonsense all year round.

"You're not going to see Aunt Sally. You shouldn't even bother Spider. It only makes them feel bad," Tanya said as she poured herself an orange juice.

"They won't feel bad. They only feel bad when you go see Aunt Sally cause Aunt Sally is much more of your idol than mom is."

"That's just total bullshit Spider and you know it."

"Right."

Amanda lit her smoke and let out a satisfied sigh.

"Amanda, are you sure you don't want to come," Spider asked, crossing his fingers under the counter.

"No, I don't think so. I gotta work, pay the bills." Amanda looked out the window and contemplated the bricks. "Spider, I'm not the woman who gets to hook up with this guy, even if all this woman is looking for is a grant."

"And why is that?" Tanya retorted. "You got it, girl."

"Um, he's got it for some swimsuit babe mermaid," Amanda said. "He's a nut, T."

"Good, you finally said it," T quipped.

"Exactly. Women like that don't exist." Spider said.

"I have a feeling that this one does." Amanda countered.

"Well too bad. We got one more seat." He turned to his sister, "Tanya, last chance?"

"Fuck off, little brother."

Spider heard the guttural sound of the Yugo pulling up around the side. He kissed Amanda on the cheek lingering slightly and kissed his sister on the forehead. Neither of them looked up at him when he waved from the door.

14

Blockhead drove at a steady 62 miles an hour, the steering column shaking in his massive hands. Zac doodled on his arm with a ballpoint pen and Spider nodded his head to some DJ Blockhead discovered on Soundcloud. Boston lay a good six hours away, seven if they hit traffic. The Yugo rumbled underneath him, and Spider imagined the car falling apart bit by bit as they inched northbound. Somewhere ahead of them Nick Adams drove. They hoped he'd leave a trail they could follow. They had no idea what awaited them outside of Providence, Rhode Island.

15

Abdullah kept his foot on the pedal while George fed Rufus a pack of Meaty Dog. Rufus had chewed a hole in the seat of George's truck, and the stuffing lay about the cab like the fur of a dead rabbit. George held the can up to the dog's face who eagerly devoured the food in great slobbering tongue-fulls. Abdullah drove fine, almost as if he had been doing it most of his life; he'd demonstrated a penchant for it on the shore. Wilmington lay before them like a knot.

"Now as we get closer to the city, watch the right and left lanes as traffic merges. We spoke about it, remember. Are you sure you can handle this?"

"Master, Abdullah is sure," Abdullah said as he pointed to his head and then pointed to the road. "I'm good buddy. Ten fore. Stay off my tail, shit for brains," Abdullah laughed and filled his mouth with air, puffing his cheeks out like a blowfish.

All during the drive, George had a feeling that he was going to find Lilly and Nick at the same place. That he was going to be able to hold Lilly in his arms and rock her to sleep. It puzzled him, the image. It had come to him as he paid the toll on US 1 before letting Ab take over. Now it haunted him.

"Master, I know what you think."

"You do?"

"You think of Lilly, luscious flower that is her, Lilly, as you say it."

"Yep. You got me."

"Master, Abdullah is sure she is fine. Lilly is, A-OK."

"Are you sure?"

"Positive. She's with mother, right?"

"Yes, that's what she said."

"Then, Master, what is there to worry about?"

Plenty, George thought. *Plenty indeed.*

BOOK FOUR: JUNE 22

"The New World is a place of beauty. A place of riches. For God, Netherlands, Queen, and family, I will bring the glory."

—from Jon de van Hazen's ship log,
dated June 20, 1607,
courtesy the Mariner's Museum, Amsterdam

"Technology has given us the ability to record supposed paranormal phenomena. Skeptics, such as me, are given the challenge to refute these findings. That orbs, and spirits are nothing but dust caught on a lens. That ectoplasm is nothing but smoke, that ghosts are hoaxes. But as more and more evidence is gathered, I am forced to reexamine my world view, and wonder what nature is trying to show us."

—Zachary Widgeon,
criminal pathologist & writer,
from a lecture to the Edgar Cayce Society,
Virginia Beach, June 30th, 2003

"Virginia Hayes continues to show an elaborate detachment from reality. The underlying trauma will be difficult to root out."

—Dr. Savannah Garvan,
personal notes

CHAPTER ONE

1

Mick Ellis was stumped, no one wanted to talk about Mulch Hayes' wives. There was no record of them, anywhere – no pictures, no notices, even the copies of the marriage licenses were missing.

Hayes occupied a corner of his mind, and he could not shake it. Part of it was reading Virginia's journal over and over. Her writing left him drifting in a pool of anxiety. Mulch Hayes, farmer, and local businessman was a corrupt and awful human being. His daughter's boyfriend had been working for him and what Virginia described disturbed him. Of course, Virginia could be exaggerating. He'd been fooled by journals before. Add to his consternation was the fact that none of the locals would talk about it. When he interviewed the old men at Sea Hag's they had told him to contact old Bob Watterson.

Watterson, from what he could gather, was something of a collector. His number was in the phone book, but when Mick called no one answered. *Probably no machine,* he thought. So, he hopped into his car and drove to Cheapside.

2

The one thing Mick Ellis loved about the shore, and probably the only thing other than his kin, was the curious names of the towns that occupied the seaside and bayside of the shore, the old railroad names.

Cheapside was one of the oldest towns and along the road into it, telescope houses and old plantation farmhouses were mixed in with the cape cods and the saltbox homes. Watterson's address was 181424 Sanity Lane, which ran perpendicular to country road 23. Mick expected a long street of homes like in Parsley and Cape James, but Watterson's house was only one of four homes on Sanity Lane, as far as Mick could tell. The boys down at Sea Hag's fritters had given him Murdock's name. He hoped the boys had called ahead as they had promised.

Watterson's home was a single trailer whose yard was unkempt but tidy. An old weathervane was perched on the roof and cigar butts lay scattered under the folding chair on the cement block porch. Watterson answered the door before Mick raised his hand to knock, his withered lips trembling with age.

"What the hell do you want?"

"I'm Mick Ellis, I run the Ace Detective Agency."

"I figured that'd be you. Capt. Murdock called and said you'd be coming over."

Bob stood in his doorway, leaning, and wheezing. He wore an old pair of paint-spattered jeans and a white T-shirt. His glasses were thick and greasy as were his hands, which held a gnawed cigar.

"Alright. Come in then. Don't mind the mess."

"Thanks."

The trailer smelled sour and old. On the coffee table lay three shotguns and several boxes of shells. Covering the walls were several layers of built-in shelves, each stacked and bowed with old newspapers, magazines, bottles, and signs.

"Murdock says you are looking for information on Mulch Hayes."

"Yup," Mick said as he eyed the guns on the table. Watterson sat on his sofa and began loading shotgun shells into his guns. "You going hunting, or something?"

"Hunting season isn't until fall."

"Yeah, but the guns."

"I'm expecting nobody, but I like to be prepared," he said pausing to cough into his arm.

"I see."

"No. You don't. That's your problem. Look, you're an outsider trying to get an insider's view on that missing girl."

"Yeah, so?"

"So, son, all I can give you is some cursory information. Nothing that's going to help you in your search. If you ask me, that girl is already dead to the world."

"How do you know that?"

"I hear things."

"Like what?"

"Rumors. About Mulch. About his father."

"Look, you've gotta tell me. I'm up against a real tough spot here."

"Well, then you've gotta help me clean these guns out first."

"Why?"

"Just to keep me sharp. Jesus, guns need cleaning, I need to clean them. What's with the questions. I'm old and slow. You're young and quick. I think."

"Uh-huh."

Watterson kicked about his living room as he told his stories. Mick felt like he had bought a ticket and come to town for a show with old Watterson as the star for he spat and modulated his voice as he retold the old farm hand's tales about the strange native Mr. Bill and the other odd happenings on the Hayes farm. Generally, Mick thought it was all horse manure, your run-of-the-mill town gossip supercharged with superstition, what with the mysterious fog and all that. *But hey you're in the country now Mick, here's your required helping of backwater crazy told as redneck versions of your everyday Urban Legends.*

Watterson eventually settled into his chair and just chewed on his cigar and continued to spit one after another of these crazy folk tales at high speed towards Mick who was the one doing all the work cleaning the guns, at Watterson's command, and fumbling about doing so like a greenhorn getting ready for his first hunting trip.

3

"The way I heard it was Ruth Hayes, Mulchie's mother, was nuttier than squirrel shit – a real batty woman, loose, too. Old Mike Watkins, passed last Sunday, God rest his soul, worked there then. Said Ruth was always coming into the barn and rubbing up on all the young men until they gave in to her out back," Watterson said as paused to look Mick over.

"Yup, she was straight crazy for men. Probably has a scientific name for it these days. But the way it was told to me was butterflies was what did it. Yeah, I know. Butterflies? People said that they kept coming into the house and that it was the flowers that brought 'em in. The only thing Ruth ever accomplished outside of being out of her head sick for days on end was a little cultivating. She was real good with flowers – God bless her. See those flowers of hers, over the years, grew patchy and thick and dripped off the plant and the butterflies were attracted to that ripe smell. It just so happened that once they'd get into the old house they'd follow Ruth around the place.

"He'd tell you all about it. Well, Mike would if he weren't dead just now. But I know it for a fact that what he said is true. I was with Old Mike when Mulch recounted the tale, almost two years ago, at our yearly oyster roast. Heard it fall from his mouth as sure as I stand before you."

"I don't understand," Mick interrupted.

"What's not to understand, boy? The damn butterflies flapped and flipped and sputtered and fucked with her head so much she thought she was hearing voices. Probably did hear voices too, schizophrenia, I think. She talked all about learning how to levitate, according to Mulch. Can you beat that?"

"Well, I... uh... dunno."

"Damnit, boy. Listen to me, she had a thing about all them butterflies. Mulchie said the butterflies made her crazy spells worse."

"Spells?"

"Yeah, when she'd get loopy for weeks on end. Sam would tell me the Indian, excuse me, the Indigenous Native American would try to heal her, but she just go off and do something stupid, again, like sleeping with another farmhand, and Eb would find her and beat her near to death. There's a word for it, named after a hostage situation."

"Stockholm syndrome? Eb, Mulch's father? Beat her?"

"Every goddamn week."

"Really? Damn, that's a little more brutal than..."

"His brother was sleeping with her too. Up until she vanished in a late winter snowstorm, maybe a few months before Leon vanished. Coincidence? I think not. They were in love, or so they say. Ran off. With Ruth. Ha! As if. They're both out in those fields there somewhere, I bet you that much. Same with Mulch's first wife. She's in the fields too."

"The fields? What fields?"

"Damnit, boy. Ain't you done none of your homework. Here take a look at these."

The Eastern Shore News June 12, 1982 A-7

Local Woman Missing?

Oysterhaus, staff writer

Authorities will not speculate on the missing wife of local farmer Mulch Hayes. Mrs. Clara Marina Hayes was reported missing by her husband last week. Deputies, coordinating with State Police and local volunteers, passed out fliers and canvassed local communities. Mrs. Hayes had recovered from her pregnancy. She delivered a healthy baby girl two months before her disappearance.

Police describe her to be 5'8, 138 lbs, with blond hair and blue eyes. She was last seen walking south in Oysterhaus, away from Hayes Feed Store, towards the southern end of town. Anyone who thinks they have information about Clara Marina Hayes is encouraged to contact the Sheriff's department.

The Eastern Shore News August 19, 2019 C-2

Smoke signals on Oysterhaus horizon, work of drug dealers or cults?
Oysterhaus, staff writer

For those that live in Oysterhaus, smoke rings varying from 10 to 25 feet in diameter are weekly, sometimes daily, occurrence. Many residents believe that they are the work of delinquent teens, or drug dealers, or perhaps even a Satanic cult. Last Tuesday dozens of eyewitnesses reported seeing strange smoke shapes rising from a far-off field. 911 was called and the Cape James Fire Department investigated. The smoke had dissipated by the time firemen arrived on the scene. They did report finding a small campfire, which had been recently extinguished on the property of Mulch Hayes, farmer and business-man. Hayes told the fire department that he didn't know who would be setting fires to his property, but that sometimes migrant workers burn trash on the out-skirts of his fields. Hayes was warned that if the fire got out of control, he could be fined for starting a brush fire, which is a minimum $1000 fine. Still, locals insist that local law enforcement do more. "It's a shame young people have no respect for nature. A serious fire could result. This needs to be taken seriously," said local Captain Murdock, retired.

The Eastern Shore News May 21, 2020 A-4

Farmer and businessman to buy five-hundred acres of land, including Federally leased watershed property
Oysterhaus, staff writer

Mulch Hayes, a local businessman, and a farmer has secured a contract for five hundred acres of land in Cape James, a deal that includes Federal leased land, and a deal to buy old Great Goose Farm. Hayes outbid seven other parties for the deal, including submitting written promises to continue renting any structures on the land to current clients. Warren Kellam, the current owner of Great Goose Farm says the deal couldn't have come at a better time. "We've had one helluva time lately. Last year's drought hurt us badly. Plus, the political situation with China, I'm just glad it's going to another farmer." Kellam isn't sure if he will continue to farm, but Hayes has at least offered to keep Kellam and his farmhands employed, putting locals at ease. Hayes' purchase will allow the local businessman the right to restructure certain aspects of the government's lease.

"Mulch buries people in the field?"Mick asked. "These articles do not..."

"Some say that's why his tomatoes are the best," Watterson said, cutting him off. "You're missing the point."

"This doesn't prove anything," Mick said.

"He'll squash you like a bug, Mulch will." Watterson farted into his couch cushion and smirked. "Excuse me," he said. "What I'm trying to show you, boy, is that no one can get anything to stick on Mulch. Everything is a dead end."

4

Ruth Hayes stared at the butterfly's eyes and antennae as it rested on the windowsill. She thought that it might be contemplating the color of the rose, which had turned three shades darker over the last two days. Ruth was sure that her new plant-food mixture was right on the money this time. *This time they won't yellow and fall sick*, she thought. Her stomach turned, she felt sick. The horrid rancid gas of her dead roses from the previous spring haunted her. She had added way too much fertilizer, and they seemed to shriek as they yellowed and turned bronze in the sun. This year's garden was thick and rich with color and body. *Maybe this year things will work out*, she looked at the Eastern Tiger Swallowtail entranced by its fiery orange coloring, like eyelashes she had seen in a dream.

In the yard, a stray hen squawked in the morning sun. She heard Mulch's voice as he called out to Bill to help him with his homemade beer. Eb and Leon were out in the fields, the zucchinis ready for picking as she sat on the couch, the newspaper folded open across her lap. The morning light made the house seem clean even though Ruth knew that it wasn't. They were supposed to hire a new house girl, one of the migrants. She returned her attention to her magazine but found the print blurry. *Not another migraine.* Ruth yawned. *I'm so tired.* She thought about getting up and accomplishing something, and then she couldn't. So she turned back to the swallowtail who stared at her with dumb abandon.

Ruth was almost asleep when the butterfly flew *through* the glass window.

In a daze, she found herself unable to tell if what she had been thinking was real or something from her daydream. *Had someone called my name?* For a second, her mind juiced into a panic. Eb would not catch her off guard again. She shot straight up, her heart hammering. *Eb?* She couldn't breathe for a second, and then it passed. In her panic, she looked at the butterfly, and the butterfly rose and flew through the window into the house and rested on her arm. She knew the butterfly was real because its feet felt like cat's whiskers against her skin. She felt its light wings flapping lightly like a baby's breath on her arm.

"Well, hello," she said to it.

"Hello," it replied.

Ruth didn't reply because she heard the voice clearly in her head. It was both her voice and the voices of her mother and of every woman she had ever loved as one voice, and she knew this with such confidence she did not dispute her reasoning, and for a moment a queer thought entered her mind, that she felt all her ages at once, inside her, a tickle.

"Hello?" she repeated, dreamily rocking her eyes back in her head.

"Hello," the butterfly said again, only this time the voice sounded amplified and deeper, like a young man's voice. "Nice morning, isn't it?"

"Yes." She almost laughed. "Yes. It's quite nice. Perhaps I should open the window to let you in?"

"No need. I'm already on the inside," the butterfly said as it began to clean its appendages like a fly.

"Yes. Indeed, you are."

"But you might want to open the window for yourself. You know, catch a breeze."

At first, Ruth didn't want to reply. She had a horrible vision of herself trying to explain to Leon why she was talking to herself and that Eb would then come to her in the dark and beat her for talking to insects. Her breath seized up. Panic fluttered in her mind. She took a deep breath. *One, two, one, two.*

"Perhaps," she said to the butterfly.

"Very good. I sense that there is a fresh cut flower in the kitchen if you don't mind," the swallowtail said as it flapped its wings and paused until Ruth understood that it was being polite.

"Oh, I'm sorry. Of course."

"Why thank you," it said as it fluttered into the bright kitchen.

The next week the Hayes house filled with butterflies. They appeared everywhere at once, it seemed. Ruth first saw them in dizzying flocks on her walks around the farm, a small cloud of them behaving like starlings, pulsing almost, forming eyes and ovals and circles and spirals in the air. Later, she combed them out of her hair and found them dozing in her shower. They appeared in the attic even, startling her as she opened the attic door and turned on the light which stirred a thought of black swallowtails, softly battering her face as they fluttered and followed her out and down the stairs and onto and the porch. The next day when she went into the barn to nuzzle the horses, she found them lining the walls of each stall. The horse kept on swishing its tail out of habit, unaware, or uncaring. Swallowtails and monarchs and morning cloaks, and question marks, they didn't speak to her but to each other which she heard as a low growling whisper, their collective voice haunting, chorus-like, and warped, like the voice of Legion itself.

5

Mick held onto the small johnboat as they navigated Patterwucks creek which was thick with marsh grass and sandbars. Every ten feet or so a sandbar rose out of the water like the back of a beast. Mick kept thinking they'd run right into one of the sandbars and he'd go bucking out into the water, headfirst. Old Bob had grown up on the creek and the map of its shifting sandbars lived in his hands as he guided them up around towards where Patterwucks creek merged into Chessahexex creek, which would take them to where he claimed Mulch dumped his bodies.

"Oh, we won't find nothing," Bob had said. "Let me get that out of the way, first and foremost."

"Why are we going, then?"

"If you see his stomping grounds, you'll get the feel of his game."

"Maybe."

"Plus, I can't go out on my own anymore – Doc's orders. I suffered two mini-strokes in the winter. I got to be supervised. I got crab pots I need to catch on the way back. That's my price, you pay it with your muscle."

They spent hours floating in the creek, Bob doing all the talking. No sooner had they tooted around a piece of land that Mulch supposedly owned under a fake name, when the sun began to go down. There was no place to get off, not really. The land was overgrown and littered with broken tree limbs that Bob couldn't get close enough to the bank to pull them out. Mick wasn't going to ruin his shoes by walking in the mud, so they didn't go ashore and just putted around. The setting sun cast the sky in an orange glow and made the searching a lot harder and like Old Bob had promised they didn't find anything and soon turned home. Back to the land, and to check his crab pots on the way home for a late dinner.

Mick didn't notice how quickly the darkness had overcome them because he was thinking about Macy and how it didn't help that all the locals felt she was dead. At this rate, he was expecting to find her floating face up any minute now. He didn't notice the darkness until the engine stalled and Old Bob's whispers pulled him out of his head and back into the world where he suddenly found himself staring down a massive fog bank rising straight out of the creek, fifty feet in the air.

"Jesus fuck me on a skateboard," Old Bob whispered.

"What is it?" Mick asked.

"I don't know."

"Oh, my God," Mick whispered as the boat nosed into complete darkness.

6

They drifted with the tide until they came to rest against a sandbar. Old Bob wasn't saying a word, but Mick knew he was there because he heard the old man's heavy breathing behind him. It was the only sound Mick heard in the soup, a gunmetal gray that absorbed even the sounds of the tide coming in against the thick marsh grass.

"We've stopped," Mick said aloud, his voice echoing back to him. "Do you have a light?"

"Here," Old Bob threw his zippo towards the front of the boat, and it banged against the frame. Old Bob had never seen fog like this before, had only heard about it from other watermen who had lived through the strange weather known around these parts. Inside the air temperature had dropped at least ten degrees.

"I think I got it," Mick said, fumbling for the zippo. "I don't think it will help, though. I can't see shit."

"This ain't right," Old Bob said. Somewhere in his throat, there was panic. "This ain't right at all. There still should be some sundown left."

Mick's skin drew in on itself. *It was the fog*, he thought. Mick's finger brushed the lighter and he scooped it into his palm. When he struck it open, he thought he saw something slither by in the air, something leathery moving against the flow of fog. Then he saw that it was only the fog itself moving in ropy currents stacked upon themselves like a city clover of traffic.

"Jesus, this is thick fog. We don't get this kind of fog in Jersey."

"Fuck Jersey, city boy. Help get us off this sandbar."

"I don't know where the sandbar is…."

"Get a fucking oar and push us off, boy," Old Bob felt his heart popping in his chest. He hadn't been this scared in a long time and the hairs on his neck were stiff with fear. "Do it, now."

"Jesus, Bob." Mick found an oar, leaned over the bow, and sunk it into the sand. He grunted as he pushed. He felt the boat move some, but it remained perched on the sandbar.

"More!" Bob shouted.

"I'm trying."

"Faster! Do it!"

Mick rose off the john boat's seat, shifting his weight to one side, all the while pressing down hard on the oar, and he felt the boat move back into the creek. He felt sudden relief, for the fog felt alive against his skin. His instincts gunned his adrenaline and even as he sat down, he felt his body rush to respond to the thick gray slate that was the fog before him.

"We have to go through it, boy."

"We could go back?" Mick heard himself stammer.

"Maybe."

"What do you mean, maybe?" Mick's tongue was thick and coppery. "Tell me that, Bob."

"This is winter fog. Ain't right for this time. I don't know what's happening, but I don't think we're safe anywhere on this creek."

"What the fuck does that mean?"

"Don't shout at me!"

"Fuck off, old man."

Just then, as if on cue, a deep grunt came from the bank, then a chorus of grunts – thick guttural sounds of a large beast. Old Bob froze up. He had grown up with stories of the ghost deer and how they traveled in the fog.

"Jesus." Old Bob hissed.

"What is it?" Mick asked.

The grunting came again, this time louder and concentrated.

"Nothing living, I can tell you that."

Somewhere above the muscled flight of wings a stamping of hooves came from farther up the bank.

"What is it, Bob?" Mick's fear centered in his stomach, and he felt like throwing up. His knees knocked and his body broke out in gooseflesh.

Old Bob didn't answer, he only started the motor and plunged them into the fog howling all the way.

7

Old Bob screamed for a good thirty seconds as he pushed the johnboat deeper into the white hell. They hadn't gone thirty yards when they ran smack into another sandbar and Mick was thrown headfirst into the shallow water. The world went blurry as the fog and sandbar came up to meet him. He found himself face first in the water. He struggled to sit up and spat, throwing his arms against the sandy bottom. Mick managed to get himself upright, saltwater burning his lungs and throat. Coughing and sputtering, he stood. The water was perhaps two feet deep if that.

"Bob!" he whispered.

No reply.

"Bob!" he said again.

The sounds of grunting and stamping came from all sides of the creek. From above Mick felt the rush of wings. A garbled bird cry pricked his spine and fear spread through his body as he thrashed through the creek mud back towards the johnboat.

"Bob, Bob!" he gasped as he fumbled around until he tripped over the hull and fell forward into the floor of the boat and over the old man lying there, knocking himself unconscious.

When he awoke the stars were bright above him, and Old Bob was urinating into the creek. They both complained of headaches but were unhurt. They puttered home under the light of the constellations, neither of them speaking much. The fog had lifted leaving the air chilly and damp.

8

Nick dangled his legs over the side of the billboard, half amazed he wasn't in jail, as the traffic below him zipped and converged on the horizon in one giant humming blur. The sun was beginning to leak over the eastern side of the billboard and beyond that, the Atlantic Ocean crashed unseen onto the shore, though Nick smelled the salty bite in the air. He had no idea how long he had been up on the billboard. He guessed hours for his arms hurt and his sides throbbed from reaching high to paint the upper half of the advertisement. Next to him, a small ladder was folded and leaning against the billboard scaffolding. It looked skeletal in the fuzzy light. His breath came in ragged heavy sighs. He'd been smoking in his sleep too, he could tell. By now he was attuned to his sleep body and his sleep brain. It was easy for him to imagine standing there high above the interstate painting billboards because he could feel it in his body's memory. Heck, he could almost see it. It made sense to him seeing how his brain rested and someone else took control when it happened. How *she* took control since it was *she* that was leading him to *her*. He wasn't sure who *she* was, but he felt that she had already moved on past Boston. At least he thought *she* had. He didn't know how he knew these things, but he knew them as sure as he knew if he didn't get off this billboard soon the cops would have him.

Boston, a giant magnet that pulled him north, farther north than he had ever been in his life, northwards and outwards towards some edge in himself. Now that he was close his whole body was beginning to change becoming thin, transparent almost. Once he was a man, now less than.

Nick sat down on the small stoop railing and dangled his feet over the edge. Down below someone honked, and Nick waved, unsure if the honk was meant for him, the mustang he'd stolen glowed under the billboard in the early pre-dawn light. The billboard lay five miles outside Providence, Rhode Island, on the side of the interstate, his car pulled up under it like some kind of toy. He stared down at its hood, not believing that he'd come this far. Of course, he had been asleep. Even the white roar of passing cars had not penetrated his trance.

The truth is that he had begun the painting at three AM, and it hadn't taken him long to finish. The moon had hung pregnant in the sky on its cord and watched Nick as Nick had moved in his sleep like a graceful dancing robot, the cars zooming under him at seventy and ninety miles an hour. Nick hadn't dropped one dollop of paint – not one. His hands had willed the brush to paint, to mold, to sculpt her face over the tired billboard advertising the new Honda Accord. The Honda had vanished quickly under the heavy paint. Nick had brought but so much, and somehow, miraculously there were buckets of it at his disposal. As he had painted, the paint had kept coming, as if it needed only the will of the painter to exist. It shouldn't have been possible. When he started, he didn't have enough paint to make her face the face of heaven and all the cut-up stars. But he had, and he did.

His body had worked as if it had been suspended from invisible wires, reaching into the void that was the Honda Accord advertisement and rendering the deep lush folds of Marina's hair, his hair whipped up in the knotting wind, his skin rippling with goosebumps. The moon's light was like a coating of ice on Marina's face, and he remembered winking out of his furious sleep, just for a second, for a brief second, when he had come out of his trance and looked up at her great big eyes and smiled, wanting to fall into them, wanting to fall into the painting and be lost there forever.

The passing drivers who did see him saw him as some dark and quick Michelangelo, painting not the ceiling but the sky itself outside Providence, Rhode Island, going North on Interstate 95 towards Boston. Only those driving north that night would be able to see the painting as it unfolded, many thinking that it was unusual for someone to be painting a billboard at such a late hour, in Providence, even.

A young boy, just beyond the interstate, would wake up in his tiny room in the middle of the night absolutely sure that some strange creature was watching him. In the morning he'd glint out into the sky and see, beyond his crappy little neighborhood, the face of a woman staring at him from the interstate. An old man driving north, insomniac, lonely and deathly so, would almost lose control of his vehicle as he came across her hair as Nick completed it, his breath sucking in and out of his withered mouth – hair that reminded him of his dead wife.

Even a state trooper would see the painting in progress and shrug thinking he didn't understand advertisements anymore, that it was too ironic, too funny. Ads never said what they were for anymore and that annoyed him. He had passed under just as Nick worked the enamel of the mermaid's teeth, working with speed, his arms a blur as he passed the brushes back and forth between his capable hands.

A young girl, unknowingly snatched from her mother's house by her father, her father making a mad dash to Maine from Connecticut, would look up as the trooper sped by her window, her father muttering and smoking as the hour grew later, the girl nervous and awake because she was afraid, her instincts alive and throbbing. The girl would look up and decide right then and there that she would become a dentist because the nice man on the sign looked so happy working on the big lady's teeth.

The newspapers would miss it. The Honda people would miss it until it came time to re-up their ad, but the painting would remain for a while, at least.

Nick reached into his bag for a cigarette. He lit it and leaned back, his elbows on the walkway looking out over the gunmetal macadam. Above him, winking in the soft glow of four 1000-watt outdoor halogens was the face of Marina. At least he knew what she looked like now. He'd hadn't been able to see what she looked like in Spider's phone, or little hand-held digital camera. Heck, he hadn't even been able to see her in his little scant drawings and graffiti, and by the look of it, she was a looker. He looked up, his neck craning back, her face upside down to him, thinking, *I could love her.*

No, I do love her.

He knew that. He also knew that she was a fish, a mermaid, a magical creature. He knew he felt stupid thinking like that but couldn't help it. Nick's heart knew she was human, knew she was real, but something in his higher brain gave him pause. *What if I couldn't love her. What if it was impossible?*

9

Of the many cars that cruised up Interstate 95 the face of Marina would always remain one of the most beautiful billboards many had ever seen, her face, set aglow by a light pink coral color, showed her high Roman nose and her Spanish cheeks. Nick had somehow captured her complexion just right and somehow captured the emerald-ebony shade of her hair, how it glowed green in the right light and how the hair somehow moved of its own volition. Ryan Stills saw it, and his girlfriend saw it.

She was about to tell him it was over, but when she saw Marina's giant face, she quieted and bit her lower lip. She'd been dreaming about a woman the other night – a powerful woman with hair that had a mind of its own. The woman on the billboard looked like that woman. The words were on her lips when she saw the hair move, thick ropes of it swaying as if caught in a breeze. Ryan saw it too and muttered a low, "Whoa. That's some kind of holographic ad?" Neither of them knew why but a silence settled on them, and Ryan's girlfriend decided to wait thinking she should bring it up some other time.

Thomas and Irma Myers nearly ran into the tractor-trailer in front of them. Marina resembled their granddaughter and for one second, they both thought that she might have gotten herself out of rehab and gotten a modeling job or something.

Selma Irwin saw Marina's hair twist and twirl and make a tornado out of itself and she made a wish. Nick had just been putting the finishing gloss on her hair and Selma thought it was the work of an earthly angel and that the moving hair rising off the billboard were angel's wings and she prayed and hoped her husband's lung cancer would go into remission. Mr. Bill saw Marina too, as he traveled through Providence, and he turned off at the next exit and doubled back toward the billboard. He was sure it was her. He reached out with his mind to touch the mind of the painter who worked in furious strokes atop a small ladder. All he got was her face, her face like some moon that eclipsed all the man's thinking.

That was how Mr. Bill knew to seek out Nick Adams.

10

Nick clambered down the billboard's scaffolding, his arms stiff. A dull ache spread over his back, and he felt like the spring inside his body had sprung, his insides pulled like strained coils. Nick was famished. His mouth filled with a sticky film that he recognized. It tasted like creek water. A light salty, muddy film coated his teeth and pallet. He hopped the last two feet down onto the soft earth. Already the sun was creeping up the sky and soon Interstate 95 would be boiling with cars. Nick supposed the early morning rush hour would begin soon. He'd never really seen rush hour traffic before, and he didn't care to start now.

Glancing down the Interstate he spied for Rhode Island State Troopers. He didn't see anything. Down a bit, an abandoned car was parked under another billboard, a white t-shirt tied to the antennae. He counted his blessings and got behind the wheel of the stolen mustang. The car he'd stolen in New Jersey would surely have been reported by now. He thought it unlikely that Rhode Island Troopers would be looking for it, but he didn't like the idea of driving around in a stolen car. *What if I am pulled over? Ditch it in Boston, Nick,* he thought as he pulled out into oncoming traffic.

Behind him now, a grizzled arm removed a white t-shirt from the antennae of an abandoned vehicle and the car moved into traffic. Mr. Bill, on the chase, slumped in his seat, his eyes fixed ahead.

11

Between Providence and Boston, Mr. Bill's mind opened like a flood gate, ready to receive all the water that flowed into it. The water happened to be any person alive and awake on the Interstate that fine June morning. It was like someone had turned up the volume, for it was like he was being hit in the nose with a basketball. *Smack. Smack. Smack.* In front of him, the man driving the blue impala was musing whether to tell his wife that he had stolen funds from his firm for their honeymoon. Their dog, who was curled up in the back, thought about rabbits. Ahead of them, an old man thought about taking his life savings and gambling it away in Vegas. He'd been a good gambler in his youth, brimming with luck until it ran out. He`d been away from the game a long time now and felt like his luck had recharged and he was ready to cash out.

Ahead of that old man, Nick Adams thought about fish – raw fish – and not sushi either. Mr. Bill was struck with the idea that Nick was of two minds. One of them was his. One of them was Marina's. Nick's thoughts submerged under the weight of Marina, who Mr. Bill saw through Nick's eyes, scared and trapped somewhere in a dark place.

Bill focused on Nick's head, the black blob ahead of him, heading north as Rhode Island became Massachusetts. But as Bill monitored Nick's head, he could not see how Nick knew about Marina. He could not understand how they knew each other and though Bill reached deep into Nick's memory all he could see was a dark room and flickering lights – the smell of smoke, a buttery grease coating everything.

There was nothing there. It was as if Nick's mind had been wiped clean. As if someone had taken out all the filing cabinets and office furniture of his brain and dumped all the trash in an alley somewhere.

Reaching into his shirt pocket, Mr. Bill fumbled for his pipe. There was a bit of smoke left inside and he chewed on the end, lighting the slightly charred ball of homegrown. When Nick pulled off in Boston, Bill would follow. They had much to discuss.

CHAPTER TWO

1

Marcos' body was found by a nursing student detouring home through the alley where he'd been jumped. Her name was Marina Stanokovic and in the palm of her hand, she held a syringe and morphine vial. Both were wet with her sweat. She'd stolen it before leaving work, and as soon as she disembarked the 57 bus she'd planned to fix. Her whole body sweated. She didn't think she had so much moisture inside her. Marina knew it was her hand sweating, but it felt to her as if it was the morphine that was sweating and if the vial of morphine got any hotter it would explode in her hand. She had just pumped the drug into her vein when she looked over at Marcos' body smashed up against the alley wall. Trash had already covered the body like a blanket. As the morphine worked its itchy magic through her body, she walked calmly out into the street and into Cafe Brazil Rio. There she politely told the hostess that there was a dead body in the alley across the street. When the hostess looked down to find the phone behind to counter to call the police, Marina had already walked out again. She had to get home to fix again.

Boston PD found little evidence at the scene other than a partial shoe print in blood where Hector had stepped after kicking the body to the side. Marcos was sent to the morgue as a John Doe where he lay for two days before an autopsy could be performed.

The Ugly Mother did not sense that Marcos was dead. In her hard round belly, she felt Marcos and hoped for Marcos' safety, at least for now.

Loco smiled and sipped his coffee, his hangover cracking over his face in the bright morning sun. Already he had *Ride the Lightning* pumping in his truck. The Ugly Mother remained in the back seat. She kept herself busy by darning her socks.

Loco's truck rattled as they approached Providence, Rhode Island. Lilly remembered that Connecticut sat on top of New York like a hat and skewed like a feather in the hat was Rhode Island. Massachusetts seemed like it should be right over the horizon. She didn't think that there would be so much space, long stretches of 95 where the trees took over. Only Loco had been this far north before. He drove up once a year to visit his relatives who lived in the squat brick brownstones around Brighton and Allston and the taller brownstones outside Roxbury. Loco knew that eventually, the trees would plane away into the guts of Providence, which was the last landmark before Boston started its slow rise from sprawl to suburb to urban decay to city. Loco liked driving through the cities. It gave him a thrill. It was like he was passing through a movie.

"It makes me feel as though I am in the center of something great," he growled. "Like I am back home again, in Mexico City. Look, over there, so many people engaged in so many endeavors. And over there, the same. The sprawling wave of humanity. It is awesome."

Lilly nodded. The Ugly Mother did not speak.

"You'll see. It's exciting – the lights, the people, so many kinds of people. Not just Mexicans, or Puerto Ricans, but Dominicans, Germans, French, Portuguese, Brazilians, everyone. It's very nice."

"Not like the shore," Lilly said.

"Where everyone treats you like aliens."

"But Loco, aren't you an alien?" Lilly laughed.

Loco chuckled. "From Planet Mexico City. I've come through the vast sea of stars. They look like scrub bushes, these stars. I've come to the Eastern Shore to take the minimum wage jobs from the rednecks and blacks," Loco licked his lips, smiling at the jape. "One day I'll either move back to Florida for good or come up here and try to finally make something of myself."

"There's not much farming up here."

"No, but there's work. I could open a Mexican restaurant. Call it El Loco Pollo. What do you think?" Loco's laugh was infectious.

"I think that's all crazy talk," The Ugly Mother gruffed from the backseat.

"You'll see Madre Fea, you'll see."

Lilly stared ahead. She spied the beginnings of Providence – little gray specks against the horizon. She felt sad again.

"We're coming up on another borough," Loco said as he scooted up in his seat to get a better view.

2

When Sea Hag was younger, back when trains steamed up and down the shore's ruler-straight line of track, and tourists had packed their camping gear to come to the Eastern Shore to hunt, to bird-watch, and to fish, when Smith Beach, Silver Beach, Hungar's Beach, Sanity's Point, Jefferson Hollow and Cove, Oysterhaus, Onancock, Wachapreague, and even Quimby had some kind of beach, or harbor, or both, for folks to explore the languid waters of the sea and bayside, back when Cobb and Hogg Island were turn of the century PLACES TO BE SEEN, when New York Bistros and Long Island restaurants paid top dollar for Eastern Shore game, fish, shellfish & bird, the shore had been alive with cottage industry and local energy. Sea Hag hadn't been much of Hag back then, the nickname more of a term of endearment from one crusty old sailor whose eye had been gouged out by a swordfish's lance during a particularly nasty nor'easter, which he had been struggling with the beast as he came in from fishing, the swordfish caught up in a rushing wave that broke the bow and brought the monster over the top of the rail. The sailor, Edmund Herricks, had caught the point of the fish's beak in his eye. Jerking back, he had saved himself from certain death and watched in pain as the surprised swordfish disappeared over the side again, with his one eye lanced on the tip. Then when Edmund Herricks came ashore, bleeding, in shock, hacking seawater and phlegm, Sea Hag, then only a wily teen girl, who even in those days dressed in over-sized rags and manly clothing remarked, "The next time you go out the fish will see you first." Upon which Edmund Herricks took to calling her Sea Hag, as well as many other expletives.

Before she was known as Sea Hag, she had not known the pleasure of a name. Her mother had simply called her daughter. Sea Hag's mother died, just as Sea Hag was approaching puberty, Sea Hag never once heard or saw her given Christian name written out on any document. Her mother had often teased Sea Hag that she did have a name and that she was withholding it till she was old enough to deserve it. Sea Hag and her mother were not Christian, nor were they educated in the traditional sense. Sea Hag, born on Hogg Island out in the marsh-grass, had known only the basics of life – tough practical clothing, how to live bait a line, how to swim, how to clean wounds, how to field dress a deer, how to tell poisonous mushrooms from those that were not, how to make mosquito repellent from mint and aloe and seaweed. How to be happy with what is given to you.

From a very young age, her mother had taught Sea Hag that she possessed some control over the basic elements: earth, air, fire, and water and that if she, Daughter, and sometimes Sweets, or Doe, or even Guppie, could tap into the invisible river that flowed underneath everything, then Sea Hag might just survive the harsh world that her mother only knew as Hogg Island. When Sea Hag grew up on Hogg Island, Hogg Island was only inhabited by a few fishermen and their families and the lighthouse personnel. That being said, Hogg Island was a desolate place. It was barren in most spots and open to the weather. In the summer, the sun scorched everything crawling underneath it. Sea Hag had never seen a desert before, but she would certainly recognize the searing heat and ghosts shimmering up from the sand. In the winter the marsh often froze and the winds, more often than not, blew away the roofs from the houses. Rime coated anything close to water, an icy afterthought that lingered for days till the sun melted it away again.

On Hogg Island, Sea Hag and her mother, marginalized by poor hygiene (that took Sea Hag years to correct – thus having her name stick with such a ferocity that sometimes it would come with the added "smelly Sea Hag" or "stinky Sea Hag", or even "boot-shit Sea Hag," and quite accurately, some might add) and by the fact that Sea Hag and her mother did not attend the local Methodist church, or the chapel, as it was called locally. To the good Christian women of the island, Sea Hag and her mother were simply sand witches that lived in the dingy shack in the marsh grass.

But they were happy in the marsh grass and lived on fish tonic and happy melodies strung on driftwood and dried stinging nettles. The marsh grass provided them with a thatch-like roof for their shack and even insulation. The sea provided driftwood which they burned nightly, just outside the lean-to in the back of the shed. The sea provided them with fish and the land provided corn and tough cabbage, and turnips and carrots and wild onions, which grew through winter. Sea Hag, in her defense, simply did not know any better and followed her mother's teachings because she had been instructed to do so. Years after her mother had died and Sea Hag, blown off Hogg Island like the rest of the inhabitants, refused to modernize, even the least bit, so as not to shame her mother who could still be watching from the other side. But that was not to be forever. For love, it seems, has the power to transform anyone, even a sand witch like Sea Hag, into something other than what it was to begin with.

As it turns out, Sea Hag, for a reason she could not even figure out, fell in love with wretched Edmund Herricks. This after Herricks originally dubbed her the Sea Hag. Herricks, who was then married to one Sarah Stewart Herricks, as pretty a blonde as there was, even though her face was sort of smashed up at the nose, liked to sneak out of his bedroom at night and secretly drink rum and freely walk the dunes and tough grassy meadows of Hogg Island, kicking at the hogs that ran half-wild, and for which the island took its name.

Sea Hag, now orphaned and newly christened, would watch the sad shadows of Edmund Herricks traipse around, drinking as he became more and more leaning, his voice low and smooth as the bay was when it is calm, lamenting the loss of his eye, praising his ship and his wife Sarah's firm bottom. Sea Hag fell in love with Herricks as she listened to his poetry he'd recite to the hogs, to the sea and stars, wishing in verse to make his way over the great line of horizon far away from where the stars dim and twinkle and seem to rise and fade into forever. Because of Herricks, she began to pull from the river of elemental, emotional, and spiritual forces, and, for the first time,perform magic.

When Herricks went out on his boat for the first time since he had lost his eye, Sea Hag, while digging for clams in the shallows near her shack, saw Herricks face reflected in a pool of water below her. At first, she thought Herricks was behind her, and she jumped back, slipping and falling into the shallow water, and she felt something inside of her lift and take flight. Her first case of the butterflies, which to her was the flight of her heart out and over the rough and choppy waves of the ocean beyond her.

When she looked back down at the tide pool, there staring back at her was the handsome face of Herricks. Sea Hag made it a habit to watch Herricks from afar, in her little tide pool.

When she could, Sea Hag studied the sky, the sand, and water for a way to help Edmund. The Edmund, who by the way was rather ugly, kind of shriveled looking, since birth, and now made uglier by the eye patch which made his face seem larger on one side than the other. She was able to see Edmund and all his movements in her little tidal pool of water beside her cooking fire; she hoped to help him, in any way she could.

It was on the eve of Herricks' fourth night out when Sea Hag, gazing at Herricks' face in the pool beside her fire, fell into a heavy sleep. What she saw in her dreams amazed her. Out there, in the Atlantic, she saw the swordfish with Edmund's eye on the end of it, jumping and turning and flipping.

During that night as Sea Hag slept, Edmund returned home, exhausted, beaten, and utterly baffled as to why he had caught nothing. On an island the size of Hogg Island, word travels quickly, even to sand witches like Sea Hag herself. While digging for clams she overheard Old Codger Jackson and Sammy Sample, out on two separate dinghies, pole fishing, shouting about the failed trip. Immediately Sea Hag gathered herself up and walked over to Edmund and Sarah's house.

When she knocked on the door, Sarah refused to answer it.

"Oh it's nobody," she said.

But Edmund, pulled by something he couldn't explain, found himself at the door.

"What do you want, smelly one?"

"I know why you didn't catch any fish."

"You've cursed me, is why is all." Edmund fumed.

"What?"

"When I lost my eye, you cursed me on the docks, with your tongue and your ugly cheek."

When Edmund Herrick got mad his body straightened and enlarged.

"I didn't curse you; the fish did."

"The fish?" Edmund looked back to Sarah, who leaned against the wall, seething, already planning some kind of all-chapel offensive against the witch. "Listen to this Sarah," he said pointing to Sea Hag, "this Sea Hag has come here to tell me it was the fish that got me eye that keeps me from catchin' any fish."

"Well you can tell her that sand witches need to be careful, or sand witches will find themselves in more hell than they can bear. God bless, em'," Sarah replied.

"Listen," Sea Hag said, her voice cracking with earnestness and love, her heart having taken flight. "The swordfish who has got your eye is using it to see you before you come for the fish."

Sea Hag didn't see the backhand coming. She only felt the hard ground beneath her, her lip bleeding from the corner and tears gathering in her eyes, which stung.

"Get out of here. If you'd have kept your mouth shut, I'd be out there catching fish like everyone else."

"Not true, "Sea Hag whimpered and scrambled off, much like a crab.

Edmund never did catch another fish, ever. Though Sarah did manage to get the chapel riled up against the sand witch, all they did was joke about her and plot mundane cruelties. Most of the islanders tolerated Sea Hag and didn't buy Sarah's zeal.

A few months later, the hurricane that brought down Hogg Island brought Sea Hag to Oysterhaus, the seaside town directly parallel to Hogg Island. Most of the residents that had remained on Hogg Island were drowned. Sarah's body washed ashore in Wachapreague, bloated and pecked apart by crabs. Edmund, listed as missing by the Coast Guard, was presumed dead, but many claimed to have seen him riding the roof of the chapel as it were some kind of raft. Sea Hag had simply blown across the water, carried aloft by her patchy rags, like a giant balloon made of seaweed. She had landed in a tree, right above the site of her future Fritter Shop.

After the hurricane, hurt and wishing to pay homage and tribute to Edmund, hoping to draw him out of her heart somehow, she opened her first restaurant: Eye of the Swordfish, a floating fish and fritter restaurant built into a long and wide fishing boat, that drifted up and down seaside or bayside, whichever she chose for the week, forever unmoored, but always easy to get close to. Sea Hag would either row to you, depending on the water's depth, or you walked out to her, or you boated over to her.

The restaurant was a huge success. People brought beach chairs out in low tide and Sea Hag rowed over to them and served them fritters, and fried fish, and baked fish, and clam fritters, and crab cakes, and duck, and sometimes shrimp, but always littleneck clams. The newspapers touted it as a novelty and success and people traveled from Philly and New York and Charlotte and Atlanta to either wade to her, or be rowed to, eating out in the open, drinking cold home-made beer, all the while soaking up the sun. Customers remarked that Sea Hag's eyes were quick, and kind and her hands moved with the speed of three women. It never occurred to anyone that while her eyes darted while talking and preparing dishes and fetching beer out of the floating cooler attached to the side of her boat, that her eyes were looking past you and through you to the beach, looking for a shriveled old man with an eye patch that made one side of his face look larger than the other, for it was him whom she brought the fish to, so he wouldn't have to keep looking in vain.

3

In the sunny boroughs of Boston, Nick dreamed. His body pitched and his eyes ran back and forth under his lids as traffic began its slow lurching stop and go through the streets. He slept on peacefully, despite the horns and brake squeals. Inside his head, he was somewhere else.

"Look I'm sorry we had to leave it like that," Nick said to the woman.

"Like what?"

The woman turned her head towards him, her neck bent so that the tops of her eyes floated up to meet his own. He straightened to meet her gaze and felt her heat and the tingle of her lips, even though he hadn't kissed her yet.

"You know, I'm not sure," Nick said.

He had the sick dream feeling he'd done this before, in another life.

"I feel drawn to you like a firefly to a blossom. Everything else is cloudy to me."

She giggled, her black hair flashing green in the light. Nick couldn't see where the light came from, but he knew instinctively, in dream knowledge, that the light came from an open window. She took his hand and pulled him up and away from the other tables. Nick noticed for the first time that he was in a cafeteria – gray walls and bland furniture. She pulled him close to her body, her black clothing clinging to her curves. He saw for the first time, felt for the first time, how tall she was. She sat him down at the far table, away from his friends. He glimpsed George and some tall fellow, but both faded into the background.

"Come," the woman whispered.

Her hair spilled over her shoulders and a strand of it dangled to his fingers. Her hair felt cool. It was the feel of the sea and of kelp and all green things that call the sea home. Her devilish smile made her straight perfect teeth seem all the more kissable. He leaned into her and felt the tingle of her lips, the light taste of salt on her tongue. Her hands squeezed his forearms and locked him into place. She kissed him back, hard, and he enjoyed it. He grew aroused and she ground her body down onto it. When she pulled away, she licked her teeth.

"Who are you?" Nick pleaded.

"Don't you know?" she teased.

"I've seen you so many times before, I think," Nick said, though he knew immediately that he was wrong.

She shook her head.

"No," She giggled and bit the end of her right pinky finger, the red fingernail clicking against her perfect teeth. Light fell over her shoulders and lifted her in its arms and made her face shine.

He thought to remember this later. He wanted to remember all of it later – to suck on it and live off it, like a cub to a bone, but Nick still didn't know her name.

"I'm in your heart and in your head," she said, giggling the last word into her the crook of her elbow.

"Are you sure?"

"All your memories are safe."

"Memories?"

Nick's head filled with light air and the smell of the sea. He reached closer to her and remembered in dream language the feel of her hair as it brushed his skin like cool silk, cool seaweed. When they kissed again, he closed his eyes and felt her shudder through their lips, her hands squeezing his own.

"Time to go," she whispered.

Then Nick's lap grew wet. At first, he thought it was because he was aroused, but when he jerked out of sleep, he saw it was because he had spilled coffee into his lap.

"Shit," his body hummed, the previous night's work burning inside his muscles. Outside his window, a sweaty attendant exited a restroom tucking his shirt in as he went around the front. Across the street from him, the Krispy Kreme Donut shop buzzed with activity. He had considered parking over there before he took his nap, but there was no shade. At least when he had gone to sleep there had been some shade from the canopy over the pumps, but no longer, and the sun's clocking gaze had found him once again. There was no shade in Brighton.

Approximately two hours ago, Nick Adams exited Storrow Drive and got off the raceway in a place called Brighton. He didn't know Brighton from Boston, but the name appealed to him – a bright place. The gas station attendant filled his car up, gave him directions on how to get to the harbor. Then Nick pulled around to the back and parked his car. Next to the gas station was a computer store and next to that a Store-24, which Nick assumed to be something like a Shore Stop or 7-11. Traffic had been bad when he pulled in and feeling groggy, he got himself a double coffee, which was now all over his lap. His stomach grumbled and Nick thought about the Krispy Kreme and grimaced at thought of the sugary meal.

"Don't do it Nicky boy. Donuts make your stomach twist."

The gas station attendant had said something about an Irish pub, on the way out of Brighton, on the way to the harbor, that served a good hot plate for lunch and strong coffee. He checked his wallet. He'd spent all his money in New Jersey which seemed like a million years ago. But he still had his credit card. He was a stranger here.

His stomach grumbled and Nick decided he'd probably fare better on a full stomach. When he pulled out he lowered his eyes briefly to switch on the radio and he missed a glimpse of a Native American pulling in behind him into the left-hand lane.

4

Sloping up, the street was peppered with tall row houses and long railroad apartments with wide, roomy porches that seemed out of place in the city, at least to Nick. To one side skyscrapers towered and the darkling harbor waited.

St. Columbkill, a large stone cathedral dominated the landscape on his other side where children played on the playground next to the church's expansive parking lot. He'd never seen such a large church before, he was used to the small clapboard chapels and brick Methodist affairs doting each shore town.

"I don't know what I'm doing." He said aloud and suddenly. "I have no idea what I'm doing."

He felt like screaming. The blonde in the van next to him hardly glanced at him as Nick shouted and slammed his fists against the steering column behind his closed windows.

Soon the church joined the long parallel lines of blurry buildings and cheap storefronts behind him. As he passed, Nick's heart beat a little faster. He was alone, in a city, a real honest-to-god city, not even a Dial-a-Nurse to talk to. He missed his buddy George, a nagging hook of guilt still scraped at him about his screw-up at old lady Enfield's a lifetime ago.

"I am all alone," he said to no one.

Nick felt better when he said it aloud – alone, in a scary world d. He didn't know anyone in Boston. At least in New Jersey, he had met Amanda. At least in New Jersey, there had been...*nothing – an illusion of camaraderie*. He had been alone there too, only it didn't feel so bad because he had found someone to talk to. Yesterday seemed like a million years ago. George was from another country, another lifetime.

The street came to a curvy ending, his car rattling at the red light. Behind him an old man hunched forward, gripping his steering wheel. Nick's head enlarged as he waited, the walls of his mind falling away. An old-fashioned pharmacy stood on the corner, its windows boarded up, its doors soaped over. Steve's Donuts looked busy and there was a crappy little hardware store that looked like it was bathed in dust.

"Look for the green awnings, oxidized copper," the gas attendant had said. "That's the pub."

What was the name? Green something or another. The buildings weren't too tall, but they gave the street a compressed feeling, cars zipping by. Nick had never seen so many people on the street before – even in Cape James, or Onancock. Those streets seemed homely, deserted, even on busy shopping days, compared to what it was like here in Brighton, where the sun laid everything to waste.

People clustered and moved with heavy shopping bags, hopping on and off buses, hurried with hastened eyes to some unseen spot. Sweat rolled across his eyes. *When had it gotten so hot? Wasn't it supposed to be cooler up North? It had been cool last night. Last night when I was painting.* Nick thumped the steering wheel with his thumbs.

On the opposite side of the street, a hairy taxicab driver peered at him from behind the steering wheel. Three girls crossed the walk-in front of him. One of them looked directly into his eyes. She said something to her friends, and they giggled. The red taxi revved his engine and a bus pulled up behind him. The taxi driver's eyes bored through the glass.

Nick had forgotten who had the right of way. The light had been red for an impossibly long time. Too long. It was going to change real soon, it had to.

He turned the radio on and over the airwaves heard a cackle, that of an old woman whose voice sounded like that of onion skins rubbing together.

"Come and get your fish, fish-girl!"

Nick's hair stiffened. His sweat froze to his skin and his balls crawled up into his groin. He went to change the radio but paused, it wasn't a radio anymore. The pushbuttons had become teeth, gray fangs, rotten molars, and all.

The cackle continued, "Fishy. Fishy, fishy. Smells like an old pussy in here. Is your brain dry, yet?"

Nick's throat closed up and he felt his chest tighten like a drum. And then in what felt like forever, the light turned green.

5

When the light changed, the hackles on Nick's neck rose and he almost floored the accelerator, but the old woman's voice gave him pause, and in that short second the red taxi lazily crossed the street and passed him. Nick's mouth tried to produce spit. He wanted to bite his tongue to get something wet flowing up there.

The old lady's voice continued, "Come on you little bitch. Come and let me take you to the water."

The teeth on the radio ground together and for a second, Nick thought the car was going to explode. His arms jerked the wheel and Nick felt like the girl, the woman, the mermaid, whatever she was, was in control of him. He thought maybe that he was somehow near her and that she had taken him over to bring him to her, like in those space movies where aliens take over the ship and pull the unsuspecting space travelers to their doom. She was inside his head, only this time he was awake.

As soon as he turned the steering wheel and pressed his foot on the gas, the feeling evaporated. His mouth loosened and produced a thin veneer of spit on the roof of his mouth. The radio turned back to normal, the exotic voice of the DJ announcing that something called the Kabisa was in progress. The cackle had faded and crawled back under whatever rock it had come out of. Nick knew, as his hands shook, that the girl was close. She had reached out and touched him and let him go. But the thing was also close, the thing in the woods, the voice. This thought made his skin crawl.

Nick passed the Green Briar for the first time, turned around on Winship Street, and found the side parking lot. No longer did his stomach feel hungry, instead it felt scooped out, erased. Nick thought if he were to see himself in the mirror now, he'd only be a shade, something like a vampire's reflection.

6

Overall, Mr. Bill thought the Northeast had a big sky. Above him, the electric blue afternoon reminded him of the Eastern Shore and how the sky seemed to take over areas of land where deforestation gave way to farming. There was a lot more of the sky here than there was on the shore. The shore's trees swallowed the sky, so unless one was on the creek, on the highway, or in the middle of a field, the sky was always broken, laced with branches and leaves. But here, in the parking lot of the Green Briar Pub, one could look up and be dazzled by its electric blue – in the middle of the city. For kicks, he walked down to the end of the parking lot. There he noticed that the neighbors lived a redneck life. An engine sat on concrete blocks. Laundry hung on improvised lines. Beer cans piled up in the recycling bins. Tomatoes grew in weedy patches, separated by paint thinner sticks. The back yards of Brighton reminded him of the backyards in Hexmore, Oysterhaus, and the hundreds of other crumbling vales on the shore. There was an alley of sorts, leading down to Winship Street, where his prey had turned around. Mr. Bill still couldn't get a read on the guy. This both bothered him and didn't bother him. His prey had the smell of Marina on him which made him important to Mr. Bill. He was certain he would find out all he needed to know in a matter of minutes.

Mr. Bill kicked down the street and looked up at the white statue of St. Elizabeth, her arms open wide on the hillside across the street and the triangle parking lot of Mutt's Garage. The hospital in her name sat on a hill and overlooked Brighton like the good saint. The sun was squarely overhead now, and it blasted Brighton like Brighton was a beach town, vacant of trees and full of high sun, sky blue, and beach fun.

Walking left on Winship, Mr. Bill paused in a storefront to check his appearance. His hair was wind-blown from driving with the windows open. He supposed whoever he was following wouldn't know or recognize him anyway. Turning the corner, he walked up to the entrance of the Green Briar.

7

The waitress' face held a moony smile and for a second there was a static-like flutter across her lips and eyes and Nick stared for one brief second into the eyes of the woman he was searching for, the face of a mermaid. Then the static flutter rippled across her face again and the face of the mermaid vanished and became that of the waitress again. *It's her,* Nick thought, *in my mind again.*

"Just one?" her question lingered in the air.

Nick nodded and followed the woman into the recesses of the pub, her dark hair falling behind her, and in the green hue of the pub, the black shimmered between ebony and pitch. The waitress's tall frame glided between the tables, leading Nick to the back, her green eyes flashing at him. From the kitchen, a squat redhead emerged brandishing silver in one hand and a gold-rimmed pitcher in the other.

"Thank you," Nick managed, his arms and legs trembling as he sat down in his booth. "May I have some water?"

"Sure."

She slipped between the double kitchen doors and immediately Nick felt utterly and completely exhausted, fatigued. *If I don't fall asleep in the booth, it will be a miracle.*

8

Hector knocked against the box's wall in front of him. He wanted to get in and run his fingers through the catch, like an eager young boy with his first kill. He pressed his ear to the wood and listened. From inside came forth a low moaning like that of a wounded animal.

"What the fuck," he whispered.

He twitched, jerking his head back as if a shock had jolted through him. His mind clouded with images of a dead man, a stranger, his boot slamming against the man's bones with a stomach echoing crunch. Then he saw the face of his mother as she rocked on the porch of her home and the first girl he ever kissed. A sharp jolt of pain hit him between the eyes. He shook his head, clearing like a bell. Hector looked around. *Had I been doing something down here? Knocking on wood? That sounded familiar. Where am I exactly?* It took a second to register that he was below decks, but he had no idea why he was down there. *Knocking on wood? Yeah, right.* There was nothing down here but the smell of hashish and long rows of boxes and shipping crates. But he had been down here to check something. Something he had brought inside. *But what?* He stared at the box in front of him and stalled.

Hector's stomach felt like he'd had too much to drink. But he knew he hadn't had anything to drink. *Had he?* He placed his hand to his mouth and breathed. He didn't smell alcohol. *Had he been smoking again? What was he doing down here anyway? How could I have forgotten?*

Then suddenly, Hector felt a shock, a jolt ran through him, and his mind filled with the images of the box. It was like he had switched channels. That's how he would remember it right before he died – his life-changing channels. A white itchy feeling came over him and his head was buffered in a low-grade noise, white noise, like static, like the sound of sleet falling on the roofs of the sedans outside his mother's house. It reminded him of snow and when he and his father would go into the garage to listen to radio Havana on his short-wave radio.

He didn't know what was inside the box, but in his mind, he saw a woman clutching the floor of the box with great tenacity, her fingers dug into the wood.

Marcos. That had been the dead man's name. *An errand boy from somewhere down south, an errand boy who would have caused trouble.*

Hector's hand skimmed the side of the box looking for a latch. *There would be some kind of hatch, some way to get inside.*

Ripe. A taste rose in his mouth like sour fruit. For a second Hector thought he felt fruit pulp between his teeth. He remained calm. Something was happening to him, something unnatural. A small part of his brain reared up like a reptile on a hot rock, but that part of his brain was too small and no match for the sweetness in his mouth.

By the time Hector had found the latch handle, his teeth felt loose. He beat on the small hatch with his hands. He kept thinking that his teeth were going to fall out soon and he had to get inside to have at her flesh. Hector fumbled with the latch and having no luck, knelt to force the bolt open.

Metal banged against the hardwood and echoed against the ship's steel hull as the small hatch door creaked open and the box shimmered. Hector's eyes burned. Stumbling back, he snapped back into himself, the white noise fading from his brain. He had tripped one of the magic traps. Panic seized him, the sweetness in his mouth turned to fire and he jammed his fingers into his mouth to gag. He spat out gobs of bloody spit. His teeth felt soft and loose when he ran his tongue over them.

I must get inside, Hector thought.

Hector squinted through the hatch, trying to make out any shapes in the darkness. At first, he saw nothing, but soon he was able to make out the bed, lying up on its side, bolted to what must be the floor, and there, wearing torn and shredded clothing, the girl, who looked haggard and fried.

She seemed to sense his desire and looked about for a place to hide, only there was none. When he spoke, his voice was not his own. What creaked and cackled out of his throat sounded like something out of a horror movie. And to his surprise, his teeth moved around in his mouth, loose. He felt an incisor come free of its socket, the slow steady flow of blood seeped into his mouth and down his throat.

"Hey girlie, girl. Fish girl. Come and get your bait, bitch," he croaked. As he spoke, the bloody nerve ending of a molar came loose and a rotten smell rose out of his mouth in a great haze.

"Fish girl. Hey there girlie. Time come for you to get dried up. Don't worry, we'll keep the scales for Daddy."

The girl looked up at him with revulsion.

Hector pressed his face up against the small square opening. *I could probably get an arm inside,* he thought. *Drag her up a bit. Kiss her mouth. Give her some of the acid she'd given me. Bite her lip off and chew, chew, chew. That's what I want to do. Eat her lips and move on to her tongue.* He could bust the small opening, crawl in and tear her apart. But instead, he pressed his face into the opening of the hole, eclipsing the little light that drained inside.

"Stew time, Fish girl. Skewer you and roast you over an open pit. You'd like that, wouldn't you? A fat stake running through your body. Huh? How do you like them crabs, fish girl?" Hector said as he flicked his tongue out at Marina, lapping and licking the air. "I think I'd like to make a fillet out of you." Hector liked the sound of his new voice. He felt power there.

The girl moved away from him or at least she looked like she moved. It was hard to tell in the dark. No matter, he'd make her come to him. Pulling his face back from the opening, Hector pushed his arm through the aperture, fingers flexing for a grip of hair or a bit of arm. He felt iron strength rush through his blood and his heartbeat and pound against his ribs.

9

Marina's brain had frozen. When the box had pulled up and out of the water her thoughts had jumped to thoughts of her dry skin. When the box had come down in the dark, dry cargo, her nose had caught the smell of dry rot and death – a slow death. Her brain had frozen as she clung to the side of the wall, her fingernails gripping the wood, cutting into the thick grooved planks. And there she had blanked out.

She didn't notice the hatch open. She didn't notice the person who looked very small at the doorway of her prison. She couldn't hear the man's movement against the grain of the wood. She *did* recognize the sound of the hag. The hag had awoken her from her daze. Now, the hag was reaching inside the box for her. The hand that groped for her didn't look like a woman and her brain rushed and flipped to name the thing. *A hand. A man.* It was a man's hand. She felt something like anger rise in her temples.

The hand crept down the wall, which was now the floor, toward her face. It wiggled and flexed for her. The hand seemed to have a life of its own as if it were independent of the man. She crept back and to the rear of the box, her own hands reaching for the searching hand.

She surprised herself when she grabbed the wrist. For a second, she didn't know what to do with it. Then suddenly, without thought, she pulled the hand up and out with a quick jerk. There was a pop and the echo of bones snapping back. She applied pressure and twisted the arm and kept twisting until she heard the crunch and squelch of flesh and blood tearing. The man screamed and flailed. The arm pulled away from the body with a short sharp crack. Blood splattered the wood walls and the man howled. His voice filled the box, bouncing off the walls.

Hector struggled and writhed against the side of the box. He rolled over onto his side; the pain was enormous. His head went out and he felt his new voice go with it. For a second, he thought only of his mother back home and how she would weep when she learned that her only son was dead. His mind ripped with the sounds of changing channels. His scream gurgled in his throat and Hector's brain went a dazzling white.

When Marina heard Hector fall to the floor of the ship, she flung the arm to the side of her box and collapsed into a fetal ball, her ears and eyes attuned to any sounds that would follow – sounds that would come to rescue the wounded man, who would come to harm her. But they didn't come, not for a long time.

10

The Green Briar's dim light grew brighter as a haggard old Native American walked towards him.

He stopped in front of Nick, blocking his way out. Then he leaned over slightly. For a second Nick thought the old man must be well over seven feet tall, but then thought that it was only the way the weird light waves of The Green Briar were pushing away from him to make it seem that way as if the light was water.

"We need to speak," the old man said, his voice raspy like onion skin. "It's about the girl you've been seeing in your head. The one you are searching for."

CHAPTER THREE

1

Mr. Bill thought it was Mulch's choice to do business with the Tortini brothers that twisted Mulch, rather than the weight of Leon and Eb's body. Of course, there was the matter of Ruth, his mother, but Mr. Bill didn't like to think about her. He didn't know anything about that. Rather, it was the business of dumping dead bodies in the backpaddles of the creeks and in the deep folds of his fields that twisted Mulch's mind and body.

From there it had been a downward spiral, in Mr. Bill's opinion. Mr. Bill did believe that Mulch wanted to destroy himself in one epic dissolution of his soul. Mulch had rambled on and on about it for years, a drunkalog that ended with his daughters pimped out to family members, and everything he owned destroyed.

Mr. Bill had always wondered if destroying everything meant destroying Maria. Was he on the list too? *Probably.*

To think it had all begun with love.

2 Spain. The Canary Islands.

Mulch, tired, disheartened, bereft of his mermaid lover, sank more and more into the mud of his memory. Mulch half-believed himself to be mad with guilt though in truth he hadn't thought of Leon in days, perhaps weeks, and even as he thought back to the last time he thought of him, the guilt didn't rise from the bottom to destroy him as it had done during his first weeks on the islands. Though he blamed his mood on killing his uncle, he didn't think of it. Perhaps for a fleeting second, processing it like he would remember a chore. His mind a tangled knot of repeating thoughts. He'd be close to tears one moment and ready to fight the next, his brain in a negative loop. Mostly he only thought of her.

Was she dead? He hadn't seen any sign of her and didn't dare ask. What would you say anyway? Have you seen a mermaid? *What would they think of him? Mad likely, and one for the clink.* Instead, he hunkered his feelings of woe down inside of him and tried to forget her. But he couldn't. So he spent time at the island bars.

Mikel, the German was good company. He had a ribald flavor for beer and foreigners, and he knew everyone. He introduced Mulch to the Italians who were on the islands meeting American business partners. Mikel promised to bring Mulch around the Italians more often if Mulch liked. Mikel felt akin to the Italians and felt Mulch's appearance at his resort was kismet, destiny. Because of the fascist debacle of World War II, the rich Italians who vacationed in the Canary Islands were eager to meet Americans, especially young Americans, who could inform their children of the proper contemporary colloquialisms and styles of dress. And styles of dress were important for the rich who desired to be brash Americans. Mulch recognized the fever at once. It was the same fever that had gripped Maria and her people who trucked up the winding roads of America from Mexico to find work picking fruit and vegetables for a nickel a pound. In America, one reinvented themselves.

Palling around with the German was fun. There was booze, women, men, cocaine, and music aplenty. Mulch tried everything and regretted nothing. But it was almost two weeks before Mulch encountered any Americans. There were three of them, all of them robust males in sharp, tailored suits. The Americans were palling around with a group of Italians, who in turn palled around with the other Italians, which somehow lynch-pined around Mikel, the German who had taken Mulch under his wing.

Mikel had introduced Mulch to an American and three new Italian men hours prior. Mikel knew of some French women who had arrived at the resort sans husbands. The women hadn't panned out, but it was on the beach, after too much red wine and too much moonlight, with Mulch cooing over his mermaid love, whom he simply called 'his heartfelt,' that he accidentally spilled the beans about Leon.

There had been a pause in the conversation, during which Mulch swigged on a bottle of wine. The young American next to him had said nothing. In the moonlight Mulch watched him fumble with the corkscrew.

"I hate these things," the American said. His name was Tony. The shadows of the palm trees covered his body like a blanket. Three years later he'd be lying at the bottom of Nassawadox creek.

"Can I help?" Mulch asked, wishing he could take back what he'd said about killing his uncle.

"Maybe," Tony said, popping the cork out the bottle. "But not with this fucking corkscrew."

He threw the tool out into the surf where it sank into the sea. There was silence as Tony drank from the fresh bottle. He passed it to Mulch.

"Bottoms up farm boy."

"Thanks."

"So," Tony said, "what did you do with the body?"

Mulch, sat silent, trying his best to look stoic. In the moonlight, he looked like a baby.

"Um. I left him in the caves."

"Caves?" Tony drank from the bottle.

"Indian caves on my father's land. My father and a friend were going to take care of it."

Tony grinned, licking his teeth.

"Really. They were going to take care of him?" Mikel asked, proffering a small mirror and glass straw. Mikel gestured to Mulch, but then abruptly changed directions and Mikel took a snort instead.

"Still, burying a body isn't like planting corn. Or is it?" Tony asked.

"They'd probably dump him in the creek. Weigh him down with bricks. Or they'd sink him in the swamp, or they could send him to the bottom of the Chesapeake."

"Hmm?" Tony wondered as he offered Mulch another swig of wine.

Mulch still hadn't finished his bottle and refused, sucking on his own instead. His bottle had a bit of cork floating in it and he had to spit out bits of it. He kept doing so. Mikel once again offered Mulch the coke mirror. Mulch took a short snort and passed it to Tony.

"These creeks can't be that deep," Tony prodded.

"Well, most are at least four or five feet deep."

"Oh."

"Some are seven, eight in places, some deeper. The closest swamp stretches five miles, melts into the creek. Some places in the bogs could hold a hundred bodies."

"Really?"

"Really. And not to mention all the land my folks have got. Shit, it's a regular fucking killing field out there."

Tony leaned back on his elbows. Behind him, squeals of girls pealed out of the cabana. There were high effeminate giggles and the pop of champagne. A high curling laugh ended in garbled French.

"Yeah, we go deer hunting back there. Lots of deer in the swamp."

"Popular place, your land?" Tony burped.

"Private. The swamp is on our land. Almost all of it."

"The creek?"

"No one owns the creek, but my uncle purchased a lot of waterfront property before he uh, um," Mulch stopped mid-sentence and finished his bottle of wine. Wine dribbled out of his mouth and onto his chest.

"Before you whacked him." Mikel said, laughing and looking at Tony as if to impress him. "I guess."

Tony slapped Mulch on the back, "No need to worry, farm-boy."

"Thanks."

"I'm hoping that we, my brothers and our compatriots, could enlist your services."

"Services?" Mulch looked at Tony.

"Services," Tony laughed. "Of which you'd be paid handsomely for."

"What kind of services?" Mulch asked.

"Tony's people are good people," Mikel said.

Tony reached behind him in the sand. From the cabana, there was a "Yello," from Tony's brother, or perhaps one of the other Italians, but Mulch thought there was something American about the yell.

"Smoke?" Tony asked as he brushed sand off his pack of cigarettes.

"Yes."

Tony lit them up and Mulch settled into the nicotine which roared in his wine-soaked head.

"Burial services," Tony said flatly.

"Wouldn't you want a funeral home for that?"

"Oh no, farm-boy. We're looking for someone like you."

Mikel excused himself, rising and dusting off the sand. Someone emerged from the cabana, at first a dark shadow in the lit doorway, then as he approached, came into focus.

"Robert, right on time," Tony said.

Tony sat beside Mulch on the sand, the moon breaking over their bodies. Robert had with him a bottle of Sambuca, a clear liquor he'd swiped from one of the Italians. Robert poured three glasses and passed them around, each one dusted with damp sandy fingerprints. Tony lit cigarettes for everyone, all three at once, which delighted Mulch. Robert's face was broader than Tony's; they both shared the same broad gut and shoulders, they looked like baseball players.

"We run our business out of Philadelphia and Baltimore."

Robert looked over to Tony. Tony nodded, "See, what Robert means to say is..."

"Is that we have encountered a steep hill of competition, you might say."

Robert and Tony sounded a lot alike, and Mulch found himself wanting to giggle.

"Real steep," Tony muttered.

"Well, to be blunt, we are under a lot of pressure from local authorities to clean up our act."

Mulch listened and his heart washed out to sea that night. He felt so long gone. So, he let the Italians fill him up with the dead.

"We need you to help us bury some of the competition," Tony said and Mulch shook his head to clear it and to show his new friends he was paying attention.

"Let me make this clear, farm-boy," Robert said as he edged up to Mulch, his breath mingling with Mulch's, "we don't want these bodies to surface, ever. We want them lost."

"As in out to sea," Tony said.

"See, if we dispose of the bodies locally, they could be linked to us, or one of our compatriots later on. And since we're practically neighbors, it would be very neighborly of you to help us."

"You'd be paid handsomely, of course," Tony said. "You never know, you could get yourself into another line of work."

Robert licked his lips, his right hand clapping the nape of Mulch's neck.

And that's how Mulch's Chesapeake Disposal Service was born.

3

Mulch's Chesapeake Disposal was officially registered in Baltimore County and had a dummy office set up on a plot of land next to a tributary that fed into the Chesapeake Bay. Mulch himself oversaw the shipping and disposal of bodies for the first six months until Tony's cousin took over the one-man office in Baltimore County. Sometimes, Mr. Bill went with him, sometimes other young farmhands. Bodies came down in black bags and were buried under trash bags and other refuse. The tugboat made the midnight voyage down to the shore twice a week, sometimes three, disposing of bodies in deep channels and marshes.

Additionally, Tony hooked Mulch up with an outfit in Maryland that ran bodies to the swamps on his property for disposal. Many of those dead found their final home on Mulch's land, others were tied together, weighted down, and lost far off in the Bay. It wasn't soon before the dead began to sprout in the huge and heavy corn, the wet and thick snow cotton, and the thick, red busty tomatoes. Sometimes the fruit of the vine tasted like meat.

4

Mr. Bill looked at Nick from across the table. "Hello, my name is, er, um," Mr. Bill looked up at the kangaroo poster on the wall and cleared his throat. "People call me Guinness." Mr. Bill said, his hands folded in front of him.

"Guinness, like the beer?"

"Yes," Mr. Bill said as he reached out his hand to Nick's who gripped it in return. "My mother liked to cook with it. Called it her special recipe."

"I'm Nick. Nick Adams. That's an unusual name for an American Indian, I mean Native American, right?"

"Yes. American. Nassa..um..," Mr. Bill's thoughts spun, "Cherokee tribe."

"Wow. Cool. Have a seat."

Mr. Bill slid into the booth to join Nick. He produced his pipe from his shirt pocket and put it between his lip, and as he did, he stared into Nick's eyes trying to read his reactions.

"I know whom it is you seek."

Nick chuckled, "uh-huh."

A redhead waitress passed by their table and paused leaving them water.

"Two long drafts, please," Mr. Bill asked.

The waitress disappeared into the kitchen.

"The lighting here is weird," Nick said eyeing Mr. Bill's pipe. "You can't smoke that in here you know."

"Your order is coming," Mr. Bill said.

"How do you know that?"

On cue, Nick's waitress bumped her behind through the doors, Nick's s order on her tray. Mr. Bill smiled but didn't move when the waitress leaned over depositing Nick's meal.

"There you go sir," she hesitated, looking to Mr. Bill. "Can I get you anything?"

"The sushi."

"Be up in a second."

"Thanks, dear," and as soon as the waitress was out of earshot, he continued coolly, "Her name is Marina."

"Whose name?" Nick asked as he ate a piece of cheese. "I don't know anyone named Marina."

"The mermaid."

"There are no such things as mermaids, pal," Nick replied as he looked over at the bar.

"You've been painting her, Mr. Adams, dreaming about her, I think. Though I don't know for sure."

Nick's throat closed up. A thin wire of air connected his lungs to the stale smoky air of the pub. Immediately he began to sweat. His fingers trembled and the soreness in his shoulders came charging back into his muscles.

"Her name is Marina, and she *is* a mermaid."

"Marina?" Nick said her name again, silently.

"Fitting isn't?" Mr. Bill nodded.

The waitress bumped back out into the dining room. On her tray were several pieces of raw fish, which stared back at Nick with its swirling flesh. The tender red of the tuna had yet to drain of blood and seemed to throb in the stale light.

"Here you go," she charmed.

"Thanks, sweetie."

"No problem," she hummed as she left them to their lunch.

"You're staring at my lunch, Nick."

"It's staring at me."

"Is it?" Nick repeated.

"She needs to eat." Mr. Bill said.

"Who is she?" Nick pleaded, his eyes focused on the raw meat on Mr. Bill's plate.

"Eat this," Mr. Bill said, nudging his plate closer.

Nick's eyes popped out; his face sprung up with hunger. It overtook Nick at once, from a wellspring deep inside, hunger came shooting out of his stomach and into his hands which gripped the meat before throwing back into his mouth.

Flash frozen, the sushi retained almost all of its fresh-kill taste which honeyed Nick's tongue with a cool, crisp feeling of nourishment. He ripped the fish apart with his teeth, sucking on the wet flesh, nursing on it. A wave rippled through him, and flashes of Marina's face bubbled up to the surface of his mind. He had a name now, a name to go with the face – Marina.

"She will love you for it," Mr. Bill said as Nick went on devouring the raw fish.

5

For the next hour, Nick didn't speak, his muscles swelling with renewed strength, the raw fish like a jolt of coffee to his nervous system. His body had been run-down over the last few days and his brain felt like a rubber band stretched to the point of breaking. For reasons Nick couldn't explain, the fish soothed his mind as well as nourished his body. As he ate, he felt some of his old self slip back into him again. All the while his new friend Guinness, a made-up name if he'd ever heard one, watched him eat. The stranger ordered a second and then a third plate.

"I don't know what has happened to you," Mr. Bill began. "You are involved in something you know nothing about. I know for whom you search, know her well, too. I will not ask you to give up your search. I only ask that I may go with you. To assist, so to speak. Do not answer me now. When we are finished here, I will pay, and you will ride with me. You can leave your car here as it is dangerous to travel any farther with it. You will not need it any longer."

Nick paused mid-chew, a piece of red tuna stuck in his teeth. He didn't think he should trust this fellow, however, he felt like he didn't have much of a choice either. After all, he had already drifted his way into Boston, he might as well swim with the tide. So, he nodded and ate his food. Knowing that the tab would be covered, he ordered dessert, a cup of coffee, and a fish sandwich to go.

Brighton was still bright when they emerged from the dark ebony bar and Nick had to put his hand up to see. He followed Mr. Bill down the block and around the corner to the small parking lot. Mr. Bill's car, a ratty station wagon with a large BU sticker cutting across the back, didn't look like the kind of car a man named Guinness would drive, Nick expected to be led to a Cadillac, or some other old guy car, a Crown Victoria, perhaps. For a brief second, he thought Mr. Bill was stealing this car, because of the contents of the car, which the stranger waved off as possessions of his grandson and friends, who borrowed the car on weekends. Nick was still suspicious when Mr. Bill didn't know his way around his car as they pulled into traffic. Nick half-expected the old guy to fumble behind the wheel, as he had done only an hour or so ago when his radio had transformed into a mouth. Thinking back to that horrific moment he shuddered and thrust the thought from his mind. He tried to think of the girl from his dream earlier that day. He remembered her dark hair, but nothing of the face.

"She'll be happy to see you when we find her," Mr. Bill said suddenly.

"I have to warn you, Mr. Guinness, I don't know where I was going."

Mr. Bill nodded, exhaling "ah" in a low groan. Traffic grew heavier as they moved onto Brighton Avenue.

"Another man named Marcos, a Brazilian came with her by boat. He was her caretaker of sorts. I imagine you traveled close to the water."

"Close to it? Hell, I practically walked to Jersey along the shore-ways."

Mr. Bill sensed the wear and tear the boy had been through, his hair moffed up and shaggy. His beard sketchy and prickly, his face wasn't so much burned as weather-beaten.

"Travel by night?" Mr. Bill asked.

"Yes."

"Smart thinking."

"Thinking didn't have much to do with it, Mr. Guinness."

"I see."

"I don't think you do." Someone blared their horn. Nick was sure the blast was meant for them.

"Believe me, I know what she's capable of. But I'm as surprised as you are with your...uh...your....um."

Nick didn't bother to fill in the blanks and just stared out the window.

"Don't you want to know how I found you, Nick?"

"I'm guessing you were going to tell me eventually. That crazy old Sea Hag said I was cursed."

"Sea Hag? That's an unusual name," Mr. Bill hadn't expected her to be involved. *This is a surprise. Marina sees a bigger playing field than I. Impressive.* "Do you know this woman well?"

"No, actually I don't."

Ahead of them, Brighton Avenue merged with Commonwealth Avenue. Downtown Boston loomed ahead like a spiky crown. Nick had never seen so many people before in his life.

"How did you..."

"I know her from her fritter shop."

"Ah."

Nick listened to the rush and roaring of speeding metal passing his ear-drums. Concrete and brownstones reflected the city-songs into his ear. He found the effect to be overstimulating and soothing at the same time.

"So, how *did* you find me?" Nick asked the stranger.

"I had a dream."

Nick grinned, "Of course."

"Is it so hard to believe? How else would I have known about you?" Mr. Bill countered.

"You could have followed me?"

"From Virginia?"

"Yeah," Nick shrugged, "I guess not."

"Dreams are powerful things." Mr. Bill said.

"Yeah, well it's been that kind of summer."

"How do you know Marina?" Mr. Bill asked again.

"I don't. You mind if I smoke?"

"No, not at all." Mr. Bill handed his pipe over.

"No shit?" He turned the old wood pipe over in his hands. It was hand-carved from cherry and old too. The bowl had warped from so many years of use and Nick saw that the resin inside was dense and fibrous. "You're the boss," he said, looking at Mr. Bill, who looked so serene maneuvering through traffic. Nick lit the pipe and inhaled, and his mouth watered upon contact. His lungs ballooned with potent homegrown, "Wow."

"Grow it myself."

"Impressive," Nick said, giving his thumbs up approval, Nick's head settled back into the cushy headrest.

"Is that your lipstick?" Nick said pointing to the floorboards.

"Grand-kids."

Nick opened the glove compartment, "You keep a compact in your glove compartment?" Nick asked. Folded up inside was a BU schedule, for someone named Tanya. And a travel box of tampons. "This can't be your kids' schedule, is it?"

"I'm driving, please, I must concentrate." Mr. Bill looked straight ahead, his eyes roving across Boston's rabid municipal traffic.

"And condoms?" Nick looked in the backseat, looked back at Mr. Bill, his eyes and face full of doubt.

"Boston traffic is terrible."

"You know there are Mademoiselle magazines on your floor?"

"My girlfriend."

"Is that a Boston University cheerleader's outfit?" Nick pointed to the backseat.

"Please the traffic, I must concentrate."

"Your girlfriend is a BU cheerleader?"

"I, uh, well..." Mr. Bill's mind, usually razor-sharp, did not have time to counter with magic. *Perhaps I should have been honest,* Mr. Bill thought. A passing car honked and flipped Mr. Bill and Nick off.

"Is this really your car?" Nick asked, looking backward and forwards as if the answer would materialize before him.

"No."

"Oh." Nick didn't say anything for a few minutes. "I'm glad it isn't," he finally managed.

Outside Nick's window the buildings grew taller and closer together *if that was even possible,* he thought. Mr. Bill drove him out of the Brighton borough and towards downtown, though Nick would have been hard-pressed to guess even the direction.

"So you don't know her?"Mr., Bill asked.

"No. How could I know a mermaid? I mean they don't even exist."

"Half-mermaid."

"Excuse me?"

"She's a half-mermaid. And they do exist. You know they do," Mr. Bill reached over and knocked his finger against Nick's skull as he smoked. "Marina is very real. You know that to be true. And we need to catch a freighter going east or she might not live much longer."

"East? Live much longer? What?"

"The damsel in distress is on her way to Holland. If we don't catch her before she gets to Amsterdam, we may never see her again."

"Just who the hell are you?" Nick said as Mr. Bill narrowly avoided running into an idle cab in the slow lane.

6

Lilly's eyes popped awake as Loco's truck lumbered along the train tracks. To her one side, the coast was stippled in masts and half-sails, the harbor thick with Cambridge yachts and recreational fishing boats. To the other, over Loco's shoulder, the houses shrank together and lay on top of each other like toy boxes, the bodegas, and shops teeming with pedestrians. There were many faces on the street. More than Lilly had seen in some time, some were dressed in suits, others shorts, and tees.

"Loco, where are we?"

Loco turned, his smile beaming across the cab. "We are in the neighborhood of my people. Reach out and feel the sunshine, smell the tortillas," Loco laughed.

The only thing Lilly smelled was acidic exhaust pouring across the train tracks. She looked back at the Ugly Mother who grinned and took in all the smells and sights of Boston. *What in the world was she doing here?*

Loco winded his truck through a crowded intersection. The early morning rush hour had begun, she assumed. It was not Mexico City, not by a long shot, and Lilly felt nostalgia for her home creep into her heart.

Loco's relations lived in a brownstone whose bottom floor was a Cuban cafe. The smell of turtle beans and garlic wafted Lilly's face as she stood below, stunned by the long drive and sudden dislocation. Loco, however, snapped to life. He crackled and popped his hands up and down. Balancing himself on one foot, he leaned over and rang the doorbell, ready to pop. "I can get you all the help you need, here. Cousin Tony is a cop. He busts some heads for you, no?"

The Ugly Mother muttered no and wiped her brow with a wrinkled hand-kerchief. The air seemed cooler, but Lilly knew it was only the lack of that cot-ton-thick humidity that permeated the swamps and marshland of the shore. "I have a bad feeling, Lilly. About Marcos," she said.

"Oh mother, stop it."

Loco bounced up and down on his feet. "I'm sure it will be fine. Don't worry," he said.

"Yes, mother. Things will be okay." But a feeling of dread had already settled into Lilly's bones, thick and heavy as iron, she had felt the same dread for the last few hours and its weight threatened to drag her into depression. *It's just the usual feelings of not being able to communicate with her, Lilly, just calm down.* But her thoughts continued to race.

Within the first hours of being in town, the Ugly Mother worried Lilly to death, about Marcos. Lilly felt incredibly self-conscious. Her mother made a scene and her hosts kept shooting them looks.

The absence the Ugly Mother felt was an ugly scar. Marcos was dead, she was sure of it. Lilly told her it was just the strain of driving for twelve hours in Loco's truck. But the Ugly Mother said no. She had been thinking of Mar-cos when the hollow space suddenly punched into her heart. The Ugly mother imagined an awl punch, the gnarled one her husband had once used to make holes for his belt as he grew skinnier and skinnier until at last, he was a thin slice of flesh that disappeared between the floorboards of their old home.

Lilly, exasperated. This wasn't the first time her mother had hijacked her weekend for some magical hoodoo that didn't amount to a hill of beans to any-one but the Ugly Mother. *This gets worse and worse all the time,* she thought. *This is the real problem, not Marcos, but your mother.*

7

Sea Hag's boat sputtered and coughed as it took her to shore. The gulls and herons took flight at the sound of her hacking motor when she passed. Her little boat ride into Oysterhaus every day gave her time to mull things over. *The noggin needed a little more time these days.* She had a lot to think about, Marcos, Marina, and Mulch's letter, which had been delivered by a pimply-faced teenager in 15 ft speedboat. He'd sent the kid out once before when the box was under construction, this time, Mulch sounded worried, desperate.

Dearest Sea Hag,
Mr. Bill is sick. Don't know by what. Maybe it is something you could help him with. I can't help thinking it has to do with you-know-what. Please come as soon as you can.
M.

Bill didn't get sick. She knew that. Everybody knew that. It bothered her and made her suspicious. She'd been feeling melancholy already, for her heart was absent where Marcos should be. Her mind rationalized that Marcos was okay; that he was trans-Atlantic by now – Holland bound, skipping over the pond to Europe. That he was taking Mulch's little girl to the next escort who would then complete the rest of the voyage. *The sea makes dice of men's bones.*

Sea Hag imagined a hole punch, one of those industrial jobs she'd seen at the copy store a year or so ago when she printed the new fliers for her restaurant. She imagined a giant one wrapped around her that squeezed out tiny circles through all her muscles leaving painful small holes that deflated her heart and left her depressed. *No, it isn't depression, this isn't emotional,* she thought as she tied up her dingy and stepped out on the dock, *it's loss.*

No, she thought, *this is magic. Mulch's cousins, I bet.*

Oysterhaus tingled with activity, something that was rare these days. A truck lumbered past the wharf. A blue school bus filled with migrant children turned up the street towards the old elementary school for ESL lessons. Two pick-ups, both pulling boats, rattled by. All the streets lead to water eventually. The bus turned, its axles squeaking, the shocks on the old bus gone in the teeth. Two kids on bikes whizzed by. Sea Hag walked up to her restaurant where she kept the old, battered pick-up she'd been carrying herself around in for so many years. As she climbed in and rumbled up the road past Hayes Feed Store, she noticed with great interest the GOING OUT OF BUSINESS sign tacked in all of the windows. *Yup. Things were falling apart.* There was no doubt in her mind that they were.

The tingle in the back of her mind fluttered and turned over and went to sleep. Sea Hag felt confident that if something were dreadfully wrong, her magic would let her know. She had never been more wrong.

8

"Give into Pembroke, let him think he's dominant. That's what I thought then. I was planning to fake it. Fake it till you make it, as Macy's father used to say. Give in, let him think he's in control.

"I spent most of my energy trying to keep the fireflies from coming to life. The head-box made my world complete and total darkness until they opened their wings. I don't think they made any noise, but when they were around my head thrummed and throbbed with their voices, their beating wings. I do my best to keep them still. To keep them still means I can't scream and so I don't.

"Which is fucking hard when the fog slips in through the coffin cracks and prods me. The fog knows I want the fireflies to be still, so of course, the fog pushes inside me. Enters my mouth, my vagina, my anus, my nose, it spreads out thin with hair-like feelers to enter my pores. The penetrating fog makes me cold and strange inside. It shows me that I am hollow.

"Doc, you ever feel hollow? Do you?"

9

Cilia closed her eyes and relaxed her body. Right now, her body ached to walk, but Cilia had to keep her physical body still to allow her spirit to roam the ship that contained Marina. Hector was of no use to her now. His body had collapsed in the ship's hold. There had been shock followed by a tremendous loss of blood. She had made sure the Captain had dispatched someone to take Hector to sickbay, though Cilia doubted very much that he would survive the night. She didn't dare risk one of the other two, so she was forced to walk the ship herself which was exhausting, and in the back of her mind she felt her body trying to rebel – her body wanted a break, her body wanted to sleep.

The danger in controlling so many individuals at once was the damage to her body. It was a double-edged sword, easy to keep at bay in the beginning. The trick was to establish control of a host, and every once in a while, preferably at night when the host slept, relinquish control for a little R&R of her own. But still, after a while, the body ached. The strain of controlling three men at once would have been more than enough for some, but Cilia had managed them while invading Marina's skull as well. This was no easy feat on its own, but since Marina was weakened from being out of the water, it was easier for her.

However, there was the matter of the mind she did not recognize. *A boy, for sure, a man even.* A boy whom Marina knew. *That isn't even possible,* she thought. Unless Mulch was mistaken about how socialized his daughter was. *That must be it. American sloppiness.*

But the boy bothered her. *He's coming,* her mind insisted. *Someone's coming and you don't know who.*

10

Marina held the bloody arm in her hands and listened for the man to return. There was no movement, nothing. She had the feeling that other people had been near her without her knowledge. *Have I been asleep?* Her mouth, bitterly rancid, was sore from clenching her teeth so hard. The quiet made her skin bubble up with chills. Her muscles were tight and bruised from sitting, though she couldn't remember how long it had been since she had sat down. Her legs trembled and propped up on her lap like some kind of trophy was the bloody arm of a man. The arm had grown cold, the blood congealing, forming a knobby seal around the bone and stump-end.

Have I killed him? She wasn't sure.

She wanted to cry but couldn't. She was sure men would come, men who would hurt her, men who would speak with the voice of the hag.

Think! What has Bill taught you? Calm yourself first.

The first thing she felt with her heart was cold and old and bitter. The hag's voice muttered, a chattering of white noise that swelled in her mind and filled it up. Marina curled up and held her knees, using all of her strength to manage her thoughts.

"Fish girl!" The hag's voice came from nowhere and filled her mind, and Marina was sure the hag was close.

When it did come, the hag's voice echoed in the box, and the hag voice was threaded on a needle and the needle pierced Marina's lip and sewed her mouth shut.

Marina tried to talk but could not. Fear had her.

Outside, the ship's hold was lined with dingy yellow bulbs that cast a sallow light into the open hole at the top of the overturned box. Enough urine light spilled in for her to see that her skin had already begun to flake. Skin the size of her palm had fallen off and turned to powder in her fingers. She lay on her side willing her brain to stay calm. The white noise of the hag made everything impossible. If she could only get out. The hole was too small for her to squeeze through. She could have tried breaking out, using her strength, but her muscles felt deflated, used up. She had used all her energy stores to rip the man's arm off. Plus, she didn't know what waited outside the box. *Certainly, there would be more men waiting for her outside,* she thought. She wanted to sleep, to escape into her head for a while.

The arm slipped off her lap and made a dull thump when it hit the wood. Marina barely noticed it happen, her head slipping to her chin, her body lapsing into a deep exhausted sleep.

CHAPTER FOUR

1

Doppelgänger Mr. Bill stumbled awake. His spider of a brain knew something was happening. He felt it, like the ripples of disturbed air, like a cold draft. He sprung to his feet and bounded up the stairs. Doppelgänger Mr. Bill paused at the top, briefly listening for voices, before slipping around the side and up the stairs into Maria's room.

2

Mulch had given Maria the day off and the driveway was empty when Sea Hag drove up to the house. She left her keys in the car, to facilitate a quick trip to the hospital if necessary. Mulch greeted her on the steps, and Sea Hag thought he looked like a content old man with his broad smile, his wavy gray hair, and for a second Sea Hag forgot why she was there, forgot that Mr. Bill was ill.

"It's good to see you," Mulch said, offering his hand.

For a brief second Sea Hag's neck hairs pricked and rose, then calmed.

"Yes," she said, drawing in her breath. "And under such horrible circumstances."

"Yes, it is terrible."

"I have so many questions, about Bill, about Marina."

"I know you do," Mulch said as he led her inside. The house smelled of lemon cleaner and sunshine. Sea Hag followed Mulch towards the basement door.

"Well, Marina is doing nicely. Marcos phoned me last night. From Boston," Mulch said with a chuckle. "They made it to Boston without a hitch."

"Oh good."

"Yes. As far as I can tell all is well." Mulch leaned against the basement door. "Although, I think Marcos thinks he's in love with my daughter. But we knew that, didn't we, Haggie?"

"I suppose."

Sea Hag couldn't help but notice the lift in Mulch's voice, the bright tones, like a flute.

"Love. Isn't it grand?"

Mulch smiled, opening the basement door, his hand gesturing down into the darkness.

"How's Mr. Bill?"

"It appears that he's come down with some sort of illness."

"Oh? How so?"

"Follow me?"

"Of course."

Mulch walked slowly down the stairs, careful not to alarm Sea Hag, though his heart pumped, and his brain felt like it was going to jump out of his skull, he was so excited. Mulch didn't bother fighting down the erection raging in his pants. He began to whistle.

3

"So this is Boston Harbor?" Nick said as he looked out the car window into the dirty bay.

Mr. Bill nodded, his arm hanging out the window.

"Damn shame it's so filthy." Mr. Bill chewed on his pipe.

"This is where the Boston Tea Party happened?"

"I guess," Mr. Bill nodded. Bill tried to look uninterested but wasn't so sure he was accomplishing this feat. In the rear-view, his face was a ball of wrinkles and weird lip twists. Even at such close range, he could not read Nick's mind, all he saw was static, like TV static. It was beginning to annoy him. *This guy is juiced with Marina's power.* "I hope this is the right harbor," Mr. Bill said to himself.

"You know, Guinness, I never was any good in history. Seemed so unreal, you know, the tea party?"

Mr. Bill pulled his car into the parking lot for the Boston Aquarium. They would have to foot it from there if they wanted to find Marina's boat. But Mr. Bill was almost sure that Marina had left already. She was getting harder and harder to read as well. Something about the two of them. *Like magnets drawn to each other, they appeared to be creating a field around them.* If she had left port already, hopefully, they'd find the trans-Atlantic passage that she was on. Mr. Bill slowed the car to allow families to pass. Children tugged their parents, eager to see the fishies.

Once Mr. Bill parked, they stepped out into the bright sun. Nick thought of Brighton and how the sun had come down in glorious beach-like majesty. It was equally as strong here. They were away from the tall buildings and the sun could just come straight down all it wanted. For the first time in a long while, he felt warm and confident. Though he wasn't sure if he should trust Guinness, the very fact that Guinness knew about the mermaid was enough to get him to follow along, at least for now.

All they found at the harbor were tourists and shops and tacky signs pointing this way and that. Mr. Bill got so disoriented he started sputtering around like his doppelgänger asking strangers for directions and making himself more and more confused. Most of the people he asked were tourists, and when Bill tried to read their minds, he only found distorted maps of the city, as they knew it, which made the search impossible. Nick didn't know the harbor from Adam and wasn't sure if they were even in the right part of town. He didn't see much in the way of freighters. There were a few, but they seemed far too big for what they were looking for. All in all, they walked around for a good two hours before Mr. Bill gave up and went back to the car with Nick in tow.

"We need a plane," Mr. Bill said as he opened his door.

"Don't you mean a plan?"

Mr. Bill shot him a deadpan look.

"So you don't think we'll find her then?" Nick asked.

"What do you think?" Mr. Bill sounded annoyed. "This isn't the industrial harbor. What was I thinking?"

"Well, I'm with you. I'll figure it out when I go to sleep tonight."

"What do you mean?"

"You know. When I dream. You said it yourself, that I might dream about her. Well, I do. And I'll just wait till tonight and figure out where she's going, or where's she's gone."

"I told you she's going to Holland."

"I don't see how you can know that."

"I just do." Mr. Bill said edging the car into traffic.

"Why don't I trust you? Hmm, could it be the fake name you gave me back at the bar?"

"You have to trust me."

"You have to watch the road."

"I was nowhere near that guy."

"Holy crow! This street is busy."

"No shit, Nick. We're in the city."

"Thanks, pal. Why should I go with you anyhow?"

"If we take a flight, we can head her off at the pass, so to speak."

"I don't have any money, buddy. Not that you do, if you're stealing cheerleader's cars."

"All I'm saying is that we can stop the ambush if you know what I mean. And I think you know what I mean, partner."

"Partner? What's with the western slang?"

"I told you, she's in grave danger," Mr. Bill said as he swerved around a minivan.

"Why do I get the feeling that I'm just a pawn in all of this?"

"Because you *are* just a pawn."

4

Spider looked at the image on the digital camera and felt disappointed. The photo didn't do the billboard justice. There was something so primal and raw about Nick's paintings. Spider couldn't understand it, he didn't want to understand it. That was part of the mystery.

"So what are we going to do when we find him? Kidnap him?" Blockhead flipped through his phone. He waited for a long break in traffic to pull the Yugo out into the highway.

"No. I don't know," Spider said to Blockhead. "I guess I'll try to pin him down or something."

"Sounds good to me boss."

"Thanks."

Ahead the road warped to Boston, the long arms of the suburban wasteland reached out and pulled them in.

5

At the same time, Spider and his buds were winding their way around Boston, George, Abdullah, and Rufus the dog had rattled their way up the coast to Boston as well where George swore Lilly would be found. George didn't know how to explain it, he just knew it, like he knew that he loved Lilly.

Rufus sat between them. George didn't have the heart to make him stick it out in the back. It was too far a drive for old Rufus, and he wouldn't risk the dog's injury. Besides, it wasn't too bad having him in the cab. He was big, but he didn't smell. Abdullah sat on the far side of the dog, staring out the window at nowhere. His eyes, large saucers filled with the rushing light of the scenery and traffic zipping by. George would let him drive in the city, eventually. The big genie had handled I-95 without a problem. Ab had a knack for driving. Somewhere around New Jersey, Abdullah remarked that riding in a pick-up truck on the Interstate appeared to be one of the best things one could do in George's kingdom. This was especially true when George floored the accelerator.

"This thing here is like flying carpet, " Abdullah said, banging his hand hard against the side of the vehicle. "Only better." Abdullah looked over to George, "Music master, music!"

George turned on his CD player and blasted Johnny Cash's "The Man in Black".

6

Marina's head was going to pop. Her whole skull seemed softer to her as she held her head in her hands and prayed for the voice of the hag to cease. It was as if she was rotting on the inside out. Instinctively she knew it was the lack of saltwater that she desperately needed, though her thoughts wouldn't come together long enough for her to form a fully formed thought on the matter. She tossed herself side to side, her nails ripping at the wood underneath them. Her voice wailed out of her like a banshee and the sound of her voice slipped out the hole in the top/side of the box and floated up into the ceiling. It wasn't long before the crew up above heard the shrieking and began to talk of going down there and taking care of it.

The anger Marina felt diminished the voice of the hag. *There is power inside me still.* Yet, what could she do? Waiting was getting her nowhere.

On board, rumors flew of monsters and beasts, the illegal capture of silver-back gorillas, and chimpanzees, of a lion, of some circus, reject who had killed dozens in a violent outbreak and was trying to break out of the country. Marina never even heard the clink and chunk of the cargo locks as they were winched open by some stevedore's hand.

If Pembroke had been there, he would have remarked on the savagery of mobs, as six sailors entered the hold, carrying flashlights and tire irons. One man carried a machete used for cutting rope, while another carried a crucifix.

7

Mulch peered anxiously about the basement for Mr. Bill, but the basement lay empty.

"That's odd," Mulch said.

"What is it?" Sea Hag's hand touched Mulch's shoulder as she turned towards him.

"Bill's gone. He was down here just a few minutes ago."

"Hmm?" Sea Hag did not detect the icy cool of Mulch's voice, the iron-like quality of his pronunciation, each word carefully vocalized.

"Perhaps he's better, no?"

"Perhaps he's in Marina's room," Mulch said as he walked Sea Hag to the chamber entrance and gestured for her to come inside. He pointed to Marina's bed where her quilts and blankets lay in a heap. Mr. Bill had left them as they were. The open pool of creek water made gentle laps against the sides the tide continued to come in.

"This used to be her room, you know?"

"I always imagined it would be colder."

Mulch casually turned to Sea Hag and smiled, his teeth yellow, his eyes yellow.

"You don't suppose Ol' Bill fell in and drowned, do you?" Sea Hag said, wondering for a second if Mulch might not have been mistaken about Mr. Bill.

"Oh, I don't know, Haggy. Why don't *you* go in and find out?"

Something turned on in Sea Hag's mind. Mulch's aura flashed red, and Sea Hag steadied herself, digging her heels into the ground, feeling her weight settle, her muscles forming hard trunks to the earth. But she moved, Sea Hag stepped backward. She managed to bring her arms up and Mulch's fists connected with her forearm and pushed her back. She had surprised him with her response. He hadn't been expecting her to fight back. Her arms flew up defensively as Mulch's hands shot between her forearms and grappled for her throat.

There was no time for magic.

Mulch didn't scream, didn't wince, didn't whimper or make any noise as he forced his way into her space. She was strong, but not as strong as he. His hands slapped and backhanded her rough skin. He fought to reach her throat to wring it like a chicken neck.

"Get off me you animal!" Sea Hag managed.

Her jaw rocked as Mulch slammed a fist into her. It felt like someone had taken a ball-peen hammer to her face. As Mulch pushed himself on top of her, both of them fell backward to the floor. Mulch hammered at her skull. She pushed her hands up to protect her head and he batted them away. His fists came down on her nose with a series of sickening wet smacks. He'd broken it and blood spurted into Mulch's open mouth much to his delight, the coppery smell of fear and blood lust filled the air. Sea Hag felt her teeth loosen and break under Mulch's pummeling fists. He swung again and again feeling her teeth cut into his skin. He raged, pressing his knees into her breasts, feeling her ribs snap under his weight.

Sea Hag's vision blurred and the words to a protective spell would not form in her throat. She flung her hands in front of her face hoping to block Mulch. For if she could speak, she could get away. But her mouth was already filled with teeth, and they tumbled down into her esophagus. As Mulch's fists came down on her, she labored to breathe.

With one hand Mulch grabbed Sea Hag by the neck, cutting off oxygen as he punched her across the face with the other. Sea Hag had little choice, either she pries his thick fingers away from her throat or blocks the punches to her face; she couldn't do both.

Mulch's fists came down repeatedly, splitting Sea Hag's lip and nose. Her eyes swelled shut and her breath became short. Sea Hag saw the stars and pinpricks of light before unconsciousness took her over. And as she went under, she thought that she might wake up again and that nothing was lost. But Mulch continued to punch her face until all that was left was a mass of twisted and swollen tissue. It took him several minutes to realize he'd cracked the back of her skull. It had shattered like a hard-boiled egg. He then mindlessly scrubbed his hands under the creek water in Marina's pool, the smell of blood hanging in the air like a kind of fog.

After the sun went down, he drove her body over to the tomato fields. He dug a long trench five feet deep alongside a tomato row twenty paces from the access road. The moon rose and made shadows across the field as Mulch finished his work.

Now there was only Mr. Bill left.

8

If Virginia had seen Doppelgänger Bill, she would have said that he looked like a cisgender person's idea of a drag queen on crack. His bra hung half-out of his blouse and his purple panties were on top of his pantyhose, which was visible under the nightgown he'd chosen to wear. Furthermore, they were Virginia's clothes, which were more feminine than Maria's, but smaller which made him look ungainly, the elastic cutting into his skin, his skin pressing into the fabric that wasn't designed to shape a man's body. Something in Doppelgänger Bill's brain had told him to change, to disguise himself. And of course, he hadn't looked in the mirror when he high-tailed it out of the house, wearing mismatching pumps, his nightgown trailing behind him like a bridal train.

Also, he didn't know how to drive, but his mushy brain recognized the steering wheel and the pedals and generally what they were used for. He wasted no time leaping into Sea Hag's truck, the keys dangling from the wheel like an invitation.

9

As Mulch climbed the stairs and re-entered the light, he heard the rumbling of Sea Hag's truck. In his mind's eye, he saw Mr. Bill at the wheel. Mulch leaped and hopped towards the front door, his hands swatting at the knob. He opened it just in time to see the truck tailing away, gravel and dust rising behind like some kind of plume. He shouted and screamed as he stepped off the porch and into the yard. The blood lust flooding his system, he ran after Mr. Bill, screaming and pumping his hands in the air.

10

"Before Pembroke came to me that evening, I never really knew what it was like to give oneself up to another, not for love, but something else. To give one's body to another, as a gift. I have to say that Pembroke gave me that, at least. Do you understand, Doc?

"He opened the coffin and helped me out, the fog making my skin cold. As I shrank away from it, it hissed and followed, whispering rude remarks in my ears about my nipples as I walked. I felt Pembroke's breath lap my skin. He held my hands behind me and led me out of the room and down the hall, my senses reeling in the blackness. He whispered that I had been inside the coffin for forty-eight hours. It hadn't felt like forty-eight hours. As he whispered, he touched my breasts, my ass, my body as if it were his. His energy was incredible. Not his sexual drive, his heat. I realized he was drawn to my scent, that of fear, but not just fear, either. My body had started to turn sour in the box. He fed on me, my energy, my essence, my spirit.

"I didn't so much walk as float on top of the fog. The fog carried me like I was on a treadmill in an airport. It was the fog, that ever-present fog, that was licking my skin. Pembroke's erection hummed through his pants as he pressed into me.

"Now let me make this clear. I was freaking out, but not how I thought I would. I had expected panic, you know, like how people in the movies act when the killer's got them by the hair and all. But I felt, I don't know, numb, already dead. Partially it was that goddamn head-box he'd clamped on top of me. Part of it was shocking, I guess. Now, I was being taken out to be played with, before probably going back in the coffin, for god-knows how long.

"Pembroke laid me gently on the bed and removed my clothing. Somehow, I found myself handcuffed to the far posts, my legs tied back, naked and open. I don't remember having been handcuffed or tied up.

"Pembroke's fingers fluttered above my skin like that of a hummingbird's wings over a flower. He whispered to me. Nothing about love, or lust, but my skin and my hair. He kissed me once, on the mouth. Then came the sound of the winch.

"He'd gotten an old farm winch from some antique store and mounted it to a bed. He told me so in hushed tones. The winch raised my handcuffed limbs so that I was lifted partly into the air to allow for maximum access – total Marquis de Sade move. And remember, I'm still in my head-box with leather and buckles and shit.

"My body, deprived of primary stimuli for so long, reacted in ways that I didn't expect when given sexual stimuli. Fueled by fear, I found myself aroused when he began to explore me.

"His penis rubbed my clitoris for a long time, allowing my fear to run off into even more arousal. I tried not to respond. Then he fucked me. After he was done, he left me to hang up there for what seemed like hours before putting me back in the coffin, cold and numb.

"Surprised as you may be, I wasn't angry, I was resolved. I promised that I was going to live and I was going to burn his world to the ground, all of it."

11

Pembroke stared at Virginia as she hung like a slab of meat on his winch. He was pretty sure she had fallen asleep. Her breathing had slowed, and her body had not twitched since he came. He remained naked, as she was, and thought about making love to her again. She possessed a strong, young, responsive body. The plan was to take her down and place her back in the coffin for another few days before taking her out again. Already her body and the coffin shared the sour stench of her voided bowels. It would grow worse. She didn't seem to notice.

He would repeat these steps, again and again, varying the "punishment" or "behavioral stimulant," as he called them, each time he took her out. Next time it would be pain.

The fog whispered at his feet. "Let us inside, again." It wanted to slip inside her like gas and fill her mouth with obscenities. "We can make her like a machine," it promised.

He waved the fog off, *perhaps next time.*

The fog liked that idea, it whispered and coiled and curled and thickened. How lucky Pembroke was to be the host of such a being. When he left Virginia, the fog followed, almost like a dog.

CHAPTER FIVE

1

When Captain John Smith first looked up at the seven-foot-tall Indians of the Nassawattucks tribe he nearly wet his pants. Some of his men wrote home that he did in fact wet his pants, and it even made it into a particularly nasty tabloid back in London, much to his chagrin. At the time Captain Smith didn't believe his eyes and stood there rubbing them as the giants moved and spoke, staring back. There were four of them, each of them naked, save for a long loincloth and moccasins. Their longbows were as tall as Captain Smith's men and had been jabbed defiantly into the sand. The largest Indian, the one who seemed to be the leader, for he stood before the rest, ground the end of his bow into the sand as if he were not happy to see them.

"Hakum," the Indian's voice, deep and rich, shook Smith out of his trance.

"Um, pardon?" Smith replied in imperfect French.

"Hakum," the Indian repeated.

"God di gen to you sir," Smith said in the Queen's English.

The Indian did not reply but licked his upper lip.

"Um. Hmm," Smith mumbled, estimating that the Indians were at least three heads taller than the average man, himself not included.

One of Smith's men nudged his way out of the boat. He coughed and spat white sputum and wiped it on his jacket. "The savage doesn't speak English, Sirrah."

Smith curled his upper lip with distaste, "Of course not. I know that. Sir Walter Raleigh briefed me about just such things before he was locked in the Tower."

"I only wanted to reiterate that these Indians most likely do not belong to the Powhatan tribe," The man continued. "They are likely a competing tribe."

"Aren't they all the same?" *Powhatan tribe, indeed,* Captain Smith thought.

"No, Captain."

"Of course, they aren't all the same. Do you think I'm that stupid?" Smith's raised voice hardly registered with the Indians who were both admiring and contemplating the restrictive clothing of the pale-faced men. They, of course, had heard of the pale faces from various sources. Some trading farther south had told of a rumor concerning white people trying to settle one of the more remote and desolate coastal landings.

"Pardon me, Sirrah. Just trying to help," the man said as he spat up a large thumb-sized clot of black mucus.

"Get your humors in line, man!" Captain Smith sneered. He turned to the tallest Indian, "I am Captain John Smith, of the Jamestown colony, founder and leader, ambassador to this new world, sent by the Queen of England herself."

Again, the natives didn't seem impressed. The shortest one, only by inches, scratched his rear.

Captain Smith turned to his men, "They don't seem to be paying attention."

"Perhaps they have met with the Dutch privateer, your arch-nemesis, Jon Van...?"

"I told you not to utter that vile name in my presence! Ever. You scurvy knave," Smith growled as he swiped his glove at the man. "Keep your dirty, stinking, filthy head shut."

When Smith turned his gaze back to the natives, they were moving away from them in a single file. The largest one, the possible leader, had already ducked under a heavy canopy of pine trees.

2

Chief Debedeavon welcomed the English with open arms. Captain John Smith and his weary, malaria-infected (but not yet too ill) men were the first white men the chief had seen. The rumors of them had spread throughout his lands. He didn't see them as much of a threat. They were so small for one thing and didn't seem to be too bright. They could barely walk when he met them, and they seemed a bit befuddled.

Unbeknownst to Captain John Smith, his archrival Jon de van Hazen had sailed his massive Dutch ship, *The Blessed Mermaid,* into Onancock Creek, about three miles from Debedeavon's main settlement on the Chessenessex River. It took the resourceful Dutch pirate less than twenty hours to scout out both Debedeavon's location, and John Smith's camp. Jon had a nose for trouble. He also had an uncanny sense of where Captain John Smith was at all times, anywhere in the world. If Smith was in Paris for trade goods, Jon was there to foil the buy. Were Smith to sail to Ireland, Jon would manage to sneak aboard and poison the drinking water. Jon lived to torment Smith and when he found out that Smith was leading the newest English colony to the New World, he set out to destroy Smith once and for all.

Jon's plan was simple, besides setting up camps to raid the natives, he planned to masquerade as English settlers and trade with the Indians, and doubly take from the natives, give the English a bad name, and perhaps start a war.

Debedeavon couldn't tell one white man from another. Plus, Jon had the uncanny ability to mimic Smith's haughty mannerisms, a trait Jon thought all pirates should possess - mimicry. His Smith always got the crew roaring with laughter. He thought his Smith impression was so accurate that if it ever came to it he'd kill Smith, take over from him, and no one would be none the wiser, a thought he'd entertained more than once.

Jon watched the smoke rise from the roof holes in Debedeavon's wigwams throughout the night. Around those very fires, Smith had negotiated his first trade. He'd wait a few days and then appear in the creek, with his crew, and Jon would go into the village after the Englishman had left and pretended he was Smith. *This could work, Jon thought.* He grinned and rubbed his carefully shaped van dyke as a plan formed in his head.

3

Inside the coffin, the headbox securely fastened, Virginia drifted in and out of sleep. Sleep had become her only friend, for there simply was nothing else for her to do but wait and try to keep her mind from eating itself. The only distraction proved to be the fireflies. At first, the smell of her urine and feces made her want to vomit, but she didn't think she'd be able to survive if she threw up, so she had forced herself to get used to it. Instead, she watched the fireflies as they skirted and skidded along the inside of the leather of the headbox. *Slick baby leather,* she thought.

Sometimes strange thoughts would invade her thinking. Virginia thought her head was shrinking, disappearing into space the fireflies flittered off to. Her hair lay back against her skull in oily patches. With nothing to distract her Virginia was painfully aware of every bodily secretion, which sometimes led her to believe that her head is the size of a small pin, the way the fireflies danced and turned and spun around her.

Worst of all, she knew the fireflies weren't real. The sounds they made in the dark weren't real either, their high-pitched squeals or their whispers, little iron fillings of whisper that she couldn't make out. For a while she had imagined that her face was scored with lines, like a haphazard landing strip, the way they came at her, burning her skin as they skimmed her flesh. But the pain did not linger like a burn. After a while, she didn't feel them anymore. *It's just that you've been broke for some time and just didn't know it,* she thought. *Your senses are all screwed up. Pembroke walked between two worlds. If he had conjured the fog, why not the fireflies?*

Because…

Because…

Just stop it, Virginia. There's no thinking your way out of inaction, right? She felt so small as if she could fit into the palm of Pembroke's hand. The feeling of being small stayed with her even in her dreams. Twice she'd had the same dream of riding a brown effulgence of mud, like a small pea on top of a log. The other night she couldn't help but feel that she was a small bean on the seat of a swing that someone had pushed high into the air. The feeling in the dreams was one of horror, of not being in control.

Time stretched into taffy and stuck to every thought she had. Eventually, she began to see that every time Pembroke opened the coffin, the fireflies went beserk, moving at dizzying speeds about her head. Pembroke would open the coffin randomly, to fuck with her senses, molest her, let the fog have its way, or just stare at her, breathing over her body to watch her stir. The fireflies would explode into fireworks and Virginia would find herself mesmerized by them. *He doesn't realize they are harmless,* she thought. *Just another mind game. But they aren't useless either, are they?*

Once during a long stretch of misery when Virginia could only breathe through her mouth to keep from gagging on her stench, Pembroke had opened the coffin to inject more hallucinogens into her veins, and the fireflies buzzed and hummed and shot up and down the headbox *before* Pembroke had injected her. *The fireflies become active when he's around. I can use this, can't I?* And Virginia's mind answered her, in the voice of Mr. Bill, *yes dear, use this to escape.*

4

Things had pretty much been turned inside out as far as George was concerned since Nick had started to paint in his sleep, Lilly had started to glow, and Abdullah had popped out of a paint can. Still, he felt restless. Was it Nick's absence? Or Lilly's? He did not know.

Since climbing into the cab of his pickup truck and gunning it onto the highway towards some unknown future, his new dog by his side, his new genie friend crammed into the seat next to him, a genie so large that his shoulders filled the back window, as in eclipsed the whole of the back window so that someone looking from behind would only see the large and incredible back of some enormous blue man, George's interior monologue sounded a lot like Sal Paradise from *On the Road*, the only book George had ever read all the way through without really stopping, on a single Saturday, on the dock, and then later in his bedroom, drinking cherry Cokes and smoking cigarettes. George had been 18 then and his girlfriend had been an older and wiser 20, freshly home from college, with George young and robust and full of the jack that made Sally go. Sally had fed him poetry, which he had hated, and old man Marx, which he hated, but she had turned George on to the Beats, which he enjoyed, which in turn had turned George on to painting again. And though he'd taken all the art classes in high school and even won a few student varsity poster contests, he'd never once painted for fun, for himself. That summer he found himself itching to drive Sally across the country, painting her in the nude standing out front of every whistle-stop cafe they came across.

And now that old feeling was present again – restlessness – a feeling of being a part of a larger unseen. Outside his window, highways whizzed by.

"Master George?"

George hummed and drummed his fingers on the wheel.

"Master George?"

"What?"

"I believe this large and hairy dog has chewed another hole into master's seat.

"Great."

"Being sarcastic, master?" Ab looked at him with a smile that was halfway between a frown and a scowl.

"Yes!" George said high-fiving Ab over top of Rufus, who had a piece of stuffing between his forepaw and his mouth.

"I am learning. Your tone gave it away."

"Yes! When you say something that means something, but the way you say, as in the way you form the plosives, fricatives, etc, changes the meaning of what you say into something else, usually the opposite."

"I see."

"Good."

"How was that?"

"How was what?"

"My sarcasm."

"What were you being sarcastic about?"

"Just then, master. I say I see, but I don't see. Abdullah has his eyes closed."

"That's not sarcasm."

"Look master, a flying steel truck has crashed."

"Looks like we're lucky that they've moved the accident out of the road."

"Someone's master was not as skillful and direct and strong as master George and his flying steel truck."

"It's not that hard. You've driven it."

"Abdullah had master by his side, showing Abdullah all the tricks of steel flying cow."

"It's a cow now?"

"Yes, master. Abdullah just remembered what flying steel truck reminded Abdullah of."

"Cows?"

"Yes. Cows. Because they eat a lot and produce noxious gas."

"What are you doing?" George asked, one eye on the road and one eye on Abdullah as he stuck his arm out the window.

"I am, how you say, cutting wheat?"

"What?"

Rufus whined.

"Abdullah imagines his big arm is a great knife cutting away all the ugliness of New Jersey."

George nodded, "Oh."

Abdullah smiled, his big teeth gleaming in the hot sun pouring through the windshield.

"I used to do that too, as a kid."

"Make knife?"

"Yes, make the knife," George passed the slow-moving Cadillac in front of them. "When I was a kid, I used to imagine my hand was like a giant sickle...."

"Sickle? Master, were you ill?"

"What? No. A sickle is a kind of blade. On a stick. To cut wheat."

"I see now."

"Are you being sarcastic?"

"Yes, master. Abdullah is a sarcastic fellow."

Rufus groaned below them.

Abdullah looked out the window, his giant arm limp against the side of the cab. George heard the genie knocking it against the side of the truck door.

"Master, what's going to happen in Bos Ton?"

"Why did you ask that?" George asked as he scanned Ab's profile. He couldn't read an expression. "Why do you ask that Ab?"

"I do not know, master. Abdullah only knows that it feels uneasy ahead, uneasy and sad. Abdullah feels in his very round and empty belly that Nick and Lilly move towards the same place."

"Is it a bad place?"

Ab didn't say anything at first.

"Abdullah does not know," he finally said, though George had already formed thoughts of his own on the matter.

5

Doppelgänger Bill gunned Sea Hag's truck into the glow of the coming sunset. He kept to the center of the road, for as far as his brain knew, the center was the best place to be. Everyone could see you coming if you were in the center. The first car he came across was Selma Titterberry's old brown Buick. Selma, at the wheel, her old lady hat perched atop her thinning beehive of a hairdo had just left Johnsontown Church's Quilt meeting and was coming home to make herself tea and continue reading that steamy novel she had hidden under her pillow. She drove no faster than forty miles an hour and when Doppelgänger Bill barreled down towards her, she didn't panic. She couldn't see the truck too well either, but on narrow crowned country roads, where one must drive to the side, and one leans to the far left or right depending on which way one was coming, people didn't move out of the way until the last minute, or so Selma Titterberry thought and believed. So, when Doppelgänger Bill was seconds from colliding with her car, she was forced to jerk a little to the side, and her car went headfirst into the drainage ditch, her hat, and her neck jerking forward as she came to a sudden stop.

She cussed him right good for an old lady. Selma had to wait a good thirty minutes before Leroy Kellam came around the bend. Fortunately for Doppelgänger Bill, Selma hadn't gotten the license plate.

But Susan Park had. Doppelgänger Bill had run over her son's bigwheel. Stanley Park, a brat if there ever was one, loved his Big Wheel and refused to change up to a bicycle when he was big enough to do so; bikes didn't have the skid brake that caused the Big Wheel to turn itself around, just like the cop cars on TV. Doppelgänger Bill was roaring down Seaside Road and had turned up rural route 234 just as Stanley leaped off his Big Wheel, TV action style, into the ditch, where he popped up and fired his cap pistols at his younger brother who was hiding behind a camellia bush three feet away. Stanley didn't see the truck but heard his Big Wheel crunch under the wheels of the truck as the truck roared past. Bits of ripped and torn plastic hung off the Big Wheel like skin flaps.

Susan had been watering her flowers out by the mailbox. And she thought the truck was going a little too fast. *A little too fast for this time of day, that was for sure.* Always good in school, but never good in love, Susan remembered the series of numbers and committed them to her long-term memory.

Northampton County Sheriff's Department had been swamped since Sheriff North joined the great police academy in the sky. There had been quite a few accidental deaths over the last few weeks, all of them suspicious. The victims all were suspects in the local drug trade, something Sheriff North had been investigating for two years, something Deputy Bird had investigated himself when he served as the school resource officer at the local high school. That day Deputy Bird had stayed late to check over some files. He had a nagging headache from reviewing paperwork and was down to his last aspirin when Susan called. When Susan called, it was usually just a distraction, *a pleasant distraction.* Besides he needed the drive, it would clear his head.

Turns out the truck was registered to Sea Hag. *Now ain't that something.* Oh, he'd heard of Sea Hag, but didn't think that was her real name. It was a suspicious name at that. *But hey, if you could be named Mulch Hayes, then you could be named Sea Hag.* Lord knows enough odd names were floating around the shore to keep a sociologist busy for years.

Bird's wife had assured him he was the first runner up for Sheriff. The Board of Supervisors was calling an emergency meeting this week and he had been invited to attend. All this ran through his mind as he logged out on the call sheet and wrote investigating speeding incident Rte. 234. He didn't expect it to be too long.

And when he started up his car engine to drive over to get a statement, Sea Hag's truck blasted by him, going at least eighty miles an hour, weaving all over the road like a drunk on Saturday night.

Deputy Bird had chased down the occasional teen speeder. They never put up much of a run because they knew their parents would have their hides. But this Sea Hag, he'd never met her, pushed the metal like a bat out of hell.

The truck turned onto the highway and nearly missed a tractor-trailer. Deputy Bird called in the State boys, and they radioed that they'd try to head her off near Cape James. Meanwhile, he waited for his cruiser to catch up.

6

Doppelgänger Bill saw the flashing lights in his rear-view and they delighted him. He assumed that others had joined him in his travels and wanted to play. When the second car joined in behind Deputy Bird's patrol car, Bill let his hand dangle out the window where his hand started billowing smoke. Doppelgänger Bill's magical abilities were limited, this was because his brain was inside out, but he had magical abilities all the same. From his fingers came a purplish and brown smoke which stank worse than it clouded and soon Deputy Bird and the state trooper found themselves inhaling a foul and putrid odor that billowed along the road and into their open vents.

7

"Are we going to fly?" Nick asked as he stared at Logan Airport as it stretched beyond his sight. Patrolling the lot were heavily armed security guards with machine guns and large German Shepards.

"You don't pay attention, do you?" Mr. Bill snorted.

"Well Guinness, I do know one thing and that is I can't wait until you have to show your driver's license, seeing that I don't think that's your real name if you haven't figured that out by now."

"There are stranger names in the world."

"You're right about that."

They parked, Mr. Bill paying little attention to where he parked his stolen car. He made sure to leave the keys in the floorboards in the hopes that someone else might steal the car a second time. Nick followed Mr. Bill across the lot to the elevators.

"Do you think they'll think it's weird that I don't have any luggage?" Nick asked.

Bill didn't say anything.

"I mean, I would. Especially since we have to go through customs, and all. I mean I would take one good look at my raggedy shoes, pants, my torn shirt, not to mention my sunburn and greasy hair. I do need to shower, don't I? Don't answer that. I would take one good look at me and think *t-r-o-u-b-l-e*."

"You'll be fine."

"I'm glad you think so. And don't forget you're not so clean-cut looking yourself."

Mr. Bill shot him a look.

"That's the same look my last girlfriend gave me all the time, I mean all the time."

Mr. Bill hit the down button on the parking lot elevator and turned to Nick. He sighed before he spoke and pulled Nick close, "Listen, you will find peace."

"Yeah?"

Mr. Bill snickered. "Nah, probably not. Now follow me and just shut up already."

8

Mr. Bill, having spent the last three hours with Nick Adams, after following Nick Adams from Providence, Rhode Island to Boston, Massachusetts, knew nothing more about Nick's intentions with Marina than he did before. Plus, he had no idea what he was going to do about Marina and Nick, especially Marina. *She's reaching out for Nick, but why? Marina had been out of the house only a handful of times and always with a chaperone. Why had she not reached out to Virginia? Could Marina sense that Virginia was in danger herself? If Marina was that powerful, then Cilia would have her hands full. That is if Marina survived the trans-Atlantic voyage.*

Now Mr. Bill had to concentrate to maintain the illusions. Mr. Bill always got a thrill out of masking his appearance. It was simple, really, the human brain functioned on chemicals and electricity and all it took was the well-placed bio-electrical charge to make the entire KLM desk and waiting passengers perceive Bill and Nick as well-dressed businessmen, and that Nick's phone card he'd just handed her was an American Express Platinum Card to pay for their flight reservation. All it took was a touch for Mr. Bill to send ripples of energy through the computer system, rewiring whatever Mr. Bill liked, all the while Nick watched in amazement as Mr. Bill booked them passage to the Netherlands.

9

Pembroke ordered the fog to carry Virginia, out of the coffin, tied and naked, and down into the basement. Virginia's skin broke out in gooseflesh when the fog wrapped its cold limbs around her thighs, chest, and sex, whispering nothings into her ear as she was lifted and transported below ground. Today he planned on experimenting with pain. By now the head-box would be causing severe sensory deprivation. *Time to capitalize on darkness,* he thought.

Earlier, Pembroke had laid out the electrodes he was going to attach to her nipples, crotch, her middle and pinkie fingers, her big and small toe, and belly button. His favorite was the belly button electrode and the way the electricity buzzed inside of you just like when you were cut from the womb; it made his skin jump with excitement. Apply enough electricity down there and the victim's bones threatened to leap from its skin, which was exactly what he wanted from his heir. Cilia had the mermaid to suckle on and chew. He supposed by the end of this all, Cilia would be much more powerful than she was now. But Cilia couldn't get pregnant. Cilia's body would kill the baby. Besides, even with her magic, she was getting to be too old now to bear children. But Virginia, Virginia was young enough and so far she had proved herself to be pliable enough. Give her time and she would be as twisted as he was.

10

"Doc, I grew up thinking I wasn't so special. See, what you don't know about me is how I got mixed up with that crowd in high school, and how I kinda drugged myself into a stupor most of the time. First of all, where was my mother? That was the first thing I blocked out – Mom – like not having one, which gave me that weird spiritual pain that must be like not having a limb or something. Sometimes I'd imagine that she was alive somewhere like Omaha, working in a Walmart, or perhaps married to a banker, or even a banker herself. Sometimes I'd imagine that she'd come for me under a black balloon, silent and in the dead of night. She'd have flowers in her hair and take me with her to somewhere better. Most of the time though, I imagined her dead, it was easier that way.

"Sometimes I'd block out Marina too, just forget her. She didn't think about me too much, either. I just didn't show up on her radar. I love her though, don't get me wrong. It's just that she had her mermaid thing, and I wasn't a part of it. So instead, I fell into that crowd.

"At first it was cheap beers for the boys, wine coolers, and fruity drinks for the girls. Then it was pot. And then sex. Then acid and shrooms and XTC – pills of all colors, shapes, and sizes that we could get a hold of it. I'm talking like I'm around 15 here. 15 and horny and completely off my rocker in terms of what I thought I knew – of what was important – drugs and reckless abandonment. Thing is, trouble is fun, for a while, and then it just becomes trouble.

"Doc, if I had paid attention, if I had not been so self-centered to the extreme, I might have anticipated my father's actions. I might have had the independence to move away and do something meaningful with my life, something that did not involve my family. Instead, I wrapped my family's privilege around me like a blanket and abused it, and with my friends by my side it allowed me to forget the mother I had lost.

"Now? No one knows who I am anymore. I'm free in ways I cannot even articulate."

11

"I've never been on an airplane before," Nick blinked as he took in the stale smell of the cabin and the tepid colors of first class. The stewardess regarded him with an indifferent smile. They'd been waiting for nearly seven hours, sitting, napping, magically scamming drinks and snacks from overpriced private vendors. Finally, they had boarded the plane, sometime after ten PM. "I'm impressed. How did you do it?"

"Old Jedi mind trick."

"Yeah, good one. Hey, how many Viet Nam vets does it take to change a light bulb?"

"Oh, I don't know."

"That's right man because you weren't there."

Mr. Bill looked at Nick with annoyance.

"Oh come on. That's kinda funny."

"Not to a vet," Mr. Bill sighed and flipped through the complimentary magazine, looking around for the stewardess. He wanted an aspirin. His head was going to be raging before they got to Amsterdam. Especially if first-class filled up, which he assumed it would. Mr. Bill supposed he didn't have to mask their appearance for the whole trip. The damage had already been done at the front counter.

Mr. Bill looked over at his companion and wondered how Nick got involved in this mess. Marina had some physical connection with Nick, a serious physical connection from what it sounded like. He saw that she was eating through him, insomuch as Mr. Bill could almost see Marina's eyes floating behind Nick's.

"Sometimes I get the craving to jump in the creek," Nick said absentmindedly.

"Which one?" Mr. Bill had found Nick's spaciness and his proneness to wander conversationally both endearing and frustrating. Nick gave up far more information when he wasn't pressed.

"Nassawadox creek, weird name, right?"

"You have no idea, Nick."

"Though I did leapfrog and drag myself into the Bay a few weeks ago. "

"Really?"

"I had this horrible craving, and I went and stuffed myself at Sea Hags and had some sort of episode there."

"Episode?" Bill leaned across first-class seats' expansive and comfortable leather chairs to get a clear view of Nick's face. Other first-class passengers were already eating their snacks, listening to the airplane's radio, watching recorded movies or television programs or business self-help programs. No one paid them any mind, except the ragged KLM travelers squeezing through on their way to coach.

"Yeah, I started throwing up. I puked all over my shoes and Sea Hag freaked out. She threw me in my car, and she started driving. I don't remember much, but I wanted to go to the water. I wanted to be in the water. You know, like it was a womb or something."

"Go on."

"Somehow we ended up at the beach, down on Mulch Hayes' property."

"Really? What a name."

"Anyway, I ended up crawling on my hands and knees like some freak towards the water. I caught a fish with my teeth."

"Did you now?"

"Yes, and say Guinness, do you know the Eastern Shore?"

"Um no. The Eastern what?"

"I thought I saw some recognition in those eyes of yours."

"What? No. That was a dust mote."

"Anyways, I caught this fish and she said she saw two pairs of eyes floating in my skull."

"You don't say?"

"My memory is kinda screwed up lately."

"Do tell, Nick."

"Well, I can only remember very recent events, things that happened since I started. Well since I started painting in my sleep."

"In your sleep? Painting?"

"Yes."

"I guess that explains how I found you."

"How you found me?"

"On the interstate, the billboard. It was quite a picture. Now tell me everything, from the beginning, and don't leave out a single detail."

CHAPTER SIX

1

Kego-tok had kept a close eye on his son since the English showed up. The English had a way of appearing when they wanted. The English would come at the most inconvenient times, sometimes twice in the same week. Sometimes two very different men with the same name would come to trade. Kiptocreek and Kego-tok had spent hours discussing the possibilities. The English often acted odd and shifty, their words not matching what their eyes and hearts said. They couldn't be trusted and looked to the women and children with wild hatred in their eyes, or lust, which was worse. Kiptocreek, alarmed, had taken to have the white men trailed. Kego-tok had pleaded with Debedeavon to cease all trade, but Debedeavon would have none of it.

Lately, too much emphasis was being placed on pleasing the white travelers. Kego-tok looked down at his son and tried to imagine him in a land full of white men, he could not – this was his son's land, and would always be so. His young son was not yet named, though many of the whites called him William.

Dan-ger, his stomach grumbled. *If only I knew where danger came from,* he thought. His stomach murmured, *all around. Indeed,* Kego-tok thought.

Kego-tok looked over his son whittling a chunk of wood with a sharpened river stone. He looked across to the gardens, his wife and her friends gathered the last of the spring squash. *Massawa,* he thought. *I share your worry.* Since the colonists had begun to arrive in dribbles and drab, his wife's heart had been heavy. Her night terrors woke him, and so far he had been no comfort. Her dreams consumed her. A great winged buzzard feasting on her corpse. Sometimes on their son's corpse, she dreamed of the death of the nation. *Promise me you will keep our son from the whites,* she had begged him weeks before. *Promise me.*

Kego-tok looked to his son. "Say it again," Kego-tok said curtly.

He stopped whittling and rolled his eyes, "Father!"

"Say it."

"I promise I will not follow the whites to their ship."

"Good," Kego-tok said as he patted the boy's head and smiled. "Run along."

"But I want to watch you."

"Run along."

The boy, who was almost a man, left, his cheeks flaring as he exited the wigwam. In the last year, the boy had grown a great deal. He had survived the bought of sickness that followed the white men like smoke – scores had died already. Rumors in the northern area of the nation spoke of more white men spreading out like a sunset. The Laughing King refused to oust them. Many griped that the nation had gotten lazy trading with the settlers whose numbers grew season by season. Behind him, his wife rose from her bedding. She crossed over to Kego-tok, kissed him on the cheek as she went out into another hot morning.

2

The fog had always been and would always be. It snaked through the forest and brake and came into trees as night comes into the sky. The fog's legion mind grouped and split and reformed. Fog slipped like snakes into the skinny creek run-offs, sliding onto the water's surface, and then it slid off the water's surface and followed the great herd. Sometimes it slipped along the water and traveled across the water, wending where it willed as it had when it followed Virginia Hayes to Richmond.

When Pembroke moved into the house on Monument Avenue in Richmond, VA, USA, the fog had already been there. Almost, as if it had been waiting for him. Sometimes, the fog would leave the house on Monument and Pembroke didn't know where it went, only that when it left it would leave a fine sheen of ice on the floor and baseboards. It would return, eventually, and hiss and ooze. It seemed that this fog had formed an unseemly attachment to Virginia, a vaguely sexual attachment, which for the fog meant that it was forever lifting a foggy tentacle to fondle her breast or wrap its cool damp arm up and under her sex. When the fog did this Virginia would bat it away with her hands when they weren't tied back. But since they were almost always tied back, the fog had a virtual field day with its unauthorized gropes whenever it did return hungry for her flesh.

Mr. Bill would have recognized it at once. He would have said that the fog sought Virginia because the fog wanted revenge, that it smelled her Hayes blood.

3

Marina tried fighting the thirst by ignoring it, which made it worse. She made a list in her mind of things to think about, to distract her from thinking about water.

Think about fruit and wildflowers and how they tend to bend forward when heavy with rain like the old man I saw once on television.

Think about Christmas and why in the winter the cold crisp air makes the lights twinkle like they never do in the summertime.

Think about how in the summertime the same Christmas lights look fat and pregnant and ready to pop, so heavy with light and airy dew that they hang lower than they do in the winter.

Think about how in the spring the water takes on a heavy pollen smell and the fish come up to eat more often and how their eyes look like watery balls of silver when they do.

Marina tossed and turned, unaware of the growing number of men gathering outside her box.

Captain Van Dijk however was aware of the growing anger among the crew. The ship plowed ahead at full speed, the weather cooperating, at least for now, even though meteorologists had begun to notice the seeds of a huge storm beginning to form in the Atlantic.

It did not help that whatever was in the box had killed Hector. Using the hold cameras Van Dijk focused on Hector's face, powerless as he bled out in the hold.

4

Mulch Hayes' fields lay meticulously straight and neat and each day the head migrant foreman, who that summer happened to be one Ediostro Huerta, walked the perimeter of each field and maintained the ruler-straight look that Mulch preferred. It took Ediostro about three hours to do this each morning, and he often started at four AM, so he could be in the fields by seven. Sometimes he split the shift with Loco, sometimes with Renato, each of them walking the perimeter of the field with a sharp stick or weed whacker, cutting back the weeds that grew out like forever from whatever plant had been seeded there. It wasn't a bad job, it was a tedious one, and Ediostro liked to hum and sing a little. He did this for three summers straight and into the fall when the cotton started coming in – singing and humming and whacking the fields into shape. Sometimes Mulch, seeking solitude, would find that solitude walking with Ediostro along the green edge of the fields, smoking cigarettes together and exchanging a few words about the weather. Mulch liked walking with Ediostro because Ediostro didn't like to speak. He liked to sing and the crows and blackbirds and even the noisy seagulls followed his pipes like children, from field to field. Once, as Mulch followed Ediostro along the tomato fields, the plants sprouting over the red plastic that made the tomatoes blow up into huge juicy tomatoes, even when picked green, a large blackbird landed on Ediostro's shoulder and knocked the top of its skull against Ediostro's ear. Ediostro changed tunes and the bird flew off, but not before Mulch's brain recalled the muscled feathered birds that had terrorized him one late fall morning during a hurricane long ago. For a second, he thought death was coming for him and when Mulch asked Ediostro why he changed his tune, he replied in his Mexican drawl that reminded Mulch of westerns and Saturday afternoons bijou flicks, "It was a request." Ediostro didn't mind it when Mulch came along. He wasn't afraid of the boss, he'd worked for worse, and by the time Ediostro came to be the foreman of Hayes Farms, Mulch had already settled on getting rid of everything he owned, because everything he owned was tainted and impure.

When Mulch wasn't with Ediostro, the birds, purple martins and grackles, crows, and even starlings, followed more closely, sometimes on the ground, and Ediostro made sure his voice was aimed at the ground and that the birds hopping and kicking along in front of him and beside him would hear the tune he sang, hummed, and whistled. Sometimes the birds told him secrets – nothing earth-shattering, Ediostro will tell you, but secrets nevertheless. Like how a sudden downpour of rain was going to wash out part of the field, where the field sloped just slightly, or how the corn was going to be very sweet this year. Only once did the birds tell him anything mysterious. It happened to be a lark sparrow and not the usual blackbirds, or seagulls, or robins, but a little sparrow who seemed breathless to Ediostro when it said to him the Ugly Mother would leave and never return. Ediostro forgot about it until two weeks later when someone told him that the Ugly Mother had died in Boston, MA, USA in Loco's aunt's house, on the couch, after having some kind of terrible fit.

5

Lilly spent the first few hours of her time in Metro Boston looking out the window. She had never spent any time in an American city before unless you counted VA Beach, which is more like one giant suburb sprawled out over a low-lying swamp. And it's not like Lilly's discounting Mexico City, well not completely anyway, only she had only ever been in a few boroughs of Mexico City, which sprawled away from the old lake and into environs beyond. Mexico City wasn't *her* city. *All one needs*, she thought, *is a window and a street to look down upon. I miss my apartment.* For a second she thought of calling to Hammer N' Nails to see how things were. But she didn't. Work would be waiting for her when she finished. *You might like city living, but you couldn't stay here*, Lilly thought. She looked back towards the main part of the apartment.

Loco's relatives were not nice. *Not like Loco at all*, she thought. The Ugly Mother's visage was being whispered about behind her back. Lilly and Loco were used to it by now, the Ugly Mother's bizarre face. Loco's aunt's kids, 14 and 12, Estrella and Consuelo stared at the Ugly Mother the way someone might stare at a circus freak, with amusement, awe, and horror. The Ugly Mother is shorter than the 12-year-old, but just barely. The Ugly Mother's hair is matted down and thin in patches and her scalp shines through when the light strikes it. Her face is shriveled up and she looks more like a hundred and sixty than sixty going on seventy. The Ugly Mother looks like a heap of skin thrown over a coat rack.

They were supposed to go looking for Marcos. But since they'd arrived, she'd come down with a horrible cough. Their first few hours in town all the Ugly Mother did was cough. She expelled not mucus but reddish wormy sputum that slithered down between the cracks in the wooden floor.

"Are you okay?" Lilly had asked in Spanish. "Oh sure," her mother had said before coughing up a tiny sand crab, at which the two little girls shrieked and scampered into a corner.

Lilly toed the little sand crab with her shoe. *Gross.* Lilly reached into her jeans pocket and removed tissues. As she wiped her mother's mouth another large sand crab scurried off the Ugly Mother's tongue and landed with a crunch on the floor. The Ugly Mother promptly stepped on it. "Now *that* is not a good sign," the old woman said to no one. Lilly looked deep into her mother's eyes and whispered, "What's going on?"

"I'm not sure."

Lilly shot an eye at Loco's relatives, they moved back into the kitchen area, whispering to each other.

Lilly hissed at Estrella and Consuelo, Loco's nieces, "Go get her some water."

Consuelo muttered how the old witch can go get her own, but Estrella slapped the side of her head and told her to be quiet lest they anger the old lady. The children continued to whisper from the corner.

"Mother, tell me what is going on. I've had enough of your bullshit about Marcos."

"When I was younger and prettier before you were born, I had a vision of a child born somewhere far away. I lived in Mexico then, I had yet to come to work for Mulch. I had more varied and absolute powers then, some of which I gave to you when you were born."

"You mean...?"

"Yes, I glowed when I was happy, sad, or other like you are doing now. It was such a pretty red glow. I could read other people's thoughts, sometimes, though I didn't like it and did my best to forget how. Which was how I forgot what my mother looked like. It's terribly embarrassing to forget what your own mother looked like. She lived with us, you know after my father died. When Marcos was born, I was somehow linked to him. I did not know this at the time. We share an ancestor from far back, I am sure of it. I see that look, Liliana. Brazilian he may be, but he also partly something else. I guess that he is Oaxacan or Mixtec, on his mother's side. Do not scowl at me daughter, I shaped you to be tolerant. Aware of him I was like he shared part of my soul. I felt him awaken when he reached puberty."

"Eww."

"Quite unruly, a boy's sexual brain can be. Could make a mop handle look sexy, a boy's imagination."

"Mother! Please!"

"Both of us had visions of a mermaid."

"A mermaid?"

"Yes, a mermaid."

"As in a girl with a fish's body?"

"Yes, that exactly. Anyways, when I finally met Marcos, I knew just who he was. No one had to tell me. I could tell like a mother can tell her baby from others. He was guarded at first, suspicious, I think, but soon I had him visiting with me every afternoon. And he had grown up with visions of working with immigrants in the south, imagine. He's like a son to me."

"Really?"

Lilly looked into the mirror over the fireplace mantle. She saw her reflection shudder with an orange-green light. Little Consuelo entered with hot tea and seeing Lilly's glowing body, fainted, sending the teacup careening through the air. It shattered against the wood floor, and Estrella cried out in surprise and, came in and dragged Consuelo by the arms into the kitchen where there came more cries and shouts, only whispers. Someone made a phone call. Lilly could hear them talking. No one seemed to be concerned about the broken teacup or the spilled tea.

"Lilly look at me." The Ugly Mother croaked.

Lilly turned back to her mother whose face was shrunken and pinched.

"I am sure that something awful has happened to Marcos."

"You think he's dead."

Loco's aunt, Belen, shouted a glorious cry, which meant that Consuelo had probably come to in the kitchen.

"Yes. I do." The Ugly Mother said.

"Then we came up here for nothing."

"No. I think we came up here for a reason," the Ugly Mother said as she coughed and spat out a tulip bulb. The flower's petals were coated with mucus, and what looked like pieces of breakfast. Lilly wondered how it could have come up her mother's throat so fast without tearing and ripping out her throat.

"Mother, take it easy."

"Lilly, I fear for us."

"I know mother, I know."

"Be aware of the coast." The Ugly Mother closed her eyes and opened them again.

"The coast?"

"Yes, the coast, as in the beaches and the sand and all the people there, and perhaps boats and docks and things of that nature." She waved her hand as if she were dismissing her daughter. "Be aware. If I can, I will tell you secrets. There is power there."

"In what?"

"In secrets, daughter," the Ugly Mother whispered. The Ugly Mother waved her away and closed her eyes, "I must nap now." And like that she fell asleep in the middle of the floor.

6

Mick hadn't slept right since he and Old Bob Watterson had escaped the marsh. Driving home that night he had encountered a large group of deer standing in the middle of the road. He had stopped his car to wait for them to pass, only they hadn't. They didn't budge when he honked his horn at them either.

It wasn't until Mick had grown impatient, tapping his foot on the accelerator with his car in neutral, when he noticed that his headlights didn't so much reflect on the deer as shine through them.

The effect was subtle. He had stared at them open-jawed and blinking. He took his eyes off them to reach for his phone and when he looked up the deer were gone leaving only a road that was wrapped in fog.

"What the fuck?"

He hesitantly shifted into first and pressed down on the gas pedal as his car moved into the murky white. As soon as he turned onto the main road the fog had disappeared back into the woods like an animal. Only later that night, after reading Virginia's journal for more clues, when he lay down to sleep, did he see it – a looming bank of white, dangerous for all that it held. *Particles of evil*, he had thought, *icy cold death, thick as soup, and white as ash.*

7

Lilly always felt guilty when she thought of how her mother had grown shorter and uglier with each passing week of her pregnancy. Lilly masochistically carried three photos with her at all times in her fake brown leather purse. One was of the Ugly Mother as a teenager, her hair, jet black and wavy, her face rosy, her skin a clear pristine complexion, and in the photo, she stood on a rooftop in Monterrey overlooking a busy street. She had had high cheekbones any model would have killed for. Lilly's grandfather had taken the photo and all she knew of him was his large, glossy, and blurry thumb in the right lower corner of the photograph. The second picture showed her father and mother holding hands. The Ugly Mother wore a white cotton dress. The photo had been taken outside and the mountains outside of Monterrey looked like teeth in the background. Her father's face looked happy, but when Lilly looked at it she always thought she saw (she knew she saw) sadness. Lilly hardly ever saw her father when he was around. The Ugly Mother had said long ago that her husband liked to work hard because it gave him the freedom to talk with no one, especially his wife and child. Her memories of him were of him sitting in the beat-up recliner he'd picked up somewhere, his eyes far away. The third photo was the most colorful. In it, her mother stood outside the door to the migrant cabin on the Hayes farm. In it, she looked shorter and bent over. Her skin had begun to wrinkle, and her hair seemed thinner. She looked about fifty when she had only been in her thirties, a fact the Ugly Mother would tease her about, 'when I formed you Lilly you stole all my beauty.'

Over the years Lilly had witnessed her mother perform magics of all kinds, mostly through cooking and through meditation, but nothing quite like the vomiting. Every day Lilly counted her blessings that she had not shown a penchant for magical vomiting.

The first time the Ugly Mother had vomited vegetables and plants was on her thirteenth birthday. Her father and mother were both vomiters. Her mother specialized in flowers, fruit, and vegetables, medicinal plants, while her father vomited up opium plants, exclusively. The sun had been hanging in the flat open yard outside their squat home. It had a way of lying there like water, the sunlight. It hadn't rained in a week and the Ugly Mother felt the tug of nausea in her gut. As a child, the Ugly Mother had been a sick child and she recognized the twisted feeling in her stomach the moment she awoke in her dry hot room. That afternoon in a sunny patch in the yard she had vomited a large cucumber. The amount of dirt that had suddenly appeared in her stomach and wormed its way up her throat surprised her – it hurt too. It burned and suffocated at the same time as well as it reminded her of a real nasty goat bite. The cucumber had filled her mouth and came out dry and crusted in dirt, with a bit of ragged vine at the end.

She had cried a lot and gone to cry some more in front of her mother, who had been keeping the whole family vomiting-thing from her young daughter. The Ugly Mother had no idea that either of her parents vomited, though she had often wondered why sick people sometimes came asking them for medicine, and her mother would slip off into the bathroom, make some retching noises and then come out with some kind of exotic plant in her hands. Likewise, young men, and sometimes a round man with a big black mole to the right of his nose came by and her father would go off and make horrible gut-wrenching noises in the bathroom and reemerge with some sweet-smelling plants of some kind. Her father's associates would then pay him with cash, while her mother tended to receive food in exchange for her plants. Her father's associates were also always rank with a certain foulness. She couldn't help but pinch her nose when any of them came around, and later got bold enough to light incense whenever they came around.

When her time came, the Ugly Mother had expected her mother to coo and caw and give her some kind of sweet-smelling and tasting potion when she brought the strange cucumber to her, but instead, her mother had hooped and hollered and yanked the Ugly Mother all around the yard until she began to kiss the rather large cucumber, its vine coiled and curled like a pig's tail.

"You have come into your own, my dear," her mother had hollered in delight.

Villagers who lived close enough to hear the fiesta had all crowded around the small home, the evening cooling off the desert floor with the wave of its hand. Eventually, someone brave enough had knocked. To which the Ugly Mother's mother had shouted that her daughter had finally thrown up her first. Of course, everyone wanted to know exactly what the Ugly Mother had vomited up, its shape, size, and everything else about what the first thing was. The sick had shown up to see if it was some kind of soothing plant that could be crushed to make a salve, the priest wanted to see if it were holy or not. Her father's associates showed up to see if the vegetable was an intoxicant.

Compay, a farmer, had offered the family a baby calf to be the first to see it. Her father's friend, the round man, had offered 100 pesos for the cucumber. Sister Margareta, who assisted Father Segundo, had offered a lifetime's worth of prayers, which many said the Ugly Mother should get any way for all her future troubles because of her curse. Somebody had shouted that the girl should be allowed to ride an elephant around town. Lots of other people shouted back "What's an elephant?" Which caused Father Segundo to launch into another tirade about the quality of education in the sleepy burg of San Juanita de Cochina, roughly thirty-seven miles due-south of Monterrey, Mexico, smack dab in the middle of a desert. All the fuss had prompted the Ugly Mother's mother to swing open the doors of her abode and carry out into the yard, by the pig-like-vine-tail, the cucumber that her daughter had vomited up that very afternoon. When they saw that cucumber, waves of disappointment ran through the crowd.

"It's food!" shouted Carlos, a sick young teenager whose nose bent at an impossible angle to one side.

"Who needs food?" shouted a round man who had been secretly hoping that the Ugly Mother would produce coca leaves from her magical belly purse.

"The poor need food, the poor, think of the poor," Sister Margarita had cried.

Most of the crowd broke up right then and there, except for the Ugly Mother's friends who hoped to witness the strange process of her vomiting more food from her throat. But that night she vomited no more.

But as the Ugly Mother entered puberty, she began to vomit mint leaves and then carrots. She didn't like to vomit cucumbers because they tended to make her gag, so when she felt the occasional cucumber come along, she'd forced it into a carrot, or sometimes a lemon, her mother remarking at how her control was improving.

Then came corn (another very painful veggie, and in the Ugly Mother's opinion, the worst) and strawberries and limes. Around this time the Ugly Mother also began to dream of Marcos and experience a mild hallucination every time she walked through her tiny little desert town. She felt like her head was a sieve and people there were constantly being washed through the sieve, sometimes leaving a pebble of thought, other times just rushing through, all of it leaving her dizzy and discombobulated.

"It's natural for you at this age," the Ugly Mother's mother replied.

"But I don't like it."

"You should be thankful, I was almost 16 when it happened to me, your father, a late bloomer, didn't hit his stride until he was 18, and almost a man, and from his family's point of view way too late. Don't tell your father this, but his mother thought that because of it he was soft, in the head, you know *slow*."

"Oh, mother."

"It is true. Come help me with these tomatoes. Gabriella is coming."

The summer that the Ugly Mother had come into her powers changed her completely. All in all, the Ugly Mother learned that she didn't like reading people's thoughts, nor vomiting veggies, although she was willing to admit that after vomiting vegetables her head filled with a light and that she felt like she rose above the clouds and became light and was light, for some minutes afterward.

8

"Mick, it's Old Bob." Old Bob's voice, thin and reedy, floated above ambient noise.

"Hey," Mick heard sounds of people, cash registers in the back of the call. "Where are you?"

"At a grocery store."

"Oh." Mick shook his head. He had hit nothing but dead ends in his investigation of Macy Allbright.

"Listen, I was talking to a buddy of mine. He fishes near Mulch's property."

"Yeah?" Mick's ears pricked up.

"Says you could find all the evidence you want in his house. The basement."

Mick sighed. He knew it would come to this. *Breaking and entering.* Back home he knew enough cops who'd risk it. *Easy now,* he thought.

"Listen. I don't know, Old Bob."

"You want to solve this case, don't you?"

"Yeah, but I think you want me to solve this case more than I do."

Old Bob coughed before he replied. "You're going to have to grow some balls, boy."

"Thanks, Old Bob." Old Bob was right, and he knew it.

"He's out now. Mulch. Gone somewhere. Saw him myself. Not long ago, too. Probably could sneak in through an open window."

"I don't know. I'm a what you call it, come here." Mick turned the pros and cons over in his head.

"No shit."

"Hey, Bob."

"Yeah?"

"You see any more of the fog?"

Old Bob was quiet. For a second, Mick clearly heard the ambiance of the grocery store.

"Yeah. You too?" Old Bob whispered back.

"Yeah." Mick shivered. His memory of seeing the fog on the backroads made his skin crawl.

"Well, just thought I'd drop you that info."

"Thanks."

Old Bob hung up.

Mick licked his lips and reached for his car keys.

"What the hell."

9

The Ugly Mother died like this.

Loco's aunt and cousins lived in a three-bedroom apartment, a whole side of the building, a bedroom on each corner, one in the middle, and a living room that bled into the kitchen. That afternoon, Loco left Lilly and her mother at his relatives' home, the little girls had gone to play with a neighbor.

The Ugly Mother napped on the couch, her little wrinkled mouth expelling pieces of dried vegetables. Lilly didn't like the sound of the cough, it was too rough, too harsh, too mean for her liking. Invited by the steady breeze coming in the window, she sat down on the floor, parallel with the window, and stared into her mother's face. *If Marcos was dead what next?* Lilly didn't feel like she had to live her life the way her mother had lived hers, driven by her biology, vomiting vegetables.

The Ugly Mother always got what she wanted and since she had felt compelled to come to Boston, of all places, then she was, by all means, going to go there, even if it meant dying there.

Lilly was glad she didn't expel fruits from her mouth. There was a tiny piece of something at the edge of her mother's mouth. Lilly reached over to wipe it off. It was something brown and fetid. The Ugly Mother coughed a deep muscled cough. Lilly watched her mother's muscles ripple as her mother's body struggled to rid itself of something.

"She should take some cough syrup," Loco's aunt Belen said quietly. "It sounds like she has the croup."

Lilly nodded, her head becoming light at that moment, the smell of pines filling her nose. Then, right in front of her, the walls of the apartment fell away and stretched back into the pine grove. The ripe smell of needle brush and the spice bushes, and honeysuckle that grew along with the grove's east side washing over her. From there, her mother seemed very far away from her. Belen even farther, but only for a second, for the walls of the apartment came back again and the smell of the pines and the grove folded back into her brain.

"Did you say something?" Lilly asked as she turned back to Belen, who was already halfway into the kitchen already and turned around to speak to Lilly.

"On the corner, Carmen, another Carmen, my friend works behind the counter, she will sell you some cough syrup."

"I... I don't know if that will help."

"It can't hurt. Tell Carmen to put it on my bill."

"Thank you. Thank you so much."

Belen nodded before disappearing back into the kitchen, back into the heat and sweat that came from steam, the broiling meats, and the body heat in small places.

When Lilly stood, she had the sudden sensation that she was standing on a very high cliff, right on the edge, she felt her toes hanging off the rock, the lack of support under her toes making her heart flutter.

10

Lilly floated down the street, her toes dragging along behind her, her head tilted slightly forward pulling the rest of her numb body. She felt that her lower body existed in a different place, back on the Eastern Shore, back in the pine grove, back in Hammer 'n Nails where she had to hug herself since it was so cold inside. Her upper half was in the real world here, Allston, Massachusetts, where she had gone out to the bodega to buy her sick mother some cough syrup. Some of the men on the street smiled and cat-called her, others teased her with chicken calls.

The Bodega smelled like must and old cardboard boxes, and the windows were covered with half-stuck fliers, peeling off like old Band-Aids, advertising ESL lessons, apartments, resistance rallies against white nationalists, rides to California, rides to Mexico, rides to Canada. Lilly floated into the store, her toes dragging behind her, her forehead tilted forward, her eyes, moony and indisposed, taking it all in. Behind the counter, a square woman chatted with a dark-skinned woman bagging up plantains, and sugar cane, and a few sodas and sweetmeats. The bodega's dim lighting made Lilly feel like she was going to sleep, or like she was waking up from a dream, half in, half out of her two worlds. Lilly floated down each aisle, her heavy head scanning the shelves blankly, looking for something familiar.

"Granuja." Lilly did not hear the insult, instead, she looked up to the ceiling adorned with piñatas, and Mexican and Puerto Rican flags, and smaller flags for Columbia, Peru, Argentina, and Costa Rica. When she finally turned around the clerk addressed her again.

"Hola," Carmen said bitterly as she lit up a short, hand-rolled cigarette and leaned on the counter. It didn't bother her that Lilly floated, but she didn't like the girl's manners. Who did she think she was to come into her store and not speak a word of greeting?

"Hello," Lilly said meekly.

"What do you want?"

"Cough syrup."

"Ah, Belen called and told me you were coming. She didn't tell me you are so soft-brained though."

"Excuse me?"

"Nothing, nothing. Are you okay? You look heartbroken."

"It's my mother."

"Yes, I heard, she's very ugly. Belen, Carmen, and I are close."

"She's... she's sick." Lilly felt as if she had been slapped.

"That's what Belen said," Carmen said as she rolled her eyes and pulled a bottle of Robitussin DX from under the counter. Carmen didn't like to keep pharmaceuticals on the shelf, on the account of Jerry the junkie, who squatted somewhere around her store.

"My mother," Lilly said as she looked to Carmen, and reached out for the brown paper bag. "She's coughing something awful."

"Try not to float too much. The young men around here will think you're an angel or something and try to shoot you down."

"Yes, thank you."

"And beware of the old men who sit on the corner with pipes and brown bags full of beer. They will tell you lies, and they will try to hurt you."

"Thank you. Again, thank you."

"I'm sorry that your mother is so ugly, it will not be easy for her to let go."

Lilly nodded with shame and shyness and floated out the bodega.

11

Loco stayed gone for most of the week, however, he came to bring Lilly some money, which he assumed she could need. Lilly used the money to pay Belen for food and the use of the couch and living room as a bedroom for her and her mother. Loco, at least, was having fun, but how Lilly missed his jovial presence, his relatives were not friendly. On the fourth day of her cough, the Ugly Mother coughed up a squash the length of Lilly's skull. Belen wanted to cook the squash, but when she cut it open, a rotten stink permeated the kitchen and floated out in a foul cloud to the living room where it dissipated out the window. At the bodega when Carmen heard that Lilly and her ugly mother had no money other than what Loco was bringing them, she sold tickets to Belen's living room so that the city folks could see a real country witch cough up vegetables. For a dollar, they'd get a ticket to walk up the fire escape and peek through the window. Carmen also wanted to sell the vegetables for an exorbitant sum of money, but Belen refused.

"Belen, she is dying anyway, we might as well make some money," Carmen complained.

"Liliana is a nice girl, you will be respectful to her and her hideous mother." Belen shook her finger.

"She looks like a wrinkled abortion."

"Yes." Belen could not disagree.

"That was rude of us," Carmen said solemnly.

"Many apologies to Jesus," Belen said as the women made the sign of the cross.

Lilly heard the women, no matter how quietly they whispered. Their whispers were like birds making a nest, or a rat in the walls, forever under every sound, scratching and scratching.

Lilly poured medicine down her mother's throat all week. She ran out of cough syrup twice in a few days. It didn't seem to help her mother much, but it did seem to help her fall off to sleep.

"So, I suppose I should go get you some more medicine, eh?" Lilly spoke to her mother in whispers. Outside the living room, both Belen and Carmen, whom Lilly suspected of listening to their hushed conversations, hoped that the Ugly Mother would cough up a diamond. The Ugly Mother turned her eyes up at Lilly and nodded her head, "Any word from Marcos?"

"No mother, not yet. Rest now."

Belen stepped into the living room, her hands on her hips, her finger wagging in the air. "I sincerely hope Marcos will either show up or Loco will take you both home. I'm getting sick and tired of the rotten stench that hangs around the two of you here. This is not a hospice. There are children here."

Lilly bit her lip and suppressed the urge to shout at Belen. After all, she was a guest, no matter how rude the host was becoming, she couldn't show disrespect.

"I'm going to the store for more medicine, I'll be back in a minute."

"I know you will. You'll always be back, Lilly."

Lilly slammed the door behind her and stepped out onto the dusty streets. A crowd had gathered on the porch steps, faces she recognized, people who had crowded onto the back fire escape to peek at her mother, to await the vomiting of some new vegetables. The crowd shuffled their behinds and formed a narrow path that zig-zagged along the street. There was nothing but silence as she walked down the stairs between the onlookers and turned up the street to the bodega.

Behind the counter, Carmen sat there like an ugly spider, the webs of leaflets and cigarette and lottery ads spread out around her, her eyes sharp, her hands quick.

"Hello Lilly, did your ugly mother die yet?"

"No."

Lilly waited behind a fat man in a baseball cap who bought three lotto tickets and a pack of cigarillos. Carmen motioned to Lilly behind him.

"She's the one I was telling your wife about," Carmen said as she pointed to Lilly. The old man just smiled and looked at her chest, ogling her body. "She's a country girl. She and her mother came up here with Loco too, you know Belen's nephew, to visit some Portuguese man, and the old woman is so ugly, you wouldn't even believe it. They are staying with Belen and her family. I'm sure you have seen the pedestrians lined up to peek into her home. To see this ugly witch. And this ugly whore of a woman just gets sick on Belen and stinks up the room when she's not coughing up vegetables. Would you like to buy a ticket to watch her vomit a vegetable?"

"Vegetables?" The old man asked.

"Yes, squash, tomatoes, cucumbers, all rotten. Stinking like the old woman."

The man laughed and turned, only nodding to Lilly, before exiting the store.

"The usual, Liliana?"

Lilly's cheeks burned white with hate.

12

Lilly swung the brown bag in one hand, striding down the sidewalk, half-mad at both Belen and Carmen, half desperate to get out of the city altogether. *Let my mother die in peace somewhere else, like the pine grove back on the shore.* The Ugly Mother was stronger than Carmen or Belen knew, and she would get better, Lilly knew it. And this would be the last bottle of cough syrup she would ever buy for her mother. She swung the bag casually as if the bottle were a bell and then Jerry the Junkie snuck up behind her and snatched the bag from her and ran.

CHAPTER SEVEN

1

For Cilia, in the days that followed Marcos' death, time glued and gooed and slowed and elephantine-like lumbered through her body, leaving large prints deep in her mind. Cilia, exhausted, felt the same deep-bone exhaustion that Nick felt. Through it, Cilia felt like she had aged ten years if she had aged a day. It all made Cilia's fingers twitch, her nose run, and her eyes feel like someone had stepped on them. With her stomach rumbling, her body depleted of nutrients, Marco's death tugged at her thoughts with its racine teeth.

She had barely been able to convince the crew to go back to their cabins and their duties, of course, the rum and tequila she commanded the Captain to give out didn't hurt. Most of the troublemakers had gone away, back to their holes to drink and dream of payday.

But Cilia knew more trouble would come, she just hoped the crew would remain placated long enough for the ship to port. Which by her calculations would be soon. Her investments in the shipping company had paid off.

In the meantime, all there was to do was rest, for Cilia would need it to marshal her strength should the mermaid, or the native Mr. Bill, or the mystery man prove to be too much.

2

"She's gone under now," Marina whispered into the air. Marina lay on her side looking at her mother, whose nose was the end of a shadow on the wall. Marina supposed that someone would have come along and set her box upright by now. She'd forgotten about tearing Hector's arm off. It lay in the corner, attracting rats, which scurried outside the walls, fearful of the other smell inside, her. Marina waited patiently for Mulch to come and set things right. But there was something wrong with that train of thought. She couldn't concentrate. She couldn't think.

Mother.

Her mother's woody face mouthed an O as if mouthing a kiss. Marina looked up to the tiny hole where only hours before she had ripped a man's limb from the socket. The hole seemed so far away now and receding. Marina pulled her knees into her stomach and hoped she didn't fallany farther away because Mulch wouldn't be able to find her if she did. She thought she was falling, very slowly, away from the world. It was the partial silence in her head, the exhaustion, the shock, but mostly it was because she was as dry as Halloween Indian corn.

What she wanted to hear were birds. The thick and jumbled, overlapping cries of birds that always seemed to be saying human things, things which she knew of but didn't understand. *Insurance,* she remembered one bird crying, a word she knew from her father. *Feed, feed,* another had cried, which she liked and always giggled at. A few even sounded fish-like cries, *eel, eel,* one went, and *pike, pike,* another. She missed the way the birds sounded when she back floated and the gulls and herons dived in the creek around her. They didn't seem to mind her swimming with them and sometimes they'd swooped at her tail, lapping and curling out of the creek.

Marina whispered, "she's gone under now," and turned her moony face to the wall, looking out at where the fireflies crushed hulls glowed. She had a crazy idea that her sister needed to see fireflies and that she had sent them to her. A strange thought, but strange thoughts came to her again and again, and Marina was helpless to stop herself. Instead, she gave into the fever and allowed it to bring her in and out of memory.

"I want to go to the movies," she said, articulating every syllable.

In her mind, she saw the theater, trumped up with swinging red swashes of carpet and velvet drapes, the theater dark and murmuring. *How that young girl in the bathroom had spoken with such love and emotion about mermaids, about me, about my mother.* Marina looked to her mother, a bit of shadow on the wall, and her mother whispered and blew a kiss, her large fin swishing in the whorling wood.

"Oh mother, you should have met him!" Marina's memory whirred to life.

For a few seconds, Marina opened her arms to accept a hug. Instead, her hug was filled with shadows.

"Oh mother, he was so handsome."

Somewhere in her skull, a very nervous Nick Adams stood watching what was possibly the most beautiful girl in the whole wide world. He wished he to gather the courage to speak to her, to ask her her name. Marina remembered how he stood, the wrinkles in his jacket, the nervous tension in the air – everything.

Marina's skin took on a greenish hue under the crushed lantern of the lightning bugs. She closed her eyes and then batted them open, her mind tracking image to image. She had wanted to ask her mother something about love, about mating, but Marina didn't see her mother, only a shadow, a plank of wood.

"Mother?" her voice cracked, weak and beaten.

She winced in a flash of pain like someone had swung a hammer into her gut. Marina practically folded in half, the pain burning her insides. *Hunger, fish girl needs food*, she thought to herself. A gleeful manic fit took her for a moment, and she laughed hysterically shouting nonsense. "No! She's in the top, She's in the top and won't come out."

Her voice pealed out of the box and into the ship's dark and musty hold.

Topside, a few of the remaining troublemakers, smoking and speaking of jumping ship, or planning a mutiny, a real honest to god mutiny, heard the warbled call. They had taken their booze and stored it and waited for the captain to go back to the bridge before sneaking back out to listen to the weird noises echoing up through the hull. They had spent the last few hours arguing among each other as to who would enter the hold first. Who would risk their life? "The *haint* in the cell," one said. Someone mentioned torches, another thought he'd seen an albatross hung on a nail in Boston. "Hush up," another said, "that's crazy talk." They did not see Van Dijk step out of the wheelhouse and looked down at them, his pipe smoldering, his face beat red and his eyes, his eyes the color of dim snow.

And when he stormed into the midst of their small group, the Captain simply stopped next to the man closest to him and broke his neck. Van Dijk remained silent, even when the crowd became hushed, obedient.

He pointed like an angry father and the men broke away from each other and went back to their jobs and their quarters. No one remarked on the strange voice echoing up, how at times it sounded like a giddy schoolgirl and how at times it sounded like a sick animal.

3

Marina felt like someone had stretched her and then let her snap back into place. Her body ached, her head ached, it hurt to speak. Her throat and mouth were parched. At times there was a part of her mouth that felt like it was pooled with water. When she went to explore it with her tongue, she found that it too was dry. *Where had all the water bottles gone?* It had been days since she had seen that man.

Or has it? She had dreamed men came to her with fire and weapons and wanted to kill her. The anger of it remained bitter in her mouth.

What had she done? *Think Marina. Think.* Her mind spaced and for a moment she lingered on the edge of unconsciousness. Then she snapped back to again.

There had been shouts, pounding, and pounding on the outside of her prison.

And then what? *A pulse. Yes, that's the right word. A pulse. From the box.*

The magics Sea Hag and Marcos and Mr. Bill had threaded into the wood had awoken when three crew members carrying torches and crowbars and knives had slipped Captain Van Dijk's eye and crept into the hold, their steps cautious and anxious.

Marina had not heard them approach, but she had heard them speaking in shocked whispers as they pulled the dead man away from where he lay. She heard them exclaim and curse.

When they began to pry and bang on the seams of her prison the box had reacted. A warm fuzzy hum began, one that tickled Marina in the pit of her stomach and as it built up to its crescendo Marina felt a curious thing in her mind, space doubled, perhaps tripled, and she soon found herself in a prison which had grown in size.

The spell crackled blue light up and down the seams of the box and the top of the upturned box, and the men trying to break in screamed and fell back, shocked and enraptured by the light.

To them, the box grew massive and impossible, the wood warping and bending outward as it swelled and enlarged and filled the hold. The men, whose minds had begun to crack seeing the impossible turned and fled, only one lingered, Keyshaun Haywood, a local roughneck who operated the crane. To him what happened in the ship's hold was simply more evidence that the world was coming to an end, and it stood fixated by the growth of the thing before common sense and survival kicked in and he too fled.

To Marina, the space around her grew exponentially, so that the walls receded from her the way the tide would recede, and suddenly the poor girl was swallowed up by darkness, the only thing keeping her warm the flicker from the sun carving Marcos had lovingly crafted for her months ago. A beating light that promised love, love that would never come.

But the hag, as Marina called her, was not deterred by the magic. The hag lingered, an infection of Marina's mind.

When Marina was young, she would run at her fastest speed out to the edge of the creek and fling her body into the air, changing into her mermaid form mid-air so that she hit the water swimming, gunning it out to the center of the creek. Sometimes she'd swim out to the middle and turn around and come right back, just to do it all over again, to see how far she could propel herself in a single leap. Once, when she was only a child, she swam out without permission, in the dead of night and watched her father board a large barge and speak with some large men in hushed voices about his business.

Spying on her father, Marina didn't think of herself as being delinquent in any shape, size, or form. She loved Mulch. She did not understand why her father did what he did, and when she witnessed him on the water meeting with men she did not recognize, she figured it was adult business, something beyond her understanding. It nagged her now, in the hold of the ship, wondering how her father could have done this to her.

Marina's mind flowed like seawater when the moon was full, and twice a day she remembered everything, and twice a day she focused on what she was doing in the present, the rest seeming distant, out of reach somehow. Even in her prison inside the hull where her mind came and went with the tides, she struggled for something to hold on to and wave it about like a flag, and surrender, to stop whatever it was that was being done to her.

Someone was watching her now. She felt it. It was someone mean and nasty – the hag. *Do not give her your power*, she thought. *Do not.*

Water, she no longer heard it. She couldn't remember how long ago it had been since she had heard water. For some reason Marina called out to Marcos in a half-whisper, begging for his help, before covering her mouth with her hand in terror. Marcos was dead. She didn't know how she knew, but she did. Then she thought about her sister.

Virginia made Marina laugh. She was good about that, but she also made Marina feel stupid and small in the human world. Virginia knew everything and knew how to get anything. Marina had never even kissed a boy before that one night. Virginia had gone all the way, which to Marina was a distant, primal urge that seemed deep under the surface, unreachable. Virginia had helped her go to the movies, where she had met *HIM*. He, standing there idle, calm, and quiet, his smell filling her nose and sending her blood pumping into her sex.

Virginia had been watched then. Just like she was being watched now. *By the hag.*

In her box, Marina saw and then forgot the whole of Mulch's desire, the face of his mother, who looked like Virginia, only with darker hair, and who

rocked the bed above Mulch's bed, her mind spiraling out of control one winter. She wasn't a person to Mulch, she had not been allowed to be a person to
Mulch, only a fetishized object of lust and love. Marina saw it but did not hear
it, but only saw the pictures of it, and she understood it with her weird luck, and
then immediately forgot it, and would only later understand it again when the
hag having finally come at last, when all hope was nearly lost.

4

Nick buzzed with red wine; *First Class was too much.* Nick turned to his new
friend. "Maybe I'll find this girl and I will know. You know? I'll just know what's
going to come next. Like in a dream, when you know you're dreaming, and you
know that up ahead you're going to see someone you know. You know?"

"Frankly, not really." Mr. Bill said.

"Man, I can't wait to see her. Hey, what's wrong with your shirt?"

"Um, nothing, it's just a little tight is all." Mr. Bill pulled on his chamois
shirt with his thumb and forefinger.

"Mine's in rags." Nick looked a little drunk to Mr. Bill.

"Yeah, I know."

"Check it out, the Atlantic," Nick said, his voice bubbly like a teenager.
"She's under us right now. Like if I was to jump out this window and float down
to the water, I'd be right on top of her. Can you see?"

"I can see fine, thanks."

"Just how in the world is she traveling. I'm getting serious claustrophobia
waves from her right now."

"You are?" Bill asked.

"No, not really," Nick said. "It's hard to say. This wine is going to my head."

"Oh." Mr. Bill chuckled.

"Are you sure there's nothing wrong with your shirt, you look uncomfortable like there's something very big and itchy under your shirt?"

"I'm fine Nick." Mr. Bill looked down at his clothing, which had begun to
tighten like a drum around his middle.

"Are you sure that's comfortable, I think I hear your shirt ripping there?
Yeah, that was a definite rip. I'm sure of that. Are you going to Hulk out or something?" Nick asked.

"Hulk-out? I don't know this reference."

"You are hulking out!"

"I am not hulking out!"

"Look at yourself, will you? That's hulking-out."

"I insist that you stop using this term."

"Look, I don't know what's going on but you're busting right out of your shirt."

"An exaggeration." Mr. Bill said, looking down at his clothing.

"You can't deny that wasn't a rip."

"What?"

"Right there. On the sleeve, at the joint." Nick pointed to Mr. Bill's shirt, which had split open, just so slightly.

"I hardly call that a joint."

"What would you call it?"

"The seam."

"Okay seam."

"The fabric's coming a bit loose is all."

"Bullshit, you're hulking-out on me".

5

Mr. Bill did not understand until after why on that June evening he began to expand, ripping his clothing, his shoes, his pants, his satin boxer shorts, his rings which his swelling fingers snapped like cheap plastic.

"Jesus, what are you doing?" Nick clamored.

"I am not doing anything. I don't know what's happening!" Bill replied.

Bill wasn't sure whose magic it was that affected him, it could have been Marina, she'd proven herself to be much more powerful than he thought. Or it could have been something else. *Buddy, you better get a hold of yourself real quick,* he thought.

"Jesus look at you!" Nick screamed.

Most of first-class was asleep, but Bill was sure they wouldn't be for long. *I'm going to have to fuck with a whole lot of minds,* Bill thought.

"I told you you were hulking out!"

"Would you shut your mouth!" Bill seethed.

Mr. Bill was now stuffed into the chair. His body had grown back into the form it had been in when the white man had begun to wipe out the Indian presence on the shore over four hundred years ago. Bill guessed he was at least seven and a half feet tall, at least the size of his father, his relatives, the Laughing King. For the first time in over four hundred years, the giants were back.

6

"Torture has a long history. I prefer to mix my medium," Pembroke whispered.

Virginia, her head encased in the leather-wooden head-box which kept light and smells out and sucked her voice away, didn't acknowledge Pembroke.

"I like to torture people for sexual arousal as well as to procure information. In my youth I followed the readings of the Marquis and the Countess de Bathory to the T, you might say. My sister enjoyed baths in warm human blood. She's in good hands, your sister." Pembroke continued to whisper. "Me, I'm looking forward to opening you up," he said as he ran a finger over her exposed stomach which rippled back with repulsion.

Pembroke had used the headbox once before, on a business partner in the early part of the 1960s who'd swindled him out of money and had refused to tell him what he had done with it. The man, weak-minded, had responded well to the sensory-deprived hallucinations. Pembroke had been able to break him with ease. In the end, the man signed over his company, his assets, and his bank account, and Pembroke had left him an empty man, broken from trauma and utterly humiliated.

"But first, my love, we will enjoy our time together."

7

Pembroke never thought of himself as a lover, but he was built for being a lover. His body long and lean, well over 6'6 when his feet were flat on the ground, and when he walked on his toes he rose as high as seven feet, his hideous feet suspending him. He found sex to be somewhat repellent. He had enjoyed sex in his youth, particularly with Cilia, and later his aunt, but as he grew older, he found that he only wished to hurt. But of course, sex can hurt, which is why it's so powerful a force. As he came inside Virginia's tied and electrified body he felt the first genuine pangs of guilt, ever, in his life.

Virginia was beautiful, even as her encased head hung back limply. She had long ago passed out under Pembroke's electrical stimulation. Her nipples, and labia, and fingers had been equipped with electrodes that fired voltage into her. He had entered her from behind shocking her with every thrust so that Virginia bucked and tightened her grip on his penis with every thrust and shock. He felt the shock too, though less than she did, vaginal secretions were a great conductor.

But as he was about to despoil her body, he paused. *This girl is to be your legacy.* He looked her body up and down. *Don't show her mercy. Show her strength. Remake her in your image.* Taking the long scalpel from the worktable, Pembroke placed the edge of the blade alongside Virginia's stomach. He pressed it into her flesh and blood rose to meet the blade. He cut up her stomach and stopped at the breastbone. Her skin bulged; her guts pressed against the weak skin wall.

"Well let's see what you have inside here, my dear."

8

When Virginia awoke, she was numb. Her hands and feet were tied to a steel table, her stomach cold and hot at the same time, and her heart was beating weakly in her ears. She couldn't see anything but felt something moving around inside her. At first, she thought it was a dream, but then she began to feel a sunrise of pain that spread around her belly and up to her breasts and down into her groin. She felt something inside her, moving around. She sweated into the open sores growing on her skin like mold. The fireflies had remained silent.

"Your engine looks fine," Pembroke said coolly, aroused by the bloody scalpel, the folded back flesh of Virginia's stomach, and her exposed organs.

Virginia wheezed inside her head-box.

"I opened your hood while you were out. Since I was adding oil, I figured I should check everything else," Pembroke giggled into his hand.

"Good news, you're not pregnant," Pembroke laughed. "Not yet, anyway."

Virginia smacked her lips together and rolled her head about, which caused the leather box on her skull to move slightly on the table.

"It looks like your appendix is in good shape, do you still want it?"

Virginia groaned, perched on the edge of passing out.

Pembroke's mind tugged between two poles, remove parts of Virginia's insides and feed them to her, or simply close her back up. He wanted to feed herself to herself but reminded himself that she was only to be brainwashed. He wanted her whole. Especially if she were fertile. She was a tool, and he was the forger. He felt that the scalpel would want him to do it, to cut a foot or two off her small intestine and make Virginia sausage. *Virginia sausage*, he liked that. Or perhaps her appendix, though he imagined that it probably tasted like leather.

"You look like you might be going into shock, dear. Tsk, tsk. Such a party pooper. I guess I had better get my thread. We don't want you dying on us now do we?"

And as Virginia began to fall into shock, Pembroke began to sew up his charge. Pembroke's heart shivered. *Had he damaged her too far?* His sadism had gotten the better of him before. Virginia was to bear his child, be his heir. *Perhaps a softer touch would be better? Nonsense,* Pembroke thought. *Don't get soft on me now.*

9

"Doc, let me first say I am a grade A repressor, which helps a lot. First, about the facemask, leather box. It was sick, let me tell you. The mask was heavy and ugly and made me sweat, which eventually started to cause my face to rot. It sucked. Besides the mask was infested with fireflies. I've had my psych 101 and know that 'nakedness = shame and disgrace.' It did bother me some, like how couldn't it, right? But it wasn't working the way old Pembroke, the sicko-fuck that he was, wanted it to work. Right?

"However, the fucking surgery did. When I awoke and found him fingering my guts and then later awoke, drugged, and stitched up and felt the wormy scar running up my abdomen, I resolved to get the hell out of there, like immediately. What else was I going to do? Not that I had a plan. Though at the time, I liked to think that I had one, but first he had to take the mask off, which he would do soon, to fuck with my face, which was breaking out in painful boils and pimples after weeks of being under lock and key."

10

Mick found Mulch's house sealed tight. Looking around he saw that recently several vehicles had driven away from the house at high speeds. From the treads, he could tell that there had been three vehicles involved, all within the last few days. There didn't seem to be anybody at home, however. *Better do a perimeter check before making a fool out of myself,* he thought to himself.

Mick stalked around to the back of the home to see if he could jimmy the lock on the porch. He couldn't. *Damn.* He looked up into the sky in vain. "What the fuck am I doing here?" he cried aloud. A gull answered down by the water.

That was when he noticed the boathouse. He headed down to see what that was all about. He kept looking over his shoulder and for anyone who might be watching. The opening lay before him dark and cold, and through its throat, he spied the creek. He practically jogged to the boathouse, eager to get out of sight.

He found nothing. It was musty inside, and smelled faintly of scorched oil, and made Mick feel as if he were standing in the open jaws of a predator. Mick's skin bristled in gooseflesh.

"Hello?"

He felt foolish calling out, for there was no one around. He sighed and turned to go, but as he did, he heard a sickening rustle of feathers and the smell of spoiled meat. He couldn't see the bird and for that, he was glad, too, for he was sure it was close and big.

And then out of the corner of his eye came the fog, gliding over the top of the water, hissing as it came, a thick wall of it, moving into the mouth of the boathouse from the water.

Mick's body juiced with adrenaline, and he turned and bolted, running up to the main house as the fog descended on the Hayes place.

In the mist came a screech. Mick's stomach leaped into his mouth, and he felt his flesh rising in goosebumps. The sound the bird made, a maddening mix of crow, and human, something from deep in the earth, something not of this world, made Mick shudder. Inside his mind, Mick heard the dead laughing. He knew it was the dead because his fear told him so. The twisted, stomach-dropping sensation of hearing the dead made him run from the boathouse and he didn't look back.

The fog filled the boathouse like fat bread. It filled the boathouse until the boards creaked and moaned with its wet, airy mass. There it waited.

When the Allbrights called on Mick later that week he did not answer. His cell phone went to voicemail. His office phone's answering service filled up. When the Allbrights called the police they had not seen the man either. It was as if Mick vanished from the face of the earth.

11

That night, Doppelgänger Bill drove the truck straight off the pier at Cape James – straight off. Blue heads still talk about it at the pharmacy. They gather for their coffee and homemade doughnuts and remember this and that about the Reverend So-and-So and eventually someone brings up that day the truck went into the bay and sunk, the police cars colliding like keystone cops at the edge of the pier, each successive car knocking the car at the front of the pile-up into the bay, so eventually, the end of the pier was crowded with five cars, two of them hanging off the pier, one end in the water, the front bumper resting against the low tide sand. Two cars had been knocked off the pier completely and had bubbled and sank, water filling up the cab, the officers dog-paddling to shore.

What had happened was this: Doppelgänger Bill, driving at 90 miles an hour tore down Main Street of Cape James, causing pedestrians to yank small children out of the way, causing emotional scarring to those small children yanked back by their terrified mothers, and causing many old folks to stop in shock half-afraid they'd die of a heart attack. Doppelgänger Bill then drove the truck straight for the pier, the motor gunning and the cops following behind, dovetailing and careening out of the way. The cops had been so excited over a real honest-to-god chase that none of them had noticed that they were headed for the pier until their tires left the pavement and knocked against the wood. By then it was already too late to stop. The braking caused planks to rip up, and then off went Doppelgänger Bill in Sea Hag's beat-up truck, flying high like some strange and heavy pelican into the air, crashing down thirty feet beyond the dock into the deep water, where the shelf of the bay dipped into one of its deeper channels. The two closest police cars, one Northampton County Sheriff's Department car, and one state police cruiser followed, breaking and tearing up the pier into the lukewarm waters of the bay. The vehicles that followed, two local and one state patrol car carefully edged their way along the pier to assist.

No one saw Doppelgänger Bill swim away, but when the truck was finally extracted from the bay, all that was found was a lump of hard, gray, clay, stuck to the seat. The town of Cape James, shocked and sensationalized by the chase, kept rehashing the story over and over again in the local newspaper until it had become something of an institution, a local mystery, the stuff of myth.

12

Before the Ugly Mother died, she dreamed of Monterrey. In her dream, Lilly was there, as was Lilly's husband, and a very large man whose head rose far above her sight. He claimed to have no home and as he said this, he stretched out his very broad and thick arms to the sides, which were the breadth of her childhood home. As Lilly's husband knitted a sock, the Ugly Mother felt herself drawn to the very large man who showed her a picture of a candle. The candle, he said, was very important for without the candle all would be lost in vain. The man looked familiar. The Ugly Mother could not place him.

The dream landscape shifted, her daughter and her daughter's husband fell away, leaving only the very large man, who also began to fade, first into shadow then into the shade and then was gone entirely, and the Ugly Mother found herself dreaming of the face of her husband who one day had become so thin he had slipped through the floorboards of the house and had not been seen since.

Lilly had been only four then. Memory and sickness shook hands and the landscape of her fever dream shifted and phased so that in her sickened state the Ugly Mother couldn't remember if they were in the house in Mexico City, or at the migrant shack on the Eastern Shore. It didn't matter, only that Ricardo had been drinking a good bit that day. Ricardo worked seventy-hour weeks. He worked the fields, he repaired fences, he helped the old men and women fix up their homes. He loved to help the mechanics work on the buses and trucks. When they were on the shore, Ricardo would get up at five and go to bed at midnight, stopping work only to eat his dinner at around ten. But when Ricardo had no work, as it was on that day, Ricardo would begin his day drinking home-made beer with whoever was around. Then sometime around noon they would drink bathtub tequila and smoke cheap cigars.

Something had been different that day, and Ricardo had felt it. Later as he flattened out and fell away like a loose piece of paper, he would shout out that it had been his birth-line that dictated his fate, because his brother had eaten his house.

The year before, Ernesto, Ricardo's brother, had died. He lived in his shack on the Eastern Shore, on the other side of Mulch's camp. That previous winter, as Ernesto and Rina packed their shack to head back to Mexico, Rina had dropped dead. She had complained of a cold and a fever, and the previous day had swooned into Ernesto's arms. Mr. Bill had wanted to bury Rina in one field and Ernesto had been disgusted by the idea. He had no money for a proper funeral and barely enough to get back home, he had mailed most of it to his mother in Mexico City. In the end, Ernesto helped Mr. Bill bury Rina at the back of the cotton field. Mr. Bill promised that she'd make the cotton purer and whiter the next winter and Ernesto went home to Mexico City in mourning. Mr. Bill didn't think he'd be back, but he returned and lived in the shack alone, still grieving for his wife.

Sometime in the following spring, Ernesto's grief became too much. The Ugly Mother had claimed that she saw it as a rock on his back, like an iron hat on his head. Ernesto locked himself in his shack and decided he'd eat the shack where he and Rina had shared their happiest and saddest moments.

Ernesto began eating the shack with the furniture and broke the table over the tiny bed, screaming Rina's name as he smashed the table into bits. He used hammers, axes, even Mulch's chainsaw. He broke the chairs, and then the bed itself, into small pieces to fit into his mouth. He spent hours sawing and breaking the wood into chunks and then into splinters and shavings. He ate the table and chairs without complaint, often with homemade salsa the Ugly Mother had made for him. He ate the bed without complaint, and when his stomach ached and became an explosion of needles pricking him from the inside out, he continued to eat.

The next week he began on the walls. Lucky for Ernesto the floor was dirt, so he was spared from wanting to eat that. And Ernesto had no intention of eating the stove, or the sink, or the pipework guts. But he wanted the fiberboard and plywood that made up the roof and walls of their home. He wanted those walls which had housed his love, Rina, to be in his heart forever.

In no time he had shredded the drywall, the pressed cardboard that ran under the windows, and the plain plank trim.

It took him the better part of a week to just eat two walls, for his stomach had become a distended grotesque relief map of a gut. The other migrants saw outlines of wood splinters in there. A screwhead was visible over the man's belly button, which hung out over his pants like a giant bulbous eye.

"Ernesto, why do you eat your house?" Ricardo asked, taking his brother under his arm. "I have work for us and we can make money, real money, for mother."

But Ernesto did not have a response for Ricardo, and when he did finally answer him, his answer was like a slap to Ricardo, who loved Ernesto very much.

"No one interfered when your wife used her magic to make a child out of wax, so you should not judge me, Ricardo."

To that Ricardo had no response. And when the Ugly Mother heard what Ernesto had said, she worried that her daughter Lilly would hear of it and begin asking questions.

Meanwhile, Ernesto continued to eat at his house. He had managed to eat half the roof before his stomach exploded. Ernesto clutched his gut and fell face first, splitting his gut open on the dirt floor, the skin had become so thin his intestines fell out like distended snakes.

Grief-stricken the incident haunted both Ricardo and the Ugly Mother. As parents, they feared the camp would rise against them if they learned the truth about their daughter, but over time that fear faded, but Ricardo's grief over his brother did not.

And when Ricardo began drinking out of the mason jar that sunny afternoon he slipped through the floorboards, he had squinted a lot and complained about a headache. Ricardo never got headaches and the Ugly Mother saw that he was in pain. Then without warning, Ricardo began to shrink. Not so much shrink, he flattened out like a cartoon character smashed by a steamroller, a thin line of flesh and hair and bones. The Ugly Mother had screamed out at the sound and knew at once that he was a goner. The sound was that of compressing bone and flesh and it was enough to make the little Lilly scream. She had averted her eyes, for it was the most awful thing in the world for Ricardo became thin very quickly and lost all his weight and began to waver in the stiff little breeze running through the room.

"Ricardo, my love," The Ugly Mother had cried.

"My family?" Ricardo had shouted back, his voice thin and transparent, almost. "Like Ernesto...," was all he managed to say before he slipped through the floorboards.

The last thing the Ugly Mother heard in the sweet and strange fever fugue state was the zipping sound her husband had made as he disappeared in-between the cracks on the floor. Later when she came to, she was only in Belen's house, the smell of her awful cooking hanging in the air. And when the Ugly Mother looked to her side, she saw her very thin husband standing next to her, offering up his lips for a kiss. His kiss felt like it always had, rough and tender at the same time. His mustache tickled and she felt his new stubble growth.

And of course, he was not there, for he existed in her fever world, she knew this. The Ugly Mother's forehead was drenched in sweat, and she stared into the face of her husband whom she had not seen in so long a time.

"Where did you go?" She asked.

"Between the boards," he said, his voice sounding the same, thin and transparent.

"But we pulled the floor up and looked for you."

"I was carried away by ants who thought they found a feast."

The Ugly Mother only looked, she couldn't think of anything to say.

"I wanted to come to see you and Lilly."

"Oh Ricardo," The Ugly Mother said, coughing lightly into her hand. She felt a real hacker brewing in her lungs. *It wouldn't be long now*, she thought, even in her dream.

"I wanted to come, but I was working," Ricardo said as he kissed her on the cheek and slipped away, falling to the floor like a leaf.

And then the Ugly Mother started to cough. A medium cough at first, then the gut retching cough that would end her life.

CHAPTER EIGHT

1

Lilly Aguirre had been thinking that the cough syrup in the wrinkled brown bag (which did look like the face of the Ugly Mother) would be the last bottle of cough syrup she'd have to buy for her. She thought this because as Lilly walked down the sidewalk, her feet barely touching the ground, as men and women lined up on Belen's front stoop waiting to hear news of what the Ugly Mother had coughed up now, Lilly had one of those moments where she felt right in the world. The sun felt right. The way the breeze lifted her hair felt right. The way her blue jeans rubbed the front of her thighs felt right. Her mother not even really on her mind, her mind hazy, weary, her body not hers, her hand allowing the paper bag to hang, first by three fingers, then by two.

And then Jerry the junkie stole her cough syrup.

Jerry the junkie, Jerry Mathers, his parents had named him after the Beaver, his mother, Beverly, thought it would be cute if her son Jerry turned out to be a lot like the Beaver. Sure, as a kid she'd always had a crush on Wally, but after she got married and her husband (Ward she sometimes called him when his real name was Wallace) ended up working shift work at the Deerfield Goodyear Factory, she had ended up spending her nights watching re-runs of *Leave it to Beaver* and when the old stork delivered her first baby, at last, Beverly decided that she wanted to name her first son Jerry, in hopes that her little Jerry would have as innocent a childhood as the Beav did.

Jerry did have an innocent childhood – for a while. He got to play in neighborhood parks, ride his bike all over Allston-Brighton, play stickball on the BU practice field, play basketball on the public courts. It wasn't the grand TV life but wasn't so bad either. That is until as a teenager, Jerry met Otis P. Road. Otis P. Road was the oldest of the Road boys who all shared their father's middle name – Peter. And all three of the Road boys were down-right mean. Their father didn't beat them, and their mother didn't swear at them, much. They were just mean kids. The thing was, Otis was the grade A substance abuser of the brothers. Beverly Mathers would often say that if you looked up the word 'addict' in the dictionary there would be a picture of Otis P. Road next to the definition, like in the old joke.

Every day after school Otis would ride his bike to the little neighborhood park in the center of Lower Allston (LA to the natives – as '*I live in LA*') where he'd get some bum to buy him a pint of vodka, rum, or whiskey, depending on his mood – which tended to run towards the clearer alcohols – and Otis would drink his pint of liquor with a chaser of OJ, or sometimes chocolate milk which gave him and his buddies the queasies. Besides Jerry, Otis hung out with a roughneck named Dale, who had a black belt in just about every martial art you could name, and "Siegfried & Roy". Dale and Jerry spent their afternoon drinking wine out of a big old plastic jug which Dale socked away under his house and "Siegfried & Roy" would roll fat joints they'd share while cracking jokes on the little shits walking home from the elementary school. Otis liked to shoot little pebbles at the kids as they went by and soon enough, he had the other three doing it as well. Roy wasn't such a good shot, he tended only to hit legs and arms. Dale could throw far, but they tended to wobble and miss for some reason. But Jerry could crack a kid's skull at thirty feet with a tiny park pebble the size of his pinkie fingernail, which would set Otis off. He'd laugh and laugh and laugh. By the time the four of them were juniors in high school, they were sharing a liter of hard liquor, straight, between them, in a span of four hours and smoking a quarter of grass. Sometimes they'd eat three packets of trucker speed each, which made their heads rattle.

Now when Jerry came home from these afternoons his mother would be at work at the Slaughterhouse Steak Restaurant up in Brighton. Jerry was lucky, he'd nap his drunk off and wake up around nine o'clock, eat, and maybe talk with his mother who by that time was half in the bag herself, giggling at re-runs on the boob tube. Occasionally Jerry got caught by his old man, but his old man didn't care if his son drank a little. He'd rather have his son drink close to home than have his son drink in the suburbs with the other suburban rats. *A little partying was natural for a teenager*. Besides, when the old man got home from work, he had a few cold ones himself. Never mind the hard stuff, that was weekend drinking with the boys, as far as he was concerned.

Now around Jerry's senior year, Otis discovered narcotics. He'd steal Valium from his lesbian neighbor (how he stole it is still hotly debated between Otis' little brother Ernest and his crew, which claimed Otis was full of shit) and he and Jerry would pop pills and drink Kahlua or Baileys and smoke cigarettes in the park. At a party, Jerry met Kelly Ambers who had a little crush on Jerry, and Kelly ran with the Brighton Babes, a low rent ten-speed gang run by McKenzie Adkins and Denim Carlile, two pre-teen girls who would fuck you up with a bike chain if you stiffed them. The Brighton Babes sold pot and mushrooms and two of the gang let little kids look at their underwear for five bucks. Kelly and Preston Ward (no relation) racked up hundreds of dollars from their peek-a-boo game. Kelly was tired of the Brighton Babes, mostly because she didn't like McKenzie anymore (McKenzie had told Erin that Kelly was a real honest-to-god slut who did more than let the little kids just look) and she wanted out and she had heard through the proverbial grapevine that Otis wanted to start a regular drug club. Jerry explained it was more of an informational exchange – a drug tree, he called it. Basically, if you knew someone who knew someone who could get you something, you'd get it for someone, and if that person needed something that you could provide, you'd get that special something for that someone. Kelly wanted in. Jerry wanted to get into Kelly and the next thing they knew they were helping Otis P. Road organize his little club.

To start Otis wanted to smoke opium like a cat wants to go after a mouse, and if Otis couldn't find opium through his drug tree why then he was just going to go for broke and shoot heroin like those cool guys do in the movies, Otis said. Dale said he knew how to make opium from poppy plants, but you had to have the right plants. Otis said Dale could go and fuck himself with his Martha Stewart How-to-book. Lorie, an ex-Brighton Babe, said she knew someone who could get them good smack. Otis Peter Road held out one week, three days, four hours, and about twenty minutes, then he and Lorie huffed it out to Watertown on Lorie's Mountain Bike, Lorie riding jackrabbit behind Otis. Otis got Jerry into smack about a week later when Otis showed up with clean needles and newly horked spoons and a brand-new bag of some killer China White. Jerry, always willing to party with Otis, tied off, spooned up, and shot up. He threw up, nodded off, and came to with drool covering his face. Jerry said it was like taking a nap with God and shot up again. It got better and better for Jerry and pretty soon Otis and Jerry were flunking out of their senior year, skinny and dirty.

Bev refused to notice. It wasn't until Bev and Wally and the grandparents showed up with phone cameras and a borrowed video cam for graduation and listened to Dale Dumas graduate with plans of teaching in Guam, and "Siegfried & Roy" Steiner graduate with plans to attend SCAD and even heard Otis P. Road's name called out when they realized something was wrong. Jerry's name had not been called. Jerry wasn't even there. Neither was Otis, but that observation escaped them then. It was Dale and "Siegfried & Roy" who broke the news to Bev and Wally Mathers that Jerry had failed (it was later learned that Otis was pushed out by the principals because the youngest Lord brother, Ernest was going to be a freshman the next year and they would be damned before they'd have all three Lord children under the same educational roof).

While everyone cheered at graduation, Jerry and Otis were high, in the back of Backseat Betty's yard, charging neighborhood snots ten bucks to see her naked. They split the profits three ways (Betty got the raw end of the deal if you ask me) and Jerry and Otis bought an egg-shaped bag of smack. It wasn't until the next morning when Jerry crawled home that his parents got a hold of him. Jerry had just slipped out of his shoes and socks when Wally smacked him across the mouth. Jerry got shoved into the living room, in shock, because his father had never once laid a hand on him. His track marks made everyone gasp and his father stood for a second, half-blubbering before wailing on him again, while his mother cried, and his grandmothers looked at their feet out of shame and embarrassment. Once Wally was finished yelling about grades and the ruination of his life, and AIDS, and whores, and the prices of meat, his paternal grandfather started beating him upside the head with the sides of their bedroom slippers. The slippers made a hollow, flip-flop-like thwack against his ears and neck and Jerry screamed, grabbed the slippers out of his grandfather's hand, and took off. Jerry stole his mother's Lincoln and sold it on the street for $200. The only shoes he had were the bedroom slippers, which would become his calling card. The slippers were both too big for Jerry, but he wore them anyway, and by the next summer the slippers were as grungy and greasy as Jerry's hair and were stretched out and way too big for his feet now, and made a horrible *thwaap, thwaap* when Jerry ran. And Jerry became known for his slippers, finding them far easier to steal than other shoes, and less likely to be stolen off your feet when you're nodded out on junk, plus you heard him coming which Jerry thought was cool.

And after he yanked the cough syrup out of Lilly's hands Jerry bolted down a side alley to cut over and away from the main drag, Lilly on his heels. The sound of the *thwaap* echoed in street, the sound banking off the brownstones and shopfronts and up-turned trashcans. And the *thwaaping* sound sounded almost breath-like in Lilly's ears as her muscles burned. She leaped over a trashcan and turned left down an alley as Jerry turned left down an alley.

As she ran Lilly left a visible streak behind her that remained fixed in the air for some hours after. Her body produced a dazzling display of rainbow colors that trailed behind her. A beat cop remarked that it looked like that somebody had tried to build a fucked-up maze using parts of a defective rainbow. Jerry wasn't too far ahead anymore, his muscles were pretty much cashed out, but he hoped to drink the cough syrup in mid-run before the crazy bitch behind him caught him.

Once in the alley, the *thwaap thwaap* sound magnified, and at once Lilly was seized with images of her mother breathing hard, *huuuh- huuuh*. Only her mother's breathing didn't come as fast as the *thwaap thwaap* of Jerry's bedroom slippers.

The brown paper bag flew off and struck Lilly in the shoulder. She opened her mouth to shout, but nothing came out. It was as if something sucked her words back into her esophagus and Lilly thought if she yelled, she would be able to save her mother. Minutes before she had been convinced that her mother was going to get better and now she was convinced that if she didn't stop this junkie from drinking that bottle of cough syrup, then her mother would die. It didn't occur to her to buy a second bottle. It was that bottle, the bottle in Jerry's hand, the bottle he now brought up to his mouth, his legs slowing down. Lilly was almost close enough to jump on him. She tried to scream again and again her mouth sucked her voice back inside her. Her mouth was hot and dry, and she needed to stop running soon or her limbs would fall off. She felt like a toy whose parts had been stretched way too far back and would soon snap if forced anymore. And when she couldn't shout out for the third time, she reached her arm out and yanked back on Jerry's damp, brown shirt.

Lilly heard the shirt rip and Jerry felt it rip, just as he was pouring the cough syrup into his mouth, running still, dodging an empty shopping cart, did the shirt pull halfway off him, causing him to spill the cough syrup all over his front. He dropped the bottle where the alley abruptly ended at Turner Street. Jerry collapsed and brought his hands up to his face defensively as he brought his legs in to block his crotch. Lilly looked at the fallen bottle, her legs quaking, her breath coming in short deep painful jabs. What was left inside the bottle spilled out in a little sticky pool of gooey red. The rest of it was on the junkie's shirt. She wanted to kick him but didn't have the energy. Instead, she spat on him, collapsing against the side of the wall. Jerry, seeing he wasn't in any danger, edged around the side of the alley, picked himself up, and scurried away, stumbling as he went.

Lilly didn't bother with Jerry the junkie. Her mind webbed out in a million possible directions, worrying about her mother. She hadn't been able to save the bottle. She hadn't been able to save her mother.

Looking back behind her, she saw the streak she'd left behind. It ended in a curvy, semi-reversed, f shape, the outline of where her body had stopped running. The trail, almost like glass, remained thick enough that she was able to follow it back to Belen's house, where men, women, and children were trying to chisel bits of the motley-colored light out of the sky for souvenirs.

She arrived on Belen's stoop exhausted, her muscles singing, her ears ringing, her mouth feeling like sandpaper, her head swelling up like a dog tick. Any moment her head would pop from the pressure building inside.

Loco was there, with news. Loco helped her up the steps, Lilly half-afraid he was going to tell her that the Ugly Mother was dead, kept her mouth shut.

"Lilly, that guy you were looking for. He's dead. A friend of a friend of a friend at the morgue did some looking around. I took that description the Ugly Mother gave me and I think he's dead. A Portuguese man with a tattoo over his ankle was found dead in an alley just the other day. Only a few blocks from here."

Loco gave her a hangdog smile, "I'm sorry you come all this way for nothing."

Lilly only shook her head. They were almost up the stairs to Belen's place now.

When Loco threw the door open, the Ugly Mother was standing in the middle of the floor, coughing and vomiting heaps of vines. The retching was awful, the smell worse. It hit them as Loco grabbed Lilly in a fireman's carry and proceeded to step over the tangles of vines in the floor which had already begun to sprout some kind of purplish flower.

The scene sent Lilly into shock, her mother's body collapsed in on itself with every cough, and with every cough she vomited up vines coated in bloody mucus.

Loco put Lilly down behind her mother. In the background, she heard Belen shouting from the kitchen. She was swinging her broom at a nasty long vine that continued to push itself into the kitchen like a snake. And the Ugly Mother continued to vomit, coughing up bloody vines, and branches, and the occasional limp purple flower. Lilly's mouth hung open in shock. Loco only seemed mildly phased for it was he who stepped up to her mother's back and whacked her squarely with the broad base of his palm, which brought a temporary end to the coughing and hacking. Then the Ugly Mother collapsed onto the floor.

2

Loco and Belen each threw armfuls of vines out the window. Below them, the people who had gathered collected the vines and bagged them up in paper sacks. Down the street, Loco saw children breaking apart the last remains of Lilly's light trail. The Ugly Mother felt like a limp piece of leather in Lilly's arm.

"Mother, I am here. What can I do?" Lilly held her mother's head and tried to calm her.

"You must help where Marcos and I could not," her voice was scratchy and when she spoke, she spat blood.

"Mother please."

"All I know is that you must help. You will know how and when."

Lilly felt the tears well up in her eyes as she watched her mother whither up before her.

"That American boy you like so much?"

"Yes mother," Lilly sobbed.

"Such a cute head of red hair"

Lilly pressed her mother closer to her chest and felt the last bit of her dry up like an autumn leaf.

3

Mr. Bill felt a little shame and embarrassment when he got up to go to the bathroom. He barely got his butt out of his seat. Nick didn't offer any advice and if he had, Bill wasn't sure he would have listened. After all, Nick wasn't the one who had suddenly, without warning, grown almost a foot and a half, and god knows how many inches wide, splitting his clothing apart at the seams. Mr. Bill kept his hands over his privates as he moved, his shoes flopping like mad, his shirt hanging in strips on his chest. He made it to the bathroom and was presented with new problems as to what to wear. He didn't have any luggage and even if he did it would have been stowed away in the back of the plane. Nick didn't have anything either and if he did it wouldn't have fit him. So for the first time in almost four hundred years, Mr. Bill began to make a loincloth. It made perfect sense. It covered him where it counted, and he could easily make it.

A long time ago he had been befriended by Selma A. Blaylock, a preacher who ministered to the slaves on the plantations. She had found Mr. Bill on the side of the road picking berries. He'd been wearing rags then, an old pair of moccasins that were coming apart, a jacket he'd taken off a dead soldier some years ago, and a pair of britches that were ripped at the knees. He supposed he looked okay, maybe his hair had been a little tangled with briers and weeds and maybe he'd been a little smelly with sweat, but he swam almost daily in the creek when he went fishing and that was as good as a bath in those days. Selma

Blaylock saw something else. She saw an opportunity to prove herself to God by taking a poor native under her wing and cleaning him up.

The preacher was taken aback when she found that Mr. Bill could read and write. She was even more surprised that he had read the Bible before. Then she realized that this was a challenge sent from God to prove her worthiness.

Selma had Bill build himself a little shack and he would spend time in the fields, in the hot hours, preaching the gospel to the slaves. Bill helped her hand out Bibles and would illustrate God's goodness by preaching his own story, which was a half-lie concocted by Selma that helped her sell them on her God. The story was a simple one – Mr. Bill had been a godless savage until one day he had a vision of God who told him to clean himself up so to go forth and help the white men save all the savages in the world from themselves.

Bill hadn't thought about Selma in decades. He hadn't thought about Farmer John Scopes who hired him to fork hay, or Elmer Bloodstone, a big black man who owned his farm and needed muscle to keep the white men from stealing his crop. He thought about his people, his father. Bill hadn't thought about them in a long time; they were hidden deep in his mind. Part of him didn't want to remember, but now it was bubbling up to the surface. His memory didn't want to hide them anymore and as he stood there, tying the frayed ends of his shirt into a ragged loincloth, he knew that real soon he'd remember everything. His size had come back to him and soon his memory would too. When he strolled back out into the plane, he didn't bother to mask his appearance any longer. *What did it matter?*

4

Zac didn't want to tell Spider and Blockhead that the guy they were looking for was no longer in town. They wouldn't believe him anyway. His stomach had growled "air" followed quickly by "plane" and followed immediately by "guy". Sometimes it took a little imagination to figure out what his guts were telling him, but Zac didn't care. He trusted his gut even when everybody else thought he was crazy. Blockhead was driving towards the Citgo sign which sits atop Kenmore Square like a beacon flashing its triangular orange eye. Spider directed them to head towards Boston University, an area he was somewhat more familiar with.

"The more I drive the more I think this is a stupid idea," Blockhead said his face covered in sweat. The Yugo's AC didn't work, and Blockhead seemed to be suffering the most.

"What the hell are you talking about?" Spider replied looking hurt.

"This trip."

"Did you see that huge fucking billboard outside Providence?"

"More like on the edge of Providence."

"This guy's taking it to a whole new fucking level. No more sidewalks and hotel walls for this guy. He erased an entire ad."

"More like covered it up."

Spider shot Blockhead a half-annoyed look, "I think he'll do something like that again."

Zac sat back and listened. He was pretty sure his stomach was going to say something else.

"What's the story with this guy, Spider? Why is he doing this?" Blockhead asked.

Spider half-turned to look out the window, "It sounds stupid."

"What?" Blockhead floored his gas and the car coughed and shuddered. "Spill the proverbial tea."

"It's stupid."

"Spill the fucking beans already." Blockhead slapped the loose end of a sticker back against the dashboard.

"He's chasing a mermaid."

"Get the fuck outta here Spider."

"Seriously."

"Mermaids my ass." Blockhead honked his horn.

"I don't think she's a real mermaid. More like a really good-looking girl who likes to swim, is what I'm thinking."

"That's not a mermaid," Blockhead said.

"No. It isn't," Zac said from the back.

"I know that. Don't you think I know that?" Spider didn't recognize as much of Boston as he hoped he would. He didn't recognize anything at all besides the Citgo sign.

"So where do we find this mermaid?" Blockhead asked.

"How the fuck should I know?" Spider growled.

Then there was silence in the very hot and cramped Yugo. The front of Zac's black T-shirt was completely soaked. The one thing he hated about his new body was that he sweated like a man, a fact Zac had not gotten used to even after years of T therapy. His pants felt sticky and hot. Blockhead had soaked through his shirt too. Spider seemed to be the only one who wasn't remotely sweating. Zac's stomach rumbled one word – *Beach*.

"Spider?"

"Yes, Blockhead?"

"Why the fuck aren't you sweating?"

"Cause I'm a cool motherfucker."

"Man shut the fuck up," Blockhead said.

"You asked."

"Let's get some grub," Blockhead suggested.

"I'm starving."

"You hungry Zac?"

"Sure am, Blockhead."

Spider looked ahead, not sure what he saw in the gauzy light, "There are some places to eat at up here."

"Cool."

"Guys?"

"Yeah, Zac?" Spider said, not bothering to look behind.

"The beach."

"What about it?" Spider said, bouncing the side of this thumb against his leg.

"That's where we should go after we eat."

"This is not the time nor place to be thinking about scoring chicks, Zac."

"Spider, we're here. I haven't seen jackrabbit shit. Why not go see the surf?" Blockhead countered.

"Blockhead, shut up."

"No. Guys?" Zac pleaded.

"What?" Spider sneered.

"That's where a mermaid would be, right? At the beach?"

Spider and Blockhead looked at each other.

"Can't argue with that logic," Spider said as they crossed the invisible line that separated Allston-Brighton from Boston and beyond.

5

Doppelgänger Bill had done one thing before he had stolen Sea Hag's truck and lead the county deputies and state Mounties on a high-speed chase through the county, he turned most of the Hayes home completely upside-down.

As it happened, when Mr. Bill created Doppelgänger Bill from his tissue, something had gone wrong and Doppelgänger Bill's mind had been created inside out, so to speak. And what Doppelgänger Bill had done before he led the cops on a chase was to go through Mr. Bill's belongings and turn all of them upside-down – beakers, vials, buckets, cups, ashtrays, rucksacks, trashcans, tea-cups, and teapots. He had put things that could not be put upside down, upside-down, which lead to broken glass covering the floor, or on the counter, or the worktable. He had gone through the basement over-turning gas cans, chlorine buckets, Marina's candles that she loved so much, buckets of oil, cans of oil, and quarts of motor oil for the SUV, the truck, and the tractor. He overturned old gallons of paint, new gallons of paint, paint thinner, shellac, and enamel. This didn't always lead to the mess that might be imagined. Most of these things such as the oil and the gas etc. came with tight lids and nothing leaked. Other things such as the mason jars full of nails and screws had no tops, so there was shit everywhere from these containers.

Ten minutes before he took off in Sea Hag's truck, he was over-turning saltshakers, sugar bowls, flour tins, and cookie jars. As it happened, Mulch hadn't even seen Doppelgänger Bill, so intent was he on killing Sea Hag. But Doppelgänger Bill had been in the kitchen, meddling in the refrigerator, turn-ing over butter dishes and pitchers of freshly squeezed orange juice, milk jugs, ice cream quarts (which he had left on the counter to melt into a milky pool) jars of jelly, olives, peppers, jalapenos, tartar sauce, horseradish, mustard, fancy mustard, little cocktail onions, jars of toothpicks, pasta containers, peanut but-ter, Nutella, boxes of sugar cereals, saltine crackers, and whatever else he could get his hands on.

When Mulch was escorting Sea Hag to the basement, Doppelgänger Bill had gone through Mulch's room and flipped the bed there, the desk chair (but not the desk), little containers of staples, and paper clips and pens, and pencils. He flipped over the box that contained all Mulch's legitimate business dealings (there was a hidden safe where Mulch kept papers on his illegitimate business – Swiss bank account numbers, phone numbers, and beeper numbers with the names of trustworthy dealers, fences, and contacts in Holland, Richmond, Va. Beach, DC, and Atlanta, etc.).

Doppelgänger Bill turned dresser drawers upside down, spilling clothing, random black and white photos of Virginia in compromising positions, a large wad of cash (which Doppelgänger Bill would have probably eaten as soon as spend), and a small well-oiled handgun. He flipped over boxes of old jewelry that had belonged to Virginia's mother, bottles of cologne (almost new), and then he had gone into Virginia's room.

Doppelgänger Bill farted loud large noxious clouds of gas. Mr. Bill would have called it "blowing his trumpet." He overturned her drawers too and her bed and all the vials and cups and vessels of jewelry and rings and little slips of paper like fortunes from the local Chinese restaurants, and random guy's phone numbers she had never bothered calling but kept as a keepsake and a trophy. There were plastic cups and one glass flute from various formal dances filled with thumbtacks and stickers advertising her favorite bands (which she never used), BU auto decals rolled and folded, a CD of Linkin' Park which Virginia swore Macy stole during her freshman year, a strip of wallet photos of Rick "the Dick" Bell from the automat, Macy Allbright's grades 9-12 class photos, Polaroids and Kodak prints of Jimm Belll (two ms, three ls,) Colin Bush, Ryan Sullivan, Corky Wroblewski, Mike Dodge, Kevin Lee, Mike Watkins, and some guy known only as Jeff, who were all boys who had wanted to date her but hadn't. Pictures of Maria and Virginia on the dock crabbing. Tiny bits of ribbon lay like worms on the dresser. Bits of colored string, rubber bands, scrunchies, one blue ribbed condom, three mismatched batteries (all expired), a half dozen different combs, three brushes, all packed into four promotional souvenirs from high school. Doppelgänger Bill half-crying from the stink his farts made, half-crying from the joy he felt at finding so much colored junk, had thrown the bits of clothes, rings, and paper into the air like confetti. Then suddenly he had stopped. Something had tickled his brain and that was when he had leap-frogged it outside and into Sea Hag's truck, keys dangling inside like an invitation.

Mulch had spent most of that evening cleaning up. Seeing the mess, Maria had cried and crossed herself that Mr. Bill hadn't found his way to her room, thank God. Once night had come and Maria had gone to bed, Mulch would take Sea Hag out of the house and bury her.

6

When Mulch had aligned with the Tortini brothers there had been a war going on and Mulch hadn't wanted any part of it. He had his problems to take care of and if the Tortini Brothers wanted to kill a few business rivals, then so be it. Problem was, the Tortini Brothers killed a lot of their business partners. That kept Mulch's Chesapeake Bay Disposal Service running at full tilt for some years. So busy in fact that for a while Mulch ran two trash barges a week out of Baltimore County, himself at the wheel, Mr. Bill at his side.

Sometimes, if the victim was a real pain-in-the-ass and the Tortini Brothers didn't want any trace of the guy to be found, the barge was loaded down with an entire house or apartment's worth of stuff – bags and bags of trash – bags of shredded documents, bags of fresh groceries thrown in from the fridge, old bottles and other recycling, random clothes just for the bulk, and jewelry even. The dead were placed in body bags and then placed in kettle drums marked oil. This was back when people dumped oil and grease anywhere they wanted, and they had just the drums for it, hundred-gallon drums, fifty-gallon drums, thirty-gallon drums, whatever worked. The bodies, depending on size, were placed inside and sealed with the lids crimped shut.

Eventually, one of Robert's cousins took over running the little office in Baltimore County, right on the Bay, with a view and its own kitchen and little fishing deck. For many, it was considered a cushier job on the Tortini circuit. The only real problem was the bodies themselves.

If there were a lot of bodies one week, then some were dumped about a hundred miles south of Baltimore County and the remaining bodies were taken to the Hayes place where the bodies would be brought either to the swamp or to some back paddle of the creek where it was deep like he had talked about when he had first met the brothers. Mulch eventually started to bury the bodies in his fields. All it took was Mr. Bill and himself, sometimes Huck and Buck, and a few shovels and a few hours and they could get ten feet under the soft sandy soil in no time. It was hard work, but Mulch likes to sweat for it because he felt like he was serving penance for his uncle and all the wrong he had done and was still going to do. But it wasn't long before Mulch was using the backhoe to dig holes for six men at a time. "No need to break your back, by gum," he liked to say.

In the fields, the dead didn't shift so much as they sprouted. They had to be buried at least ten feet so come spring the tractor wouldn't turn them over again and get caught on their clothes. But if Mulch dug any deeper, he would hit the water table. Soon after Mulch started to bury his dead in the fields, his crops erupted in healthy bursts of green. The dead seemed to bring out brighter flowers on the pumpkins and potatoes and the tomatoes were so juicy and sweet one couldn't help but to shake their head and wonder how did Mulch do it. Why even the cotton fields came up whiter and fluffier when a body was buried underneath. Sometimes the plants displayed the tics of the dead buried beneath it, like a constant nod of the leaves even when there was no wind or how sometimes the leaves grew in the shapes of profiles with big fat noses, or the stalk might look like the profile of a skinny man. One patch of cotton kept checking its head like it was always playing with its hair. Something Ernesto's wife, Rina, was prone to do.

7

Sea Hag's body was heavier than Mulch thought it was going to be. Her boots thumped into the small of his back as he crept up the stairs, her dead body over his shoulder. Maria was asleep but he moved quietly anyway.

The body made a solid thunk in the back of his pick-up and it bumped and thumped out to a far tomato field, which ran along a dirt access road. Sometimes the migrants liked to walk the road at night when it was too hot to sleep. Fortunately, he didn't see anybody walking that night, but there was one person out watching the stars. Maria's cousin Estrella. barely a woman laid out beside the field and stared up at the sky. She liked looking at the stars because that was her name and her name always delighted her. She didn't know much, she knew the dippers, she knew Venus, and she knew Gemini and Canis Major because her uncle had shown them to her a long time ago. But that was it and that was fine with her because she just liked to stare at the shapes and watch for UFOs or angels or think about her love life and how she was going to settle down in Mexico City and raise a family and maybe one day own her own house. She was quiet and didn't make a sound when Mulch passed her. She didn't even think to panic that she was out in her employer's field without permission. She was just casting her luck out there and wondering what she would catch. Mulch didn't see her either and parked his truck about hundred yards from where Estrella lay. He got out and picked up Sea Hag's heavy body and slung it over his shoulder and grabbed his shovel. When he walked through the tomato field, Estrella's heart nearly stopped.

All during her adolescence, Estrella had heard about strange things going on in the Hayes fields, but she had never seen anything. She doubted most of the tales told around camp, especially those concerning Maria, who was sweet and innocent and certainly not the devil's minion. But laid out beside the field, seeing the twisted shadow of Mulch Hayes she started to sweat even though the evening was cool. Her heart beat like a drum.

She inched herself up on her elbows and spied a dark figure, blacker than the night around it. It was deformed for it hunched and looked like it was too top-heavy. The beast labored, and it had trouble walking.

Very slowly, Estrella crawled away from the field, careful not to make the slightest noise. She froze when she heard a deep thud but when she didn't hear the figure crashing through the field after her she continued crawling until she was safely behind the planted row of bushes near the cornfield, where she got up and ran towards the forest edge, where she melted into darkness.

Mulch reached the middle of the field and threw the body down, crushing some of his prized tomato plants with a loud thud. If he had turned slightly, he might have seen young Estrella crawling away against the low-lying stars, but he didn't and instead concentrated on how he was going to hide the fresh grave from the morning walkabouts. The tomato plants were getting large, already two feet and stretching. Once he got started on digging, he lost his steam, he felt his age, and his bones hurt. He doubted very much that he could dig ten feet and tried instead for seven. And when he didn't get as far as seven either, he opted for five. Sea Hag fit nicely into the earth. He covered her and then did his best to patch the field by replanting his plants.

In his struggles, he missed Mr. Bill. Mr. Bill would have been able to help make things right. And it occurred to Mulch that he had never really been on his own. There had always been someone. First his father, then Bill, and Pembroke on occasion, and even Cilia. There had been the Tortini brothers in on the disposal service, a service that was no more. Now he was alone, his children scattered from him, and he liked it. He'd read once that sometimes animals go off alone when they're ready to die. He felt like that now, only that he had a few loose ends to take care of first. He was going to have a blowout, all right, one last hurrah, so to speak.

Why am I doing this? He thought.

Because all of this shit is tainted is why. The voice that spoke to him was the voice of his father. *One bad apple can ruin the bunch, you know.*

Set it to burn, Mulch thought. *Let it all go up in smoke. That'd be a proper end to it all.* It wasn't like he could go back now. He couldn't welcome Virginia into his arms, anymore. Maybe Marina, but she'd see through his shit too. In his heart, he knew his eldest was no doormat. She hated him now, that much was certain.

He'd finished packing the ground around Sea Hag's body and had done his best to smooth out where the fresh grave had been dug. His back hurt and he cracked it walking back to the truck. When he got into the truck a wave of energy came over him. Old Mulch was ready to kick ass and take names. A second wind of sorts had lifted his sails.

8

"Master, whose kingdom is this? Sometimes it smells delicious and sometimes it smells awful. There is a giant sign, this one has a very tall man on it holding a bottle! This land of giant signs."

Kinda like that billboard, we passed in Providence. But George didn't say anything. He didn't say anything when they passed it, though he had felt like he was looking at the leftovers of Nick's creepy work. The billboard had been beautiful though, greens, yellows, and that face, the hair. It looked like the hair moved, coming at them, a loamy wave of seafoam. The woman's face had Nick's eyes. He was sure of it. As sure as he was of being lost now.

"I believe this kingdom to be big and large, like mountains that have fallen."

George didn't say anything, his radar was completely scrambled, he was lost. George knew this much: he'd turned off the interstate, onto Storrow Drive somehow, and saw the exit marked Brighton, and thought, *hey I can use a little light right about now* and meant to turn off, but instead exited Storrow Drive too early and instead found himself in a place called Kenmore Square that had a huge Citgo sign that had made Ab's eyes pop out.

The traffic was intense, and his truck felt very large, too large. He felt conspicuous in his king cab with foreign hot-shot cars and beat up POS zigging and zagging across the lanes of traffic that merged and bled together with no rhyme or reason. George thought most of the traffic was coming together in a weird double helix pattern, except the double helix pattern overlapped a little, causing him this monstrous headache.

"Smelly dog, master befuddled at such big kingdom!" Ab laughed and rubbed Rufus' ears.

"Ab, I'm driving, please," George said as he barely missed sideswiping a guy on a bike whose saddlebags were packed full of stuff. He came to a stop at a red light.

"Master, excuse Abdullah. He is marveling at the Nobility store beside us now."

The Barnes & Noble bookstore was probably the biggest bookstore George had ever seen as well. It was the biggest one Abdullah had ever seen. George figured he'd almost swiped a bike messenger but wasn't sure since he'd never seen one before. With the windows rolled down, George made out five distinct smells wafting in from the streets.

"All the camels in the desert could not make such foul stench."

Vomit, piss, exhaust, hot steamy garbage, and mothballs, George thought as he watched a big man get on top of a very small Vespa scooter and slide down a side street.

"Even if all the camels in the desert got together with smelly old men with their night pots poured on their head, the stench would seem like flowers, compared to rot in my nose, now."

Rufus whined. George patted his head and scratched his ears.

"Nobility and barns!" Ab laughed to himself.

George's heart got a little lift when he saw that he was close to Fenway Park; the Red Sox had been his grandfather's favorite baseball team. For a second George had a hankering to check out Fenway Park and maybe catch a game. *Why not? He was in town, wasn't he?* But the thing that made him change his mind was Rufus, who suddenly after spending the entire drive on the floorboards, his huge body taking up most of the foot space, rose, placed his front paws on the dash, and let out a single bark. Even Ab jumped back, startled.

"Master, I think the dog wants to drive."

"What is it?" George felt like he was in an old TV show, except instead of Lassie the collie, he had Rufus the drooling St. Bernard.

Rufus let out another bark and pointed his nose straight ahead, which as far as George could tell, was straight towards several college-type structures.

"I think he wants me to go straight," George said. He was lucky that the red light had been one of the longest George had ever had the pleasure to sit through his entire life, and when it turned green, he didn't give himself time to think about where he should go, he just gunned it and headed off in the direction that Rufus's nose pointed them in.

9

Belen wasted no time kicking Lilly out. Lilly had no money to pay for the burial of the shriveled-up corpse of the Ugly Mother. The old woman looked more like an old shoe tongue than a woman. Deflated and shriveled, the Ugly Mother reminded Carmen of beef jerky. Belen also wanted her girls to come home, who had all been undressing dolls and watching TV that they shouldn't, over at Carmen's. Carmen was standing beside her and the two of them looked like wicked stepsisters. Belen, tall and round as a lightbulb, and Carmen, shorter, almost stumpy with broad football shoulders and a round belly. Belen's dress floated in the breeze as Lilly gathered her belongings. Her mother had been dead less than a few hours and already she had to decide what to do with the body. Loco had vanished.

"I'll give you one hundred dollars for your mother's body," Carmen said, her cigarette smoke branching out like a web behind her. "The other Carmen at the bodega would love to see it, she would pay handsomely for it."

"Carmen, for shame," Belen gasped as she gently smacked Carmen's arm with the back of her hand.

"All right. Fifty dollars and not a penny more," Carmen said keeping her eye on the window. An hour ago some of the men waiting down on the stoop had formed a human ladder and had sent Paquito up to peek. Belen had chased him off with a wet rag.

Lilly only stifled her cries. She had gathered her clothes into her duffel bag and packed up her mother's stuff as well.

"Hurry it up, Liliana. I want my daughters to sleep here with me tonight," Belen said, her eyes following her wherever she went. Outside little girls giggled.

"I'm telling you, Lilly, she would be great propped up in Carmen's bodega. She's all dried up, there's nothing left to rot. We will split the profits."

Lilly said nothing but sobbed into her mother's unpacked clothes.

Carmen continued, "I'm telling you, these Latinos are a suspicious bunch. We could call her the Saint of Lower Allston and people could pay to touch her and bring vegetables to be blessed. No, better yet, seeds, for a good crop, no?"

"Sometimes, Carmen, I wonder how we became friends."

"Because Belen, you recognized that part of me that is inside you."

"You make no sense, Carmen Arancha Escardino."

"Both of you, shut up," Lilly said, full of quick rage and spit. She wanted to hurt someone. She wanted to break something.

Belen said nothing, her mouth hanging open. Carmen pulled on her cigarette and sneered, "You're going to let this ungrateful bitch, this bruja, talk to you like that. Puta." Carmen said as she spat at Lilly's feet.

"Shut up," Lilly said quietly. "You both should be ashamed. I'm taking my mother and we're leaving now. Belen, I paid you yesterday for your hospitality. I am indebted to you, but your disrespect makes me sick."

"Look at this high bitch, eh?" Carmen said nudging Belen.

Belen stood stone-faced, her mouth rigid, her eyes like hard lumps of darkness.

"Belen, I wouldn't take this if I were you."

But Belen was silent and as Lilly grabbed her duffel and threw it over her shoulder, she picked her shriveled mother up and put her under her arms. As she did she thought she saw Belen shed a single, oval tear which ran the curve of her round face and fell onto the floor, unnoticed by Carmen.

"Hey, girl. You know where the bodega is. I'm sure you and Carmen and I can make a lucrative arrangement for us all, eh? Keep you in food, at least."

Carmen's voice faded behind her as Lilly exited the building into the oohs and ahs on the stoop below, the locals eager to see the Ugly Mother's dead body. Lilly felt very alone and very afraid.

10

Lilly walked aimlessly. She walked and she remembered, her mother's raucous laugh, her mother's hasty breakfast sausage, how she had asked her mother why her name Lilly had three Ls instead of two, how her mother sang when she fed animals, always. She walked towards what she expected to be the city center. With her, she carried her mother's dried corpse under her arm like a souvenir. She stopped only once and that was to wing the Ugly Mother's duffel into a garbage dumpster. It didn't seem important to keep that around, only to keep the Ugly Mother from touching the ground. And it had been increasingly harder and harder to keep the shriveled corpse of the Ugly Mother from dragging behind her with two duffel bags. It had been the worst when she exited Belen's place, the neighborhood men and women, many of whom had gathered shopping bags of the Ugly Mother's rotten vines, had reached out to touch what they were all now calling the Saint of Lower Allston. The Ugly Mother's dry body had become some kind of holy relic. Some believed the old woman was alive, others did not understand what they were seeing, only that the vines the Ugly Mother had vomited and had been thrown out the window were now sprouting feet and buds, giving off a faint odor. The locals crowded around Lilly as she pushed onward through them. A little kid by the name of Paquito had tried to cut a lock of stiff hair off of the Ugly Mother with his pocketknife, but her hair was too dry and hard and the knife only slid across the strands cutting Pequito's hand. Another woman had tried to reach out and touch the Ugly Mother's shriveled bosom which had turned to blackened stumps. A man wanted to rub her belly for luck.

But the milling crowd was behind her now and somehow, she would find a way for her and her mother's corpse to get home. As she walked, those that noticed the shriveled woman under her arms moved away quickly from Lilly. Some stared with curiosity, twice someone stopped her to ask her where she got the sculpture. She didn't think to ask these people for directions, and so she continued to wander.

11

My mother is dead, Lilly thought. *My mother is dead*. Lilly had arrived in Boston almost three days ago, the same day Marcos had been murdered and the same night Captain Van Dijk sailed to Amsterdam. The days had become one long taffy of misery. The Ugly Mother's sickness, the hostility of her hosts, and the derision she endured from both Carmens, Loco's aunt, and the shopkeep, all had been too much. Lilly wandered in shock, thinking about the past.

The pine grove had been the Ugly Mother's secret to share with Lilly alone. Many years ago, there had been others, the Ugly Mother had told her once. And now, in light of what Lilly knew, Marcos had more than likely been one of those others.

Her mother had explained it like this: there were places in the world where certain things came together, much like a Mexican intersection. The pine grove was such a place. The Ugly Mother said that oftentimes buildings of importance are built on such places, or sometimes it was the buildings of importance that created such places. Lilly hadn't understood that at all, but her mother had told her that sometimes when a government builds its capital somewhere and then everyone starts coming to this capital, first water must be brought and then fire, and then electricity and pretty soon, maybe a place of power is created. The pine grove was the Ugly Mother's special place. There was so much about her mother Lilly did not understand.

That is because you had your place for how many years now? Lilly thought. *Stop it. The guilt. Remember your mother didn't exactly reach out and love you. Not once did she come to you without having some other reason for being there, usually a good one, on behalf of someone else. Why would the pines be any different?*

All of sudden, thinking back on it all now, the pine grove, Marcos and her mother's special relationship, Lilly started to cry, and she walked blindly into a lamppost. Doing so she almost dropped her mother but managed to grapple with her mother's leg just in time to flip her mother up and back under her arm as if she were made of cardboard.

Part of the problem was that dead Ugly Mother was so shriveled and flat that none of her clothes fit anymore. Somehow it seemed shameful and mean, a mockery of her death, somehow, her body so small in the sea of her dress.

What Lilly didn't know was that the Ugly Mother had given Marcos his ankle tattoo in the pine grove when they had met, secretly. And Lilly also didn't know that her mother and Marcos had more of a relationship than she suspected. Marcos had been like a son to her and she had tried to teach him how to vomit vegetables like her, but he had not been able to manage it. His primary power had to do with wood, which the Ugly Mother had come to accept. But Lilly didn't know this. She only knew that the pine grove was where she could go, outside her neat little apartment, where she could practice glowing or not glowing or even practice levitating or some of the other fantastic things her mother had promised she could accomplish if she truly desired.

Lilly realized, carrying her mother, that she was envious of Marcos. Envious because she hadn't been included. It was bad enough that her father had grown thin and fallen through the cracks in the boards, but somehow being excluded from her mother's life was like being forced to live in the dark. She had made her mind up to bury her mother in the pine grove when she realized that she didn't know where she was.

12

"Sometime after Pembroke put me back into the coffin the floodgate opened. Doc, I suppose I thought it was shock at the time, but it wasn't. But I wasn't to know this for many more days, not until after I killed Pembroke and my father.

"Now, I believe, now I know. I had become the vessel for all the memories of all those that knew my family and Mr. Bill. And I had also become the keeper of Nick Adams memories.

"Yeah, I get that look. No one remembers me or my family anymore. Weird isn't it. And Nick, ask Nick and he'll corroborate. He remembers because he lived through it. And my sister, obviously. That look you give me sometimes isn't very open-minded and empathetic, I must say, Doc.

"I probably could have gotten out of there sooner if I knew about Nick, George, Lilly, and Mr. Bill. It wasn't until it was all over that I learned that Nick had chased Marina down and that Mr. Bill had gone to help him, and in the end redeemed himself. I would have been surprised that George would have followed his love Lilly to the edge of the United States. And I would have been even more surprised at Lilly, who after losing her mother, ended up saving my sister and Nick.

"I learned all that later, from Nick, mostly, and later George Henderson corroborated what he remembered.

"What happened to me while my body stitched itself back together and my inner organs healed from the bruises Pembroke caused when he poked and prodded and God knows what else, was that I absorbed all those memories concerning everyone in my family.

"I lay very still, my fingers tight, my legs rigid, my neck still. For the longest time, I was half-afraid that my stomach was going to explode with some kind of germ that had made its way inside while I had lain spread open. For hours I lay very still, listening for it. I heard it or thought I heard it, tiny things crawling in my body – tapeworms, with their hook mouths.

"I remembered reading once of a baby, on the Newton Farm up the road from us, who had been born with a hundred tapeworms inside her. They had attached themselves to the back of her eyes, to her brain stem, to her liver, and lungs, they were inside her intestines, and one had coiled up like a snake around her gall bladder. They managed to save the baby. God knows how. Christ, if I had been the mother, I'm sure I would have just died knowing that.

"And I thought Pembroke had snuck something inside me, something mechanical and rusty. I tried to retrieve the symptoms for lockjaw from my brain but couldn't remember them.

"Instead, I saw myself at the theater. I was looking at myself and my awkward but striking sister. She was standing stock-still, and I watched the honey-light illuminate her hair from behind, the color shifting from green to black to green again. I watched how she watched me and I felt only love for her. There was a pull in my gut to move, to speak, but I couldn't form the words. I watched me as I pulled Marina away into the rows and then I watched as I sat close behind her, my eyes on the back of Marina's head and not on my date, Suzanne Prince, who chewed her popcorn with an open mouth and tried to hold my hand with hers dripping with sweat. And as the movie played on, I thought about marrying that awkward girl with glowing hair and kissing that girl and making slow and passionate love to her on a giant bed of pillows.

"My name was Nick Adams and I had graduated from Northampton High School. Surprising everyone that asked, my favorite food was soup. I liked to drink cheap, ugly beer on the weekends with my best friends George and Renny. I had had sex with Shirley Audrey Morris the previous year and had not used a condom. Luckily, she hadn't got pregnant, but because of all the stress, I had caused she hadn't wanted to see me again, either.

"It was like having a god-damned friend in my head. I knew who he was. He was the guy Marina had fallen head over heels for. Only, what the hell was he doing in my head? And that was when I thought I was going crazy, for real. There, inside that coffin, where some guy I hardly knew had somehow found his way into my skull. Now I knew everything about him. Well, almost everything.

"His memories were a continuous timeline stretching back to the womb. It was pretty cool stuff. A lot of it warm bubbly thoughts, mostly impressions, with no vocabulary to name things. His memories extended into the present up to the day before I was kidnapped. How I knew that I don't know, but I knew. It was important to know. His last memory had been that of a dream. His memories ended with a dream. Before the dream, he had been hanging out with George. Then Nick had gone to sleep and dreamed of the Idle Hour theater. And that's where it ended, with his dream. What happened to him after, I didn't know, but I was going to find out. This much I knew."

13

When Bill was a young boy, he heard tales of the great herd of deer that ran through the lower portions of the shore feasting on the wild plants and herbs that grew up into forever. Legend spoke of an earth spirit inhabiting the great stag who led the herd. The stag's horns grew up like a thorn bush, only hard as stone and sharp as spears. No one was sure how many points were on the great stag's head. Many of the warriors gave varying reports. Kiptocreek claimed there were eighteen. Kego-tok was sure there were at least twenty-one. Others argued that no less than thirty points were extending from the beast's great shaggy skull. The stag wasn't all white, but most of his mane was. All those that had seen him said that his eyes flashed white and that he ran so fast he left a trail of light. The stag, afraid of no warrior, would stare down anyone who dared try spearing him. And the beast's eyes burned, many hunters said, with sharp red points of light. It was also told that the great beast's breath was fog, and an unnatural fog at that, one that made warriors forget where they were. Experienced woodsmen would get lost in the beast's breath, they said, and lose all sense. There were stories of the animal invading the minds of the hunters and causing them to crumble to the ground in fear and panic, and even stranger tales of great carrion birds that appeared with the herd at times, birds larger than falcons, larger than turkey buzzards even, and more dangerous. The herd had as many as a hundred deer, and as little as fifty, given when and where the hunters saw them. Most of the deer they hunted did not travel in large herds, but family groups. Kego-tok claimed this herd traveled as they did because the herd was led by an earth spirit. When Kego-tok had been a boy he remembered Chief Kiptopeake telling the story one night, how long ago the Chief of the Nassawattucks had asked for permission from the spirit to hunt the great herd. The tribe's spiritual advisor, who had been Kego-tok's great, great, grandfather had been permitted a vision. In that time, the herd numbered in the thousands, and the stag, the great deer, had been huge then, his white mane flowing down over his great chest like sea foam.

The Laughing King loved to hear stories about hunting and feats of strength and had been listening to Kiptocreek speak of seeing the great beast drinking from a creek and how the beast looked as virile as ever. Kiptocreek had been thinking of trying to ride the animal when the deer had run off, scared not by

Kiptocreek, but by the sounds of the white men coming through the forest to trade. The white men moved like clumsy animals. Stories like that had been told before, by other warriors and by the women to the children. When the white men traveled, they made noise, lots of noise, and game and fish were scared off by it. To say nothing of the sickness following the colonizers like a cloud of flies.

The Laughing King did not believe it was the white man causing the sickness. Kego-tok disagreed. And if the earth spirit, afraid of no warrior, had been scared off by the white man, then wasn't the white man dangerous? Debedeavon didn't think so. The white men made him laugh and they called him king. Their trade had brought many great things to the village and now Debedeavon could compete with Powhatan. Why he might be able to beat Powhatan in a fight now that they had guns now, and steel.

Most of the warriors thought Debedeavon was foolish to clash with Powhatan. The Powhatan nation was strong and many. The Nassawattucks, though giants, were only a few by comparison. But they had the support of the spirit, didn't they? That was what the medicine man was for – a link to the spirits. Surely Kego-tok would be able to see that the white man was useful and that the spirits would approve of the trading. They were growing strong, and it thrilled Debedeavon. The stag had probably been thrown off by the white man's stench, not his fierceness. The white men smelled of death and rot, didn't they not?

14

Jon de van Hazen smirked into his reflection in the tide pool. With his beard trimmed just so, and wearing the latest in ridiculous English fashion, he looked just like Captain John Smith. He was thinner than Smith and a little taller, but the fact that the Indians didn't seem to notice the difference between him and the real Smith made it easy, almost too easy, for Jon to waltz into the Laughing King's camp and make trouble. Well, trouble was a *relative* word, in Jon's opinion. He traded faulty rifles, costume jewelry, cheap wine, and the cheapest of fabric for food, or even permission to fish, or even some of the shells that the Indians passed for money in these parts. He had to be careful not to cause too much suspicion. But he had a plan, and that was to gradually make the Indians hate the English. To get the Indians to start a little war with the English. And he figured all he had to do was piss them off enough to get them rolling. And what would that take?

Jon had always been a rascal. He loved to start trouble. When he was a child growing up in Rotterdam, he liked to sneak into neighbors' homes and steal food, or clothing and place them into other houses, or windows, or on the front stoop and watch and wait for trouble to start. Jon had figured out that he could be invisible if he wanted to be. All he had to do was pretend to belong wherever he happened to be. If anyone ever said anything to him (which was never) he would just bat his eyelashes and flash his charming smile.

"Oh, why miss, I'm sorry, my mother told me to come and get her sister's laundry, I must be in the wrong house.

"No sir, I'm looking for my father, he's a sea captain.

"No sir, I'm looking for my brother, he's a sailor.

"Excuse me miss, I seem to be lost, could you help me out?"

Rotterdam was a good-sized city, not as big as Amsterdam, but all the homes and people living there made life exciting. He went around pretending that he was a pirate or a thief and he caused trouble. It was interesting for him to see how other people lived. His own family wasn't poor, but they didn't have the money a lot of the merchants and tradesmen had. Sometimes, he stole for keeps – a few coins, a purse, a bit of fabric for his mum. He liked to sneak aboard docked ships and steal the Captain's log and place it below deck, in some sailor's quarters. Usually, the sailor was flogged. The sounds of pain he heard from piers made Jon laugh. Besides, on ships there was always something laying around – a knife, a pistol. Once, while rummaging around in a ship's hold, while most of the sailors were off to get a good drunk on, Jon had found a shrunken head of a man. The eyes were as hard as beans and the closed lips were like jerky. The skin felt like horsehide. *But horsehide was skin, too, wasn't it?* He stole the head and would stare at it late at night when he was supposed to be sleeping, rubbing the dark hair for good luck, counting the whiskers that had prematurely stopped their growth. The head didn't look scared, rather the head's expression was one of passivity. The head became something of a good luck charm, and he wished on it throughout his young life, and he had luck, lots of it. Why if there was money to be found, young Jon found it. If there was a girl he liked, then the girl liked him back. If his mother baked a pie, she would bake his favorite kind. Miraculously, he'd almost always escaped trouble as a child, though once he'd been smacked hard by a drunken sailor who caught him below deck.

When he was old enough Jon became a sailor in the Dutch Navy where he advanced quickly up the ranks. His father was a miller with no love of the ocean. His mother disliked the sea, said it made scoundrels of men, but they didn't disapprove when he joined. He had a knack for getting people to do what he wanted, parents and superiors included. Eventually, he worked his way up to Captain and had his ship for the better part of a year before retiring. He'd noticed that one could make a lot of money as a privateer, robbing from the French, or English and giving most of it to the King and Queen. He talked his way into a captainship and found a swarthy crew and began robbing with a fervor unmatched by any Dutchman, and perhaps any man (privateer, pirate, or otherwise), save Bluebeard who would come to use Jon de van Hazen's hideouts on the Atlantic seaboard generations later.

Jon met Captain Smith while he was robbing Smith's private boat. Captain Smith, before heading up the Jamestown Colony, had invested in the tea trade. Smith envisioned himself as something of a hero and insisted on commanding the vessel, despite his investors' worries. Smith was to travel from Dover, England to the south of Spain to meet with a Turkish tea merchant who had set up an outpost on the coast. On the way, Smith got lost three times. The first time Smith overshot Spain and landed in Oporto, Portugal. When he tried to correct it, Smith went too far up and landed at Brest, France. The third time Smith ended up on the island of Sao Miguel, in the Azores Islands, some eight hundred miles west from his destination. Overcome by despair in his incompetence, his men were on the verge of mutiny but were too sick to do much about it. Smith had packed a limited supply of oranges, and scurvy had infected most of the crew, so by the time Jon de van Hazen intercepted the ship on its way to Spain (finally on track thanks to one of the crewmen who'd snuck up into Smith's quarters and altered the route Smith had mapped out, which would have put them around Bordeaux, France) the crew was too weak to defend Smith and his cargo of gold and silk. When Jon's men boarded the ship, they recognized the smell of scurvy at once: fever, and rotted breath from the men's putrid gums. The men wobbled when they walked if they could walk, weak in the knees from the disease. Smith, Jon remembered, grabbed the cabin boy and blocked Jon's advancement to the hold where the gold was kept.

"Keep back, you knave." Smith had commanded, his voice breaking up. Smith brandished a rapier and held the cabin boy by the neck.

Jon simply knocked the skinny blade aside with his cutlass and when he advanced on Smith, not to harm him, but only to scare him, Smith had cowered under the boy and cried.

Jon had simply knocked Smith unconscious and took all the gold from his quarters. When Jon took leave of Smith's ship, the half-a-dozen of Smith's men who could still walk came with Jon and joined up. And Jon would have probably forgotten Smith, if not for a week later when Jon had read of his exploits in an English paper, in Paris, and how the 'hero' Smith had stood his ground against a Dutch privateer, and even though he lost a paltry sum of his gold, he had scared the privateer so bad that the privateer's hair had turned forever white. Plus, the report continued, it was the privateer's fault, Jon's fault, that Smith's men got scurvy because this privateer had robbed his men of all the fruit that they had onboard, and it was this privateer's fault that Smith had lost everything of his investors. All of which made Jon want to humiliate Smith more.

He began by first sending a letter to the London pamphlet The Courant, telling of Smith's botched captainship and how he, Jon de van Hazen, had found the ships' crew on the brink of starvation and mutiny. And no, his hair hadn't turned white. Smith printed a rebuke, claiming Jon de van Hazen was a liar and a dishonorable cur. Then Jon printed a rebuke of the rebuke claiming that Smith couldn't sail his way out of London and that Smith smelled like a donkey stall during the heat of summer. Smith rebuked the rebuke of the rebuke and claimed that Jon had peed his pants like a little boy when Smith raised his sword to Jon's throat. Jon rebuked the rebuke of the rebuked rebuke by retelling how Smith's men really got scurvy and what a bad navigator Smith was. Then Smith challenged Jon to rob the next ship he was to take out of Dover. To which Jon publicly agreed.

Smiths' investors naturally became nervous. Smith balked at their attitude, claiming that he was the greatest sailor his majesty's country had ever seen. To protect their cargo, and save their standing of trust and loyalty, the investors instead hired a mercenary to follow Smith when he set sail the following month. The mercenary was none other than Jon de van Hazen, in disguise.

Jon spoke English like a gentleman, and a good amount of French and German too. Jon had managed to present himself to the board of Putmans & Williams Teas and Spices as a mercenary for hire who had heard that there might be some trouble awaiting one of their newest sea captains, the adventurer, and friend of the King, one John Smith. Jon explained that he owned his ship and that his parents had been killed by a French privateer, and even though Dutch privateers were feared above all privateers, he was sure that this privateer that haunted Smith could be beaten, and that if given the chance, he, Marcellous Drivel, would both protect their investment of gold, tea, and spices and redeem his dead, murdered, parents.

Agreeing to Jon's scheme, Putmans and Williams paid in cash and in advance. They didn't want to see anything happen to their investment in either their cargo or their ship.

So Jon robbed the men of Putmans and Williams twice, once before he left England with their cash in advance, and then once more when Jon boarded the ship at night and made off with all the goods and left Smith tied to the mast wearing a ball gown.

Jon then hit Smith's ships twice more that year, once while they were being protected by the Royal Navy. Each time Jon got away with the loot and Smith's pride.

The following year he published three letters in the Courant calling Smith a fool and an incompetent sailor who had no business being on board a ship in any status. When Smith went on holiday in the South of France, Jon and his men robbed the passenger ship he was sailing on, again tying Smith to the mast. When Smith got to France, Jon had him followed and pickpocketed. At Smith's tavern, Jon seized his carriages to which Smith had cried out, "And now on land must I endure these humiliations?" Once, on a detour, while Smith was on a diplomatic mission to Wales, Jon managed to get Smith drunk on Welsh ale, and then gag him, and tar and feather him and leave him in the center of town. It was such that now Smith ran away when he heard a whisper of Jon's name.

15

And so it was that when Jon went into Debedeavon's village that afternoon he hadn't decided on what he wanted to do to Smith. At the last minute, he decided to trade faulty muskets for special hunting rites. When he asked permission to hunt the Laughing King's land, a great hush fell about the warriors and those gathered to listen, even the King became quiet. *This was the ticket,* Jon thought.

Jon didn't like the spiritual advisor, Kego-tok, for he always looked at Jon with suspicion. If any of the giants were to discover the ruse, it was sure to be him, for the man looked through him as much as at him and that made Jon's hair stand on end. His men didn't like Kego-tok either and felt exposed around him. Jon's right-hand man, Douwe, claimed that normal Dutch people were bigger than the English people and that the medicine man had come to know it. They had also noticed that the warriors spent lots of time looking at their skulls whenever they visited the Laughing King. And that afternoon, Jon felt it too, the attention the warriors gave them. How even the children, who were as tall as he and his men, seemed hostile. *They know,* Douwe had explained.

Upon hearing of his request to hunt on his lands, Laughing King had called Kego-tok, and another, over to counsel. Jon was told to wait. It didn't take too long, but Jon saw that the warriors were not happy, Kego-tok in particular looked as if he had eaten something sour or rotten. The Laughing King seemed amused at best, or perhaps indifferent.

"Smith, Captain of England, Jamestown. I will grant your request to hunt lands of Debedeavon, the Laughing King. You will be guided by Kiptocreek and four other warriors. They will tell you where you may hunt and *there* only are you allowed to hunt."

"Thank you, gracious King. May your heart live forever and may your belly never grow out." Jon smiled as he patted the pillow he wore under his clothing.

The Laughing King grinned in return, but he did not laugh.

16

The warriors took Jon and his men deep into the forest, down the seaside of the peninsula, towards the tip. The warriors did not speak much. Some of the men carried not only bows and spears but also cudgels and sharp stone hatchets, as well as steel knives they had traded for. Jon and his men were armed with blunderbusses and pistols and even a few muskets. He had taken five men with him and with the warriors they made eleven men. Jon's men walked carelessly, making noise, more concerned with wiping their faces of sweat than being quiet. They walked most of the morning, stopping to dig for clams and mussels for lunch which they had with their pemmican. The warriors did not act overtly friendly to the white men, but neither were they hostile. Kiptocreek did most of the talking throughout the day.

To Jon, it seemed as if the warriors were leading them on a wild goose chase. That afternoon they killed a fifteen-point buck, which Kiptocreek had hoped would satiate the white men.

But Jon pressured him to keep going.

After a few more hours of walking, the band approached a densely forested swamp. The water stank and the air grew thick with flies and mosquitoes. The warriors seemed nervous, slowing their pace as if they did not want to go any further. Eventually, the band moved west of the swamp towards the pine dense forest. It was there Kiptocreek approached Jon and told him, "We cannot hunt these woods."

"What?" Jon asked, his face wet and hot.

"This is sacred land."

"Earth spirit, I bet. The English do not believe in the earth spirit." Jon hoped to get a rise out of the savage but didn't. "Is this the stag who is tall and broad and afraid of no men?"

Kiptocreek did not answer. His handsome face remained stoic, but his warriors shifted on their legs, their eyes scanning the forest around them. *This is the place,* Jon thought.

"Not afraid of men? A deer?" Jon laughed, but this did not phase the young warriors.

Kiptocreek shook his head, "No. Come I will show you some good hunting grounds."

Jon followed but noted the surrounding area and the angle of the sun, the types of trees, and how they grew. He nodded to Douwe to do the same, Douwe a master with sandglass and the astrolabe and the logline took mental notes, nodding to Jon as he did so. To get the Indians to attack the English, Jon and his men were going to hunt their sacred herd to extinction.

17

The next day Jon sailed his ship around the southern tip to the other side of the peninsula, and by afternoon he and his crew were on the trail of the great herd. This time, he brought most of his men, and they were armed to the teeth. It wasn't hard to spot the deer tracks or their scat. There were too many of them to not notice. They left trails miles long and they found them drinking from a freshwater creek twisting through the woods dense and dark with shadow.

It was almost too easy.

Jon lined his men up in the forest, spread out to cover the massive herd. The animals' size impressed the Dutch. Jon immediately spotted the great beast, as Kiptocreek had called it, an enormous deer standing as tall as the Indians, more than seven feet high with a massive head and a crown of points. Jon guessed there were at least twenty points on the horns, but probably more like twenty-five. The animal's shaggy mane was thick with fur and there were thorns and brambles from where the animal had torn through the bush. Jon planned on eating the earth spirit for dinner.

A fog had gathered, rare for the time of day, but Jon thought nothing of it. There were at least fifty animals that they spotted, but he couldn't be sure, as they mingled among themselves and made it hard for Jon's men to count, especially in the growing mist which had appeared at the forest edge like a dream.

Jon looked down the length of the line, felt pride rise in his heart, and he raised his musket and fired. His men followed suit.

Most of the men carried two muskets that day and Jon had his cabin boy, Douwe's cousin Joost, re-loading his guns. All the men partnered up for the same reason. It turned what might have only been a killing into a slaughter. The great stag took one in the flank and reared its thorny head, defying Jon. Jon had only to note the change in the animals' position when he fired his second musket into the beast's chest, dropping the earth spirit in two shots.

All told, Jon's men killed twenty-three deer, the rest scattered into the woods. The men did not bother tracking the wounded animals. Jon wanted the woods to be filled with blood. The Dutchmen skinned and dressed the animals and took their horns as trophies leaving the guts and the bones and plenty of good meat to rot in the woods. Their field dressings were careless and quick, and Jon purposely left a rifle of theirs and a wineskin to make sure the Laughing King knew it was the English that had killed the earth spirit. Douwe ordered his men to drop coins and buttons, he wanted there to be no mistake in the blame, that Captain John Smith had been the one to kill off the herd.

Jon, himself, only took the great stag's head and left its massive body in the killing zone with the others. He left the white hide on the beast to mock the natives. Jon wanted the Laughing King to laugh no more.

18

Kego-tok's young son and his friends found the slaughtered animals. They had run down to the swampy rut where the herd often spent the hot summer afternoons, and when they did not find them, the children continued to roam and play, and eventually stumbled across the killing grounds. The great stag's body had bloated with gas and flies, but there was no mistaking the corpse, for only one deer had such white fur and such a white mane, and that was the great beast. and had run crying to Kego-tok and the Laughing King that someone had killed off the earth spirit and left his body in the forest.

The Laughing King and his warriors immediately set out, taking with them the rifles and pistols, their bows and spears, and their anger and fear, and visited the site of the slaughter.

Shock followed. Then anger. Many of the warriors cried. Many of the warriors swore revenge. Kiptocreek and Kego-tok counseled the Laughing King to retaliate at once, and so shortly after, the Laughing King ordered a raid on Jamestown. A decision debated hotly among the elders. Debedeavon wanted Captain Smith's head. The warriors of the Nassawattucks tribe dressed as Powhatan's men painted with Powhatan's markings, and took canoes, and traveled down to Jamestown, by way of the Bay. It would take the small party a few days to hunt and then return. But they would be successful. They had to be successful.

19

What Jon de van Hazen couldn't know was that Captain John Smith had gone back to England for some weeks to take care of business. He had left the night Jon and his men had killed and eaten most of the herd.

In the raid, the Jamestown settlers were attacked by a small band of natives. While the Nassawattucks had sent twelve men in four canoes, loaded with weapons, but the muskets either blew up in the natives' faces or simply did not fire. In the end, it was blind-stinking luck that the small raiding party even managed to kill ten settlers and wound another six, and managed to get back to their village with their dead. They had not been able to get Smith's head, and the guns Smith had sold them cost them lives.

Meanwhile, while the raiding party returned to the shore, Jon de van Hazen was planning to set sail for Holland but was spotted by a hunting party while he and his men gathered freshwater for the voyage. The Nassawattucks immediately recognized him and his men and shouted treachery in their language (a new addition to their vocabulary) and shot arrows at him and his men, while sending swift-footed warriors back to the settlement with word to the Laughing King.

Within days Jon would be fighting for his life, and like it or not, helping the English with the problem he created. Though history would tell it differently, it was Jon de van Hazen who raided the Nassawattucks village and not the English. It was Jon de van Hazen who killed the mothers and children. It was Jon de van Hazen and his men who stole the young women aboard their ship home. And it was Jon de van Hazen who killed Kego-tok in front of his son.

CHAPTER NINE

1

Mr. Bill did not only regain his height and youthful strength on the KLM flight to Amsterdam, but he would also regain his memories from his youth, from the days when the colonists first came to his world and began trading with his people. He remembered their smell, their way of speaking, their funny clothes. He remembered the goods they brought to the village. He remembered how they killed off the great herd, and most of all he remembered how one of them killed his father.

Mr. Bill, now the size of a professional wrestler, at seven-foot plus and god knows what weight, stewed in his seat, his memory unwinding in his skull. Nick watched the man in jaw-slacked awe as he adjusted his loincloth that was made out of the remains of his shirt and tried to sit comfortably still. Mr. Bill looked younger too if that were possible.

"Um, how do you, uh like feel and stuff?" Nick finally managed after picking his jaw up from the floor.

"Fine, thank you, Nick. Just have to uh, get used to the idea of wearing this … loincloth. Haven't worn something like this since I was a kid."

"Okay. I'm just going to drink my red wine now and pretend that this isn't happening."

"That's fine Nick. You can have mine too."

Nick grabbed Mr. Bill's wine which looked small and doll-like on his table, now that Mr. Bill was twice the size he had been.

"Talk about cabin pressure," Nick said, gulping his red wine down to drink Mr. Bill's.

"I guess," Mr. Bill said as he closed his eyes.

"I'm just going to call the flight attendant over and get another glass if you don't mind."

"That's fine Nick."

574

"That's good because I'm feeling a little, uh, off might be the word, fucked-up another."

"Okay, Nick."

"I mean am I ever going to be normal again? I don't think so?"

"No, I don't think so either."

"I thought so."

"There's something I have to tell you, Nick."

"Oh yeah?"

"My name is Bill, Mr. Bill, not Guinness."

"I did think Guinness was too Irish for your type."

"I work for Mulch Hayes. It's his daughter that we're tracking."

"His what?"

"I'm going to try to relax. Enjoy the wine."

Nick rang for the flight attendant. Mr. Bill didn't move; he was looking around the inside of his head. They had another three and a half hours left in the air and then there would be the landing and customs.

2

Mr. Bill was not relaxing. He had work to do, tearing down and tearing out his old coping mechanisms. To do this, he must enter his mind where his memories lay. In his mind, Mr. Bill discovered a hole in a black wall of denial that was cold and made of stone. He knew that beyond the wall lay the rest of his memories – his childhood. He had seen snippets of flashes over the years, microseconds of remembrance, but he needed to get beyond the wall to find himself. And here was the hole.

It appeared more like a depression in the black wall and Mr. Bill walked towards it feeling the wall press up against his face. It felt like burlap as it scratched his skin, the depression, which sank farther back as he walked towards it, and as he walked, he saw that the blackness moved with him. He stretched the wall by simply moving into it, and darkness covered his body, and he thought that the elastic-like wall of denial would suffocate him completely. This was what he saw when he tried to remember his childhood – a void, blackness like that of death which is forever and endless and empty. Beyond the wall, he saw effulgence coming from trees, and beyond that, he saw wilderness. Pressing up against it the wall came apart with a loud rip and Mr. Bill found himself standing in the middle of a forest where he had found the slaughtered remains of the great herd.

Back in first-class, Mr. Bill gripped the sides of his seat. If Nick would have seen it, he would have seen his companion's knuckles go white, his fingers leaving marks in the hard plastic of the seat's arms. Mr. Bill felt like a lightning bolt had struck him square between the eyes. A ripping flood of images cut a hole in the black wall of his memory and flooded his mind, opening his pores full gauge, his heart pumping, his eyes rocketing back and forth like he was in deep REM. But he was awake, and his past played out before him. At first, there was elation, then sadness.

He and his friends had been out playing that day. They each had taken their bows and stone knives and planned to go fishing in the creek, but something had brought them to that particular wood.

A bird.

Not just any bird, but the great ravens who ate the spirits of the dead and carried them around until it was time to take the spirits to the spirit world where the ravens would vomit the spirits out. His father had told him about the large birds who'd sit on the tops of trees, their cries mimicking the warriors' war cries. Kego-tok believed some of the blackbirds to be dead warriors who had come back in the form of ravens to watch over the people. Mr. Bill had believed that too because the ravens were always following the hunting parties, and the hunters always allowed the ravens to pick at the bones. Some of the older men told stories of the birds following the great war parties up to fight the Delaware tribe, or the even farther south, before Powhatan's time.

That day the dark bird had flown in front of them and lighted upon a rock. It had let out one singular caw, which caught the children's attention. They had known, somehow, that the bird was talking to them. Mr. Bill had been the one to speak to it, barking back a single caw of his own. The bird then made a gesture with its beak and flew off a little farther and cawed again. One other boy followed first, then the rest of the children followed. The bird would land its muscular body on a rock or low branch and wait for the children to catch up before flying off.

They followed the bird for some time, not caring how far they were being led away from their fishing because the bird had called for them, the little ones, not for the warriors, not for the chief, not for Kego-tok, but them – the children of the village.

That day they had been anxious. The taste of adulthood, if it had a taste, was in their mouths that day. It tasted like meat, like salt. As they followed the bird, they all thought that around the corner would be some adventure, some beast to be killed, perhaps a message from the spirit world, or perhaps even an angry bear.

When they came upon the killing fields, the stink rose like a wall. They moved through the smell before seeing the pile of corpses, some beheaded, some cut down to the bone, some skinned and quartered, and some untouched. Mr. Bill and his friends had stood there, perhaps seconds, perhaps minutes, the smell of the rotting meat making their stomachs turn. Mr. Bill remembered feeling a yanking pull in his stomach, while another boy groaned, clutching his chest. It hurt to look at them, the waste, the dishonor. Winking in the sun, like an eagle's eye, was a shiny bolt on a rifle, lying in the high grass, dried blood patching the ground beneath it.

When they found the body of the great beast, the white stag which had stood as tall as a man, the children ran home as fast as they could, leaving the ravens where they were, stripping the dead of flesh.

"What now, did someone's fish get away?" Kiptocreek had yelled after them as they passed by him, heading for the chief. Within minutes the whole tribe knew what had happened. Most could not believe it.

Mr. Bill's head stewed with images as he rocked back and forth in his seat. The woman behind him stirred in her sleep. The businessman across the aisle, dead drunk since take-off, awoke from his stupor and felt perfectly sober. Two Japanese men, fresh from a business trip to Boston, suddenly came down with migraines. One woman sitting in the first row of coach claimed to see fog gathering over the wing, not clouds, she told the flight attendant, but the fog that climbed and snaked about of its own accord. A teenage girl in the rear of the plane, excited about visiting her first coffee shop, turned to look out over her seatmate's body and saw a giant crow. At approximately 11:30 PM EST the captain radioed Schiphol about unusual weather patterns in their flight path. Schiphol didn't have anything on the radar, and neither did the crew. But there was a weird cloud pattern swirling in front of them – not quite a cloud, neither fog. When they flew through it, the captain had his fingers crossed, a superstition he'd given up in flight school, or so he thought.

One Saacha de Graaf, in first class, returning home from a year living at an expensive private ESL boarding school in Boston removed her protective veil for the first time in weeks and decided she would never allow her nelophobia to interfere with her life again. She'd been dreaming about a ghost that had haunted the dorm she lived in and how the ghost's touch turned her bones to glass when she heard a comforting chant, a chant that she related to her psychiatrist later that week, a chant that freed her from her paralyzing fear of glass.

The chant sounded like that of an American native, she would later say. Her psychiatrist would chuckle. Saacha would try to chant what she remembered and although she didn't remember the chant right, what she did remember of the chant enabled her to look at ordinary glass and clear plastic without her mouth drying out and her throat closing up. She had found her magic.

Even Nick, dozing in his wine drunk saw a beautiful mermaid rise out of the sea and beckon him to an island where she embraced him and made love to him through the wine-dark night.

When the flight descended into Schiphol, the crew looked on in awe as three large ravens, or perhaps crows, flew onto the nose of the plane just as it began to open its landing gears, the three animals gripping the plane in flight they looked directly into the eyes of the pilot and co-pilot before flying off again.

Through the flight and twitchy dreams, Mr. Bill remembered the village massacre, an attack that happened just days after a young Mr. Bill and his friends had discovered the corpses of the herd.

The weather had been hot, and the lack of rain had made the forest jump with noise. Mr. Bill and the chief's son, a boy a year younger than young William, had been fishing that day in the tidal creek, taking long repasts to swim and eat. When the smoke started to tattoo the sky, they feared the worst. By the time they got to the village, most of the damage had been done. The women and children of the tribe had scattered, and warriors lay among the dead white men.

Neither of the children spoke, they didn't need to.

The chief's wife appeared under a column of dust. She fled three white men who were following her to the edge of the village. If she saw them, Mr. Bill could not tell. They called out her name in vain, but she hadn't heard them. Then Mr. Bill saw his mother running towards the woods, fear in her face.

In the woods, they would have a chance.

Where was his father? Mr. Bill did not know. Confusion made its masterpiece as the battle raged on.

Jon de van Hazen had ordered the attack during the hottest part of the day when many of the Indians would be asleep or in the field or hunting, a pattern he'd noticed as he stalked Smith. Jon had simply outfitted one of his rowboats and landed on the shore a mile from the village and trotted in, his crew behind him, and began the slaughter.

In the heat of it, Jon and three of his men rounded the king and the warriors who guarded the king into the horse corrals. The warriors were shot, the king left to cry in the dust. Shortly after, someone had started a fire on the far side of the village, and it began to consume the village.

This attack was meant to make a fool of the Laughing King. Jon had hoped one of the younger tribal hotheads would be forced to take over, and maybe get things stirred up between the natives and the English. Or maybe the Laughing King himself would stir things up for when Jon spotted the chief's wife running towards the hiding spots in the woods, he decided to kill her. He later recalled the event over ale on board his ship, as being one of the easiest targets ever. She was so big you see. Her son proved to be just as easy of a kill. Jon rode up behind the chief's son and simply blown the back of his head off. He raised his second pistol and fired. The air was red with dust and blood and when the roundball entered the back of her skull a murder of crows took flight from the trees at the end of the field. Jon heard a horrible scream and when he turned, he was shocked to see another young boy, taller than most of his men, bearing down on him. He was shocked, not at the fact that the boy wanted to kill him, but that he had not seen him when he rode up behind the others. He swung out his saber in time to deflect the boy's spear. There was a thump and a small cry and Jon saw the boy no more. Dust swirled about his horse and through the dust he saw another woman, one he thought might have been Kego-tok's wife, but of that he was unsure. No matter, Jon ran off after her and took her head off with his sword.

When Mr. Bill had run towards the white man, a cudgel in hand, he'd hadn't taken into account the strength of the white man. They were smaller than the Nassawattucks but were stout, strong people and Jon's blocking swipe sent Bill into the dust, who disappeared under the curling clouds of dust. When young Bill regained his composure, his mother was dead, and the white men were gone.

Kiptocreek's hunting party returned an hour after the crows descended on the corpses of the Nassawattucks men, women, and children. The Dutch were long gone, and the fires raged uncontrollably around the settlement. Anger and hate marshaled the warriors, but Kiptocreek forbade them to rush immediately to revenge, for the survivors, already returning from the forest and salvaging the remains of their lives or mourning their dead, needed their strength first. And as their anger grew so did the wailing, for the mothers and wives and husbands and sons and daughters of the dead and dying let the air and earth know how angry and sad they were, their tears fell into the bloody dust and grass and trampled earth.

The Laughing King had been tied up to a post in the corral at the edge of the settlement, and there Kego-tok found him when he returned with a fishing party from the north. Kego-tok could not find his wife, not at first, but he found his son collapsed in a heap. He had broken to his knees to mourn his young child, but to his relief, he stirred in his arms, a feeling that returned to Mr. Bill over four hundred years later, a feeling that brought even more memories for him, a feeling of being found and loved.

Kego-tok and Debedeavon urged the survivors to gather food and weapons and take them to the forest where they would be safe, for a while. A half dozen warriors took food and led the wounded and weak and broken into the forest where at least they could hear the approach of outsiders or family, where at least temporary shelter could be erected and then defended.

Mr. Bill remembered wandering the village in a stupor, the smell of blood drawing flies and mosquitoes. The fires for dead lit the sky. That evening two young women took their own lives; their rape having been too much for their spirit to bear.

The losses staggered the survivors. To make matters worse, the Dutch had been seen with several hostages, a fact that grieved parents and neighbors alike. A restless depression had settled over the nation, hearts lay heavy.

Kiptocreek knew the Dutchmen anchored on the seaside, while the English preferred the bayside. He'd had the English followed by his best trackers, whose scouting reports been ignored by the Laughing King. The Dutchman's reasoning, Kiptocreek figured, was to avoid running into Englishmen while pretending to be one himself. He had not been fooled, not once, and though he had begged Kego-tok to allow him to speak to the Laughing King about it, Kego-tok refused, for he had already tried himself and had been rebuked, for Debedeavon thought the English brought luck and wealth, and nothing was going to change his mind about that.

The evening they burned the dead the Laughing King held a war council and plotted revenge, and his first action was to give Kiptocreek command, to allow the strongest of their warriors to lead in his place.

Kiptocreek's first action was to suggest that they should send for help from either the Magothas or Assateague tribes. Both Kego-tok and Debedeavon said it was a long way to their village, not an impossible task, but also one long enough to delay swift action. They had yet to deal with the white man, yet, and perhaps they wouldn't, not if they succeeded. Others disagreed, but in the end, the war council decided to send emissaries with news as the remaining warriors would attack the ship within the next two nights. Three young warriors dispatched with dugouts to navigate north to make contact with allies were given strict orders to not engage with anyone other than the allies. In addition, five young warriors were dispatched on foot with the same mission. The other tribes needed to know the risk of engaging with European colonists.

In the end, even the children went to fight the Dutchmen, the pretenders. All in all, a hatred of all Europeans settled into the people's hearts and minds. A great dark wall of pain walled up inside their hearts against the Dutchmen. Blood, it all boiled down to blood.

3

In memory, events pick up speed, they gallop.

After the slaughter at the village, a spiritual cloud hung over the survivors. Many had died. Many more would die. For days the groups of survivors retreated into the woods to heal and be healed and find some comfort with the living.

Buzzards and crows gathered like sentinels in the trees and Kego-tok explained that they were eating the dead so the dead may live again. His son found little comfort in it, and neither did the other children. Grief consumed the young, but grief would convert to rage as time packed the pain into the spirit. The dead were everywhere, and the burial fires continued, the singing and the remembering of the dead continued. Kego-tok vowed that if he lived through the coming days, he would see a new stronger nation rise out of the dust, one his son would oversee as their spiritual advisor. One that could withstand the advance of the white man.

And finally, the night of the attack arrived, the moon slipped behind and through the ragged clouds, the ragged clouds as weary as the hearts of so many of the warriors who advanced through the forest, marked for fierceness, marked for blood. The men and women and children who chose to fight heard the shouts of the white men on board their ship, their ship anchored in the deep creek between two points of low-lying land, and when the war party emerged from the forest, they saw that the white men had despoiled both shores, as large campfires had burned within a few days on both sides of the creek. The ship lay anchored in the middle of the channel, deep enough even at low tide for the ship, which was lit like a honeycomb. The air still but cool, carried the occasional waft of the white men to the warriors, which acted as a stimulant, the warriors holding back their rage, channeling their anger, and their hate.

Occasional drunken squeals and cries from their women bubbled up over the main deck and out onto the landscape. A breeze picked up, then, the smell of roasting venison floated out to the war party creeping out of the woods like a fog. The warriors' blood boiled.

On the KLM flight to Schipol, Mr. Bill's brain popped with activity.

4

Jon and his men had planned to ship out immediately, but one of Jon's men had come back from a Jamestown recon trip and reported that the British Navy had set sail for the colonies to sort things out with the Indians. Smith was returning on one of those ships.

This interested Jon immensely. He hadn't known that Smith had gone back to the old country. And maybe before he set sail for Holland, with a few savages as slaves and some booty for his country, just maybe he'd hit Smith one more time.

Or maybe they'd stay in the New World, Holland be damned. His men liked the idea. They liked it in the colonies. There was no law but the law of their own voice. It was not like Europe, and though they didn't know that many of them were coming down with the first stages of malaria, they were having their fun – murderous fun.

Jon's ship held fifty with ease, fitted with cannon, deep cargo holds, and plenty of food storage, Jon and his crew could lord over wherever they liked. He'd lost ten good men in the fight with the natives. Down to just under two dozen, his men mourned and celebrated with fruit and meat they gathered and traded in the new world. And he had slaves, ten young women. They had killed four boys and dumped their bodies in the water. They had come across them north of where they were anchored. They were children really, out playing in the surf and sand. Taking them had been so easy. And now the young women were too beaten to put up much a fight and by the time they got them to Holland they'd be right as rain. *And how much would an Indian princess fetch? How much indeed?*

5

When the first arrows sank into the side of the ship, Jon's first thought was John Smith. He had been thinking of Smith and new ways to humiliate him when the war party attacked.

The first arrow sunk deep into the side of the ship with a thunk. Then the rapid pellets of stones and rocks cascaded against the hull. When Jon looked out into the murk, he saw nothing but shadow upon shadow.

Then, one of his men caught an arrow in the shoulder, another one in the chest. He toppled over headfirst into the creek. It was then Jon shouted for his men.

"Attack! Attack!" Jon drew his cutlass and felt his blood rise.

A horrible cry rose from the sea; the natives had begun scaling the sides of the ship, their voices rising over the vessel like a wave.

Then someone rang the alarm bell.

"Hendrick, good man!" Jon shouted as he ran down into the lower decks screaming and banging the butt of his pommel against anything solid in his way. He picked up a pistol and a satchel of powder and shot and slung it over his shoulder as he cried, "Wake, wake, Dutchmen, the savages are attacking, wake, wake!"

Most of Jon's men were drunk. And if the Indian war party had been fighting the Dutch Army then they might have killed every last one of them. But most of Jon's men had served in the Dutch Navy or had been a privateer all their adult lives. They were used to being attacked at sea. The men went into automatic fighting mode, muscle memory unleashed upon the machine that is a fighting ship. Two men downed their rum and began the long painful process of bringing up the bow anchor, thankfully the only anchor Jon employed. With only two men working it would take them a half-hour to have the anchor completely secured, but Jon didn't need it secured to sail away, and if the men could lift the anchor out of the water and he could get his sails up, they could gain an advantage. Someone shouted for the cannons to be moved so they could blast the shoreline. Jon's pride in his crew enlarged.

Topside, the Dutchmen scrambled to raise sails while engaging the enemy.

The first native onboard took out a Dutchman from behind, slicing his throat from ear to ear, and flinging the man's blood upon the deck as if to curse the ship forever. Securing the climbing gear, the hemp ropes and bone grapples, warrior after warrior climbed aboard, silent or shouting, appearing to the Dutch sailors almost like ghosts.

And then two things happened at once, the foresails began to lift as the deck of the ship exploded into flame.

In seconds, Jon's ship burned in chaos. His men were split into two factions, those that sought to raise the jib and foresails and those that fought the natives on the top deck. There was far too much noise for any of the Dutchmen to organize and rally beyond small pockets of resistance.

The fire spread up and down the deck, but Jon's men fought back, stamping out the fire and calling for water.

Next to Jon, a young Dutch sailor fell face forward into the deck. A stone hammer had hit him from behind. All around him, the deck exploded into cries and action. Jon lost sight of Douwe but killed two native warriors, the first with shot and the second with a swift chop to the neck.

When the ship lurched ahead, the wind had picked up enough to push the great vessel up the creek, Jon fell backward into the wall. All around him Dutchmen and warriors alike fell back, their balance thrown into disarray as the ship began to move. And all along the hull the second wave of the war party, that still clung to the sides of the ship, held on with surprise as the boat lurched ahead.

Back on the KLM flight, Mr. Bill remembered the fear of holding onto the rope, how his hands burned as he swung. All around him, other warriors struggled to hold onto their grip, below him, a young woman kicked off from the hull to avoid being knocked loose, and before Mr. Bill fell backward into the creek, he saw how his people were being shaken off the rigging, the slack fly ropes, the pitched oak hull. They fell into the creek below as the foresails pushed the ship ahead.

His fate was no different, flailing as he went backward, the young Mr. Bill splashed down into the creek and began to swim towards the shore where the third wave of the war party waited, firing flaming arrows into the boat's side. Kiptocreek's best bowmen had split into two parties and occupied both shores. The children carried horsehide pails of pine pitch the men dipped, and women lit, and the bowmen fired into the ship, aiming for the sails, or the sides, and any fool who showed his white face.

Back on board, Jon's cabin boy gurgled as an arrow blew through his throat sending flesh out in a chunky bloody spray. Joost's mouth foamed blood, and for a second Jon thought he was going to be next. But he wasn't, for his cannons got off one good shot which annihilated the marshy beach where the bowmen stood on the western shores. The natives would have to re-group. Jon's luck was holding out.

However, the remaining war party outnumbered them two to one, and even with the odds somewhat made even by firepower, familiarity, and setting sail, the white men were nearly wiped out. Spurred on by the piles of deer hides piled on deck, and the head of the earth spirit rammed on a spike beside the wheel, its mighty rack desecrated with empty rum mugs and what appeared to be a pair of soiled underpants drying in the night air, the war party muscled forward, swinging clubs and jabbing spears at the Dutchmen. The natives breached the Dutchmen's line of defense, time after time. His sailors held their ground.

Of course, the war party's main job was to keep the Dutch occupied, leveraging something that Kego-tok and Kiptocreek had counted on, white arrogance.

Kiptocreek and his best four warriors had already penetrated the lower decks, seeking their people and revenge.

The fire spread from the side of the ship down the length of the hull, the burning pine pitch crackling and flaring to life as the ship prowled the waters. During the melee, Douwe and his cousin abandoned the wheel and climbed up the foremast into the rigging above the smoke which hung about the decking like a fog. They climbed into the mid-sails, to raise them, hoping either to pick up enough speed to ram the ship aground and unseat the natives or to pick up enough speed to make into the Atlantic where the wind and the waves might give the Dutchmen enough speed to save the ship from flames, and give the Dutchmen a tactical advantage over the natives. Douwe and his cousin first pulled the three jib sails tight, which along with the foresail pulled the big ship forward like a needle on a thread. When the mid-topsails were raised, which gave the ship just enough speed for the pitched flaming arrows to beat out, burning faster from the ship's progress through the guts of the channel, the Dutchmen's hearts grew stronger. The air began to clear as the fight continued.

Kiptocreek's strategy had a second objective as well, to steal from the stores, or if they could not steal anything, destroy the stores with fire. In truth, Kiptocreek wanted the cannons which would certainly deter any further English or Dutch interference, but the warrior had not figured out how to make that happen.

So, while the war party muscled forward on deck, swinging their clubs and jabbing their spears at the Dutchmen, they did so with tempered fury, seeking to contain and hold and occupy the Dutchmen. *Play with them,* Kiptocreek had said, *play with them while we strike at their interior.* And play with them they had.

And back on the KLM flight, Bill's body jerked in his small seat. His body juiced with power twitched and flexed with the memory of swimming to shore to meet up with the remaining war party who fired flaming arrows into the side of the ship. Cannon fire had scattered the warriors on the opposite side of the shore, but already they were regathering strength even as young Mr. Bill climbed out of the creek and onto the beachhead.

And before the ship passed out of range, who did Mr. Bill see on the poop deck of the ship, the flames rising behind like a flaming maple, but his father, his buzzard war dress crisp and clear in relief against the orange and red inferno which was already flaming out as the ship sped up. When the stark shape of a white man appeared behind his father, Mr. Bill and the others watching thought that Kego-tok saw the figure, for in the shadow it was not clear what direction Kego-tok was looking. In truth, Kego-tok did not have a chance, for Jon had danced between his men and through his line of defense hoping to sneak into the rigging and get behind the natives to cut them apart from behind. When Jon saw the big warrior, he slipped behind him and cut open his life by swinging his cutlass up at the giant's neck, tearing a chunk of flesh and opening the man's jugular. Arterial spray shot up into the sky, a dark relief against the fire's orange and red light.

Kego-tok had simply turned his back at the wrong time, perhaps to marshal his men forward, perhaps to look back for his son. The natives had not anticipated the Dutchmen's abilities to get the ship moving.

When Jon struck him, he dropped his cudgel and fell forward, a huge gash in this neck that tore around to his throat. He dropped to his knees and fell forward and bled out on deck.

What Mr. Bill remembered of that moment was that his head suddenly became very hot and his eyes throbbed. His arms no longer hurt from the climb, his fingers no longer felt raw and bloody. His mind screamed for his father, but he could not speak. Across the channel, on the other shore, two Dutchmen had emerged from the water, coughing and spitting. And in his rage, Mr. Bill found himself leaping into the creek, swimming towards the Dutchmen who were only now realizing they were in danger. The white men put up their hands to surrender and when Mr. Bill swam over, his young body pulsing with anger, he did not hold back, and none of his peers held him back as he pummeled the first man, who stood as tall as he, before taking his knife from his belt and stabbing the Dutchman in the chest. The other Dutchman screamed in fear, begging for his life. He stumbled away in the melee, but the young Mr. Bill ran him down and cut his throat from behind. His spirit enlarged by hate and anger deflated as he watched the Dutchmen die.

From the belly of the ship came the sound of thunder as two forces battled and fought. The air popped with musket shot, musket balls pinged and ricocheted, the cries of Dutchmen and warriors alike rang out through the ship as it began to speed up, the jib sails fully raised now, the wind picking up the ship and carrying it out towards the Atlantic, the fires along the side of the hull streaking along the side and flapping out.

Somehow below, one of the deckhands inadvertently fired the cannon onto the lower deck railing when a warrior buried a hatchet into the man's neck. The cannon, pushed to the side by the force of the fight, exploded the lower deck into a hail of splinters leaving a gaping hole in the port side. It was through that hole, that the prisoners and the warriors escaped, diving headfirst and feet first into the creek. Once the prisoners had leaped through the opening in the side, the warriors tipped casks and chests and bags into the water. And finally, after a series of barrels had been dumped overboard did the last of the warriors finally escape, stealing muskets and holding them high in their hands and leaping into the water, arms raised, into the creek below.

Kiptocreek's war cry as he landed in the creek below was the signal for the warriors remaining on the upper deck to back away into the dying flames and smoke, to drop off into the water, one by one, leaving the Dutchmen to cry and scuttle to save their ship and their dying shipmates.

Jon's ship sailed off into the night as the Nasswattucks gathered on the western shores of the creek, celebrating and lamenting, and eventually receding into the treeline, as The Blessed Mermaid headed towards the mouth of the creek, on fire. The sound of dying men and exploding gunpowder echoed across the dark water.

6

Debedeavon considered the raid a victory.

Losses were staggering.

The Laughing King swore they would rebuild, and spent the remaining summer strengthening his local allegiances, but already the damage had been done. Kiptocreek remained the dominant leader, the Laughing King simply a figurehead, an outlier among his people.

Then sickness started to spread.

7

The combined stress of the fighting amplified by close contact with the Dutchmen, their rats, their fleas, and their germs, sickness spread through the entire breadth of the tribe. It surprised no one but the Laughing King. Death followed death and Mr. Bill's people, thinned out by fighting, was reduced to a passive puddle of manpower by winter. By then the English established a small colony some miles from their village and convinced Debedeavon that peace would be kept if the Nassawattucks stayed out of their way. The Laughing King had no choice. The nation splintered into factions, Kiptocreek led many of them north to marry into sister tribes among the Delaware peoples.

Mr. Bill's time was marred by fever and grief and a crushing sense of powerlessness. Unmoored without his parents, he stayed with the Laughing King's faction because his father would have stayed, or so he thought. A hard cold winter led to a colder spring. Their numbers decreased further.

When the first African slaves were brought to the Eastern Shore, the slaves were housed at a new plantation close to the natives. The large expansive farm had multiple out shelters for the slaves. The natives saw this as their fate, and as the white men's presence grew and the white man's power grew, the natives faced decisions, marry with the slaves or vanish, for their numbers had dwindled to nearly nothing. And one by one, women and men paired off with Africans or slipped away north to ally with other nations, so soon there was only one lasting survivor of the Laughing King's nation, and white men called him William, and the fiery young man lived alone on the creek where his people once had a great nation, where William lived as a hermit and avoided all human contact.

8

Jon returned to Holland with only five men. Twelve men survived the battle in the creek, four died en route to Amsterdam, the remaining died of fever as their wounds festered and swelled. The return voyage nearly killed them all, for the crew was so exhausted and few that they could not raise all the sails for they did not have the manpower to lower them if a storm came upon them, so they limped home, hoping to meet another Dutch ship while en route, a fruitless hope that weakened Jon.

Jon took a break from privateering. Only until he heard of John Smith telling wild tales of how he saved the Jamestown colony from Indian destruction, only then did he take up privateering again, just to be a bee in Smith's ear.

Eventually, he did retire in Rotterdam though, where he married a nice Dutch girl and had a child, a boy named Kasper, who remained fascinated with his father's tales of Indians, privateering, sword fighting, and sailing, and would first become a rum runner, and then move to the peninsula of the Virginia colony, where he would build a house and change his name to Haze, which would evolve in one generation's time to Hayes.

Mr. Bill sitting in first class, barefoot, clad only in a loincloth, covered by a very scratchy and not very warm KLM blanket, knew why he had stayed with the Haze family for so long, where else was there in the world for him to go except into the belly of the beast, the very line of the descendants who had slaughtered his family and started the long slide into oblivion for his people. Revenge would finally be his.

9

"Doc, Nick's memories, packed into my head like pipe tobacco, made me smoke. Doc, let me tell you, I was burning with conversations. Having all those other memories inside my head helped me forget about the itch in my stomach where Pembroke's fingers had been inside me.

"I laughed a lot. That might surprise you, me, sitting in that fucking box, sometimes in a coffin, sometimes in a bed, god knows where. I learned to laugh in my head. It was easier on my throat, but harder on my body. If by chance, a laugh escaped it became a twisting wheeze.

"Thinking Nick's thoughts was like living a lifetime in a moment. A completely different lifestyle and point of view packed into my mind and unzipping a great speed."

10

Upstairs in Pembroke's house, Virginia laid perfectly still inside her coffin. Virginia felt an itchy burning in her stomach where Pembroke had opened her up and fingered her organs. Her insides, bruised but healing, felt like someone had kicked her in the stomach, repeatedly. The first night, when Nick's memories poured into her out of some invisible hole in space, Virginia could have sworn she had been stomped on by an entire football team, cleats and all.

What Virginia didn't know and what she would never know was how Nick's memories came to be inside her in the first place. If she had known she would have said that it was impossible. The fog carried Nick's memories from the Eastern Shore to Pembroke's house. Fog, a trickster of the old world, fog, a conductor of sorts, stealing Nick's memories and sliding them across the bay and up the James River and into Virginia's head.

The morning Virginia escaped, Pembroke opened the coffin, he stared down at Virginia's pale body and thought for a second that he had killed her. She lay there like a board, her fingers flat against her side, her legs straight out like she was in rigor mortis. *Fuck,* he thought. *This is Albania all over again.* His mistake was that he took the head-box off; as much to see her breathing with his own eyes as to see the damage to her soul, should she still be alive. His fingers shook with anticipation as he prayed and hoped his charge still lived. And when he removed the head-box and lifted it off her pale and puffy face, he drew in his breath. Her eyes were closed and still, and for a split second he felt his heart stopped.

I have killed her, he thought.

Then the buzzing began.

11

Virginia had been having a discussion with Nick's memory when the fireflies started whipping around the head-box. She had almost forgotten about them, the fireflies. If they were a hallucination, the pain had kept them from appearing. If they were real, then they had been resting, waiting. The fireflies remained a mystery to her so many years later, when she tried to make sense of the world where no one remembered her or her father.

Nick's memories became concrete images to her. The experience was disorienting, much like looking at a double exposure. Her memories overlapped his. And once again, Nick's memory of that one evening at the Idle Hour Theater came popping up with balloons, firecrackers, and champagne corks, the memory practically celebrating its joy. That was when the fireflies in the box began to burn so bright that the whole of the head-box lit up and Virginia spied the pits and pores of the leather about her eyes, and if she looked down, she spied her upper lip and the rough dark stains of the leather box encasing her face. They glowed with fury and began to fly at impossible speeds about her face, between the spaces between her skin the fireflies flittered and fluttered and made Virginia's head hum.

When the coffin swung open, Virginia's skin cooled from the sudden exposure to air, and then she felt his long fingers on the headbox, unbuckling the straps that wrapped around her shoulders and arms. And when the box began to come off her head, Virginia closed her eyes and for a second the fireflies stopped all movement.

A great pause hung in the air before the fireflies, or whatever they were, exploded upwards into Pembroke's face. They buzz sawed through the air like the hum of a giant swarm of bees and pelted Pembroke's face, scoring his skin. He screamed and swatted at them, stepping back, surprised and horrified. He recognized the smell of hot flesh. It smelled of his basement torture chamber. *There are thousands of them*, he thought. A firefly zipped into his open mouth his whole face flared with pain, the soft tissue of his palette burned as it burrowed into his skin and died.

Virginia opened her eyes as soon as she heard Pembroke cry out. The sudden light forced her to squint. Through her fingers, she saw that Pembroke was covered in them, the pulsing tiny bits of light. This was her one chance. She had no plan. She instinctively held her stomach. As she climbed out, very slowly, the pain blasted her at the knees and in her breast. Her whole body braced for it, the pain of walking and the pain of running. By the time she managed to stand and wrap her arms around her belly, Pembroke's toes had retaliated against the fireflies, swatting them from all directions. They snapped and hissed, and his nails opened like the mouth and snatched the hot little lights inside. Pembroke dropped to his knees, his hands covering his eyes. When the toes snapped the fireflies in their jaws, she could see their little veins, and what appeared to be teeth; one of his pinkies smoked.

She wobbled out into the hall, forcing herself not to look back. The cold hallway sent her flesh into ripples against the chill. Not sure where to go, she headed towards the stairs. It struck her as she fled how vacant the house was, how tomb-like it felt. But the fog had gone, which comforted her, but when she reached the stairs, her hope drained through a hole in her stomach. The stairs would slow her down.

Behind her, she heard Pembroke curse. A bright flash of blue light lit up the back hall.

She didn't have time to think.

CHAPTER TEN

1

"Doc, this is so cool. I remembered, or rather Nick remembered how he played on the stairs in his house when he was a kid. He didn't slide down the banister, instead, he crabbed down the stairs, on his butt. So, I slid to the floor, holding my stomach the entire time. I kept thinking that instead of some alien-like creature popping out of my stomach, my stomach would pop out of me, and my guts would go sausaging down the stairs, pulling me with it. But my stomach held, thank God. Using one hand, I scooted down the stair, using my butt and legs to propel me, my hands as balance. Fear drove me, and adrenaline pumped through my veins and my heart opened like an engine. I guess that's why he didn't see me, because I was on all fours When Pembroke came out of the room shouting and cursing in Dutch, the smell of fried onions permeated the hallway.

"I heard his toes hissing in the air. He must have gone the other way down the hall, towards my old room, for I expected him to appear over me like some kind of devil moon, but he didn't. There was the sound of doors opening and slamming shut and more cursing. He moved quickly on those toes of his, and surprisingly enough, I moved quickly too. When I got to the bottom of the steps, he had yet to appear. My legs burned, my stomach throbbed and the arm I used to balance felt rubbery and useless. I managed to get into the living room when I heard him call after me.

"Virginia, my dear, where are you?"

"His toes carried him down the stairs faster than I would have expected. He was in the living room by the time I made it to the study where I collapsed in the desk chair. At that point, I didn't think I was going to make it. I was in too much pain, for one thing, and I had no weapons, and I was scared. I didn't know how scared I was until his snaking toes appeared. Fear spiked inside me, and I opened the desk drawers and found a handful of pencils and pens.

The letter opener was plastic. It didn't look like it would cut butter much less flesh. Grabbing a handful of pencils, perhaps six, or so, and several black ink ballpoints, I gathered them in my left hand and hid them behind my back. I was sure he saw me, but Pembroke didn't. Rage can blind a person to details, so when he rushed towards me, his head held high, his toes hissing and burnt, his face tightened, his cheeks scorched with lines from the fireflies looked like shadows from his protruding bones, he didn't pause to even think that I would attack.

"You did this," his hand hovered over his face which was scored with four deep red lines from where the fireflies had hurt him. "You did this to me!" He said as his lips curled back over his teeth. "I am your master, and you would do *this* to me!" He came closer and for a second, I thought he was going to see my weak weapon, but he stopped a few inches from the desk, his mind prying into mine. All I could think about was a hand going into the cookie jar. That's where he froze. The anger drained out of his face and his lips became loose. He was confused. He sensed Nick inside and didn't know what to do. I know that now, Doc. I didn't know it then. His eyes became glassy.

"Stand," he instructed me, and I felt the invisible strings on my bones pull me out of my seat. I did my best to keep the handful of pencils out of sight. His face retained its vacant look as he moved closer to me, his toes smelled like burnt popcorn kernels. In those seconds I did my best to bring up all of Nick's memories, and for a second, I thought I could read Pembroke's mind, that the line of thought went both ways, that I felt his pain and his confusion. *Something was dreadfully wrong here,* I could see him thinking. Then I drove the bundle of pencils and pens through his neck.

"I swung my tight fist in a swift downwards arc right into the fleshy part where his neck and shoulder meet. There was a wet slocking sound as the pencils and pens punctured his flesh. As he screamed, I hung there for a moment, my weight pressing them deeper into his body. He threw me to the wall. When I slammed against the wall, pain erupted in my stomach, but I kept my eyes open. I did not shout out. A wide arc of blood spurted up into the air from his wound. I tasted him on my tongue.

"Pembroke fell to the floor and his toes snaked out towards me. For the first time, I saw them in hideous detail. Each of the toenails opened in the middle with a tiny mouth. The skin on the toe was patched with diamond shapes, like snakeskin. They aimed to kill. The first one tore into my shoulder and I had to let go of my stomach to bat it away. The others grappled with my feet, trying to drag me closer to Pembroke, who was up on one arm, his eyes popping out of his skull in pain, his neck torn open in six places. I had managed to shove one pencil into his body almost up to the eraser.

"Swatting the snapping toes away, I crawled around the desk and threw whatever I could at him. First more pens and pencils, then paperweights, papers, and even paperclips. Grabbing a drawer, I yanked it free and rushed over to where he knelt. He only looked at me, his arms trembling to keep him balanced, his toes hissing at me and beating against my skin. One of them bit me on the thigh as I stood over him for what seemed like a few seconds before I brought the hard corner of the desk drawer down on the top of his skull. There was a wet crunch, and the desk drawer came apart, the bottom popping out, the frame collapsing around the one-inch corner sticking out of Pembroke's head.

"That's when I turned and ran."

2

Cilia, unable to sleep, stood in her kitchen and opened her cabinets, and reached for the sugar bowl. She poured three teaspoons into her tea and stirred, pausing only to say out loud, "My brother is dead." For a second, she felt grief, then relief. *That is one potential problem out of the way*, she thought and began to hum.

3

"Doc, I didn't have any clothes, but I didn't care. I ran into the streets and the night, the heat, the sweater-thick humidity sucked the energy right out of me. Adrenaline pumped and sweat began to pour out of my body as if a faucet had been turned on. I didn't think to holler or scream, I just ran, more like jogged, with my hands to my stomach, my feet skimming over busted glass and bottle caps. When I saw the first alley open to my left, I took it.

"Ah yes, the good love a park, and the rest love an alley. I wasn't thinking about anything other than finding somewhere to curl up for the night. I didn't care where. My body needed to rest.

"I passed several cross streets and several groups of night owls saw me. Somebody even said, 'Is she naked?' Another remarked that I looked like, 'hell running to catch the devil.' Eventually, the buildings grew more ramshackle, and prostitutes began appearing on the corners. I saw them intermittently through the alley-breaks in the brownstones and old homes, the student section of Richmond. I grabbed a neon orange tank top from a back porch railing.

I snatched a pair of boxers off a clothesline that hung across the back of another porch. I estimated it was after midnight, though I wasn't sure. I slowed to a walk, my feet hurting. I grimaced, imagining the dirt and grime collecting in the open wounds, *infection city, here I come,* I remember thinking.

"Then Nick helped me out again. This is so fucking cool, Doc. When he was sixteen, he and his buddies hot-wired a car.

4

If Nick Adams were to try to recall the details of how he had hot-wired a car when he was sixteen, he would have only been able to give you vague details, his mind riddled with holes. But Virginia remembered the wires that she had to cut and peel back and tie together. After he had shown her how all those years before, Virginia had no trouble boosting the rusty Honda Accord, which had a full tank of gas, which she hoped would be enough to get her to the Eastern Shore.

5

Nick was more than a little drunk when he deplaned at Schiphol, the stewards and flight attendant giving him screwed-up looks and sideways glances. They were an odd pair, the giant muscular Indian wearing a KLM blanket around his shoulder, his loincloth swaying between his legs, somewhat obscenely, and Nick disheveled and smudgy, reeking of wine and garlic. Neither of them had ever been to Schiphol, but neither of them let that fact intimidate them.

"We will walk until the crowd thins." Mr. Bill explained.

"You hoping to just disappear?"

"We are much too suspicious-looking to disappear." Mr. Bill nodded at a passing KLM attendant.

"You know, you could always just wave your hand, and you know, make us look like normal people." Nick half-whispered.

"Never again," Bill said.

"What?"

"I've hidden too long."

"Who's hiding? I don't want to get arrested."

"It's been a long time since I felt so invigorated." Mr. Bill clapped his hands together.

"Good for you. Glad the Viagra's working."

"Funny. We will pretend to take another flight and slip out a side door." Mr. Bill gestured ahead.

"And then what?" Nick asked.

"We'll find our way to Amsterdam."

"And how the hell are we going to do that?"

"Walk. Of course." Mr. Bill said.

"Ah, yes, the old foot."

"Nick."

"Yes?"

"Never mind."

"No, what?"

"I'll tell you later. Through there," Bill said as he pointed at a door.

They slipped out an access door that led them to the tarmac. There they got a few curious glances from pilots sitting in their cockpits. None of the pilots reported the strange duo since the pilots saw no one giving chase and heard of no such irregularity on their radio, they assumed they were crew members from one of the newer airlines, one that hadn't quite gotten their dress codes in order yet, for certainly, no respectable airline would allow an employee to come to work in rags, or a cape. But it took all sorts, didn't it?

5

When they got to the surrounding fence Mr. Bill threw his blanket over the barbed wire top and hiked Nick over the top. Mr. Bill followed, making it up the chain with no problem. Ahead of them was the freeway and Mr. Bill thought he could make out a sign for Amsterdam, some 30 kilometers away. Nick sighed and followed his giant friend who seemed to grow more and more energetic with each step. Nick still felt like he had fallen asleep in a wine barrel. The thought that he had slept one night without painting something in his sleep hadn't crossed his mind.

6

It took Captain Van Dijk approximately thirty-six hours for his mostly unladen cargo ship, traveling at 37 knots per hour, to plow through the calm Atlantic waters to Amsterdam. He'd never in his life made such good time, part of it was the weather. The Atlantic waters lay slack before him, the chop easy and almost negligible as the ship clipped ahead, the sun and moon looking down on them with favor.

In the hold, in her box, Marina's skin lay in piles of dust around her body where she existed in a hallucinatory state, half-dead, moaning occasionally. Marina lay curled in a fetal position in the throes of a fever dream where she rode above the clouds next to Mr. Bill dressed as the Jolly Green Giant.

7

While Marina steamed towards Amsterdam, Nick and Mr. Bill walked aimlessly, more or less in the direction of Amsterdam, while Cilia prepared her home for her guest. They were forced to lay up in a maintenance shed near the FedEx hanger so that Nick could sleep. But sleep did not help Nick and after a few hours.

While Nick and Mr. Bill wandered towards the city, Cilia's energies, once depleted from her control of the Captain and his men, had re-surged and Cilia's adrenaline and focus allowed her to prepare for her charge with great speed.

Long ago she had installed a rack, made of thick planks, steel, and leather straps as wide as her thigh. She kept it on the second floor of her home, in the backroom, where she hung dark drapes and set up shop, her potions, her herbs, her library. Marina would be strapped down and then Cilia could begin drawing her lifeforce from her, before harvesting her hormones, which Cilia would then consume, and like her brother transcend her human form.

If Marina were awake and had somehow miraculously retained her strength, she'd have to do something nasty to the poor girl, *something nasty indeed*. This was a possibility, she thought because someone had killed her brother. The mystery man? Unlikely. Mr. Bill? Possibly. Cilia didn't trust the native. Suddenly there were too many variables she could not account for. This was supposed to be simple.

A long time ago a man had cut her ears off, and Cilia had to choose between the deformity or surgery. Needless to say, she chose deformity which she wore like a badge. Her ear holes gave her courage. Her ear holes reminded her of her past. Her ear holes scared the children. She had hoped Marina would be scared. She had every reason to be.

Marshal fear. Gather up all that anger and sharpen your blades, girl. When Cilia dressed herself to go to the harbor, she realized she'd been making fists since she'd woken up. The old instinct for blood welled up in her; her senses sharpened and enlarged.

8

Lilly almost walked to Cambridge with her dead mother under one arm but instead got turned around several times trying to avoid the traffic and barking dogs. She didn't have the patience or temperament for barking dogs. She supposed the dogs smelled her mother's jerky-like body. Though the dogs could have been barking at just about anything.

That evening she eventually walked far enough to spy the blazing Citgo sign cutting through the hazy Boston night. Without thinking she marched towards it as George and Ab sat at a Burrito Max joint drinking cokes and eating beef and chicken enchiladas. Rufus sat upright in the car watching the men eat. Rufus had pointed them in this direction, towards Allston, and then just when Rufus thought he had Lilly's scent in his nose, the men had wanted to stop and rest, *to look around, to kill time,* or so they said. George seemed to think something big was going to happen that night. Ab didn't know what to think, he was more concerned that his stomach was grumbling like unoiled machinery. Smelling Lilly, Rufus suffered a kind of doggie headache at being kept in the truck cab that was matched only by his hunger. Rufus barked through the glass at his companions.

"Master, look. Dog makes noise while we stuff our mouths. He looks so hungry!"

George nodded and waved at Rufus. The other people in Burrito Max thought it odd that Ab kept calling George, "master." Each time he said it, eyebrows raised, and people looked away or found something to look at on the floor.

"What now, master?"

George instinctively sniffed his underarm.

"Does master smell, too? I don't think so, sir," Ab's voice rang out loudly in the Burrito Max.

"Well, honestly, I don't know, buddy."

"Abdullah thinks the dog has led to us on a goose chase. But Abdullah sees no gooses."

George drummed his fingers on the table. They could either: give up, start asking around if anyone had seen a woman who glowed, or find a hotel and get some sleep. George didn't think he could afford any of the hotels around here, but there was a Howard Johnson's not too far off. They had passed it when Rufus had led them to here, *wherever here was,* a hot, tacky strip of businesses, restaurants, and stores packed, absolutely packed, with people of all types.

Lilly could be among them, somewhere, George thought. *Yeah, right, Lilly is probably sleeping.* He yawned and grabbed the napkin on which he had laid out strips of chicken and beef for Rufus.

"Come on Ab, let's go see a man about a hotel room."

"Yes, master," Ab said as he rose and grabbed George's tray. "Master sleeps on the bed, Abdullah will sleep on the floor," Ab continued.

A woman behind the counter molded her face into one of disgust at hearing their conversation.

George let out an audible groan as he left Burrito Max and stepped out towards his truck. He fed Rufus through the window and later even managed to move his truck without dinging someone's car. Boston forced him to practice his defensive driving skills, which he hated.

As George and Ab puttered towards the giant Citgo sign, Spider, Blockhead and Zac sat in the brisk breeze rising off Carson beach, beers in hand, each one wondering what was to come next, not realizing their artistic prey wasn't even in the US anymore but was walking aimlessly along a Dutch highway towards Amsterdam.

Blockhead sat on one end and Zac on the other, Spider sat in the middle. Blockhead expected Spider to give the order to sack out at any second. His mind played with the idea of ripping out the backseat of his Yugo to sleep on the beach, under the stars when it was cool. He had some mean gas building up in his pipes and was sure if he was forced to share the car with Spider and Zac, he'd stink them out. Spider thought about hitting the streets, checking out what kind of street art they could find in this crappy neighborhood. Zac's stomach grumbled over and over again as if it were trying to tell him something. Zac began to think his friends were right, that he was crazy, that nothing was going on down here.

"You know guys maybe I'm wrong," Zac said into the mouth of his beer, its brown bag looking like the bottle's wrinkled skin.

"I think one day I want to live in the desert," Blockhead said blankly. He burped a second later and smacked his lips as the taste of Mexican food rose in his mouth. "The desert is cool."

"Fuck that desert crap," Spider replied as he reached into his pants pocket for his one-hitter.

"What if I've led you all here for no reason at all?" Zac wondered.

"The desert is for hippies. And Blockhead, you are not a hippie," Spider said grinding his fake ceramic cigarette into the dugout chamber filled with finely ground Mary Jane.

"Maybe," Blockhead said as he watched Spider light up. "I got nothing against hippies. Except for you know, the music."

"Really, Spider, Blockhead, if you want to go, I'd understand," Zac stated.

"I hate the hippie music shit. Phish and the Dead. Classic rock crap my Dad listens to in his workshop. And he's not even a hippie. I hate that crap," Blockhead said.

"I'm being serious and open here, guys. If you don't want to listen to my stomach I understand. I have to listen to it," Zac explained.

"I'm a heavy-metal guy, no offense Spider. I also like hip-hop, especially the hip hop chicks." Blockhead did not hear Zac.

"But you guys *definitely* don't have to listen to my gut. It's weird I know. But my stomach saved my life. Like really saved my life. I can't just, you know, ignore it."

"Hip hop chicks *are* the best," Spider said as he passed the newly packed one-hitter to Blockhead. "My wife is going to be one fine woman, a beauty who can rhyme and dance and make beats, no cap."

"But in all fairness, heavy metal has always been what Blockhead is about. Sathoven, PEN 1.5. Fucker, Junk Fetus."

"Sathoven, as in Satan?" Spider asked.

"I'm being frank and open in regards to my stomach gentlemen, I know it's odd and a little, well, unusual to attribute your health and safety to a series of spongy tubes that turn food into, well, food." Zac continued even though no one paid him any attention.

"Sathoven rocks, Spider. It's totally evil and fucked-up shit."

"I mean the intestines are really long. Twenty-something feet. I've looked it up. But I've forgotten the number. There could totally be something inside my intestine, I don't know, like a sentient being of some kind."

"Do they worship Satan?" Spider asked.

"No, they more like acknowledge the Satan in all of us," Blockhead said, looking ahead into the ocean.

"I guess I'm thinking that maybe there's a guardian angel in my stomach."

"Wow. That sounds bitching," Spider said as he handed the one-hitter to Zac who lit it up and inhaled without missing a beat.

"My grandma always said I had a guardian angel and maybe, just maybe I ate him somehow or he just slipped into my stomach for some reason. They're really small you know? Guardian angels."

"Isn't that crazy guy from Junk Fetus from our neighborhood," Spider said as he took the one-hitter from Zac and slid it into his pocket. "I heard that somewhere."

"How does that old saying go? You can fit thousands of angels on the head of a pin." Zac said to no one.

"Yeah, the Piss, the drummer. Heard he used to pee in trashcans if the teacher refused to let him out of class."

"No shit?" Spider said.

"I'm thinking I ate my angel. He or she must have been on something I ate."

"Yeah, Mr. D'Angelo, the horticulture teacher, wouldn't let him go to the bathroom on purpose. Then Piss watered his begonias. On the windowsill in the classroom." Blockhead explained using his hands to frame the square opening of the trashcan that Piss supposedly pissed into.

"White people are weird." Spider said.

"I hear angels like pizza, and I eat a lot of pizza." Zac continued.

"Spider. What the hell is with that name?"

"And you're saying Blockhead isn't at all unusual?"

"I mean when I say I eat a lot of pizza, I eat a lot of pizza. There are marathon pizza-eating nights in my household. Especially since my Ma took that job at Papa Johns." Zac looked up at the stars, which he could not find among the growing weather phenomenon above them.

"Blockhead is because when I was a kid I looked just like Charlie Brown, bald with a squiggle of hair on my head."

"Spider's just a cool name."

"Ma does work too hard, though. Dad never liked the pizza. Guess that's one of the reasons he left. Grandma said angels often sleep on your pillow next to you at night. Maybe he crawled in and I swallowed him by accident."

"I'm being serious here, one squiggle of hair, only one." Blockhead raised one giant finger to emphasize one.

"I bet I swallowed that fucker whole." Zac clapped his hands together.

"What the fuck are you talking about?" Spider said to Zac, his beer raised to his lips.

"Oh, nothing. Nothing at all." Zac sighed.

Zac had been almost entirely ignored up to Boston that day. Blockhead would say something to him occasionally, but Spider pretended that Zac wasn't there. Not that it bothered Zac. He was used to being on the fringe with Spider and the guys. Even though he had more in common with the guys from the website than say Blockhead did, who hung with them cause graffiti was cool and there were always drugs floating around. Spider's crew tended to be a motley crew, had been since the old days. Blockhead had been ghosted by his jock friends when he went through a period of genuine questioning and self-reflection about his gender identity, something Zac related to. And Zac had to admit Spider's website had really taken off lately. Plus, his freelance pics were everywhere around town, little crap magazines that you pick up at the coffee house, stuff like that. Zac's photos weren't any better or worse than Spider's, in Zac's opinion. And Zac continued to listen to Spider and Blockhead talk about the ins and outs of hip hop and punk and kept his eyes open. His stomach growled once more, a single word it growled twice before it shut up for the evening. "Wait," it said. "Wait."

9

Lilly walked through the depressed, and often tacky, residential sections of Boston that ran like a brown scab near BU. It dominated the landscape for miles. The Citgo sign was bigger now, and it gave her a lift. She didn't know why, but she supposed it reminded her of her mother in some strange way, like how her mother was a beacon of light and truth to the community of migrant workers who lived and worked the Hayes farm. And perhaps because she thought of her mother, who she carried like flattened baggage under her arms, she began to glow a little herself, not realizing it. Lilly knew that eventually, she'd have to sit down and have a real long cry. Her stomach hurt, her legs still hurt from where she chased Jerry the Junkie, and her chest felt like she had smoked a thousand packs of cigarettes; it was tight, wheezy, and sore. She was going to let it all out, she knew she was, but she didn't know when or where. She walked, concentrating on her feet, concentrating on her pace, thinking only when she had to cross the street, or if she felt her mother begin to slip under her arm. She couldn't let her touch the ground, that would be too much. She walked towards the Citgo sign because it was the only thing she could think of to walk to, and as she walked, she glowed, and maybe because she knew she had to let her pain out eventually, the glow from her body increased until she shined as bright as the Citgo sign herself.

Children pressed their faces up the car windows to view the light. Old women thought the streetlamps had gone haywire again like they had during the hurricane of '57. As the T rumbled above ground people pressed their faces to the windows to see if some UFO had landed in the middle of Boston. Some didn't even notice, others took pictures and later discovered that Lilly burned so bright all they got was a white blurry picture, no definition, no shape, no form, only light as if they had taken a picture of the sun. And as Lilly came closer and closer to the Citgo sign, she closed upon Commonwealth Avenue, plugged with cars, buses, the T, and pedestrians, all who stopped, paused, or gave a glance at the sad woman who looked like she was walking inside a bubble of light. Those that found themselves too near her shielded their eyes, fetching their sunglasses out of purses and bags. Someone began to sing Corey Hart's "Sunglasses at Night." People gasped and guffawed. Someone called the Channel 7 news team. Someone else called their pastor to tell them that 'an angel was walking down Commonwealth Avenue.'

On the T-subway-cars, conversation flipped back and forth as to what was causing the light.

"It's an alien, I know it," one man had said.

"She's the light of my life," another one chimed.

"No, no she's eaten too many fatty foods. She's got cancer, I tell you," An old woman insisted.

"You're all wrong, she's a witch," a young man with black fingernails said, before slumping into his seat, his eyes behind his blue hair.

"No, definitely not a witch. An angel."

"Maybe she works at the nuclear plant in Medford."

"There's no nuclear plant in Medford."

"That's what they want you to think."

And so on.

Lilly didn't notice the people veering out of her way, or hear the honking horns, or see the bicyclist tumble headfirst off the overpass into the interstate traffic below, his yell ballooning out like in a cartoon before landing in the shrubbery in the bushes below. She didn't notice the cars that dinged or banged into each other as they headed into Allston from downtown Boston, her light blinding the drivers making it impossible for them to see where they were going. She didn't notice the few summer college students wowing and woahing from the benches in front of the PA building. Lilly was thinking of her mother and that if she could somehow reach the giant Citgo sign, its giant pyramid flashing out into orange and then flashing into black again like some weird eye, then she'd be okay – she'd be right as rain, somehow. Lilly didn't hear anyone and the faces she saw were all blurs. She didn't hear Rufus barking, or George calling her name, or the confused babble coming from Abdullah's mouth.

"I don't get it. Is she deaf now or something?" George asked as he placed his sunglasses on his head while Abdullah covered his eyes.

"Looking at the woman who glows like the sun makes Abdullah want to cry."

"She is very bright, isn't she?"

"Little woman is like a desert at noon."

"You sure gotta way with words, pal."

"Burns brighter than a pimple of the backside of camel in the middle of a sunny oasis."

"Why aren't you a poet?"

"Burns eyes from dead beasts and kings alike, woman over there does."

"What's she carrying, anyway?"

"Master, it appears woman who walks in an umbrella of searing-eyeball-light carries something thin and leather-like."

"Maybe it's a suitcase?"

"Perhaps she carries a rug, Master, to pray to her heathen gods of sun and moon?"

"Doesn't look like a rug. She's got a bag over her shoulder."

"This woman clearly carries horrible, burnt-offering to gods."

"I'm pretty sure I see feet."

"Abdullah sees no feet except for the ones who hurry to get around bright umbrella of light."

George found an illegal parking space in front of some kind of newspaper office, an affiliate of some sort of the college. He didn't think anyone would want to park there, not at this time of the night, but what did he know? He ran across the street, mindful of cars. George wasn't too fond of Boston's drivers, which on the whole had not really scared him, but hammered home the fact that George didn't belong in heavy traffic. He heard Rufus barking over the honking and shouts as he paused on the wide median strip which served both as a pedestrian safety zone and a subway drop-off/pick-up point. Lilly had moved farther up the street now and George had to run diagonally across the road to cut the distance.

"LILLY!" He cried.

She didn't seem to hear him.

"LILLY!"

The intensity of the light burned through his cheap sunglasses. George realized now how the folks in Lewandos had felt when they were on their first date. Heck, their only date.

Lilly paused, the heavy traffic stalling at the sight of her, but she couldn't tell why. She aimed herself towards the giant Citgo sign. She knew in her grief that she would only feel comfortable when she was standing under it, wherever that might be. Then someone jumped in front of her.

When George entered the bubble of light he thought, for a moment, that he would explode, the intensity was so great. But he hadn't, though, for a second, he did feel burning as if Lilly's love could destroy a soul. He said her name calmly and with love.

Lilly didn't see him at first. When she finally looked at him, she didn't say anything for a second, but then she began to cry, her shoulders slumped, and her bag fell to the sidewalk. She kept her left arm stiff, the Ugly Mother's rigid flat body pressed under her arm, cutting into her flesh. She cried and cried, even as George hugged her.

10

Cilia's ship arrived in record time. The humidity had vanished, and the wind vanished completely and from her window, the Atlantic lay as flat and still as she ever saw it. She had laid in magics to make it so, and so when she arrived in the harbor to meet her captain and to claim her prize she did so with confidence. She did not notice a dark line of clouds far to the south of the harbor, on the horizon.

The port bustled with activity, and Kasper Van Dijk's ship, the Idle Watch, occupied a lonely spot on the western side. They had berthed in the early dawn hours before the sun began its slow climb. The captain had ordered the men to clear a few shipping containers before bringing the box up on deck. Already one of the crew had bravely descended into the hold and cut the box away from the trawler which was to remain in the hold until the box was secure, a fine claim for the Captain, the trawler.

Throughout the tedium, Cilia felt the caginess of the crew. They were frightened of Marina, and when she saw Hector's body being carried out under a sheet, she stifled a fit of glee. *That mermaid took him apart,* she thought, *the power, the power!* Her body prickled into goosebumps. And when the Captain allowed it, finally, after clearing space on the pier to allow for a lorry to maneuver under the crane, did Cilia slip below into the hold.

It lay like a treasure, bathing in the sunlight streaming down from the open hold. It was more impressive in person, its oiled wood reinforced with steel gleamed in the low light, and the magic scrollwork along the seams glowed in her presence. She ran her fingers down the length of it as she walked very slowly to where the top of the box lay upturned. The little door Marcos had fed water through was covered in dried blood from where poor Hector had died.

Marina moaned from the inside, a soft almost imperceptible moan which made her nipples grow hard. *Poor girl is dry as a bone, tsk, tsk.* She ran her hands over the wood, her body tingling and filling with power. The fear and confusion emanating from her prey thrilled her. The box was more beautiful than she believed possible. She bet the inside was a real kicker if Marcos and this Sea Hag were half as talented as Mulch bragged. Cilia liked the way the box looked Medieval somehow. Through the small hole in the top, the zoo-stench of a starved girl sleeping in her madness rose like a perfume. *How pitiful. How wonderful.* She almost didn't want to bust it open. It would look nice in her basement just the way it was, pontoons and all, but sadly it would not fit. *And when I bust it open all those magics will be mine.*

Up on deck, she heard the winding arm of the crane coming to bear over the hull's opening, and soon the good captain would be unloading her cargo.

Cilia bent low and stuck her mouth right up to the opening. "Psst. Fish girl," she hissed. "I hope you slept well during your travels, girl. You're almost home."

Inside, Marina's head whipped up at the sound of the voice, flakes of skin falling from her shoulders and arms like white powder. She groaned, not with pain, but with recognition.

"That's right sweetie. You'd better gather up all your skin, you're gonna need it."

11

Less than fifteen kilometers away Mr. Bill and Nick finally entered the outskirts of Amsterdam, Mr. Bill pausing occasionally to sniff the air, his senses had sharpened since he had regained his strength and size. They had spent the night in the scrub brushes near a canal and had woken up early to walk into the city. Nick, no longer hungover, had grown more and more exhausted.

Linked as he was to Marina and her dementia and her weakness, and drawn by his own heart's yearning, Nick now slinked his body along, trailing Mr. Bill's pace. Nick assumed that his exhaustion was a hangover and jet lag and the overwhelming sensations of being in a foreign country with the strange Mr. Bill, but he knew that it was Marina's sickness and starvation that was eating away at his body with sharp teeth. He moved by will, one foot at a time.

That morning he made Mr. Bill stop and rest several times, and each time Mr. Bill paced anxiously.

"Bill, it's like my attic door is shut, and somebody's playing tunes inside and I can hear the music through the door, but I can't make it out. And I think if I try to remember, I'll just get a headache," Nick said as he scratched his arm; he was downright dehydrated.

"When we find her, you will remember," Mr. Bill said calmly. "Come, we must keep going."

12

Virginia made decent time to Virginia Beach. Once she was on the Bay Bridge Tunnel which separated the Eastern Shore from the sprawl of Virginia Beach by seventeen miles of bridge and two underwater tunnels, she felt better, she felt relieved, her brain spinning plots of murderous revenge.

13

"Doc, I figured I'd crash at Rick's house. He wouldn't care. I'd get his aunt to look at my stomach, maybe find a way to get an X-ray. Then I'd sneak home and see Maria. I'd have to confront my father, but I didn't think I could kill him, you know. I wanted to. I did. But still...he's my freaking father for one thing. As much of a bastard as he was, I didn't think he deserved to die. I sure-as-shit was going to disown him for sure. He wasn't going to be my father anymore. I figured that would be enough. Right?

"When I did get into town, I laid low for a few days. I found out Macy was missing, and that Sheriff North had choked to death in my house, looking for me. Mulch must have killed him; I just knew it.

"The feed store burned down while I was sleeping at Rick's. He woke me with the news. Rumor had it that Mulch was inside somewhere and that there was nothing left but teeth. I didn't believe it.

"The firemen reported that it had been an intense fire, compounded by all the fertilizers in the store. Some flammable materials caught the storehouse behind the main building on fire. They'd found a body in the office, but it was at the coroner's office getting identified. The insurance folks were looking for Mulch. The cops were looking for Mulch.

"But I had to be the one to find him."

14

The afternoon before, Mulch had discreetly checked the Feed Store storage facility to make sure there was plenty of fertilizer and pesticides stored in the back of the storage shed, which happened to be adjacent to his office, the way the Feed Store snaked around itself with the out-buildings and loading docks. In addition to the fertilizer, his crop duster pilot kept extra fuel in the hold under the loading docks. Mulch figured there was enough explosive material to disguise the poor soul he'd picked up on the road, running away from his property, the look of fear and horror burned into his face, haunting his eyes. The poor kid didn't even put up a fight when Mulch punched his lights out. When Mulch tied him up in Mr. Bill's room, the kid looked like he had expected it. When Mulch killed the poor son of a bitch, all he did was whine and whimper like an animal. The kid's ID, from New Jersey, would melt in the fire, and so would his phone. The fire would destroy the rope he used to tie the kid to his desk, the ruse would be enough, for a while.

Before he blew the store he'd climbed on top of the storage shed's corrugated roof, and walked along the length of it, pouring gas. He made sure he'd walked over to the hanger where the crop duster remained parked. He paused thinking he'd spare it, then poured the remaining container over the corner of the hangar roof. *If it survives it survives*, he thought.

When he finally lit the storage building up like Christmas dinner, he watched like a kid as the flames shot up, first along the sides, then along the top, as the flames grew ten feet. When the fertilizer sparked, the explosion knocked Mulch to his feet, but he didn't mind. A flaming piece of the roof of the storage shed flew overhead and landed on top of the store. Fire spread like gossip.

With the storage building gone, there was going to be no more work in the fields. Mulch had Bessie, his accountant, cut unusually large checks for workers two days prior, the day after Mr. Bill had driven his stolen truck off the dock and into the bay. 'Gonna give them out and see how they like it, Bessie,' he had told her. Bessie thought he was crazy. 'An operation like this was a dying breed,' she had said. 'Bessie,' he told her, 'You don't know half of it.' When he had given the checks to the migrant foreman his eyes went wide; he'd almost cried, and Mulch had to explain, lie, even claiming that business was collapsing. In the end, the foreman exclaimed his luck, and together they had handed them out in camp to all the workers.

As the fire diminished in his rear-view mirror, Mulch took a swig off his hip flask. The liquor was hot, bitter, and foul. Even his poison had lost its taste.

"It's all turning to shit." He said to no one. "No. It's always been shit."

CHAPTER ELEVEN

1

Amanda Blackstone's phone rang just as she was falling off to sleep. She rolled over and swiped her hair out of her face.

"MmDial-A-Nurse mmis Amanda."

"Baby, I have something that needs nursing."

"Spider," Amanda bolted up in her bed. "You shit."

"Yeah, good to hear from you too."

"What the fuck are you calling me for in the middle of the night."

"I was bored."

Amanda yawned.

"And I wanted to see how my sis was doing."

"She's fine, she's sleeping like normal people."

"Yeah, well." Spider said.

"You saw her this morning, I mean yesterday."

"Was it only yesterday that I left because I feel like I've been gone for a very long time." Spider's voice echoed.

"Are you okay Spider? You sound weird."

"I'm fine. Nostalgic, I guess."

"You're drunk aren't you."

"Looking at the muddy stars and sitting on the beach."

"I can tell because you're slurring your Ss." Amanda sighed.

"It's real romantic, you know. You could be here, with me."

"Now you're slurring your Ys, which is new to me."

"Amanda, you can slur any letter."

"Why are you calling me?"

"What do you mean?"

"You called my phone." Amanda retorted.

"Oh yeah, I forgot. But really I need your help."

"Why?"

"This is going to sound weird."

"It's been a weird week. Try me."

"How do you make a tourniquet?" Spider asked.

"Oh my god, are you hurt?" Amanda exclaimed.

"No..."

"You know alcohol will make you bleed faster..." Amanda warned.

"...is hurt, babe.... like you wouldn't believe." Spider's voice cut out. "Relax," he said. "Amanda, I just need to know, in case."

"Why?"

"Let's just say a little birdie told me."

"What?"

"Well not me so much as a companion of mine, you see. And since none of us here are Boy Scouts, heaven forbid, we need to know." Spider pleaded.

Amanda reached over to her bedside table for her cigarettes and came down on a pack of Nicorette. She'd made Tanya hide the smokes after dinner with Nick, two days before.

"Hold on Spider, I need a smoke. Wait just a sec."

Amanda went into the kitchen and found them almost immediately. Tanya always hid her smokes in the same place, in the flowered wine pitcher her grandma had given her when she graduated college. Tanya figured Amanda would quit when she wanted; Tanya was an isolationist in terms of quitting. Amanda saw that it was after midnight.

She lit up before she closed the door and let the nicotine run through her system. She felt a flash of heat run through her body. *You should get your head checked girl.* She picked up her phone. "Spider, still there?"

"Yeah."

"You gotta pen?"

2

Zac woke up around midnight to his stomach's growling instructions. Spider's singing had stirred him, but once he was up his stomach wouldn't let him be. Zac couldn't make it out at first, but after much patient listening, and after plugging his ears to hear his stomach better, he thought he was being told to make sure he knew some First Aid.

Zac tried to forget about his stomach for a while and go back to sleeping in the Yugo, but he couldn't. He kept thinking back to the day when his stomach told him not to go to school and his lab partner blew the classroom up. After that, Zac quit drugs and drinking and hoped to god that his stomach would stop talking to him, but it didn't. Therapy didn't help in that regard, though it did help him with other aspects of his life, drugs or no, booze or no, his stomach kept on talking to him, and lately, since the weird mermaid graffiti started popping up, it seemed like his stomach had a lot to say. *Like a lot*, he thought. *Too much for me, man*, he whispered to himself.

Across from him, Blockhead laid out, flat on his back, snoring, his big chest breathing in and out, snorting when he was ready to exhale. If Zac hadn't been so worried about what the hell his stomach wanted out of him, he might have found Blockhead's snoring humorous. But Zac wasn't in a humorous mood. Spider, however, was.

"Yo, Zac. What's up with your bad-ass gastro-self." Spider said, dreamy, stoned.

"Um, do you know First Aid?"

"Should I? Friend of yours?" Spider said.

"What?"

Spider laughed, "I crack myself up sometimes, I do."

"I'm serious." Zac pleaded.

Spider swung himself around to face Zac. Spider drank from a fresh Tall Boy and offered Zac some. Zac took a swig and then launched into his story, to which Spider listened, alert and attentive.

"Look. I think your stomach is some fucked up shit. But it saved your life. I don't think there are angels and shit in there, but hey, what do I know?" Spider said.

"It's telling me that I should know First Aid, but I don't know any. Do you?"

"Nope, but I know who does." And Spider picked up his phone.

3

Amanda couldn't believe she was getting up out of her very warm and cozy bed to drive her grandmother's crappy car to a beach in Boston because one of Spider's friend's stomach spoke to him and told him he better know how to make a tourniquet. And Amanda was almost *not* feeling like a complete loser again. She didn't know what to pack, the stomach hadn't been that forthcoming. She was going for one day, two at the most and she was going to be there strictly for nursing purposes. She added a hand-held video cam to her clothes in case she had a brainstorm on how to capitalize on Nick's sleep painting. A phony gesture, she would later think, looking back on how powerless she was, how swept up she was in the magic that drew her to Boston.

Spider had pricked her curiosity. She wrote a quick note to Tanya and grabbed her pepper spray. She'd need it in her neighborhood after midnight. She'd called her grandma to borrow the car and her grandmother said yes and was completely wide awake, "Oh you know dear, watching television," her usual response to why she never slept.

On the way to her grandmother's, she picked up a carton of cigarettes and a large coffee. With supplies laid in, she walked the two blocks to her grandma's place. Grandma let Amanda use her car anytime she wanted because she didn't use it anymore, like never.

Amanda knocked on the door, she smelled bacon and coffee.

"I've got road food for you, sweetie," her grandma said opening the door wearing a short sleeve shirt and her apron that read TAKE THIS JOB AND SHOVE IT, with a print of a cook with a spatula flipping the bird. She greeted Amanda with a kiss on the cheek.

"Hey, grandma."

"You're up early. Bacon?"

"No thanks. How are you doing?"

"Fine dear. Your father wants me to move in with them and sell this place."

"Really?"

"I told him to stick it. No offense, but I hate your mother's cooking."

"Me too."

"Well. Keys are on the counter."

"Thanks." *Grandmas always know,* Amanda thought.

"But you gotta tell me the story first."

"Story?" Amanda said.

"You know, is he a cutie?"

Amanda blushed and sat down. She decided to have some bacon and coffee, but passed on the homemade donuts, on account she knew she'd be driving for a good four hours, and donuts would rest like lead in the bottom of her stomach. Then she told her granny the story or almost all of it.

An hour later Amanda was heading up the interstate towards Boston. She hadn't been back since she graduated from school. She hadn't seen her old college friends in years. Ashley lived in Paris via Rio, and Raven worked in DC, if she remembered right, Rayne was an administrator of a school somewhere in Maryland. She assumed Virginia was home in Virginia, wherever that was. Amanda thought how nice it would be to live in Beantown again. Amanda couldn't afford housing in Boston; it was too rich for her blood. Jersey had been much more affordable. She didn't recognize the street address of the beach Spider had given her, but she was guessing it was in Revere, or near the harbor, or one of those godawful parts of Boston. Everyone knew medical waste washed on metro Boston shores like seaweed. And a kid was as likely to get a syringe in his foot, or find a body part, as find a cool shell to take home. *What the hell was Spider getting her into?*

4

Nick didn't feel so hot and stopped walking and sat down on a phallic short metal pole that was emblazoned with three small Xs. Whatever he sat on hurt his butt, but he didn't care. His head felt like someone very heavy had sat on it. His stomach felt worse. He'd drank three bottles of water already and it hadn't put a dent in his thirst.

Mr. Bill had flagged a carpet salesman down on the highway and the guy spoke enough English and gave them a ride into the city for kicks. His name was Wilhelm, and he was from Belgium, but now lived in the 'city of sin,' as he called it. Wilhelm dropped them off on a street corner. Wilhelm had drawn Mr. Bill a very crude map. The shipyards were only a twenty-minute walk from there, give or take. Seeing Nick stumble out of Wilhelm's truck Bill didn't think Nick would make it. Mr. Bill pretended to look around, pretended to take in the sights. Nick only looked at his shoes, what was left of them, and tried not to fall. Mr. Bill then used his magic to get a nearby newsstand clerk to hand him over some water and some fruit.

"You look like the bottom of my feet," Mr. Bill said to Nick who didn't answer; he looked as pale as a ghost.

"Look buddy you have to walk with me. If we find her, I can save you both. But you have to keep up," Mr. Bill said.

Nick nodded and stood up from where he sat and took a step, and then fell face-first into the pavement.

5

The spirit of the Dutch draws many a genius mind, and Amsterdam is home to a great many artists and a wild music scene. Theater, especially street theater, thrives in the city like no other. The city is used to wild passionate displays of oddities, such as those during Carnival, on Gay Pride Day, or Her Queen's Day. So no one paid much attention to the half-naked giant carrying a very pale, younger man across the city, towards the shipyards, to where Cilia watched the giant box being lowered onto the wharf from below deck of a massive cargo ship.

6

Lilly had cried herself to sleep. George felt sad for her. Losing your mother is devastating, and the poor thing had exhausted herself carrying her mother across town the way she had. They had parked in a parking lot across from the Howard Johnson's. There had been lots of tears and lots of hugs and kisses too. George couldn't believe his good fortune, Lilly was with him, and they were together, in a parking lot in Boston, MA.

Abdullah stood outside the truck, holding the jerky-like corpse of the Ugly Mother high in the air, out of Rufus' reach, who barked and whined and begged to get a piece of the poor dead woman's foot. Lilly had said something about having to go to the beach tonight and George doubted he would get any sleep. He had to figure out what was going on, he was going to use his second wish to see what his friend Nick was up to.

Finding Lilly had been a relief but as soon as she was in his arms, he felt a compelling vacancy in his heart for his friend. Add to the fact that Lilly had been glowing again and that her mother looked like a Slim Jim didn't help matters much. For George, it all traced back to Nick, the genesis of weirdness in George's life.

George took his army blanket out and draped it over Lilly before slipping out of the truck. *She looks like a princess*, he thought. He let her sleep and was craving some shut-eye himself but knew that rest would be far off.

"Abdullah, I will make my second wish now."

"As you command." Abdullah cleared his throat, and waited, his hand holding the dead woman's corpse out of reach of Rufus who wagged his tail playfully. Twice already the dog had tried to chew on the dead woman, luckily Lilly had not seen it.

"I wish to know what my friend Nick is doing, right now."

"Your wish is my command."

7

George's head filled with light. The smells of the sea filled his lungs and for a second, he thought he was inside the head of another dog, but he wasn't, George was flying.

The ocean appeared as a wide bright blue giant below him, and George dipped and flew downward towards a large, blurry blotch of gray and blue. He recognized the shape as a harbor and boats. Far off against the horizon, he saw a line of the darkest storm clouds he'd ever seen in his life. As he got closer the details of the pier came into view, a group of people gathered around a large box. His nostrils filled with the smell of fish, and saltwater. As he came closer and closer, a sound filled his ears, a cry, and George's heart skipped a beat. He thought his buddy was in trouble, but it was only the sound of a seagull, the seagull whom he now inhabited.

The gull dove by Cilia and the captain and three of his crewmen who stood around the box, slack-jawed. Captain Van Dijk's headache ceased as soon as the box touched the ground and suddenly, he couldn't remember getting to Holland from Boston. Three crewmen stood behind him with crowbars, awaiting orders to open the box up.

The gull dipped into the sea beyond the pier and rose into the air again, a small fish wiggling in its mouth, a fish that sent a cold shock through George's body as he swallowed the wiggly meal whole, and then George saw how enormous the box was, how strange its markings were, reinforced with steel and resting on pontoons. Through the seagull's eyes, the faces of the men and women were bowed and bowled and bent out of shape. The sight distracted him so that he didn't see the hulking shape of a very large man jog into the shipyard, just beyond the group of people and the box. As George's gull turned to wing-back over them, things went black.

Cilia killed the seagull with a thought. She smiled as she watched the gull fall into the water. That one had seemed especially nosy. *Patience,* she told herself. *Expect to be attacked you are all alone now.*

And just beyond her sight, a giant lumbered around the shipping containers, a body thrown over his back. And looking out towards the box, Mr. Bill eyed Cilia. *That's right,* Bill said to himself. *Focus on the seagull, Marina, and the box. I'm not even here.*

8

When George snapped to, Abdullah was driving his truck into oncoming traffic. A large bus loomed towards them.

"What the hell are you doing?" he screamed. He yanked the wheel hard to the right, causing the truck to swerve back into the lane. Horns bleated and people shouted curses at them. The car behind them almost smashed into George's bumper.

"Master, Abdullah so sorry, but Rufus began to bark, like before. Dog leads the way." Rufus had his big paws up on the dashboard and stared out the front. He barked as Abdullah steadied the truck. Lilly lay in the back of the cab, asleep on the jump seats.

"Pretty lady who burns people's eyes is sleeping in the back."

"And her mother?" George asked.

"Abdullah has folded her into the bag in the back of the truck."

"YOU DID WHAT?"

"Master, Abdullah would not allow her mother to touch such dirty ground, even in such a big kingdom."

"Jesus fucking Christ, Abdullah."

"So sorry. It was all I could think to do."

Rufus barked and like before, leaned his head to either the right or left to signal a turn. He leaned his head to the right, and Abdullah almost squashed a little old lady in a small Honda driving next to them.

"Sorry," George shouted out the window. The old woman gave him the finger. "Ab, you have got to be more careful."

Abdullah grinned, "Sorry, master George, I feel like a powerful genie in a truck of flying steel."

"Yeah, well, don't kill us."

"Master find out what master needed?" Abdullah's speed tended to be between 85 and 35, depending on how far apart the red lights were. George had no idea where they were going.

"What is it with you and animals, anyway?"

"Master did not like the seagull?"

Abdullah laughed.

"I couldn't see Nick. At least, not unless he was inside the huge freaking box on the pier," George explained.

Lilly slid across the jump seat and fell onto the floor, bumping into the other side of the truck. She kept on sleeping, a cartoon look of surprise on her lips for a second before whistling back into a snore.

"Watch it!" George shouted.

Rufus barked twice and nodded to the left where the road split and headed uphill.

"Are you sure he knows where he's going?" George asked.

"Smelly beast is a very good navigator."

"Yeah, well I wish I could say the same thing for your damn seagull."

"Seagulls like to dive and turn."

"Yeah well, I couldn't tell what the hell was going on, wherever he was. It was light there and warm, like it was afternoon."

"Master, Abdullah wishes for a truck of his own."

"Maybe you could start your own cab service," George muttered under his breath.

"Cab? What is a cab?"

"Never mind. I think Nick is in trouble. Big trouble. There was this box, kinda like a prison," George said as he tried to remember it as it was. "Everything was kind of bowed out. Like through a fish-eye lens."

"Master, seagulls have no fisheyes."

"Yeah, I know. Never mind. It looked like one of those boxes you might see on a war movie or something."

"War movie?"

"Yeah, you know like TV, only bigger."

"Box bigger than TV."

"No. Never mind. The box looked like something I'd seen once. They keep prisoners inside them for long periods."

"Yes, Abdullah has seen these before."

"You have?"

"Yes, master. When in the secret city of Petra, thieves and liars were dropped into deep pits which were like a box."

"Yeah, that's it, only...."

"Only what, master?"

"Only the box was... carried somewhere," George snapped his fingers. "That's it! Nick must have been in the box, kidnapped!"

"Master is very smart," Abdullah said as his big foot squashed the accelerator and floored the truck to 95.

"Only why would anyone kidnap Nick?" George said.

"Master, I believe, we are here," Abdullah said as he slowed down.

They were on a street running parallel to a beach. A dingy sign that spelled Carson Beach hung at a slight angle. George looked around him, the city rising behind him, its lights like a jagged line of Christmas lights.

9

Zac heard them first. His stomach had told him to *watch out*, and he supposed that meant he had to keep an eye out for that Amanda chick – the Dial-a-Nurse – Spider's sister's roommate. *Yeah, whatever.* Zac was more worried about cops and not whether some nursing school reject would get to the beach in time for whatever was going to happen. Night was coming to an end.

Zac had decided that nothing was going to happen and that his stomach had been shooting off at the mouth, so to speak, when he suddenly saw four dark figures approaching along the beach. One of the shadowy figures was very small, the other very large, and between them there walked two average-sized people. At first, Zac thought one of the figures was a midget, but it turned out to be a dog instead. The very huge figure on the other end was bigger than Blockhead, by a lot, which meant that the guy had to weigh in over three hundred pounds and stand at least seven feet, maybe seven and a half feet tall. He was about to go get Blockhead and Spider when the dog barked and trotted up to him in the darkness, his slobbering tongue dropping huge globs of spit onto his bare legs.

"Gross!" Zac put his hands up to his face. "Man, like, get away from me and stuff."

"Rufus!" One of the middle figures snapped. The dog barked once and seemed to gesture with his big head towards Zac.

There was a series of muffled whispers before they stepped up to him and for a second Zac was sure he'd seen them before, but once he got a good look at them the sensation faded.

"My name is George Henderson and this is Lilly Aguirre."

Zac had trouble seeing their features, but he could tell from George's voice that they were from the South. "This is Abdu...Ab. Call him Ab. This is gonna sound like an odd question, but, um, uh...." he said as he turned to Lilly and whispered something in her ear, then back to Zac. "You haven't, by chance, seen a giant box floating anywhere around here lately?"

10

Virginia Hayes spent less than twenty-four hours in Rick "the Dick's" spare bed letting her stomach heal as much as it could before striking out for her own house. Rick "the Dick's" mother, Mabel, had worked her nursing magic which consisted of lots of chicken soup, and antibiotic pills horked from the hospital supply. Rick was pretty upset about Macy and hoped that if Virginia could make it back, she too would be found soon.

Virginia knew her father had to be involved in Macy's disappearance and the death of the sheriff, at her own house no less. So yes, Virginia was worried about Macy too, and Marina, whom she was sure was in more danger than her.

It was what Pembroke had said about her, something having to do with his sister, Cilia, and if Pembroke's sister was as screwed up as he was, then Marina would be in big trouble, with a capital B and T.

For all these reasons and more Virginia decided it was best to go home in the early morning. And if she was lucky, Mulch would be tied up with the insurance people all day, perhaps even arrested for fraud, if it turned out to be her lucky day. *Yeah*, she thought, *that would be just great if that were to happen.*

Quietly thanking Mabel Bell, Virginia took the car she stole in Richmond and drove it to her house. The sun began its climb above the trees. Virginia thought of bloodstains, something about the way the sun diffused through the clouds.

CHAPTER TWELVE

Oysterhaus 6:00 AM EST

Mulch Hayes had dismissed the migrants two days prior, telling them they could stay in camp for another week but that they had better be gone soon after that. It didn't take long before many of the workers loaded up in trucks and packed themselves off to the Smith and Taylor farms up the road, looking for more work. Within hours the first families had already moved. Mulch had given them a generous severance check, much more than any of them had ever seen. Still, work was work, and working meant staying in the US legally. Camp buzzed with talk. Estrella, Maria's cousin told stories of the strange person she had seen in the tomato field some nights before. No one paid it much mind. What Estrella had seen wasn't even all that weird, for the Hayes farm anyway.

Ediostro told stories of the bird who told him that the Ugly Mother was dead, which sent shockwaves through camp, and many believed that because the Ugly Mother was dead that was the reason Mulch was getting rid of them despite the fact there was much work to be done in the fields.

"The luck had run out of this place," Manuel said to his wife, "can't you feel it?" She nodded, packing her clothes as she did. Like the other migrants, Manuel and his wife were going to work elsewhere on the shore. Many of the migrants would not see the house burn or feel the sudden and violent storm that was to break over the shore later that morning when Virginia chased her father into the woods and killed him, but those that stayed remember the day it happened despite what everyone else claims.

2

Mulch watched Maria from the shadows in the hallway, his breathing low, rancid with whiskey and rum. Every day for years Maria rose before dawn to prep the day's meals. She'd cut all her vegetables and ingredients and plan lunch and dinner, even if she only cooked for herself and Mulch. It was her way, and on the last morning she would ever spend in that kitchen Mulch stood in the dark hallway watching her cut onions, chopped bay leaves piled to the sides. He smelled cilantro, garlic, and onions which made his mouth water. Part of Mulch wanted to see her live, the same part of Mulch that believed he could change his ways and redeem himself through love and action. Mulch knew better. He had taken the first step on his path a long time ago and he couldn't step back from it now. Mulch thought if he had not have seen his path laid out before him like a timeline, then he would have been able to reverse his speed and turn back. As a young man, he'd witnessed the brutal smacking his father delivered to his wife, Mulch's mother, the winter morning she disappeared. Snow and ice fell in sheets. When Mr. Bill found her the next day in the cornfield, she was frozen solid, bruises on her cheek and face like dark bubbles trapped in ice. Ruth had been caught sleeping with one of the farmhands the day before, and Eb, taken aback by her wantonness, dragged her back to the house and beat her senseless. The farmhand had been beheaded by Mr. Bill some days later. Ruth's skin cracked and split under her husband's knuckles. Neither Leon nor Mulch said one word to stop it, despite having seen Eb drag the poor woman by her hair and into the house. The next morning Ruth had apologized like a weak broken child and Eb slapped her again and again, his fury unchecked. After crying and retreating into her room, she had vanished in the storm later that day. Mulch had followed her and sealed his fate.

When Maria began cutting up the peppers, he came warmly behind her and turned her around to hug her. Perhaps it was the way the sun struck Maria's face that morning or the way Maria stood. In surprise, she dropped her knife.

"Mulch, you scared me!" She shrieked with joy and began to laugh, but it froze in her throat when she saw Mulch's face reddening. His mouth pulled back in a tight intense smile. Maria had seen that look before on Eb when he would set upon his wife in the kitchen. Suddenly, very afraid, Maria's hands searched for her knife behind her.

For a second, she thought she had a chance, but Mulch's backhand whipped across her cheek and blood rushed into the open cut. Maria cried out for help, forgetting for a second, she was the only one in the house. Then Mulch was upon her.

Amsterdam 11:15 AM GMT

Mr. Bill rested Nick Adams against a shipping container on the eastern side of the wharf. Nick's forehead burned with fever.

"Water," Nick throated, his voice nearly gone.

Mr. Bill handed him another bottle of water. Nick drank it in three long gulps.

"I hope you'll regain some of your strength back. That is if I can get the girl into the water, if only for a little while," Mr. Bill looked down at Nick and continued. "And when you do get your strength back, I need you to go for the girl. Do you understand? Make sure she gets into the water. Do you understand?"

Nick didn't hear Mr. Bill. In his mind, Nick wasn't even on the dock. He was sitting at home in front of the television watching things from afar. His house felt very hot, and he was very thirsty. He looked around his room and found no water. *Water was still free, right?*

"Do you understand?" Mr. Bill asked.

Nick nodded, unsure of what he agreed to. *Why wouldn't this man give him some water? It was a reasonable request.*

Mr. Bill adjusted his loincloth and stepped out from behind the shipping container. He'd forgotten the free and easy feel the loincloth gave him and after years of jeans, he found the feeling somewhat distracting, even now as he prepared to summon magic more potent than he had ever wielded in his life.

Captain Van Dijk's men on the dock still hadn't seen him, they were too busy trying to figure out where to pop the box open. Cilia was gesturing to the sides of it as the men waited for their instructions. "There's no seam," the Captain was shouting as Mr. Bill stepped up between them, throwing the whole morning into confusion.

"Need any assistance?" Mr. Bill barked, half-laughed, his arms rising into the air.

The reaction was instantaneous and expected. Cilia threw her arms out in front of her, and Bill felt her push through the air between them. And he pushed back.

This is going to be fun, Mr. Bill thought.

When he was a boy, he and some of the other children would grab hold of a stick and stand on either side of it and push until someone fell. Only now there was no stick, but an invisible wall of wills between Mr. Bill and Cilia van Hazen.

"Get him," Cilia screamed, her voice coming out papery and throaty.

Captain Van Dijk wasn't sure what he was looking at. On one side of him stood a very attractive older woman whose only blemish seemed to be that she had no ears. On the other side of him, a huge muscular man, wearing only a loincloth made of what looked like a shirt, held his hands out. The man looked like something you might see on an old American Western movie, except much, much bigger, and the duo looked like they were holding something between them. He felt the power but did not understand, his brain paused searching for meaning so that it took a moment for the Captain to order the men with crowbars to swing at the big man, which did the men no good.

Mr. Bill seeing the stevedores close in, broke his hold on Cilia and pivoted, turning to kick attack the closest stevedore in the gut, all the while keeping his left arm stiff and out, raised like a shield against the man with the crowbar on the other side of him. The kick sent the man down the wharf where he skidded against the decking. The other man adjusted his swing to hit Mr. Bill midsection. Mr. Bill grunted and took the hit without so much a grunt and then grabbed his assailant's skull with his giant hand and broke the man's neck with a single short turn.

Cilia, seeing her moment, grabbed the Captain by the arm, and together they pried at the box's seam, but they could not make the crowbar budge. Urgency boiled up in Cilia's blood and she took her right finger and placed it as high as she could reach on the corner and ran her finger down the side like her finger was a blowtorch. Ozone crackled and popped. Magic crackled and blue fire crawled along with Cilia's touch.

Mr. Bill pried the crowbar from the dead stevedore and threw it like a tomahawk to crack the skull of the other stevedore. The poor man had recovered enough to turn and run but didn't make three feet before he met his end. Mr. Bill's blood pulsed through him, and he felt his lungs billow for a great cry. The final sailor, having more sense than others banked away from Bill and bolted. But Mr. Bill did not allow him to escape, instead he picked up the dead stevedore and throwing the corpse like a stone which clipped the man in the legs, sending him face forward into the hard deck with a bloody crack.

The Captain didn't know what happened when he was lifted off the ground into the air. At first, he thought he had slipped, for he must have, but then he began to fly in circles he thought this must be what a stroke feels like. Mr. Bill had snatched him off his feet from behind and whipped him around like a toy. Mr. Bill's hawk-like cry was enough to make the Captain wet his pants, and the smell of piss and fear filled the air. Bill smacked good Captain Van Dijk against the dock before bouncing him into the harbor's oily water, the ground stained with wet blood smacks from where his tender body scraped and tore.

Mr. Bill turned to Cilia, and Cilia, focusing on cutting the box open with her finger, didn't notice until Mr. Bill struck her from behind.

Cilia blew back against the decking like a gust of wind had taken her by surprise. For a second her power faded, she even had to catch her breath, which gave her pause. When she rose again, she did so with anger.

What Cilia saw that no one else saw was a giant raven whose feathers wormed with lice. The great bird stank of death and when it batted its wings the smells of the dead blew into her face. When the bird raked her shoulder, its claws drew blood.

Cilia ducked her head and swatted her hands about her head and ran around the box to catch her breath. She called her magics and the air above the raven clapped and at once a grotesque mouth clamped down on the bird and flung it aside before turning to Mr. Bill standing below.

What Mr. Bill saw that no one else saw was a giant red ear, its helix lined with teeth. From the hole in the ear tore a funnel of wind that blew against Bill's skin and battered at his flesh.

If anyone innocent to the proceedings happened to be there that day, they would have seen a box on the docks and two people locked in a staring contest. The customs officials that lunched in their office on the other side of the wharf, the few sailors and captains and crew who milled around on their ships in the harbor nibbling at cheese and rolls and waiting for afternoon coffee to finish brewing were all concerned about the coming weather. A bulletin had been issued not an hour before Bill and Cilia began their staring match that warned of a large storm system building over the North Atlantic. The system had appeared on everyone's radar suddenly, about an hour before the alarm bells rang. Meteorologists were somewhat baffled but explained the system away as being something complicated and Canadian. What was interesting was that the storm system was forming a straight line across the Atlantic and looked a lot like a mermaid with what appeared to be a finger pointed directly at Boston, MA USA, and what appeared to be a head of hair located somewhere south of Greenland. The tail formed the last bit of the system and swooped up the coast of France and ended above Amsterdam. The storm system was pulling moisture and wind and already existing systems into the long body that looked like it might have breasts. All over the world, satellites and meteorologists trained their eyes on the mermaid system and the seas in-between.

Scientists who had been up all night in California popped trucker's speed and gulped coffee watching it develop. Someone in Alaska broke out a vial of cocaine, usually saved for those winter storm systems, and snorted up a line to crunch the data of this strange phenomenon.

Two hours from Boston, Amanda Blackstone heard the weather report as she sucked down her fifth smoke in a row. She doubted herself the first time she heard it, and when she switched channels and heard it again. *Mermaid storm system,* she thought, *my spider-sense is tingling.* She accelerated, pushing the car beyond its speed limit.

In Amsterdam, ship captains and sailors and old sea dogs wondered if the storm system meant anything – rain being the common consensus. Many of the older sailors told stories of mermaids that their fathers had told them many years ago, stories handed down from generation to generation. All the while a real mermaid lay inside a box, in the Amsterdam harbor singing a song she had heard in the womb when her mother had swum the distance from the Canary Islands off the coast of Spain to Virginia's Eastern Shore.

Inside the box, Marina saw the sparks from Cilia's finger and thought of fireflies, and for an instance assumed she was back at home, lying under the stars and watching the world go by above. But even there, dreaming herself back in her creek, she knew that something was wrong, very wrong. Her eyes had trouble focusing and she couldn't move, she had no strength. If she were to have stood up, she would have found that she was indeed several inches shorter. When the sparks stopped, Marina too heard a storm gathering outside. She heard the clouds rustling together, rubbing against each other, their friction sparking lightning. *It's going to rain soon*, she thought.

The raven had taken a hit from the ear which had torn into the bird's skin with its teeth. The shape of the ear made it hard for Mr. Bill to concentrate because it was such an odd thing to be doing battle with. Mr. Bill had to concentrate not only on fighting but also to keep the silly notion of an ear far off in the back of his mind. To do this Mr. Bill remembered the past, especially the oldest memories he had forgotten for so long. Mr. Bill remembered the day he and his friends found the slaughtered herd and how the bird had led them to the site. How the raven ate the dead and took them to the afterlife, the stench, the blood-soaked grass, how the trees were hacked and damaged by musket shot, by the Dutchmen, by liars and thieves.

But the ear heard him thinking and sucked Mr. Bill's power away. He couldn't concentrate while fighting an ear, it was absurd, and all sound vanished around him in a clap. Mr. Bill thought he might be in a soundless bubble of space where nothing existed and for a few terrible seconds his sight was gone and the voice inside him was sucked out into the void of the ear. And then the ear wasn't an ear anymore, but a blackness that pulled voices and sounds out of the living and into its maw where it chewed them up with its teeth. Mr. Bill knew if he was to win against Cilia, he would have to call upon the power of the dead. The ear would not be able to steal from the dead, he was sure of that.

Cilia had spent all her life listening to other people's thoughts and planting her own where their thoughts had once been. She had never before had to call up so much power at once and she was thrilled to see the grotesque shape she had conjured. The ear was perhaps ten feet tall and five feet wide. Teeth circled its folds, and through the hole the ear snarled and bit like a wild beast, sucking all power from the air and into the hole of the ear. Even her thoughts slipped away from her. *If a man can't talk, a man can't think, and if a man can't think, he can't withstand me,* she thought joyfully.

Neither Cilia nor Mr. Bill noticed the dark clouds building overhead, and for a second Cilia thought she had won, for her ear had swallowed the bird whole and plucked feathers fluttered around Mr. Bill's pale, defeated face. Then the massive stag appeared above Mr. Bill and Mr. Bill began to change.

Boston, MA 5:30 AM EST

Zac, Spider, and Blockhead listened as George and Lilly explained who and what they were looking for. Spider couldn't believe it. "So, you're looking for the same guy we're looking for?" Spider wasn't sure what to think. He hadn't expected anyone else to look for his discovery. He hoped they weren't from another magazine.

"That's what they said, boss" Blockhead confirmed.

Blockhead figured if he needed to he could take the big guy, though he would want to get a good look at him first. From where they stood in the morning dark, the guy was jacked. The sun, it appeared, wasn't coming up. Storm clouds, a different shade of black than the rest of the sky, covered all of Boston in darkness. Blockhead had a strange thought *like it's a fairy tale kind of story.* He shook his head clear and stared straight ahead to project machismo, its own kind of glamor.

"And you saw the billboard sign?" Spider said as he calculated figures in his head.

"Yup," George said. "That's my buddy, Nick."

"You don't by any chance have a camera on you?" Spider asked suspiciously.

"Nope," George said, bouncing on his heels. For some reason, he felt like he belonged here, beside Lilly with this strange company in a strange city.

"I have one. At home." Lilly said. "I mean besides my cell phone camera. Did you mean a cell phone? Or a fancy camera?"

"Good one," Blockhead laughed.

"Yeah," Spider chuckled nervously. "No, don't worry about it. I meant you know fancy camera."

"Professional camera." Blockhead interrupted.

"Professional camera, that's right," Spider said. "Now what exactly did you want with this guy? I was a little groggy when my associate here woke me up. See I had several beers last night," Spider explained as he checked his watch. "Only a few hours ago."

"Oh man, is your head going hurt Spi," Blockhead chuckled.

"What do *you* guys want with Nick?" George asked, he didn't feel like talking anymore. Something was going to happen here; the air buzzed.

Spider wasn't sure if he could trust them but since they showed up at the same place they did, he supposed it would be foolish not to try and use them. After all, the big guy looked like he could eat Blockhead for breakfast if it came to that. He towered silently over them all.

"And you're not all from some website or newspaper or magazine. You know, one of the local free ones," Spider thought the dog looked a little too cute to be just a country dog. *If they were from Virginia, why bring a dog?*

"No. We are not from a magazine," George's Southern accent sounded just like Nick's. "Are you?"

"Hmm. Yes, we are. Okay, let me get this straight, I'm a businessman, first and foremost," Spider said as he began his story, this despite Zac and Blockhead's sarcastic giggles and snorts.

Amsterdam 11:35 AM GMT

The stag appeared above Mr. Bill's head one foot at a time, its front feet first, then its head and its long middle, and finally its hindquarters, as if it walked out of some foggy swamp bottom. Cilia expected the beast to charge, but it only stood there, its strength in its steely eyes and many horns. Mr. Bill twisted and grunted on the ground below the stag, his body bulging, his skin rippling like water. *What the ever-living fuck is happening to him?* Cilia thought. She hadn't expected this. She had met the Indian once before and knew he was powerful, but this transfiguration was beyond her power. *First, he arrives double his size, no small feat, and now this!*

Cilia swore to herself and began to chant, to manifest her energy. She gathered herself as an athlete might gather themselves before a feat and fired her magics towards Mr. Bill and the great beast above him.

Her magic ear howled with wind, sucking and blowing through its mouth before it swooped down upon the stag, trying to envelop it, but the stag remained stock still. Only its nostrils flared and when the animal exhaled, a rolling fog blew out of his nose that curled and fell in long rolling tides around Mr. Bill so that the decking faded behind its curtain and the air grew damp with its breath.

The ear flapped like a great maw, the teeth sharp and yellow tearing at the stag. Only the stag's body did not rend, which incensed the ear causing it to quicken. It cared not if it battered itself against its flanks or if it caught itself on the jagged prongs and Cilia felt her shoulder rip and bleed as her avatar attacked and took damage as it did so. By the time she realized that the stag was only a shield to protect Bill, Mr. Bill had slipped away under a blanket of mist. Above her, the cloud bank of black storm clouds curled in like a wave.

2

Mr. Bill's body popped and bled from where the exhaustive shapeshifting tore through his skin. As a child he loved hearing tales of the great herd and how they moved without sound, leaving the ground untouched. He loved how the stag's horns twisted up towards the sun like a plant reaching for the light. And now as he flailed in the fog, he felt his head grow and twist, antlers protruding from his head. Bone pressed through scalp, and a great ripping sound unwound in his ear. His fingers and hands began to fuse, his skin darkening and growing tufts of hair. His feet hammered into hooves struggled to stand as his face warped and pulled out like clay. The protrusions on his head stretched and stretched until they were a royal crown of tines and horns and Mr. Bill for the second time in two days had changed; half man, half stag, he possessed the strength of the spirit and with the ghost of the stag above him, protecting him, he possessed the strength of a nation.

Boston 5:50 AM EST

Spider finally finished his story. Possession? No one was sure if Nick was possessed as Spider said, but no one argued with that logic either. It appeared to all that the paintings were Nick's way of processing the information given him, somehow, by the captive mermaid. Blockhead, Spider, and Zac were doubtful that there was a mermaid, but they did not understand yet that George's big friend was a genie, and none of them had seen Lilly glow, and none of them had touched the wrinkled and jerky-like skin of Lilly's shriveled up mother. They had all seen the paintings. George, not wanting to call attention to Abdullah, pulled him aside. Enthusiastically Abdullah replied, "Oh great and wonderful master, how can I serve you?" Abdullah's loud voice and cheery smile got the three young graffiti hunters elbowing one another and whispering.

"Ssh. Keep it down, Ab," George didn't think discretion was in this genie's capacity.

"Yes, master," his whispers sounding like a low shout.

"Good," George wasn't sure how to begin. "Listen, for my third wish...."

Amsterdam 11:55 AM GMT

The ghost of the great stag vanished with the fog, the fog itself billowing and thickening and spreading across the wharf. Cilia staggered back; unsure of Mr. Bill's location, she braced herself and dispatched her ear to attack. She had suffered wounds, but they only spurned Cilia onward.

She had not seen Mr. Bill's complete transformation and assumed he was vulnerable to her magics so that when the ear made its move, she expected it to take the top of Mr. Bill's head off, but the Native American stood up from the foggy decking half-man and half-beast, his arms distended and gorged with muscle, his legs thick and trunk-like. His hooved hands pawed at the air as his great lungs snorted and blew out a breath so thick it curled and swirled and thickened in front of him like a shield, and when the ear came down with a snarl, Mr. Bill simply rolled his head, and the great horns took the blow. With a great bellowed cry, he threw off the ear and screamed a noise that sounded both deer-like and man-like and not of this world. His face bulged with rows of tiny teeth made not for flesh but greenery, but his face maintained both the haunted look of a man and the starved look of a dangerous animal, and that face searched the fog for its adversary. And when Mr. Bill caught Cilia in his gaze, Cilia paused for a moment, just before Mr. Bill lowered his head and charged her.

Cilia jumped out of the way as Mr. Bill rammed Marina's box behind her, splintering it and sending it careening towards the edge of the wharf, tilting it towards the water.

I was lucky, Cilia thought. *I won't be so lucky next time.* She dispatched the ear again to wrap its hideous mouth around Mr. Bill's monstrous shoulders who was now beating the box with his skull. *The damn fool doesn't know he missed me!*

But Mr. Bill hadn't been aiming for her at all, the side of the box now looked like something had bitten into it, and Mr. Bill continued to break apart the walls using his massive rack of horns. He simply shrugged off Cilia's avatar and continued to smash.

"Enough!" Cilia shouted, angered, dissipating the ear with a wave and rising into the air, her body charged with electricity. She expected Mr. Bill to grab the girl but Mr. Bill only swung his hooved hands at the box, pushing the box to the edge of the wharf dock.

"Stop!" Cilia shouted. *He's fooled me!* She readied herself to fire her magics into her adversary. And as the air crackled and sparked around her, the box poised over the side of the dock, wobbling for a second before falling into the water with an undramatic sploosh.

"NOOOO!" Cilia shrieked, her body seething with anger. *Damn fool!* Her window to control Marina had just closed. Still, if she acted quickly, she might be able to overtake the mermaid and Mr. Bill.

The effect of the seawater on both Marina and Nick was instantaneous. Energy and strength snapped back into them both. Marina's body enlarged with water, the Atlantic swelled into her and she grew like a dry sponge brought to life. Whereas Nick's fever washed away and he discovered his mouth was no longer so dry. When he managed to stand on the dock where he had been left, he saw Mr. Bill transformed, grotesque, standing now at eight feet, ten or more with his rack, the antlers spreading out like the crown of a king. Nick stared up in disbelief at his new friend and Cilia, floating three feet above the dock. The woman looked vaguely familiar, and after a second a shock ran through his body from his skull to his feet. *The old hag. From the woods,* he thought. *The thing in the woods! Where was Marina?* Without thinking, without hesitating, he ran for the edge of the dock and dove without looking. The box had not sunk, instead, it settled on its pontoons, and Nick splashed into the water and caught its sides with his fingers and hauled himself up. Water had rushed in through the gaping hole in the side, and Nick followed, climbing over and then dropping into the interior. There Nick found Marina, on her knees, looking down at the oily water covering the box floor. She didn't see Nick, only the water. She looked as if she was praying.

Boston 5:57 AM EST

George cleared his mouth. "I wish you would pluck that box out of wherever it is, the one with Nick and his mermaid, and bring it across the world to us, here, on this beach," and with that declaration suddenly a great relief washed over George. He didn't know if he had wished for the right thing or not, but he felt like it was the only thing to do. But thus far Abdullah's wishes hadn't exactly worked out the way he had thought they would. He hoped this one would be a straight shooter. Abdullah nodded, a serious look coming over his face, which made George doubt himself. *Are you ready for this, George?*

"As you command, master," Abdullah said, the air above his head swirling as the genie's magics formed. George's hair rose with static when suddenly, out of nowhere, a golden fishhook appeared, and before anyone said boo it shot out over George's head and across the sea. Behind it trailed a golden fishing line that un-spooled from a golden reel appearing in the air by Ab's head. The line popped and crackled with energy as it zipped across the water. When George turned around to see his new friends' reactions, Spider, Zac and Blockhead looked on with amazement. Even Lilly's face softened with surprise as the goofy genie watched his fishhook speed across the water.

Amsterdam 12:05 PM GMT

Cilia wanted to get the box back on solid ground, but so far, Mr. Bill hadn't let her. Each time she tried to stun him with her electricity he countered with his antlers which caught her magics and repelled them away. Each time he tried to attack her, she countered, using the ear as a great shield around her body.

The old man is full of spirit, Cilia thought. She fired a blast after blast of magic, but Mr. Bill did not budge.

Below them, in the box, Nick held Marina from behind. The box bobbed on its pontoons, and Nick heard it scraping against the pier's pylons. Marina had slid into his arms and kissed him hard on the cheek as soon as she saw him "We will have to swim to get away," Marina coughed. Her skin had regenerated and Nick felt her scales re-freshening and melting into her human skin underneath him; it tickled his flesh. He held on tighter.

"Yes," Nick replied. "But how?"

"Wait," Marina said. "Patience."

Though neither Nick nor Marina saw it from inside of the box, Mr. Bill could see it coming. His transmogrified body paused for a second and opened himself up enough for Cilia to strike him in the chest with a bolt of electricity, searing flesh, drawing blood. The attack drew Cilia in close and Mr. Bill dropped to his knees as if in supplication, and when Cilia bent over Mr. Bill to deliver a deadly blow, she saw his smile grotesque and full of small deer teeth.

Bill's eyes focused on something beyond her, and she turned, but it was too late, for the box sped away from her out to sea, pulled by a giant glowing fishhook.

"No!" Cilia screamed. She turned and fled, following her catch. She hit the water running, her feet skittering furiously across the surface of the ocean. Behind her, back on the docks, Mr. Bill shook and snapped to. His shoulder bled where it was torn, and by the time Mr. Bill started to follow, Cilia was already a speck chasing a tiny cube over the horizon.

Somewhere over the Atlantic

Nick and Marina fell back as the box jerked. Shouting in surprise, they found themselves pressed against the wall. The speed at which they traveled alarmed them. Air whipped through the hole in the side, and occasionally water would rush through the seam Cilia had burned open. Marina continued to regenerate; Nick continued to grow stronger.

Both Nick and Marina had given up control of their lives some weeks ago, and both had been driven to breaking points and neither had the strength to court more adventure. *Just let me sleep, right here.* Nick thought, holding a woman that he hardly knew. But if Nick could have seen the whitish figure chasing him, he would have peed his pants. Then he would have put all his prayers and luck and hopes into the speed at which the box was being yanked across the open waters. And still, he would have worried.

The box skipped over waves and the two of them were bounced around inside. The pontoons plowed a deep groove across the sea; the highways and byways of the sea tying a knot behind the box as it moved across the Atlantic towards Boston. The great mermaid-shaped storm gathered darkness above the Atlantic, and inside, together, Nick and Marina cuddled for warmth and strength and stared at each other with their own eyes. Nick pushed Marina's hair out of her face and then the ocean spray would knock her hair back into her eyes and Nick would gently push it away again, grateful for the moment, grateful to be in her presence. He saw strength in her bones, felt them, her body's dense mass against his own. His own body was empty and powerless as he held her, his own body empty of her mind. The seawater that ran across her legs and her thighs reacted with Marina's skin which flashed color, pinks, and baby blues, and purples as the scales were refreshed and repowered by mother ocean's caresses. Nick stared off into the colors of her skin, his mind fractured, but whole.

"Nick," she said, her hand reaching up to his face. "It was almost too late. You almost missed me."

Nick didn't know what to say, he was dumbfounded. *Shock, buddy, shock.* Instead, he leaned over and kissed her forehead.

Through the bite-like hole in the wood from where both Cilia and Mr. Bill had broken the magic, seawater continued to foam and spray. The cracks along the box from both Cilia and Mr. Bill allowed sunlight to break through and the sun revealed great gouges in the floor, claw marks. Nick shuddered as he held Marina in his arms. *How had she suffered? How much had she suffered?* He didn't think he would have survived her ordeal.

"We've met before, haven't we?" Nick said, not knowing how to be charming.

Marina's skin continued to quicken with color and life. "You will soon remember us," she promised him.

Nick kept his mouth shut, holding his doubts deep down inside of himself. Now that he was facing the woman who he had chased, he didn't know what to say. He fell into her eyes like they were a pool and he saw himself as her, and her as him, as he chased her across the world. She had mingled their spirits together like a sailor making rope, and he still felt her magical hold on his body.

The golden hook pulled the box along at a frightening speed. The box skipped over waves as waves turned over and over and as the currents peeled back and swirled, the waves themselves rolling back into the squall building and careening behind Nick and Marina. Neither of them felt it. Even Cilia didn't notice the storm. The sun disappeared as her quick feet turned the water below her into steam as she raced after them. Her legs powered by magic, left a foamy salty path behind her that Mr. Bill had no problem following in the form of the great raptor, even with one of his giant wings swollen and bleeding into the Atlantic. He was the only one of them who noticed that the clouds were forming into the shape of an enormous mermaid, the storm chasing them, almost, as if drawn by great magics.

Oysterhaus 6:01 AM EST

Mulch bit into Maria's neck like a wild dog, his eyes tearing, his face stretched tight around his skull. Mulch's teeth tore a chunk out of her neck and blood covered his lips and chin. Luckily, he missed the jugular, and simply tore muscle and fat from the poor woman who had only ever loved him. Maria screamed and cried and batted Mulch away, but her former lover weighed far too much and possessed far greater strength. Maria managed to turn and get a knee into

Mulch's groin, which perhaps delayed the inevitable, but allowed her to run for the stairs, her shirt soaked in blood.

When Virginia opened the door to her home, Mulch lay at the foot of the stairs, his face contorted in pain as he recovered from Maria's attack. He did not turn at first, but when he did his face grew pale with shock and slack with disbelief. Virginia's face turned white when she came to face to face with the bloody visage of her father who had gone insane, his teeth bloody and his hands curled up into fists. Virginia's hair rose on her neck, the air was so charged with hate and rage. So, when Mulch finally lunged for her, mouth peeled back in a rictus of pain, she had barely enough time to close the door on him. Mulch slammed into the wood. *Virginia was home*, he thought. *Something had gone very WRONG.* His thoughts came in short bulletins and Mulch slammed his fists into the door in frustration.

"Doc, I ran around the side of the house, my heart exploding in my chest. The clothes Mable leaned me, bless her soul, were baggy and I had to hitch my jeans up so I wouldn't trip. For a second, I thought I was in some kind of movie because my father howled like a werewolf. I heard crying from an upstairs window. It was Maria. The blood everywhere must have been hers. When I got around to the back of the house I barely managed to get into the kitchen before my dad was on top of me."

For Mulch, the morning had merged with events from his past, the killing of his uncle, and the death of his mother. Shame and hot anger boiled over. One second, he knew he was chasing his daughter, in the next he thought he was chasing his mother. On some level, he knew they were two different people, his mother, and his daughter, but in his rage, he only saw one person, his mother, Ruth.

All his guilt and anger foamed out of him as he slammed into Virginia. He smacked her across the face, knocking her to the kitchen floor. Too mad to speak, too enraged to hold back, he raised his hands to beat the woman underneath him. In his father's house, words always came *after* the beating, never before. His daughter kicked at him and landed one solid kick into his groin, her foot connecting with his testicles which sent a sharp pain through his abdomen. Virginia scrambled out from under him, desperate, fighting for her life.

"'MARIA!' I screamed. 'Lock your doors!' After I kicked Mulch, I had enough time to get a weapon. Maria did not answer me. I hoped she had already called the police. I had only time to reach the cutting board, the knife just out of reach when he yanked me from behind.

"Mulch hit me square in the base of the neck, which sent stars reeling in my head. I had to get the knife. I had to protect my stomach. Fighting a blackout, I thought of Marina, Macy, and Adam.

"My father pulled me back by my feet and bit at my shoulder and pummeled at my back. When he grabbed me by the neck, I felt like an insect caught on a pin.

"My throat closed up and the only thing I could do was kick, so I swung my legs out at my father, but they missed. Again, it was Nick's memories that helped me. I remembered Nick kicking off from the side of the Moose pool when he was a kid. That's all it took. I steadied my legs and kicked out sideways, striking the side of the counter and pushing my weight up and over Mulch and he fell over with me on top. As I fell, I moved my elbows out behind me, hoping I'd elbow the son of a bitch in the ribs and break something as we fell."

Mulch saw his daughter and his mother merge into one blurry adversary. He kicked out at her and tried to laugh, only the laugh didn't come out. It slammed against his clenched teeth. When she kicked against the side of the counter he didn't expect to be propelled so easily to the floor. And as she came down on top of him, her elbows slammed into his thigh and stomach. And though the air rushed out of him, he could not cry out even if he had wanted to. And for a second his anger left him, but that impulse faded, and Mulch rose and followed Virginia, his hate burning in his body like a fever.

"I didn't waste any time getting off of him before he could reach out for me. I screamed for Maria and ran out into the sun. What felt like minutes was only seconds, and Mulch was after me, screaming at me. "You can't get away from me! I'm your son!" His voice gave me goosebumps. I knew I could outrun him and headed towards the barn. I knew there must be something in there for me to use as a weapon. I just didn't expect him to be so quick."

Mulch saw Ruth Hayes run out of the kitchen and into the snowy, icy yard. He watched her from the windows, watched his father run after her into the cold. His father screamed at her, "You can't get away from me!" Mulch both hoped that Eb would catch her and lose her. Eb dashed off into the storm. Mulch only looked back at Mr. Bill who was already walking away. Divided, Mulch ran out after her.

He called out to her only once.

When he blinked, the world cut away from snow and ice to grass and sunshine. The barn was the only warm hiding place, and that was where Mulch went first, with a speed that surprised even him. As Mulch ran, he expected to slip on the snow and ice because he wasn't wearing his heavy snow boots with the thick treads. Instead, he was wearing his summer clothes.

The barn was a quick sprint, and he often ran it as a child, timing himself by counting off the seconds in his head. *One one-hundred, two one-hundred, three one-hundred, four one-hundred, five one-hundred*. He usually made it under eight seconds, but uninhibited in the snow he made it there in under seven. He pushed the heavy doors open with his fists. He didn't notice the blood on them or the throbbing pain in his stomach and thigh. He had to find his mother before Eb got to her. And low and behold there she was, hiding in the barn.

"Doc, I barely had time to look around the barn before my father knocked open the door with his fists, his face drenched in sweat, Maria's blood in his mouth running down into the collar of his shirt. Behind the barn, in the stalls, we had some horses and a few cows. I hadn't ridden any of them in a long time and I hoped I'd be able to handle one. The animal smells added to the electrical charge Mulch brought into the barn with him. They lowed and stamped their feet through the barn wall. If I could make it to the door, I could get on a horse and it would be: *So long Mulch, and thanks for all the fish!* But Mulch didn't want me to go anywhere."

Mulch's mother bolted for the stalls. He knew it. *Let his father search the snow. Let him. Just let him.* He had her dead in his sights. He sniffed the air. It was musky with horse smells, and cow smells. The hay in the upper loft was warm and it was there where his mother had fucked that dirt poor white trash farmhand. 'The indecency. The shame.' Eb had told Mulch. Mulch knew exactly where to find his mother and what to do with her. Mulch could take care of his father's business.

"Doc, my tongue rolled around in my mouth, and I chewed on it out of nervousness. I wondered what my father looked like when he killed Adam. Was it like this? Rabid, silent, calculating? Part of me wanted to think of him as my loving father. To tell him that he needed help, that he was sick. But I also thought that this was his true face, the face of a demon.

"I turned instead towards the hayloft, where I thought I might be able to jump up on the ladder and get away from him in the hay or jump out the window onto the stall roof below."

Mulch saw his mother move toward the stall door at the far side of the barn and then he saw her twist toward the hayloft ladder. He knew she would go there. She might even think she could hide from her son. She was up on the ladder and already disappearing into the loft. But in a few short pulls, Mulch was at the top and narrowing his eyes on his mother's back.

The air in Virginia's lungs went out of her when Mulch tackled her. She went sprawling into the hay where he pinned her down with his knees and began to slap her. Stars filled her head, and her stomach became a pit of red-hot fire. Her pores opened full-barrel and sweat-soaked her through immediately. She felt her bladder let loose before she passed out.

Mulch aimed for the bruises his father had put on her face, little targets for his hand. She struggled under his knees, her arms pressed into the hay, her legs kicking and wiggling. Soon, her arms went limp under his weight and he began to undress her. Over the years, Mulch had learned about the birds and bees from spying on his mother and uncle's love-making sessions. His father had never told him anything about it and it didn't make much difference to Mulch; he knew what he had to do. Once Ruth was undressed, he was quick with it. If Eb caught him, he would surely be killed. No one must know, not even Mr. Bill, especially not Mr. Bill. If Mr. Bill ever found out what he had done to his mother, he was sure that Mr. Bill would make something worse than death happen to him. The snow outside fell thicker now, he saw it through the loft window as he entered her. The loft smelled of blood and sex and fear, of copper and protein.

He wasn't sure where the idea came from, but Mulch threw his mother over his shoulders and climbed down the loft ladder carrying her. He exited the barn through the stalls, past the cows and horses, and out into the storm. He needed to leave only one set of footprints in the snow. He doubted Mr. Bill would be able to tell who made the tracks because as he walked they were filled quickly with snow, a real winter nor'easter. He'd leave Ruth in one of the fields. Mulch knew Eb wouldn't question it because he was drunk. They'd all think she died in the storm after running from Eb. No one would question that logic.

Mulch made sure he was far enough away from the house and the barn before he dumped her. There in the snow, he took her again. When he finished the second time, he found his hands around her neck. Her neck fit so easily into his hand. He laid her out like a doll and kissed her cheek once before heading back to the barn. There he would wait till his heart stopped pounding before going back inside the house, where he would pretend to wonder what had just happened and where his mother might be.

2

Somewhere in the Atlantic, approaching Boston, MA USA, Cilia came to the assumption that Mr. Bill had caused the box to fly from the docks; *it was a good trick.* He'd tricked her twice in the last half-hour, but she would make sure he'd pay.

A sailor on the deck of the oil tanker, 'The Allano,' out for a little nip before what promised to be a whale of a storm, looked over the deck and blinked. A woman ran across the water chasing after what looked very much like a giant wooden cube. The giant cube appeared as if it was being pulled by a golden rope. Steam rose from where the woman ran over the water, her spray flying up in a foamy fog tunnel so that a line was drawn in the sea along the path she had made. The sailor, thinking it must be the alcohol, emptied his flask and swore never to drink again.

Not ten minutes later, a Coast Guard plane on a deep-sea training mission, noticed two small fast-moving objects but was unable to investigate due to the gathering tempest. Two NOAA weather research planes dispatched into the unusually shaped storm clouds, radioed back and forth that something was moving at a fast pace below them. One pilot dropped his altitude to get a closer view but only saw a line of hissing water that stretched out towards the horizon. They were ordered back to base.

The National Weather Service issued a severe storm watch for Boston and the surrounding coastal areas between the hours of 6-10 AM. A second storm system gathered strength below the mermaid-shaped system, this one over the coast of Virginia and Maryland, and although there was no odd shape reported, several radar watches noted that the storm system in Virginia appeared to have many horns, like that of a deer.

Poor Cilia, her catch flying away from her at a speed she could not fathom, grew restless and angry. Her energy reserves, depleted, caused her to slow down. She was forced to pour on the strength to just barely keep up. Behind her, some hundred miles and closing, Mr. Bill's raptor soared almost blissfully, using the storm's gale winds, hundreds of feet up in the air to whip him along faster than any bird could fly. There was not a single report of a giant raptor flying at extremely high altitudes and speed, despite several weather research planes, and sensitive radar aimed towards the Atlantic.

Oysterhaus 6:42 AM EST

Maria waited several minutes, unsure of what was going to happen. She expected Mulch to pop out of the shadows at any minute. She made the sign of the cross and gripped a letter opener in her fists. The phone in her room didn't work. She was pretty sure the others in the house didn't work either. There was a singular cry from the barn which made her shrink to the floor. He was out there. *Get it together, Maria. He's gone crazy. You need to get help.* Grinding her teeth together she unlocked her door and threw it open. The hallway crept with silence.

"Hello?" she called out, her voice weak and cracked.

Running downstairs, she yanked the landline from the cradle and pressed them to her ear – nothing, dead air. Running back upstairs, she didn't waste any time getting her things. Maria grabbed the money stashed in her mattress by the handfuls and shoved it into her suitcase. She grabbed some clothes, a jacket, a pair of sweaters, not knowing what she was taking, but only that she was taking things. *Where was her phone? How long had Mulch been gone?* She didn't know. Her whole body hurt, and she was sure her face had swelled up to a balloon by now. She managed a quick look in the mirror before hauling herself downstairs. *He got you pretty good, Maria. At least the blood had stopped flowing to your bite. Time to make your exit.*

She couldn't find her keys. They had been on the little hall table nicked and knocked from the many years of key tossing. Leaving her bags at the door, she ran through the house, looking on the kitchen counter, and in the back sun-room. She searched the coffee table in the TV room and even went back into her room, her mind shattering into a thousand fragments. She chattered and chittered, her teeth knocking against each other as the physical and emotional pain roped together with fear. In the end, she found them in her pocket of all places, along with her cell. She had put them there because she needed fresh ginger and she was going to go out to get it as soon as she finished her chores. That had only been half an hour ago or so. She remembered because she had looked at the clock right before Mulch had struck her. *He could be back at any minute*, she thought. *You must get out!* Every nerve in her body screamed.

She began to dial 911 and as she opened the door, she found Mulch standing there. Her heart stopped and for a second, she saw herself die of fright. His eyes burned a bright yellow, his face tight with madness, his hair rising in spiky clumps. Someone had clawed his cheek and a large flap of skin hung down his cheek. His lip bled from the corner. Whose blood it was Maria could not say. His voice sounded far away. "Hello Maria," he said as he grabbed her by the hand. "I'm home."

She didn't have time to scream. Her phone flew out of her hand and against the wall. He dragged her inside and threw her to the floor and delivered a short kick to her ribs. She smelled the gasoline on his shoe leather, and when he tried to move, she held onto his foot and dragged along. Mulch screamed at her and kicked her in the legs until she pushed herself away from him. He stopped half-way out of the door and grabbed his red gas cans, one in each hand. For a hot second Maria seized up fearing Mulch was going to douse her, but he walked past her, pouring gas all over the first floor, and when Maria began to crawl away, pulling on the one Turkish rug she had always loved as if she could save it, he yanked her back and pulled her into the kitchen and broke both her hands with a cast-iron frying pan.

Crying, in shock, her hands dangling down, Maria collapsed into a ball. She didn't flinch when he covered her in gas, the fuel running into her cut and split face.

Flickering in and out of the past, Mulch believed himself to be in the present. Though he couldn't remember exactly what had happened. He'd been thinking about the day his mother died, but that was fuzzy, grainy, that could wait till later, right now he had some trash-burning to do. First, the feed store and the storage shed, and now his own house. And to end it all, the barn where he would make sure that his mother would never shame him, or his father, again. If he saw Maria, he did not show it, although she was screaming when he lit the match. Soon the back half of the big house crackled. It would not take long before the fire grew laterally along with the telescopic home, as each addition went up in smoke.

Inside, the house burned from back to front. Flames shot up the gas-trailed stairs. Maria struggled for a while to use her broken hands like hooks to fill pans of water to save the house, and the rugs she loved so much, but each time Maria grabbed at the pan, she dropped it. Her hands were broken across the back, but she had use of her pinkies and partial use of her right thumb. By using both pinkies and one thumb she was able to hold one pan, but she didn't possess the strength to carry the pan to save the burning rugs. Her arms flared in pain as she tried to lift them. The pans would spill again, and she would have to stoop and grip them with her broken hands and take them back to the sink to try again. She'd spill the pan again and again until the rug in the hallway was consumed by flame. There were too many rugs, and the pain in her hand was too great. Instead, she grabbed her bag, and ran into the yard, her home for many years burning behind her. Screaming into the sky, her hands raised like a praying mantis, she cried out for rain.

Boston, MA 7:07 AM EST

Spider took a dozen photos of the strange golden thread that had spun outwards across the Atlantic and was now pulling something very big back towards shore.

"This is going to be some good shit." Spider said.

Blockhead nodded, he had his camera phone out, but his face looked like he wasn't pleased with his picture.

Zac did not have experience fishing, but he could tell from Abdullah's strained face that whatever he was reeling in was huge. *Bigger than huge*, Zac thought. For a while the only noise was the winding reeling sound of a golden fishing line, occasionally thunder boomed. Blockhead thought the thunder sounded like some guy with combat boots kicking an empty dumpster and said so, twice.

George gave Lilly some distance. She looked forlorn but cute as she nibbled on her breakfast bar purchased in a dim convenience store. Rufus sniffed around the beach, his tail wagging, turning his head upwards to bark at the clouds, or a passing gull. Both Spider and George remarked that Rufus seemed to be waiting for something, for the dog, after a time, would sit by Ab's side patiently as if any minute something was going to appear on the horizon. George wasn't surprised. Rufus had been calm to Boston, cramped in the truck with Abdullah, who could be hard on the nerves. Once they had arrived, Rufus had shown them where to go through a series of Lassie-like barks and nods. Maybe George could get Rufus a spot on TV as a pet chow spokesdog and retire. Blockhead gave up on filming and sat on a picnic table near the bathhouse watching the group mill around, wondering what Abdullah was reeling in. He kinda hoped George would get lost so he could put the moves on Lilly who kept digging small holes in the sand with her cute little toes.

Carson Beach was cold that morning and they were the only ones around for miles, it seemed, and none of them knew that the threatening storm clouds above them, the purple and black and smoky ones, somewhat shaped like a finger, were about to break. If someone were to have told them that the storm clouds were indeed the finger of a giant mermaid-shaped storm system, with everything that was happening, they would not have been surprised at all. At this point, Zac was seriously considering giving up marijuana and all recreational substances, his eyes wide open to the possibilities of the world, his stomach continuing to growl out the words, 'wait, wait, wait'. Zac's brain had trouble getting around the fact that an honest to god genie was standing there in front of him reeling in a very big catch. "This is way weirder than anything I could ever imagine," Zac thought. The promise of it being a mermaid stupefied him.

Spider and Blockhead had pretty much had their minds blown. Blockhead was watching the beach around him with curiosity, a tight ball of anxiety rolling around in his stomach. Sometimes it felt like he was nauseated, sometimes hungry. He had already thrown down a pack of zingers and a bottle of OJ and now his stomach was coated with sugar. It was the same feeling Blockhead got every time he asked a girl out on a date. Girls seemed scared of his large frame and build. One girl, Chloe Keily Westwolf, a pretty girl with cool hair had more or less run away in fright when he had asked her to go to a movie with him. Blockhead's heart had sunk into the depth of his stomach when she turned tail and scampered off, saying that she was late for a meeting with her friends, a trail of smoke threading the air behind her. Waiting for the box, or whatever the hell that might be, made him feel as small as a bean, just like girls did.

Spider, who had only in the last two years begun to think about his future in the world, waiting with his hand on the camera trigger. He was going to snap photos, put them online, and wait for the money to roll in. If no money comes, then for sure there would be fame. And if no fame, he could sock this away as something wilder than urban decay in the post-post-modern world he so enjoyed cataloging and turning into 'art.' Spider's gut felt full of cobwebs, all his emotions bouncing off the web's string and sending reverberations up inside him. When Spider had been nine, he had looked into the corner of his room, directly into the eyes of a huge wolf spider that had taken refuge from the fall weather. Even before his nickname was Spider he knew all kinds about spiders, it was his hobby after all, and he knew that this spider was poisonous. He had stayed home from school with a fever and after finding the little fellow had begun talking to the spider. Whenever his mother came into his room, he would clam up and wait for her to leave. *She wouldn't understand.* That afternoon when she went to the store for more orange juice, he held his hand out to the spider, who could have made him even sicker and possibly killed him in his weakened state, his hand steady and his eyes steady, his voice calm and soothing. The spider leaped onto his palm, and he jumped back at first, but the spider looked up at him with its many eyes and Spider knew that there was an understanding between them. He took the spider down into his basement and placed it in a dark corner where it would spin a giant web and lay its many eggs. From that day forward, Spider decided to have people call him Spider. Now he remembered that feeling of disembodiment, like when he had talked to the spider from another part in his brain. It was as if he had been somewhere else. The fever had contributed to the un-realness then and now he felt the same un-realness wash over him, sitting in the damp, cold sand, his camera ready to take as many pictures as he could aim at and snap.

Lilly spotted it first.

George didn't know how Lilly could see it, but it grew in size as it approached, and they could certainly see the golden fishing line pulling it in.

"Master," Abdullah said, strained, his eyes popping as he held onto the reel, "something is wrong."

2

Cilia had thought, for many miles now, that the box would slip over the curve of the edge of the earth entirely. Then she remembered that when she had been very small she and her brother had been playing in the street with a rubber ball. When he threw against the street, Pembroke could bounce that ball as high as the row houses. Cilia couldn't get it to go as high. She could play jacks as well as her brother, but she couldn't bounce that stupid ball as high. Up and down the street all the boys could get their little rubber ball to bounce as high as they wanted, while the girls waited around the stoops for their brother, or cousin, or neighbor to quit fooling around and get back to the business of jacks or skip the ball, or whatever ball business that was not bouncing they had planned for the afternoon.

Pembroke, being the snot he was, teased her about it. It bothered her and so for the next few days, she practiced with the ball. This was something that did not involve magic, this involved practice. The more frustrated she became, the more the ball seemed to bounce at erratic angles away from the houses. She couldn't get it to bounce up, higher than any house, not the way her brother had been able to do. Frustrated, she had gone inside. The next day, instead of trying to push the ball to the ground, she casually bounced the ball and found that she could, without concentrating, get the ball to bounce higher than all the houses along the street. She discovered that she had always had the strength (for it didn't take much to bounce the ball super high), but it had been her aim and the angle at which she threw the ball and the speed at which the ball bounced that had caused her so much trouble. Here she had been feeling stupid for not being able to bounce a silly rubber ball a few stories in the air and it had been her technique holding her back. It had been her frustration that had clouded her concentration. She experienced that same frustration now.

The box zooming away from her reminded her of that rubber ball. It reminded her of being a child. And before she had ever been a child she and her brother had killed their father from the womb. And so, she let her consciousness be filled with the power that had coursed through her veins while she had been just a tiny baby in her mother's womb. It was the power she had been born with. Sometimes it was just a matter of turning your head off and letting the body do its work. And so, with her body flushed and warmed, she imagined her feet having wings and she felt her legs pick up speed. And magical mercurial feet popped out of her flesh and spread their wings and began to flap as she ran, and then Cilia relinquished control to her body and let her mind wander the twisting turns of her memory. She stopped thinking of trying to catch the box and thought only of breathing in and out and filling herself up like a lung. She imagined her heart kicking into a smooth overdrive as she closed her eyes and breathed.

From inside the box, Nick peered out of the hole in the top corner of the box, Marina breathing heavily behind him. With the saltwater spray covering her, Marina's health had improved, but she was still weak.

"She is coming," Marina said.

"When you mean *she*? Who exactly are we talking about?"

"The hag. The hag is coming," Marina said. She tried to stand, but only wobbled and sat down. "I'm so sorry I had to bring you into this."

Sometimes she looked a lot like a normal girl with really shiny hair that flashed green to black under the light; Nick's smitten heart ached for her.

"I had no choice, you see," she said clearing her throat and spitting a large loogie onto the floor.

"Hey? You okay?"

They held hands.

"Yes, I'm okay. Just a bit dehydrated."

"Perhaps you should, you know, dive in?"

"I must regain my strength first. And besides, I can't leave you to fend yourself. You would never make it."

"Why not? I mean I could handle her, couldn't I?"

"Give me a little time and I will carry you away from her through the water."

"I have been in bar fights before, you know. It's not like I'm a total wimp or anything. "If I lost you, I don't know what would happen." Marina reached out and touched Nick's mouth with her fingers.

"Cause, I can hold my breath for a while. YMCA record, right here baby."

"Kiss me," she said.

Nick gulped, and heat rushed to his extremities.

"It is time for me to mate, you know?" Marina leaned into Nick, her body pressing up to his.

Nick gulped again and fanned his face, *damn*, he thought. *How did I get so lucky?*

"You were the first boy I ever saw, and I knew then when my time would come it would be with you."

"Um. Well."

"So you see, I am sorry that I possessed you the way I did."

"Uh, well. See, I don't..."

Marina pressed herself up against his body. For a second Nick thought he was going to pass out. *Please don't let her be freaked out,* Nick thought as his body reacted, his erection pressing into Marina's stomach, but she didn't seem to notice. Then the box began to shake and splinter, a shudder from under like that of a wave crashing into the already fragile vessel.

Cilia had not only caught up to the box, but she had also passed it and closed upon the American coast. Ahead, the lights of the Boston harbor and skyline looked faint and far away. Above, storm clouds descended like a hand, its index finger pointing towards the beach ahead of her. The water churned and chopped, and the storm brought up the greens and the blacks and the sea's darker colors. Cilia steadied herself in the gale, flying above the sea's rolling surface, and when Cilia reached and then grabbed the golden, humming fishing line, the box rocked against her and tossed about.

For a second the magic golden line almost threw her back, but she held onto it and flew closer to the box, hovering above its surface, the fishing line slack in her hand. Sensing the magics that bound it she did not dare to land on the surface, she had already lost too much to the native, and she didn't dare step into a trap.

He'll expect it, she thought, *but he won't expect me to skewer them.* The wings on her feet flapped and flapped and Cilia slipped to the front of the box and this time she grabbed the hook in both hands and feeling it true as steel she pulled it free with all her might and swung it in a wide arc. The hook tore into the wood and cracked it open further, ripping another huge chunk out, and as she swung the hook to smash the box entirely something powerful ripped the hook and line back from her hand. All at once she was in control, and then suddenly she was yanked backward, and if she hadn't let go her arm would have ripped out, she was sure, so strong the magic was that wielded the golden line.

3

Abdullah fell backward into the sand and sand flew up in clouds around him. The big man's fall shook him, and he looked up in surprise, his one big hand still on the golden reel, the other gesturing upwards as if to say, I give up. The golden hook and line still sizzled through the water as it returned and slowed and curled as it slacked, still carried by the Genie's strength; the slack looked like a live wire against the sand.

"Ab!" George shouted as he raced over to Abdullah who stood, brushing sand off him, his face confused, worried "What happened?"

"Master, something cut Abdullah's line."

A thunderclap echoed above them, and they all jumped, including Abdullah. Rufus barked and whined and ran up to Lilly, trying to hide beneath her legs, but to no avail. Lilly continued to eat, as if she were on a mission, working on her fourth breakfast bar and her second orange juice. Lightning clawed across the Atlantic, a bright blue shock. Then it started to rain.

4

"Thanks," Amanda said waiving to the clerk behind her as she got into her car just as the rain started to fall. The Store-24 disappeared into her rearview before she even pulled out of her parking space, the rain fell so thick.

"Carson Beach," she said aloud. Her cell phone had nearly half its life and she hadn't brought a cord. *One thing Dial-A-Nurse is good for is teaching some kick-ass interpersonal skills,* she thought. She'd even gotten a free pack of gum out of the deal. *A smile can come in handy.*

When she had been a student, Carson Beach was where men went to have clandestine sex in the little park near the beach. Her dorm had been co-ed and one of her floormates cruised the park often. The memory made her nervous, not exactly scared, but cautious. *Needles and drugs and perverts, oh my.* The guy behind the counter said it was a nice place now, not as sleazy as it was ten years ago. The water not as dirty since they had cleaned the harbor up. Though it was still the opinion of the clerk that if one wanted beach, a real honest-to-god beach, one had to leave the city.

5

The rain fell in sheets, and the magics of the box though strong against Cilia, could not stop mother nature from swamping it. The waves had intensified as the storm continue to gather; the great black clouds that gathered in storybook heaps promised a gale. With the crushed fireflies no longer burning, the box had filled with storm darkness. Nick held onto the bed as the box tilted towards the prow. Marina lay against the side of the wall, growing stronger with each breath, simply by biding her time. She and Nick had locked gazes when they separated from their embrace, and Marina's body pulsed with desire. Her scales rippled across her body, and her legs had already begun to flash from blue to purple to red to orange to yellow to green and back again.

"Soon," Marina said.

"I'm so tired," Nick said.

He broke their gaze and looked up, hearing a swoop of wind, and for a second Nick thought that some horrible monster was going to appear above them, out of the clouds, eager to eat them. And when Cilia exploded through the roof, he peed his pants.

Floating in the air, her hair trailing out behind her catching the wind, Cilia's fingers tore at the wood. Her magics cast a bright orange glow as she pounded and grasped and clawed. Her fingers cut on the ragged and rough splinters and her blood dripped off her fingertips like poison dripping off a wasp's stinger. The box began to sizzle, a slow popping white noise that gained force and grew so loud that Marina and Nick had to cover their ears to block the sound of Cilia's magics tearing away the power of Marcos, and Sea Hag, and Mr. Bill. The carvings pulsed with heat and light, a furious red followed by a furious orange as if the carvings of all the sea creatures and the carving of the sun's flame reacted. Nick shuddered.

Cilia no longer looked attractive. Her skin had wrinkled, and her hair had turned whiter, almost translucent, and her spotted scalp showed in ragged patches, her teeth, egg yellow, even in the darkness of the storm. The sizzling of magics ceased as Cilia busted through and sprung towards Marina with the dexterity of a big cat. She grabbed Marina by the neck and yanked her up against the wall, and Nick saw thick black ooze running from where her ears should have been.

"Little bitch!"

Marina's feet kicked below her. Rain poured down their faces through the damaged box, and Nick moved to tackle the hag from behind, but she stopped him by simply raising her free hand. Her voice echoed in his skull, "I'll deal with you next, fish bait."

Nick flew back against the box, the wind knocked out of his lungs. *She batted me away as if I were nothing at all. What the fuck am I going to do?*

Above, the wind tore over the hole as the box took on more and more water, and above in the growing wind, far beyond Nick's sight, a large raptor circled the box, waiting, waiting, waiting.

But the box had one more trick left.

6

Lilly suddenly sat bolt upright in the sand. She had laid down in the rain some minutes ago, her mouth open, drinking in the falling rainwater, thinking of her mother. All her life all she wanted was to feel a connection to her mother. She supposed she was jealous, on some level, of all the attention other people received from the Ugly Mother. *Just once I'd like for us to do something alone,* she thought morbidly. *Guess that's never going to happen.* Her mother had always put other's burdens upon her shoulder, and Lilly's shoulder for that matter. *You must use your gifts with English to help everyone at camp.* And she had, hadn't she? *You must know when to shine, Lilly.* She used to say that to her all the time. When she sat at the card table in the kitchen and studied her math and her English. *You have a chance to show the world what you got, Lilly. We need you to be the bright one around here. You must know when to shine.*

"GEORGE!" She shot over to the shelter where everyone else huddled from the downpour. They didn't look all that dry to Lilly; they were all as soaked as she was.

"Yes," he was at her side in seconds, his face slick with the weather.

"You all have to GET ME as HIGH as you can."

"What?"

"GET ME UP HIGH!"

"YOU WANNA GET HIGH?" The wind howled so fiercely; he barely heard. He put his hand up to shield the rain which hurt his face. He looked back at Spider and Blockhead sure they would hook her up with some of their medical-grade weed.

Lilly screamed in his ear, "NO, I NEED TO GET UP AS HIGH AS I CAN." She pointed up.

George looked around. The tallest thing was the bathhouses, but they were open to the sky; she couldn't stand on them. Huddled in a group under the shelter's corrugated steel roof, Abdullah, Blockhead, Spider, Zac, and Rufus looked like a blob in a gray haze.

"There's NOTHING HERE!" George shouted back.

"I HAVE TO GET UP ON SOMETHING."

There was the truck, but that would probably get mired in the muddy sand. The rain had turned the beach into soup. The surf roared and crashed, and on top of it all, the tide was coming in. George looked around and over to the blob of people to his left. *What to do, George, what to do?*

7

The box, Mulch's twisted possessive spell had a final surprise, one Mr. Bill had woven into the magics of Sea Hag and Marcos. A kind of bear trap for magic, and when Cilia entered Marina's prison and used her power the box became a pocket universe, albeit briefly, and the interior tripled in size while the exterior remained the same size, now half wrecked in the Atlantic, the genie's line cut and already returning to its master. The box began to take on water, not enough to swamp it, not yet, but enough to fill the now expansive interior.

Cilia noticed none of it so intent she was to kill Marina. She'd given up on capture, her blood raged through her. The witch had flown right up to Marina as she lay on the floor, her body in an inch of water, and sinking fast. She ignored Nick who had climbed away from the hole in the side and clung to the walls. Nick did not notice the spell either, his body running on reserves, his senses simply did not see the box expand as Cilia grabbed Marina and lifted her off the floor.

She dug her fingernails into Marina's neck. Marina lashed out with her feet, striking Cilia in the chest. The witch did not move and squeezed harder.

"Let me go!" Marina wheezed. Blood flowed from where Cilia's fingers dug into her skin.

Cilia began to choke her with both, and Marina reached up and grabbed Cilia's wrist and used them to pull her body into a powerful kick that struck Cilia in the chest.

The crack shook Cilia, she felt her ribs break and she let go of the mermaid and stumbled back.

When Nick shouted all Cilia did was look his way and blow him a kiss and Nick felt his feet squirm and when he looked down, he saw that his feet had turned to jelly. His toes were translucent digits, the bones barely there. Nick felt sick.

That was when he noticed the box had changed. Suddenly he was very far away from Cilia, and if Nick were to guess he would have said he was now a good sixteen feet from Cilia, who in turn was another sixteen feet away from Marina.

Suddenly there was a lot more water, and Cilia was now up to her waist, her face a twisted scowl of surprise. Marina's body splashed and thrashed sending spray everywhere, she had found the deeper water and slipped under, while Nick continued to stare in abject horror at his toes which now looked like jellyfish's tentacles, which he loathed.

The number one reason Nick didn't go to Chincoteague beach was because of the possibility of Portuguese Man-O-Wars that floated like bloated sacks of blood in the deeper waters. His feet began to separate into long strands of tentacles. He thought of melting snowmen. *Fuck, what the hell did she do to me.*

Nick slipped, his feet no longer holding his weight. He landed face-first in the floor, and though he was on the higher end of the swamped box he lay in six inches of water and immediately began to thrash, turning his body over, desperate. His body continued to transfigure into goo.

And then the box shuddered with a crunch as something on the outside struck what remained of the top; Nick looked for it but could not see it. Cilia fell backward into the water, shocked. Nick could not see Marina. Then the box began to move once again.

Cilia screamed with rage, her body temperature roared with her anger, and all about her the rain that had begun to fall boiled off into steam, and the ocean water about her lower body turned to steam and the box filled with a hiss.

Nick began to scream as his body continued to turn to jelly, his ankles had become translucent, and a cold numbness crept up his leg that tickled the pit of his stomach. His thoughts ran out of his ears like water, and he knew they were feeding Cilia, he knew in his gut that he was giving all of his power to her for all of a sudden he only wanted to float to feel his elongated toes stretch into tendrils floating in mother ocean.

Outside the box, Mr. Bill gripped the front end of the box and beat his enormous wings pulling the box towards Boston. He flew in ink, the storm now lashing and whipping about his body. Boston's skyline lay before him dim, shrouded in heavy fog and storm clouds. The thought of failure hung in his mind. Intellectually he knew his strength, weakened by the fight with Cilia, might give out on him. But the raptor had served him well, and Mr. Bill poured all hope and love and promise into his flying. He imagined Marina happy, living on her own away from Mulch, he imagined Virginia happy with a family and the love she deserved. He imagined Maria happy on her own, living a life beyond the shore, and he imagined himself with his parents and his childhood friends, living a life away from the English and Dutch and all colonization. He had no choice but to hope and keep on going. *Please swim,* he thought. *Swim!*

Inside, Cilia's mind probed the box, aware of the magic working against her. She sensed the movement and wondered if Mr. Bill had caught up with her. Her mind too focused on Marina and sucking Nick's life force, she could not sense the native, but she knew something pulled them forward again. *The mystery man? Too many enemies now. Oh, dear brother now I miss you!*

Cilia narrowed her eyes and sought her prey and spied Marina in the murk of the ocean water. The sea continued to pour through the box as it moved forward. *Damn this box!* Cilia thought. *At least she hasn't transformed yet.* She spied the girl and took her chance; Cilia lunged for Marina, crossing the gap in space with speed and force, her ankle wings beating furiously in the water.

When the witch grabbed Marina's left hand, she snapped it back, breaking it. The mermaid screamed.

8

George's shout drowned in the thunder and wind. On their hands and knees, facing the ocean, Abdullah and Blockhead continuously spit out the water that rolled down their face and into their mouth, adding to the white noise of weather. Both big men ignored George who continuously gave directions to everyone else. As best as they understood it, Spider and Zac would be forming the second level of the human pyramid.

"SON OF A WHORE RAIN." Ab shouted at Blockhead.

"THIS FUCKING BITES!" Blockhead shouted back.

"SAND SINKS BELOW US. ABDULLAH HOPES THERE ARE NO SCORPIONS."

"YOU BETTER BE RIGHT ABOUT THAT, FRIEND."

Blockhead grunted when George helped Zac on top of him. Zac's bony knees dug into the meat of his back. Blockhead felt his hands and legs sink into the muddy sand beneath. But when Blockhead saw that Abdullah didn't complain, he decided not to bitch about it. Besides Zac weighed considerably less than Spider, Blockhead was most sure. Spider had already steadied himself on top of Abdullah. George hiked himself up on top of their butts and pulled Lilly up behind him. Unlike Blockhead and Ab, Spider and Zac vomited expletives as George hiked his skinny behind on Zac's lower back and pulled Lilly up and who then steadied herself on Spider.

George hoped this would work. He was bigger than Spider and Zac, but he was only going to put his weight on them for a short while, just to get Lilly setup, and then he would drop down to rest on the asses of Abdullah and Blockhead, mostly on Ab, and act as a support to hold Lilly who planned to stand on top of Spider and Zac. Worst case scenario, the wind would knock them over into a pile.

9

Nick heard Marina's cry, it broke through the water like a funnel. From the surface, it sounded warbled and broken, but Nick knew that it was the sound of

Marina in pain. Nick wanted to call out, to show his support, to distract Cilia, something, but he could only think about floating, about dissolving single-celled organisms in his fatty tissue. Nick had turned into jelly from his upper thighs to his feet and pretty soon his manhood would be jello-like too. His stomach felt ticklish and when he looked up he saw that he floated across the great expanse of the box toward the hole where rain and seawater poured in. Below him, his feet and legs had turned into thousands of nettles. In the darkness, he thought his skin looked a little too clear for his good. *It wouldn't matter anyway,* he thought. *Why I could just push myself out the top of this box. And I can pull myself up and float away, float to the moon.*

Above, Mr. Bill fought the wind. Blood matted his feathers in a sticky patch. He could not afford to look back but could feel the box descending into the water behind him. Exhaustion burned in his wings, and he could feel numbness in his wingtips that he did not like, not one bit. But they were close, they had to be. The storm had reduced his visibility to zero, he could only keep hoping and keep flying.

Where are you, Marina? He probed with his mind but sensed nothing but the spent magics of the box and Cilia's pulsing power. *This has been for naught,* Mr. Bill feared.

For a brief second, he faltered, Mr. Bill, no longer capable of maintaining his form, briefly began to transfigure back into his human form, and he fell, some twenty feet. The box dropped back into the sea with a splash and Mr. Bill dropped into the sea only to burst out of the water with renewed vigor. Pain erupted throughout his brain as he continued to fly towards the beach. *Use pain, use it.* The oldest magic battery in the universe gave Mr. Bill enough energy to clutch the top of the box and plow forward once again.

Inside Cilia and Marina did not notice the fall back into the ocean, nor did they sense Mr. Bill picking up the box and resuming his flight for the pocket universe had flooded with seawater. Nick noticed but gave it little thought as he watched with fascination his waist, half translucent, pulsed with a deep blue, almost like a blossom, almost like a bulbous eye, one that stared directly back at him.

And Mr. Bill had not flown more than half a mile before he began to falter once more. The wound across his chest and shoulder could not heal and sustain the transfiguration. *I'm don't think I'm going to make it. Sorry Nick, kid, it's been real.*

Then, a flickering light began to beat on the beach in front of him. Like a moth, Mr. Bill's eyes were drawn towards the steady pulse, which became a bright exclamation point of light that focused its searching beam out towards him, towards the box. *Keep it up, keep it up!* The light shined so bright he had had to close his eyes, but he felt it on his face, through his feathers, through the storm which now had turned the seas into a roaring chaotic soup. He flew straight ahead towards the light which burned ahead of him like a giant candle.

Oysterhaus, VA 7:45 AM EST

"Doc, I woke up in the cornfield, flat on my back, my nose itching. Corn pollen flew in the wind's currents and eddies. Giant purple lightning rollers rolled in. Thunder clapped and shook the ground underneath me. The corn pollen gave the sky a yellow haze and it took me a moment to remember where I was. My stomach hurt like hell, and I didn't know how I got here, in the field. I remembered that my sister was in danger and that I had been in danger. For a second my skin exploded in goosebumps.

"I could feel that it was going to rain and that was fine with me. My swollen face could use a cool shower to clean out the bruises, the cuts, to clean it all out. I smelled smoke and shot bolt upright. The thunder wasn't thunder but cows and horses stampeding towards the fields tearing up great clots of sod under hoof and the storm clouds were purple billows of the smoke of my home going to ash and cinder.

"Mulch couldn't be reasoned with. Mulch had set fire to the house. The house was burning there before me, and the barn too, and beyond it all, there was the creek with all the water anyone needed to douse the fire. Far off to my left, I spied the haggard shape of Mulch moving away from the house.

"Getting up was difficult; I hurt, my stomach, my groin, and my arms hurt. They were bruised where his knees held me down in the barn loft. From where he raped me."

2

Mulch headed for the crops, a slow plodding jog. He didn't need to hurry. If there happened to be people in the fields when they shouldn't have been, well too bad, they deserved to suffer, to die. *That's why I paid them to go away, didn't I?* Mulch thought. *It's my party and it's going to end the way I want it to.* Heaven forbid some little cunt cut in on his fun. *That's for damn sure.* His head hurt like hell, a pulsing spike in his forehead. He did not hear Maria, crying and shouting to the sky, her body exhausted and laying against her car, her face a rictus of pain, and he didn't see Virginia who followed. He smelled the gas on his boots and hands, and the remaining can he carried sloshed and slurred.

The access road ended in a large donut shape just beyond a grove of hardwood trees. None of the usual pickups were parked along with the donut, but the shed door stood open a crack, and for a second Mulch bristled with adrenaline, fearing that someone lay in wait inside. He balled his right hand into a fist and barreled in, the gas can in his left ready to swing at anything that moved. But there was nothing, just dust, and tools. He grabbed an old tomato stake from the floor and wrapped a polish rag from the shelf around the stake and swung it in the air.

The torch felt good in his hands. *A piece of wood feels good in my hands – old and primitive. Hell yes.* Last week he had turned off the sprinkler system which stretched along with the fields like a serpent. And it had been hot, blazing hot. *Let's hope it's ripe for destruction.*

Striding out, he paused long enough to light the torch. He walked forth pumped full of purpose and adrenaline.

He walked along the rows blessing his plants and sprinkling gas and dribbling gas and making sure he didn't break the chain before touching the torch to the corner to set the wild flame loose among his crops. He lit the horse corn next, and the crackling fire spread, sounding like a big animal moving its great mass through the dry husks. He laughed and kicked at the dirt, his skull boiling. Past and present mixed into a soup in his brain and when his daughter came up running up behind him and called him out, he only saw his mother, whom he had killed once before a long time ago and then killed again that very morning.

"MULCH!" Virginia's voice threaded across the field. She didn't have a weapon. She only had her strength and the strength of Nick's memories. She balled up her fists and felt her blood rush in her ears, *paboob, paboob, paboob.*

When Mulch turned, his skin went cold, and his stomach dropped into his groin. His mother stared back at him. *A ghost, a fucking ghost! How many times do I have to kill you, mother?* His skin rippled with cold. It took only one look at the screaming ghost of his mother for Mulch to turn and bolt, he dropped the torch into the dirt and aimed for the forest. *He might be able to lose her if he ran hard enough,* he thought. *The forest. The caves.* He ducked his head and ran.

Virginia's rage boiled up and bubbled over, her mind thrumming with Nick's memories and her own. She poured on the speed.

"When Mulch took off for the woods, Doc, I didn't think I could catch him. Still, I ran. I let my pain fall away, the pain in my stomach, my arms, my groin, my legs, and my head. I didn't think about anything, not of Maria, not my sister, not myself. There was only the chase and I imagined myself to be one giant lung, no legs, no feet, no body, but only a lung, breathing in and out, steady as a heartbeat, in and out, in and out, with the woods melting through me.

"There was a moment there when I thought I was coming undone. I thought I felt something powerful touch me, right on the forehead. So strange. What do you make of that? I don't know what to think. All I know is that I ran faster than I have ever run in my entire life, jumping over branches and deadfall and twisting through nets of brambles and deadfall and ducking to avoid limbs whipping back from where Mulch broke through them. When he looked back at me, he looked like he'd seen the devil.

"And I caught up, I did. I don't know-how, not with my stomach all stitched up from where Pembroke opened me up and sewed me back. I should have died running after him."

Boston 7:48 AM EST

George couldn't see Lilly's body anymore. All George saw was light and he saw that through his eyelids, a flame shooting up into the sky and across the water. She looked like a candle. *Just reach out to her. She'll be okay.* He kept his good hand steadied on Spider's butt cheek, and with the other, he reached up to touch her leg. He had to know she was okay. *I hope she doesn't fall.* He felt something in front of him, but it didn't feel like a body. Lilly's leg felt waxy, warm, not hot, but warm, like love. He kept on holding onto her leg, hoping he wouldn't distract her, he kept his eyes shut.

"WHAT IS HAPPENING?" Ab screamed at the top of his lungs. "IT'S SO BRIGHT!"

"HOLD ON!" Spider screamed.

George no longer felt the rain, the wind-battered them, but the rain had slacked off.

When Amanda pulled her grandmother's car into the beach parking lot, she wondered how she was going to find them, but then she saw the beam of light directed at the ocean that punched a hole through the storm. "What in the ever-living fuck is that?" And then she saw, in the beam of light blasting over the Atlantic, a giant raptor flying low to the water, its talons sunk into something that remained nearly under the surface, she caught glimpses of it as waves crashed across and over whatever it was that the bird carried.

For Nick, everything in his field of vision had become white, and then shadow. *So this is what it means to die?* His genitals felt both warm and cold at the same time, and when he pressed his fingers to his upper stomach all he felt was a cold gelatinous mass. *Floating would be so nice. Float out and away, like a dream attached to a string.*

Below Nick, underwater, in the sunken bottom of the box, Cilia and Marina were locked together. Cilia's magic splintered, but she showed no signs of slowing. Part of her sucked Nick's lifeforce and fed the magic that allowed her to breathe underwater. And part of her magic focused on grappling with Marina. Had Marina been a human the battle would have been quick. But mermaid biology worked against Cilia. For one thing, Marina's strength re-surged as she remained underwater, despite Cilia's poundings as she thrashed the fish girl back and forth. For a while, Marina did seem stunned, but mermaid's throats are thicker, to endure the pressure of the ocean, and though Cilia would have crushed a normal man, she simply did not have the power to kill Marina, especially a mermaid regaining her strength.

Why won't you die! Cilia raged. *A few more minutes and I'll drain you too, girl.*

Marina simply flowed with the hag's thrashings, her body dragging like dead weight. For a moment she could not breathe but she did not panic and simply went limp until Cilia let her go in frustration, and when she raised her hands to bring forth her power she was hit from all sides by dozens and dozens of small sea animals.

The first littleneck clam smacked her against the eye, and Cilia felt the contusion's knot rise on her face, and for a hot second Cilia assumed that the young man whom she feasted on had thrown something at her, a pitiful attempt to get her to stop absorbing his life force. Then she was hit again. She whipped around prepared to bring her magics against Mr. Bill, but there was no one in the box but her and her prey. When she spied the far wall of the box rippling and warping as if it were the back of a living beast stirring from slumber, she paused, unsure of what she was witnessing.

On the far side of the box's expanded space, Sea Hag's carvings had begun to squirm and wiggle and lift out of the wall as if they were not carvings but instead the very animals themselves. The wall where Sea Hag had carved and chiseled now thrummed with life as the animals began to fire themselves through the water and across the air at Cilia, battering her from both sides.

All at once, it seemed, Cilia's body peppered with pain. Tiny sand crabs, tiny sea horses, and tiny mussels bit and burrowed into her skin, sending her into a rage. Her body pulsed with light and heat as she fought back; her magics bubbled up from inside her breaking apart the brittle sea creatures as they bit and chomped and smacked against her body.

Mr. Bill! How I will skin that native alive, she thought.

Still, the animals kept coming, fish as large as her hand flung themselves from where they were carved, small-sized whales and sharks aimed for her head and back. Cilia ducked, and moved, splashing through the water that continued to grow deeper and deeper as more ocean water flowed in through the cracks in the box. A squid careened onto her head, and the witch thrashed to throw it off. A whale pummeled her in the gut while an octopus wrapped its legs around her leg and sought to bring her down

Damn that man, her anger swelled and for a second, she almost let loose all her power but restrained herself. *Patience, think!*

She could not concentrate to counter the spell, not while she drained Nick. And before she could react the carved flame on the opposite wall of the box began to pulse with heat, a dull orange that grew brighter and brighter until Cilia winced from its brightness. For a second, she did not react, for the heat invited her, but then she began to feel her energies drain from her. *Damn him!*

The light pulsed brighter as it drew power from her. Cilia knew if she didn't throw everything she had against the box she might find herself drained, vulnerable.

A blue light pulsed from her body as she bucked off the spell. The box shuddered and shook with her power. The heat from the sun carving faded, dulled, and finally went out, the fish carvings fell away and broke apart into ether and became carvings again, but in the momentary confusion, she lost sight of Marina.

The attack had forced her to drift closer to Marina's bed and feeling her age upon her, Cilia needed a weapon. Grabbing a bed leg Cilia strained. A blue fire surged through her body and out her fingers and the driftwood bed exploded. Splinters and limbs flew outward and feathers from the mattress and pillows formed clouds in a huge swelling eye of white. Through it, Cilia grappled for and took up a spear-like limb of the bed frame and swung it like a club. Had she used it as a missile, it might have changed everything, but she did not, instead, she waded through the water, chopping down with the three-foot branch, beating the water, and sending spray up into the air.

The feathers from the exploded mattress and the chop from her fury provided Marina enough cover to evade. Marina, already bleeding from a raked shoulder, her left hand broken, continued to swim in tight circles, using her human feet, her full strength nearly returned. Cilia swung at her again and again, and again and again, Marina dodged it. When Cilia got close enough Marina braced her legs against the side of her prison and prepared to pummel the old hag and bust out of the box for once and all. But as she readied herself, light from the outside world cascaded down the wall, and for a second Marina and Cilia both thought the carved flame had roared back to life, but it was not Marcos' flame. The light streaming from inside was as bright as day, and it broke through the water's surface, and for a second Marina and Cilia, both looked up towards it.

Outside, Mr. Bill worked his wings. As he flew closer to shore, he began to get some lift on the sunken prison. Who or what awaited them on the shore, he did not know. They were powerful, that much was certain. *The Ugly Mother*. Her name had come to him while he strained with the box. At first, he shook the thought off, and then he warmed to it. *Of course, who else could it be?* Something about the light radiated love, a feeling he often perceived when he spent time around the migrant camp's spiritual advisor.

The shore came up suddenly. Mr. Bill had been closer than he thought and called out a cry of relief. On the beach, there appeared to be a very bright but very short lighthouse focused on them, and them alone. He could not see what it was made of, not exactly, for the light obscured his sight. *Soon enough.* His strength slipped out of him the closer he drew the box towards shore.

Inside, Cilia prepared to defend herself from another magical attack, and when that did not come, Cilia became curious for the outside light both drew her attention and drew her ire. *It better not be the Indian.* And fearing Mr. Bill, she flew up through the water and up towards the hole in the box, her ankle wings flapping.

Cilia did not mean to tear the box open, but as she rose and focused her power to ready for the offensive, she broke it open. The box weakened by Mr. Bill's attack on the pier, weakened by Cilia's attack, and weakened further by the immense pressure of water flowing in and out of it as Mr. Bill carried it to shore, the box finally cracked apart, destroying the pocket universe and spilling Marina and Nick into the sea, while Cilia flew up into the storm.

Mr. Bill felt the vibrations in his talons and when the box broke, he let go just in time to avoid Cilia's rage as she flew up into the sky, her ankles wings once again flapping and carrying her far above the sea.

Marina tumbled into the ocean, free at last of her prison. She turned around in a circle as she swam, her body rippling with power, her legs merging to form her great fin which powered her away from the wreck, and then back around to look for Nick.

The gelatinous blob, vaguely human-shaped, the torso and shoulders and head all present, but featureless, translucent, pulsed as the ocean waters carried Nick upwards. His lower half had become colored nubby nettles, purples and black and violet and blue.

In the air, Cilia gathered her strength. If Cilia was going to win, she had to take care of that light and *take care of Mr. Bill.* Then she could find that little bitch and fix her good. *Where is that native?* She flew upwards into the storm, the storm now bristling with lightning. The wind threw its arms every which way, and Cilia fought her way up to gain height to look towards the beach without losing all sight. *What is this? Is this the Indian's doing?* She felt great power and behind that power an even greater power. *Too bad you can't be here, brother!*

She focused her energy toward shore. Cilia did not see Mr. Bill above her, the raptor circling in a wide eye. When she flew forward towards the light, gaining speed for the attack, she did not see Mr. Bill break from his pattern and follow, dropping altitude as he approached.

When Lilly had begun to shine, she had been thinking of her mother. She stopped thinking when she began to shine. Images would come to her. Emotions would come to her. She saw her as a young mother, just like from one of the photographs she had of her parents. In the images, her mother shaped something very soft in her hands. Perhaps clay, perhaps not, she did not follow the tree of thought and simply allowed the images to wash over her. Her father appeared to her as well and together her father and mother were shaping what appeared to be something small and doll-like out of dough, or clay, or wax, she could not be sure. The heat she radiated felt good to her. She felt her mother's love in that heat. *Do not think, Lilly,* she reminded herself. *Let go. The key was knowing when to think,* her mother had always said, and *when to let go.* This was a time to let go. And when she did, her body burned and drew in on itself to use as fuel, and the light that shone forth from her was brighter than she ever had allowed herself to shine. The light exploded into a powerful beam as it left her body to cut away at the darkness as if the light were a steel blade. She burned with love for her mother and for all of the mothers there ever was and for George and his friend and Loco and even for Loco's aunts, and she beamed with wonder at love, thinking *how could I ever keep this to myself? How could I ever be so selfish?* She thought about how George looked right into her heart, and how he made her feel comfortable and safe and she thought about her mother and how she once came to her elementary school to fetch her for an errand, and how scared she was for some reason and how frightened her mother appeared in that moment. Lilly wept and laughed and mixed up the emotions so that she vibrated with goodness, and when Cilia floated up in the currents of the wind, placing herself directly into the beam light, Lilly only felt a bump, a skip perhaps, in her beam of the light.

The ear grew out of Cilia's back and inflated with the wind of the storm, and Cilia rose. The ear's fossa and concha bloated with air that carried her up, up, up. *Perhaps I can steal this magic*, she thought, *this light*. She'd already drained the mermaid's companion, his lifeforce had replenished her reserves. If she stole the light's magic, she might have a chance against the powers waiting for her on the beach. *The Indian, and something else. Something huge. A leviathan. Waiting behind the light.*

And as she prepared herself, the ear erupted into long saurian teeth along its helix and antihelix. She would eat up the light and then go for the girl.

When Mr. Bill's raptor tore through Cilia's ear it tore through the fossa and tore the top of the concha off. Cilia screamed; she banked in confusion, angry, determined. *Where is it? The Bird!*

The raptor, caught on the hideous skin, tumbled forward and careened out of control towards the sea. She summoned the storm's electricity and fired off in every direction, looking for the bird that had torn her avatar.

Below her, closing on the beach, the raptor glided across the sea. It had regained its flight path, but it had slowed long enough for Cilia to spot its dark shape against the chop.

The bolt exploded, catching Mr. Bill in the tail feathers. Shifting into human form, he tumbled head over heels towards the sea, his arms splayed out like a cartoon falling. And when he hit the water he vanished in the surf, the beach yards from him.

Speeding towards shore, victory in her veins, Cilia edged up closer and closer to the beam of light which came from some structure on the beach. She held her hands to her face, at first, but the light was still too bright, so then she closed her eyes and flew directly into Lilly's light. Cilia experienced only a moment of shrill happiness, victory pulsing in her blood before pain ripped up and down her body as everything she knew broke inside of her, and Cilia van Hazen knew no more. The light shattered her into a million pieces.

A thunderclap resounded over the beach, lightning forked the sky, and the sea became the color of stone.

Amanda Blackstone, late to the party, her first-aid kit slung over her shoulder, soaking wet from rain, was the only witness as Cilia van Hazen exploded. At first, Amanda wasn't sure what she saw. At first, she thought it was the bird, but the bird had gone if there ever had been one. Or perhaps what she was the whatever the bird had been carrying. Whatever it was fluttered in flight and then scattered like a swarm of birds, or exploded, Amanda could not tell. The next second the light went out and the darkness of the storm overtook the sky again, as the strange human pyramid on the beach collapsed.

Oysterhaus 7:50 AM EST

Mulch ran deep into the woods, which had been thicker and wilder when he was a boy, and thicker and wilder still when his father had been a boy, and even thicker and wilder when Mr. Bill had been a child and had played in the same wood following the sounds of the crows and the great herd which once roamed the forest. Mulch's brain raced along the length of memory, and as he raced deeper and deeper, turning to spy his mother following him, he saw that the fog crept out of the woods, and the fog filled the spaces between living things, the fog hanging close the ground, close to the trees. The fog appeared everywhere. Still, he ran, eager to keep his mother's ghost behind him. Then the great stag appeared, stepping out of a wild pine thicket, its white mane thick and tufted with brambles and leaves, a god, regal and proud and still.

Virginia, following her father, saw the fog too, and slowed, her mind triggered into trauma response. But the fog snaked around the bases of the trees, and she heard it hiss and call for her father, for Mulch. Then, erupting from the trees above her, the fluttering of many wings. The forest grew dark with feathered bodies, hundreds of birds gathered up and over her and behind her and all around. Virginia's heart grew cold, her focus buckled underneath her, and she slowed to a walk. Thick muscular wings beat above the forest and through the forest, shutting out the sun and stirring up a breeze that became a wind that pulled and pushed the trees back and forth. *Birds. Thousands of them*, she thought. *How is this?* She didn't finish the thought and instead began to run again.

Above her the birds held court. She did not recognize their shape, but they appeared to be monstrous crows or ravens. Ahead of her, Mulch had stopped, his body obscured by fog. *What is he doing?* She thought.

Then Mulch began to scream.

Standing three feet taller than her father, the largest buck Virginia had ever seen in her life loomed over Mulch, its great rack of points like a crown. At any moment it would bring judgment down upon her father, and then her. She stopped running, her body juiced with fear, and waited.

What is he doing?

Mulch had thrown up his hands as if to shield himself from the deer's attack. And the forest above her father crawled with birds, who cawed and beat their wings, their flapping and their chattering building in intensity. The wind they created whipped Virginia's hair around her, and in the wind, she found she couldn't move, frozen as her father was by his fear and by the dead stare of the stag. Her skin bumped into gooseflesh and her stomach numbed into ice.

The stag, the deer, the god of the fog, snorted, his body shuffling on its hooves. The beast did not seem to notice Mulch or Virginia. And as Mulch looked up, all his body shuddered. He lost all control. His hands shook as he stared into the eyes of the animal which snorted, its great rack vanishing in and out of the fog. Mulch pissed himself, and in doing so felt all his anger leave him and cold fear rushed in to fill the void.

All at once, the bird noise increased, their cries and calls reaching a crescendo where the birds began to lift off their perches, their wings spread wide. All at once, they flew in diving passes towards her and her father. Virginia screamed, ducking, putting her hands up to block their flight. Upon her skin, Virginia felt rain, but when she glanced down, she saw only small white worms upon her skin. They wiggled and squirmed, and she screamed.

Without thinking, she picked up the nearest stick, thick as her wrist and three feet long, and she began to swing it above her and around her to scatter the birds back into the forest.

All the while Mulch continued to scream and the stag lowered its great head and for a second Virginia thought her father was going to be impaled, and she felt her body react with adrenaline and rushed ahead, the birds flying between them thick and sick with worm and rot. And when she reached her father, she did not swing the stick at the animal god above him, but at Mulch's head.

Virginia felt the wood vibrate as it struck bone. Mulch howled and turned to her, his face pulled into a terrifying grin, his mouth white with foam. She swung again striking Mulch in the jaw. She'd cracked him good, and blood flowed from the wound, and for a second Virginia thought Mulch was going to strike her, for his hands were raised, but before she even brought the stick back up to defend herself, the bird's terrible racket clapped about her as the birds swarmed her father. Mulch didn't have time to react.

The birds covered Mulch in an oily black cape that tore at his skin and pecked at his flesh. Virginia could not discern him from the feathered mass, and their noise filled her ears like a passing locomotive. Dropping to the ground, she hugged her knees to her chest, afraid she was next, holding her ears down with her palms.

And her father roared in pain, his hands and arms stripped of flesh by thousands of hungry birds, birds that picked his body up and lifted into the air all so the birds could better strip the man of flesh as the fog thickened and whipped and swallowed them up.

And then at once the noise ceased, and Virginia peeked through her fingers expecting to see nothing but birds, her father collapsed on the forest floor, but all she saw was the stag, the fog receding into its nostrils, and her father's body some three feet off the ground, at least. And when the birds began to lift Mulch high above the forest floor to some other place, the great white stag had vanished, the fog slithering back into the woods dark with the coming storm.

Boston, MA 8:03 AM EST

Warmth. Absolute warmth. Through him and in him, warmth. Nick had been his name, but he was Nick no more. *Float on.* Something itched in his mind. *Float.*

No. Girl.

There had been a girl.

Yes.

The warmth. All of it for you.

His body had spread out, his forearms rising out of his new gelatinous body. How long he floated he did not know. Of course, later as he would recall thinking almost nothing, his mind occupied with a single idea, *to float in warm mother ocean,* to be carried by her. How long he floated he did not know, but then came a bright light, its warmth and intensity attracted him. *Float towards it.* And when he felt his form pick up speed, he did not think about it. *Float this way,* he thought.

And for a while he thought he was floating, he felt the water lap against his tendrils, he felt the water on his belly. And then a warm itch began to crawl down his lower half, and then he felt stillness for a while, until, as if waking from a dream, Nick began to see, and then he felt tingles below him, and tingles became tiny shocks. And his eyes began to differentiate between clearing sky and the ocean, which rolled and roiled, the storm above dissipating into dark shreds.

Something warm pressed him from behind.

A voice whispered.

For a moment fear spiked, and then panic, for he felt nothing. And then the voice again, soft, warm against his skin.

Marina found Nick with little difficulty, and she had carried him away from the wreckage of her prison and the old hag's magics and when the old hag exploded into fragments, Marina had been half a mile away, already in shallow water, Nick's gelatinous body in her arms. When the hag died, her spell broke, but Marina did not know this, and when she reached the shoals and rose with Nick's body, his neck, and head almost completely gelatinous, already morphing into the man of war, she wept for him and her and for all they had gone through. Her body, pushed to the limit, let go of all grief and she shouted and screamed and beat the water. And as she cried, she noticed the strange pulsing purple charge of magic as it unmade itself, a slow dizzy light that eventually brought hope to her. She cradled Nick in her lap and sang to him. She shielded Nick's eyes from the sun, and she waited and hoped.

And finally, when Nick's color began to return and when Nick's hair began to separate and rise from the jelly and become once again hair, fine and dark and soft in her hands, did she begin to touch him, first his face and then his shoulders, her legs underneath his frame. And they sat there for some time, in the shallows, the water rushing over them, Marina holding them true.

Oysterhaus, VA

"Doc, I watched my father's body fly off into the forest, the fog rolling back with the birds and their eerie flutter. My father's body was gone, but I heard his screams. There were no signs of the deer and if I had looked, I doubt I would have found any.

"Then there came the jerk. It felt like someone had taken a hook and had snagged me at the base of my neck and then jerked me as hard as they could, down and up. I snapped. I flailed. For a second, I thought I was going to die right there in the middle of the forest after all I had been through.

"And I was okay with that, the dying part.

"But instead, images filled my head like a slide show. You know the kind I'm talking about where some family member whips out vacation slides and next thing you know you're sitting through ten hours of trips like Uncle Bob goes to Smith Mountain Lake, and the Trouble with Trailers, and it's awful and somehow so informative at the same time. You see how pathetic some people are and how interesting they are too. Like somehow Aunt Julie's obsession with spatulas becomes clear when you see an inside shot of the camper van and the crappy Coleman stove, with Uncle Art lording over her like some toad king with a bad temper. And suddenly Aunt Julie is somehow humanized because she likes pink, tacky t-shirts with deer and shit on them. After all, they are tacky, and because they piss Uncle Art off who shuffles his feet under his chair each time a slide of Julie pops up and she's wearing some kind of pink tourist-trap shirt on that says: The Smokies are Smokin' and Cherokee Indian Reservation is Chief on FUN! And you see Aunt Julie wearing dozens of trashy shirts like that and Uncle Art is furious at that fact, and somehow Uncle Art who'd been so friendly when he hugged you tight and asked you to fetch him a drink now seems controlling and annoying, and you realize it's poetic justice that he works as a shoe salesman instead of just a simple fact.

"Except what flashed through my head was thousands of slide shows all starring my father and his father, my grandfather Eb, and I saw for a few frames my great uncle Leon who mysteriously disappeared. Mr. Bill was there too, and Maria, and a woman I recognized as Grandma Hayes, only she was a young woman, a knockout in a simple housedress and no make-up. I saw our house go from its original box to the telescope house it is today. I saw the boathouse built in seconds. Images zoomed by and played like a movie in fast-forward. I saw my father as a child and as a young man. I saw him with a beautiful woman in a wedding dress who must have been my mother. I saw my father kiss her as she lifted her veil. I saw the farm triple its size. I saw the migrant shacks go from bug town, which was what they called it in the old days because there were no screens on the windows, to the camp that it is today. I saw peach and apple trees grow from seedlings to full grown. Cotton popped like popcorn and was plowed down and under and was planted again and popped like popcorn all over again. There were sounds too, screams and shouts, words my father said to the bankers, hellos, and goodbyes, and more. There was the sound of my grandfather's voice and my mother's voice. And there were sounds of towns-people and anyone who might have come into contact with my father, or with Mr. Bill, or with myself, or with anyone in my family. It took me a while to figure this out because the sounds were overlapping one another like a tapestry and sometimes it was hard to hear what people said, but I heard someone talk about me, my high school teachers. Every thought they had about me, every word they ever said to me, or about me, flooded my ears. And it wasn't just me, either. Whatever they had thought about my family wormed its way into my skull, all of it. There was so much that I couldn't make heads or tails of anything.

"I just knew.

"And that was what scared me. Because I knew now that people had believed that Grandpa Eb killed Grandma Ruth and Uncle Leon, that Mulch had killed my mother, that Mr. Bill was some kind of demon, that my father had forced other farmers to sell their land for pennies, that Uncle Leon had done the same, but had been smarter and kinder and better about it. That the smoke signals coming from the Hayes farm meant that there was a body to be buried, not that there were drugs. That Sly, my father's friend and accountant of sorts, had told people when he was drunk that Mulch sold drugs out of the Feed store. That I was a whore just like my mother. That I had not worked to my potential. That my father and I didn't look at all alike and that I must look like my mother, God rest her soul. That only the church could save our twisted family. This is what was thought of us. People from all over the shore. The manager at Hammer N' Nails, businessmen from New York, a pair of aged brothers each named Tortini. In an instance, I saw hundreds of dead bodies in bags on boats, and my father carrying some of these bags and sinking them into the swamp. I saw my father and the truckloads of drugs and where he hid them in the storage shed. How some of his trusted farmhands got paid big bucks to keep their mouths shut, some time ago. How they knew they would be visited by Mr. Bill if they fucked with Mulch. I saw my father whip a man to death. I saw how Mr. Bill scared little kids. I felt how the old women felt about my Uncle Leon. Some of the memories and feelings were gray and faded with age and some were hot and fresh.

"I felt the hate. It seethed and took on a body of its own and gave me muscle, and my heart thrummed, it beat so fast. My head felt like someone had pumped me full of air. I felt the fear and the indifference and the utter contempt for the Indian savage known as Mr. Bill. I felt the almost mythical evil attributed to my grandfather, how they hated him but loved to talk about him. How they hated all of us but loved to talk about us all. How they wanted to be us, to be Mulch Hayes, to walk a mile in his shoes and fuck all the women he fucked and make all the money that he made. They wanted to be me too and smart off at the mouth as I had in high school and primp and fawn over myself and be so pretty that I didn't need any make-up. All the petty shit you can think about a family, Doc. I held all their memories. All of them. Like I had with Nick.

"I understood why they hated us so much, or loved us, or feared us. It was the prices of corn that fell just when they needed it to be high and the new clothes their baby needed. It was how young people looked at their parents when their parents had no work left because Mulch had bought the farm or shut the oyster shucking house down and invested in the new shucking house down the road. How that dignity had been stripped away from them. And instead, there was the Hayes family to contend with, always the Hayes family, like some dark cloud over everything, both touching everything at once, and not touching anything at all. How our family affected other families. I hadn't realized what effect we had, but they all knew. And I felt how just a small part of a town can cause so much hate. Like puzzle pieces, they fell and linked together. Because my father killed Sam Mules over the price of dope, Sam Mules' mother had had a heart attack and Sam's younger brother had to drop out of school to go to work to feed his brothers and sisters. Hate stemmed from the cocky way Mr. Bill walked through town and the things he made happen. Like to Eartha Jones who called him a red nigger one Saturday afternoon. And as Mr. Bill walked away, her skin turned bright orange like she had eaten a million carrots. And no matter how much she scrubbed she couldn't get the orange off of her. How she was then forced to wear clothing to cover her entire body and how she had been too ashamed to tell her friends and how she was voted off the committee to elect the new preacher, which was the only thing she had lived for because she refused to come to meetings because she was stained orange. And how the orange skin had gone away after she burst into tears in front of the bank as Mr. Bill had passed, a wry smile of satisfaction on his face. She didn't know for sure if Mr. Bill had made the orange go away, or even caused it, but part of her did know and hated him for it. For making her need to hate him, somehow. And somehow, they all became part of me, and I knew what they knew and felt and shared, and somehow, I didn't hate them back. Even my friends in school were envious of me because I was so rich. And that I attended a rich kid's school with doctors' kids and lawyers' kids, but they pointed their anger at me because somehow they knew the root started with me, with my family.

"Their memories were all sharply focused spears aimed at us, aimed at me. All the memories of us filled my body full and I felt as if I were full of hot wind and was all the hot wind in the world that ever was, and there came a clapping, a great echoing boom, and like that all the world's memories of my family disappeared from the earth forever."

EPILOGUE

When Nick next awoke, he was lying in the back seat of a familiar truck. He sighed. *George?* He thought, but then paused. He wanted to call out for his friend but did not. His throat felt slippery. His head hurt.

"He's awake!" Marina cried, and then Marina was looking down at him, and George, who looked like he had been crying, reached down and squeezed his hand. Marina's head was patched with gauze above her right eye and her hand was bandaged. George's hair looked singed, but Nick thought it was his imagination. Nick was still soaking wet. Outside the storm continued to clap and roll.

"George," Nick smiled. "Good to see you."

"Good to see you. Holy shit you gave us scare."

"Where are we?" Nick managed.

"In a parking garage," George said, his voice breaking into quiet sobs.

"What happened?" Nick asked. And then George told Nick the story in broken sobs.

Spider, Blockhead, Zac, and Amanda huddled together outside the truck under the parking garage. Zac agreed to drive back with Amanda, just to keep her company, to keep her awake, and make the trip shorter. Even though Amanda had only arrived recently, she was exhausted. Amanda had patched up the strange girl who had dragged Nick from the sea and mended Nick's various cuts. She had wondered why she had been called when Spider, taking as many photos as he could, spotted a very large man washed up down the beach. In the rain, it had taken Blockhead, Abdullah, and Amanda to bring him completely out of the water. He was as tall as Abdullah and broad and naked. His torso was cut in several places, shallow cuts that she bandaged, but the large wound running down the man's shoulder and around the side to the back would need to be stitched. She didn't have enough on her to do the job; however, she would try.

Amanda had barely finished wrapping the giant man up when George had cried out for help. Lilly had collapsed. She had been breathing fine when

Amanda left her to tend to Nick, and what she assumed was Nick's mermaid, whose left hand she splinted. The mermaid, a very awkward but striking girl had carried Nick out of the surf despite her injury. When Amanda had splinted her wrist, she had been surprised to feel a very different mass of muscle and bone under her fingers, a fact she kept returning to over the next few days. But she did not have time to process it that morning for George had called out for help, and the many mysteries she found herself in the middle of would have to wait.

"She's not breathing," George had gasped, holding Lilly to him, the color and heat drained from her. "We were going to get some food across the street when she passed out on the beach."

And as Amanda pressed her fingers into the young woman's neck her first thought was that the young woman was far too warm, but all that changed when her fingers pressed *into* the young woman as if her skin had been cast with the softest wax.

"Jesus!" She cried and withdrew her hand.

George's face became a complex O of shock and surprise as Lilly began to melt into the sand. George barely had time to jerk back before Lilly's body dissolved completely into a gooey mass. He broke into sobs, his body started to jerk and spasm with grief.

Amanda watched George's fits and then out of nowhere Abdullah stooped to her side and whispered in her ear.

"Help me pick up Lilly so she can be buried with her mother."

And Amanda, who for the first time that morning began to contemplate Ab's blue skin, said yes without thinking and rose with Ab and gently began scooping pools of already dried wax into a bag that was filled with something dry and leathery and smelled faintly of beef jerky. Ab had promised her that it was the right thing to do. And though she didn't understand it, she did it, and with love.

And now Amanda was tried. Very tired.

Now it was time to go home.

"To think I didn't get one good picture." Spider said to no one. "Amanda, we'll meet you at the gas station and we can caravan it home."

Amanda nodded, and having already said goodbye, Blockhead got in his car and started it up. Spider got inside without a word and the two of them slowly chugged off into the wind and rain.

Shortly after Zac shouted out. The giant naked guy had vanished.

Perhaps he had melted into the sand too, Amanda thought. But later at home, Amanda discovered her bandages missing, her kit stripped of scissors and thread and needles. *Whoever he was, he was less hurt than he let on* she would later assume. But that morning all she could do was shrug.

As Amanda and Zac drove away Zac's stomach grumbled, but only with hunger. He didn't think it would speak again, but he didn't know how wrong he was. And on the way home Amanda and Zac tried to hash out what they had seen, and she shared her own belief that they had been orchestrated by the strange girl with luminescent skin and hair that changed colors in the light, that the mermaid had brought them all together.

"Damn," Zac said. "I didn't even get to see her change."

"Yeah, neither did I."

Hours later, the mermaid-shaped storm system broke apart, the cloud formation separating and drifting across Europe and the North Atlantic Sea. It became a curiosity in the records, and for a while trended on social media, inspiring conspiracy theory after conspiracy theory, till that too faded from the public mind.

When George, Rufus, and Abdullah got back to the shore they didn't go straight home. Instead, they drove along a back road George had used to take Lilly home the first night they had gone out. It took George a while to find where he thought the path had appeared, but he found it. George had a feeling that Lilly and her mother would have wanted to be buried there. With a little help from Rufus, the three of them made their way through the wood to the grove of pine trees. The path itself was covered in shatters, and here the sweet resin floated on the air. George didn't know where the women prayed or did whatever it was they did, but he and Rufus found a spot in the soft earth and there they dug a shallow grave and buried Lilly and her mother side by side. George said a few words, Rufus let out a few barks, and then they went home to George's. And George fell into the deepest sleep he'd ever experienced.

The next day George hardly believed that he stood in front of his big friend who was hitting the road with his paint can. The now-empty can was tucked under his arm. The lid had been lost somewhere; George suspected Rufus had buried it.

"You are a good man, my former master," Abdullah said as he bent over and lifted George off the ground in a bear hug. "It is time for new adventures."

"Abdullah thank you. I don't even know what to say."

"Dog and I will be around your kingdom. He has told me that I should open my own business."

"Really?"

"Yes, perhaps I will hire you."

"What kind of business exactly?"

Rufus barked three times and panted heavily.

"Abdullah was thinking something in men's fashion, but the dog does not agree with Abdullah."

"I agree with the mutt."

"Cheer up, George. Love has a way of changing things." Ab said.

"Yeah, yeah. Time heals all wounds and all that crap."

They stood for a while and chit-chatted and George realized that he was sad to see them go; he hadn't expected Abdullah to take the dog, too. And after they had gone, he found the lid to Abdullah's paint can on the kitchen counter.

"Well how about that. He forgot his lid."

Or he didn't he thought. And he tossed the lid in the trash can.

2

When Marina swam away into the surf, Nick had hoped that one day he would be able to see his child. George had dropped them off in Connecticut on some lonely stretch of beach and over a few days, Marina and Nick talked and cuddled and kissed. She had swum him around some rocky nook to a rough place among the beach where they could be alone.

Far away from the tourists, they made love. And when they joined together Nick's head filled with all the memories he had forgotten. As they held each other and their mouths explored each other's taste, his mind sparked back to life, his old life and new life mingled and fused. For days they spoke of their past and what was to happen in the future. She would have her child, which she felt growing inside her. Nick wanted to go with her but knew he couldn't. When she was ready, she told him, she would find him.

And after days of lovemaking and days of rest, he watched her swim off. Every so often she turned in the water and waved at him and he would wave back. He watched her until she vanished into the horizon, and then he continued to watch for her. He fell asleep on the beach and when he woke up, he felt happy and fresh, and as crisp as a lemon peel.

3

"Doc, Since I killed my father no one remembers me. Not even Rick "the Dick" Bell, not even the Allbrights. Not even Maria, Maria who was like a mother to me. I wanted to apologize to her for all that she'd been through, but when I got back to the house she was gone. I didn't call 911. I just left in my stolen car. I let the house burn to the ground.

"I checked myself into a hotel and laid on the bed. My head hurt; it was crammed full of shit that I didn't need. Two days later I ran into Maria at Great Goose Farms, you know those mini-mart/farm stands? Yeah. She didn't know who I was. She wore a manager's apron and was stocking vegetables.

"I just stopped in my tracks. I saw no recollection in her eyes. None. Her hands were bandaged from when she had saved two children from a fire. When I asked her about her former employer, she told me that she wasn't able to recall the man's name. When I asked her if his name had been Mulch, she chuckled. Maria had never worked for a man named Mulch. "What a silly name," she said. And she didn't know anyone by the name of Virginia.

"It seems I have been erased.

"No one remembers Mulch either and when I drive by the fields that were once owned by my family they are not as I remember them. The crops are there, cotton, corn, tomatoes, soybean, and everything else. The fields are in the same place, even down to the way the peach, and apple trees look so thin between the fields – like a thin line of hair on an old man's skull. The migrants still spend their lunchtime eating the fruit. I've seen them do it. The way they form a thin line that stretches across the field and appears to evaporate at the ends. It is all the same.

"The house is there. The driveway is there with its crushed oyster shells. The porch sags in the middle and the newer parts of the wrap-around look cleaner and less ratty than the original front porch It's a wonderful old house, built in the late 1700s. My great-great-great-grandfather built the house. Or maybe he didn't in this new world.

"Now it's somebody else's house. It doesn't belong to me anymore.

"It's as if fire never touched it. But if you look closely, you can see that the roof looks smudged with ash. The last time I saw the house it was collapsing in on itself with flame.

"After I killed my father, everything changed. When I call out to people I once knew their faces screw up and their mouths drop open like I'm the answer to a question they don't quite understand. You've probably seen people get this way watching game shows, or the news as if they are trying to guess what's about to happen but fail to make the mental connections that will allow them to answer correctly and promptly. People tell me that I look familiar, but no one knows for sure. No one from here remembers me.

"My friends from away-from-here remember me, the ones I traveled through Europe with. Amanda Blackstone remembers me. She's told me that she's dating a man who talks to his stomach. Isn't that strange?

"And now with this life inside me...

"Excuse me, doc, I'm feeling a little emotional.

"Whew, boy.

"I didn't meet Nick Adams until recently. When I thanked him, he gave me a strange look.

"We're having dinner tonight, at Heron's, which I remember as Lewandos. I hope we can exchange information. He says he knows my sister. He painted a picture of her, a few of them. They are in an online gallery somewhere. If I can find it, I'm going to get a print made.

"Doc, maybe I should move. Get out of Dodge. But you know, I can't. If I move away, what if I forget myself, and what I've gone through? If I stay, I know I'll remember all the shit, and all the wonderful things too, and the reason why I hate my father. I can't forget him because then it will have all been for nothing.

"I mean, would anyone in my situation want to forget it all?"

4

Rockfish sizzled in the frying pan as Bill's mouth watered. Behind him, the tidal creek kept on breathing as the tide rolled in. What little beach there was suited him just fine. Far off, just around the bend, he heard some teenagers splashing about. The sound of an outboard motor broke the silence. On the horizon it looked like rain; the blue haze hung above the surface and Bill saw a fine curtain of moisture spreading out in the atmosphere like a curtain. He didn't care either way, not one bit. He supposed the rain would spoil the kid's fun, but no matter. There would be other days. Bill didn't mind the rain. If it did pour, he'd take his meal and eat in the caves. A long time ago he and his friends had played in those caves, a very long time ago. Now there was only him, and for the first time in many, many years, Bill felt youthful again. The scar on his shoulder itched, but he didn't pay it any mind. It had healed itself nicely. *Eventually, the scar would fade*, he thought, and that was fine too. He didn't need to remember it, though he supposed he would be the only one who would. But he wasn't sure about that either. When Bill got right down to it, he wasn't sure about anything anymore but for the smell of fresh fish, the salt on his cheeks, and the feel of his skin covering his bones like a drum.

5

On Carson Beach, twelve-year-old Mickey Sullivan found a leather satchel digging up sand for his very big castle. He wiped his sweaty forehead and brought the satchel back to the lump he was going to shape into a fort. Once while digging he'd found a quarter. Mickey hoped that this time he might have found a pirate's treasure that would get him out of school. He was teased a lot at school. A pirate's treasure would certainly buy him out of school. He knew people only went to school to get a job, and if he was rich he wouldn't need school. Those mean kids could suck a fart for all he cared.

His hands shook when he worked the drawstrings of the bag. The bag itself felt strangely dry, though it was stained as if it had been wet. At first, he thought it was empty and Mickey muttered "shitbird" to himself and he almost threw the satchel over his shoulder, but he didn't.

He felt something inside stir.

Using his index fingers and thumbs he pulled open the bag, making the mouth wide so he could turn it over and spill out the guts.

When the two ears fell out of the satchel and onto his lap, he didn't scream, not even when they began to wiggle.

It's fine he thought, *it's fine.* He then thought to tell his mother, but when he looked back at her sipping on her Diet Coke, on her towel spread out wide, he thought he should leave her alone. She needed to relax. Besides, they were kinda cool, the ears. He liked gross things – monsters, snakes, eels, and spiders. They couldn't have been real ears, anyway. Real ears don't wiggle unless they are on a person, and these ears weren't on anyone, they were in his lap. On a lark, he placed one ear to his own and suddenly his hearing became so clear and focused it made his teeth hurt. The surf came in louder and crisper, he heard crabs scuttling across the floor of the silent sea, he heard the light clicking of gull's beaks as they chewed cracker bits left in a discarded saltine package, he heard the shifting rustle of swimsuits, blood rushing through swimmers' veins. He heard all the conversations up and down the beach – sports talk, sex talk, complaints about husbands, wives, and kids, discussions of movies and books. Underneath the talk, he heard the whispers. The whispers were hard to hear at first, like TV static, but when he pressed both ears to his own, they became loud and clear. He heard everything so clearly, even the thoughts of the old beachcombers along the beach and the swimmers out in the water. The sensation thrilled him, and it was just like listening to the radio or listening to the TV in the next room. He bent back over his lump of sand and began to build out his castle. Mickey didn't notice the light-sucking feeling as the ears attached themselves to his head, covering over his ears. He didn't feel their small teeth dig into his skin; he was too busy listening to all the whispers of the world around him.

FIN

AUTHOR BIO

Stephen Scott Whitaker's writing has appeared in many journals including *The Rumpus, The Maine Review, Gargoyle, Fourteen Hills, The Shore, The Atlanta Review, Oxford Poetry,* and *The Southern Poetry Anthology IX: Virginia,* from Texas A&M University Press. They are the author of four chapbooks of poetry, a broadside from Broadsided Press, and the winner of the Pink Prize for Poetry, from *Great River Review.*